121881

D0065066

c.1

Pfarrer, Donald
Fearless Man, The

DATE DUE			

Rostraver Public Library
800 Fellsburg Road
Rostraver, PA 15012
724-379-5511

1-06

GAYLORD M2

ALSO BY DONALD PFARRER

Cold River

Neverlight

Temple and Shipman

THE
FEARLESS
MAN

THE

FEARLESS

MAN

A Novel of Vietnam

DONALD PFARRER

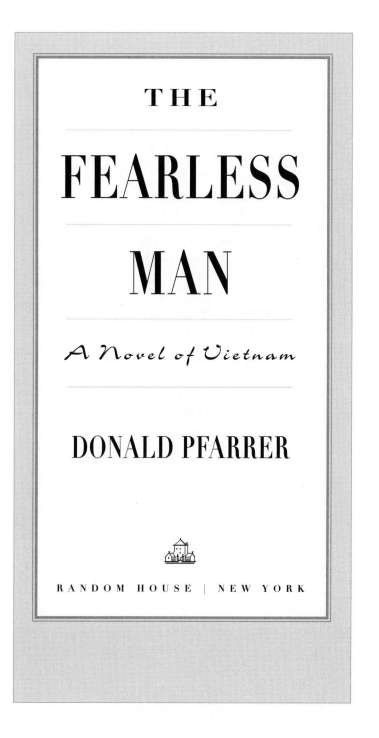

RANDOM HOUSE | NEW YORK

Copyright © 2004 by Donald Pfarrer

All rights reserved under International and Pan-American
Copyright Conventions. Published in the United States by
Random House, an imprint of The Random House Publishing Group,
a division of Random House, Inc., New York, and
simultaneously in Canada by Random House
of Canada Limited, Toronto.

RANDOM HOUSE and colophon are registered
trademarks of Random House, Inc.

Library of Congress Cataloging-in-Publication Data

Pfarrer, Donald.
The fearless man: a novel of Vietnam / Donald Pfarrer.
p. cm.
ISBN 1-4000-6267-5
1. Vietnamese Conflict, 1961–1975—Fiction. I. Title.

PS3566.F3F43 2004   813'.54—dc22   2004041884

Printed in the United States of America on acid-free paper

Random House website address: www.atrandom.com

2 4 6 8 9 7 5 3 1

First Edition

AUTHOR'S NOTE

This novel is set in Vietnam and the States. The places are real, the characters and action fictitious. I have changed historical chronology in one instance to compress the narrative.

As a Navy lieutenant I served in the 7th Marine (infantry) Regiment as naval gunfire liaison officer and gunfire forward observer. Three others who fought in the war have generously shared their knowledge with me. They are: my brother, Steve Pfarrer, formerly first lieutenant, U.S. Marine Corps; Mike Stilwell, formerly lieutenant (junior grade), U.S. Naval Reserve; and Jim Birkenhauer, formerly corporal, U.S. Marine Corps.

I dedicate the book to the 58,305 Americans who perished in the war; to the 153,000 American wounded, including the 74,000 who endured multiple amputations or survived as paraplegics; to the missing; and in particular to my friends

Art Brumagen,
second lieutenant, U.S. Marine Corps,
killed in action 26 November 1966, and

Vince Capodanno,
lieutenant, Chaplain Corps, U.S. Naval Reserve,
killed in action 4 September 1967

THAT THEY BE NOT FORGOTTEN

Happy are they and charmed in life

Who through long wars arrive unscarred

At peace.

— MELVILLE

CONTENTS

THE
FEARLESS
MAN

Chapter 1

Mac and Paul

"Sit down, Mac," said the 5.

The only seat available was an artillery fuze box and Mac sat on that. He had no idea why he'd been summoned but he expected the worst. Probably somebody in the operations shop had gone to the 5 begging for a change in the plan. Having spent hours arguing for the plan in its present form, and having already been forced into one major concession, Mac went on his guard. But the 5 had something else in mind.

"Mac," said the 5, "you're coming up for R and R. A week out of the mud. Bangkok, Hong Kong, Japan, take your pick."

"Honolulu," said Mac instantly.

"Oh yeah, there too. If you went to Hawaii your wife could meet you. I remember her, yeah, by all means, Honolulu!"

"We're counting on it," said Mac. "We're going to start a family."

"By God! By God! Little redheads running around the kitchen whistling the Marine Corps Hymn! I remember your wife," said the 5. "We met at the Marine Corps Birthday dance at Lejeune two years ago. A real lady. I said to Jeannie, my wife—"

"Sir, I remember her."

"I said, 'There's a young couple for you, there's a man-wife team, Kid, a man and what a wife, by God.' Ha!"

3

"Yes sir. Thank you."

They were sitting under a big lightbulb in a little tent. The 5's field desk was piled with as much paper as if he'd been working in the bowels of the Pentagon—except that it's been said the Pentagon has no bowels, only brains. The Pentagon is *pure brains.*

"So Mac, I'll tell the One to find you a Honolulu slot after this little caper's done. O.K.?"

"Sir, that's more than O.K. That's my main fantasy."

"Yeah. So—how do you feel about the operation?" He pounded a rolled-up map on his desk and it made a *bong bong* sound. "Ready for it?"

The 5 did not talk with his mouth only, or even his eyes. He had a long, drooping, mobile face, pale as dishwater, and the whole creation expressed itself when he spoke. He awaited Mac's answer as if he were dying for it.

"I feel damned good about it," said Mac. "And we're ready, yes sir."

"You've got some good people. How's Hitchcock working out? Kind of a rough son of a bitch but a— How's he doing?"

Gunnery Sergeant Hitchcock was Mac's company gunny, the man above all others who made the right things happen.

"We're lucky," said Mac. "I'd hate to think the other side had anybody like Hitchcock."

"Yeah, yeah. We've sent you some good people. I wish we had more."

"The company's tightening up, sir. It's coming along."

"Yeah, but Honolulu! Start a family! God if I—but listen, Mac—keep your eye on the ball, O.K.? This little excursion's no walk in the sun and we've got a whole goddamn *battalion* just waiting for you to whistle. Then we pile on, by God, and spin the fuckers like tops. So Honolulu and the arms of your beloved and little babies and whatnot—that's for later, way later. Eye on the ball, Captain. Concentrate. Light up your whole board. You'll be all alone out there and nobody to tell you what to do cause we don't friggin *know* what to do. See?"

"Yes sir, I see."

"That's why the Six said, 'Send Clare.' He had his eye on you when you were the Three Alfa up here. He said, 'I want Clare on this one.' It wasn't my idea although I fully concur. No, it was the Six. I thought you should know."

"Thank you sir," said Mac, who had seldom heard sweeter words.

"Yeah, but Mac, new subject. Did you ever see a chaplain humping the boonies?"

"No sir."

"Don't be offended if I say I've been in this outfit since you were a pup, and I never have either. I heard about one at Chosin. You should have been at the Frozen Chosin, Mac."

"No thank you, sir."

He gave Mac a long, sympathetic stare. His pallid features were lit from above but it was still possible to see he was smiling down there among the craggy shadows.

"But wouldn't you think a chaplain belongs out in front with the troops? Or would you say he should limit his flock to the rear-echelon pogues in places like this? People eating A rats and drinking cheap booze; safe people. What would you say?"

"Obviously, forward, sir."

"Forward." The 5 brightened a little when Mac gave the right answer. "And who do you think just flew in from Da Nang?"

"A chaplain?"

"And what do you think this chaplain, who is nothing but a civilian who just put on a uniform, who was in San Diego a couple days ago—what do you think he said to me five minutes after he got here?"

"I don't know sir."

"He said, 'Colonel, this is the rear with the beer, am I right?' And I said, 'Rev, you are a fast learner.' And what I didn't say was he's also a tough-looking little boxer or wrestler kind of guy, an Italian made out of re-rod and cement. And no worries about rank either. Next thing I hear is, 'I'm not staying here. I'm going out where the troops are.'

"So I gently informed him that people in this regiment, Navy and Marine Corps alike, go where the Six tells them, and he said he understood fully, which I thought was very open-minded of him. And then: When could he meet the Six? I congratulated him again on how quick he's picking up the language—Six equals commanding officer—and he laughed and said, 'Thank you, Five,' and then told me in so many words, 'Take me to the Six.'

"I guess if God is your copilot you're not awed by a mortal man with little dead birds on his collar. So I took him to the colonel and they spent an hour together, and in that hour this civilian wearing a Navy lieutenant's railroad tracks got further with the colonel than the president of the United States could in a year. Of course the president is a prick.—But you're wondering."

"Yes sir, I am," said Mac.

"O.K. here it is. The guy's waiting for you at the O Club. Go down there and get him. His name is Paul Adrano, lieutenant, Chaplain Corps, U.S. Naval Reserve, and he's more Catholic than the Pope.

"The colonel told him about your little caper." The 5 bounced the rolled map on his desk with a *bong bong bong*. This map outlined the area of Mac's search in the jungle. "And of course," the 5 continued, "Father Adrano likes the sound of it, 'recon' and all that—jumping off day after tomorrow—and he says, 'That's for me.' But the Six is thinking, 'Company-size, he'll be relatively safe while believing he's struggling against the forces of darkness.' And the Six, I have to tell you, is also kind of happy that the officer leading this thing has got an Irish name like Clare and is therefore undoubtedly a Catholic."

Said Mac, "I am not, sir. I never paid any attention to that."

"Careful talking like that around here, Mac. The regimental staff is crawling with Catholics. We've got two kinds of officers in this regiment: believers and wild men. We've even got some Protestant believers if you can believe that.

"Well there's a third category too, the guys who want advancement in rank with physical safety. But what do you mean, you pay no attention? Were you born a Catholic or not?"

"How can you be born a Catholic?" Somehow Mac failed to put a "sir" on that.

"Look Mac," the 5 said almost pleadingly, his features assuming two or three expressions, all of them full of tolerance, regret, and insistence—"Look, can it. For me it's enough the Six thinks he's putting this guy in the hands of a capable officer who also happens to be a Catholic, O.K.? Is it enough for you?"

"Yes sir, it's enough."

"Good. Now another thing. I said he looks tough, unlike some of the Herbie Popnecker types the Navy sends us, but even if he's the Pope's welterweight champion he is not accustomed to the climate, and he is minimally trained—classroom trained, totally inexperienced. Never humped the boonies a mile and doesn't know a howitzer from a hydrogen bomb.

"I said to him, 'Father, do what the troops do. The guy in front of you hits the deck, you hit the deck.' He says he certainly will. I said, 'By God, you better.' He says, 'By God, I will.' I says, 'Woops, took the name of the Lord in vain.' He says, 'No sweat.' I say, 'Exactly how long have you been in the Navy? *No sweat,* for Christ's sake.' He says, 'About nine weeks. You did it again but I'm sure you are forgiven under these wartime conditions.' I said, 'Woops, sorry about that.' He says, 'If you're Catholic I'll confess you. If not, you're going to hell anyway. Ha ha ha!' Man, has he got a devil of a laugh. I couldn't tell, was he mad? Will he curse me in his prayers tonight? I say again, he looks like some kind of tough bastard for a priest.

"Incidentally, the Six said it's up to you, but of course he means: Take the guy along and don't let him get killed."

"Yes sir, I'll take him if he can walk."

"Yeah, well, I thought about that. Can he keep the pace?" The 5 lifted his thin white eyebrows mournfully and gave a smile that creased his whole face.

Just to show he had some rights, Mac said evenly: "If he falls behind, we medevac him out."

"Right," said the 5, "but—you hear me? But." Meaning: *Don't let it happen.*

The 5's face was even older than his body. He was old enough to have fought at Okinawa and in Korea, and looked old enough to have fought at Belleau Wood. He was waving the rolled-up map around as he no doubt used to wave his swagger stick in the Old Corps.

"He won't hack it," said the 5 gloomily. "How could he? The heat, Jesus. But let me tell you, Mac, be thankful. You get a choice of a war in a hot place or a cold place like Chosin, take the hot one, buddy. Good luck on this caper"—and he *bong bong bong*ed the map on his desk.

His sagging eyes followed Mac out.

Mac ducked through the flaps and stood outside waiting for his eyes to adjust. He listened to the stuttering sound waves running up the valley from a diesel generator down below. The sky was closed over with blocked moonlight. Had his wife been standing beside him and taken his hand she could not have been more intensely present. Honolulu! Sarah! He did not see her naked, but dressed for sunshine and beach breezes. He didn't actually see her clothing, but the wind pressed against her figure.

For a moment he dwelt on this illusion, this vision. Then he started carefully down the path, trying to see its boundaries. He passed the 5 and 6's outhouse, then the 4's tent, which was dark as the outhouse but smelled better, then the comm tent, where the flaps were half open and the light shone out, and men were laughing and one man shouted something about how stupid somebody was—and at length he reached the bottom, where the surface changed to sand.

Here he had to pump along, lifting his knees and leaning ahead. He passed tents on either side now. These were the staff quarters, pyramidal tents called "prams," poking their black points up against the sky. He passed the one where he'd lived during his assignment as assistant operations officer, or 3 Alfa. Dead ahead lay the Officers' Club with its latticework sides releasing a delicate diamond pattern of yellow light. He could hear the "truck-drivin son of a gun" singing his happy song about "six days on the road and I'm a gonna make it home tonight."

Mac thought: "I'll be satisfied to make it back to Delta Company."

He was still with Sarah. Sarah was with him.

"He cometh! The quiet Commie killer."

"A man, a forked mammal with balls."

"Beware of Captain Clare."

"Dirt pile Delta Six!"

Mac had worked with these men until about two months ago, and had known some since Basic School. He shot back an insult or two and hung his pistol belt on a nail, then advanced toward the bar, toward a short chesty man with bulging shoulders in a too-tight set of jungle utilities, who faced him with a self-confident smile.

"Father Adrano," said Mac, holding out his hand.

The other's hand slapped into Mac's and took it in a vigorous yet slow, hard grip. "Captain Clare, I presume."

"Mac. Call me Mac."

"And you call me Paul, please."

Paul's utilities were straight out of the box. They stretched over his chest and shoulders and clung tight around his biceps. His trousers were bloused at the boot-top in Marine Corps fashion but his haircut was too long. The glistening black hair swept to one side. His face was surprisingly big on top of his short body. It was a hatchet-shaped face, pale, and marked at the eyebrows by sharp streaks of black. His eyes were even blacker, and sharp, hard, not completely serious. Maybe he was amused at the ridiculous idea of wearing the bars of a Navy lieutenant on one lapel and a cross on the other.

The handshake was going on a bit longer than usual—Adrano's forearms were bare, white, covered with black hair. When they broke, both men were still looking at each other.

"We've got to roll," said Mac.

"I'm ready."

"But first I need a drink."

Mac ordered a Hennessy from the man behind the bar, a staff NCO working for wages, who could be trusted to keep the secret that some of the officers on the regimental staff were fools, drunks, and chronic gripers.

Paul Adrano went behind the bar and came back carrying a seabag over one shoulder and a small haversack on the other. Mac took the haversack. He threw back his head, scorched his throat, and glimpsed the lightbulbs strung on a wire along the ridge pole. He closed his eyes and saw orange spots turning yellow-green. He ordered another and drank a glass of cold water. He put down fifty cents in military payment certificates, looked at Paul, and downed his second cognac. He jerked his head toward the door.

A man called: "Hey Mac, have another drink, buddy!"

"Can't," said Mac. "Got to fight the war."

"Lord! Don't *kill* anybody!"

"Kill a Commie for Christ," a man called out, then cried: "Yikes! Sorry, Chaplain."

Mac stopped for his gun belt. He put it on with a twist and a click of the locking device, then went back to the bar and asked for another glass of water. It was cold—cold water! He drank, and asked for another. A major at his side said: "Either leave or take off that pistol."

9

Mac said, "Aye aye sir," and finished the water knowing it would be the last cold drink or cold anything he would taste for days or maybe weeks. He nodded to the major and thanked the bartender.

Mac and Paul went out into the darkness.

"Ready?" asked Mac.

"Ready," said Paul Adrano. His voice was both high-pitched and husky.

They started down a sandy track and Mac immediately broke out in a heavy sweat. "The booze," he thought. Yet the haversack was light; his dispatch case was weightless, and his pistol belt with its pistol, spare magazines, K-Bar knife, first-aid kit, and two full canteens was like a belt of sweat; but he didn't mind the weight of it.

Paul was laboring, so Mac cut the pace and listened to Paul's breathing.

"Just get here?"

"You mean in this country? I got to Da Nang day before yesterday and flew here today."

"Notice the heat when you hit Da Nang?" asked Mac.

"We didn't land at the air base. We landed in an oven somewhere."

Mac chuckled and said: "I see you don't have a helmet or flak jacket."

"Should I?"

"Unless you're bulletproof."

"I've got a body like any other." And Paul thought: "So did our Savior. I'm going to die here."

"Then we'll get you a helmet," Mac proposed, "to keep the rain off, and a flak jacket to give you heatstroke."

Paul didn't comment; he trudged on, hoping the other man could see where they were going. When Paul was twenty, a premonition of death, the voice in the head—"You will die here"—would have thrilled him. To leave this world and see God! Now this same message had a different impact. Why should he alone feel this terror when everyone else— But were they really so fearless? Hadn't he seen a row of body bags on the airstrip? That sight was still in his eyes.

Mac was saying, "You're lucky. This is a good regiment."

"So they said at Division."

"I'm glad they know it.—So, you can go anyplace you want?"

"The Six said I could, within the regiment. Just tell the Five and he'll talk to the battalion commander, and off I go. I want to go where the men go."

"Where you're going right now is Delta Company, my company. I'm the Delta Six."

"Where is Delta Company?"

"About four miles that way."

"What!"

Paul stopped. After a pace or two Mac stopped and looked back.

"I've got to lug this bag four more miles?"

Mac said, "If I say yes, will you let me carry it?"

"I surely will. Here, take it."

"Keep it. We've got a six-by at the road."

"What is a six-by and how far is the road?"

"It's a truck and the road is maybe two hundred meters away."

"Why meters? Why not yards?"

"The maps are in meters," said Mac. "Artillery uses meters, so do we in the infantry. Naval gunfire uses yards."

"Six-by?"

"Six wheels driven by six wheels. Six-wheel drive," Mac said. "It's cool enough now but when the sun comes out and you're humping the boonies you won't believe it."

"So I've heard," said Paul. He was starting to puff.

"It took me months to get used to the heat," Mac continued. "I lost twenty pounds and then the monsoon came and shook my bones."

They talked about the problem of marching day after day in the monsoon, never dry, sleeping in wet clothes and sometimes in water. Mac described his method, which was to forget about trying to create a dry place at night.

"It's a waste of time," he said. "Sometimes I roll up in a shelter half and let it rain on me. Pretty soon I've got my own private puddle. You'll love it."

"Do you get any sleep that way?" asked Paul. Paul's voice was edged, with a New York sound to it.

Mac said it was cold if you disturbed the water. He realized he'd never written to Sarah about this and made a note of it. There are many ways to go to sleep. One is to lie in monsoon water and warm it with the finite energy of your body. Another is to slip between clean sheets beside Sarah.

They slogged along and the noise of the generator faded to the rear. They were now on a road through the sand, with dark low bushes on both sides.

Mac called loudly: "Captain Clare, Delta Company!" He switched on a red flashlight and shone it back on himself, walking two or three paces with his eyes closed, then turned off the light.

A man from nowhere moved quickly into the road. He held his rifle across his chest.

"I'm Captain Clare and this is Chaplain Adrano."

"Aye aye sir. The captain's six-by is ready. Gunny Hitchcock is waiting for you."

At the truck a man took Paul's seabag and heaved it up. Another man came out the passenger door and hit the surface of the road with both feet. It was too dark to see whether this man saluted Mac, or if they shook hands. Paul strained his eyes to see the man.

"Father Adrano, this is Gunnery Sergeant Hitchcock."

Paul held out his hand. At first he made no contact, but after a moment the two hands met, and gripped. This grip of a hand he could not see, belonging to a shadow, was Paul's first sign of Gunnery Sergeant Hitchcock.

"I'm happy to meet you, Gunny," said Paul in a tone marked by a sort of democratic attitude.

Hitchcock's response: "Happy to meet you, sir." There was no tone in his voice, just words.

"Are we ready?" Mac asked.

"Yes sir."

"All right, then. All aboard."

Some men Paul had not seen scrambled aboard the truck. Paul started to climb up, trying to figure out how they did it so quickly.

Mac said, "Father, you take the seat in the cab, please."

"It's O.K., I don't—"

"Please," said Mac, and Paul understood. He opened the cab door and climbed in.

"What have we got?" Mac asked Gunnery Sergeant Hitchcock.

"Two sixties, two seventy-nines, four rifles," the gunny answered.

"Holy shit. O.K., put a man in with the chaplain."

"Aye aye sir."

Hitchcock called a man down from the rear and the man climbed up and squeezed in by Paul with his rifle poking out the window. Hitchcock climbed up a rear wheel and jumped into the truck bed.

Mac followed him up and said, "CSMO on outa here."

Leaning toward the driver, Hitchcock said softly, "Move out."

The truck rolled. The road and its shadowy borders were revealed by dim headlights.

Paul thought: "A sixty must be an M60 machine gun." He was trying to remember a slide show on weapons he'd seen at chaplains' school. "What's a seventy-nine? I forget what a seventy-nine is. What is CSMO? What in God's name am I doing here?"

Chapter 2

Whap!

To get inside this tent you parted two flaps, then securely closed them; then you turned and parted two more, entered the tent itself, where a gasoline lantern burned, and securely closed the second set of flaps. The atmosphere inside was stifling. Paul broke out in a prickly sweat and his lungs soaked up the gasoline fumes. His head pounded. The others seemed oblivious as they crowded around a map.

A light so white it bit the eyes—hissing, sputtering—and they huddled around it over a map spread on a footlocker. On the green-painted wood Paul could read "MacHugh Clare CAPT USMC" stenciled next to a blue diamond and a number. Now these disappeared as someone covered them by a chance movement of the map.

Something, Paul didn't know what, was badly wrong.

To a young man who looked frightened MacHugh Clare said: "Try again."

The young man nodded to a man who sat somewhat outside the inner circle. This man held a microphone on a spiral wire. So far as Paul could see he didn't do anything, and he certainly didn't say anything, yet everybody strained to listen. Paul could hear radio background and the hissing of the gasoline lantern. The youth with the frightened eyes watched for a moment, then turned to Mac.

"Nothing, sir."

They bent to the map again: Mac, Gunnery Sergeant Hitchcock, the frightened youth, who was a second lieutenant, and another officer, whom Paul had met on arrival at the company area. He had not caught the name, but the man was Mac's executive officer, second in command in Delta Company.

Mac took a set of stainless-steel dividers out of a plastic case; he stepped the dividers over the map—one, two, three, four steps—and looked up at the exec.

Mac said: "You filed the patrol and ambush plan with Battalion?"

"Yes sir," said the exec.

"And you've looked at the H and I's? You checked the night defensive fires?"

"Yes sir."

"Show me."

And the two bent over a transparent plastic sheet which the exec placed carefully on the map.

Paul wished they would use plain English. He knew somebody was in trouble but who it was, and what H and I's were, he had no idea.

Mac looked up at the frightened youth. Mac's face shone red in the cruel light; his hair was red or reddish brown—his eyes were calm yet somehow severe. He looked at his watch and studied the map for another half minute. Paul consulted his own watch: 2 A.M.

"O.K.," said Mac, clicking the dividers shut. To the exec: "I'm going out." To the frightened youth: "Get a squad and two guns. We walk in ten minutes." To Gunny Hitchcock: "You come."

Paul Adrano cut in quickly: "May I go with you?" He had never felt so ignorant or so frightened. He was over the fear of the truck ride with lights distorting the humpbacked strange vegetation on either side of a white trail. But now his voice quavered. Or did it?

"Say it again!" He heard this as an internal command. Aloud he said: "I want to go with you," and this time his voice was steady.

MacHugh Clare was big and rugged, not unnaturally big like a football player but big enough to stand out. He was about a head taller than Paul, but Paul was used to that. Every competitor he had ever known had been taller than he. "It's not his height, it's his face," thought Paul. He saw Mac's face as a sketch of power, of physical strength, or power over objects, and inner strength, power over himself. His skin was sunburned, his eyebrows bleached by the sun, his blue eyes a deep, not a pale blue, and his nose almost as wide at the bridge as at the nostrils. The nose shot straight down from its bridge. Mac broke into a smile that showed big white teeth.

"Do you know where we're going?"

"I do not," said Paul defiantly.

"But you want to go?"

"Yes."

Paul considered adding some organ music about his reasons for coming to Vietnam and all that, but he saw the smile growing on Mac's face and held his peace.

"O.K., come," said Mac, still smiling. "Gunny, is there a flak jacket and helmet around here for the chaplain?"

Gunnery Sergeant Hitchcock said there was; and to Paul: "Come with me, Chaplain."

Mac said, "Nine minutes."

"Aye aye sir," said Gunnery Sergeant Hitchcock.

Then they were marching in a sinuating course between dark tents, moving incredibly fast. The gunny had assigned a man to stick to Paul, and Paul had overheard the last part of the instructions the man received. He had heard Gunny Hitchcock say, "He's a chaplain. Doesn't know shit. You're his guardian. He dies, we kill you."

This man, this guardian, was walking behind, so Paul Adrano dropped back, took him lightly by the arm, and whispered: "Do you know where we're going?"

"Yes sir, don't you?"

"No. Tell me."

"There's some guys from First Platoon out on an LP. They ain't answering the radio check."

"What's an LP?"

"A listening post. You snoop and poop. You take cover and listen. You keep quiet and you don't talk, and you better know your way back in the dark."

"If you don't talk how can you answer a radio check?"

"Easy. The guy at the CP keys his mike. He don't *say* nothin—"

"What's a CP?" Paul cut in.

"A command post, sir, a headquarters area. But we gotta be quiet. So the guys at the LP key their mike twice and it means 'All secure.' Three times means 'I want my mamma.' The main thing is, we gotta be quiet, sir."

The column stopped. Men adjusted their gear. Somebody whispered back: "Five-meter interval," and Paul's guardian whispered it on down the line. Then he said: "Stay five meters behind the man in front of you, sir, and I'll follow five meters behind you."

They went steadily ahead. They passed beside a rectangular hole, a darker smudge in the ground, with two men standing in it exposed to the waist. These men lifted their weapons in salutation—and the column left the tents behind.

Crossing a dry rice paddy, Paul was caught between exhilaration and fear when the sky cleared and a three-quarter moon showed itself, riding sedately through a zone of virgin black. The column was fully revealed and Paul thought: "They can see us. They'll know exactly how many we are. They'll see me."

Because he carried no rifle he'd be identified as an officer. He had sweat in his eyes, his shirt was drenched with it. His helmet squeezed his skull and the flak jacket constricted him. "They shoot at officers," he thought. And a nutty tune went through his head: "In the cool cool cool of the evening . . ." He wiped his eyes, squinted, and struggled to keep up. The man ahead was drawing away and Paul trotted to close the interval. He heard his guardian's breathing. Never in his life had he felt so far inferior to so many men.

The man in front jumped to the right and walked along the narrow top of a dike separating the dry paddy from one that was flooded. Paul made the leap and walked along, fearing the wall would give way under his feet.

"If I fall I'll make a big splash," he thought, "and I'll never live it down." He lengthened his stride but took extreme care.

The trooper ahead jumped to the right but there was no splash. When Paul approached the turning point he saw what must be dry ground and a path dimly visible under the moon, leading away to the right and ahead. He jumped blindly, found his footing, and churned on up the path after the trooper. The man seemed to be trying to shake him. Yet he was doing better. He began to believe he wouldn't die. For a second the whole thing felt like a movie. He wasn't a priest now, not a man of God. He felt a thrill. The ground was rising and he was keeping up. He was finally "humping the boonies." He was eager for the dawn, but not from fear of the dark. He wanted to see more. He wanted to see it all, because it was no movie.

Captain Clare was somewhere ahead. The gunny was controlling the rear. There was one machine gun ahead and one behind him somewhere. And somewhere the frightened lieutenant was stumbling along.

He tried to piece together, from lectures he had heard at Navy chaplains' school in Newport, what this could possibly be all about. If the enemy had taken the LP, wouldn't they set a trap for just such a rescue mission as this?

On the left Paul saw an armed man walking a parallel course no more than fifty meters away. It was distressing to realize he was the first to see this man. He started to run, to warn the man ahead.

He had taken four running strides when he saw another armed man on the right, also pursuing a parallel course and also fifty meters, more or less, from the column. Paul checked his stride and thanked God. "Of course! They're—"

He forgot the word but they were surely our men. The moonlight showed him how similar they were to everybody else, especially in the shape of their helmets.

His mind played out the consequences. Should he have made that blunder: ridicule, contempt, some awful nickname like "Scout" or "Eagle Eye." These consequences justified him in bothering God with his gratitude. He said: "Thank you, God, thank you." Clearly it was God who had let him see the second man—and Paul glanced quickly again left and right. He was thinking that he didn't give thanks for his ego's sake but for the sake of his mission. This was a special kind of congregation. There were a thousand ways to prove you were worthless but only one way to prove you were not.

His feet told him they had left the trail. Just as the moon darkened and disappeared in a gray sky he saw that they were traversing rolling, open, dry country dotted with bushes and small trees. Then he could see nothing. He was amazed at how fast they still moved and how quietly. No talk, no clicking or rattling of equipment. The column and its flankers conquered the terrain like a long reptile with short legs thrusting out on either side.

Paul felt as if he were walking a foot above the ground and over all the little obstacles that must be there. They could not impede him. But he did sweat, and he did struggle for breath. He seemed to skim over any ankle-twisting obstacles and yet his legs were all but dead—his chest began to ache.

"I will—die—before I'll—Walk! Walk! Walk!" he cried to himself. This was no time to pray, this was a time to—walk! And he did, like a prisoner in a death march, a man without a will of his own, chasing the half-visible form of the man ahead, slouching away from Bethlehem.

Suddenly there was a great white flash in the sky. The man's body stood out in silhouette.

Paul's mind knew—this was death! And it told his body. His guts expanded and his heart exploded. His face prickled with terror. To die so soon! To die in the first few minutes, without giving a stroke of help of any kind to any man—to die in the very condition he was trying to remedy by coming here—to die *right now*! And he waited for it—

He was not just mad with suspense but ripped apart in his mind by the failure of his mission. Yet nobody hit the deck. Thank God he did not either. Everybody kept on humping.

Paul had seen a ragged hill line in the flash, but he could not see anything now. When his eyes recovered he saw dark forms gliding forward, the flankers humping out on the sides, everything the same as before; and he could hear his guardian's breathing behind him, then *whap*! A wave of sound rolled over the reptile and snapped in Paul's ears—but everybody kept going!—and a new kind of sound chased the *whap* like a hollow twisting tail chasing its body. And everybody kept going, and so did Father Paul Adrano, lieutenant, Chaplain Corps, U.S. Naval Reserve.

Whatever it was, it had exploded beyond the hill line. Thus its light silhouetted the hill and, reaching into the overcast sky, this same pulse of white light diffused its power down on the column. Yet it seemed so close! That *whap* sound seemed—

Paul did what everybody else did. It was the only thing he could do. If MacHugh Clare was marching these men to their deaths, then he would march with them to his own.

Now came pale distant flashes in the sky and at length a series of pounding detonations from the left—then a second series of perhaps a dozen more unstoppable eruptions following a pale flashing. These caused a change in the men.

The man in front turned, raised his fist, and pumped his arm in anger or triumph. Paul turned around and saw his guardian also pumping his fist and dancing a jig.

Then on and on, and the sweat streamed into his eyes continually and the headband of his helmet seemed to tighten around his splitting brain. He craved water, and his strength was spent—yet he had been humping only about fifteen minutes. He wished he could check his watch. Fifteen minutes or two hours?

They halted. His guardian motioned him down and he sat, and panted and longed for water. The guardian crawled forward and handed him a canteen, and this was his first experience of guzzling warm water.

The guardian crouched beside him and they waited in silence. He wanted more water but dared not ask. The sky flashed again and a few seconds later the *whap* and its multi-toned rustling tail passed over them like a whisk broom.

His guardian put a hand on Paul's shoulder and drew him close. Paul strained to listen.

"That's just our H and I's," said the trooper as if to a child.

Paul felt as if he knew less than before.

The moon found an opening and cast its "dim religious light" over the rumpled hillside, magnifying every rock and bush. These objects seemed to be moving, creeping—and behind every one there crouched an enemy gunner waiting to annihilate the marines and their chaplain. Maybe! Maybe not!

A man approached swiftly, crouching and silent, and knelt beside Paul and his minder. To the minder this man whispered: "Where's the chaplain?"

"He's the chaplain."

And to Paul, leaning so close Paul could smell him, whispering so softly Paul could barely hear: "The skipper wants you, sir. Follow me."

Three men crept forward—this messenger, Paul, and his guardian. The messenger motioned them down, and all three went snaking forward on their bellies to a clump of bushes.

"Sir, crawl, don't walk," the messenger said to Paul. "Go around this bush and you'll see a bunch of cactuses."

Paul thought: "Cactuses!"

"Go there," the runner continued, "and you'll find the skipper. Quiet. Quiet."

Paul wormed around the bush. The cactuses were just ahead about six paces, and he reached them by planting his elbows and pulling, drawing one knee forward and pushing. During this crawl a single bright flash lit up the cactuses and the forms of three men flat on the ground. One turned to face him—he recognized Captain Clare. Then darkness. Worming through the dirt. "Quiet," he thought. "Quiet."

Paul realized he had made a mistake in coming without a canteen. The minder had noticed and shared his water. Paul thought: "The gunny should have—no, no! You are responsible for yourself. Just crawl, just shut up!"

A hand fell on his shoulder and encouraged him forward. He came shoulder to shoulder with Captain Clare, both men prone and propped on their elbows. Mac handed him a heavy—thing—that looked like a weird pair of binoculars. Mac pointed, and Paul put the glasses to his eyes.

Right in his face he saw a strange bright picture—squat trees, humps of earth, round lobes of cactus, a pale line that must be a trail—and all of it displayed in blinding yellow light tinged with a mellow green, chartreuse.

He lowered the glasses and tried to match what he saw now with what he had just seen. His eyes were still dazzled and all he could discern were vague shades of gray in the darkness.

When Mac did not demand the glasses back Paul looked again. What had been distant now jumped into his face—and he recognized something. He lowered the glasses and with his naked eyes saw the faintest visible trace of light that marked a trail. He raised the glasses and saw it jump to chartreuse life right in his face. He took a correct measure of the distances, and soon found himself able to match the image in the glasses with what his naked eyes beheld.

Leaning forward and placing a steadying hand on Paul's shoulder, Mac whispered: "Take a look. Five meters short of the point where the trail disappears on the right."

Paul lifted the glasses again, and the more he looked the harder his eyes felt, as if the device were turning them to marbles. He scanned the same area with his naked eyes. Raising the glasses again, he breathed: "My God."

He began to pray fervently but silently for the souls of three marines. "Heavenly Father, forgive them the sins they had no time to repent or confess. Forgive them for the sake of your Son Jesus Christ, whose sufferings on this earth . . ."

Down the slope before him, thirty meters away, lay a depression invisible to the eye but quite conspicuous in the night-vision glasses. In this depression lit by a color never before seen lay three bodies. Under the yellow-green light Paul saw one man, who lay with his head thrust back and his mouth open. A dark shadow of blood ran down from his throat to his belt. Paul thought: "His throat has been slit." His rifle and earphones lay across his body.

The other two were on either side, one lying on his right and the other on his left side. Paul could see the back of one of these men and it was soaked and dark. There were two helmets in view. That these were the men of the LP there could be no doubt. Their radio was propped against the sloping side of the depression.

Paul stared at the man with the open mouth. He imagined that those lips were his own and that the marine's blood was his blood. He prayed: "This man's blood is the blood of Christ and my blood is this man's blood."

He passed the glasses to Mac and half-heard what Mac said.

Captain MacHugh Clare, U.S. Marine Corps, whispered to the frightened youth who lay on his left, "What are you going to do?"

The youth said instantly: "I'm going down there." His voice all but failed him and he spoke too loud.

Mac shushed him and said: "A good way to die."

But the lieutenant had no other idea. He was dumbfounded, paralyzed, or so it seemed to Paul. And Paul had no idea either.

"Why don't you throw a rock?" Mac suggested.

The frightened youth ran his hands over the ground within reach but couldn't find a rock.

Mac reached into the pocket of his shirt and took out two rocks. Paul heard them click faintly together.

Paul thought: "He carries stones around in his pockets?" Paul felt perfectly hopeless, ignorant.

Paul heard the soft *whup* as the lieutenant threw. They all heard it land, and nothing else. He threw again with the same result. Mac passed him two more rocks.

The next throw produced a grunt, a scrambling noise, and a sound of metal dragging on metal. The two officers looked through the glasses, then Mac passed them to Paul.

He saw the three marines. Now they were hyperalert, weapons poised, scanning their surroundings from the rim of the depression. The one whose mouth had sagged open had the earphones on his head now—no helmet. Their faces, or at least the one Paul could clearly see, were distorted not just by the yellow light but by fear.

Said Mac: "Give'm a radio check."

A radioman on the far left keyed his mike—Paul imagined—and made a sign Paul could just barely see, a thumbs-up.

Mac said: "Don't move. We'll wait here for daylight." And bending to Paul he said: "Don't move. Get some sleep."

Paul forgot to say his prayers that night. He took off his flak vest and arranged it as a pillow. He heard Captain Clare speaking softly into the microphone:

"We are twenty meters north of you, by the cactuses. Maintain a listening watch. Be ready to move at first light."

Paul stretched his body on the sandy ground and found it to be the closest thing available to paradise. His slab of a pillow was quite all right. He sat up, took the new leather prayer book from his shirt pocket, and placed it in his helmet, which stood beside him like a bowl. This book had been given to him by his aunt, his father's sister, who was the only mother he had ever known. He pulled out his keys—he was still carrying the keys to his car and the rectory in Fall River. He placed these soundlessly in the upturned helmet.

He didn't suspect that if he closed his eyes he would drop off so quickly. He lay down and let the relief and gratification fill his legs and soothe his mind. Immediately his mind trotted off in pursuit of strange unnatural images; he listened in surprise to the voice in his mind as it trifled with the question of his life.

Paul was here for a reason. It was not only relief from boredom and it was not only to serve, although he intended to serve with all his strength. No. The reason was doubt. Paul did not believe in devils but he understood why others might. His doubt had a personality like a devil's. He could not ignore it and he could not live with it. Others did; he could not. And exactly like a dwarf devil it would follow him forever.

"Not follow," he said. "It will lead me. It already does."

Since he could not tolerate this and since he intended to continue as a priest, he must—kill it?

"I must make it go away."

And when the war started he saw how he could do that. The plan itself came in a flash, but it took him a long time to see that he had actually to do it. He reasoned that if God is anywhere—if He can be found—He can surely be found on the battlefield. Therefore go to Vietnam and search. It was a good idea, but nearly two years passed before he put it into action. He joined the Navy on the condition that they send him to serve with the marines in Vietnam, and they were happy to oblige.

Now he lay here with a sweet lassitude invading his limbs. His mind at the same time was loosening its grip on reality and saying some peculiar things about the "theme" of his life. He would never know what was said; the drama left no trace or text. But in the morning he did remember that it had been strange, and that it related to his—search. If God does not appear to men dying in battle, to whom does He appear?

"Chaplain, wake up." This came in a quiet voice, but a voice, not a whisper.

He opened his eyes and saw a marine standing over him. He closed his eyes.

He had not recognized the voice or the man but then he realized this might be his minder, a man he had never heard speak except in a whisper and had never seen except in the dark. He opened his eyes again and they burned as the sweat poured in. He squinted. There stood a marine with a rifle slung over his shoulder, his helmet cocked at an angle, offering a canteen.

Paul sat up and his head hurt. He closed his eyes and his brain cracked, but he knew he had finally come to the place where you must go on.

The place was unknown. There was nobody except himself and the marine.

"Thirsty, sir?"

Paul eagerly took the canteen. It tasted of iodine but was cooler than last night's drink.

"Finish it," the man offered.

Paul did, without first asking if the man had any for himself. Then came a bolt of guilt and he said: "Did you drink first?"

"I'm fine, sir. We'll be at the CP in an hour anyway."

"Where is everybody?"

"They're saddling up, sir. We gotta *di-di* on outa here."

Paul slipped the prayer book into his pocket and buttoned the flap. He pocketed his keys. He stood up and the headache punished him severely—and he stood there, hoping to calm it down. He was not quite a steady man standing there. He dreaded stooping to pick up the flak vest, and the idea of placing the helmet on his head was—

With the headache beating inside he had no need to fret about brushing his teeth or shaving. He turned and saw the cactuses, low flat ear-like things half the size he remembered. For the rest of his life these plants associated themselves in his memory with pain and nausea. He looked down the sandy slope at the depression, the LP, and he stooped for his helmet and flak jacket and paid the price. He had no urge to urinate and was not hungry.

"I'm ready," he said.

"The skipper wants us in the middle of the line, sir. We'll keep back from that antenna."

Paul said that would be fine, and did not ask why. He thought: "I can't say 'Why why why' every time the man tells me something."

"You go first, sir. Just go down the line and I'll show you where to slip in."

So Paul started down the file of waiting men and the first he came to was Gunnery Sergeant Hitchcock, who gave him a half-smile. Each man looked at him as he walked the file, and he felt as if he were the object of a ritual.

A man said, "Thanks for keeping the rain away, Chaplain."

Paul thought of his upturned helmet and for the first time saw the possibility of its filling with rainwater and floating his new prayer book. "You're entirely welcome." Paul heard this and the cocksure tone of it, and couldn't believe it was he who said it. Could the men be seeing the man he pretended to be—stocky, fearless, and flip?

Some of them were standing—they were spread out at intervals—some were down on one knee with their rifle butts in the sand—some sat on their helmets. One man spat between his legs and Paul thought: "Is that meant for me?" But this same man called out: "Welcome to Dirty Delta, Chaplain." Others spoke: "Morning, Chaplain," "Hello, Father." On down the line, and Paul greeted each man.

They had something in common besides youth. It seemed to Paul that they were—sincere? Honest?

The minder steered him into a gap in the middle of the file. Paul could see the antenna well ahead, where Mac was speaking to a marine carrying a radio. The marine spoke into his handset. Mac's eyes met Paul's, then Mac raised his right arm and held it—the men got up.

Mac dropped his hand and the column moved.

Paul started to recite his morning prayers. And when, later that day, he tried to remember where he had gone astray, he had no idea, but he never finished the prayers. He felt he was walking on the rim of the world.

There was nothing to be afraid of, he knew—and he was not afraid! He marched in this column with the antenna bobbing at the head of it. He saw the broad shoulders of the captain, turned and saw the men following him—and nobody showed the slightest sign of fear—walking with weapons dangling in their hands or propped casually on their shoulders, smiling, some of them nodding at him as though they knew exactly how he felt—tramping along five meters behind the man ahead, turning to smile at his keeper. He felt something exceedingly strange. He didn't want to be anywhere in the world but here.

Thirst, headache, heat, bugs—danger? Was it dangerous? "Who cares!" This came as a shout in his mind. "This is the place! I'm glad!" The whole column pressed forward, following Mac and the antenna carried by his radioman, who marched just behind him. And the men near the front sometimes turned to see those following. And a man near the middle—Paul himself, the newest man here—could watch the sinuations of the column as it dropped with the terrain.

Paul began to notice the order of it. It wasn't a bunch of guys out for a walk. He saw near the rear a man carrying a gun noticeably bigger and longer than the rest. He had a belt of brass cartridges slung across his chest and was certainly a machine gunner. The men before and behind him carried smaller rifles and heavy metal boxes. Just behind this group Gunnery Sergeant Hitchcock marched, as effortlessly as if he were strolling a gravel walk. Paul churned through the sand. Hitchcock seemed to glide over it. And Hitchcock was the nerve in the tail of the reptile. And this nerve had an instrument of destruction. Let no one forget it. The reptile had a stinger in its tail.

They halted long enough to reintegrate the flankers. Then the lead disappeared in a slit in a jungle wall, a solid growth only about ten feet high. And the trail began to curve; Paul could see only three men ahead, then two. It looked like: three men—alone—confined on the sides and above by green. He looked back. His guardian's face wore a newly serious expression.

They had not come through this brush last night and Paul didn't know why they were in it now. He kept the pace and the interval. Here came the headache with new fire. His knees grew weak. "How much can a man sweat?" he thought.

The alley, bored through the greenery, cut off vision and air. Breathing was like gasping for a worthless mixture of hot gases without oxygen. The chest expanded, the air flowed in, but there was no relief, no kick.

Had you been poised over the column in a helicopter you would not have seen it. And if your eye were situated just six feet above the ground you might have missed the thing that had drawn MacHugh Clare into this green alley.

The soil here was true soil, not sand. The ground had a gentle lift to it, and tilted to the right; and on the right just at the edge where the growth encroached on the trail there appeared from time to time a linear mark—noticed up to now only by Mac, Gunnery Sergeant Hitchcock, and one or two troopers.

Paul Adrano saw one of these marks and it meant nothing to him, perhaps because it was so familiar. It was only when he saw another that he realized it did not belong here. He edged nearer, keeping the pace, but the line was broken and he could see nothing that resembled what he had decided it must be. He concluded he had been mistaken. He marched. He kept his place in the column and kept his surmise to himself. But he was aroused now. Had he seen a pair of black eyes staring silently at him from within the bush he could not have been any more—aroused—than he was. He marched and his knees turned to jelly. "I'm tough. I'm strong!" Then why was he collapsing after fifteen minutes of easy walking? Was it the helmet and flak vest? He knew that when his body had exhausted its capacity to perspire, the real trouble would begin. He wanted to pray: "God, let me make it to the CP before—"

His untrained ear registered a noise, a bang. Not a *crack* but a small hollow boom. Suddenly everybody was down and the man in front of him was rolling with his rifle clasped against his chest. Paul watched in amazement. He did not hit the deck. Then a terrific blow struck him from behind and knocked him clear to the ground. He was in the dirt! His helmet was in his face—he couldn't see. Some terrible weight bore him down.

"Stay down!"

It was his guardian. Paul struggled but his arms were pinned. "Stay down!" Paul lay there, moving just enough to pull his face out of the helmet and now he saw the roots shooting out of the trunks of the little trees. How strange they were: roots that shot out of the trunk in all directions a foot above the ground and went down slantwise, digging into the earth.

His guardian clapped Paul's helmet back on his head (no headache, but Paul didn't notice) and the two lay still and Paul thought: "Where are they?" By *they* he meant the enemy.

Now Paul felt gratitude and was about to say something when he heard a shout being relayed down the line: "Corpsman up! Skipper's hit!"

The message went right past Paul and his guardian. Then a man with a pistol (no rifle) and a pack on his back ran past, going up the line.

The Gunny shouted something from around the curve in the green alley and Paul heard some scraping and rolling. The man ahead squirmed around and faced one way and Paul's guardian faced the other.

The guardian said: "Stick by me."

But Paul rose to his feet. He knew he was doing it but didn't know the man doing it.

The guardian hissed: "Down! Get down!"

But Paul began to run forward, winding along the tunnel-like path, passing one man after another, all of them prone and with weapons ready. He saw them staring, amazed, at him as he passed. And maybe there was something wild in his eyes, which they reflected back to him. As he thought of it later this seemed to explain the wild strange looks they gave him, each man rolling a quarter turn to watch him running up the line. His brain was shut off. His senses functioned. He saw the faces one after another, and recognized that two men lying side-by-side, both pointed the same direction, one of them holding a belt of brass cartridges out of the dirt—that these two were a machine-gun crew—but this recognition was the heaviest work his brain could do. All his powers were shut down except: Go!

Then he saw the antenna, but it was pulled down on a cord of some kind; it was not up and straight but down and doubled. Odd. What's that mean? Then he came upon Mac.

Mac too was bent over, and the Navy corpsman was kneeling in front of him. The radioman stood beside him, upright. Paul was suddenly there among them. He read the name Clare penned in black on Mac's camouflaged helmet cover. He put his hand on Mac's shoulder.

He felt the wet cloth, and the great shoulder encased in armor. He started to bend, to see what they were looking at, and he saw blood—but Mac straightened and turned (he was wondering who would touch him like that)—and their eyes met—they were not a handsbreadth from one another—and Paul saw those—burning—confident eyes—

"Father!" Mac cried and smiled.

"Are you all right?"

"I seem to be just fine."

"What—"

"Take a look," said Mac.

"Your leg!"

"That's nothing. Look at our friend here, Miss Bouncing Betty."

Paul saw a dull-green cylinder with a kind of chimney. He sniffed an odor, sharp and sulfurous.

Mac's trouser leg was ripped. A stream of blood diluted with sweat trickled down to the top of the boot. The Bouncing Betty lay at Mac's feet like a discarded beer can—but big.

Murmuring "Just let me get some pressure" the corpsman began winding a bandage around the leg.

The radioman whispered: "Jesus, Skipper."

Chapter 3

Sarah Clare

Sarah Clare and her friend Denise were arguing.

"You turned out to be a quitter!" Denise lamented.

"Watch your step," said Sarah, ready for combat.

"You gave up too soon."

"How would you know when too soon is? What do you know about it?" Sarah burst out.

"Everybody praised you and everybody was predicting a great future for you and now you tell me—"

"What do you know about it?" Sarah pressed on. "There was only one person—"

"I did know. I was in the cast too if you'll be good enough to remember."

"Of course I remember. Neither you nor anybody else knew what I know."

"What was that? What's the big secret?" Denise demanded.

"I was faking it, that's all," said Sarah ruefully. "I wasn't acting, I was just saying memorized lines."

"Acting *is* faking," Denise fired back. "You were terrific but I—"

"Cut it out!"

"—but I think you lost your nerve, is what I think."

"Ohhhh no. Pardon me for boasting but—talk about nerve—the thing I did was the nervy thing. To keep at it, to lie to myself about my so-called talent, that would have been chicken."

"Sarah, you are full of it. You've got real talent, the whole cast said so. You should have heard us when you weren't around."

"It's a good thing I didn't."

"You've got that body, those eyes, that smile, that voice."

"None of that is acting. I was a mediocrity, Denise. You are a great friend but I know what I know. I decided I wouldn't waste my life as a mediocre actress just to live the romance of the stage."

"You could have been a movie star."

"It was the stage I cared about, just as you did."

"Sarah, be realistic. Fat women get nowhere in the movies or on the stage, either one. I never even dreamed."

"Yes you did and it was you who had the talent, Denise, damn you. And you are not fat."

"Please don't turn this around. I was getting nowhere fast. You were the rising star."

"I might be pretty good—at something else—at least I hope," Sarah murmured meditatively.

"What?"

"I'll tell you sometime. I'm testing myself right now."

"What! Tell me. I told you about Tommy—and my supposed pregnancy and all that earthshaking drama."

"I'll talk when I'm ready. I don't jump till I'm ready."

"O.K., then I won't talk about my life, either."

"Yes you will. You are incapable of being silent about your troubles."

The two women had studied in the same drama program at the University of Wisconsin. They encountered each other by accident in the commissary at Camp Lejeune after a separation of four years. They discovered they even lived in the same tract housing for junior officers, called Tarawa Terrace. Sarah had been amazed at her flood of good feeling when she and Denise embraced beside their grocery carts. Now they sat in Sarah Clare's half-bungalow on Hagaru Drive in Tarawa Terrace drinking coffee and debating the astounding news— to Denise—that Sarah had quit acting right after her great triumph in

Mrs. Warren's Profession. This had been the last production of the women's last year at Madison. Sarah had told nobody of her decision at the time, but Denise's questions this afternoon forced it out of her.

Through high school and college Sarah Woodley—the woman who would become Sarah Clare—had called herself an actress. She uttered the word to herself alone, never to others. In the theater of her mind this was what she was. She never had an "identity crisis," even though that was a popular pastime in those days, because if she ever suffered a doubt about who or what she was, the answer came right up: "Actress." She kept it to herself because she feared that she was not a natural. She studied, trained, read, practiced; she played in student productions. And if people praised her and suggested she had a future she laughed and assured them that she enjoyed it, and that was enough. But secretly she burned for a career on the stage.

In her senior year at Madison a student director chose her to play the daughter in *Mrs. Warren's Profession,* a play she had read twice for pleasure. She saw this as her big chance—and dreaded it. The source of this dread was a deeper dread that if she were not, after all, an actress worthy of the name, then her future was an awful blank.

Her character in the play was an ahead-of-the-wave feminist and free spirit determined to "do something" in the world who discovers that the money that has paid for her upbringing and education, and given her the exhilaration of being free to direct her own life, has all been extorted from girls who sell their bodies on the streets of Europe. Mommy is a madam. Sarah was perfect for the role physically. When she moved the whole stage came to life around her. Her voice carried a strong, vital music to the farthest row. The connection, through her mother, to prostitutes covered her character with a glow of sexuality.

But she began rehearsals in fear. And as she went deeper into the role she saw what was coming. She was like a prisoner walking the plank. It turned out as she expected. She didn't fail; she even succeeded in a way, but she never made the critical shift from understanding her character to merging with her. From beginning to end she remained Sarah Woodley.

Yet everybody praised her performance, Denise was right about that. It seemed that Sarah alone knew the secret. On this point it was

Sarah who was right, of that she was certain. Her performance had been all technique. The spirit and energy that animated the stage were Sarah's and not that of Mrs. Warren's daughter.

She also noticed that most of the praise was connected somehow to her physical body. Denise was right on this point too. Sarah was tall and finely formed. She had startling dark eyes, and a surprising, expressive smile; and she had "presence"—but she came to believe that this only meant they wanted to look at her. If she aspired to be an actress that would never be enough.

She arrived at a painful conclusion. As a woman on the stage she was a middling talent at best. She told this to no one but her mother. And in three long dialogues the mother and daughter determined it would be foolish for Sarah to spend the decade of her twenties waitressing in New York or L.A. and auditioning for her big chance when she knew the outcome already. Her mother had seen the performance three times. According to Sarah's own standard there could be only one outcome that was satisfactory; she had to be sensational or she'd walk off the stage.

She married Mac because she loved him, but it was also a convenient time in her life to marry. She had thought of marriage from the moment she stood watching him at a party in Madison. She smothered the actress flame; she still sensed herself at the center of a theater, but this time the script was reality. Not just a wife, she was now in the process of defining herself as a human being, one who is not acting in a play but living a real life. She was happier. She felt for the first time the happiness of self-discovery, or a particle of it. She saw it as her duty, her life process, to wait watchfully for a clearly defined role. She was alive to possibilities, or strove to be. Mac was in the Marine Corps for a good long time, so she had all the space she needed to roam and search. She thought of his release date, June 1968, as her deadline. That was when they'd embark on a presumably normal life, one they had never lived, because Mac was already a marine officer when they got married. So—what did "normal life" mean?

When the Marine Corps sent Mac to Vietnam she had stayed at Camp Lejeune. What was the point of moving to his new unit's home base in California, simply to live in the same atmosphere at Camp Pendleton? But she was bored at Lejeune, living in Tarawa Terrace.

She got a job typing at a law firm in Wilmington. She already knew half the jargon from her father's table talk. But it turned out that even the most dramatic document, such as a threatening letter to opposing counsel, thrilling as it might be to write, or scary to read, was drudgery to type. She started going to the O Club on the base, a country-club kind of oasis in the woods, but this could be dangerous, even if she were accompanied by a friend. She certainly couldn't go alone and drink even one drink without feeling the eyes of the men on her, and fearing the gossip of the women. Victorian concepts like "scandal" and "reputation" were not anachronisms at Camp Lejeune. If she didn't watch out they'd begin asking, Was she sleeping with Captain X or Major Y while Mac risked his balls in Vietnam?

So she never went alone to the club or even a movie. Being sometimes unable to find a female partner she spent too many nights at home in her half-bungalow. She grew tired of music, even Beethoven or Brahms, and of books, even the best. Maybe that explained her joy on seeing Denise pushing a grocery cart in the commissary. Now they could go out together and—as Denise said—get plastered like they used to do in Madison. Actually it was Denise who got plastered and Sarah who drove home. But Denise was cover, and Denise was her old pal. She was fond of her. Denise's husband, Tommy, of course was in Vietnam too.

But during the pre-Denise phase at Lejeune, with boredom and sexual hunger distorting her mental life, and with her hatred of typing quickly overpowering the feeble belief that everybody has to work at a job, she began one night to write a scene in a play. Like acting, this was make-believe, but if reality was represented by typing, she was happy to escape it.

She assembled a set of girls from a rich Milwaukee suburb, River Hills, and put them into a mammoth clique-ridden high school, Nicolet High School, and listened to their ridiculous chatter. Pretty soon it was making a joyful noise in her head. She tore up the scene with gusto and started over, and it got better. It didn't lead anywhere, it was just a bunch of pampered adolescent brats struggling in a collective identity crisis, but to Sarah it was alive, funny, and almost real.

She gave the best lines to one particular girl who was obviously herself. And she delighted in the paradox that a suburb and school designed by wealthy parents to solve all their children's problems should create others for which there was no solution. To these girls their school was a mental hospital and their suburb sterility itself. There had to be a better life somewhere, one that meant something, and they would find it—or would they?

"It'll be a better play if they don't!" she said one night.

Denise was launching a new assault on Sarah's decision when the phone rang and put an end to silly chatter for that day and for several more to come. Sarah pulled the plug on the coffeepot. The women put on their coats, turned right at Sarah's front door, and crossed three yards. A lieutenant in uniform answered Sarah's knock.

The lieutenant opened the door wide and Sarah entered the house. Behind him she saw two women of her own age, who rose and came forward to greet her.

The lieutenant had now recognized her and was shaking her hand. He was the youngest-looking officer Sarah had ever seen. His neck, hands, and fingers were long and limber. Sarah and Mac had met him at the O Club just before Mac went over. The lieutenant on that occasion beat out a message on the bar with his Naval Academy ring and challenged Mac to decipher it.

Mac said: "Easy. You're telling me you went to Canoe U."

Now the lieutenant said: "We're getting organized. Two ladies are in there now."

Denise looked up from under her black bangs, staring at Sarah, waiting. There came a murmur of feminine voices from a nearby room.

Sarah, turning to the lieutenant, asked: "What can I do?"

"We're figuring that out," he said. "Her mother's coming in tonight from Pennsylvania."

And Sarah asked immediately: "Where will she stay?"

"Here, I guess. I don't know."

"I mean where will she sleep?"

"Beats me," said the lieutenant.

Sarah opened the refrigerator and surveyed its contents. She said to Denise: "Well here's one job. Why don't you make a grocery list."

Minutes later Sarah found herself staring out the picture window in the back at the jungle gym, monkey bars, and barbecue pit in the common area. Here the children of marine families stationed at Camp Lejeune cavorted in good weather while the parents blackened burgers over charcoal. Now there was a light rain falling on autumn grass.

Sarah had introduced herself to the two women, and forgotten their names. No one was talking so it didn't seem to matter. The lieutenant brought a chair from the breakfast nook and Sarah sat and asked the women if they lived in Tarawa Terrace. They did. That was as far as the conversation went. Denise slid down a wall and hugged her knees.

Sarah paced and kept returning to the window. She thought it might not be so very helpful to take away all the little jobs that serve to occupy the mind; but she felt the momentum. The lieutenant seemed to imply that the "ladies" would soon issue forth with a work plan for the assembled volunteers.

Sarah dreamed up two jobs. She could get groceries and she could pick up the mother at the airport. She went down the little hall—the floor plan was the same as in her house—and knocked.

"Oh, hello, Sarah. We didn't know you were here."

Again Sarah found somebody falling back to admit her. She stepped into the room; two women moved aside like curtains and Sarah faced a young woman seated in a soft chair, nursing an infant.

Sarah and the mother exchanged a glance—the woman's eyes were enlarged, almost glassy.

The infant's color was a compound of pink and blue pigments from another world. The baby slept even as it sucked the breast, and Sarah drew closer and saw a blue vein in its head, and the pink depressed center, and the thin streaks of hair. The child's eyes pressed out against the blue lids, and its fingers curled against its own cheek. It was alive—taking nourishment, sleeping.

"Hello, Sarah," said the mother, and her expression and voice declared she had known Sarah would come.

"Mary, I am so terribly sorry," and Sarah bent to kiss Mary's forehead and then the baby's, so much hotter. As she straightened she took in Mary's stunned face, as full of mixed color, almost, as the baby's; and her eyes too seemed to press outward—from the swollen red lids.

Mary gave a little shudder, which she covered by a smile.

"You'll need groceries, with your mother coming," said Sarah. "So Denise and I'll hop in the car and go to the commissary and stock up for you. Is that O.K.?"

Sarah bent down close, looking hard into Mary's eyes.

"Yes. Thank you. Do you notice how she's grown?"

"I certainly do. In just a week! It's amazing, and she is beautiful, Mary."

"She's my little sweetheart." And Mary kissed her child and looked again at Sarah, distressed, and then aside.

Sarah left the room but looked again at Mary and saw her blank eyes staring aside. The image stayed in Sarah's mind and the eyes began to show pain and fear.

She told the lieutenant her errand, and she and Denise walked through the rain to Sarah's house along a curving street with bungalows scattered along either side, and cars, tricycles, and bikes in the driveways. This time they walked in the street to keep their feet dry. Sarah opened a drawer in her kitchen, took out her checkbook and car keys, and said to Denise:

"Ready?"

"Your house is the same as Mary's," Denise observed critically.

"Yes. Aren't they all the same—two patterns, left and right?"

"Mine's different. But so's yours in a way. You're so organized. Mary's a shambles, Mary and her house both. You are not a shambles, Sarah. You're an inspiration to us all."

"Of course. Get your place squared away, Denise, right now."

"That's me. A. J. Squared Away." But at the car Denise began stammering. "I'm glad to help you. I just don't want—for God's sakes, I just don't want to—talk about it!" She jerked open her door and slumped into the car.

Sarah replied: "I have exactly nothing to say about it."

"Neither do I! You know where Tommy is at this very friggin minute?"

"Yes, he's where Mac is."

"Yes!" Denise wrapped her coat tighter around her chest and flung herself back in the seat. "So let's not talk about it, O.K.?"

"We'll talk about groceries instead."

"Wonderful!"

"I'll push the cart."

"Right."

"You get salad makings, vegetables, and fruit. How's that?"

"That's just terrific, Sarah. I'll find you and dump it all in your cart. I am also an ace at getting milk and butter. What's Mac's RTD?"

"June fifteenth," said Sarah naming Mac's rotation tour date, several months in the mists of the future, when he could start home.

"Tommy's isn't till September."

"Oh. Well. Clock's ticking. What happened to your job?"

"I quit. I'd rather swing on the monkey bars."

"I quit mine too," Sarah said.

"I knew that already. You told me and I said if you can, I can, so I quit yesterday and now I'm looking, and everybody says they want permanent people only—'You military wives never stay.' "

"Yes. But I'll have to find something," Sarah said.

"Me too. Do you worry about Mac?"

"Of course. But not, you know, every single minute. Mac isn't going to do anything stupid."

"Tommy is. He's the daring young man on the flying trapeze."

"He'll get over that."

"Tommy says you're safe with marines because of the discipline. He says if they made him a lieutenant in the U.S. Army he'd draw up his will."

"Mac says the same thing."

"Liars."

"I think they have a point," said Sarah. "The Army's a pathetic mess, everybody says so."

"Yeah, the marines say so. If the marines are so hot why is Mary nursing an orphan? Woops! Talked about it."

"After you get the vegetables," Sarah said, "get milk and butter. Let's stick to the grocery business."

"You're right. Strictly groceries. Did you see her face?"

"Yes, I saw her face."

"And you can think about groceries?"

"I can and you should."

"Right! Cauliflower, broccoli—funny names when you think about it—asparagus! Cheese, milk—I'm reading my list."

"Like lines in a play," Sarah observed.

"Apples, oranges, onions. I am grocery-obsessed."

"So am I," said Sarah as she pulled out of the drive and crossed the railroad tracks and headed toward the commissary.

"Cabbage, radishes—more funny names."

"Denise, shut up please."

"Eggs! I forgot eggs. They're over by the milk. Are you paying for this?"

"Somebody has to pay for it."

"I'll help. Here." Denise opened her purse. "Ten dollars. Get the *ladies* to fork over and pretty soon this act of human benevolence'll turn you a profit."

Sarah took the bill, folded it, and slipped it into her shirt pocket as she drove.

"You have a dog, don't you?" said Denise.

"Yes, our boy Clinker. He was sleeping in my bedroom."

"Where'd you get the name Clinker?"

"CLNC," Sarah explained. "Camp Lejeune North Carolina. We found him starving out by the artillery range."

"You know, Tommy did something secret in the woods down by Onslow Beach once, I have no idea what. Do you know Tommy's men killed thirteen rattlesnakes once before they settled down to beddy-bye? Tommy said one guy screamed he had a snake in his sleeping bag."

"What fun."

"But it was a lie. He wanted to scare the ones who were already scared or something. Do you know what I'd do?"

"I suppose you'd go shooting out of the bag like a rocket."

"No, Sarah. What I'd do if Tommy was killed."

"I don't think anybody knows what they would do. You might think you know."

"I do think I know."

Sarah waited, not very eagerly, and at length asked: "O.K., what?"

"I'd get blind drunk."

"There's a novel idea."

"I'd take care to be vomiting drunk at the funeral, and scandalize his family. And I'd eat candy bars and soda pop till I threw up. I'd get fatter, and sleep late, and live on my pension, and go to movies, watch TV—and I would in every way go to pot."

Sarah looked at Denise's profile—so eager and forward.

"I would make myself so disgusting," Denise continued, "that even I would be unable to stand myself. Pasty skin, body odor, bad breath, lazy, fat, useless, watching TV, and I wouldn't send for my mother. Not *my* mother. And when they threw me out of Tarawa Terrace I'd move to some dirty hole in J'ville. What would you do?"

"If Mac were killed?"

"Yeah. Mac and Tommy blown to smithereens."

"Actually," said Sarah with hesitation, "I don't think about it. I'm not fit for anything the world needs."

"You could be a lawyer, with your stage presence, not that the world needs lawyers or actors, either one, but you'd be terrific. You'd command respect in the courtroom. 'Ladies and gentlemen of the jury, I am the grave and sincere Sarah Clare. I threw away a brilliant career on the stage to be here today guiding you to a truthful finding. Not just another beautiful face with clothes to fit my body. I am the eagle of the law. You can trust me.' Or: 'Ladies, pay no attention to my opponent. He's a man. Listen to a woman for a change.'"

Having watched her father perform in court, Sarah had, perhaps too easily, concluded she could do that part of the job well enough.

"That's a good idea," Denise resumed. "Lady lawyer—wool suit, leather briefcase. 'Hey, men, shut up and listen to a woman.' Or why not be a movie star, for the money."

"I could enjoy the part about listening to a woman," Sarah conceded.

Denise seemed to brood on this. "Tommy listened to me," she said, "when I told him please don't go over, and he said, 'I'll be *sent* if I don't volunteer.' But they don't send everybody and maybe, if he'd just kept his head down, he'd be at Onslow Beach right now killing rattlesnakes. But he did listen, I'll say that much. He listened, then went right ahead. Did Mac listen to you?"

"I never tried to stop him," said Sarah.

"Jeez, holy cow. Why not? Are you some kind of witch?"

"The same reason. We knew he'd be sent. Then they told him he could have Stateside duty if he extended for a year, but he already extended once, for officer training. Now he's ready to get out, and we want to start a family. He's got this dream about farming or logging or something, it's all pretty vague, but the one clear thing in his mind is, we start a family."

"What!" Denise cried, looking at Sarah sideways. "You can't be pregnant!" And she began counting on her fingers.

"No, no, we do it when he gets home," said Sarah, looking askance at Denise.

"So he's home in June. My God, you lucky woman. So you're starting a family in June? There goes your career. But you're not making sense if you'll pardon my saying so. He'd get out at the same time whether he went over or not, right?"

"Well they offered Stateside orders and nobody *said* his other option was Vietnam but we guessed as much. And he said if he didn't go over he'd forfeit the privilege of despising draft dodgers."

"Well that's worth something, I admit. I hate the revolting little shits myself."

"To Mac apparently it's worth something, if you take it at face value."

"Do you?"

"Of course not. The Marine Corps was going to send him and he volunteered for an assignment he wanted."

"I'm kinda lost, Sarah."

"I haven't told it right. He wanted to go. He doesn't hate draft dodgers but I'm sure he thinks of them as less than— What do I want to say?"

"Obviously, real men."

"Probably," said Sarah.

"Tommy wanted to go too. So he went—after 'listening' to me and my silly quibbles like 'you might get killed' and so forth. But didn't you care?"

"If he went? Sure I cared but he said it was something he had to do. He couldn't sit around Lejeune guzzling beer at the O Club when guys he knew were going you-know-where. But it's not entirely Mac's doing," Sarah went on.

"No, it's our genius leaders in Washington."

"I mean," Sarah persevered, "it's my fault as much as his."

"Oh sure! I can just see you kicking his butt out the door and screaming, 'Get your ass over there and kill me a thousand gooks!' Sure."

"Actually," Sarah hesitated, "I mean it."

"Your fault that the Marine Corps is in Vietnam? You are some powerful woman."

"No," Sarah said. "I was instrumental. Maybe I didn't intend to be, but I was.

"We were at Wisconsin," she continued. "This was before I met you. I was a junior and Mac was a second-year law student, having drunk his way through Letters and Science three years ahead of me. He's thirty now, I'm twenty-six, but somehow he was three years ahead in school. It doesn't matter. I do know it was 1962 and the war hadn't yet begun, or if it had, nobody knew it. But you could get drafted even then. Men who were not in school were called up."

"Don't I know it," Denise said cryptically.

"So I went to a party with my frivolous group and I can set the scene by saying that not a single person had lifted a finger for civil rights or any other cause, and I include myself. We were all from the suburbs of Milwaukee and I do not mean the southern suburbs either, where they make earth-moving machinery or something. No, the northern and western suburbs where there is no dirt, grease, or noise. If you grow a set of crooked teeth you'd better have them straightened or out you go. Old, sick, and smelly people are not admitted. You should visit River Hills or Whitefish Bay or Fox Point sometime and see what I mean. I was a rebel against all that conformity. It was pleasant being a rebel in Letters and Science while my father paid the bills and I seethed with contempt for River Hills and went back at Christmas to see the same friends I saw all year long in school. Am I making this clear?"

Denise said: "I lived in a place like that near Chicago."

"So you get the picture."

"Sure. You're talking about the smothering suburbs."

"Right. There were some law students at the party, which is one reason we went, to see these future Big Men who were already becoming what our fathers were, certainly what my father was. He is a generous reliable man and I love him—but at the time I thought: lawyer, that's no life! And I will tell you—perhaps you can imagine— among these future men of the business elite one caught my eye the moment I walked in, and that one was Mac.

"First was his voice, actually, that baritone. I heard it and went looking for the source of it. You don't hear a voice like that very often. What you hear is male actors straining to sound like that. Then his, call it projection, presence or something. There were twenty people there and as far as I was concerned, there was one. There was this MacHugh Clare figure, and myself gazing. I don't believe he noticed me, although he later claimed he did. He claimed he was smitten the instant he saw me but of course that's a lie, but I lapped it up, together with all his shockingly specific compliments. I fell for it! The truth is he never noticed me until I voiced my opinion when nobody asked for it. Then he did look at me and I knew at that moment, and so did he, that something had happened."

"Opinion about what?" Denise asked.

"Well that's the thing that rings down the centuries, or at least years. Mac was sitting on a couch in the middle seat with a male friend on either side and a bunch of other people, law students and kids from the college, and I was riveted, because Mac had just said he was thinking about quitting law school. And all my life I had listened to my father talk of 'the law' as a noble profession. Quit law school! Nobody did that! Then the guy next to Mac said, 'You can't quit. You'll be drafted.'

"There they sat in their outrageous male way, legs spread apart and a beer can clutched in the angle. The world had already begun to change, I mean we had at least heard of the civil-rights movement and of some trouble in Southeast Asia. Kennedy was talking about a country he called 'Lay-oss,' but we were the privileged, we and our younger brothers and sisters, the most privileged bunch of spoiled brats the world had ever seen. Mac groaned, 'Drafted, Jesus.'

"And 'The Army,' one guy said. 'March around with a bunch of morons while an officer screws your girlfriend.' To which Mac said, 'That won't happen.' Meaning? I thought he meant either he had no girlfriend, or if he did nobody would dare touch her. A message to me? 'Why quit law school? You'd be crazy,' one guy said. 'Think of the money.' And Mac said, 'I don't like it.' 'Don't like money!' 'Law school.' 'Don't like it then. Who does? Law school is a means to an end.'

"Somebody said means to what end and this man says, 'First, stay out of the Army. Then money.' 'Right,' said Mac, 'and end up in Whitefish Bay.'

"I've got to tell you, Whitefish Bay is the most boring, safe, and stupid suburb. That's when I stepped in, when he said something I could have said myself. Because I grew up right next to Whitefish Bay! But I didn't speak directly to him. I said to one of the crotch-men, 'A person, then, I guess you're saying, should take fatal poison to stay out of the Army?' You see what I'm getting at I guess. I had a vision of a certain kind of man and decided on the spot that Mac was that kind. I was smitten just because this Mac character was talking like—'Go on, draft me!'

"An hour later we were walking on Picnic Point and pretty soon we stopped and I remember saying, 'I am a patriotic woman and if they're going to draft you I want to express the appreciation of a grateful country.' It was a stupid spiel but I was embarrassed and I could hardly keep my hands off him—and Mac just laughed and—well, he didn't just laugh, he took his opportunity."

Said Denise: "I see. You let him lay you and therefore it's your fault he volunteered for Vietnam. Yes, logical."

"I just about said, 'Go ahead, quit!' "

"So?"

" 'And be drafted!' "

"You have a sick desire to feel guilty, Sarah."

"They drafted him into the Marine Corps and took one look at his mountain shoulders and listened to his rumble-thunder voice and said, 'Hey, mister, how'd you like to be an officer?' And it meant at least *two more years* in the Crotch, but I said, 'Take it!' And he took it."

"So why'd you do that?"

"Denise—we were mad for marriage."

"Oh. Oh. Day and night love, playing house, you wake up in the night and the dear boy has thrown his leg over you. I see what you mean. The blissful and carefree state of marriage."

"You see," Sarah said and her eyes narrowed as she thought about it, "had he said no to officer's training we could not have married, but he would have been out two years ago. *Out.*"

"He could have been killed in Vietnam two years ago," Denise parried.

"Not likely. He would have been nearing the end of his obligated service and it's unlikely he'd have been sent over."

"Well, Sarah, I have to agree, it wasn't Johnson and McNamara and that bunch of statesmen, it was the *lust of a woman* that sent Mac to Vietnam."

Said Sarah: "You've got it."

Returning to Mary's house, Sarah and Denise found two civilians from the Household Goods section assembling a cot in Mary's bedroom while Mary herself walked with slowly hesitating steps, like a bridesmaid, and sang in a low voice to her baby. But the baby was inconsolable. Sarah saw its little cheeks bunch up and its lips stretch as it cried out its desperation or pain. Then it paused in its shrieking long enough to gather breath for an even more terrible complaint.

The other women had gone and the lieutenant departed as soon as the cot was put together. Denise and Sarah made it up with sheets and blanket and a quilt that was the work, so Mary informed them, of the woman who would sleep under it tonight.

Looking out from the kitchen, where she and Denise were preparing supper, Sarah was fascinated by Mary's dancelike steps, consisting of a normal walking step followed by a slow dragging of the other toe, till it met the forward foot, when it moved into the lead, while the other came up quite sedately to join its mate, never losing contact with the floor. Mary sang and hummed to her baby in low gentle tones of wordless consolation. The baby calmed down, and her lids closed over the blue-white eyes, in which a deeper blue formed the center, and she went altogether still and slept on her mother's shoulder. The three women ate quietly, but Mary assured them the baby would not awake.

Sarah had little to say anyway and the quiet suited her. She did volunteer to meet Mary's mother at the airport. Denise also volunteered, and in the end they decided all three would go, plus the baby, if the baby did not start crying again. For the present it slept in peace on its mother's shoulder, and Sarah watched it with a keen interest, as a creature destined to become such as she was herself, who until last week had lived in a different universe, to the accompaniment of the maternal heartbeat.

When she was a little girl Sarah had imagined life in the womb—the jostling, darkness, muffled sounds of voices, heartbeat—and had discussed it at some length with her mother. She asked whether her mother, while carrying her, had ever stood near a whistling train, or fallen down the stairs, or gone out in winter without a coat. Her mother narrated two incidents—a shocking fall on the ice and a bird hunt with her father, where men were firing off shotguns all day long. Sarah searched her memory and tried to believe that she remembered both. Why had she not registered, or why had she lost all recollection of such noteworthy events in the first phase of her life?

Her mother's answer was that birth and early childhood were harsh and frightening, and it was for the best that we could not remember. Seeing the tortured countenance of Mary's baby, Sarah understood her mother's meaning. She felt a wave of love—and almost wept at the memory of her mother's care. She turned her face from Denise but in so doing revealed herself to Mary.

Mary smiled from her stricken heart and squeezed her hand.

"She thinks I'm crying for her husband," Sarah thought.

When the time came, the baby cried again, so Denise and Sarah left without Mary.

"O.K. now," said Denise when the passengers began filing through the gate. "Short, plump, white hair, blue hat made out of shiny straw, which she always wears when traveling—sounds like an all-American momma from the culture that is now being smashed by peaceniks and hippies."

"Here she is," said Sarah with certitude, and they moved forward to meet Mary's mother.

"Oh—you're Denise and you're Sarah," said the mother after the introductions had been made, pronouncing it "Say-rah." And she asked, "Are you girls marines?"

During the ride she asked if Mary was all right. Was the baby all right? When would the daddy's body come home? Was the body all right? Sarah's imagination ran with that one, and she pictured bodies that were all right, and some that were not.

Although this woman was not at all like her own mother, Sarah felt an immediate and surprisingly strong affection.

Denise drove into the driveway and Sarah carried the lady's suitcase, and they all three approached slowly, keeping pace with Sarah.

She listened, and heard no crying from within the house. Denise knocked and opened the door. The mother went first, then Denise, and finally Sarah, with the suitcase. Thus Sarah was still outside in the dark when the mother and daughter met in the lighted inside.

The door was half-blocked by Denise. Sarah reached it, set the suitcase down, and saw the embrace in the lighted hall of the mother and daughter, and heard Mary cry "Mommie!" in a breaking voice. The cry was the cry of a child, and the sobs were a child's sobs.

Sarah saw Mary fling her arms around her mother's rounded back, saw the light reflected on the lacquered blue straw hat on the mother's white head, and listened with pain to Mary's cries of "No, no" and "Mommie."

Sarah carried the suitcase to the bedroom, bent over the sleeping baby, and almost missed a strange scene flashing through her mind—of this baby grown to young womanhood, explaining to somebody at a party why her last name was different from her mother's. But Sarah caught it, the scene, by the last trailing ribbons of its image. She straightened but could not take her eyes off the baby, who was too simple to have developed any faculty so touching as trust. She was innocent even of that.

Sarah and Denise left quietly. They stood by Denise's car.

Denise said, "But there's one thing about her I envy."

"What?" Sarah was shaken and wanted to be alone.

"Her mother," Denise replied. "If I had a mother like that—"

"Your mother is difficult?"

"Ha! I could take anything, and I mean anything, if I had been raised—with love. By a mother I could call Mommie."

"I had a good mother," said Sarah. "She's gone, but I had her."

"I'm sorry she's gone, but you had her."

"Yes, until quite recently."

"Well, you're lucky."

Later, walking alone on Hagaru Drive, Sarah was conscious of the stars and seemed to know they were there before she looked. When she did look up, and paused, the immensity of the heavens impressed itself upon her mind without diminishing her. She did not feel puny merely because the heavens were vast.

On the contrary something seemed important, perhaps more important than before she looked up. The "something" was perhaps just her life, this life that she intended to live. She was flooded with a sense of significance and need. It was the opposite of recklessness or self-surrender. It was a need to grasp life.

Letting herself in the house she stood motionless for several seconds, thinking in the dark, going back over one thing Denise had said: "Did you see her face?" And Sarah tried to imagine the woman whose face she had seen, Mary when nursing her child and looking up at Sarah, transforming into the woman who cried out "Mommie!" and "No, no!"

And Sarah thought: "What will she do?"

The pension for lieutenants' and captains' widows was very meager. Next she thought: "What would I do?"

She saw herself on a dimly lighted stage, rocking, nursing a baby, the father dead—Mac dead—herself destitute but giving milk.

Looking back, Sarah could see two moments when the future was trying to reveal itself to her. The first was the party in Madison that she narrated for Denise. She saw a man and responded as she never had to any other man. The party itself was somehow more important than their lovemaking afterward on Picnic Point.

The other scene took place more than a year later, in the time between Mac's quitting law school and his being drafted into the Marine Corps. That was Sarah's senior year in Letters and Science. Mac had spent it drifting around the West, earning a living by the skills he had gained working for his father in the house-construction business in Stevens Point. He was a carpenter and heavy-equipment operator in California and Colorado, returning in his final summer to help his father expand the business.

Stevens Point is in the "Golden Sands" of central Wisconsin. Farmers and scientists at the university had discovered that sprayed fields in that area drained the water quickly and more or less straight down to a water table remarkably near the surface. Except for evaporation loss and plant nourishment the water could be lifted by electric or gasoline-driven pumps and sprayed again, the same water wetting the same fields and the same crops repeatedly. The irrigation boom was beginning, and land that was covered with worthless jackpine was being cleared, wetted, and sown in vegetables. Mac's father, Jim Clare, borrowed $40,000 to acquire a drilling rig, an extra crawler with backhoe, and three used trucks. He hired drillers, electricians, and laborers and started searching for farmers with good money or good credit.

Mac's draft notice arrived in the middle of the summer. Knowing his days were numbered he expended whole tank cars of gasoline driving to Milwaukee to see Sarah. She was in love. He could tell that, but she was also in doubt. That was equally clear.

Seeing her father's house in River Hills, having met the quietly formidable Warren Woodley, and having tried to explain why he had quit law school, Mac began to see the source of Sarah's doubts. It seemed to Mac that Sarah had listened to the dialogue between him and her father with acute sympathy—for Mr. Woodley. What puzzled Mr. Woodley was why any promising young man of reasonable intelligence would quit the UW Law School. He asked Mac if he had completed his second year and Mac said yes. He asked if he could go back for his third year, after he did his military service, and Mac said that he could, but would not. This darkened Mr. Woodley's face by two or three shades.

Mac decided to meet Sarah's misgivings head on. He invited her to Stevens Point to see where he came from and meet his father. She consented. So—he had two weeks left, and he was driving her to his father's house, which, together with six others like it, would just about fill the ground floor of the Woodley domicile in River Hills.

They were approaching Stevens Point via Waupaca and Amherst when Mac veered left and aimed the car toward the Wisconsin River on a county trunk road. The land rose and dropped gently from the level while the car went straight west.

Mac said: "Raise your right hand."

He raised his own and she said:

"I'm not taking any oaths today, mister."

"Ha! Who's asking? Hold it like this," said he, with his palm toward his face.

She complied and he said:

"Close your fingers like mine, spread your thumb. That's good.

What a quick learner. Now, you see, we've got a map of Wisconsin. The space between your thumb and index finger is Green Bay. See it?"

She ran the index finger of her free hand around the shores of the bay and ventured: "Here's Lake Michigan and over here on the left is the Mississippi."

"Right. And the palm, the hollow, is where we are right now."

She touched her palm and said, "This very spot."

"And if you look out the window you'll see we're at the bottom of Lake Wisconsin. Go on, look."

"Yes, I see. When are we going to drown?"

"We're driving on the bottom of an ice-age lake, Woody, and that's an important fact."

She watched the road slipping under the car; she let her gaze wander over the bright green fields, divided here and there by woodland. Seeing a great wheel and a spout she asked: "What's that monster wheel?"

And he said: "That's what we call a center-pivot irrigator."

He accelerated. It was a bright day and they were tooling along a dirt road colored light tan, that glared almost white in front of the car, while a billow of dust chased them through fields whose rows of greenery glistened with moisture. Sarah exclaimed on seeing another pivot system standing in a rank of great wheels. Nearest the road was a wheel eight feet high, with a spigot shooting pulses of silver over the road. He drove headlong onto a mud slick and into the jet of flying water that crashed against the windshield. Mac hollered like a maniac and Sarah gasped as the cold spray reached through her window and splattered on her shoulder.

She looked back and saw a series of wheels crossing a field side by side, widely separated by segments of a long pipe, and clouds of sunlit spray hovering along the entire length of the colossal pipe.

"Stop!" she cried.

But he drove on, saying, "There's one down the road that my dad and I built."

Looking back again Sarah saw the anomalous dust cloud reinventing itself as the car creased along the dirt path. They passed through a shaded woods and the cool air spread a pleasant chill over Sarah's wet shoulder and arm. Then they burst into the sun, and she saw another irrigated field ahead, and now Mac was slowing the car, then stopping. He cut the engine and sat there as if in reverence, watching the shoot, shoot, shoot of water jumping from the nozzle above the wheel nearest the road. This one didn't quite reach it.

Mac said: "That one's set right. It's not supposed to hit the damn road."

"Is that the one you built?" She watched it too and couldn't pull her eyes away after she had caught the rhythm of it.

He said that he, his father, and his father's crew had built it. He got out, went around and opened her door, and they looked at each other and she saw the excitement in his eyes. She took his extended hand and they set off down the road. They jumped a dry ditch, rejoined hands, and waded together over rows of thigh-high plants. Mac said they were potatoes or snap beans or something; he didn't know one plant from another.

They turned to travel along, instead of across the rows, holding hands, separated by a single row. The sandy earth gave off puffs of dust, which Sarah imagined rather than saw, down there under the foliage. The clouds of silver spray billowed before them, and pretty soon their legs were soaked and Sarah felt her feet squelching in her shoes. She was cool from the waist down while the sun scorched her shoulders and burned into her dark hair. They stopped at the edge of the watery billow and Mac said:

"If we watch for a second we'll see it move." He said the farmer could adjust the speed depending on weather and season. Sarah turned her eyes to the great steel spokes of the nearest wheel, and waited for evidence of movement. The wheel crept stealthily forward.

As Mac discoursed on the system she was more focused on him than on his facts. He said the water table was just five feet, certainly not deeper than fifteen feet below their shoes, and that the well he and his father's men drilled here was just ninety feet down, but deep into the earthen sponge. He called this system a 360-degree center-pivot irrigator.

Sarah looked down the row toward the center and the wheels seemed to march away from her eye in a cloud of active vapor. A great pipe carried the water from the center outward through the middle of each wheel. Mac said the spigot on the outermost wheel watered the corners of the field, and the billows along the pipeline covered the rest. All this time she observed not just pride but nervous passion in his voice and eyes, as if he were a scholar of some narrow subject who discovers some new thing that seems trivial to others but to him is a new source of inspiration. Never before had she seen a man of any age reveal, quite unconsciously, such emotion about a piece of machinery.

But she checked herself. It wasn't just machinery but a machine working within nature. She gazed at the silver brilliance coruscating before her, and felt the cool spray reaching her face on a puff of the breeze; and she looked around and behind her at the undulating field, whose rise and fall were only just discernible to the eye; and at the dark wall of jackpines. Shading her eyes, she bent back to let her gaze go into the royal blue of the limpid sky. She felt as if she were over-arched by the blue color, and she gripped Mac's hand tighter, with a rush of affection for him.

He was saying that he and his father would soon drill the well for a 180-degree system called a "wiper," where the arm described an arc instead of a circle.

"But I won't see the end of that job," he added.

She raised his hand to her lips.

They stood for a minute, listening to the gentle dripping from leaf to leaf.

Mac looked around, squinting against the sun, and said: "This field is a hundred and sixty acres, and the well pulls up a thousand gallons a minute. There are hundreds of these around here, and we drill more every year. A thousand gallons a minute, out of a shaft thirty inches in diameter. Woody, that's *water!*"

"I've never stood at the bottom of a lake before," said Sarah.

"You are now. How do you like it?"

Sarah smiled and said it was very beautiful. He watched her smile. She watched his face, his eyes, and saw that he loved her. She felt almost that he was offering it all to her, and therefore she had to speak immediately and honestly.

She said: "It's beautiful but I could never live here."

He held her eyes and waited patiently. The look of love in his eyes did not change.

She continued: "If I were a farmer, of course, it would be ideal. But—" She wanted to release his hand but some impulse restrained her and she held it more tightly and swung his arm nervously.

"That's all right," Mac said.

"To me this would be nowhere. I appreciate the beauty, the openness, the fertility and abundance of it, but—"

When she didn't finish he said again, "That's all right," and he smiled with something like encouragement in his eyes. "To most people it's nowhere, especially people from River Hills, I imagine."

"It's not that."

He surprised and disconcerted her by responding: "Not what?"

"Not whatever you meant by that remark. I can understand that you might think I'm somebody I am not, because of what you think of River Hills and all the—atmosphere of it. I hope I'm not a product of that. I hope you don't think I am."

"I don't," he cut in.

"I hope I'm a woman in my own right regardless of where I came from."

"I didn't mean to insult you," said Mac. "I meant that coming from that kind of place, and all that—should I say it?"

"Please do."

"—all that money—that you'd probably see yourself living somewhere else. That'd be natural enough. This is pretty elementary. But I never said we should live here."

"You never said we should live anywhere."

"No. I haven't said that yet."

She pondered the "yet" as they walked back to the car, still holding hands. Facing the irrigator again, they watched it for some minutes while it patiently bathed the sparkling crops, and Sarah felt the gratification of finding her hand in his. Whether their joined hands meant that she was giving, or taking, she did not know. She was conscious also of another impulse, of pride and confidence.

She said: "You have seen only one side of my father. He is proud of what he's achieved and he is trying to protect his daughter. I cannot blame him for that and neither should you."

"Protect her from what?"

"From a mistake. He was extremely poor as a boy and he doesn't want me or my sister to sink back into the poverty that he and my mother escaped."

"He's got a right to protect his daughters," Mac allowed, and she heard a gentleness in his voice that she loved. "But there's more than one way to live a good life."

"He understands that. He's a man of very wide experience."

"I'm sure he is." Mac paused.

"All right, so what are you saying?" Sarah said.

"No. What are *you* saying—that he has to protect you from me? Because I quit law school?"

"He may feel that way, it's possible. Which doesn't mean that I do."

"I hope you don't."

"You probably don't know—I mean really understand," Sarah said pressing her words out reluctantly, "how I love you, how you fill my whole mind when you're away, and how I love it that I can just think about you. I bet you don't know that!" She added the last in a burst of laughter.

"I guess I don't but I'm glad—"

"Oh how I wanted you to come back from out West last spring to see our play. I—you want me to see all this, and meet your father. I wanted you to see the play because I was an actress then. I wrote you about it and you didn't come."

"I'm sorry. I didn't—you're right, I didn't understand. And I thought there'd be other times. I was clear out in California."

"That was the last time."

"I didn't realize. I wish I had seen it."

"I didn't beg you because that would be stupid! You'd think, 'What an ego this person has.' "

"I'm sorry. I wasn't listening carefully, I guess."

"Don't apologize anymore. You didn't care enough, but maybe it's a good thing. I was too much in love with myself as an actress. I'll be more practical from now on. I talked to my mother about it and I am sure she talked to Daddy, I can see the relief written all over him, *thank god* just breathing out of him, but of course he hasn't uttered a word."

Mac said: "If you loved it, why quit? How can you know? I mean, doesn't it take years, and then you find out when it's too late to change? Isn't that the way it works?"

"For me, yes, it would have worked like that. Make the commitment when you don't know enough, and learn when it's too late. But yes, I'm certain. All I have to do, to confirm it, is to listen to you describe this machine, and I can compare your case and mine, and I see the difference right away. I was right and have no regrets, except that I did love it, but that was ego. Applause! Praise! I have only the regret that you never saw me on the stage because I know you would have praised me, whether I deserved it or not, and I would lap it up like a thirsty puppy."

Mac kissed her, and they went deep into each other's eyes for the reassurance and the joy of it.

"I am certain," Mac said, "I have no doubt at all, that we could make a good life. Your father's not the only one who cares about you."

"Mac, I know you care."

"O.K. then. Will you wait for me?"

"Yes."

Chapter 4

S-Curve

You have to fight the Marine Corps before you can fight the enemy.

After drawing up his plan for the operation at the S-curve, Mac took it to his battalion commander. This officer, his immediate superior, approved it in its entirety. Mac then had to present it to a meeting of the operations section at Regiment. This was the meeting he had attended before he talked to the 5 about R and R and before he picked up Paul Adrano at the O Club.

Mac told the meeting he would insert his troops at a point just west of his objective. This would allow him to advance to the search area without traveling on Route 5B, or any other road. He could surge straight east from his landing zone to the hill mass that he had been ordered to search. Route 5B was a north-south road bisecting a valley lying just west of the hill mass, Nui Gio, or Mountain of the Wind. The LZ lay between 5B and the foothills of Nui Gio, at 9 o'clock from the center of the op area. If he inserted there he could proceed directly to a tableland low on the west slope of Nui Gio, which he considered the most likely place for the enemy to depot his supplies. Mac's job was to find and destroy supplies.

Mac was keen to demonstrate the advantages of this LZ because he expected somebody at the meeting to propose another that he did not like. The other one lay north of the hill mass at about 12 o'clock. To reach his prime search sites from the 12-o'clock LZ, Mac would have to walk his company around from 12 to 9 o'clock, and the obvious route of march was along 5B—and through a defile with hills looming on both sides.

If he dispatched a small force to secure the hills before passing the rest of the company through the defile he would consume all his first day. If he did not secure the hills first he would risk ambush. If he swatted the hills with heavy ordnance he would announce his path of march to the enemy commander.

The 3—the operations officer, a major—polished his magnifying glass and bent to the map. He said he believed Mac had made a pretty good case for the 9-o'clock LZ. (Mac had not mentioned the other.)

But then the air liaison officer, an aviator and, like the 3, a major, and therefore Mac's superior, raised the objection Mac had anticipated. He asked in all innocence whether Mac's proposed LZ lay within the artillery's fan of fire.

The artillery liaison officer, another major, placed his thumb on the U.S. Army Special Forces camp, where the two Marine Corps howitzers were being positioned at that very hour. The map was drawn to a scale of 1:50,000, so by spreading his hand and rotating his long finger, using his thumb as a pivot, he traced a fan-shaped arc 11,000 meters in radius. The 105-millimeter howitzers could hit targets within this fan of fire, but not outside it. The artillery liaison officer said one word: "No." The LZ that Mac wanted lay outside the fan of fire.

The aviator said the helicopter squadron would prefer and perhaps insist on an LZ that could be protected by artillery. What if the first bird to land were hit and disabled while discharging its troops? Could the sixteen men then on the ground defend it against a machine-gun or rocket attack? He said: "Don't forget, this is a Sea Knight." The CO of helicopters would scream bloody murder if he lost a Sea Knight.

Mac said the helicopter gunships covering the insertion, and fixed-wing planes orbiting above, could protect the LZ against any such attack. The aviator dismissed that as a fair-weather argument. Mac agreed it was, but countered that if the weather were truly foul, the whole lift would be postponed anyway. The aviator said again: "These are Sea Knights."

Mac conceded that a Sea Knight was a valuable piece of equipment, but said the enemy could have no intelligence on this operation because it was purely a USMC show—no ARVN to leak it. The aviator said: "We're lifting the 105's right now. The enemy is not blind."

"The fan of fire from that Special Forces camp covers hundreds of square kilometers," Mac said. "He can't possibly know what we're up to. We have no reason to believe he would preposition troops or heavy weapons at this or any other LZ."

The aviator insisted on minimizing the risk to the Sea Knights.

Mac said: "I'd rather minimize the risk to my troops." Then, hearing the conspicuous absence of the word "sir" in that sentence, he added: "That's my point, Major."

The major started to reply but the 3 held up both hands—and kept them up. Everybody waited. It was the 3's decision.

The 3 asked Mac how he'd feel about an LZ to the north of the hill mass. He pointed to a paddy area at 12 o'clock. This was exactly the LZ Mac had expected they would designate.

Everybody bent to the map and there was silence in the 3 Shop.

After an interval Mac said: "From that LZ I have to hike my people along Five B between these two hills"—pointing them out. "We could have enemy on high ground on both sides."

The aviator snapped: "This whole thing is a surprise, remember?"

"Yes sir. But Charlie could pull together a squad or two while we're landing."

"Trivial," said the aviator. "We'll cook the bastards"—meaning lay on a napalm strike.

"In fair weather, yes sir."

And the aviator shot back: "If the weather's foul you'll have artillery"—because the beetling hills lay inside the fan of fire.

Mac said carefully: "Except for the reverse slope, sir." And he touched with his fingertip the parts of the menacing hills that would be in defilade, and thus could afford the enemy safe ambush sites. Mac looked at the aviator with a "Do you get it?" meaning in his eyes.

"You can't have everything," the aviator said with indifference.

Mac turned to the 3 and stared at him patiently.

The 3 rendered the judgment that the point about protecting the

Sea Knights was a weighty one. "They are new birds; we've been waiting for those birds for a long time."

He bent to the map. He scanned it with his magnifying glass. For this peculiarity he had been named "Sherlock Holmes" by the staff. And then he took a grease pencil from his shirt pocket and made an X. The aviator had won. The conference moved on to other topics.

It was this concession, or defeat, that plagued Mac throughout the day that had begun with his brush with a Bouncing Betty. He was fully occupied with preparations for the next morning's lift, and this busyness prevented his thinking about an LZ he did not like, and a road he liked even less. But by late afternoon, when the platoon leaders reported their readiness to operate, he found he had made a decision. The regimental 3 had chosen the 12-o'clock LZ under the assumption that Mac would take his chances on Route 5B. But Mac now told himself that nobody had actually ordered him to march that way.

He assembled his "brain trust." This was the group Mac relied on to challenge his thinking and ratify his decisions. It was also his instrument for commanding the company. Its key members were his exec, the leaders of his three rifle platoons and the weapons platoon, the artillery forward observer, the forward air controller, and Gunnery Sergeant Hitchcock, whose moral authority exceeded that of any officer except Mac.

These men had already been briefed on the original plan and were expecting to insert at the 9-o'clock LZ. Mac gave them the bad news and they took it as such.

Then he said: "Gentlemen, two beers each and B rats for dinner. But first look at the map one more time. We haven't paid much attention to this wall." He touched it with his pencil. "Look at it now."

The wall, a crumbling but mammoth barrier, ran east-west and passed just north of the foothills of Nui Gio. It separated the LZ from the objective, but there was an opening where it ran along the edge of a village.

Mac said Route 5B was too exposed, with or without air and artillery. It would force the company through the best ambush site on the map, and it could be mined as well. It did offer an easy walk to the west side of the hill mass, but that was its only virtue.

A second route was offered by a trail that rose near the LZ and climbed the shoulder of Nui Gio (on the west side), passing through jungle most of the way. This was an even more direct route but the gunny called it "Ambush Alley." And there was a third choice.

The company could press over the west shoulder of the hill mass, through the jungle, parallel to the trail but not on it. This route avoided ambushes and mines, but it would take all day and exhaust the troops' energy and water.

Mac said: "There's a Local Force commander around here somewhere, and his job is to harass us if we approach a cache and to alert his boss at Main Force. Let's say the local man has a light platoon. Let's say he can pull it together in an hour, and reach an ambush site in two hours. If we take Five B he'll find it out in less than half an hour and send two or three snipers north to slow us down while he sets his ambush. We brush off the snipers and march into the ambush.

"We take the trail, same problem. But if we march straight south from our LZ, through the village and through the wall"—Mac paused, and touched his pencil to the map—"if we go through the wall, he won't know exactly where we're headed. I don't like this defile"—he meant a trail running between the wall and the base of the hill mass—"and I don't like this stream"—it was a pretty big year-round stream—"but maybe we can zip through before anybody knows we're there."

Mac saw mostly heads as they studied their maps and pondered. Following the principle of junior first, Mac bent his patient gaze on Gunnery Sergeant Hitchcock.

Wearing a faded green T-shirt, leaning forward with his elbows on his knees and his map spread before him, the gunny peered at the skipper and then back at the map. The tanned hands holding the map were large compared to his arms. His head and face were rounded and large upon his rounded shoulders. His eyes as they met Mac's were cynical, almost playful. He said:

"We could throw a couple snuffies in the stream and see how deep it is."

Mac smiled and turned to the exec.

"That's my question too, Skipper," said the exec. "Crossing that stream."

"A question," said Mac, "that none of us can answer."

6 1

Staff Sergeant Reggie Graves, known as "Graves Registration," was junior. He said: "I'd go through the wall if I was you, Skipper."

The gunny, seeing Mac's eyes on him, said: "Through the wall."

Mac shifted his gaze to the next man.

"Through the wall, I guess," said Lieutenant Kim Kolias, who had thrown stones into the sleepers at the LP.

And they continued in reverse order of seniority till Captain Kindred, the forward air controller, said: "I go where you ground pounders go."

Paul Adrano, a spectator and guest, watched Mac.

And Mac declared: "Through the wall."

"To the skipper's balls!" Captain Kindred proposed, lifting his beer can.

"On those two things I'll stake my future," said Mac agreeably.

Gunnery Sergeant Hitchcock smiled and turned his eyes before he turned his head, and looked at his captain. They all drank.

Their table was an ingenious construct of metal fuze boxes and wood ripped from pallets and 105-millimeter howitzer ammo boxes. These could be knocked apart or fitted together to make any number of appliances to ease the life of a marine in a static position. Shelves for shaving gear, mirrors, and candles; duckboard to lay a path through oozing mud; stools, tables, floors. If a company had to surrender these amenities to a relieving force, as Delta Company would do at first light, it could do so willingly, knowing that wherever it should go, when it finally settled down again it would find the previous owners' furniture intact; and if there were none, then a new supply of 105 cases would be available from the artillery.

A low sun was throwing beer-can shadows over the table. The men had already praised the sun and begged it to shine for the next week, an unlikely event. A man lifted a beer can and called on "Nimbus" to keep shining.

They ate and drank with the eagerness of men who expect to subsist on C rats for days or weeks, men who would next taste beer at the far end of some indeterminate stretch of unpredictable time—men who would have preferred cold beer but had convinced themselves that the warm kind is O.K. They were feasting on B rats—canned beef stew, canned tomatoes, all of it heated in a bucket—and John Wayne crackers.

"What is a man without balls?" queried the forward air controller, Captain Kindred.

"And what is celibacy without balls?" This shot through Paul's mind before he could stop it.

"On the other hand," the FAC continued, "the dead need no balls."

"What the dead may need I do not know," Mac said, "but I plan on putting my balls to good use."

Observing Mac's face down to the smallest detail—its livid color, the wide bridge to the squarish nose, the smile of big regular teeth—Paul saw or thought he saw a kind of darkness in the eyes, something dark in the deep blue of the eyes as Mac looked at the officers gathered around the table. Was he asking, "Will you make it?" as his gaze roamed from man to man.

"I've got another question," said Paul, addressing the whole table. "Sorry."

"Hey, ask!" Mac cried.

And Paul looked at him and thought he couldn't be drunk on two beers, so—

"O.K.," said Paul, "this is a dumb one, but why didn't it go off?"

"You're disappointed?" Mac asked.

"Hardly." And Paul saw in his mind what would have remained of Mac if it had gone off. The picture held him for a second till he said: "I understand that the propelling charge lifts it two or three feet off the deck—"

"Deck!" exclaimed Kindred, the FAC. "We got us a salty chaplain."

"O.K. the ground. Lifts it to the *right height*."

"And blooie," the FAC cut in. "Dear Sweetheart, the Commandant of the Marine Corps regrets to inform you that certain spherical essences—"

"But why, I mean, mechanically and so forth," Paul persevered, "didn't the explosive charge, if that's what you're calling it, why didn't that one go off too?"

Mac turned to the artillery forward observer. "Ollie, can you answer the chaplain's question?"

63

"No sir. Corrosion, dampness, a mechanical disconnect, a bad primer . . . If you'd brought it home maybe I could, but if I can't take it apart, no."

They hadn't brought it in. Mac had said to Gunnery Sergeant Hitchcock: "I don't want to look at it, Gunny. Blow the fucker."

The gunny blew it and it produced a solid *bam* in the morning air. After that the heat seemed heavier. They marched home, a walk in the sun. By seven they had reached the company command post. They got two hours' sleep and began preparing for the lift. It was now five in the afternoon and the company was ready for tomorrow.

"Do you mind?" Paul asked.

"Another question?" said Mac. "Gentlemen, do we mind?"

Cries of "No! Ask away."

Again it struck Paul that these men who had drunk two beers were acting as if they had drunk five.

Mac continued: "Chaplain, any one of us might someday ask you— a question—see what I mean?—a devilish question—and to us you are not a nuisance but a—I was going to say a warning, let me change that to a reminder—of everything we are usually happy to forget. So, by God, ask any question you want, and if we don't know the answer we'll make it up."

"O.K.," said Paul, "I've learned that those flashes up ahead, behind the mountains, were H and I's, 'harassing and interdiction fires.' Our side shooting artillery. But why? At whom?"

Said Mac: "Ollie, it's another artillery question."

"H and I's are fired on trails, trail junctions, known listening and observation posts, roads, bridges, and all that," Ollie explained. "The idea is to disrupt the enemy's system of supply and deny him sleep."

"Doesn't it deny us sleep too?"

"Ollie, the chaplain has a point," said Mac.

"We get used to it," said Dan Shaw, a platoon leader.

"We don't need sleep," somebody said.

There was no distinguishing these men by rank. They wore no insignia, only faded green T-shirts hanging on them like wet rags thrown over sweating shoulders. Paul alone had a white T-shirt, but Mac would loan him two green ones for the operation.

"But," Paul protested, "the men doing the firing, surely it disrupts their sleep."

"Yes sir," Ollie assented willingly.

"Well?"

Said Mac, "There is no 'well.' This is the Marine Corps, and Ollie has given you the Basic School answer. You might also ask if the H and I's ever harm the enemy."

"Do they?"

"Ollie?" Mac prompted.

"We don't know," said Ollie.

"And there you have it," said Mac. "Next question."

"All right," Paul went on, "this is very instructive. Now those big flash-and-boom things on our left, far away, those—"

"Ah yes! Thud thud thud. Captain Kindred, our forward air controller, air liaison officer, and toastmaster, will take this one. What about it, Kinny?"

"B-52's. U.S. Air Force. What you saw was probably five-hundred-pound general-purpose bombs."

"*General purpose*," Paul repeated with a straight face.

"Delivered for the general purpose of changing the specific gravity of the earth," the FAC continued. "A radar-guided strike."

"On what?" asked Paul.

"Some target assigned by U.S. or ARVN intelligence," Kindred surmised.

Said Mac, "A jungle. You witnessed the U.S. Air Force in a merciless assault on defenseless trees."

"And if I ask why," Paul began, "you'll say this is the U.S. Marine Corps."

Mac responded: "I will say that 'why' is your own department, Chaplain. 'Why' is theology."

"What's that?" This in a low voice, from Gunnery Sergeant Hitchcock—velvet, but very low. It was the first word Hitchcock had uttered. He faced Paul and Mac from across the boards, his eyes moving from one to the other, and the sun was just behind his head.

Paul shaded his eyes and got a clearer view of Gunnery Sergeant Hitchcock's face, of his steady—unconvinced—eyes. This was what Paul thought. That the gunny's expression was that of a man who cannot be convinced.

"You're asking what theology is?"

"Yes sir." Low, quiet.

"Theology is the study of God, the 'queen of the sciences,' the search for God's will."

The gunny regarded Paul in perfect silence.

While he locked eyes with the man, Paul had a sudden intuition. He realized that Hitchcock was in his right and only role, that he'd be unfit for any other.

"Theology is what I am supposed to do, and what nobody *can* do," said Paul.

From the gunny the same silent stare, with the sun behind him.

"All right," said Paul in a changed tone, "this is my last one. I am certain I saw bicycle tracks on that trail this morning."

Mac turned to the "frightened youth" and made a slight movement of his head toward Paul.

The young lieutenant explained: "The VC and NVA have porters, civilians conscripted to carry their supplies. They lash a long pole to the main up-and-down bar of a bike and a short one to the handlebar. They lash their load to the frame and they push on the load and guide it with the pole coming off the handlebar. They can carry maybe two hundred pounds that way."

"Carry it just about anywhere," Mac added. "You'll notice when they destroy a bridge, they often leave a narrow path, a board or girder or something, so it can still be crossed by a man pushing a bike. Same when they crater a road."

Paul glanced aside and found he was under the eye of Gunnery Sergeant Hitchcock—and Hitchcock met and held his eyes, and allowed himself a flicker of a smile.

"I didn't want to ask this at dinner," Paul Adrano began.

Paul and Mac were in Mac's tent, on two cots jammed into a crowded space by the center pole.

"Ask what?"

"What will happen to the men at the LP?"

"They'll be shot at sunrise."

Paul's breath stopped. He tried to absorb the shock and see his duty all at once. He began: "I'm the chaplain and I can't let you—"

"You can't stop me either," Mac cut in. "The Uniform Code of Military Justice is perfectly clear on this. Sleeping on watch in the presence of the enemy is a capital offense. Why bother with formalities? Three bullets and the problem's gone, and think of the effect on the others."

It was dark in the tent and Paul wished he could see Mac's face because he began to suspect. Paul said: "Better yet, strangle all three and save the bullets."

"Good idea. I'll do one, we'll give another to the gunny, and you can have the third."

"Fine," said Paul. "I haven't strangled anybody in weeks."

"Me either. So we'll get up five minutes early—four fifty-five."

"I forgot my alarm clock," said Paul.

"No sweat. I'll wake you, four fifty-five, stranglers' reveille."

Paul spoke of something that worried him. He said: "I can't get a grip on this S-curve operation. We're going to search for enemy supplies, I understand that. But you were telling your so-called brain trust that there's a hill that could block our communication with Battalion."

"Only if we're deep in a ravine on the west side of the hill mass, and I don't intend to get into any such fix."

"But suppose you have no choice—we get into trouble."

"And we're driven into a ravine to get into defilade, where the artillery can't hit us. Is that—"

"Something like that."

"Like we run into a battalion of VC Main Force. Holy fucking shit."

"Exactly," said Paul.

"Excuse my language."

"Don't alter your language on my account."

"Good, we got that out of the way. O.K., we're in a ravine on the west side of the highest hill around there, Hill 263, and we holler like hell and nobody answers. Well if there's an AO, an aerial observer, buzzing around, maybe he can hear us, and we relay to Battalion through him."

"And if there's no AO because of bad weather?"

"Chaplain, you are thinking like an infantryman. If there's no AO, and that'll be the case ninety-five percent of the time, we send an officer and radioman up a hill. When he's high enough he'll contact Battalion on his prick twenty-five."

"His what?"

"Portable Radio Communicator, PRC, prick. The twenty-five means the transmitter-receiver weighs twenty-five pounds, a marked improvement on the old prick forty-seven. Imagine hauling one of those, plus your rifle, ammo, food, and shelter half. The twenty-five is an FM radio, which is sometimes a problem, a line-of-sight signal."

"And," said Paul, "if this officer and radioman can't climb high enough?"

"Because they're intercepted. Then we destroy the whole enemy force by ourselves and return to a heroes' welcome."

"And if—"

"If it's a battalion of enemy we die like marines and you go to heaven."

"I see."

"Don't worry about that, Chaplain. Worry about the artillery. We've got just two tubes of 105, and a good piece of our op area lies outside the fan of fire."

"Meaning?"

"They can't reach us. Ollie hollers for artillery and they say, 'Sorry, friends, use your organic weapons.' Then we pray for flying weather so the airdales can help us."

"And if the weather is bad?"

"Figure it out! And Paul, about those shitbirds at the LP. I gave'm a choice. I file charges of sleeping on watch, enemy present; sleeping on watch, no enemy present; or they take their chances with Gunny Hitchcock."

"And they chose—"

"The gunny."

"And he can do anything he wants? He seems like the kind of man I would not want—I am sure he's a good marine but—"

"He is."

"Nevertheless if I were the offender I'd choose—some other hangman."

"They made their choice. They know my limits."

"What do you mean?"

"Nothing physical, nothing to impair them in the future performance of their duty, but whatever it is, it has to be a deterrent."

Paul asked: "So what will it be?"

"I'll let the gunny decide. Nothing till we get back from the S-curve. Then they'll burn shit, they'll dig bunkers, they'll dig a tank trap, drink no beer, pussy corner's off limits. If we shot everybody who falls asleep we'd have a congressman or a chaplain down here."

"And a chaplain obviously would be a nuisance."

"No, but a congressman would, or letters from one. Paul, these are my guys. Orders are no good—you may have noticed that already. You don't bark orders. Marines do, or do well, as a general rule, what they want to do, what they are inspired to do. Those three guys are all good men. I need good men, but I also need'm to stay awake on an LP. Two should have been awake at any given moment, one to listen and the other wearing the earphones. They could sleep when they came in, and they knew it. So when we get back they'll be punished hard enough to take the joy out of life, and long enough for everybody else to notice. A week, two weeks."

"And they're going with us to the S-curve?"

"Everybody's going to the S-curve. So you're not impressed with the gunny."

"I am very impressed with his steel eyes."

"Ha! And somebody described you as a wrestler made out of cement and re-rod."

"What?"

"Reinforcing rod. It holds cement together."

Said Paul: "Whoever thinks so is mistaken. I thought I was pretty tough till I got here."

"It's the heat. You'll be your old self in no time, a year. But Chaplain, please, when the troops hit the deck, you hit it too. I can't have you running around drawing fire."

"I thought you were hit. They said, 'Skipper's hit.' So—"

"If I was hit what I'd need is a corpsman, not a chaplain."

"Excellent. You don't need a chaplain. Congratulations. But how did you like it?"

"How did I like Miss Bouncing Betty?"

"Yes. If you don't object to the question."

"No, it's your privilege. My whole life flashed before my eyes."

"Seriously."

"I did have one clear thought. 'This'll take my balls and legs.' It wasn't a scream, just a fact. The term 'death' wasn't there, just: 'Goodbye balls, goodbye legs.' "

"And you didn't fear death?"

"I didn't have time. I knew the 'fact' in one heartbeat and in the next I knew it was a dud. I didn't feel the gash in my leg till later. And when I felt it, believe me, I didn't care. Pain, O.K., give me lots of it, pour it on."

"Are you saying it had no effect on you? That you are not afraid now?"

"What have I got to be afraid of?"

"You know that better than I do," said Paul.

"No, I am not afraid, of yesterday or tomorrow."

"If you stepped on a Bouncing Betty that was a dud, surely the next one will blow you up."

"You can't cheer me up that easily, Chaplain. What if I don't step on another one? Trip it, actually, you don't step on it, you trip the wire."

"And there are—bullets, grenades, mortars, and so forth," Paul continued.

"All of which," said Mac, "I assume, is what is scaring you."

"Yes."

"Listen Paul, I salute you for admitting it. All I can tell you is I have never been afraid. They say everybody is, but it's not so. I am not, and I doubt that Hitchcock is. Put me in the middle of Stalingrad, starve me, freeze my feet, put dysentery in my belly, point ten rifles and a machine gun at me, kill all my buddies, and I'm sure I'd be terrified. But not yet."

While Mac was saying this, Paul heard the pop of a star shell over the perimeter. At the top of the tent there was a hole where the pole passed through, and in the hole Paul could see the brown light of the descending flare pulling its parachute to earth. Then the light blinked out and took the hole with it.

Mac's voice said: "Most people are afraid. That's what everybody says. Were you afraid when you ran to the point?"

"To reach you?"

"Yes."

"Oh no, I didn't have time."

"So remember that."

"I will. Why do you think—why are you immune?"

"I have no idea. It's certainly not courage."

"You said you were planning to meet your wife in Hawaii, and—"

"Yes, when I get my R and R, we start a family. I think of that every minute. I wrote her a letter today. I got a Honolulu slot yesterday when I went to Regiment for the meeting on the operation. Here it comes, little Clares crawling around the kitchen, a wife, normal life. So I wrote Sarah and said we don't have to wait till June, we can put one in the oven in Hawaii. One month, mister."

"Less," said Paul observing Mac's happiness and feeling some of the warmth himself. "So you are thrilled at the thought. Her name's Sarah?"

"Her name's Sarah and I am wild. Sarah, babies, home, peace, love, and good cooking."

"You see a future, you and Sarah and a child. You speak of a normal life. So you're not staying in the Marine Corps?"

"I've been in five years. That's enough. In June I'll be a civilian, whatever that is."

"So," said Paul, pondering, "you have a vision of the future. A normal life—I don't know what that is."

Mac let this pass and said, after some deliberation: "Our idea of normal is, we go to Vermont and work and make a family and a life. When Sarah was a child she went to summer camp up there. That's where we'll live."

"Yes, it's a beautiful place, isn't it?"

"Don't know," said Mac. "I've never been there. But we signed a peace treaty. I don't want to live in any city and Sarah won't live where I want to live. I planned on helping my dad build up his business, which is drilling wells and building irrigation systems on farmland—row crops, potatoes, beans, and what have you. In Stevens Point, central Wisconsin.

"But Sarah says that's nowhere, which it is, so we compromised on Vermont, which is the kind of country she loves and yet it's close to Boston and New York, sort of. Therefore Vermont is not nowhere in her book. And hilly, she likes that. Three hours to Boston. That's our Treaty of Perpetual Peace."

"And what about your father?" Paul asked.

"Yeah," Mac said and thought it over, visualizing the irrigated fields. "He'll be disappointed, but he's a tough character."

"And you?"

"That was what I wanted, to work with my old man, but I want Sarah more. We're going up there and search for a place where the farmland and forested mountains meet. Whatever I do for a living, that's where I'm going to do it, and as soon as Baby One is a year or two old, we'll bring along Baby Two."

"That is a future," said Paul, still more earnestly, "that will never come to pass if something happens to you."

"I understand that, but for now I am the Six of this company."

"Yes," said Paul, ruminating. "For now you are the commander of all these men. I wonder if that's why you aren't afraid."

"I can't explain it but it's so," said Mac. "What about you? Do you have a vision of the future? In your line of work, does a man—"

"Beyond doing my job here, pardon me for interrupting, no."

"All you can see is yourself doing your job, and nothing beyond?"

"I never knew it till now, but no, I can't see beyond this—war," said Paul as if confessing a transgression.

"So you're afraid to die and lose a future that has no meaning for you."

"I suppose I am, yes. Life is sweet, even if you—" Paul didn't complete his sentence but Mac understood.

"Why are you here?" Mac asked. "I don't have a right to ask, you're the chaplain, but—I could guess—"

Paul said: "I doubt you would guess right. Why are you here?"

"Ha! You wouldn't understand. I'll tell you when you tell me."

As the relief company moved in to occupy Delta's position, the men of Delta prepared to march to the lift zone. First they assembled for a briefing. At a word from the exec they downed their packs and weapons. Then the exec signed to the platoon leaders, and the whole company, arrayed by platoons in a semicircle, converged on its center. When this was done the exec could have reached out and touched the closest man.

He called: "Listen up."

Silence went through the company in a single pulsation, and the only sound remaining was the idling of the motor on a mechanical mule. A man dashed back and killed it. He trotted to his squad, and his footsteps ceased, and all was silent. The exec retired and Mac stepped forward.

"Some of you," said Mac, "have asked me why we are humping so much weight. I think you may have guessed the answer. There could be days, maybe three or four in a row, when it'll be difficult to resupply us.

"So don't waste your ammo. A man who blows up his ammo just to lighten his load may be letting the rest of the company down. There may come a minute when we'll need every round for every weapon. We can't advance by bounds, we can't lay down an effective base of fire if we've pissed it away to make life easier. Marines—use your ammo wisely, never piss it away, least of all on this operation."

Mac spoke in a baritone that rolled easily through the dense mass, but no more loudly than necessary, and he paused as if to express a meaning that went beyond his words. Most of the men could look directly at him, and those who could, did. The rest, whose view was blocked by the men in front, stared as if into a book where they read for the first time some engrossing message. They began to understand why they carried so much weight, in both food and ammunition, and why every man who was able had been tasked to carry extra rounds for the machine guns, the 60-millimeter mortars, and LAW rockets.

There were smart-asses, gripers, faultfinders, bigots in black and white, haters of the Corps, cowards and shirkers and con men—scattered thinly through the 130—but even these now melted into a creation called Delta Company. Although this would soon dissolve, and many would be dead or flying to the World in a month or two, at this moment even they and Delta Company were a single imperishable world unto themselves. If it were offered, very few and perhaps not a single man would take a pass out of the S-curve.

Mac turned to an easel and picked up a black grease pencil and drew a lazy S at the left side of the sheet. He turned back to the men. He was wearing no helmet, and his reddish hair took on a redder hue in the light of the rising sun.

He said: "Charlie and his bosses from the North are preparing an attack. That much we know. One possible target is the place we call Shit City, Quang Ngai City, but it's not shit to the VC Main Force and the NVA. To them it's an important target because it's a provincial capital and headquarters of an ARVN division."

He drew a cross at the extreme right of the sheet.

"You all know Quang Ngai City. And you know the river that flows out of the mountains, past the city and into the South China Sea. That river is the Song Tra Khuc, and we've been there before. But that time we were close to the ocean and we had naval gunfire support. You remember what Mr. Stilwell and Sergeant Hamner and the naval gunfire team did for us? Sorry, but you won't see them on this operation because we'll be thirty klicks up the river, inland and out of the range of naval guns. All we've got is two tubes of 105 howitzer. O.K., here's the geography. This is how the river curves through some hilly country west of the city."

Then he drew a meandering line from the top of the S east to the X that marked the city.

"And this is how it flows, past the city, east to the ocean. From the top of the S-curve the river goes pretty directly to the sea. There's also a road that parallels it. But concentrate now on the S-curve itself. Look at the lower loop—*especially* the lower loop—because that's our op area. Now look at this."

He drew a north-south line that all but enclosed the west opening of the lower loop.

He said: "You see, gents, the loop is closed on the west by this line. This line is Route Five B. So you've got a big loop of river running all around a hill mass—it's called Nui Gio, Mountain of the Wind—and on the west there's this all-weather road called Route Five B. So think of this lower loop as a rough circle bounded by the road and the curve of the river. That's where we're going."

He looked at his audience for a significant moment then turned to the easel, and drew again over the S, darkening and thickening it.

"Inside this open loop," he continued, "is mountainous jungle. Thick, green, and hot. So you can see, we've got an op area clearly defined by conspicuous terrain features. They'll look good to the pilots when we holler for air strikes. They won't have any trouble finding us."

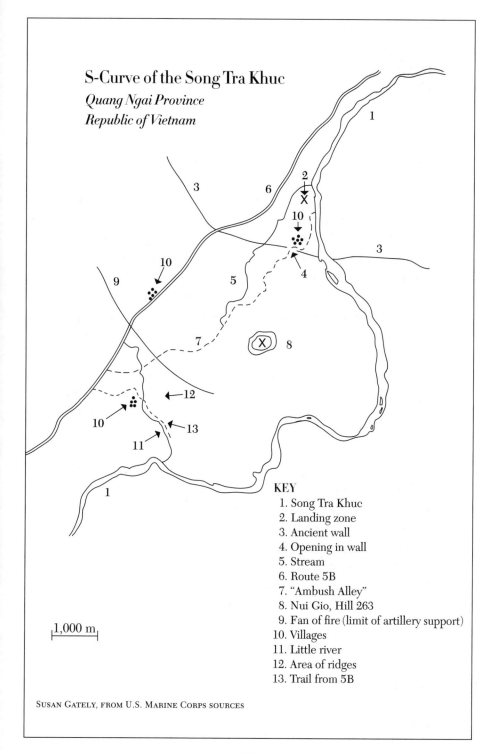

S-Curve of the Song Tra Khuc

Quang Ngai Province
Republic of Vietnam

KEY
1. Song Tra Khuc
2. Landing zone
3. Ancient wall
4. Opening in wall
5. Stream
6. Route 5B
7. "Ambush Alley"
8. Nui Gio, Hill 263
9. Fan of fire (limit of artillery support)
10. Villages
11. Little river
12. Area of ridges
13. Trail from 5B

1,000 m

Susan Gately, from U.S. Marine Corps sources

Mac tapped the sheet with his knuckle and turned again to watch the men for a long moment.

"So this is our area, about five klicks by five—mountainous, mostly jungle with some of what the map calls 'clear forest,' with fishing and farming villages all around its periphery at the bottom of the hill mass, and sloping ravines and draws giving access to it all along this road—" and he again traced Route 5B as if he had a fondness for it.

"In other words, if you were piling weapons, ammo, food, and medicine, and you were coming from the Ho Chi Minh Trail, you could take Five B, turn right, and walk right up one of these draws to a good hiding place on the west slope of Nui Gio.

"So if Charlie and his masters are bringing in supplies for an attack on Quang Ngai City, this is a good place to drop'm. Only thirty kilometers from the city, by river or road."

He paused and asked for questions. Hearing none, he went on.

"We'll have two tubes of Marine Corps artillery at the Army Special Forces camp—here"—drawing the map symbol for artillery at a spot northeast of the S-curve—"and we'll be inside the artillery's fan of fire so long as we're humping the east side of the hill mass. But there are portions of the west and south sides that are outside the reach of artillery; we will not be able to call on the big guns. We'll rely on what we carry, plus air.

"This may not be a coincidence—that the best place for us to search is the worst for supporting arms. If I were Charlie and I had to preposition an ammo dump, this is where I'd put it, right here"—touching the west slope of the hill mass. "Direct access from Route Five B—gradually sloping draws leading up into the hill mass from the west—some of it in defilade. The west side of the hill mass is a closed book. Our job is to open it and see what's inside.

"There's one more conspicuous terrain feature. There's this gigantic fucking wall—" He carefully drew a line running east-west just north of the hill mass. "I haven't seen this wall but I've seen others in the same neighborhood. They are generally twelve to twenty feet high and almost as thick."

Mac paused and let the silence stretch out, then continued: "We drop north of the wall and hike south. We go through the goddamned wall—there's an opening—you'll see—but first we prep the south side

76

of the wall and make fruit salad out of the jungle. So when we go through, believe me, there'll be nobody waiting on the other side." He called in a louder voice: "Is that right, Captain Kindred?"

Kinny shouted: "You bet your ass, Skipper!"

Mac went on: "I think Regiment did a good job in choosing this terrain here, they did well to tell us to search it. That's our mission. Search or fight, or search and fight. If any element gets into a fight keep this in mind: your platoon leaders and platoon sergeants know that an enemy force trying to break contact may not be really running, they may be in tactical retreat to pull us away from a cache that could be closer than we know. So we will have to fight smart. None of this 'hi-diddle-diddle right up the middle.'

"Yes, kill the bastards. But our primary mission is to find caches, or to come home having established that there are none worth finding."

He again invited questions and a man asked: "Sir, will they know we're there?"

"Yes. But remember: he can harass us but he can't move his caches."

Mac stood silent, shifting his intense gaze slowly here and there among the men. He said: "The whole battalion is on standby. If this thing gets big, we get big."

Turning again to his diagram Mac reviewed the geography: "So the op area is this hill mass crowned by three peaks, covered by jungle, enclosed in the lower loop of the S-curve of the Song Tra Khuc, bounded on the west side by Route Five B, which is allegedly an all-weather road and is the enemy's route from the mountains to his possible target area. The hill mass is ringed by fishing and rice-farming villages at the river level. The elevation difference is—the river's thirty meters and the peaks are about two hundred sixty; the highest is Hill 263—so we'll have to do some climbing."

Bracketing the op area from top to bottom with his thumb and index finger, he said, "North to south, five thousand meters." He shifted his hand. "East to west, five thousand meters. The key idea— the hill mass is approachable around its edges by gentle slopes and ravines. If there are any big caches, that's where they'll be.

"So—we land north of the wall. We move south through the wall, at this opening; we turn west—we turn right—and hump along the edge of the jungle—along the base of the hill mass—then we turn south and start searching for Charlie's big PX."

Paul Adrano was watching from the edge of the group. He saw how Mac stood perfectly composed—saw him hand the grease pencil to a man who took down the diagram and rolled it—heard him say "Thanks, Slater" to this man—and saw him turn again to the company and let his eyes roam freely, touching nearly every man, pausing to let his eyes stay on Paul for a moment. What was communicated between the two in that moment neither could express in a word. What Paul felt in his heart was a sort of—heat—an increasing—something. Surely not joy—he—

Mac continued: "Someday, somebody is going to ask you what you did in this war. You can answer, well, one thing you did was go to the S-curve of the Song Tra Khuc and try to disrupt an attack. When the enemy goes into a city or village he murders civilians. He has done it from the start and he will keep doing it until one side or the other wins this war."

Mac turned as if to refer to the map, remembered it had been removed, and faced the men again and created another silence, while he looked at them.

"When the army we are fighting takes over a city or village they round up the politically incorrect, take them out somewhere, and, just like the Nazis, they put a pistol to the back of their heads and pull the trigger.

"We are here to try to stop that. So remember, marines. Teamwork. Help your buddy. Clean that M16 whenever you get a chance. Use your bug repellent. Never drink untreated water. Keep one heavy in your pack—never eat your last heavy. Take your malaria pills. Dry your feet whenever you can. Show your superiors and subordinates that you respect them. Teamwork. Fire discipline. Fire discipline. Semper Fi." Mac nodded to the exec.

The exec stepped forward and shouted: "Platoon leaders! Saddle up!"

Paul Adrano prayed for a good death—should death come. He begged forgiveness and asked for mercy. He even uttered the words

"I beg forgiveness" but his mind was not the mind of a man who can beg. He was "stiffnecked" as he marched toward the valley of the shadow of death. "Me? Die? Not just yet!" He looked around him and said, "Who can touch me?"—in the midst of so many armed men. Safe, this is the safest stroll anybody ever took.

They were marching toward the pickup zone and the choppers were clattering in the gray sky like a flock of mad hens.

The idea—of burning in the crash of one of those grotesque dragonfly machines—and even now he saw them high in the gray featureless empty—sky—here they come! His guts heaved. Now they were close enough to be counted—one, two . . . eight of them. Paul heard, within the heavy droning, a throbbing trying to break free, growing louder, sending out a stronger premonition, and here was Paul, a man of peace, marching in the center of this company toward—someplace!

The trail led downward, winding through waist-high brush toward a flat pan of red earth bounded on the other side by a wall of coiled green vegetation, trees of a kind he'd never seen before and didn't care to see now.

He knew he was going to do it—he'd run with the rest of these eager beavers with their heads ducked down—the rotor blades were above head height but the men ducked anyway—running to climb into one of these hearses modeled on the dragonfly—and then (he'd seen it on television) you get whooshed up, and the thing hesitates and drops its nose and pauses to think, then zoom off it goes in a straight line with its tail up, till it makes a banking turn and begins its upward spiral, after kicking sand in everybody's face and sending its thudding waves of sound through your insides, and off you go to some "LZ," which always reminded Paul of Lazarus, and there you'll be met by lethal men you can't see, darting flames of death at you because—you made one hell of a mistake in coming here.

For now his feet were hitting ground.

He thought of the rectory in Fall River, of the interminable evenings, the stupid ads on television, the threadbare carpet, of Father Connolly, his superior—the paradigm of a life of service—or a wasted life—of the emasculating "parish events" and parish business, of the old women who would believe—anything! And in that flash it seemed to him he had two choices, both of them representing death in one form or another.

The choppers kept coming and Paul kept marching.

On Mac's advice Paul had removed the silver railroad tracks from one lapel. The cross on the other he did not remove. But for the cross, he might have been the most dangerous-looking man in the command group. He was thick and dark-looking, as if he'd stepped out of the wrestling ring, put on a flak jacket and helmet, which he did not need, and assumed a place among these men to guard them from a menace he alone could overpower—except for the pallor of his face, made to seem even paler by the stark black eyes and heavy black eyebrows, and the new growth of black stubble—except for the cross—except that he carried no weapon.

He wore the expression of a man who swims underwater too long, who breaks the surface and gasps and looks at the world and breathes its precious air—but he was muscular—oh yes, he was a tough bastard, priest or no priest.

And that phrase "no priest" was all too interesting. He remembered pure belief as a stage, like adolescence and the struggle against masturbation. He knew its hallmark. During his phase of pure belief he had never feared death or anything else. He knew no fear whatever; for he was God's servant and death by definition and by faith was the opening to a better life.

The logic was all too simple. If pure belief drives out the fear of death, then the fear of death must have driven out pure belief. Paul Adrano, the tough guy, was a frightened chicken. He didn't have pure belief but rather belief compromised by negation (there is no God) and this was happening just as his father had predicted it would. What a quarrel that had been. What a thrilling and horrifying end to all love between father and son. What had they said that was unforgivable? What had they not said?

There was moisture on his face, the sweat of fear. Then he felt a drop of rain, then several cold isolated drops. He tried to lick them but they were too few. He thrilled to the rain. Several more spattering drops cooled his face. He heard a man behind him shout: "Lock it up, Nimbus!"

But Paul thought: "No, open it up, Nimbus. Rain!"

80

A wave of thin scattered drops struck his face with a friendly splattering; against his flak vest they made little dull sounds; on his face they spread a cooling relief.

Other men were now cursing Nimbus and the rain. Not Paul. He was absurdly happy! Thank God for the rain! It caressed and cooled his face and made him slightly crazy. Marching! To war at last!

A few more big drops, then the crescendo of roaring engines descending—then a new wave of light rain in his face—and as he reached the flat ground the first two birds squatted down, raising clouds of flying dirt, weeds, and trash. Their rotors slowed but did not stop, and a line of men jogged toward the anus of each of the two monsters.

The first man was, of course, MacHugh Clare. He was not with his command group—Paul was there and the man in charge of the command group was the exec. Mac was with 2nd Platoon. He would set in with 2nd Platoon in the first two birds, Mac in the first, the platoon leader in the second. With these thirty riflemen Mac would secure the LZ and then call the rest of the company, Paul included, down from the sky. So now Paul watched him jogging easily toward the first bird, the men following him, and another file running to the second bird now on the deck. Six others orbited.

In a few seconds the two on the ground sealed up their hatches. The gunners peered out their openings and swung their guns left and right. Paul read the word "Marines" and the word "Rescue" (with an arrow) painted on the helicopter, he saw the windshield wipers sweeping the broad curved glass of the cockpit, the helmeted head of the pilot nodding, and the first bird revved up its two long drooping rotors—which lifted and stiffened and disappeared in a blur. The dust and trash and wind swept over Paul and the noise pitched higher, but deeper as well. It had a drenching hydroelectric power that assailed Paul's eardrums and tried to chip the supersensitive little bones in his ears.

He stopped his ears and squinted against the storm—but he didn't close his eyes. He wanted to see it all. He thought of Mac "unafraid," crouching, holding his rifle, thinking, thinking inside the belly of the big mechanical dragonfly. And the thing lifted with Mac inside, slowly, seemed to take a misstep, then rose smoothly with its engines drenching the flat land with skull-shaking sound, and a separate wave of swishing noise reverberating off the green wall across the field, and the bird rose, dipped its nose, lifted its tail obscenely, and sped away in a fright. Then Paul watched two more as they circled down and squatted carefully, like ruptured hens, kicking up a new dirt storm and opening their anuses for the next group.

Two files duly fed themselves to the noisy trembling birds who clapped their anuses shut, vibrated with the thrill of it all, shuddered unsteadily, and rose a foot, then leaped straight up and played their part in the ballet of departure.

Paul was watching the third pair land when somebody slapped him from behind. He heard the exec cry, "Command Group, move!" and everybody around him suddenly was gone. He sprinted to catch them as though death lay on this side, not the other. Had he paused to think he would have seen it: he feared being left behind in safety more than he feared death.

He charged up the ramp and found himself inside a metal box with a bloodstained floor. He searched for a seat—men made an opening for him on the canvas bench, but the exec took him by the arm and pulled—and he followed the exec up a slight incline to a huge gun sticking through a window about three feet square.

The gunner smiled and shouted and Paul heard nothing but the engines. Paul moved closer, actually touched the gun and leaned forward as far as he could, looking out, then with a great lurching heave the floor rose and buckled his knees. The gunner supported him, and the ground flew down deeper in the clouds of swirling dirt.

The bird lifted itself, and the thrill was that Paul still conceived of himself as a ground creature, while the bird lifted him higher and his guts protested. The bird tipped as if to throw him out the window. He watched the trees diminish, watched as his view grew ever larger, and saw the paddies wheeling below, the hills, the dunes—and in the midst of the big turning he saw the ocean swinging into his view. On its rippled metallic surface lay a ship shaped like a sword, sharp at the bow but with a complex superstructure like a cliff dwelling—and long gray guns poised skyward fore and aft. Then the swinging of the bird showed him the whole coastal plain divided into hundreds and thousands of rice paddies, and strewn over the paddies, like unhealed wounds, hundreds of bomb craters, which seemed to open their ragged circles wider as Paul looked. Then he saw the pathetic little narrow strip of "highway," cut and crimped every few hundred meters, patched and refilled; and finally Paul observed the railroad, less the rails, decorated with discarded overturned boxcars thrown indiscriminately to either side of the right of way, and an overturned locomotive; no bridges, just wreckage and damage gaps.

As the bird whirled up Paul realized he was cold, shivering. The bird had risen beyond the reflected heat of the earth, and a cold wind blew so violently through the window that when he opened his mouth his cheek billowed out.

It was a cool ride at 150 miles an hour. Nothing but that strange coldness, and noise like rushing water. Mac's eyes were closed and he might have been anywhere or nowhere. Then he was in Sarah's presence, as intimately as if they had stepped into the shower together. The noise in his ears was the shooting water, the hands dangling before him as he leaned on his knees were placed on the swell of her hips. And he saw her loving eyes looking up to him, and anticipated her kiss on his lips.

A tap on his shoulder. He opened his eyes and saw the air-crew gunner beckoning. He staggered forward as the craft banked left. The gunner removed his helmet, lifted its wire carefully over his shoulder, and handed the whole thing to Mac.

Mac pulled it over his head, and the chill of the man's sweat mixed with the ice of his own. He heard the pilot's voice.

"Hey there Delta Six, hear me?"

"Yes, I hear you."

"O.K., your company's all airborne. Your gunships are approaching the LZ. Looks like you're going to war."

Chapter 5

Through the Wall

"Sir, he wants you to jump," the gunner shouted.

Mac thought, "The bastard," and jumped. His eyes were blinded by splashing muck—but he struggled to his feet, sinking in, and it came to him that the pilot was within his rights; his wheels could bury themselves in the paddy if he dropped the full weight of the bird.

"Jump!" Mac called to the men poised on the edge of the ramp, and they sailed down like big geese spreading their wings, and pitched forward and came up like Mac, half-blinded, wiping crud from their eyes and hollering.

Mac grabbed the platoon leader—Lieutenant Dan Shaw—and faced him toward a line of brush growing up along an irrigation ditch. Holding out both his arms in a V, Mac indicated the arc he wanted and said, "Go."

As the rest of the men flopped down into the bent green stalks and the waves of agitated water Mac noticed that the water was being driven away from the area just below the huge after-rotor. The men of 2nd Platoon flopped down in twos and threes and Mac sent them after Lieutenant Dan Shaw. The lieutenant and six men were slogging toward the brush line and suddenly they started firing in short bursts on automatic.

"There's somebody over there," said Mac (nobody could hear him). He gave a thumbs-up to the crew chief and the huge howling machine revved up to a wild pitch, the prop-wash beat upon him, water splattered his legs, and the bird rose, slowly curving. The crew chief waved and shouted something, and Mac heard, or thought maybe he heard, within the engine blast, a few rounds of rifle fire—not his own—incoming.

He staggered, pulling his feet out of the holes he had sunk in—and moving fast toward the other bird, where men were flying out the back, hitting awkwardly in splashes, Mac saw that one man had managed to dig his rifle muzzle into the muck.

"That'll take ten minutes to clean," Mac thought, as if seeing the man assembling his ramrod and cleaning the bore—because if he fired now the barrel would explode and maybe blind him—so as Mac drew near the second bird, which was still hovering and waiting for all the men to jump, Mac shouted, "Clean that weapon," and the man cried, "Aye aye sir."

"Dougherty!" called Mac, and Dougherty, a squad leader, raised his hand and came pulling toward Mac.

"To the right of the lieutenant, remember?"

"Yes sir," said Dougherty.

The bird sent down a gale of watery wind and created concentric waves of green rice and white water, flying out from the place where two or three men still struggled to free themselves from the muck. Dougherty formed his skirmish line and they began waddling toward the platoon leader's men, and Mac heard six or seven shots and a burst of automatic fire from an M16. Turning to the brush line he was just in time to see a marine twist and fall. A man from Dougherty's squad began loping toward the fallen man, holding his pistol close against his thigh. Mac pulled through the ooze and reached the fallen man at the same time as this other man, the medical corpsman. Mac lifted the fallen man, pulling him up by the arm hole of his flak jacket to get his face out of the water.

"Stay low, Doc," Mac said and pulled on toward the brush line, where the firing continued.

He felt the pressure wave as a bullet flew past his ear with a snap that strained his eardrum, and he distinguished (perhaps) the weapon that had fired it, for the unusual loudness of the report mixed in among a cacophony of sharper smaller cracks. He knew what he had heard. It was most likely a U.S. M1 rifle—which suggested his troops were under fire from Local Force guerrillas, probably a squad equipped with World War II–era weapons. He still felt the bullet ripping past his ear.

Reaching Lieutenant Dan Shaw, who was crouched behind a dike, Mac flopped in the mud and was overswept by a wave of water as a man flopped behind him. This was his radioman, PFC Graeser, who was following closely. Graeser held out the handset and Mac took it and keyed it.

"Bingo," said Mac to the aircraft commander, "this is Striker Six. Better stay up there for a while. We're taking sniper fire."

Bingo said: "Roger, Striker. I'm gonna *di-di* outa the way of your gunships. Don't worry, ain't goin nowhere."

Mac shouted over his shoulder: "Hey Kindred!"

The forward air controller crawled along the dike toward him, like a pregnant amphibian with his pack, map case, and glasses. His radioman followed. The radioman had his short antenna rigged. This made no difference now since Mac's radioman was using his long antenna. Whoever was firing on the marines would now concentrate on this conspicuous marker.

Mac and Kindred held a short conference, which Mac interrupted to shout a few words to the platoon leader. The volume of friendly fire diminished. Mac poked his head up, then crouched down, then removed his helmet and put it on the end of the rifle, and lifted it. He pulled it down promptly and waited, and nothing happened.

Kindred, the man who had proposed they drink to Mac's balls last night, assured Mac he could do the job.

Said Mac: "O.K. then, shut'm the fuck up." And he thought: "That bullet!" But there was no shiver, no quaking; just an exclamation.

Kindred got on his radio and a minute later two Huey gunships with rocket pods bulging at their sides charged in slanting, sending forth slender javelins of black metal rushing eagerly down at the head, each one, of a long liquid flame, all this with a rush of sound as if the sky was being torn open by a giant wearing canvas mittens. The rockets (275's) detonated with dull thuds that sent shock waves through the humid air. The gunships lifted up and away, and came back to do it again. The platoon leader shouted and waved the "advance" sign. The gunships lifted away and spiraled up in a corkscrew pattern, straight up, as if they were ascending the only shaft of safe air in the neighborhood, which they were.

Four marines crouched firing short hot bursts into the brush line while another four advanced in darting zigzag lines toward the smoking beaten zone. Then they knelt. One launched a 40-millimeter grenade from his blooper, and another hammered away with the M16 on automatic, and they waited.

Mac called Bingo and said: "Send two more down please."

Two Sea Knights spiraled serenely down the safe shaft like butterflies trained in ballet, and within five minutes Mac's force on the ground had doubled. He could now lay out a hasty perimeter defense and call down the rest of the company. He sent the skirmishers to the beaten zone of the rocket strike, pushed the opposite arc of his perimeter a hundred meters out, and started toward his command group which had just assembled near a junction of dikes at the center of the landing zone.

Shaking like a man in a malarial fever, Paul Adrano set his chattering teeth, spread his feet, and shrugged off his pack, and let it fall to the deck behind him. An icy glaze spread across his back and he would have retrieved the pack but he thought: "He'll think I'm a nut"— meaning the gunner.

Paul braced himself against the bulkhead and peered out the window, clamping his jaw fiercely and gripping the edge of the window hard to keep his hands from trembling.

The gunner's eyes changed—he suddenly got a faraway look—and he pressed his helmet close against his ears, then he turned to Paul and shouted, "It's a hot zone. Snipers."

Paul nodded and watched the ant-sized figures on the ground, who seemed to move very slowly, if at all. The first two birds had lifted off and were whirling away northeast—Paul was sure of that because he distinctly recalled the orientation of the river here, the S-curve stretching out like a serpent, its tail pointing southwest and the fire-breathing snout reaching northeast. The first two birds rose, one following the other, spinning away to follow the river toward the coast, and rising in sharp revolutions as they slanted out of the imaginary safe shaft connecting Paul's bird with the landing zone directly below.

The black dots were doing their tiny little jerks and crawls in a green space between the river and the road (Route 5B) just at the stretch where the road came closest to the river, which was also the place where the river ran north-south, before branching off into its great swing northeast. Paul could now identify—as the bird swung around and his view opened south and west—the hill mass that was to be their operation area, Nui Gio. One of the officers called it "Little Italy," for the "Gio" and for a hut or two up on a slope that had earned a name on the map: Godari. Italy it was not. Italy was a place where Paul had been welcomed by his cousins, aunts, and uncles. He did not have any relatives on Nui Gio.

As the bird swung he got a clear view of the wall. He had been unable to say what it was on the first swing, but now with this revolution he could clearly see it, topped in green but brown on its sides—running east-west across his view. From this altitude—above small-arms range, up in the arctic chill—it almost seemed to hug the earth, but measuring it against the village houses clustered along the river, he judged it to be higher than an American farm fence, and it ran as far as he could see eastward, while to the west it disappeared into vegetation at the foot of the mountains. It was a thing of colossal length, stopping at the river's edge on this side and resuming on the other. He saw it disappear into jungle and then reappear on its eastward journey. It ran along the border between the paddies and the mountain marches. It lay between the antlike figures and their objective on Nui Gio.

Then Paul leaned to the gunner, who had placed a hand on his shoulder. This made Paul think of a bishop he had met.

Paul had attended a conference, and the bishop had addressed the assembled religious. After the speech Paul approached the podium, hoping to speak to the bishop. Among those gathered around was another priest, a monsignor known to Paul. The monsignor placed his hand on the bishop's shoulder while asking him a question.

The bishop's reply: "Father, I will say this once and never again. Do not lay your hand on my person, ever."

Now Paul in return put his hand on the gunner's shoulder and they leaned together and the gunner cried:

"Here we go!"

The bird wheeled, and spiraled down the shaft. The revolving earth rose with remarkable velocity. Paul saw fretted waves spread across the bending rice as another helicopter preceded his in its descent. Then the deck heaved beneath him and Paul felt a change in orientation as the tail lowered and the nose rose up, and then all was motionless, except for a vibration stronger than any he had felt since takeoff. The gunner shouted, "Good luck, Chaplain!" Paul stooped for his pack, and fell flat when the deck heaved again. Dragging his pack he lurched aft to a vast opening into a new world, where the rice and water fled in waves, and where men jumped in twos and threes and disappeared. On the threshold his guardian—Paul now knew his name, Michelson—Michelson waited—they looked at each other with big eyes, and jumped.

Each gripping a corner of a sagging poncho, four men labored toward the chopper through the sucking muck. The engine noise abated and the rotors slowed. The wheels sank in the muck. It was almost possible to hear the slogging steps of the four as they carried their burden closer.

MacHugh Clare led them. The medical corpsman, pale and desperate—his face shadowed by the helmet which was tipped forward—the corpsman strove to keep up. The four bearers arrived. Paul stepped close as the four spread the poncho on the ramp. The man lay flat, pale, almost blue; no helmet or flak jacket, his arms flung out, the fingers curled and twitching.

"I better go with him, sir," the corpsman said, looking at Mac in doubt and terror.

Paul stood at the wounded man's head, a little above it to keep out of the way. He placed his hand on the blue-white skin, bent near, and whispered: "I am Paul, a chaplain." There was no reaction, except the skin of the forehead may have jumped under Paul's hand, as if the man had lifted his eyebrows. Paul moved around enough to be seen—the eyes were open but vacant—but Paul still left the corpsman free access. He leaned even closer and said: "Let's pray a prayer of thanksgiving that you survived."

No response.

"And let us pray a prayer of supplication to our merciful Father for a complete recovery. Shall we pray?"

A low gurgle agitated the blue lips.

Paul became aware that MacHugh Clare stood beside him, very close. Mac bent and gazed into the man's eyes. So did Paul. The eyes did not gaze back.

Mac and Paul were so close the rims of their helmets clinked. Paul lay his palm on the wounded man's forehead, his fingers extending into the soaking hair, and began to pray in a soft earnest voice.

The corpsman cried: "I gotta go with him!"

The captain, looking full in the corpsman's eyes, raised his arm and pointed toward the perimeter, where the corpsman's platoon was crouched behind a dike.

"He'll bleed," the corpsman cried.

"Go back to your platoon."

The corpsman cried out: "He's dying! Bleeding!"

And the corpsman lifted his leg to climb onto the ramp with the wounded marine.

Mac took him by the shoulders and spun him around. From behind, Mac extended his arm and lay it on the corpsman's shoulder, so the man was looking down Mac's arm as if he were sighting down the barrel of a gun. Across the flooded paddy, huddled in little groups against the dike, with their flak jackets curved by their crouching posture, and their helmets round and curving—there his platoon took shelter.

Mac's finger pointed. The corpsman could see the red hair on the captain's wrist. Mac spoke into his ear:

"Go to your platoon."

The corpsman staggered off. One of the bearers pulled the bloody poncho free. Paul Adrano lifted his hand. The gunner dragged the wounded man into the Sea Knight. Mac signaled. The big rotors stiffened and accelerated, and the noise rose to its crescendo. The two great rotors strained and the engines howled and sucked the black wheels out of the muck, and the bird rose up trailing streams of wind-blown water, and sped away. It took a straight course, like a grouse, then spun up and began ascending the safe shaft in tight circles.

Mac said to Paul: "Stick with me till we're through the wall. Then we'll talk."

The wall! What a colossal thing—running for miles over the land, between paddy and hill, and it must be higher than it had seemed from the air. Paul saw a desert space across the paddies, a brush line, and elsewhere palms, and a solid front of green—and beyond this, mountains. He watched Mac closely.

Two more birds landed but Paul was unaware. He was watching Mac with intense interest. He kept seeing the corpsman stumbling toward his platoon, and the marines huddled under the paddy dike.

Paul and Michelson followed Mac, and soon the command group had reassembled near the center of the LZ. Watching Mac, Paul saw a man he could not understand. He believed he understood what he had done. But what it was like to be the man who did such a thing Paul could not know.

The skirmishers returning from the beaten zone brought a blackened, charred rifle and a sheaf of soggy mimeographed papers. Mac took the rifle and turned it this way and that, and some of the charring rubbed off on his hands and streamed between his fingers. It was an M1. Mac gave the papers to the exec and asked one of the skirmishers:

"Did you see any bodies?"

"Yes sir, one, and a blood trail into the ditch. We didn't go into the ditch, the water looked deep."

"This thing," said Mac, turning the rifle at various angles and inspecting it with curiosity, "was probably given by the U.S.A. to the Chinese Nationalists in the forties, captured by the Chicoms in '49, given by them to their friends in North Vietnam, humped down the Ho Chi Minh Trail by a porter in sandals with a stocking stuffed with rice over his shoulder—and given to our friend in the ditch. Now it's yours if you want it."

"I do, sir."

"Here. We get one rifle back."

Mac said to his radioman: "Platoon leaders, form up." The man repeated the order to his handset, and Mac said to the ever-present Hitchcock: "Gunny, I'll go behind First Platoon. You be the stinger."

"Aye aye sir," said Gunnery Sergeant Hitchcock, looking his commander directly in the eyes.

In ways Paul could not fathom, the gang of marines scattered around the LZ changed its form and moved south. Passing through a stand of trees, palm and bamboo and others, it entered on a wide dry path with paddies on either side.

Climbing a sandy bank, the company's lead platoon, and then its command group, including Paul, turned into a well-trodden trail and entered a village. At about the same moment Paul saw two Huey gunships above the trees, slanting down, perhaps 300 meters away.

Fascinated by the village and its strange small houses—looking at the well with its wet flagstones and asking, "Where are the people?"—Paul was yanked out of his concentration on these—peaceful—details by a clatter of machine-gun fire, a multiple *chat-chat-chat*, extraordinarily loud, hard on the ears. He saw smoke puffing along the side of one of the gunships, and soon the second followed along, and it too began barking a sustained stuttering of individual reports that all but blended into a stream of sound. The gunships were firing ahead of the company and across its course, and not too very far away. Paul heard a voice call "Double time!" and everyone began trotting—no easy task, loaded down as they were—trotting—directly toward the machine-gun fire. The picture in Paul's mind of the wounded marine and of his own fingers entering the man's curly black hair—the sight of the well and its wet flagstones—even the grass-roofed and mud-walled houses he was passing on either side—all this disappeared without his knowing it, and Paul saw only the trotting forms of the men ahead, and their packs jouncing up and down, and, most conspicuously, the captain, recognizable by his wide shoulders and something about the way he seemed to dive ahead as he ran.

The gunships had turned. Paul was gasping for breath and his legs were barely able to support him but he kept going. Here came the gunships, and of course they were much closer now. They spewed out a horrific volume of fire. They were ahead and just above the treetops. And Paul ran with everybody else directly toward the ear-splitting destruction.

Then he saw Captain Kindred, the forward air controller, crouching against a tree, a coconut palm with big shaggy plates curved against the trunk. Kindred had a handset, and his radioman squatted beside him, gazing up toward the gunships. Mac came close, the two men exchanged a few words, and Kindred spoke into his handset. The gunships lifted and spiraled up. Mac stood to full height and raised both arms, and lay them parallel to the ground and forward, and 1st Platoon ran forward into a breach in the gigantic barrier.

The platoon ran in two parallel files into and through, and the men peeled off, one left and one right, beyond the wall, so that for a few seconds Paul Adrano gaped at an empty space where the platoon had disappeared.

It was a big opening, wide enough to admit a cart pulled by a water buffalo—and indeed the track was strewn with buffalo droppings.

Michelson said furtively: "Don't step in no shit, Chaplain. Mines!"

But all this was like data flung too fast into some semi-intelligent machine, too fast to be absorbed, for Paul was still marveling at the wall.

It was constructed of roughly shaped brown stones, so massive they could only have been placed there by being dragged up earthen ramps by buffaloes or elephants—the ramps being removed later, and the wall standing free and rising twenty feet high or higher. Where the cart path went through it seemed to loom even higher. The opening was irregular as if stones had been pulled away by people far less skillful than the builders had been, a semicollapse occurring; and then the debris was cleared away a few stones at a time.

The wall ran along the edge of the jungle, just at the foot of the hill mass. The top sprouted with a teeming tangle of vines and ferns overhanging with a fringe—but Paul's examination of this ancient thing was cut short. The command group went through—and here were the two parts of 1st Platoon deployed in defensive positions left and right, and the ground chewed up as by a big harrow, and trees gouged and clawed by the gunships' fire. The ancient brown stones were chipped white in a thousand scattered places. Little branches hung down from the top, half split; and some of the large leaves had allowed slugs to pass through unresisted, and now stood as before, but for the holes with their weeping inner edges.

The rest of the company passed through in order; 3rd Platoon passed through the defensive formation laid down by 1st, curved right and deployed. Then 2nd passed both and deployed on either side of the trail running beside the wall. Finally the command group placed itself behind the lead platoon (2nd) and the whole company resumed its advance with Gunnery Sergeant Hitchcock's "stinger" marching as rear guard. Hitchcock had two riflemen, a two-man machine-gun crew and a blooper man. The "frightened youth" led 1st, and Paul noted him—that he was very youthful indeed, but no longer frightened.

So they stepped out to the right, along the base of the wall, soon leaving the beaten zone behind, angling somewhat uphill, heading toward a place where the wall plunged into trees so thick that Paul imagined they could be called "jungle." This word took its part in overwhelming his mind. Never before had he approached a jungle. Would they be forced to hack their way through with machetes? Could one walk upright in a jungle? Was it infested with snakes and bats? Paul did all he could do, he marched on, he kept up, he thirsted, he drank. One canteen was already empty! He marched, glancing back at Michelson, wondering: "Is he scared? Does he think the captain knows what he's doing? Does the captain?" Paul marched, and while marveling at the giantism, the hugeness and endlessness of the wall, and while remembering that it ran straight over the land for miles—while part of his mind was thus bewildered he saw again the chalky face of the wounded marine, and saw his own hand—and heard again his prayer, which was both a sincere supplication to God and a performance for the sufferer, on the assumption that he could understand it: "O Father, Father, merciful and loving Father, grant, we beseech You, that this man, Your servant, brave but afflicted—may he live to see Your divine light."

They were pressing right up against the base of the hill mass and starting to curve left around it with the wall. The company was moving fast. The rain had stopped. The sun was climbing behind them. It had not been rainfall but rather a filling of the still air with molecules of water. Now these were gone and the sun claimed their space with malevolent power. It beat on Paul's back. He spun as he walked and saw the sun.

They were tending west, across the northern arc of the base of the hill mass—they were almost running, confined in a narrow pass between the base of Nui Gio on their left and the shaggy wall on the right. Surely this was as bad as 5B. Paul ran with the rest, urgently. Although they had left the beaten zone far behind, Paul still scanned the wall for those little bright chips—and saw none. There was nothing bright there. The wall had endured rain, wind, and sun for four hundred years. It still stood and exuded vines and hanging creepers, and Delta Company, 1st Battalion, Nth Marines, rushed along its base. There was a clicking and muted jingling of equipment, but no words.

Lance Corporal Purdy stripped to his skivvies. He sat on his helmet, opened his ruck, and pulled out a pair of beat-up sneakers. He laced these, stood up, and lifted his arms while his partner looped a messenger line around his waist. In accordance with well-established routine, Purdy tied the knot himself. The partner paid out the line as Purdy, casting a glance back at Captain Clare, waded in two long lunges into the stream, gasping and looking back yet again, with his skinny arms lifted clear of the water.

Purdy dived, emerged and stroked hard, then bounded off the bottom, lunging ahead into the current, bobbing up and down, stroking when he must, jumping when he could, gaining but also being swept along in the silent stream.

By this combination of stroking and jumping he gained the opposite bank, grabbed a branch, bent by the current, and pulled himself up. He staggered, found his footing, and began working his way back upstream along the rugged, branch-clogged bank. Mac grinned and gave him a thumbs-up. When Purdy stood opposite, bending his slender pale body forward—every rib showing, his lips and nipples going purple against the white skin—trembling and making a parody of a freezing man—holding his hands straight out, shaking and muttering "Brrr, man, brrr!"—as Purdy celebrated in this way, his partner guided the big rope out of its coil, Purdy drawing in the messenger line with several long pulls, but still wobbling his knees and saying stiffly, "Brrr, mister."

Finally taking the main rope in hand, Purdy untied the messenger. He reaved the big line twice around a tree and gave a signal. His partner pulled it taut till it leapt out of the water, then secured it around a tree and said quietly to Mac, "O.K. Skipper."

Leaving his rifle, flak jacket, helmet, and dispatch case on the bank, Mac took the rope under his right armpit and stepped slowly into the stream. The bottom sloped away, and Mac moved carefully, and the water rose above his knees to his thighs, and he stopped. He still had about six or eight yards to go to the middle. With the next two steps he was in to his chest. He paused to test the current. It was weaker than he expected. The rope was bent downstream by his weight, but not much. He took another step, and the water grew cooler as it surrounded him and rose to his shoulders. But the important thing, he told himself, was the current. "It's O.K.," he said to himself. Striding against the weight of the moving water he gained the opposite bank, where Purdy held out a hand and drew him up—surprising power for such a skinny man—and Mac said: "Good job, Purdy."

The next man across brought Mac's and Purdy's rifles. This man stepped out along the trail and dropped to one knee.

The next man brought Purdy's ruck, his clothes, and equipment, and he too went a few paces down the trail and dropped. In ten minutes the platoon was across and the command group followed.

They rigged another line upstream, and the columns crossed and then joined later, and Mac consulted his watch. The company had been on the ground as a unit for forty-five minutes, and Mac felt safe. He stretched the leading elements forward to make space on the trail for the rest. Now the whole company was across except for the stinger. Mac's eyes and those of Gunnery Sergeant Hitchcock met over the stream, and the gunny gave a half-smile. He started his men across, keeping the machine gun on his side till the only ones remaining on the bank were the gunner, assistant gunner, and himself. He sent the assistant, then the gunner, who held the big gun high, with one hand at the balance. The gunny, who had knelt and faced the rear, seemed to sense the exact moment to rise, and he did rise, with a slow smooth motion, turning also.

Looking across at Mac he showed his teeth, almost as if he were smiling, placed his rifle carefully on the ground, and loosened the rope. He wrapped the bitter end around his right hand and held the rifle high in his left and entered the stream, and allowed his weight to tend backward, and his body to lean that way, as Purdy pulled him across, and the rope stayed taut all the way.

Gunny Hitchcock splashed up the bank and said to the nearly naked Purdy: "You're out of uniform, marine."

Sitting cross-legged by the trail, Paul passed unconsciously through an interval of comfort between the chill and a new state of oppression under the heat. Wrapped in a suit of water from chest to feet, and even though the water had chilled him a moment ago, he still knew a choking heat was coming; he took deep breaths that yielded no oxygen. His head threatened sickness, as if some sick pain were gaining there; and the heat—he shook his head and looked around him.

But there was a curious fact. Here he sat in a jungle that must be home to snakes, lizards, insects, and leeches, and he didn't care. His legs had commanded him to sit, and he sat, and the relief was unbelievable.

Then the exec said quietly: "Command Group, move out."

Chapter 6

Lost

When Purdy finished dressing, and the company had put the stream behind them, it was time to *di-di-mau,* and Mac said to his radioman: "Beat feet." The company doubled its pace and snaked along the trail, as the troops said, like shit through a goose.

The point man's buddy had been instructed to count paces and slow down at 700 meters, and halt when the point reached an upslope. The halt came. Mac and Graeser, his radioman, stepped briskly and, passing through the lead platoon, joined the point and his buddy where they stood several meters out front, just within sight of the main body. Leaving the others, Mac went a few paces ahead, and ascended the trail, which was clearly presented on the map even though it was over-topped for most of its length by sun-suffused vegetation. This perhaps meant it was less traveled now than when the map pictures had been taken. Maybe the peasants had been told by the local Communist boss to stay off the trail. There was a certain excitement in this thought, and Mac stood and looked around him, and the strange thrill rose in him.

Shoots of bamboo as thin as a man's wrist rose by the thousands all around, and the sunlight filtered down. On his right he could no longer see the wall, but he seemed to sense its ancient presence. He opened his compass and tilted it to calm its whirling, then gently lay it flat.

If the point man had estimated correctly, the first draw lay just to the left on a bearing of about 180 magnetic. Mac peered as deeply as he could into the jungle, and listened. He turned—with something like a shiver—and went back to his point.

He sent the lead platoon, 2nd, out on a south bearing into the bamboo thicket, moved the other two platoons forward, and waited. The men took up defensive positions either side of the trail. Mac signaled silence. He conferred by radio with Lieutenant Dan Shaw, commanding 2nd Platoon, and after the search had proved futile, Mac drew 2nd back into line, and moved the company out on a southwest bearing.

Mac expected the point to break into sunshine in about 200 meters, and it did. With the sun at his back Mac crouched in tall grass with the point man and looked across the stretch of open paddies 300 meters to Route 5B. Through his glasses he watched a little boy riding a water buffalo and a mama-san humping a shoulder-bar down the road. The baskets at either end glided smoothly along as if the woman moved on wheels. The boy's fingers lifted, fell, and curled above a little wooden whistle. Lowering his glasses, Mac listened. He said to the point man, "Hear anything?"

The man said: "Gook music."

Mac passed him the glasses and the man studiously set each lens on a number, then raised them to his eyes.

The marine gave back the glasses, saying, "Yeah, sir, cute."

Mac drew close and whispered: "Stay just inside the cover. Never let yourself be visible from the road. Follow the base of the hill south. Don't go up; don't go down."

"Aye aye sir. Contour line. It'll be kinda slow."

"That's fine. You get to Thrust Point Albany, stop."

"Aye aye sir. Semper Fi."

"Semper Fi," said Mac.

Michelson spread himself in the prone firing position, propping himself on his elbows, pointing his M16 outboard—his face a burning red, and his blond hair darkened with sweat and clapped close to his skull. When Paul spoke, Michelson looked at him sidewise but did not change position.

"I am entitled to an assistant, a man to provide security and"—Paul had thought this out and decided it wouldn't do to say "a bodyguard." So he said: "I need a man to help me set up prayer services, Bible discussion groups, help me set up to celebrate Mass—are you a Catholic?"

"No sir, I'm a Swede, you know."

"No matter. I'll be running prayer meetings for all faiths. There's also some paperwork. Can you type?"

"No sir."

"No matter. I'll do the typing myself. A man to help in all ways, go with me to forward units by helicopter or jeep. There'll be no days off. You'll get R and R of course but otherwise we go where we're needed. That's the whole plan. Do you want the job?"

"You mean a new MOS?"

"I don't know about that bureaucratic stuff, MOS and whatnot. I mean this is a full-time job, chaplain's assistant. I'd like to work with you."

"Yes sir," said Lance Corporal Michelson in a solemn whisper as if he were taking Holy Orders.

"You want it?"

"Yes sir."

"Good. I'll speak to the One at Regiment. It'll mean you'll leave your platoon, you know."

"Oh! I didn't figure—"

"You can reconsider. You are not pledged to anything."

"No, I'll go with you," Michelson decided.

"Good," and Paul extended his hand. "One thing let me say now. I am aware there is no personal servitude in the Marine Corps. I dig my own hole, light my own fire, heat my own C's."

"I'll help sometimes," said Michelson.

"Another thing. There will be times when I must be alone with a man, to pray or hear confession, or talk things over."

"I'll stay back," Michelson offered.

"Right. If I go like this"—Paul made a down motion—"just hang back, keep us in sight, but far enough away so the man knows he won't be overheard or watched. And never talk about my conversations with anyone."

"Yes sir, I won't."

"Now help me out. I can't remember where Second Platoon is."

"Lieutenant Shaw's? Back a ways," and Michelson raised a thumb over his shoulder.

"Let's go," said Paul and they went down the line toward the rear. The men were spread somewhat more closely than the usual intervals, so each could see at least two others. The company was now off the trail and the men seemed to have relaxed a little. Paul smiled calmly and sometimes lifted his hand in a gesture barely visible. He was searching for the medical corpsman.

When he spotted him he gave Michelson the down motion and moved quietly forward. The man was sitting cross-legged, rocking, with his arms over his chest—drenched—his shoulders visibly trembling.

Paul crouched and the man took no notice. He just rocked, and made a faint sound of crushing vegetation as he did so. Paul had heard of the "thousand-yard stare" but this man's great eyes were focused very close-in, almost crossed.

"I'm Chaplain Adrano."

"I know who you are." Rocking, and the eyes pulling in closer.

"Paul Adrano. I am a Catholic priest, and chaplain to serve all faiths."

The corpsman did not respond.

"Tell me your name."

"Bartholomew, HM Three."

"Hello, Bartholomew. Your first name I mean."

"People don't have first names."

"I would like to call you by your first name."

"Fine. Go ahead."

"What is it? Please."

"O.K. it's Henry."

"Hello," said Paul. He did not know what to say next. Especially as Henry Bartholomew, hospitalman third class, U.S. Navy, did not stop rocking, like a rocking-horse loser.

Paul said, "I want you to know, Henry, that I will find out if he lived, as soon as I can get on a radio, and I'll tell you immediately."

"Fine."

"Because I care about him too."

"Well that's your profession. The skipper, his is a different profession."

"Yes it is."

Doc Bartholomew's gray, or white, skin seemed to jump up and down on his cheekbones; his shoulders twitched as he rocked. His voice too seemed to stretch out on a thread. People whose bodies are still, perhaps, don't understand what it's like to live inside a shaking body that will not be still.

Paul whispered: "God is everywhere."

Bartholomew showed no sign of assent or disagreement.

"He is here with us too," Paul affirmed.

Bartholomew increased the tempo of his rocking, glanced at Paul quickly and looked back at his point in near space.

"If God is everywhere, He must be here," said Paul softly as if to keep it secret. "I came here because I knew He would be here of all places, to feel His presence."

"Ha," said the corpsman. "You're new. Just wait a few days, Chaplain." They were bold words but the speaker took in a shuddering breath like a sobbing child's.

"Yes," said Paul. "I am praying for the courage to bear what a chaplain must, or a corpsman."

"You'll need it," said Bartholomew without any force.

"I am sure I will."

"And I'll ask you later if you still think He's here."

"Wherever I go in the Regiment, I will come back to Delta Company soon and find you, and I promise I will tell you."

"Tell me—"

"Whether I have changed my mind."

"So you think God must be here of all places. Is that your little joke?" This time he met Paul full in the eyes. He said: "I am terrified, helpless, useless."

"I am praying for you, for myself and for all of us," said Paul, knowing this was what must be said at that moment.

Bartholomew said: "And for him too, that marine."

"For him too."

Paul had been sitting beside Bartholomew. Now he rose partway and leaned close and said: "God holds us in His hand."

"He holds us and the gooks kill us."

Touching his shoulder Paul sought to go deep into his eyes to where the terror was, then he turned and picked up Michelson and they trotted forward along the line of sprawling troopers.

Paul imagined that he himself had been spun around by Captain Clare. And Paul imagined Mac's voice in his ear. "Go to your platoon."

Bartholomew was thinking: "Great. Now everybody knows. Christ let me out of this place."

And you try to move your feet, but they are seized in the muck.

Gunnery Sergeant Hitchcock came strolling up the line. He cradled his rifle and carried his helmet in his free hand.

Henry Bartholomew, hospitalman third class, U.S. Navy, saw movement and turned to see the gunny's eyes on him and the man himself approaching him—not just trooping the line but coming toward one man.

The gunny had left his stinger behind and walked alone. What Bartholomew saw was a short easy-stepping man compactly built, with thin arms, large calmly aggressive eyes, a rounded head and shoulders, thinning brown hair receding from his forehead, and invisible eyebrows, and a set expression—set on him, Henry Bartholomew.

The gunny came close and stood still, a little behind, so Bartholomew had to turn his head. Even then it was hard to get a full view, and so Bartholomew shifted his body and awaited what was to come. He was full of a new kind of fear. The gunny could do anything, the officers would not know or care. Bartholomew believed the gunny could kill him with a lawful order if he chose, and might well choose. Bartholomew knew himself to be a coward when he looked at Hitchcock, standing there over him knowing he was looking at a coward; that was why the gunny came and stood there cradling his rifle, and not quite smiling, but almost.

But seeing that the gunny's eyes were slightly rounded like his head Bartholomew had a bold idea, that the gunny looked vaguely froglike.

Hitchcock said: "Anything bothering you, Doc?"

When the lead element reached Thrust Point Albany, Mac halted the company and pondered his decision. To a remarkable degree the plan in his mind was being transformed into reality on the ground, perhaps more important, on the face of his watch. It was not yet 1100 and here they were at Albany. They had already searched the first draw. The terrain and trees were proving difficult, but no more than expected, and the weather was quite tolerable. Mac hoped his tremor of doubt was connected to something rational like the departure of the gunships and then, soon after, of the air observer, who had been orbiting a few miles away, never directly overhead. That would have revealed the company's route. And Mac had cause to believe that his adversary could not as yet know precisely where he was. He wanted to set into a night position unknown to the enemy at least for the first night, if possible.

Another fact: Delta was still within the fan of fire. So what was wrong? Maybe he was just pissed because the change of LZ had wasted two or three hours. Here he stood at Albany, and it was 1100; and he could have been here by 0900.

He concluded this was the bug in his brain and he might as well forget it. And he laid out his course up an undulating ridge that led to a hilltop that he had chosen for his CP and night position. He sent two platoons forward with detailed orders on where to search; he took the other platoon and began climbing toward his night position. All three platoons would reunite ninety minutes before sunset, at the CP, which by then would be half-prepared for night defense.

Thus the company split into three components. The chaplain asked to accompany one of the search platoons; Mac told him to stay with the command group. So Paul Adrano walked with the command group as it beat its way up the ridge. This was not the first order Paul had ever received in the service but it was the first he took as a rebuff.

The vegetation on the ridge was thinner than anybody had hoped, and the command group and 2nd Platoon reached the hilltop by 1400. Here Mac got a surprise. The summit was but thinly wooded. Charcoal burners had worked here this year or last, and the visibility stretched to two hundred meters across the uneven summit.

Mac began setting up a 360-degree defense and clearing fields of fire. His talks with the two platoon leaders below were all O.K. They had found nothing but they were making progress in covering the draws and ridges Mac had assigned them. The two platoons were in good proximity to each other for mutual support should that become necessary.

Mac told Ollie, the artillery forward observer, to pound a hilltop across the valley (the valley of Route 5B), and after firing two adjusting rounds Ollie began thumping his target with accurate fire, giving the troops something to feel good about. This target hill was only about eighteen hundred meters west of Mac's CP. Mac was now where he wanted to be, on the west side of the hill mass, digging into a defensible position. The artillery was limbered up, and his communications were excellent. His troops were running out of water but he anticipated a moderate if not a heavy rainfall soon, and then they could spread ponchos and collect all the water they needed.

He looked about him and then his eye came to rest on the summit Ollie had pounded. An observer up there would have seen his men as they broke into the area thinned by the charcoal burners. But as had often been said, you can't have everything.

He dug a shallow hole—he would deepen it later—and sat down to study his map, from his adversary's viewpoint.

The man he imagined was a captain in the NVA, and he commanded a company of VC Main Force stiffened by a dozen or two NVA regulars, many of them experienced corporals and sergeants. They were billeted in one of the vills along 5B, perhaps within a few kilometers, on the main route from the Ho Chi Minh Trail. They were well armed with AK-47 assault rifles, machine guns, rocket-propelled grenades, and one or two 82-millimeter mortars. And there could be mortars in the hills already, perhaps even above and behind Mac's CP, or across the valley, on the reverse slopes.

Mac believed that this man, this creature of his imagination, was at that very moment marching north on 5B with most of his company, having left orders for the rest to follow without delay.

He believed this man had already sent a runner—probably the one who had informed him of Mac's landing and breach of the wall—north to alert the Local Force commander, and to give orders to assemble the guerrillas and to gather ammo. This assembly point would be in or near one of the vills below Mac's position.

All of this could be true, or none of it.

The digging progressed, and the atmosphere grew too thick to see the valley floor, and the hilltop across the way disappeared. If there was an observer posted there, and if he were still alive, word of Mac's position would reach the vill before the NVA commander did. Therefore Mac made the assumption, as if inscribing words in the tissue of his brain, that the NVA commander would soon know his position.

While imagining his adversary, Mac went deeper and imagined himself. He saw an officer bent on accomplishing his mission, even when it required going outside the fan of fire; a man whose principal weakness was impatience. This was not imaginary; it had been proved. Therefore: "None of this hi-diddle-diddle right up the middle."

He put it into English: "This is a contest of will and skill."

And he tried to imagine what could not be true, that his adversary knew his weakness and would seek to exploit it, to goad him.

He conferred with Ollie on the night defensive fire plan. He accepted Ollie's recommendations, then added one thing. He wanted the artillery to fire two or three illumination rounds per hour throughout the night near a small hill that lay two thousand meters southeast. If his position were known, this would complicate the enemy's thinking. If it were still unknown, it might cause the enemy to think he was two thousand meters away.

Mac's position, while it lay within the artillery's fan of fire for high explosive, was too far out for illumination. Except for small fast-burning flares, Mac had no way to light his perimeter.

Finished with the FO, he started for the place fifty meters away where the chaplain stood in a hole swinging an entrenching tool.

"What a surprise!" exclaimed Paul. "Throw away your helmet, flak jacket, shirt, and T-shirt and it's like diving in the ocean. And this breeze, blowing water molecules, this is good, mister, this is number one!"

Said Mac: "Glad you're enjoying the trip."

"I haven't used these muscles in weeks," Paul exclaimed and took another lick at the edge of his hole with the bent E-tool.

Mac thought: "Christ what a muscle-man." Adrano was pale as a sheet, with black hair spread over his thick chest and curling on his arms, and he had a farmer's suntan—only his face, wrists, and hands had as yet taken any color from the sun; the rest was ghostly white.

He was flinging dirt, loosening new bushels of it with a few hacks of the tool in its angled position, then shifting it to straight with a few twists of the ring bolt, and flinging out more dirt, piling it neatly beside the hole.

Mac advised, "Spread it on the uphill side, to catch the drainage."

Paul caught the point. He braced his thighs against the edge, leaned out, and began scooping dirt into a low wall.

"It'll help a little," said Mac. "Give me the tool a second."

Mac scraped a shallow channel around the outer edge of the parapet, commenting that Paul would still be living in water before the night was over. "But this gives your hole a touch of class," Mac said. "You want to build something that'll impress the neighbors. This is deep enough but you need a grenade sump."

"Oh, a grenade sump! Since I'm a 'friggin new guy' I suppose I should say 'a grenade *what*?' "

"Come here," said Mac enigmatically, and held out his hand.

Paul saw what he meant and grabbed the hand, and Mac hauled him up. Mac took the E-tool, sailed into the hole, and began digging a small-diameter hole at one end. Paul watched the operation suspiciously and said:

"So that's my grenade sump."

Mac looked up at him and said: "You don't believe it?" and pawed in the dirt till he came up with a fist-sized stone. "Grenade," Mac said, holding it aloft. "In your bedroom," and he dropped it. "Kick it!" He did so, rolling it into the sump. "Ball up and hold your ears," and Mac. "*Boom.* You almost die of shock and you lose a foot, but you live, and you write me a thank-you letter, O.K.?"

"Now I suppose people are going to stop by and say, 'Hey Chaplain, cool grenade sump.' "

"They might," Mac agreed, raising his hand.

Paul heaved him out.

Paul folded the E-tool and tossed it in the pile of his other gear.

Mac said: "But do yourself a favor, Chaplain, don't fill it."

"Never. Live in a sumpless hole? How could I face the neighbors?"

Mac stood still—not in hesitation, but as if to change the subject—and looked at Paul with a look that made him draw back within himself. For a few seconds neither man spoke, but Mac seemed to be communicating a warning.

He took a paper from his shirt pocket and handed it to Paul, who unfolded it, feeling the dampness on his fingertips. It nearly fell apart. There were three names on it. He looked at Mac and waited.

"The man who was wounded at the LZ has died," Mac said. "Those are the names of the men in his fire team."

Paul read again: "Jennings, Bisbee, Hararra." He looked up.

"The platoon leader is expecting you. Over there. The corpsman, maybe you didn't know, the corpsman who treated him is with the same platoon."

"Aha," said Paul.

"I think maybe a few words—" Mac began tentatively.

"I'll conduct a service for the whole platoon."

"No. No. That's for later. Now all you can do is gather the fire team for a few minutes, no more. I hope you understand."

"Of course. I was forgetting the situation."

"You were thinking as a chaplain, but I have to think differently."

"You do think differently. I take it the man bled to death."

"Probably," Mac said.

Paul's whole body stiffened and his chin lifted, and Mac saw the change come over him all at once.

Mac said slowly, holding Paul's eyes: "The corpsman, Bartholomew, is a good man."

"You use that term pretty freely. Maybe the man who was bleeding was a good man too."

"There is no maybe about it," said Mac and stood silent.

Without further speech Paul got his flak jacket and shrugged it over his bare torso, and strode away toward the platoon leader.

The rain thickened. Instead of molecules wafting over the face and body it was now a form of water fully subject to the pull of gravity. Ponchos spread throughout the perimeter like dark blossoms opening, served by the rain as flowers are by the sun.

Mac returned to his hole, where he and his radioman combined their ponchos and started a steady silver trickle of water that filled their canteens in minutes.

Mac called the leader of the platoon searching the low promontory that jutted two hundred meters into the paddies.

"What is your position?" Mac asked and the officer said he was right on top of Thrust Point Rochester.

Mac looked at his watch, and at the darkening sky, and at the trembling of the stretched ponchos. He said:

"Execute your second order." Meaning come home.

The officer said: "Roger."

Then Mac called the other platoon in; then he opened his E-tool and set about deepening his hole. He spent more time than was actually necessary fashioning the grenade sump. The labor and the embellishing of his hole this way released his mind to go back where it had already gone several times since Delta reached its hilltop.

Mac thought: "He could have a platoon above me, or a company."

He straightened and looked toward the summit of the hill mass, toward Hill 263, which loomed 150 meters above and 1,600 south of him. He could not see Hill 263 for the rain and the shifting ill-defined clouds.

"Possible," he said. "But not likely." And he paraded a few reasons it was not likely. "Possible that I'm between two forces, one up there"—again looking into the gray sky—"and the other down in the valley."

Without leaving his hole he hollered to Ollie. The artilleryman came over and Mac said:

"Pound Two-six-three. I mean zone and shift. I mean ruin it. And hit the reverse slopes."

"Sir, we've only got two tubes."

"O.K. half-ruin it."

"Sir, it's on the night defensive fire plan as a preplanned concentration."

"I know that, Ollie, but I mean do it now."

"I've given myself over for life—I am not a free man like they are, I must be what I am, a priest. I am not free to fall into a rage and blame people for—Judge not that you be not judged. I have to—"

All unaware, Paul was grinding his teeth; his anger came pouring out as sweat, his frustration as a pulse thudding madly.

"If I were not a priest, if I were able to speak my mind—but a priest must hate the sin but love the sinner, that's the formula, impossible and—"

He went from hole to hole trying to find the platoon leader. The piece of paper was disintegrating in his hand. The rain went into his eyes without his feeling it; he just blinked it away and kept going.

"Drunk with power, that's it. Dangerous! He'll feed men into the meat grinder and call it his duty. He is a—God, what's the word?"

Paul stopped with a jolt and the mantra about "judge not" flashed through his brain. He tried, he strained and struggled to pour all this venom into a jar and roll it into a sump.

"That's the word he used, 'probably,' the kid was 'a good man' and unfortunately he 'probably' bled to death! Bartholomew too is 'a good man.' And what is a good man? Anybody he'll send to hell!"

The image of the dying marine filled his mind—the feel of his forehead, the skin wrinkling under Paul's hand as if the man were looking up to see who was touching him and why. He was conscious!

"Chaplain."

"Yes, yes, what is it? What? Oh!"

"I'm Lieutenant Dan Shaw. I think you're looking for me."

Like Mac, like all the officers, Dan Shaw wore no badge of rank. He was just another guy in jungle utilities darkened and heavy with rain.

"Yes, let's find those men, the fire team. Let's find Bartholomew, let's go."

The fire team had dug two two-man holes spaced about thirty meters apart on the perimeter. The man who lacked a partner had gone a little forward to rig a trip flare. Lieutenant Dan Shaw waved him back, and soon all three marines were sitting on the rim of a hole while Paul sat opposite, and found his attention divided between the team, who sat in stony silence, and the empty hole off to his left. His eyes darted to it several times just as if he had been accustomed to seeing the missing man in that hole. He waited for the lieutenant to say what all knew he was going to say. After the lieutenant had spoken no one else spoke or stirred.

The fire team—Jennings, Bisbee, Hararra—were two black men and one white. The dead marine was white.

Paul wanted to say: "I am not your equal. I am well behind you in grief." But it came to him that he, perhaps, knew the dead man better than they. Had he not placed his hand on his forehead, had his fingers not sunk into his warm wet hair? Had he not looked into his eyes in a vain attempt to awaken a response? And had he not prayed to the ever-present God for his recovery? And did he not know what they couldn't know, the manner and cause of his death?

He ached to pray as a Catholic priest but disciplined himself as a chaplain to all faiths and prayed as follows: "Merciful and all-loving Father—" He spoke in a low voice that was unmarked by his characteristic rasp. The men sat close, with their shoulders slumping and their muddy boots dangling. "We commend to you the soul of our comrade"—Paul's heart jumped as he realized he did not know that man's name—"so recently departed from us, so suddenly taken away, and in asking you to have mercy on him we also ask mercy for ourselves. For we all have sinned, and therefore we dare not ask for justice, Heavenly Father, but rather forgiveness."

He looked at the men, and all were now looking straight at him. Did they expect some kind of answer? To what question? He said:

"I spoke with him, a man I had never met till that minute, and I do not know if he was conscious. Did he understand me when I said 'Let us give thanks that you are alive, that you have survived this wound'? Did he hear me as I prayed, with my hand on his forehead, for his recovery? Did he—was he afraid?"

Suddenly Paul looked at one of the black men and repeated: "Was he afraid?"

The man cast his eyes up to Paul and said: "He was out. I helped carry him to the chopper."

"You think he was unconscious?"

"That I do. I shook him. Whispered in his ear."

To another Paul said, "Did you help carry him too?"

"Yes sir."

And to the third he addressed the same question and the man affirmed it.

"But I believe he was trying to respond to me," Paul declared. "I felt his forehead—wrinkling—under my hand."

"Maybe," the first black man conceded. "But he's gone now."

On a sudden inspiration Paul asked: "Does any one of you think the bullet was intended for you? Were you close to him?"

The white marine shrugged uncomfortably.

The black man who had been speaking said simply: "It was his bullet. If 't was mine, I'd be where he is."

Paul said, "Yes, we cannot understand chance, or what looks like chance. Faith is the only answer." He wanted to say: "I can feel his forehead, his hair, his life in my hand. I can see his unresponding eyes."

Paul bowed his head, closed his eyes, and began a silent recitation of the Our Father, then a Hail Mary, but he was distracted by an acute consciousness of his own hand. As he prayed he heard a two-beat thud from the hill above. This moved his senses from his hand to his ears, or the brain within. Still praying, he heard another double detonation up there in the steady rain, audible but not loud, and later—he had gone into an Act of Contrition without intending to—later, as he said ". . . because I dread the loss of Heaven . . ." another double detonation touched his brain, and he thought: "What is that?"

He opened his eyes and found himself staring at the grenade sump, just below the dangling muddy boots of the three marines.

He stood in the hole and shook the hand of each man and promised to conduct a memorial service when the company returned to the rear. But the thudding from the hills unnerved him. Something was wrong in his mind, affecting his body. He was jumpy and short of breath. He didn't know what it was, but it seemed to be taking charge.

To fight this he said to Lieutenant Dan Shaw: "I'll find the corpsman myself," and he went in search of Bartholomew.

"So you already know," Paul surmised.

"I saw you and the lieutenant talking to his buddies," said Doc Bartholomew.

"I see. Was he a friend of yours?"

"I knew him like I know the other guys in the platoon. He seemed like a pretty good guy. He treated me O.K."

"Nobody has told me his name."

"His name was Blalock—Bob Blalock."

"Where was he from?"

"Kentucky. He said he was a hillbilly with nowhere to go but the Corps."

"And did he like the Corps?"

"Well enough I guess," said Bartholomew reluctantly. "He wasn't a lunatic jarhead but yeah, well enough."

"A 'lunatic jarhead'?"

"You'll meet some; maybe you already have."

"How do you tell one? I mean what are you saying?"

"I am saying, Chaplain, that you will come across men over here who want to be here."

"But I myself want to be here!"

"Sure, of course, you have a mission, you told me."

"Yes, why else would I—"

"O.K. These men I'm talking about have a mission too. It is not the same as yours. You think they're looking under the rocks for God? They came here to relieve suffering? I know you learned all about sin in the seminary so—"

"Certainly," said Paul abashed, trying to grasp what kind of man he was dealing with.

"Well," asserted Bartholomew, "sin is a silly fairy-tale word, excuse me Chaplain, for the real thing. If you haven't seen it yet in this company just keep your eyes open. I don't mean the sin of eating meat on Friday either."

"You're a Catholic?" asked Paul the priest.

"Oh no. I used to be. Very different thing," Bartholomew replied. "In fact I spent two years in the seminary and I do mean 'spent.' Gone. And when I walked out, my draft board sent me a little notice and I squeaked into the Navy just in time, so I'd never have to sleep in a mud hole."

He was in fact sitting on the edge of a mud hole—but he was not rocking now. He added: "If I still believed in the fairy tale I'd say God was pissed because I quit."

"You intended to become a priest?" Paul asked.

"Sure. And now I need one, or would if I still bought the story."

"The—you call it a story?"

"The whole rigamarole. 'God loves you' and all that."

"You say you need a priest. Here is one with you now."

"I *would* need one. I didn't say I do."

"You know," Paul advanced tentatively, "there can be no guilt when one is unable to—when you could not—guilt is there only for what lies within your power to do, or not do."

Henry Bartholomew, hospital corpsman third class, U.S. Navy, a small, closely built man with inquisitive blue eyes, a man who was not trembling now, looked quizzically at Paul and awaited an explanation.

Paul said: "You wanted to go with him. You would have—"

"Blalock?"

"Yes. You were required to obey the captain, and leave Blalock. It is not your fault that you did. You had a duty to—"

"Oh shit, Chaplain, what are you talking about?"

"You wanted to save him," Paul persisted with patient gentleness. "You did your utmost. You need feel no guilt. Had you jumped into that helicopter you would have risked court-martial, and no reasonable man would expect you to do that."

Bartholomew was watching Paul with an expression that changed by degrees as he comprehended the argument.

"Chaplain, for Christ's sake, I'm not responsible for Blalock. He was bleeding internally. What do you expect me to do about that without a set of MAST trousers?"

Paul stared, and tried to explain himself, and decided to keep quiet.

"I told you, Chaplain, I was scared out of my mind. And in case you're wondering, I may be normal right now, but in the dark I turn to jelly. Maybe you will too."

"That is nothing to be ashamed of. Anyway, God will—"

"Oh, can it, Padre. God will or God won't, what's the difference?"

Paul bowed his head but not in prayer. He tried to think. What was his obligation to this man?

"And watch yourself," Bartholomew advised. "No rifle, no ammo belt for the machine guns, no mortar rounds hanging from your pack straps—traveling light—they'll think you're some big shot sent out here by some general, some staff pogue. Did you notice? Even the skipper carries a rifle. So I ask you, Chaplain, who are they going to aim at?"

"I guess," said Paul quietly and calmly, "me. And you."

The corpsman suggested: "Maybe you should borrow two ammo belts and make a cross over your chest like Pancho Villa."

"I can't do that," said Paul gravely.

"No you can't. 'Man of God' and all that. Well you're in God's hands, and you'll get all the protection God gives to his chosen ones."

"Yes," said Paul just as if Bartholomew had said it straight. "And so will you."

"Ha!" the corpsman exclaimed.

The ground up here was level but lumpy; so if you flopped on your belly anywhere inside the perimeter and gazed off in any given direction you'd see nothing beyond the nearest heave of the earth. To gain a view of, say, fifty meters, you had to stand (not in your hole but beside it); and to see clear across the CP you'd have to mount one of the heaves, which rose irregularly two or three feet above the flat. Then in the gusts of the monsoon you might not see very far no matter where you stood.

MacHugh Clare was getting to know the terrain as he trooped the line with his exec and radioman. He found no signs that guns or mortars had registered on this hill. A crater or two would have been something to worry about. In fact he found nothing to give him pause. There were fire sites scattered all over but they all appeared to be the remains of charcoal fires.

On its west side the hill dropped away quite sharply and he was obliged to station a fire team well down the forward slope. But it was just here that the unbroken jungle approached nearest to the crest. The effect was to place those men closer to the solid tree line than he wanted. But to pull them back would bring them virtually to the military crest, and that was no place to leave them.

He asked their platoon leader (the same Dan Shaw who had met the chaplain an hour before) to get them some help in clearing fields of fire; and he continued his tour of inspection.

"Sir," his radio operator called, holding out the handset.

Mac took it. One of the search platoons was coming in. Mac sent the exec to make certain nobody shot at them, and continued his rounds. But here was another little question. The platoon on its way in was the one that had been farther out. It was the other platoon (1st) that should reach home first. Mac stopped, took the radio again, and called 1st Platoon. This was the one whose team had slept on LP duty.

Mac asked the lieutenant (Kim Kolias, the "frightened youth") for his position. He plotted the result. To do this he bent forward to shelter his map from the downpour, and placed a blue mark on the streaming plastic map cover, then checked his work, because it looked doubtful. What the lieutenant had told him was that he was on a height of land leading straight east, up a rise to the CP.

On this course 1st Platoon would approach the CP at a place where the level ground jutted out like a ship's prow. This was as it should be, so Mac suppressed his doubt and resumed his tour. He spoke or locked eyes, during the next fifteen minutes, with every man in that sector, and glanced at every fighting hole. Often he would crouch on his heels and bend into the shelters the men had built out of their ponchos and shelter halves. Some of the hooches covered the fighting holes; others stood beside them so a man could sleep on the ground and roll into the hole in case of incoming mortar rounds.

Mac never said much in these visits, sometimes nothing. He would nod, or lift his chin in a kind of silent message of greeting and approval, then move on.

The arriving platoon (3rd) passed through the line and took up its assigned sector, and began digging in. This was the platoon commanded by Staff Sergeant Reggie Graves. Their work was well advanced when Mac again called 1st and asked for his new position. The answer—encoded as a range and bearing from a thrust point—was obviously wrong.

Mac and his radioman crawled into a shelter, first asking the owners if they minded a little company, so Mac could study the map more carefully. Taking the handset he said: "Striker One, check your position again."

Four men crouched under the outstretched canvas, with the rain thrumming and gusting in unpredictable puffs. It would be necessary to put out a few more listening posts and to repeat the standing orders about shelter. This is what made LP duty on such a night so arduous. To sit all night enveloped in the "molecular rain," sleeping at best half the hours from dark to dawn, was bad enough. To do the same job under the medium downpour was exhausting. Some men retained their edge through four or five days; others lost it sooner.

The next voice on the radio was not the platoon leader's but his radioman's. He gave the same position as before, and Mac said: "Let me speak to Striker One Actual." When Kim Kolias came on, Mac told him that he doubted the accuracy of his report. Mac said calmly: "If you had started climbing that height of land when I told you to, you'd be here by now."

The lieutenant said "Roger," and nothing more. Mac listened to the sound of the rain, like the exhalation of a monster that has no need to inhale, and looked at the two riflemen who were his hosts. There was a candor, a patience in their faces that gave him confidence.

Mac knew the platoon leader's plight. He was standing in a jungle in a downpour, able to see perhaps five meters in any direction, and his company commander was asking him to check his position. How? Mac spoke into the handset:

"What is the direction of your march?"

The answer: "East."

Said Mac: "Keep climbing. You are not where you think you are, but just keep climbing."

Mac checked his watch. It was now an open question whether 1st Platoon could reach the perimeter before dark. Mac told the exec to assemble a working party to begin digging the defenses in the sector the platoon had been assigned. Men who had already dug their own holes were now to be asked to dig somebody else's as well.

Next Mac took a call from the lieutenant. He said that if he followed the steepest route he would have to deviate right from his set course. Should he keep on course or take the steepest route? Mac answered: "Climb, as steep as you can. Tell me when you come out on top."

Dusk came but 1st Platoon did not.

"I'll be O.K. Chaplain. I don't need it."

"No, no," Paul insisted, "take it, please."

And Paul started to tear down the little shelter and give Michelson back his shelter half. Michelson had been ordered to the perimeter, to man the hole left half empty by the death of the marine shot at the LZ. Lieutenant Dan Shaw had come and given the order.

"Skipper's orders," Shaw said.

Michelson stayed Paul's hand. He said the man he was joining had rigged a very good hooch. Paul reluctantly assented, and thanked Michelson.

"Here, take this," said Michelson. Crouching over his pack he pulled out a little contrivance made of the stiff wire from a box of C rats: one of those cardboard boxes labeled "Meal, Combat, Individual." Under Paul's inquisitive eye Michelson pulled the twisted wires and they jumped ingeniously into a box-shaped frame. Michelson placed the frame on a flat rock and lay a heat tab inside it. He said:

"Gimme your heavy, Chaplain."

Paul handed over his main course for dinner, a can of ham and lima beans.

"Wow, this is the best," exclaimed Michelson without irony.

He opened the can with the John Wayne hanging on the dog-tag chain around his neck and set it on the wire frame, then lit the tab. All the while the rain was skimming off the roof of the hooch.

"Don't breathe the fumes," Michelson cautioned, but it was too late. Paul's nose and throat were seared with an inhalation, and Paul leaned out into the rain, squinted the tears from his eyes, and took a deep breath.

Michelson propped open a vent with a stick he had picked up earlier. He bade the chaplain farewell, saying, "Just stay in this hole, Chaplain."

And so Paul was left alone with his dinner, and realized he had not been alone for many days, except while falling asleep.

But he did not use his precious solitude to pray or to contemplate his strange situation, or to try to decide whether he owed the captain an apology. He had learned that MAST meant "military antishock trousers"; and he surmised from Doc Bartholomew's outburst that the wounded man had been a poor risk from the moment he was hit. He saw a rivulet carving itself a deeper channel on the edge of his hole—saw it in the fading light—and left the shelter to scrape out a better drainage ditch around his parapet.

Returning, he saw that the rivulet had stopped running. This started an absurd little wave of satisfaction coursing through his chest. He stirred the ham and lima beans, took a long drink from a full canteen of cold water, and watched the lambent blue flame mantling the heat tab. He tried to figure out how the wire frame worked, so he could fold it up correctly, but the light was too feeble.

Under the glow of his red flashlight he read his Daily Office, asked God to help him control his tendency to judge others harshly, and finally finished off his meal with the piece of pound cake and a cup of instant coffee that was both bitter and weak. When he had finished he was ready for a meal. He wondered why this solitude which he had craved was so unsatisfying.

He found he had let the little packet of toilet paper from his C box get wet. It was now useless.

"Absolutely, worry about that!" he cried. "How do I wipe myself? Cosmic question! Forget your evil temper, your propensity to judge others by standards so much harder than those you apply to yourself—your total failure to respond to Bartholomew's cry for faith—forget your—just—just worry about that!"

Restless, unable to sit still, he closed his book, returned it to his pack (the book and pack contents were still nearly dry), twisted into his poncho, which was not easy to do in a stooped posture, and pulled up the hood. He sat there ready to go out, listening, and he might have been alone in the world. For a few seconds it seemed he was, just himself in this rain, and "just himself" meant that exactly. No other men, no animals, no God. He believed this for a few seconds and there was nothing to do but die.

Then with quick energy his mind hopped from one point to the next, and so to the end. If he was afraid, his faith had no meaning, and was nothing but a vain hope. If that were true, his whole life rested on an error. Little corrections cannot set a big error right.

His father had howled against him in sorrow and fury. Adrano Senior was much more "Italian" than his son, whose mother had been Danish. "Don't be a fool! Believe it if you need to, but don't give your life to it. Even if it was true you wouldn't have to give your whole life." And when Paul had stated his case: "Paul, you could be anything you want—with your intelligence. If you do this you will be nothing. You'll spend your life trying to convince dying old ladies they're about to enter the gates of Paradise, and why are they scared shitless? Paradise for Christ sakes!"

And so he sat on what Michelson called the firing step (Michelson had remodeled the hole), within a feeble shelter that the wind could carry away with one sweep—Nui Gio, the Mountain of the Wind!—realizing or fearing that he was not alone, that out in the jungle men who could neither be seen nor heard were crawling closer; men who would kill him without hate or remorse; kill him as if he were one of the marines; kill him with mortars, grenades, rockets, or rifle fire. Maybe tonight, his first night. But if he should survive tonight, so what? There were other nights to come.

He crawled out and hesitated. Then he saw moving figures in the dark. Under the shelter half he couldn't hear their steps, but up here he could both hear and almost see the men passing him, carrying rifles slung over their shoulders and entrenching tools swinging in their hands. They did not speak, they marched, and perhaps the reason he could see them was that the rain beat a silver nimbus around each man's helmet and shoulders. But he did see them, six or eight passing near him and seeming to ignore him. They did not act like the friendly marines he knew in the daylight. They walked into the dark and disappeared in the rain.

Paul stood at the edge of the nucleus of fighting holes that was the command group, situated near the center of the perimeter. If he simply went in a certain direction he would find Captain Clare and the exec and their radios. He had imprinted their location in his memory during daylight. Now he began tentatively on a twenty-pace march, rising over the small humps in the earth, touching a tree trunk now and again, and leaving the problem of finding his way back to his hole for another time. He knew he was close to something when he began to hear the sound of rain beating on stretched canvas or rubber. He stopped, and stood still, listening. He took a careful step, using his feet as feelers, then another.

He crouched down and said, "Hello, it's Chaplain Adrano."

A voice an arm's length away said, "Hello, Chaplain."

"I'm looking for the captain."

A man came out of the ground, a man he could not see very well, whose voice was unfamiliar, and took him by the arm—he recalled the bishop—and guided him through one or two twists and turns, just a few paces, and then said:

"That's the skipper's hooch."

Paul could see it, and hear voices inside. He went down on his haunches and duck-walked, and saw a flicker of red that disappeared instantly, but he had seen it for certain. He reached out and felt the cold canvas and said, "Gentlemen, may I come in?"

"We are talking about—"

Mac glanced up into Paul's eyes, saw the intense interest there, and turned the map for Paul to see.

"—this point here—" said Mac, touching the map with his grease pencil.

To Paul, who could not have found the CP on the map to save his life, this gesture was cordial but not useful. He said, "Put it in Latin and I could read it."

Mac replied: "You'll see in a minute." And turning to Gunnery Sergeant Hitchcock he continued: "I've told him to start digging. But I'm telling you I'd like to bring him in as soon as we can. Tonight if possible."

Mac spoke in a low voice and Hitchcock nodded slowly, turning the map and playing his red flashlight on it. Hitchcock's convex eyes looked liquid and colored in the rich glow.

Mac continued: "He doesn't know where he is and neither do I, but I think—"

He made a blue mark on the spot he had indicated to Paul and said: "This knob, right here. I think he was coming up this ridge and I told him to report when he came out on top, and he did, and this is where I hope he is."

Now for the first time Paul heard more than a few syllables from Gunny Hitchcock, who said:

"So I go about, looks like five hundred meters, at about one six zero."

"Right," said Mac. "Just don't go down any hills. If you feel yourself crossing a contour line, you're off course. Make a ninety-degree right turn—"

"—and go maybe four hundred meters," said Hitchcock—

"—and the ground should start to rise," said Mac.

"If it don't, I come back."

"And if you hit thick jungle—"

"—come back."

"Right," said Mac. "Bring him in if the going was fairly easy on the way out."

"Like, if it was—what?"

"Say you find him where I think he is, and it took you no more than an hour or hour and a half."

"Then I bring him in."

"Yes."

"Otherwise dig in and wait for the dawn's early light."

"Yes, and Guns."

"Yes sir?"

"Call anytime. Always glad to talk with you. But for sure, call every thirty minutes."

"Aye aye sir."

"Do you need my red light?"

"No sir, these batteries are fresh."

"You've got a compass?"

"Yes sir, sure."

"Then collect your troopers. A squad plus a gun and a blooper. Carry some flares but don't use'm without explicit permission."

"Not on your life, Skipper."

"So get your squad and report back to me in ten minutes, and we'll call him and tell him to man the net, that you're coming; and please don't let's have any U.S.-only firefights. But Guns, listen. Approach with caution. Those guys'll be anxious to shoot."

The gunny glanced at Mac, gave a quick disappearing smile, crawled over Paul's legs, and waited at the flap for Mac to douse the light, then lifted the flap and was gone.

"What's up?" Paul asked.

"First Platoon's lost."

"Oh. It was the lieutenant from First Platoon who had the trouble with the sleeping LP."

"Yes, but it could happen to anybody," said Mac evenly. "He'll be all right. We'll get him back."

"You mean the gunny's going out there and stumble around in the pitch black and try to find—what's his name?"

"His name is Kolias, Lieutenant Kim Kolias, with thirty men."

"He's the one who threw the stones at the LP?"

"Yes."

Paul pondered this, and wished tonight were like the other night, with an intermittent moon and open country and H&I's flashing all around. Certain words stuck in his throat. He tried, but could not say what an impulse told him to say. It was a mad impulse! Don't say it! He choked it off and said:

"I came here to apologize."

As he spoke a match was struck and flamed into life, and moved toward a candle. For the first time Paul saw a third man, Mac's radioman, who crouched beneath the canvas and leaned closer to place the candle on a little disc of yellow wood.

Paul cast a mortified glance at this man, who looked studiously down at the wax dripping from the candle to the yellow wood. And Paul looked at Mac, whose blue eyes looked steadily at him.

"We can discuss that later," said Paul hastily.

"If you wish, but so far as I'm concerned there is nothing to discuss."

"I misunderstood something," Paul continued hesitantly, and looked again at the radioman, who was still occupied with the dripping wax. "I spoke without thinking. I am—"

"Forget it," said Mac. "I don't even know what you're talking about."

"Exactly. I have to clarify that. But some other time."

"O.K. Whatever you say."

"And now," Paul plunged on with mounting desperation, "I want— I want to go—with the gunny."

"That wouldn't be—"

"Yes! I, my job—"

"You mentioned 'stumbling around in the dark,' and it could amount to just that," Mac declared. "This isn't the same as our hike to the LP."

"Clearly. This is—" Paul was thinking of darkness and death— death striking from nowhere. Mac had been looking carefully at the chaplain's face and listening with extremely close attention to his voice, and determined that he was terrified. Mac said:

"It is not my prerogative to define your job for you, but—"

"No it is not. And my job is to go where I am most needed. Or likely to be. So I am—going. I'll get my flak jacket and helmet and be back here by the time the gunny shows up."

Said Mac: "Stay where you are, Chaplain."

The radioman set the candle stub in the pool of wax, held it for several seconds, and withdrew his hand. He did not look at either officer but sat staring into the flame with wide-open eyes.

"No," Paul said again louder, "it is not your prerogative. You said it yourself. The colonel told me to go where I was needed and that's what I intend to do," and he made a motion to leave, but Mac said as quietly as before:

"Stay where you are, Chaplain."

After stumbling around and shivering in the dark Paul finally located his hole and slipped under the canvas, landing in a foot of water. This set off one of those hated heart-explosions in his chest. He struggled out of his poncho. He wished he had a candle. How nice it would be to see something. He slumped sideways on the firing step, held his feet up for a while, then gave up and let them drop in the water.

"I need sleep," he said quietly but aloud. "I didn't sleep enough last night. How many days is this going to last?"

There was no place to rest his feet. At this rate he'd be frozen in an hour. Sleep, he needed to sleep but trembling men do not sleep very well. He had always thought that if you are really tired you can sleep anywhere but what if you're stuck in a slippery hole filling up with water—and anyway, what if this firing step just collapsed into the pool?

"So what, I've got a grenade sump!" he exclaimed in his mind and laughed. But the drumming on the roof—"I understand now. They can't hear a thing. The gooks could be—"

He said *gooks*!

"So I'm a bigot as well as a coward. But who says so? Cowards do not volunteer to go out on hazardous missions! No, but they are sick with relief when told they cannot go. At dark Bartholomew turns to jelly." All this ran in a turbulent stream through his fear-struck mind.

Paul was not jelly, he was stiff and rattling as if he were nothing but freezing bones.

"For all that so-called skipper knows, we're being surrounded this very minute by a hundred gooks, and what does he do? Sends the only real soldier in the group out with twelve men and a machine gun, a gun we may need, out to chase an incompetent adolescent who has wandered down the wrong mountain. They will—kill us! All of us. They will overrun this place and blast it to hell and then—

"Well then as a priest you'll be saved! You are not in a state of mortal sin unless cowardice and shame are mortal sins, but Christ comforts the cowardly, surely, so you die and whoosh! Off we go to Paradise to meet all those frightened old ladies and say, 'See, what did I tell you?' The gates of Paradise!"

He stood erect and ripped the hooch apart, took a shelter half, spread it on the ground, and rolled in the watery muck till he had wrapped himself twice around with the heavy cold soaking canvas. And then he lay shivering, intending to give his heat to this little puddle of his own.

What if somebody yelled "Incoming," which way would he roll? Where's the hole?

"Fuck it!" he cried and was utterly shocked. Had he said *gooks* and *fuck it*?

He said in a silent dialogue with himself: "Am I really a priest? Dad would say, 'More, more!' He'd say, 'What are you anyway?' He'd say— What do I care what he'd say? Shut up! shut up!"

He awakened in warm water. It was daylight and he heard voices around him. He unfolded the canvas and rolled out, and stood. There were men huddled in twos and threes over their fires of heat tabs and C4. Paul knew they burned something called C4 but did not know that with enough of it you could blow the whole mountain flat.

He loosed a prodigious stream against a tree and watched with interest as the scattering drops caught the horizontal rays of the rising sun. What a pleasure to let it go like this and to look around in daylight and see the marines shaking out their ponchos, wringing their T-shirts, heating their breakfast.

Here came a man stepping carefully, carrying a small dark-green C-rat can that was steaming, with its cover folded to make a handle.

It was Michelson. He said, "Good morning, Chaplain. Here's your coffee."

"Michelson, you are a prince. You are the King of Marines. Tomorrow I make the coffee. Is it a deal?"

"O.K. sir, deal."

He saw several men he knew by name. He was getting to know a lot of these men. Looking around with avid curiosity, he saw the "frightened youth" talking with Mac out on the perimeter. This gave him a lift—and then he saw the gunny.

Gunnery Sergeant Hitchcock was squatting with several men circling a small blue flame, and as Paul watched him he rose slowly and steadily from his squat, with a true and effortless motion, like a gymnast. He saw Paul watching, and gave him a nod of greeting that involved scarcely any movement of his head, and then he gave the usual Hitchcock smile, if that's what it was.

Paul pulled his pack off the firing step and dug in it till he found an envelope of coffee. He went over to the hole where Michelson, Hararra, Jennings, and Bisbee were cooking breakfast.

Chapter 7

The Fan of Fire

Mac wondered: Should he wait for clear weather and air support before pressing his search outside the fan of fire?

The sky was the same dark gray, charged with the "molecular rain," so unfriendly to aviation. Watching more closely he saw an ominous variety of tones and colors of gray—color, or lack of color, and it was moving, dispersing, intensifying like a display of northern lights in the negative.

Mac strode across his CP to talk with Lieutenant Kim Kolias, chiefly to be seen speaking with him and, importantly, listening to him. Anybody who happened to be looking was sure to see from Kolias's expression that he was not being chewed out.

Mac looked at the boyish red face and tried to reconcile the naïveté with the impulse that had led him to join the Marines. There were very few draftees in Delta Company. Mac was one, but he understood Kim's decision.

"Come to my hooch in ten minutes," he told Kim Kolias. He sent Pickens Freeman, his runner, to summon the other officers.

The meeting convened over C-rat coffee: Mac, the exec, the three rifle platoon leaders, the forward air controller and artillery forward observer, the weapons platoon leader, and Gunnery Sergeant Hitchcock.

All these had traced an arc on their maps showing the limit of artillery support, a line running through the paddies southwest of Nui Gio, piercing the villages along Route 5B, and rising into the hills on the opposite slope.

Mac said: "Unless the weather clears we operate inside this line today."

"Thank you, Skipper."

"I'm writing my mother and telling her I'll live another day."

"Very good idea, sir."

And so forth. Then Mac resumed:

"First Platoon, CP security. Second, search from Rochester to N.Y.C. Third, N.Y.C. to Buffalo. We're looking for any sign of heavy foot or wheeled traffic from Five B into the woods. Ollie, one FO team per platoon, and you stay with the CP."

"Aye aye sir," said Ollie.

"We displace the CP at zero eight hundred. New CP at Four One Four, Seven One Seven. Everybody in the new CP by sixteen hundred. Got it?"

They located the new CP on their maps and were happy. It was closer to their search areas.

Mac said: "Who can give the gunny six men that he'll like?"

Nobody volunteered, so Mac designated 3rd Platoon. He explained: "The gunny's going on an overnight recon around Syracuse. He and his men walk at fourteen hundred."

To the weapons platoon commander Mac said: "Cliff, can you scrounge up three or four LAWs for the gunny? Give him some rocket power?"

"Yes sir. I'll have to pull'm from—uh—"

"Second and Third," Mac suggested.

"Aye aye sir."

Mac looked pointedly at the leaders of these platoons and they nodded assent.

"O.K. here's what the gunny's going to do," Mac continued. "Take a look at Four Zero Four, Seven Zero Four."

When they had located this spot on their maps, Mac went on:

"You see a trail leading off Route Five B, passing through a little vill, going around some paddies and curving south and crossing that little river, the Song Xa what's-it's-name. See it?"

They studied their maps and looked again at Mac.

"See where the trail crosses the little river?"

They said that they did.

This river lay south of the hill mass and flowed east into the Song Tra Khuc.

Said Mac: "Gunny Hitchcock is going down to the edge of the jungle and rest in the shade of the trees. He'll watch that crossing till dark. If he sees a water buffalo pulling a cartful of ammo he keeps quiet and we give him a week's R and R in Bangkok. If he sees a big Dodge truck lumbering along he blows it away with a LAW. If he sees nothing interesting before dark he waits in the woods till about midnight, then—Gunny, you tell us what you do then."

"Ha." This soft and low sound escaped from Hitchcock's curved bristling lips. His nearly hairless eyebrows lifted and his forehead wrinkled as if in an effort to remember. "Ahh," he breathed, "at midnight I break out the beer?"

"That's a different assignment," said Mac.

"Oh yeah."

"You see why I chose the gunny for this job, gents," Mac said.

"Yeah. I'm the man all right. Sir. Captain. At midnight sleepers wake up, which includes me. We look up and we don't see the moon. We hope. So me and my snuffies walk into the open down there by the creek. We have left the gun in the woods with the gunner, assistant gunner, and one snuffie with the night-vision glasses who has briefed me before I go out. Keep my eyes in good shape. I hate those fuckin glasses. So with big eyeballs and little assholes me and my friends go strolling out like we own the place and we come to the bank of the little river; moon in the last quarter and anybody here prays, pray for a night as black as the hinges of hell. So there we are, where the little river crosses the trail, or you could say the trail crosses the river, and we got enough rope to hang ourselves."

Mac cast a glance at Lieutenant Kim Kolias and saw a man utterly transfixed, staring at the gunny with disbelieving eyes.

"And being outside the fan of fire," Hitchcock continued, "we won't waste any taxpayer dollars shooting those noisy artillery projectiles. We snoop and poop to the river and we try to find the answer to the skipper's question, which is: Have the gooks built a bridge at the level of the summer pool?"

"Exactly," said Mac and everybody looked at him and waited, "because if they have, there's dynamite down there somewhere. In short, gents, if the gunny finds an underwater bridge, at the level of the summer pool, he's found the route to a major depot. If there's a bridge down there we go to that sector tomorrow in force."

"With or without my help?" asked Captain Kindred, toastmaster and forward air controller.

"I'll decide that tomorrow," Mac answered. "I should have said we go for certain if we have gunships or Phantoms. And if we don't, maybe we go, maybe we wait for clear skies."

The group was perfectly silent. Lieutenant Kim Kolias asked: "Sir, summer pool? I don't—"

"The water level during the dry season. They build bridges six inches underwater so they can't be detected by aerial photography," Mac explained.

Said the gunny: "Anybody want to know how far down the summer pool is?"

How far below the present monsoon surface of the river was the summer surface?

"Anybody?" the gunny repeated.

"Yeah, Guns," said Captain Kindred. "Tell me, O wise one."

"Sorry sir, nobody knows. I'll tell you when I get back with both balls and all limbs." He gave Captain Kindred one of his disappearing smiles.

As the meeting broke up Mac spoke privately to Lieutenant Dan Shaw of 2nd Platoon.

"Say, Dan. Before you go."

"Yes sir."

"The chaplain's been feeling pretty bloodthirsty. He's dying to escape this boring command group."

"Yes sir. Y'all want me to invite him along when I go down the valley?"

"Yes, and tell him I said it was O.K. In case he asks. And take Michelson."

It was 0800 and Mac and his command group, marching with Kolias's 1st Platoon, headed for the new CP. The way being uncertain, Mac took the point. The footing was not difficult but the shapes and slopes of the land were puzzling, and Mac preferred to navigate from out front, rather than from the center of gravity of the main body, where the commander usually marched, and where he is told in all the books that he should march.

So Mac walked point as 1st Platoon went down over the crest, after the men had buried their trash and the radio operators had pounded the terminals on their spent batteries till they were junk. Gunnery Sergeant Hitchcock with his just-assembled recon team marched rear guard. When the platoon reached the new position these men would be allowed to rest.

But the new position was easier to find on the map than on the ground. The forest grew thicker and tangled with vines. The sky clamped down. Fine rain swept across the ridges in invisible waves, and soon Mac's visibility was cut to ten meters. He stopped now and then to check map and compass, and to estimate how far he had come, like a sailor on dead reckoning. He made his pivot from southeast to southwest when the ground felt level under his feet. If he had placed the pivot right he was aiming right.

He followed his bearing, working his way steadily through a woods that was more brown than green. Even so, he came upon a wild banana tree with its six-foot leaves showing a deep green and its little stunted fruits shining in the shadows, pale green. If he kept to the bearing he should not encounter the stream on his left nor the rise of land on his right. He should soon—in about six hundred meters—feel the ground begin to rise straight ahead. Then he would know where he was.

With a subtle change of light something else changed. He no longer believed he was in a completely wild place. Something ahead suggested a clearing. He slowed and went more carefully. He stopped and listened. He turned to the man behind him, who joined him in listening. Back one more interval he could see his radioman, whose expression asked whether he wanted the mike.

Mac felt that if he made a negative sign to the radioman he would confuse the man standing in between; so he turned slowly back to the front without communicating anything to either man, and for a second this made him feel a kind of distress—that they had shown they were with him and he had not responded. He listened. He took three more steps and the light grew perceptibly brighter ahead. The woods were still shadowed under the monsoon sky but something changed with every step. He shifted his rifle from Safe to Fire, took two more steps, and crouched. Nothing, only the dripping of water from leaf to leaf.

Mac went forward; then it was apparent that the area ahead was more open than where he walked, and perhaps open altogether, a clearing. With two more steps he was crouching at the edge, staring at a house. It stood alone in an open space about the size of a basketball court. It had mud walls, vacant windows, grass roof, mud porch. Mac could see a black fire pit on the packed earth of the porch, under the projecting roof, and a trickle of water dropping from a runnel above.

He brought two men up and sent one around to either side while he approached the door. It occurred to him that if a man fired from behind the house the bullet could pass through the wall and hit him, and with this idea added to his thinking, but not changing his intention, he strode swiftly forward and stood in the doorway. He could see the rear wall grow a little darker when his body blocked the doorway, but he could not see much else. He knew that a person inside might not realize how blind he was, so he stepped forward and swept his rifle clear across the room, and dropped to one knee, and searched the gloom with anxious eyes.

He saw a plank bed, a handful of nut shells scattered over the earthen floor, a bunch of wooden boxes, and an open kerosene can with "Gulf" on it. There was nobody home.

When Mac came out a man told him there was a trail behind the place and a kind of shed, or something, down the trail. It proved to be a rick of half-burned wood beside a grassed-over dirt pile. The ground had been cleared of trees. Wood chips darkened by two or three seasons lay everywhere.

It was a charcoal-burning site. The rick had half fallen down but still stood six feet high. The dirt would have been put there to smother the fire when the carbonization was complete.

Mac saw the rick and house together. Here a family had lived while making charcoal. Here they worked early and late, built their ricks, fired the wood till it was almost pure carbon, then threw dirt on the fires, broke up the charcoal remains, and loaded each other with roped bundles big enough to brush the sides of the trails as they went bending down to the valley.

The rick trail curved off to the left and Mac guessed it would lead him to the big "shoulder trail" that the gunny had called Ambush Alley; so Mac abandoned it and kept to his bearing, and walked upright now and swiftly through the culled forest.

With his rifle back on Safe and slung over his shoulder, and his compass in his hand, he pressed blindly on. It seemed to him the trees grew smaller and thicker, the leaves more numerous and small, and almond-shaped, and the sky felt closer above. He was sweating and breathing heavily but he felt strong, as if he could hump like this for days or weeks, given enough water. And then the ground began to rise under his feet. He looked again at the compass because it seemed too good to be true. But he was moving on a heading of 250 magnetic and it was exactly here that the ground should rise. Now he knew he was following a true course to the new CP, where the company would gather again before dark. And he kept on humping and the ground kept on rising, just as it should.

He signaled for the radio. He spoke to the exec: "I'm climbing now. Next time I stop it means I'm checking the position. Go into a hasty defense and wait."

Returning the handset to his radioman, he couldn't suppress a smile, and the man smiled too—his sweating, ashen face breaking into silent mirth and congratulation.

Mac pushed on, climbing, and something absurd flashed through his mind. He imagined troopers pausing in their digging, and one said: "The skipper really hit it." Everybody agreed that the skipper had got it right. And he imagined, not that they would cheer or anything so improbable, but that there would spread through this platoon, the one that had been wandering lost just twenty-four hours ago, the conviction that they were satisfied to be in Delta Company. All this played in his mind quite involuntarily.

His pride usually found a way to communicate itself to Sarah. But this wasn't normal life and he couldn't tell her. He wanted her to understand not just this feat of dead reckoning—like a sailor's, who counts the turns of his screw and watches his compass, and so makes

1 3 3

his way unerringly through fog—not just that he was as good on the point as any man in Delta Company—but also—

But they would meet in Honolulu and throughout the whole five days he knew he could not inject it, however subtly, into the conversation. Might as well be an incompetent fool as brag to your woman about something like this.

Then—he must have kept to the bearing, he must have moved silently, he must have stayed alert—but if so, all that was the farthest thing from his mind, because then he was conscious only of her intimate presence, a trembling awareness of each for the other.

She appeared as his dancing woman, in a nightgown with lace straps going over her shoulders and down her back in parallel lines. That she wanted to dance before him, that dancing excited her, she had never denied. She had said she danced for herself as well as for him. He would stand before her, turn her body by suggesting she turn, revealing his wish with a gentle pressure of his fingers on her waist, and when she had turned her back he would lift her arms and join her hands over her head. She began a sinuating but unpredictable motion of her body, and her height and the fullness of her figure were accentuated by this motion.

So he let his fingertips slowly go down, tracing the outline of her wrists and forearms, moving as he descended to the long muscles of her upper arms, and so down her sides to her waist, then coming to rest with her hips undulating against his palms as he seemed to hold her in a controlling grip from both sides, yet did not really hold, but only sensed the motion within the orbit of his palms.

When she turned he drew her nearer, kissed her lips (but a chaste kiss), and embraced her as if to join the dance as an equal partner. But it never happened that way. He was a poor dancer and his impulse to watch her lose herself was always stronger than any desire to try to harmonize their movements with his body pressed against hers. So it happened that she danced for him, in a hotel in Honolulu, so close that they often touched, but what aroused him was her unconcealed desire to affect him through her own arousal.

These dances usually were lit only by candles. Often she would strike the first match herself and then he knew what she was thinking. They would set up a row of candles and they would each light one, then light the others from the first, moving toward the center and sometimes as if by chance bringing both their candles to bear on the one nearest the center at the same time.

It was these converging candles that Mac saw just before the scene changed. He was again pressing through the jungle on a lower slope of the Mountain of the Wind, in the country of those people whom the nobles of the Kingdom of Champa had called savages. The Chams had ruled for a thousand years down in the lowlands, where they grew rice in flooded paddies and raided the Pacific shipping lanes. Their armies and their thousand-elephant battalion were invincible until the Viets (who themselves had been disparaged as savages by the Chinese) invaded from the north. They conquered the Chams and then, showing the same fear and contempt for the mountain people, built the wall that Delta had pierced yesterday. They called it the "wall to pacify the barbarians."

That was four hundred years ago. Knowing some of this, Mac advanced into the clearing on the hilltop—his new command post, he hoped—with a keen sense of being a stranger, and of danger.

He dropped to his right knee, propped his rifle against his side, looked over his shoulder, and crossed his wrists over his head. A fire team came forward and he sent them left to search the periphery of the hilltop. He repeated the signal and sent another fire team right. He brought up an eight-man squad, formed it in a wedge, and led it straight across the plateau.

It was a defensible position. He laid out a perimeter and the men of 1st Platoon began digging and setting out trip flares and claymore mines.

Walking the perimeter, Mac thought that the enemy could catch one of the squad-sized search teams down near the valley and fix it, and begin to kill marines. The squad would call for help and the platoon leader would charge into an ambush en route to the squad. The platoon would be fixed in its turn, and thus piece by piece Delta Company would rush into the fire.

Mac thought: "Every day we stay out here gives him more time to assemble his troops and figure out my pattern."

But Mac would change his pattern with the gunny's mission tonight.

"And maybe," he thought, "the sky will clear and the planes will fly."

And in some recess of his mind he knew there was another world where he would be changed from the creature that he was. He had forgotten how the change would happen. But if he could only stop for a minute, if he could only detach himself from this—from this—if he could only—

As 2nd Platoon descended from the hills to the flooded paddies, Paul Adrano prayed for the soul of the marine killed at the LZ.

Paul marched in the command group, consisting of Lieutenant Dan Shaw, platoon commander; his radioman and a runner; an artillery FO named Corporal Sedgwick and his radioman; and the medic, Henry Bartholomew; and Michelson and Paul. There were thirty-six men in 2nd Platoon. They were descending the west slope of Nui Gio to search for a supply route leading from 5B to the foothills.

Paul's mind was sunk in prayer. "Father, I entreat You: had he been warned, would he have repented of his sins?—the sin of 'solitary relief,' of anger, meanness, lack of charity, selfishness, spite and cunning? Whatever his sins, I entreat You in Your omniscience, judge him on his best potential. Treat him as if he had wept over his sins and trembled before Your judgment."

Then Paul prayed for Bartholomew; for Michelson; for Ollie and Kindred (the artillery FO and the FAC, the death dealers). He believed these men especially needed his prayers. He prayed for MacHugh Clare but here he found he was actually praying for himself, for tolerance. He prayed for an effective ministry, that he might do his duty not just for the troops but for the leaders too, to set before them a beacon of light, for their better sight.

With his mind and heart so engaged he did not notice that the platoon had reached the level ground, and was now walking just inside the cover of the greenery, with open paddies in view.

"Chaplain up."

He heard and did not hear this. He was trying to answer the question of sincerity. If he prayed for a man whom he feared was a power maniac, who would feed men into the fire and call it his duty, was he sincere? Or was he praying for this man because he knew that God demanded generosity of spirit from a priest?

But then, even as he observed in a flash that the paddies lay like a sheet of lead beyond a screen of thick trees, he tumbled forward into the terrible question: Would God condemn the dead marine to hell because of an accident?

Actually two accidents. The snipers happened to be at the LZ and the marine died without time to prepare for death. And why should his, Paul's, prayers have any effect? If God had to be reminded, or begged, to deal with the man mercifully, would He deal harshly with others who had nobody to pray for them?

"Chaplain up," came the whispered message again. At the same moment Michelson tapped him on the shoulder and whispered, "Sir, Lieutenant Shaw wants you."

He found Lieutenant Dan Shaw, crouched at the edge of the woods, looking expectantly over his shoulder, smiling when he saw the chaplain running forward in a poacher's crouch.

"Have a look," said Dan Shaw, giving his binoculars to Paul.

Paul knelt and took the glasses. They were 6 × 30 spotter's glasses with adjusting scales etched on the lenses. And so the chaplain for the first time saw the world through the "death dealer's" eyes, with the left-right and up-down gradations crossing his view.

"Over there," Dan Shaw whispered and pointed. "See the two ladies?"

Without lowering the glasses Paul said, "I see a woman working, stooping. She's in black pajamas and one of those conical straw hats."

"Why man, they all dress like that," said Dan Shaw in accents from south of Mason-Dixon. "No, I mean two ladies straight across, standing up out of the water on a dike. You'll see'm kinda swingin, kinda rockin."

And Paul replied: "Here! Yes, with a rope. They're swinging a rope or something. What are they doing?"

"Ain't it something? Man, they're shifting water like it was ten thousand years ago."

"What? You don't mean—" Paul's voice faded as he tried to accept the only possible explanation.

"Right, Chaplain, yessiree. They're moving the water from that paddy to the one next higher. I've seen this before. I have seen'm go at it like clockwork, hours on end. I have got tired myself watchin'm, believe me."

Paul saw two young women, each holding an end of a rope that ran from one to the other. At the center was a basket, which, by an effortless movement, they threw into the flooded paddy, then dragged with a deliberate motion toward the dike on which they were perched. As it neared them they gave a graceful but powerful flip, the rope straightened, and the basket jumped the dike and spilled its contents into the higher paddy.

They flipped it back and did the same thing over again, and as Paul watched they did it again and again, and they made it seem more like a game of jump rope than a piece of work. And he even believed he heard cheerful women's voices.

Surrendering the glasses he said to Lieutenant Dan Shaw: "I never saw anything like that."

"You never saw men diggin a ditch back home?"

"Yes, but not this."

"I've seen'm use pumps too," said Dan Shaw. "A pump with a motor as big as a bowling ball. It'll take those two ladies a while to fill that upper paddy, I bet."

"Man!" Paul exclaimed, looking across the paddy.

"Yep. What the heck, it's a job. Now I got me a job of my own. I could call the skipper and ask him but maybe I'll just decide, you know, on my own discretion. See what I'm sayin?"

Said Paul: "No."

"O.K. here's the case. Looka that tree line."

"Straight across?"

"Yes sir. You'd say a hundred fifty meters? Two hundred meters?"

"About that," Paul agreed.

"So we hump along a dike a hundred fifty meters straight across the paddy and there we are, on the other side, in five minutes."

"Yes," said Paul tentatively.

"The peasants'll act like we're invisible. I guarantee you that, mister. They won't see, smell, or hear, much less touch us."

A dike ran straight across the paddy and connected on the other side to the dike where the two women still slung water. It would be an easy stroll, like crossing a little lake on a causeway.

"Or," Lieutenant Dan Shaw continued, "I take the platoon around to the right, around the curve, through these popples or whatever the hell they are, and curve around, so to say, go around the lake instead of across it, and it takes two friggin hours. See the question?"

"Yes. Why are we going over there?"

"Well, Chaplain, just beyond that tree line"—there was a wall of jungle across the paddy, and the women were posed against it—"is ole Five B. I gotta search for supply routes over there."

He had to take the platoon to an arm of dry ground beyond the paddies.

Paul asked: "I don't get it. Where's Five B?"

Said Dan Shaw: "We just cross the paddy. We poke through some woods maybe a hundred meters straight west and we'll be lookin at another paddy field and Five B'll be on the other side of that."

"Straight west?"

"Yes sir. A ten-minute walk from here if we go right across this paddy. Two hours if we circle around the thing.

"See, Chaplain, we're still inside the fan of fire," Dan Shaw mused, "but just barely, you know?" The lieutenant lay one hand flat and played a piano on it with his other hand. "At this range," he said and the tempo of his drumming fingers increased, "the artillery's gonna splat all over the map. I mean I wouldn't want it falling anywhere near my guys. But I gotta—"

He went silent, pondering his decision. Paul let his gaze wander over the people, ten or fifteen in number, stooping around the paddy. The rain had stopped and the air was getting close.

"The thing is," Dan Shaw began, and looked with his earnest blue eyes full into Paul's, "how much do they already know? See what I'm sayin?"

"You mean, do they—"

But Dan Shaw hadn't finished. He went right on: "Cause if they already—oh—frig it!"

He stood up quickly and stuffed the binoculars into their case and snapped it. He lifted his arm and held it, and looked down the line. Paul saw a man watching the lieutenant with burning eyes, who lifted his own arm in imitation of Dan Shaw.

Shaw said in full voice: "Willie, point. Straight across."

Dan Shaw dropped his arm smartly. The marine down the line

dropped his. Then 2nd Platoon filed into the paddy, balancing on the dike, and the Vietnamese paid not the slightest attention.

"Sumbitch, where'd that little bugger come from?"

Lieutenant Dan Shaw was staring at a figure in black pajamas scooting along a dike that led toward Route 5B.

"No weapon," said Dan Shaw, lowering his binoculars and looking perplexed.

"What's the matter?" asked Paul.

"Don't you think it's early in the day to quit your work as carefree tiller of the soil? Holy Moses, here's two more."

Two new figures in black had appeared and joined the runner. The platoon stood halted at the edge of the woods, and they could see 5B across the paddy.

Several more people appeared and Dan Shaw said, "Lookit. Buggers sure know how to *di-di-mau*."

Dan Shaw sent a fire team back into the woods. In ten minutes they returned with word that the paddy the platoon had just crossed was now empty.

Said Dan Shaw: "Sumbitch. They done quit early it seems to me. Makes me wish I was a PFC. Anybody want my job? Great job, good chance to show leadership. Chaplain?"

"I'd better keep the job I've got," said Paul smiling.

"Michelson? Platoon leader job?"

"Michelson's got a job," said Paul, "keeping me alive."

"Oh. Important," Dan Shaw conceded. "Well, what the livin hell."

He was turning in a slow circle scanning the woods and then, as he completed his turn, gazed intently at the rice paddy that lay between him and 5B. This paddy too was empty of people.

When Paul looked across it (with his back to the woods) he saw, a mere three hundred to five hundred meters away, the flat line of the roadway, also unpeopled, and, beyond that, a cluster of houses in a grove of coconut palms and leafy trees. This grove was thick enough to provide shade and shelter to the houses, six or eight in number, but not to conceal them from Paul's inquisitive eye.

Behind the houses the land rose in steeply graduated levels, clothed in brush and small trees, till it eventually turned to jungle-covered mountains. This was the hill mass that had been visible from Delta's first CP. One of its summits was the one Ollie had pounded on Mac's order soon after Delta arrived.

Lieutenant Dan Shaw, as if he too had been thinking about that, called his artillery forward observer, Corporal Sedgwick, a solemn, towering black man with bones like reeds, with more skin on his head and face than he really needed.

Dan Shaw asked: "Am I right, Sedgwick? We're still inside the everlovin fan, are we?"

"Yessuh, but we on the very edge," said Sedgwick wrinkling his corrugated face like a man who had run his fingernails across a slate.

"So—"

"So iss erratic aroun heah."

"Oh boy, great."

"Also," said Corporal Sedgwick portentously, and stopped.

"Also what?"

"Also for any target aroun heah, we on the GTL."

"Oh boy. Really great. What if I want to hit that paddy behind me."

"This heah one?"

"No, the one we just crossed where all the gooks were."

"We close to the GTL."

"How close?" asked the lieutenant.

"Say two hundred meter."

"Oh boy, Sedgwick. Thanks for all the good news. You're a real swell guy."

"Yessuh. That road? Ole Five B? Two hundred fifty meter from the GTL."

"Well, goddamn it, I mean darn it. Excuse me, Chaplain. God bless it, Sedgwick, could you hit Five B if I ast you?"

"Well suh, if Lieutenant Oliver cle-ahs it, but fust I wanna be in the bottom of a ten-foot ho."

"Oh boy, you are a real help and an indispensable member of this platoon, Sedgwick."

"Iss call geometry, Lieutenant, and ain't nothin I kin do. Know what I mean?"

Turning to Paul and squinting to see if Paul understood, Lieutenant Dan Shaw said in a whisper, "We are on the gun-target line."

"Which is not good?"

"It's O.K. anywhere in the fan of fire except in the extreme range band."

"And we are—"

"Yeah. Oh frig it! Willie! Point. Saddle up you bastards! Eyes open. We're lookin for tracks, wheel tracks, buffalo tracks, smashed trees and weeds. Tracks, you marines."

The platoon began moving, with flankers in the woods, along the edge of the paddies that lay on the right. Paul walked between the medical corpsman Bartholomew and his assistant Michelson. He traveled with light feet and he kept looking with quick, hungry glances to his right at the paddies, Route 5B, and the little vill, and the green hills rising beyond. These gave off a luminescent color even in the absence of sunlight. The visibility was pretty good in thin haze.

Henry Bartholomew turned, paused, and when Paul reached him, said, "Do you feel the divine presence, Chaplain?"

Paul made a toy gun with his right hand and slowly shot Bartholomew. As he walked he thought: "Actually I do. I feel the presence, the immanence, of—of that which must be called God—if you call it anything—the power that—I mean—"

The platoon leader was whispering into his handset: "O.K. for Christ sakes get on the point yourself if you don't trust him, and I'll get on mine, and if anybody shoots anybody I'll shoot you."

Dan Shaw replaced Willie on point and the platoon continued its march, more slowly. A whisper went back: Paul in his turn relayed it: "Friendlies ahead. Third Platoon ahead."

The column halted. Dan Shaw halted the flanking squad with an arm signal. He took a few cautious steps.

Looking over Shaw's shoulder, Paul saw a marine emerge and grin hugely at Dan Shaw, and Paul could read his lips as he said:

"Hi, Lieutenant."

This was the staff sergeant in command of 3rd Platoon, a man salty with his years in the Corps but having no more combat experience than Dan Shaw. The two conferred, Dan's platoon did a 180, Dan took his command group forward to the new point, put Willie forward, and set the whole formation moving.

But he soon halted and motioned for Corporal Sedgwick, whose face, which looked like that of a hundred-year-old philosopher, took on an ever more somber hue as the lieutenant set forth his wishes.

Then Corporal Sedgwick got on his radio and called Ollie, the artillery lieutenant at the company command post. Paul heard Sedgwick rattle off two or three sets of numbers and then say:

"Request you cle-ah these as preplanned concentrations."

There was a pause during which Corporal Sedgwick stared at the ground, slowly moving his face, mournfully, from side to side.

He said to his handset: "Roguh. Wait." And to Dan Shaw: "Negative."

Shaw: "Negative! Negative? What the fuck! Gimme your radio, Sedgwick." And to the handset: "Ollie, gimme these friggin concentrations." Dan Shaw listened, breathing hard, so that his pack rose and fell on his shoulder straps. He said: "We know all that. It's fuckin geometry and there's not a damn thing I can do about it." He glanced at Sedgwick, then continued to the radio: "No. By the Lord Harry no. I want the FDC to work up the data, that's the whole point, you friggin cannon cocker. Now! I mean give'm the missions now." And a moment later: "O.K. fine, adjust from the top of the friggin mountain, adjust from the Laotian border for all I care."

This seemed to settle something and the column moved again, and Paul was thinking: "What's an FDC? What was that all about?"

Soon they reached the place where they had halted to watch the scurrying peasants. Lieutenant Dan Shaw motioned Paul up and said:

"I see, said the blind man as he picked up his hammer and saw. Know where we are?"

"Yes, where we saw the people in black pajamas."

"Yes sir. Know where else we are?"

"No."

"We are on a line"—he bore down on *line*—"between that little vill there"—indicating on the west the hamlet among the palms, and on the east—"and the paddy where the two ladies were swinging water. See what I'm sayin?"

"No, I—" Paul began.

Dan Shaw's face went wild, then froze with eyes bulging, and he dropped flat, bellowing: "Incoming!"

Paul happened to catch a puff of dark smoke in the vill and then a yellow streak, and he stood there staring at it—"like an imbecile," as he later thought—and was knocked senseless as Michelson's great Swedish body and all his pack and equipment crashed against him. And Paul would never know what happened in the real world in the next ten minutes. It was hard enough to fix in memory the impressions of his mind.

Michelson landed with his full weight on top of him and drove the wind out of him as if with a blow in the chest from a cannonball.

Paul's brain recovered only gradually from what must have been complete unconsciousness and all he knew when he came back was a noise without a peer in his life, a hammering of deafening power directly overhead and all around, but mostly up there—or off to the side—everywhere! He was in the center of it. He heaved Michelson away and rolled onto his back and beheld a brilliant white flash, then a series of many flashes all around and above him, some yellow, and a hideous cacophony of devilish lethal noise—and somebody pummeling him in the chest with powerful pointed blows like strikings of a ball-peen hammer. He knew what this was. Fragmentation beating on his chest, on his flak jacket. He thought: "Will it hit my face?" But he didn't seem to be worried, just—

He rolled and there was a mocking series of sharp ear-killing cracks. He rolled first one way then, hitting some obstacle, rolled another. Suddenly he realized one of the "obstacles" was a man and he thought: "Help him." He rose to a crawling position and saw Michelson rise up like a maniac ghost and hurl himself forward, on top of Paul, and all was again darkness.

"Let me go!" cried Paul.

But Michelson spread himself over Paul's body and the flak vest he wore crushed Paul's face. He jerked his head aside and tore his nose against Michelson's body armor, and he felt something hot streaming over his face. Then he felt the warm wet blood on his legs. All this while the treetops shook with sharp-edged noise; fragments and branches and sticks and leaves rained down. Great red "goofballs" sailed in shallow arcs from the vill over the paddy and into the trees overhead, where they splintered and showered sparks among the green leafy canopy.

Somebody shouted, "Shoot it for Christ sakes!"

Paul recognized the lieutenant's voice and this seemed strange because he had concluded the man was dead.

Paul began to squirm toward the man he had hit while rolling, but this same man rose up on his knees—it was the artillery forward observer, the skinny tall black man with the deeply wrinkled haunted face, Corporal Sedgwick.

Sedgwick now stood up to his full height, an act of pure madness. Paul rose too and dragged him violently down, and Paul felt a sense of temporary refuge from the cracking flashing death threats.

Corporal Sedgwick pulled loose and stood up again—he didn't speak.

Paul watched him with—terror. And Paul for the first time (since the last time) felt that death-fear in his guts and heart. He flattened himself and watched Corporal Sedgwick raise his binoculars and spend a good three or four seconds scanning.

Then Sedgwick dropped and grabbed the handset being held up for him by his radioman, who lay as flat as Paul.

Corporal Sedgwick spoke in a loud but calm voice. It reoriented Paul's whole world, and Paul thought: "This man's not afraid"—while Sedgwick was hollering into his handset: "Reckless rifles, eighty-twos, one or two fifties, RPGs maybe; but they all high. But they got the bearing. Gimme concentration number Sierra Charlie One Six Dash Three rat nah mudda!—fo they click down and kill my black ass."

Now Paul realized the marines were firing too. Dan Shaw was shouting. M16s barking on full automatic made Paul cringe with the shock of their ferocity. And after a few more seconds there came a voice of greater authority as a gun crew brought an M60 machine gun into action and marines on either side of Paul cheered and hollered obscenities. Paul did notice that nobody whistled. But they hollered like madmen and cursed Charlie and wished him to hell and offered to fuck him with a red hot poker and blind him with Willie Peter and rape his mother and blow his miserable hooch to dust—and all this while the volume of marine fire grew greater and more irresistible. It was at this moment, as the marine fire rose to a new pitch of intensity, that Paul believed the enemy fire was decreasing and that he might live. He looked around. Everybody was firing.

Somebody yelled "Ammo" and a marine jumped up and began a

crouching run down the line, the brass ammo belts flashing and flapping on his chest. And it was about now that Paul set himself to understand all this. What exactly was happening?

He rose to his knees and looked around. He looked to the rear to be sure nobody was sneaking up on the platoon. He looked up and down the line and saw, among others, a small man with a red face and exulting eyes who was screaming, "You fucker, you fucker," and next to him another man calmly, carefully letting off short bursts. This second man shouted, "Shut up and aim, you moron."

Corporal Sedgwick was standing, glasses on the target, and he shouted: "Drop four hundred." His radioman, flattened near Paul, repeated into the handset: "Drop four hundred."

"Two guns, you fools!" Corporal Sedgwick shouted, still watching through his glasses. And the radioman repeated this too, complete with "you fools."

Then a sudden calm descended on Paul and he rose, utterly without fear, and approached Corporal Sedgwick and touched his shoulder. Sedgwick slowly lowered his glasses, looked at Paul, and said, "Hello, Chaplain," raised the glasses and called to his radioman: "I said tell the mudda drop four hundred or I kill him when we gets home."

Paul distinctly heard the radioman say: "What's takin so long, you fuckin moron?"

Paul saw a black eruption in the jungle just above the vill and flying debris, swinging branches, and rising smoke.

"I said two guns," said Sedgwick. "Gimme two blessed guns in adjustment like I axed you."

The radioman repeated this, then told Sedgwick: "He is using two guns."

"Well I dint see no two pops. O.K., left one hundred, drop two hundred, and tell him quick, fore these here Communistic peoples kills me."

Then two black bursts flew frantically up from the jungle, down the hill, and nearer the vill, and Paul saw with a kind of joyful horror where this was leading.

Corporal Sedgwick said: "Drop one hundred."

There was a burst in the trees and Sedgwick fell. Paul felt a terrific ripping at his ear drums and a bang on his helmet, and he was on the deck and a voice inside said, "I'm down," and he and Sedgwick lay there together looking at each other, one calmer and more nonchalant than the other, then they got up—rather, Sedgwick got up groaning, and as Paul was rising, Sedgwick held out his hand, Paul grabbed it, and Sedgwick lifted, and there they stood, in time for the next fall of shot.

One landed in the vill, the other in the paddies right in front of them, scarcely a hundred meters away.

"Platoon eight, fire for effect!" cried Sedgwick. "Hey you muddahs of Second Platoon—you muddahs heah me? Eat dirt, muddahs!"

He dived and took Paul with him, and the earth began to shake, and the air to scream, and nobody cheered or offered to fuck anybody's grandmother.

"Tay ya, man, I can walk! You boys gonna bust a spleen carryin me. Chaplain done lost more blood than me, I should be carryin you, Chaplain!"

"We're doing just fine," said Paul.

"Anyway, you fell on your face, Sedgwick, so shut up," said Henry Bartholomew to his patient.

With Paul on one side and Doc Bartholomew on the other, Sedgwick swung along, planting his good foot, shifting his weight to his two human crutches, then swinging forward.

"I got me a Navy escort," he mused, swinging.

They were setting forth on the trek uphill to the new CP.

"Birds be gone," Sedgwick mused, looking above him.

"Everybody wants to get off the GTL," said Paul. He was starting to feel pretty salty.

"Yes man! You see the hole where them girls was pitchin water?"

"I saw it," said Paul thinking: "Thank You, Father." To Corporal Sedgwick he said: "Give me your hand." He grabbed Sedgwick's hand and rearranged the grip, drawing the bared black arm in its torn sleeve closer across his shoulders.

Paul called: "Are you with us, Michelson?"

Marching behind, carrying the extra packs and looking like a forlorn peddler, Michelson said he was making it.

"That boy got him a job," said Sedgwick. And he called: "Hey Michelson! You can throw mine away. Ain't nothin in it but love letters."

The two platoons, 2nd and 3rd, marched together. There were enough men to help the wounded, to guard the flanks, and form a squad-size vanguard. The hardest humping so far had been the slog through the paddy, where the men not tramping the dike sank in and had to pull their feet free with every step. Now they had mounted to the firm ground and the chief obstacles were thickets and brush. The steep slopes and thicker woods were still ahead.

"Hoo-ee! Did you see that one crater, the one, you know—"

They knew, for sure. It was the one that almost swallowed them all.

"You know why we *alive*? You and me, Chaplain, you Bart, and Lieutenant Shaw? Know why?"

"Yes I do," affirmed Doc Bartholomew, but Sedgwick went right on.

"We alive, mistah, cause a the ooze! You know a *fuze* in the *ooze*— I be writin a poem on it someday and read to my grankids. You grandaddy alive, babies, cause God done put all that mud in that there paddy. Tha *projectile* come a whistlin, babies, and bury hisself in the ooze before the fuze done pop, so Grandaddy get all splatter with mud and water steada bein *killed*.

"Same with the lieutenant, the doc, the chaplain. God done save our miserable lives by means a *muck*. So babies, the lowest thing on God's earth done got a noble purpose! Thass why ole Doc gonna bind up some more wounds fore he go, and ole Chaplain gonna sing hallelujah. Causa muck!"

"You're a dangerous man, Sedgwick," came a voice from behind.

All six legs stopped, the men turned, and watched Lieutenant Dan Shaw churning and catching up.

"Me?" cried Sedgwick. "I the one shut them gooks up. I the one done neuterized my target."

"And damn near neuterized me," said Dan Shaw, puffing and striding. "And anyway it's *neutralized*. If you neuter somebody you cut his balls off."

"Maybe I done that too. Less go back and do us a damage assessment, Lieutenant."

"No, man, we're going to the new CP. Eight hundred meters that-away." Dan Shaw pointed up the hillside and humped on up the line and his radioman hastened to keep up, and the antenna whipped crazily over their heads.

"You a rickety little thing ain't you?" Corporal Sedgwick commented and turned to Henry Bartholomew. "Little glass bird, ain't you?"

"Yeah," Doc Bartholomew muttered.

"And Chaplain, he a boxer. Got him boxer shoulders and ditch-diggin arms. Jus feel them muscles! You ever box, Chaplain?"

"I wrestled. I was a pretty good wrestler in my time."

"In the days a yo youth. The golden days gone by, eh?"

"Yes, they're gone by. But I still feel young."

"You do? But you a wise old man a God now, wise beyond yo yee-ahs. Ain't you?"

"That's right," Paul conceded. "Now I know I don't know anything."

"Except what the Bible say."

"Of course, except for that."

"But thass all you need! How bout you, Bart? You know anything at all?"

"Yes. I just found out something really groovy. God put that muck there to save my crappy life."

"That He did, Bart."

"And by the same reasoning," said Bartholomew, suddenly sounding like a college man, "He left the muck out of that vill, and you and your 105's *neuterized* the place! Right?"

"Now you way beyond me, Doc."

"Maybe clipped the balls right off those Charlies, knocked the brains out of some little baby girl sucking on a piece of sugarcane. Right?"

"I jus don't know, Bart. I think her momma take that baby girl down the tunnel, don't you? If there's a baby girl."

Said Bartholomew: "I don't know who saved my life, Sedgwick, and you don't either."

"Well now, whass all this?"

They went swinging on for a while like three men practicing some clownish form of gymnastic exercise, and Corporal Sedgwick said:

"Musta knock down another hundred meter, boys."

"We're making it," said Paul Adrano.

"Good thing he's a skinny bag of bones," said Bartholomew. "If I'm a little glass bird, Sedgwick, you're a sack of brittle bones. I dressed those frag wounds and I know. There's nothing to you, Sedgwick; you're hardly there at all. That's why you didn't bleed to death, you're too skinny. How much do you weigh?"

"Fore I come to this here country I weigh a hundred an forty pound. Now I skinnier. One boy in Chu Lai, at Charlie Med, he say, 'Happiness is a dry fart.' I ain't been *happy* since I got in country."

"It must be—" the medical corpsman began, and hesitated.

Paul glanced at him, looking across the pain-wracked face of Corporal Sedgwick to the straining, exhausted Doc Bartholomew.

"It must be God's will," said Doc Bartholomew with a trace of venom, panting. "The vill was *neuterized* by the will of God. Right?"

"Iss war, Bart. Thass all I know."

"Yeah. How bout it, Chaplain?"

"I understand you, Henry," Paul said quietly. "Stop a minute."

He grabbed Sedgwick's wrist and pulled his arm taut again, caught a deep breath that sounded like a sigh, and nodded to the other two, and they resumed their wobbling march.

"I know what you're saying, Henry," Paul repeated looking straight ahead at a particular tree with its roots shooting out from two feet above the ground.

"Oh? What am I saying?"

"I have the very same thoughts myself," Paul acknowledged.

"O.K. then, say it. Or are you afraid to? They're just *thoughts* but if all of a sudden you get the courage to—"

"God," Sedgwick cut in, "ain't no boxer. You ring the bell all you like, Bart, He ain't comin outa His corner. You cain't challenge God like Liston challenge Patterson. He don't play no human games."

"What about it, Chaplain?" Henry Bartholomew said.

"He's right," was all Paul would say.

"But you've been ringing the bell, haven't you? That's how much faith you've got. Am I right?"

"Yes," Paul said. Now they had passed the screw tree and he looked ahead and didn't give his attention to anything in particular. They were in a woods with blackened chips strewn over the ground.

"Hoo-ee! Bout six hundred meter and we be at the fireside."

Paul looked at Sedgwick's face. It was sweating and distorted by pain. Paul held Sedgwick's left wrist on his, Paul's, left shoulder. He circled the man's body with his right arm. It was true, there was not much to him.

He looked past Sedgwick to Doc Bartholomew but the doc drove forward, oblivious, grim, eyes fixed on the ground.

Late in the day Gunnery Sergeant Hitchcock was pushing his gang of cutthroats southward down the slope of the hill mass.

He had not chosen these men carelessly. He had not chosen individual marines for their excellence, whether bravery, quickness, docility, or resourcefulness. What he chose was a fire team of four riflemen all of whom knew one another better than they knew themselves (you can always surprise yourself); and a gunner and ammo carrier, also like a hand-and-glove combination. The gun crew came out of the same squad as the fire team. Not just men. A single animal composed of men.

Golden Greek walking point, then the fire team, the gunny, and the gun team, with its permanent hard-on, the M60.

First stop, Ambush Alley. Cross it. Don't even think about using it. Then a stream to worry about. Then around, not over, two hills and down a "clear forest" draw, and back into jungle at the bottom. Choose a place and set in. Set up the gun. Post a watch to cover the place where the river and trail cross. Go to sleep. Listen to the maniacs in the brain as you slide into slumber.

That was the difference! In sleep you had that oddball performance of the maniacs spouting loony language, in their crazy clothes and big brown hats like derbies. But when you walk and look around and pick your route and all, somehow you're—empty—

". . . yeah but I mean, sure it's normal, but where do I go when I go there? I mean," mused Gunnery Sergeant Hitchcock, "is it a blackout? like I'm drunk? It's not sleep, what is it? I keep on walking or whatever, like just now I was humping with these characters, the Golden Greek up there and all these—ha, killers—but for Christ's sake where was I?"

Wherever Gunny Hitchcock had been in the "blackout" he was now walking with the "characters."

"Yeah, maybe what happens is you lose your personality, but isn't that like death? You sort of die, and by a miracle you come back to life, or whatever it is, and your terrific precious personality says hi. Because it's the brains, those cells, all that slop formed into a lumpy shape, some kind of vegetable or meat, yes, an organ of meat, boned, that's your brain. Ha!

"And your self always says, 'Where you been? You got to do this, do that. Get off your ass and do it.' Like now, the bridge. Great idea. Total dark, it's pitch black, listen for the river, maybe some gook playing his radio in the vill, news of the world in gook talk, or that stupid music, and dark, man, real dark. I'm taking off my clothes, nobody can see my cock, although anybody's welcome who wants a peek, what the fuck do I care? A Mark One Mod Zero dork, you know? Nothing special, except to me.

"Works pretty good though. Hey miss, I promise you, this cock's a hard worker.

"What the fuck. Yeah, bridge. Night. Dark water. Maybe gook music from the vill. Gun in the tree line. But water, yeah, gonna be cold, gonna be balls up when I hit that water. Hey you! Any gook fucks with me, show me his face when he gets it in the chops from the M60, seven-point-six-two millimeters of instant fuckin death. Haa.

"There I am, naked as a striped zebray, here comes Mr. Charlie to kill me. Sorry Charlie, I just scream 'Shoot this slope' and it all comes at once, muzzle flash, brain-busting ratty-tat-tat, gook whimpering, and he's off to see his ancestors. Then I dive in and my dick's in my belly.

"That skipper! I wonder if he'd have the balls, or is it all he can do to think it up? Looks around and sees a hero, and here he comes, 'Hey Guns old fella, how'd you like to take a little dip and find me a bridge at the level of the summer pool, eh?' And hell yes, Skipper, I wouldn't do it for anybody but you. Truth is, I wouldn't. He's one marine, that guy. What the fuck's that?"

He heard the sounds of a firefight from somewhere below the mountain. Propagated by the molecular rain shimmering on the breezes, baffled by intervening hills, faint familiar sounds reached the gunny's eager ear. He picked out of the distant fusillade at least two 50's, plus rockets or recoilless rifles screaming like stuck pigs, a chatter of small arms, and, after a minute, a marine M60 going chug-chug-chug.

The 50's sounded like big machines that had got stuck in some fucked-up industrial process that kept them banging one piece of steel against another. Bang bang bang-bang.

On the point Valas the Golden Greek stopped and turned back. His skin really was a polished gold color and his brown eyes now widened and grew inquisitive while he listened to the noise. His eyes didn't go narrow; they grew, to take in more. He listened—then his eyes interrogated Gunnery Sergeant Hitchcock with: "What the fuck, Guns."

In fact everybody was watching the gunny to get his decision. That's what the gunny really liked: when everybody looked to him and said, "Huh?"

Signaling "down" and "quiet" he went to Hippo the radioman and squatted behind him and adjusted the Prick 25 to lowest low. He tapped Hippo's helmet and Hippo passed the handset over his shoulder.

"Striker," Hitchcock whispered, "Buzzbomb. Request guidance." (Meaning, "Hey, Skipper, let me turn around and save the day.")

Now came the captain's voice. Gunnery Sergeant Hitchcock wanted to be a classic marine. The command voice was part of it. He didn't have one, he knew it; this guy did. The gunny's voice was O.K., nothing to worry about, but he would kill to have this one.

MacHugh Clare said, "You already have my guidance"—kinda rumbling shadowy tones, easy, careless, deep, king talk.

"Roger," said the gunny, thinking: "God damn, I could save those bastards, I could sweep in from the flank and claw the eyes out of the gooks. I could—what the hell."

Hitchcock stood up and brought his men to their feet, and they rose from the brush as if the gunny had the power to conjure soldiers out of the earth. They watched, and you could see what was going on in their minds. Every one of them was asking: "Do our guys need us?"

The gunny with his odd rolling gait approached the Golden Greek, and his walk was perfectly soundless. Also effortless. He whispered:

"We are real close to fuckin Ambush Alley, Valas. Don't fall into it. Slow. I don't care if you take an hour."

Lance Corporal Chris Valas opened his lips in a huge smile. His teeth were pure white, movie-star teeth. And shiny gold skin. He could have posed for a picture advertising suntan lotion. His pushed-back helmet released a lock of hair to make a black mark on his fore-head. He had a nose befitting a Caesar. His dark brown eyes bored in on the gunny.

"Move your ass," Hitchcock ordered.

Chris Valas let his eyes get bulgy and his smile grow wider and cra-zier. His first steps were those of a comedian moving with exaggerated stealth, looking over his shoulder at the audience.

The team moved toward Ambush Alley.

No sweat, really. They weren't planning on using it, just crossing it. A little caution was called for. No big deal. Only trouble was, where the fuck is it?

Push push, slow-walk, look at the ground and plan every step for si-lence, but don't forget to look around too. A guy plans every step and don't look around is as good as blind, he'll miss the muzzle flash and the shaking of the leaves.

The ears hear it—but it feels like it happens in the middle of the brain. Two far-off detonations, almost simultaneous, and the gunny's mind knew instantly that one of the FOs was calling in 105's, probably Sedgwick. He didn't think the CP was under attack. With the hills and all, nobody could say exactly where these thuds originated, but he thought the skipper would summon him if the gooks hit the CP. No. This was 2nd or 3rd Platoon over by 5B tangling assholes with the gooks. Two more raps. Drop one hundred, fire for effect, blam blam blam, end of target, target destroyed.

And it happened pretty much like that. Two more adjustments, then a sixteen-round fire for effect, then more small-arms fire, but no more rockets—and no more 50's. God lets His light to shine upon howitzers.

Gunnery Sergeant Hitchcock appreciated artillery, air and naval gunfire; he really appreciated the big stuff. Too bad. A few more min-utes walking on this bearing and we cross that line. Yeah, too bad. He hated to operate outside the fuckin fan of motherfuckin fireballs.

"Hey Gunny," the machine gunner asked, leaning close in the dark, "what do I do about the hooches?"

The gunny and three others were ready to crawl out of the woods and approach the little river.

Hitchcock responded: "Nothing. You don't do anything. What are you asking me?"

"Well if I have to open up with the sixty I might hit the hooches. They're right in the line of fire."

"Oh!" cried the gunny—whispering, amazed. "You mean if the gooks have got me surrounded—is that what you mean?"

"Yeah, you need help, I mean if you—"

"Easy! Let'm kill me and the Greek and Collins and Hippo. Just so you don't hit some old gook sleepin in his hooch. What a question!"

The machine gunner tried to rephrase it: "Uh, I don't mean—"

"You dumb fuck," said the gunny. He turned to Chris Valas, Collins, and Hippo, and said, "Leave your helmets. Wear your flak jackets. Two minutes and we hop."

He disappeared under a poncho, where he lit his red flashlight, checked the time (it was 0008), and took a last look at his compass. Since the kerosene lanterns had gone out in the Vietnamese hooches across the creek an hour ago, he had nothing to steer by. The sky and the night were a single void.

Coming out of the poncho he asked: "Collins, you got the rope?"

"Yeah, Guns, I got the line."

"We got three LAWs?"

"Yeah," said Valas.

"O.K., LAWs, rope, socks, and cocks. Everybody got two grenades and a full ammo kit?"

"Yeah."

"Yeah."

"Yeah."

And to the man with the night-vision glasses: "Stay here with the gun. Keep us in your goggles." To the gunner and assistant gunner: "Don't touch the glasses. Let him go blind, you two keep your night vision. You gotta fire, fire at their muzzle flashes. *Adios, muchachos.*"

Three men stayed: the machine gunner who had asked about the hooches; his ammo bearer, armed with a blooper; and the man with the night glasses, with a rifle.

Four riflemen emerged from the jungle onto the darkling plain: Gunnery Sergeant Hitchcock, the Golden Greek, Collins, and Hippo.

Hitchcock walked ahead and the others followed in a line abreast three paces back. They could sense the gunny's body if not see it. He stumbled on something and removed all doubt about where he was. They took exaggerated steps, lifting their feet well off the ground. Everybody's face was blackened with stick paint except Hippo's; his had been blackened by God.

The goggle man had described the terrain to Hitchcock, so the gunny stepped off the paces and paused, and it did seem that there was a shaft of a coconut palm looming right about here, as there should be, right before his straining eyes. Opening his compass, covering the radium dial with his cupped hand, he determined that he had done it right.

Even if he couldn't see the treetop he could hear it, palm fronds rustling in the breeze. That's why they had left their helmets behind, so they could hear like dogs.

Now he touched the shaft, rough, rugged, plated, hairy.

"Hot shit! O.K. now we just—Jesus Christ I can hear the river. I hope it's not fast, what if it's a goddamn Niagara."

He took some steps and halted to listen. A gurgle, a glug-glug, but not the sound of breaking water. It sounded narrow and deep and un-broken. Deep; goddamn that deep. A voice said in his head: "Don't kid yourself. He'd do it."

The skipper would walk over and jump right in. But the skipper didn't have the father the gunny had; or used to have.

It was odd, it was not quite right, his dad dead.

Stop right here!

"Don't fall in for Christ's sake."

The ground was disappearing. Going somewhere. He sat carefully down, holding his rifle high, and let his feet dangle. Jesus Christ, the river.

Stripped down to nothing, Hitchcock took the bitter end of the rope and circled his waist and secured it with the knot Collins had taught him. Collins was an ex-boatswain's mate on a destroyer. He knew all kinds of knots and he wouldn't let you call a rope a rope, you had to say "line" or "sash cord" or "six thread." And a rope didn't have an end, it had a "bitter end" and a "standing part." Whatever that might be. Collins had left the Navy for the Marine Corps so he could see the people he killed. Anyhow now Hitchcock was on the bitter end and Collins had the standing part. "I'll keep a strain on the line," Collins whispered.

"Yeah, a *strain* on the *line,* and I'll dangle on the *bitter end.* Just don't let the river dump my ass in the ocean. Now you creeps keep your eyes open."

"That'll do a lot of good," commented the Golden Greek.

"Well, good-bye, world, here I go."

Thinking: "Why did I leave that blooper behind? If that character shoots a grenade he'll kill us all." A mistake. "Well I never said I was perfect, just close. Why does he always call on me? Eh? Obviously I'm the best he's got. Like bringing that pussy lieutenant home. Lost, lost in the jungle! Waaaa waaaaa! Dark! Ooo! Glad to see you Guns, but I'll just dig in right here. Hell you will. We're gonna CSMO right now, Lieutenant. Waaa! Captain said dig in! Right and now I'm tellin you saddle up!

"God—cold! Hey throat, make room for the balls. The case of the disappearing cock. Jesus Christ, I thought this was a tropical country."

He waded in and stumbled and recovered and slipped on a slimy log and splash, face in the water, then he sort of slid sideways and in, in deep, and no bottom. Open your eyes, close your eyes, it makes no difference.

"O.K. how deep is this sewer? I'd rather not try a surface dive, head down, feet up to push you where it's cold. Bridge, what bridge? Is this just a hunch? I freeze my dingo for the skipper's hunch?"

He was a kid, practically a baby, and his father was saying, "Come here, old man, and I'll give you a ride," and like a trusting fool he ran to his father's outstretched arms, into his huge hands, and zoom! Up we go! Spin, and face front, and straddle his neck and hold his hair, and he says, "Hey old-timer, don't pull my hair," so being an obedient baby—

"I let go of his hair and cup my hands under his chin and the whiskers prick my skin, and this is my daddy! Whoopee. What a ride! This is the stuff I now know is called *power,* and way up high! Into the pool with his lurching, kinda jolting steps, scared hell out of my innocent little heart, but he's my pop. And there are kids all around swimming and having water fights and hollering, big kids, scary and loud and tough, who can do stuff I can't do—

"And flip, over I go backwards, and he lets go of my ankles, feet flying, fuckin terror—and splash in the face, a snootful, no air, I'm suffocating, drowning, and dying of terror. That's my daddy all right, teaching me to swim."

The goggle man watching from the tree line saw the gunny rope himself up, saw Collins brace himself and pay out the line as the gunny stepped toward the water—and it occurred to the goggle man that the bare-assed gunny and the sailor in his jungle utilities and flak jacket were the same pee-yellow color; real bright. O.K. so everybody's the same, the gooks and us. Odd thought.

Then the gunny slipped and was gone and Collins took the shock on the rope, payed it out slowly, and at least he didn't act like the gunny was drowning; and the Greek and Hippo knelt down back to back and peered blindly out into the greenish yellow, ready to defend the honor of the U.S. Marine Corps. The river was below the lip of the ground so the goggle man couldn't see the gunny's head, which he assumed was bobbing around in the river.

He swept his glasses over the cluster of hooches across the river, then upstream and down, then back to Collins who might have been fishing for a really big fish. And Collins payed out more rope and he didn't seem worried.

The machine gunner asked the goggle man: "What's going on?"

The goggle man said: "Nothing. I think I'll lob a grenade into the river. The gunny can collect the fish and we eat fried perch for breakfast."

"Yeah. Do that," said the machine gunner.

"What?" whispered the assistant gunner. "What are you going to do?"

"Oh shut up," said the goggle man.

"Fuck," the assistant gunner complained. "I don't like perch. Trout—give me—"

"Shut the fuck up you fuckin rube."

"Hey smart-ass, what's a rube?"

"You," the goggle man said informatively. "You are a rube.—Christ, somebody's coming."

Down where Hitchcock was, nothing but dark, nothing but nothing, unless you count the cold.

Thought the gunny: "This is where cold begins, where death begins. I could die down here, get caught in some branches or vines—fuckin vines! What if—"

His stroking groping hands came to something like weeds, like a willow. He grabbed it and held himself down, opposing his natural buoyancy with his unnatural determination to stay down here—his kind of furious need to touch bottom. "Gimme the damn bottom!" Pulling on the weed stalks, he struggled against the tendency of his body to invert. His head was down and his feet rising. He tried—

"I'm running out of air!"

Fast, do it fast, or else jump for air and try—no—"Goddamn it, go deeper, pull, goddamn—"

He stroked away from the weeds. He was afraid of the weeds. Who knows what's in there? He tucked his knees, stroked, and broke into the air and gasped, trying to do it quietly but not really succeeding. "Air, by God, give me air!"

Sailor was pulling on the rope, keeping the tension on it, and the gunny looked at the bank, and pressed the water out of his eyes and tried a closer look.

He could see Collins holding the tether; he could not see the Greek or Hippo. But obviously all was well.

He faced into the current. So there was the fuzzy presence of Collins at the end of the rope, backgrounded against the sky—he could just about see the sky—and farther right a darker wall. That'd be the tree line and the M60 and goggle man down there somewhere—and to the left, a sloping ramplike bank where the trail entered the river, maybe three strokes away—and on the right, he could almost discern the trail rising out of the water. "Yes, I can see it."

Positioning himself now more accurately over the trail, feeling the steady reassuring strain on the line from the sailor, and heedless now of the cold—"Ha! Not cold anymore"—Gunny Hitchcock flattened his body facedown, put his hands at his hips, and stroked down and forward, and raised his legs into the air as his trunk headed down. The weight of his legs drove him down.

He descended the length of his body and began stroking to go deeper, and he felt the pressure in his ears but he aimed down and stroked, and ignored the knocking and popping in his ears—funny sounds, but then he had to be down pretty deep—and still couldn't find anything with his hands as he reached way out with each stroke. Christ, where's the bottom! And his ears protesting with those strange *wop-wops* and *wopwopwopwops*—

And just then a little wedge of fear, a very little sharp wedge, in his heart, fear of the cold, the dark, the watery cold dark like he was entering the borderland of a different world, fear of the weeds, of vines, holes, swirlings—the rope tangling on something—

"Hold me down, keep me down . . ."

Not even a combat death, not even that. They'd call it an accident. A stupid *accidental* death.

No bottom yet, and too late. He tucked, flipped, and stroked with all his might for the air, for the world. He was desperate and his brain was throbbing—terrified at how deep he had gone, or was it sideways?—how many strokes to air, with his throat, brain, and ears about to burst. He broke out and rose into the night and barked (he heard it) and opened wide and pulled in the first quick breath, expelled it with joy and pulled in a long, satisfying one even as he sank again up to his neck, but he kept his head clear and breathed the best air he had ever tasted.

Then he saw white flashes. He thought he was hallucinating and thought: "Jesus, I stayed down too long."

Two rifles on automatic, obviously M16's, obviously no hallucination—firing like crazy and the gunny was right in front of it, the slugs screeching five feet over his head, that fucking Greek and Hippo—a hammer of the 16's cudgeling his ears and his brain, then a short pause and a cry of "Grenade!" and Gunny Hitchcock rose vertical in the water clear to his waist, brought up his arms to meet over his head, and was gone, down and down, and he stayed down there in the shelter of this former death trap as long as his breath lasted.

He heard a sort of muffled echo of a hammer, or something, some odd puffy sound like a hammer striking an anvil in a world where sound waves had a sense of mystery. He thought: "Don't try a LAW for Christ's sake"—because if they aim it low the rocket would hit the lip and—death death death.

Hitchcock rose again and grabbed air, and by God that fool was firing the 60, red tracers sailing over the gunny, and the noise alone was murder. If he raised his arm he could let one pass through his hand. "Don't think I'll do that."

A streak of yellow went sliding over from the gook side, a big streak, and the gunny stayed on the surface to listen, and heard a muffled detonation obviously too high, in the jungle, fine, good. Waste your RPGs, you fucking slopes. Anyway, the gunner was still pumping away on the M60, scaring the shit out of the guys on the bank, for sure, till the gunny decided:

"What the fuck, here I go," and he did another surface dive.

He was surprised to feel the rope adjusting to his depth. He had forgotten the sailor! Where was the sailor? The question gave Hitchcock a shot of juice and he went deeper, fearlessly. Without thought of fire or ice he plunged deeper still into the black cold medium, stroked down, his feet high and his strokes powerful, and when his ears began to hurt, his outstretched hands—his fingertips actually—they—

Bottom! He surfaced and gulped air, watching the sparks and flashes and listening to the whams and cracks.

The breathing. What felt better? Not eating, drinking, fucking—nothing! Plain air. He gulped a deep one and dived again. He kept his wits and his breath, and began pawing the bottom. He scraped and scooped and found, beneath the sand about two inches down, a flat surface.

A flat surface, by God. Then a crack an inch wide. He stuck his finger in and slid it along—a straight smooth fissure. Another surface and another crack parallel to the first. And another.

He thought: "Goddamn. Goddamn."

Planting his feet he vaulted off the bottom and rose in the black river like a happy porpoise. All was dark and silent. He smelled muzzle gas even as he did his breathing through his mouth.

He pulled himself home on the rope and crawled up the muddy bank. He got a report of a kind from the sailor. He took his M16 and held it high as he slipped silently back in, and he rolled onto his back and did a slow underwater kick till he had crossed the river. He placed his rifle carefully on dry ground, untied the rope and wound it around a little stalk of woody brush, and crawled.

He peered over, he heard a man sighing, he waited to see if anybody would come to help the guy. He waited several minutes and his troops were utterly silent. Good job, characters.

Hitchcock wormed his way over the lip, slithering on his side to keep his privates out of the brush. He could feel the sticks and thorns tearing his thigh and hip. "Rip my legs, fine, but save the cockand-balls."

He crawled around, and finally stood and walked, and found four bodies, no weapons, but some long tools like spades and mattocks. He searched around, waving his feet like feelers, and when his foot touched the sighing man the man sighed again.

When it touched a long barlike thing he thought he had found a rocket launcher but it was some kind of farm tool. He dropped it and searched some more, but he didn't want to get too far from the characters. He decided not to shoot the groaner. Maybe he'd draw some of his pals. Anyway, the patrol was compromised.

He walked back to the river, reeved the rope around his middle, and yanked on it twice. He entered the water and felt the rope go taut as Collins pulled him back across.

When they were all crouched in a circle back at the gun, the goggle man said: "Hey Gunny, no shit, retrograde attack, man, how bout it?"

"Yeah," the machine gunner seconded him. "*Di-di-mau beaucoup.* Tactical retreat, Guns."

"Keep your goggles on those bodies," said the gunny, ignoring them, as he pulled his clothes on—no easy job with his body still wet and his legs torn by the thorns.

And Hitchcock said: "Hasty defense, fuckers. We watch those bodies and we move at first light. Nobody sleeps. Got it?"

"Sleep?" said the goggle man lowering his glasses.

Gunnery Sergeant Hitchcock said: "Gun and goggles stay where they are. Collins, four meters across from the gun. Hippo on that side. Greek over there. I'm in the middle. Something pops, keep down so I can fire over your worthless heads. Got it?"

"Yeah, Guns," said the goggle man, "but I'm so sleepy, I'm so fucking bored."

"Sleep tonight and I remove your balls with my K-Bar."

"Yeah but Gunny," said the machine gunner, "did you find anything?"

"Almost forgot," said Hitchcock. To the goggle man, who now carried the radio: "Call the CP. Tell the skipper: Paragraph One. All secure. Four enemy KIA. Compromised. Syracuse, east-southeast three hundred. Paragraph Two. George Washington."

"That's not a thrust point," the goggle man protested. "We don't have any George Washington on the map, Guns."

"No, it's not a thrust point. George Washington is a bridge. Just tell him, George Washington."

Chapter 8

Surf City

This was out of her control. Her fantastic mind slipped into a scary drama, and she could hardly tell if the "Mary" playing in this scene was Mary or herself. The character was supposed to be Mary but her terrors were equally Sarah's.

In the real world Sarah Clare was standing at a counter in Mary's kitchen packing a box, wrapping long utensils in newspaper, and cramming them in as tightly as she could, to get a well-packed box. In a moment she would tape it and write "Kitchen Misc." on it and place it on the stack that already rose so high it cut off the view out the front window. But this real world did not reach into Sarah's mind. Certainly she didn't notice the conversation from the living room, where Mary and Denise were also packing.

She was engrossed in the fantasy of Mary's waking up in the middle of the night in a dark room looming with stacks of cardboard boxes. At first this fantasy-Mary didn't know where she was. The space was dark and nothing had its proper shape. She was not aware that her husband was dead. She moved her leg, expecting to be reassured by his body, and then the word "body" registered its awful meaning in her brain. She gasped and clutched her throat. But she had the baby! She flung away the blanket and threw her hands forward and felt her way blindly to the little travel crib that she had placed in the middle of the room, away from the piles of boxes—a box might fall and hurt her baby—and she found it. Here was her baby in her arms, warm and stirring—the baby's scent touched Mary in so deep a place that she began to sob with joy, and embraced and rocked the baby, weeping with gratitude that God had given her this beloved little child. The baby began complaining. Mary opened her robe and gave her a breast, and sat on the bed—the only piece of furniture that had not been disassembled and made ready for the movers. The movers were due in the morning. She would then drive to the airport to meet her mother, and set off in the car for Pennsylvania with her aging mother and newborn girl.

"I love you!" she whispered to the unperceiving baby. She loved its knowing way of taking her breast. True, it reminded her somewhat disturbingly of her husband's licking and sucking the very same breasts, but so what! Let that mystery remain unsolved. "I remember, I will always remember!"—thinking of him with a love that was almost happy. So they both nourished themselves on her body in the same way. She eagerly gave herself to both. For a long interval she had neither fear nor sorrow, and it was a relief like none she had felt since the news came.

In Sarah's distracted mind it seemed that Mary descended a black shaft of despair and fear—when she let go of the baby—

But interrupting this sudden twist in the scene, of Mary falling in a dark shaft, Sarah's reason argued that despair must rule out fear, despair being the end of hope. Nevertheless, fear and despair embraced over Mary and crushed her.

A banal memory intruded. Pausing over a half-packed box Sarah remembered herself, Mac, Mary, and Mary's husband, and Denise and Tommy, watching *Shock Theater* late on a Saturday night before the men went over. It was a horror show usually more funny than frightening. They used to sit all six of them piled on the couch in Mary's living room, now laden with taped and labeled boxes, and drink beer and cry in unison: "Shock, shock, shock!"

Looking into that very room Sarah saw Denise labeling a box "Your Desk." This must contain the letters Mary had received from Vietnam. She heard Mary and Denise talking about giving the mailman a forwarding address. Sarah felt a need to escape.

She opened the front door and grabbed the parallel handles of a wheelbarrow full of trash and began pushing it down the drive. Gaining the street she turned left into a fresh wind and pushed two hundred yards to the Dandy Dumpster. She flipped its lid and began throwing trash in. The wind caught a slip of loose paper and Sarah chased it, and felt the force of the breeze as she turned again to the Dumpster. She looked at her own house—she was practically in front of it—and saw it as a place of refuge. It was a low bungalow divided in two. Hers was the right half. There she could cook, read, play music, write letters, and try to keep her hands where they belonged. The two-ton rusty monster Buick given her by her father hulked in the drive. They had sold Mac's old heap when he went over. Inside, on her couch or bed, Clinker would be snoozing away in a dream. When his toes twitched and his legs ran in his sleep she knew that a dog's life wasn't all kibbles and gravy.

In that refuge too she kept adding scenes to her play, which grew more complex and disturbing each time she touched it. It was still a comedy about high school girls whose imaginary problems caused real anxiety, and it still lacked direction, it just wandered over their psychic moonscape; but it was writing itself, it required no energy of her own, it flew—and she was keen to learn whether its pointlessness concealed a truth.

There were two kinds of girl in it, the fearless and the frightened. The first had no cause for fear since they knew nothing about life. The second were, apparently, cringing under a rain of blows that hadn't yet fallen.

In the wheelbarrow there was a box with flaps open. Sarah pulled out armloads of magazines and tossed them over the rim, and the pages fluttered. She came upon a soft-covered book, colored olive drab, with red letters, titled *Guidebook for Marines*. Because Mac owned the same book she paused to look.

The chapter on squad tactics had been heavily marked by Mary's husband with red stars and boxes. Sarah flipped pages and came to a part on the M14 rifle, where the names of the various parts struck her fancy. It all seemed to be about sex. She laughed at the first one, the connector assembly, and proceeded unbelievingly through the operating rod, barrel and receiver, gas piston, gas cylinder, hammer, and spring plunger. She threw it, grabbed the handles of the wheelbarrow, and began to push.

But she felt held back. She stopped and dropped the handles, aware that something was going wrong. The wind was freezing the sweat that suddenly covered her body and soaked her shirt—in an instant. She shivered and began to weep, with her arms hanging at her side. The tears led to a convulsive sob that bent her spine, then another, and she dropped feetfirst down Mary's shaft. She was spinning and the water was rising at the rate of a thousand gallons a minute, yet her fall forced her down through it toward the bottom. She knew she must freeze and drown and it terrified her. The terror roiled her stomach and bowels. It was death, and a death undeserved and too early. She opened her lips to protest but at that instant she saw Mac's mutilated body floating in another shaft. He had neither limbs nor eyes. Everything that could not possibly happen to a girl from Nicolet High School was happening to her. These things happen, but not to her. It was inconceivable!

"Sorry, we won't let you," said Sarah lightly.

"We sure won't," added Denise, taking Mary's hand.

"But I want to," Mary insisted but not too vigorously. "I'll be O.K. here, it's just one night."

"Of course you would but we've decided," Sarah declared calmly. "We meet here at six o'clock. We carry the travel crib, I mean Denise and I carry it, and you carry the baby, and we go to my house. You get the baby ready and nurse it and all that while Denise goes out for pizza and I make a salad and select a bottle of two-ninety-five vintage, and we eat and drink and forget the charming world for an hour. Denise goes home, you and I climb into my bed, and we saw some Z's before the movers come at seven."

"Eight," said Mary, weakening.

"Movers are always late," Denise pronounced.

"O.K., we set the alarm for seven, but no, wait," Sarah said. "You'll be up to nurse her at five or something, right?"

"Yes. Three, four, or five, and again at seven or eight."

"O.K. fine," Sarah went right on. "I get up at seven-thirty and come here to meet the movers. When they come I take the baby and you supervise the move."

Mary hesitated, and Denise told her it was all set. Mary had to struggle to keep control of her face, and Sarah repeated the rendezvous time of six o'clock and went out.

Walking rapidly toward her house she saw the mailman approaching her door. She passed the Dandy Dumpster, gave it a glance of recognition, and strode on. The wind had risen and it buffeted her. She kept it out by crossing her arms over her chest, but the sweat that had soaked her an hour ago still dampened her back, and the wind glazed it. She hurried on.

She accepted her mail, which included a letter from Mac, and told the mailman that Mary had filled out a forwarding form. She felt the thin letter between her fingers. She heard Clinker crashing against the door from the inside, howling his wild greeting. She thought, "So you both love me," feeling the letter. As she approached her door one function of her brain regretted the thinness of the envelope and another planned her table for tonight. She pressed forward the admonition that a thin letter, maybe just a quick scrawl, was better than the void between letters. But every letter was bitter and sweet, it was Mac and it was the absence of Mac.

Sometimes he wrote to warn her that she'd receive no other mail for a time. She had figured out that he gave these warnings to a friend with instructions to wait three or four days before sending them.

At the kitchen table, rumpling and folding Clinker's ears, she read: "Earthquake Woman: Meet me in Honolulu for Christmas! No bull! Five days' R and R. If we score this time the baby arrives just three months after I come home. You! Me! Baby! Human happiness, love, dance! Now I'm taking the company out to the boonies. *Do not be alarmed* if you get no letters. This is no big deal. —Mac"

"I'll bet!" she cried. "No big deal, I'll bet!"

The letter wasn't dated. If somebody had held it three days, and it took six to reach her, then he was in the middle of something right now. An "operation," a "search-and-destroy" mission, a "reconnaissance in force." She knew the lingo. He was out there in the jungle or the rice paddies right now. She sat there stunned, not from surprise but from this new confirmation of a persistent surmise, that there was no safety. She tried to push the dog away but he thrust his nose deeper into her lap and regarded her with reproachful eyes. She bent, and took his narrow head in both hands, rocked it from side to side and cried: "Honolulu!" She rocked the slender head harder and Clinker's eyes grew doubtful and nervous as she cried, "Honolulu! Honolulu!" He licked her wrist and she jumped up and cried, "Come, boy!" which to him meant a delightful game about to happen. He leapt straight up and chased her down the hall.

In her room she pulled off the wet shirt and found the thick flannel shirt that had taken her through the harsh winters in Madison. She put this on, plus a sweater, and got a windbreaker from the hall closet. Clinker was racing from the hall to the front door, barking madly, and Sarah drove him crazier by barking back. She flung open the door and he bolted, dancing around the car like a dervish. When she opened the door he scrambled in, taking the driver's seat for himself, panting with emotion. She pushed him. He refused to surrender the seat. She forced herself in, bumping him over with her hip, and he sat just as happily in the passenger seat, looking forward vigilantly.

"Off!" Sarah shouted. "Off to Honolulu!"

She started the big engine and backed out the drive for the hour's trip to Surf City, sent the monster rumbling over the railroad track, and drove out through J'ville, and south past Folkstone and Holly Ridge. She crossed the Intracoastal Waterway, turned left, and parked at the north edge of the village. She climbed a barren dune and ran down to the sea shouting, "Honolulu!"

A wave crashed in. She danced away just in time, and so with feet still dry Sarah Clare walked the belt of firm sand impacted by the surf. She thrust her freezing hands into the pockets of her jacket and of course there was Mac's letter, but it was more than a letter—it was—

She began to run, but running with her hands confined like this was no good. She pulled them free and ran along the strip of hard sand where the surf turned, where the receding water left a disappearing sheen. Her eyes began gushing. She wiped away the tears with her free hand. The letter was still in the other. Windborne sand peppered her face, and cold drops carried shoreward from the spindrift cooled her skin. She licked her lips, and it was like tasting sweat from his body.

She stopped and retraced her steps and was amazed at her four-foot strides, as they were marked out by her footprints. A wave inundated the tracks and chased her up into the deep sand; she descended again, pursuing the receding wave, and walked fast along the surf line.

Wind—sea—and a firm path to tread—the rush and crash of the waves—and—this letter—this man!

She was going north with the Atlantic on her right and thatched dunes on her left. Out here nothing was built to last and nothing did. Every few years whole villages would be covered by water and even sand. She was on the Outer Bank, between Cape Fear and Camp Lejeune. She passed through the pilings of Barnacle Bill's Fishing Pier, with the pier overhead, and watched the sea reach up the sheathed poles and drop to reveal the encrusted barnacles and slime. She faced an untamed coast where snakes abounded in summer and where, in the autumn, hurricanes had their way with the ocean and the island.

There was plenty of light but no sun. The turbulent sea lifted logs, branches, seaweed, and scum into view when it sloped toward the beach, and then concealed it all with each successive fall. The island had survived another hurricane season; all that remained of the autumn's fury was a wintry desolation that thrilled Sarah and made the letter in her hand all the more electric.

"Earthquake Woman: Meet me in Honolulu for Christmas!"

Happiness, yes; his weight upon her breast, yes; the long slow slide taking them nearer their own hurricane season, yes! But there was this other—this—

Clinker—rangy, black and white and thoroughly mongrel—suddenly appeared at the top of a dune, skidding down in the sliding sand. He rushed her, jumped up, and sought her with his forefeet and friendly jaws. She reached out to repay this wild affection but he was already satisfied. He spun around and headed off with quick chopping steps, scattering water that the wind carried away. Then he loped up the steep dune, disappearing in the grass at the top while the sand he had set loose was still running down.

She walked and pondered and let the wind buffet her body. She was warm, protected against the gusts. "Rest and recreation," fine, and she was already naked in his arms—but—a baby?

It was true they had agreed on the Treaty of Perpetual Peace, a plan, a life, a definition of happiness, a male-female pact in the midst of potential conflict. Have children as soon as Mac got out of the Crotch in June, live in the boonies, accept poverty (for a while), struggle, and sooner or later make a regular kind of life, but never compromise on the fundamental principle of freedom.

It was for this he had quit law school. He said law school was so insulting that anybody who stayed in it just to avoid the draft deserved to be sentenced to a lifetime practicing law. "With apologies to your father," he added. But when Mac called to tell her he had decided to quit law school, a thrill ran through her. When he said, "If I quit I'll be drafted for sure," she had said, "Do what you must do."

They both wanted kids, Mac perhaps even more than she. So they saw kids coming when Mac got out. It was now November 1967 and he'd be released in June.

But here comes this startling proposal of a meeting in Hawaii at Christmas. She began to understand that the thrill blowing around inside her was not simply the arousal of desire to a new pitch. She broke into a run and shouted for Clinker.

He appeared on the dune with his ears lifted and head cocked inquiringly. Seeing her running, he leaped eagerly off the rim and came wading down the stream of moving sand and joined her, taking the water side and splashing along close to her knee.

"Right, that's the plan but—good God!"

"I have to make a decision and make it quickly," Sarah said.

Sarah and Denise sat over coffee in Sarah's kitchen. It was five o'clock and the movers were long since gone. Mary and her baby were gone.

"I don't have time to consult Mac, although I have to take him into consideration," said Sarah.

Denise blurted out: "Why, for God's sakes? Did he consider you?"

"No," Sarah admitted serenely, "he just announced it. But he assumed that since we were going to start in June we might just as well start at Christmas since we had the chance."

"Assumed is right! You love him and all that but gee whiz, pardon my profanity," said Denise. "He as much as told you you're getting pregnant at Christmas. I guess he's like Tommy and enjoys giving orders."

"Denise, it's me, not you, if it's anybody getting pregnant at Christmas." Even as she said this, however, Sarah felt that Denise had expressed her own complaint quite succinctly. Sarah then acknowledged: "This does have a different feel to it."

"I'm amazed you're so cool and calm."

"I am actually not very cool and calm," Sarah said.

"You were always a fine actress."

"We want a family," Sarah said as if passing it all in review, "we are of one mind on that. But I have to say that this letter"—it lay on the table before her and Denise had done her best to read it upside down when Sarah had gone for the coffee—"this letter throws me."

Denise said: "When Tommy went over I missed my period and I just knew I was pregnant. I saw myself with a baby and no husband, or a baby and a paraplegic husband screaming drunk in his wheelchair. I obsessed about taking care of two helpless beings, neither one of them giving an ounce of appreciation in return. Oh, I was a selfish, weak, and self-pitying maniac for two weeks. Then I had this hideous clotty discharge that went on for hours and finally it was obvious that whatever ailed me, it wasn't pregnancy, but all I could see was myself at this grim ceremony with some marine playing on a bugle and me sniffling while a general presents me with a nice folded flag for my trouble."

"You have a very sympathetic mind," said Sarah, and their eyes met, and Denise saw Sarah's large dark eyes grow warmer and darker, it seemed, under the current of her thoughts.

Sarah added: "But there's a way out."

"There sure is."

"The doctor said—"

"Good for you! You went off like a shot to—"

"I went this afternoon. He said I have to start immediately, this cycle, and I'll be almost a hundred percent safe at Christmas."

"Almost!" Denise cut in.

"Yes, almost. He said on the first cycle I'd better use a diaphragm too."

"Your fire wall."

"But if I do, Mac may know."

"So he knows."

"No," Sarah intoned without explaining.

Said Denise: "Of course they don't like to bump their roddies against the wall. O.K. here's your plan," Denise declared decisively. "Take the Pill, you're ninety-nine percent safe, fly into the big guy's arms and you've got five days in paradise. Come home clean as a whistle."

Sarah said: "No."

"Why no? Are you so regular you can predict now that you won't be ovulating at Christmas?"

"Denise, I am not going to discuss my female functions."

"Jeez, why not? I discuss mine all the time. So I ask again, why not just take the Pill and tell him you love him."

"I may do exactly that. That's why I got the prescription. It's in my medicine chest right now."

"Explain please."

Said Sarah: "I don't want to get pregnant till Mac is safely home."

Denise nodded with a quick jerk of her head, accepting instantaneously what Sarah had taken hours to work out.

"But I don't want to—"

"You're afraid to—excuse me—disobey him," said Denise with some pride in her candor.

"Denise, don't be stupid."

"Then what?"

"I am not the least afraid to go against him and that's probably what I will do, but I am not very pleased about deceiving him. He has never deceived me, and I prize that in our marriage."

"O.K. don't deceive him. Tell him 'Merry Christmas, lover, no baby till you come home.' What's wrong with that?"

Sarah spoke carefully, working through her emotion, as if to clarify it to herself. She said: "If I take the Pill it will be out of fear." She stressed the last word. She paused and Denise again gave one of her quick signs of understanding.

Sarah continued: "Mac has told me he is not afraid, and I believe him."

"I thought everybody was afraid," Denise said skeptically.

"That's what I thought but Mac says otherwise. So if I confess my fear that—he'll be killed or maimed—it might pass to him. Do you see? I might infect him." Sarah looked up from her coffee with great seriousness and waited.

"That's silly," Denise said. "These men face death every day, and you're afraid to point it out to him?"

Sarah asserted quietly, "If I were going under for brain surgery I surely wouldn't appreciate Mac's saying, 'This scares me, you may never wake up.' "

Sarah was now standing and staring into the street. Denise saw her in half profile and admired her unusual height, slender waist, and full breasts, and the rich contrast of her dark glossy hair and pale but flushed complexion.

"Sometimes I think he relies on me to be the rational one," Sarah ventured. "He thinks I'm practical. Where he gets the idea I don't know."

"Well," Denise allowed, "that's better than being treated like a baby doll."

"Is that how you are treated?" Sarah asked on a sudden intuition.

"Not exactly but Tommy often breezes right past me. I'll be holding up my hand and saying, 'Hey, stop,' and he's already gone."

"Gone where?"

"Wherever he intends to go. I'm expected to catch up."

"Your parents," Sarah began tentatively, "were they equals in any sense of the word? Did your father treat your mother—"

"The question *there* is, did my mother treat my father as an equal, and the answer is no. But just a minute," Denise said. "First it's your unbridled lust that's responsible for his staying in the Crotch, and therefore being sent to Vietnam; now you're the rational partner of a husband who needs restraining. Which is it?"

"It's both," said Sarah without explanation.

"O.K. I'll accept that. And now the big guy is dying to make you pregnant."

"Evidently," said Sarah.

"I was really pissed at Tommy," Denise said, "as if he'd deliberately gotten me pregnant against my will. Then I—after the proof came in that I was as infertile as ever—I started missing him and blubbering and losing weight—you'd never guess it now, would you?—and I saw him walking out the door a thousand times a day with his seabag over his shoulder, and he turned and gave me a quick half-ashamed smile and a wave, and got into some car where the wife was driving her hubby off, and my Tommy was gone too. Still gone. Is. I mean *still is gone*. I won't see him till September, if I see him then."

"Stop it," said Sarah.

"Yeah, stop saying what we are both thinking."

"I am not thinking it. Just because I fear it doesn't mean I think it."

"What did I tell you?" Denise cried. "You are a born lawyer, splitting hairs like that. Listen don't make a federal case out of it, O.K.? Take the damn Pill and tell him we start a family in June as previously agreed. I don't see why these men have the right to dictate to us about our own bodies, you know?"

"They have no such right," said Sarah cooly, "but neither do I have the right to deceive him."

"Then don't, damn it! Have I made myself clear? Tell him. Let him live with the truth."

Sarah turned from Denise, whose mobile, excited features had been fascinating her, to the deserted street and the Dandy Dumpster at the curb.

Sarah said heavily: "I can't be dishonest and I don't want to get pregnant until he's safely home."

"Fine, so do what I—"

"Denise, shut up."

"Pardon me, madam, I thought you wanted my opinion."

"I did and now I have it."

In the ensuing silence Sarah wandered to the rear window and watched the children playing on the monkey bars and swings. Three or four mothers stood by, talking. The sun broke out and painted their colorful coats with its level rays. When Sarah returned Denise said:

"Does it ever strike you as just a little grotesque that it's such a real war for us, and so phony for our gallant leaders in Washington? I mean, think how real it is, for example, to Mary and her mother. Are you political at all? I've never heard you utter—"

"I am political," said Sarah, "if you mean do I pay attention, yes, I pay attention."

"I never did, till Tommy went over."

"Oh," said Sarah warming to it, "I've been more or less political since I went to Madison at age eighteen. In that town there are three streams—alcohol, sex, and politics."

"Yeah well, I just sort of woke up when they snatched my sweet Tommy from me. If he should die over there I will go to Washington and murder Johnson and McNamara with my bare hands."

"They are so inept, so dishonest," Sarah pronounced with some vehemence.

Denise replied: "I despise them," and she spoke with no trace of her customary lightness. "Tommy says they keep pausing the bombing because otherwise they might cause some inconvenience to the North Vietnamese who are trying to come south to kill marines."

Sarah commented: "Of course they say that's how they'll persuade the North to negotiate. An original theory. To make you beg for mercy I stop hitting you."

"Tommy says," Denise rattled on, "that we are fighting with one hand tied behind our back. Like, the Ho Chi Minh Trail—why don't we just friggin block it? I wake up at night seeing North Vietnamese soldiers crawling through the jungle on their way to kill my Tommy, while LBJ and McNamara and their clown group plan the next bombing pause."

"And they draft the poor and protect the rich," said Sarah, and added immediately: "Denise I can't listen to this."

"O.K. Sorry. I can't quit raving."

Then Sarah said in a voice of gladness: "I'm going to see him in less than a month!"

"I envy you."

"Yes, and you'll see Tommy soon, and someday it'll be over for all of us."

"Right. Actual life. What a shock it'll be. So Sarah, do you have any idea what you'll do then?"

"What I will do is be happy with Mac and a baby."

"I mean, do in the world, you know? Like say work. Or are you committed to the mommy business."

"It makes me feel queasy, but the truth is I can see one scenario quite clearly—but the other is perfectly blank."

"O.K. which is which?"

Sarah said: "If Mac should die I know exactly what I'd do. If he lives, I can see—yes—a baby or two—but what I myself do is a mystery."

"It's no mystery at all," Denise said. "If you have two or three children you've got your head in a toilet till you're forty, and then it's too late. But what would you do, pardon the word, if you were alone?"

"As you said, I'd become a lawyer."

"Oh wow! Pioneer woman! Took your head out of the toilet! Good going!"

"When Mac quit law school I can remember thinking, 'O.K., you don't want to be a lawyer, I respect you for it, but maybe I do.' Of course I never did anything about it, we were so mad to play house, and also I didn't have the courage. If Mac should die, I'd need money. It's pretty simple actually."

"Don't you hate that phrase, 'if he should die'? It zings through my head ten times a day."

"I hate it and I cannot silence it," Sarah acknowledged.

Said Denise: "If Tommy dies, I already told you, I go to the special hell reserved for women who can't stand on their own two feet. If he lives, it's babies and suburbs, bridge and book clubs. How's that for a vision of hell without the flames?"

"I wouldn't call it that," said Sarah. "It's what most people end up doing. It can't be so bad."

"Like hell it can't. You yourself fled your White Folks Bay or River Flats or whatever you called it like a scared rabbit."

"Yes, but one can love—love one's children and husband, even there. My mother—I've told you—"

"Sure but that was an earlier generation. Anyway you can't make a life out of loving somebody, you've got to do something. Say we're lucky and they both come home 'with all their faculties intact,' to quote Mr. Salinger, healthy and eager to jump us—"

"And we are eager to be jumped," Sarah interposed.

"—and then what? See what I mean? Babies are just an impulse, just hormones after all, but—"

"Liar," Sarah cut in. "If Tommy called you and said, 'Hey sugar, surprise, I'm at Cherry Point, come and get me, they gave me emergency leave to make you pregnant'—you'd be delirious."

Rostraver Public Library
800 Fellsburg Road
Rostraver, PA 15012
724-379-5511

"With what? Happiness or terror?"

"Happiness obviously."

"Well maybe I would but you're saying we're just baby machines? Our whole purpose is to pop little purple squealers and do the laundry forever after? That's life?"

"You're a mother, that doesn't mean you can't be something else at the same time. You can do something in the world." She was thinking of her play, which suddenly seemed important, not to the world perhaps but to her own life. "You don't turn off your brain—"

"Hormones, that's their mission, turning off your brain. Anyway," Denise added, "you already threw away your big ambition."

"I told you why." Sarah flushed with anger—but she did not mention the play.

"And your mother," Denise said. "Just because she was happy doesn't mean you'd be happy, or I would, doing the same thing."

"All right, damn you, what do you want?" Sarah almost shouted.

"I want my Tommy!" Denise wailed.

And Sarah thought: "I want Mac." She wanted his arms around her, to receive him into her body, but she did not want to become pregnant at Christmas.

While walking on the beach she was so in love that her feet skipped along. The love was still the same but now she was far above the surf line, pushing heavy-footed through the deep sand. She imagined the little wheel-shaped card containing the pills, standing in the dark of her medicine chest. She imagined popping one out of its bed and holding it in her palm. Above her she saw the shaft, the one with Mac in it. She gazed stupidly at it.

Chapter 9

A Waste of Assets

It was a request she had never refused.

Mac said: "Lie on your back. Stretch out your arms. Let your hands come to rest palms up."

And the second part: "Let your fingers curl gently. Do not close your fingers. Let them stay open."

Her eyes were half-closed, her lips slightly parted, her breast rising softly, then falling—and he watched her hands, as the fingers came to rest.

He looked at her face, her pale skin, her dark dark hair spreading over the pillow, her dark eyebrows and lashes. As he hovered above her, her deep eyes met his—her eyes, deep, in that they accepted and invited him. She lay, as it might seem, passive and yielding, yet not so passive. Her fingers were still curled and motionless, but she moaned and her eyelids lowered.

He detected a new heaviness in her breathing and a vague motion of her legs that he could not see.

He said, "Sarah" and bent to kiss her lips.

He sat up as if propelled by a spring. In the candlelight he saw that his radioman, Private First Class Graeser, had come alert too. An observer from another world might have thought these men listened with their eyes.

The rain had stopped. When Mac first heard the sounds, he thought they were the advance wave of new rain beating softly on the canvas. He rolled out of the shelter. He sensed neither wind nor rain in the warm night air. He felt the presence of another man, then another. No one spoke; they listened.

The sounds came from the direction taken by Hitchcock and his team. Through the moist vapors the reports reached Mac's ear faintly, distinctly. The sounds of a distant firefight were treated by Mac as a coded narrative. Hitchcock had opened up on a small unit, three to six men, who responded with AK-47's and RPGs. The rocket-propelled grenades sent soft booms seventeen hundred meters up the draws, and some of the force of these reports was absorbed by the jungle. Still, on reaching Mac's ear they suggested a lethal reality present at their origin.

A new stuttering intervened, and Mac knew Hitchcock's machine gunner was keeping his head, sending out quick bursts that would conserve his ammo and keep his bore cool. Next, as Mac and his companions stood like sentinels in the night, came the chuff-boom of Hitchcock's M79 grenade launcher.

And next, after about four more minutes, silence.

"Graeser," said Mac in a low voice, not a whisper, and the radioman responded:

"Here, Skipper."

"We'll listen but we won't transmit. I don't want to bother them yet."

"Aye aye sir."

And now Mac could see Graeser's form or shadow. And for a few seconds the sky opened a random cluster of stars.

Mac told the exec to get what sleep he could, then Mac and Graeser trooped the line, approaching each perimeter hole carefully and responding correctly when challenged, keeping very quiet, pausing at each hole (except the forward listening posts) and greeting the men in brief whispered messages of encouragement. "Big ears," Mac said. "Rabbit ears tonight, marines."

The gunny's call reporting "George Washington" came just as Mac and Graeser were crawling back into their hooch. Graeser repeated the gunny's message and Mac said:

"Tell him Roger. Stay and observe"—which Graeser repeated into his handset; then he lay down, placing his feet carefully on a low mud shelf that also served as Mac's pillow.

Mac settled his body, resting his head on his pack next to Graeser's feet. He began the slow job of warming the mud under his poncho. He closed his eyes and saw a blackness speckled with red and purple—and the vision of Sarah did not come back to him. He was cold.

Mac assembled the brain trust in the morning and reported on the gunny's night's work. The CP was awaking around them. Men lit fires and crouched over breakfast.

Mac put the first question: "Why were they walking toward a bridge that's eight feet under water?"

No one ventured an answer.

"I just talked to Hitchcock. He says they were carrying farm tools. Why?"

The men dug their spoons into their C rats, sipped their coffee; one man cleaned his pistol and peered into the bore. Nobody ventured an answer. Paul Adrano almost spoke up, but silenced himself. His guess was that they had been heading for a boat. The farm tools baffled him completely.

Mac said: "The gunny searched the bodies an hour ago. No papers, no weapons. One body had been pulled away in the night, which surprised the gunny. They had the four bodies in the scope all night."

"Somebody snaked out there," Ollie suggested.

"Nobody can look through those glasses all night," Captain Kindred offered.

Sitting cross-legged and drinking from a can full of steaming Red Rose tea, Mac watched the brain trusters for a sign that someone wished to speak, and saw none. He said:

"If they intended to follow the trail, then they intended to cross the river. If they were carrying picks, machetes, mattocks, and shovels, they did not intend to swim it."

"Are there any boats down there?" Ollie asked.

"Did the gunny look for boats?" Kindred asked.

Said Mac: "We'll look for boats when we go down there. How bout this for the farm tools? There is a cache somewhere on the trail or near it, camouflaged. And the camouflage is due for preventive maintenance."

"Hey! They're gonna pull a PM on their camouflage!" said Kindred with admiration. "Cool gooks!"

"Them ole boys with farm tools were farmers," Lieutenant Dan Shaw proposed. "They got their ass drafted to dress up the camouflage. The soldiers were Local Force VC assigned to guard the cache."

Lieutenant Kim Kolias of 1st Platoon, the "frightened youth," observed: "The Local Force will send a runner to Main Force. Tell him about this—"

"Discovery," Mac put in. "If," he added, "they assume we've discovered the bridge."

Lifting his chin to finish his tea Mac scanned the sky. It was gray but gave reason for hope. Said Mac to Captain Kindred: "Ask'm again."

Kindred got on his feet and walked ten paces to his radioman, who was squatting over a little blaze of C4. Mac saw the bronze fluttering glow of it, amid the surrounding gray and brown, and saw the marine's face as it lifted to see Kindred approaching.

Kindred returned and said: "Medevac bird lifting off at Ky Ha, gentlemen."

Turning to his left, Mac said: "Paul, would you do me a favor?"

"Certainly," replied Paul Adrano.

"Make sure the corpsmen have got the WIAs ready to fly in fifteen minutes."

Kindred added: "The bird'll be here in twenty minutes."

Paul rose and left the conference. Just as he passed out of hearing, Mac was saying:

"If I were the NVA commander—"

If he were the NVA commander preparing an attack on Quang Ngai City, and if he had placed caches anywhere on the Nui Gio hill mass, he would treat the appearance of marines near the bridge as a threat to his entire operation, whether they had found the bridge or not.

If indeed the NVA planned to attack the ARVN in Quang Ngai City they would attack in force. This suggested that they had established a battalion or even a regimental CP somewhere close to Nui Gio.

"Jeez Skipper, you mean close to my momma's boy? How close?"

182

This from Ollie, who made his eyes bulge. He grabbed skin at his throat and shook it up and down.

Whatever his rank, Mac continued, revising and extending his earlier ideas about his adversary, and whatever the size of his force, this officer would dispatch a quick-reaction company and later perhaps a battalion to deal with the threat. This force would probably be a well-trained NVA or VC Main Force unit—professionals.

The enemy high command understood what the American general in Saigon did not, that the "war of attrition" being prosecuted by the Americans favored the NVA. Mac did not fulminate against General Westmoreland, although he considered him a dangerous fool. He did say that the NVA commander would pursue two objectives at once. He would protect his caches, and seek to kill Americans in the greatest possible numbers.

These objectives were complementary. He would fight any American unit that threatened the caches, and in so doing he would preserve the caches and with luck kill Americans. If forced to choose, he would sacrifice the caches, using them as bait to draw more Americans into the fight.

Some people said it was racist to hold that the enemy's government was indifferent to its own casualties. However that may be, said Mac, they were always willing to lose ten soldiers as the price of killing one American. They understood how to win the war. Westmoreland did not.

"Well then, Skipper," cried Ollie, "yuk yuk yuk, let's go home."

"We're going down there," Mac replied, speaking to the whole group, "with or without air support."

Captain Kindred said the air command was predicting a clear sky and Battalion was wetting its pants over the bridge. "I think we'll have gunships today, and if we step in the shit I can get us Phantoms with rockets and bombs."

Mac asked: "Can you get us nape?"

"Yeah I think so."

"Because if they're in bunkers we'll need nape. O.K. gents," said Mac, resuming his speculations, "I think he's going to hit us, whether there's a cache down there or not. If he's anywhere nearby, he's going to hit us."

"God help him," said Kindred.

"Well," said Ollie the artilleryman, "since we'll be outside the fan of fire I'll just hop the medevac bird back to Ky Ha-ha-ha."

Mac said, "Ha ha ha."

"Well shit," Ollie changed his tack, "airplanes are not *totally* worthless." He glanced sideways at Kindred.

Kindred went to his radio again. Mac still held the empty can dangling in his hand, looking inside as if to learn what happened to his tea. Kindred came back and announced the ETA of the medevac bird and that it carried ammo, C rats, and batteries. Mac said:

"Saddle up and hold positions."

He went to talk to the wounded men, where they had been assembled in a ragged group by the chaplain. Only two were stretcher cases and the rest walking wounded, also called the "sick, lame, and lazy." Mac spoke to each man.

Corporal Sedgwick assured him: "I be back, Skipper."

Mac clasped his hand and Sedgwick repeated, "Ain't nothing wrong with me. I be back." Then he cried: "Ooooh, Skipper, you crushin my han! By golly my bones be chips now. I one a them McNamara draftees, a hunred thousan morons to fight the gooks. Ain't as strong as a regular Marine."

"Don't worry about it," said Mac. "I'm a draftee myself."

"Yeah Skipper, but you ain't no moron," said Sedgwick, still pumping Mac's hand.

"Thank you, Sedgwick. Neither are you."

"Sir, I am, sir. Don't know nothin but follow God's will."

"Then, Sedgwick, we sure need you. Come back as soon as you can," and Mac released his hand.

The brown, earnest, yet pleased eyes, set in alabaster, regarded Mac with infinite charity, and held him.

Mac thought: "If there was a God I would fall on my knees and thank Him for sparing this man." And immediately he thought: "But there are others, a hundred and thirty of them, and—"

But some authority within, so influential it didn't need language, cut off this line of thought.

The men looked up and listened. Mac listened. It was the medevac bird coming in high, above small-arms range.

Kindred popped a smoke grenade and Mac moved upwind. The chopper descended the shaft.

Mac's thinking about this adversary was mostly speculation but there was one fact: with the arrival and departure of the medevac bird he knew Mac's exact location. And with marines so close to the bridge, he could surmise that his caches were in jeopardy. He could draw a line on his map, if he chose, showing Delta's route of march from its present CP to the bridge.

Delta moved out before the twigs quit flying. Its lead element was already two hundred meters down the hillside when the bird hit the top of the shaft and leveled off for the dash to Charlie Med.

Dan Shaw's platoon led the way with the excellent Willie walking point. The command group followed, then 1st Platoon with Lieutenant Kim Kolias in command, then 3rd, under the command of Staff Sergeant Reggie Graves—"Graves Registration." The stinger consisted of Graves's platoon sergeant with a gun crew and three riflemen.

In the beginning they went deep into the shadow cast by Nui Gio. To their right, westward across 5B, they saw hills and mountains six klicks away capped with a style of early sunlight that glowed almost golden on the bright-green slopes and peaks. Below the sun line the terrain seemed two-dimensional; above it, the folds and ridges cut deep and rose into a startling prominence.

As Delta reached Ambush Alley and turned a few degrees left, to cross it at right angles, the boiling white ball crept over the top of Nui Gio and threw its bright rays into the men's eyes. The country was open parkland with high trees widely spaced and pale yellow grass rising to their knees, a country touched but lightly by the hand of man, where birds and insects flicked here and there in the slanting sunlight; where, if a man looked back, he could see the sun glint on flitting wings. The tree trunks ahead that stood out for being dark and thick turned light and slender when seen from the sun's angle. And the marchers raised billows of mist that lifted around the men's knees to create a light haze along the column.

And all the vegetation, trees, grass, vines, and bushes, was none of it stunted or thirsty. It was a November morning but it gave off the colors and airs of spring.

Willie halted and Dan Shaw went forward to confer. The two stood back to back and moved crabwise into the Alley, facing along the trail in opposite directions, each training his eyes and his weapon along the axis of the trail while two others crept out into the open and added their senses to the maneuver of crossing this ribbon of red-hot coals. Having penetrated the thick woods on the other side to a depth of ten meters, Dan Shaw came back and waved the column forward. The men proceeded with a strained attention to all that lay within the ambit of their senses, in all directions, including up.

As Mac crossed he gave the trees special scrutiny; turning toward the east he took a shot of unfiltered sun in his eyes and regretted his carelessness, till his vision returned to normal.

He began to sweat as Delta moved into a thickly wooded saddle between two rises that he could not see. The air was close, the sun was climbing, and his brain, and his heart, felt hot and constricted and pressed.

He spoke with Dan Shaw by radio and gave him a new bearing, and suggested he caution Willie against breaking into open ground, which he would encounter in about ten minutes. Willie the point man reached this landmark in fifteen minutes, and halted. Lieutenant Dan Shaw again moved forward and, again, Dan and Willie went butt to butt, like a two-headed dragon, waddling like an abortion of the divine plan, as they crossed the open space in brutally bright sun. It was now about nine o'clock and the sun was giving fair warning of the superheat to come.

But nobody objected to sunny skies, least of all MacHugh Clare. Captain Kindred had just informed him that two Huey gunships were boring holes in the sky out of Ky Ha and would arrive overhead in ten minutes' time. Who would gripe about the aviation-friendly sun for broiling a column of marines when they had just stepped outside the fan of artillery fire?

Mac now walked with his handset clapped to his ear, listening in on Gunny Hitchcock's conversation with Dan Shaw. Hitchcock was guiding the column to his gun pit and kept referring to an open space which Dan Shaw insisted he had already crossed. But the map showed two open areas in the thick woods between the Alley and the gunny's position, and Mac believed the point had not yet reached the second, but soon would if Willie kept to the assigned bearing.

So Mac said nothing. He walked like all the rest, with perhaps one difference. The men felt themselves to be humping through a blind jungle that might go on forever. To Mac it was the threshold of the open bottomland where the swollen river poured its mountain water to a depth of seven or eight feet over the "summer pool" bridge. Having a map, Mac could see through jungle so thick it made the sun itself strain to find an opening.

Delta marched on, and then stopped abruptly and contracted like an accordion. Mac heard Dan Shaw say:

"Got it, Guns."

"O.K.," said Gunny Hitchcock, whispering, but clearly audible in Mac's handset, "just walk down the hill and when you break out keep close to the tree line on your right. If I see you coming I promise I won't shoot you."

"Guns, y'all're a gentleman," said Dan Shaw, and he set the column in motion.

Mac heard—then he spun around and saw the gunships—crossing the summit of Nui Gio. Before this he had had a company of infantry. Now he had a company plus four bulging rocket pods and a couple of extra machine guns, plus two scouts whose visibility was computed not in yards but in miles.

He saw Captain Kindred watching him and Kindred's lips formed the words "You're welcome."

Mac turned until his shadow fell over the glaring plastic cover on the map.

"That's better," said Captain Kindred the toastmaster, removing his sunglasses. Being an aviator he was bound to wear sunglasses even when he marched with the ground pounders. "Now what can we do?" Kindred asked.

Said MacHugh Clare: "I'd like a quick VR of the little river, downstream to where it empties into the Song Tra Khuc. Then he could turn around and do it upstream."

"Two sweeps," said Kindred.

"Yes. So he can look from two angles."

"What are the EEIs?" asked Kindred.

"Signs of a boat or raft along either bank, signs that troops or motor vehicles ever use these trails"—the trails winding along with the river. And Mac asked: "How long will that take?"

"Five minutes."

"And can the other guy give me a VR up and down Route Five B five or six klicks either way?"

"O.K. Visual reconnaissance, little river and Five B; Essential Elements of Information, look for gooks."

"So will they do it?" Mac asked.

"Why not?"

"Why not! You never know what airdales will do and what they won't."

"Airdales will save your ass, Mr. Mac, and mine too."

"Meantime I'll be putting a squad across the little river," said Mac, "and searching for boats. I want to *di-di* from this last good place soon as I can, and I'm not turning my back on that riverbank till we've reconned it. Then you won't have to save my ass."

Collins the sailor and Purdy, the swimmer who had crossed the deep stream on day one, were already stripped and rigging a lifeline and messenger line. The sailor, as Mac and Kindred talked, was running the bitter end of the lifeline to the palm tree the gunny had used as a night landmark.

A squad of eight men were undressing down to their shorts, and lacing their boots together for transport across the little river. At length they stood ready, and a few went to the river's edge and splashed themselves and enjoyed the cooling of the gentle breeze that rolled down from the mountains and passed through an opening in the hills.

Kindred spoke with the pilots about Mac's requests and gave Mac a thumbs-up, and adjusted his sunglasses. He watched the birds diverge.

The pilot taking the little river dropped fearlessly down to an altitude of less than a hundred feet and roared along the bank, going south about twelve hundred meters to where the little river entered the Song Tra Khuc. Then skidding into a turn and coming back, he reconnoitered the river in an upstream direction.

Kindred reported the pilot saw nothing of interest. The other bird was by now a speck in the sky to the west, sweeping Route 5B. It was along this road that Mac had imagined an NVA company marching to the attack.

To reach Nui Gio from the south a marching force would have to cross the little river. Since the gunny's team had seen no such force last night, then this imagined formation of the enemy either did not exist or it had crossed at a ford somewhere. Mac was compelled to assume the enemy had a southern access route to Nui Gio. No other assumption was prudent.

A sergeant reported that the "skivvy squad" was ready to cross.

Mac said: "O.K., Sergeant Weathers, go."

Purdy rushed in to his knees, then his waist, and he plunged and began stroking furiously, drifting downstream but gaining the middle of the swift stream in three or four strokes.

Gunny Hitchcock, standing beside Mac, said: "He's right over the bridge now, sir."

And from behind him Mac heard Kindred talking to one of the pilots: "Hey, if we scream, get your ass back here pronto."

Purdy was struggling up the brush-clogged bank, and Hitchcock was saying: "That's where I climbed up last night. The bodies are about fifteen meters like that"—holding his hand out flat.

A fire team stationed along the near bank kept the lone marine on the opposite bank covered. One man rode the shoulders of a hulk, to gain a better view. The hulk strode lightly up and down the shore smoking a cigarette, while his rider, with boots crossed on his mount's back, propped the butt of his rifle on his own thigh and scanned the open ground between the little river and the vill 150 meters beyond Purdy.

Purdy was by now drawing in the lifeline by its messenger. He worked silently, hand over hand, and the big rope moved through the crowned, domed water like a snake.

"Ain't nothin to hook the fucker on!" Purdy called out.

He and the sailor held a conference across the roiling water. It appeared that Purdy could find no firm purchase on his bank for the mansaver.

Mac watched as the squad sergeant, dressed only in his shorts but with his rifle slung on his shoulder, told Collins to cross.

The sailor walked gingerly in his bare feet ten paces upstream and then waded in to his knees, and jumped. He began an awkward, unskilled, but energetic stroke and he soon joined Purdy. They pulled the lifeline taut and held it, and the squad crossed one man at a time, minus clothing, boots, and weapons.

Seeing this squad vulnerable on the opposite bank, Mac watched with a pressing, dilating fear in his belly as the men of the skivvy squad stood unarmed and nervous, silent, glancing all around them.

Now the sailor swam back, for it was believed that few men, but certainly Collins, would be capable of the next trick.

Collins was burdened with a thick uniform blanket of fat but he had no gut, and he had once demonstrated his strength by lifting and carrying the very hulk who now carried the rifleman.

That man's rifle was propped at a rakish angle and the hulk and his rider continued their patrol up and down the bank.

Graves Registration gave Collins a long shaft of bamboo with three packs attached near the top with electrician's tape. These contained the squad's boots. Holding the boot tree aloft in the manner of a knight with his lance, the sailor entered the stream cautiously, tested his footing, and advanced unevenly, with the packs swinging overhead. His left biceps bulged white, and he hooked his right arm over the lifeline.

He moved to deep water. With a sequence of fast powerful grabs he advanced one-handed along the lifeline, kicking vigorously till he found a foothold again in the shallows. He climbed and pulled his way up, lowering the shaft slowly into the uplifted hands of the skivvy squad.

While his mates were pulling on their boots, Collins brought over just one rifle hanging on the bamboo by its sling, as an experiment. It worked well enough that he brought the rest in two loads. A trooper on the near side threw several loaded magazines across; they sailed in low arcs glinting in the sun.

The squad was across, booted and armed.

The men of Delta began searching the brushy banks of the little river.

On the far bank the skivvy squad set out a fire team as a screen on its right. The others cautiously probed the bushes, receiving sharp scratches and cuts on the bare legs, and thorns in their hands. Every man was hyperalert for trip wires, pressure plates under turned earth, or the antenna-like protuberances that could mean death.

The screen kept the slow pace of the searchers as they moved downstream. Mac had told the sergeant in charge that he had fifteen minutes to search a hundred meters of stream bank, and ten more to get his troops back across the stream. "I don't want your men burning up in this sun," Mac said.

On the near side a squad conducted a parallel search with the same tense care, while Mac paced up and down the bank, his face lit by reflected light off the water. He was not able to stand still in the sun.

Father Paul Adrano had spotted a patch of shade but stayed with the command group. He had never thought of a little shadow with the same desire he now bestowed on a square yard of sandy earth.

As Mac paced, it seemed the soles of his jungle boots pulled in the heat of the sand and sent it rushing upward.

Mac turned from the river to face the jungle, to watch Kim Kolias's 1st Platoon spreading in a skirmish line to cross an embayment of open sandy ground that reached some one hundred meters into the jungle. On the left of this embayment, somewhere within a solid wall of bright green, was the gunny's gun pit of last night, now abandoned. The gunny's team had been returned to its platoon. On the right the open bay was bounded by another wall of jungle. Mac had told 1st Platoon to enter on a broad front and search to a depth of fifty meters, then stand and hold.

The platoon crossed the sandy bay with the uncomfortable tread men might exhibit if they were asked to walk in an oven. The skirmish line melted into the tree line. The men along the little river, meanwhile, talked freely, but 1st Platoon had moved in silence and circumspection.

Neither of the aerial VRs had turned up anything interesting, and Captain Kindred so reported to Mac. Mac asked Kindred to thank the pilots and hold them on station.

"Hang high, don't say good-bye," Kindred spoke into his handset. Then: "Hey Mac, they want to know if they can annihilate or destroy anybody for you at this moment in history."

"Not yet," said Mac who was passing Kindred in his pacing.

The sky was purifying to a slate blue, a color not seen aloft by Delta's men in several weeks. The sun grew hotter and it was impossible to stand still.

Paul Adrano watched the nearly naked figures struggling in the brush across the stream, now some seventy-five meters away by virtue of the divergence of stream and trail. The command group was spread along the trail in anticipation of moving out. Everybody wanted to move; stillness was misery, tension. Paul's head ached and he grew anxious about whether he could keep up when the troops moved.

He gave in. He troubled God with his petty concerns, casting his prayer in selfless terms. He said: "Father, please give me strength to endure this sun. If I collapse, my mission is at an end, just when I may be most useful to these men."

Then he heard a small explosion from across the stream.

MacHugh Clare threw his rifle to Graeser. He knocked his helmet off and slipped his cloth belt of M16 magazines over this head.

He decided: "I don't have time—" time to run thirty meters upstream to the lifeline.

He twisted out of his flak jacket and web belt; the belt and all its equipment dropped to the sand, and he lunged through the brush and dived into the river.

His face scraped bottom and his nose took a heavy blow that shocked him. The blow cleared his mind and he went off automatic into a more rational mode. He saw that he was leaving the only place from which he could control his company. He flung his arms out and pulled water, and stroked, and pressed forward by hopping off the bottom, and stroked and began to sink even as he pulled and kicked with all his strength. He saw the line where water met air, then lifted above it, saw a cloud of thin dark smoke rising from the brush ahead, and sank again.

His kick was troublingly slow—and his strokes taxed his wind beyond belief—and he kept kicking and stroking and there was no bottom. He paused, searching for the bottom with dangling feet.

He resumed the horizontal and swam, if swimming it could be called, and reached the center and again saw a glimpse of the men on the bank, and smoke and dust. There was bustling, shouting, and confusion, and the smoke lingered.

His hands were ripped by thorns—he scrambled up the bank grab-bing bushes and stalks that were like little weapons against intruders such as he—but he paid no attention. He didn't even feel it.

Later he remembered the ripping of his hands but could not, even then, recall any pain.

They gave way. He heard a man say, "Make a hole for the skipper." Men withdrew and there lay the wounded man. Mac dropped to his knees beside somebody who was trying to help. Mac spoke to the wounded man and saw his terrified eyes turn in a jerk toward him.

Naked but for his shorts and boots, the man lay spread on the ground by a smoking sulfurous black hole in the bushes. He was sur-rounded by brush three or four feet high and the smell of explosive, if not the smoke, filled the place. His white hairless chest and slender arms were marked with small rips and holes, exuding blood; his shorts were ripped and his boots—

Mac saw the left boot. He stared at it—at that moment a marine dropped at the man's feet and said to Mac, "I'll help."

Mac said, "Take off that boot. Quick."

Mac pulled down the skivvy shorts, saw the wounds, and said to the wounded man: "Your cock and balls are good, mister."

There was no response from the wounded man and the terror in his eyes did not change.

Mac's helper could not unlace the boot. He pulled at a loose boot lace and it came away, only two inches long. The marine, being virtu-ally naked himself, had no knife, and Mac's K-Bar lay on the other side of the river, on his web belt.

Mac said, "I've got to see the wound."

The marine worked at the laces and the wounded man screamed. He said that he was going to die. And that he did not want to die.

Mac did not speak. He watched the marine picking away at the half-destroyed leather-and-canvas jungle boot.

Mac said, "Get it off," and went for the big artery.

The wounded man cried out and Mac said firmly:

"Take it off, quick."

The marine twisted the boot and the wounded man cried out.

Mac said to the man who had been there when he came: "Call a corpsman." Thinking: "Let him cross somehow."

"I need to see the bleeding," he repeated to his helper.

The marine picked away scraps of leather and canvas and exposed the foot and ankle, and brushed the hideous wound as if to rid it of sand and fragments. In fact he did touch a fragment and it was, or he imagined it was, hotter than the flesh in which it was embedded.

Mac dug his fingers into the thigh muscle.

"He's bleedin, sir."

"Yes," Mac observed and dug his fingers in elsewhere.

The flow slowed. He added pressure and it stopped. He said to the wounded man, "We've stopped it," but the man did not seem convinced.

He said, "I'm gonna die, I know it."

"No you are not. Lie still and don't yell anymore."

The wounded man said he was ready to die and Mac said: "No you aren't." Then Mac cried in shock: "What the hell!"

The helper said, "It's yours sir—"

Mac's blood streaming down.

"Oh yeah—yeah—O.K., no big deal."

Mac turned his head and spat blood, and the taste called forth unpleasant memories—they went back to football. On realizing this he almost laughed. He blinked sweat from his eyes, spat again, and turned back to the mutilated foot, and saw clear muscle and bone, and no blood streaming.

Turning to the wounded man, who looked at him with desperate hope in his eyes, Mac said:

"Yes, by God, you're going to live and walk, but lie still, goddamn it."

"Yes sir."

"Right, just lie still and—"

Sudden firing from across the stream—rifles, machine guns, grenades—

"Christ Almighty," cried Mac silently in despair.

He was blind down here, couldn't see a thing, and no radio; he might as well be dead, for all the good he could do.

But he bent closer and said, "You will live, mister. Just keep your mind on that. Say it. Say 'I will live.' Say it."

The man said it and Mac listened to an M16 blatting away on full automatic across the river. He cursed and didn't know what to do, swim back or stay.

A new figure knelt beside him and said in a calmly reassuring voice: "Hold that pressure. I'm going to apply a tourniquet."

It was Doc Henry Bartholomew. He was soaked and dripping water. To Mac's helper the doc said: "Elevate that leg for me."

"Goddamn! I forgot that," Mac exclaimed.

Another form intruded on Mac's right, by the wounded man's head. This was Paul Adrano and he was bending low whispering to the man, "Thank God," and on the man's face Mac read a surprised happiness.

Doc Bartholomew examined the foot and ankle, thanked the marine down there with the same cool grace, as if by helping the wounded man the marine had done a special favor for the doc. Then Bartholomew uncoiled a length of small nylon line, pulled it one turn around the leg and yanked it hard. It bit into the muscle. The wounded man winced and then his eyes enlarged as if in terror, but he made no sound.

Mac said, "May I let go?"

"Not yet, keep the pressure," said Henry Bartholomew, running his hands over the parts of the legs and back that he could not see. He again peered with an intense interest at the major wound and made a quick inspection of the rest.

He took the man's hand in his own and said, "Squeeze my hand." The man responded and Bartholomew said, "Now the other one"— with the same evidently satisfactory result, because Bartholomew then asked the man to follow his finger as he moved it slowly across his field of vision. He pressed the good foot down by the toes and required the man to lift against his pressure.

He asked the man if he was in pain and got a negative answer, and Mac wondered: "Then why did he scream?"

Mac still knelt over the white mutilated body, holding pressure on the artery above the tourniquet, observing as in a dream how his fingers dug into the thigh muscle.

He looked into Paul's face and said, "Hi, Chaplain," and Paul smiled.

"Paul," said Mac, "can you hold pressure here?"

Without a word Paul shifted on his knees and placed his hand adjacent to Mac's. Mac pulled free and Paul's fingers pressed into the clearly marked indentations.

"I'm going back to the command group," said Mac to Henry Bartholomew. "Stay with him. I'll get a medevac bird. You stay with the company or go with this man. It's your decision. But if you go to Charlie Med, come back as soon as you can."

"Aye aye sir," Henry said.

Henry Bartholomew took Paul's hand and gently lifted it, watching for a new flow of blood. Mac ran upstream to the lifeline, calling two men to secure it as he crossed.

The shooting continued.

Graeser, Kindred, and the exec met him as he dragged himself up the bank, shedding water in sheets and streams. He listened to the exec's summary and consulted with Kindred. Hearing from the air officer what he had hoped to hear, he radioed Kim Kolias of 1st Platoon.

He told Kolias to tighten up and pull back, and to cross the open embayment and set up a defensive line in the trees on the other side. Kindred was preparing the mission. When Kolias's platoon began pouring out of the jungle and when it was consolidated and Kolias had assured Mac all his men were withdrawn, Mac made a sign, and Kindred said into his handset:

"Shoot."

The gunships swayed carelessly but somehow came abreast of one another, aligned exactly on the long axis of the tree line just vacated by 1st Platoon, dipped their noses, and came clattering in. They placed their rockets with precision, so that on the third pass they had scorched the whole of the thin finger of jungle where Kolias had found trouble. After two strafing runs with machine guns Mac called it off.

To Kindred, Mac said: "That WIA has got to go to Charlie Med."

"I'll call a medevac bird," Kindred offered.

"No. He can't wait. Let's use one of these."

"They won't do it. They're here to—"

"Do it."

"They won't, Mac. It's a waste of assets."

"Do it."

"Mac. They work together. They've got orders. They do not operate alone."

"Ask them."

So Kindred asked and was refused.

Mac held out his hand and Kindred surrendered the handset.

"What's his call sign?" Mac asked. On being told Mac said to the senior pilot: "Wrestler, this is Striker Six Actual. Do you see that squad of men on the south side of the little river? The men in their skivvies."

"I hold'm visually, Six," the pilot said.

"O.K. I want one of you to pick up a wounded man and choo-choo to Charlie Med."

"No can do, Six. This is a gunship and we work in pairs."

"I understand. Then one of you drops down for this marine, the other covers him, and off you go to Charlie Med, and come back as soon as you can."

"Negative. That's not our SOP. Our standard operating procedure is we don't waste assets. Call a medevac bird from Ky Ha."

"You don't waste assets," said Mac, "no, of course not." He spoke so quietly that some of the men standing by didn't catch it all, although they strained to hear.

One of these was Gunnery Sergeant Hitchcock, who stared at the bright sand, squinting against the glare, half-smiling, a combination that gave his pale features a look of pained irritation.

Mac continued: "This marine is an asset too, and he could die if you don't take him."

"You'll be naked," said the pilot.

And Gunny Hitchcock, still with his enigmatic smile, being able to hear only one side of the conversation, looked at Mac as if he knew what the pilot had said.

"You get to Charlie Med and back in an hour, I can handle it, we'll still be here," Mac said.

"I'd have to refuel."

For the first time Mac's voice betrayed a doubt. He lost the "command voice" Hitchcock envied, and Hitchcock heard the change.

"Listen," Mac pleaded, "for Christ's sake, save this man."

For a minute or perhaps two the only sound, as Mac, Kindred, the exec, and the gunny stood in a circle, was the engine drone of the circling choppers and the peculiar churning of the air aloft. Mac said quietly to the exec:

"Put some sixties into that woods."

The exec got the mortarmen firing on the ridge of jungle where the enemy had harassed 1st Platoon. The tubes were ready to go, and the first three *chunk* sounds had coughed out their news when the pilot said:

"O.K., Six, coming down," and Mac turned to the group and said, "He's coming down."

One bird started corkscrewing while the other widened his circle and lifted.

The mortar projectiles boomed in the jungle three hundred meters away, and Mac said to the exec:

"No more than ten rounds."

The bird raised a storm of sand and dartlike twigs as it lowered itself across the river. Four men carried the wounded marine but the chopper was so positioned that Mac couldn't see whether the chaplain and corpsman had jumped in. The bird fired up its engine and lifted.

When it was airborne a man came to the river edge and shouted, but no one could hear. He waited till the bird was higher and shouted again. He said they had found a boat.

"With respect—sir—" Gunnery Sergeant Hitchcock said as an opening, and Mac responded:

"Yes, Gunny, what?"

"Sir, if you think maybe the NVA has got a, maybe, a fuckin *regiment* around here—"

Mac and the gunny stood watching the paddles flash in the sun as the boat neared the bank with its second and last load of men. Paul Adrano and Henry Bartholomew were conspicuous among the passengers for being clothed in green and helmeted.

"Why did I send the gunships away?" Mac completed the gunny's challenge.

"Yes sir. We're outside the artillery fan, and no air, naked as a striped zebray. And we been probed by at least a squad of VC and we suspect Main Force and fuckin NVA in the bushes, you know?"

The men of Delta who had searched the beaten zone on the little ridge had found blood and drag marks but no bodies, weapons, clothing, or equipment. From this Mac and the gunny surmised that the probing force was thoroughly trained and disciplined.

The boat drew near and men jumped out to pull it up the bank.

Said Mac: "Wreck this thing, Guns."

"Aye aye sir. How bout a thermite grenade fore and aft."

"Fine."

"With respect sir, some of the troops didn't appreciate it when those gunships cleared out."

"I didn't much appreciate it myself."

"Yeah but it was your decision to make."

"Sure it was. So what?"

"You had a decision but the men feel kinda helpless."

"We'll be helpless when we quit helping ourselves."

"You know what I mean, sir. We're naked as a jaybird out here."

Mac said: "Captain Kindred is trying to find us a couple of Phantoms."

"Useless goddamn howling blunderbuss Phantoms," opined the gunny.

"They are not so very useless. How would you like it if the NVA had a couple hundred Phantoms skipping around down here? Listen, Gunny, I could do one thing or the other. You see what I did."

"Yes sir, I see what you did. That's my problem."

"No. Your problem is to support my decision."

"Aye aye sir." And the gunny shouted: "Clear out! Pull that thing up and clear out, you fuckin fairies."

He brandished a thermite grenade and yanked the pin and the men hollered in protest, cursed him, and scattered. The chaplain ran with them from pure herd instinct.

Paul saw the grenade fly and heard it thump in the bottom of the boat. And though Paul didn't know what it was, he had covered thirty meters before the second one landed.

Mac moved the command group down the trail to avoid the smoke pouring up from the boat. He and the exec bent over the map while Mac dictated orders, which the exec wrote in his little green "wheel book," one of those pocket-size government books that said "Memoranda" on the cover, which were needed only by people who considered themselves big wheels. Actually many little wheels needed the books too but the troops enjoyed ridiculing the very idea that somebody should write down what he already knew.

He had to search in one direction or another so he chose downstream, along the trail that paralleled the little river.

While Mac dictated orders that would move Delta downstream the gunny let his round brown eyes roam over the scene of last night's firefight. He saw that he had placed his gun quite well. He looked at his swimming hole, and the three remaining bodies across the river that were swelling in the sun. He saw the hooches of the little vill 150 meters beyond. No people. A few goats. He studied all this and could not discover what was odd, but something was.

He turned his attention to the near side of the river, and realized he must be standing in or near the tracks that would have been left on the earth before the monsoon by any vehicle crossing the summerpool bridge. But he saw no ruts. Then it occurred to Gunnery Sergeant Hitchcock, although he was no farmer, that he was standing in grass. True, it was anemic and marked by patches of open sand, but it was grass—and then he noted there was no grass anywhere else. The sand supported clumps of some weed or other, unfamiliar to Western eyes, and brush at the river's edge, but clear to the edges of the jungle, no grass anywhere but here.

The gunny began to walk slowly, dragging his feet, in a straight line, toward a place where the grass gave way to open sand.

"Skipper," the gunny called a minute later.

"Yes, Guns," and Mac looked up from the map.

The exec stopped writing. Captain Kindred, the chaplain, and Ollie the FO looked at the gunny.

He said, from ten meters off: "Can I have my team back?"

"Your team from last night? The Greek and the sailor, Hippo and the gun crew, is that who you want?" Mac asked. He seemed interested.

"Yes sir. Same clowns."

"Why?"

Hitchcock approached, then turned a quarter-turn and pointed with his rifle, as if making a slow jab with a bayonet. And he started explaining while still looking the other way.

"We can't hear you," said the exec.

The gunny faced the group and came closer, looking over his shoulder from time to time at the tree line where he had concealed his gun last night. He explained:

"This ground is so smooth"—dragging his feet the last few paces before stopping in front of Mac—"and that ground"—where the company was headed, downstream—"is kinda rough, and no grass."

His listeners took this in.

"Why couldn't the gooks cross the George Washington Bridge and instead of going on in the same direction downstream—why couldn't they curve back upstream toward my little home in the forest—"

Hitchcock again pointed to the finger of jungle where he had set his gun last night, and Mac saw what he meant: that the area between the river and the tip of the finger of jungle was covered with grass. Elsewhere grass was scarce or absent. This finger of jungle was the upstream boundary of the sand bay that invaded the jungle. The downstream boundary was the jungle where Kim Kolias's platoon had run into the enemy.

The gunny resumed: "And the cache, if there is a cache, could be—" He held out his rifle with a studied, slow determination, pointing toward the tree line that marked the upstream boundary of the little sandy embayment.

"So this is smooth," Mac repeated tentatively.

"Yeah sir. Maybe they drove off the bridge, curved back upstream, and dumped their junk up there somewheres, upstream."

"And they bulldozed their tracks," Mac ventured.

"They planted this rice, which ain't growin worth shit," Dan Shaw supplied.

"Rice!" cried Gunny Hitchcock.

"Yessiree," said Dan Shaw. "Was never meant to grow in this soil."

Dan Shaw squatted, rifle across his knees, examined the ground, and said, looking up at Mac: "I ain't never seen a John Deere in this miserable country but if you look at this ground, Skipper, and allow for the rain and all, it kinda looks like—you know—somebody dragged a—I'd say this here ground has been harrowed."

"We're hot!" Mac shouted. The jubilation was too much and he boomed out: "We are hot!"

He called his runner, Pickens Freeman, and said, "Find Lieutenant Kolias over in that woods and tell him I want a thorough search of that ridge. Tell him he's got an hour."

"You mean—" Freeman hesitated.

"The ridge he just left. The one the gunships hit."

"O.K. Aye aye sir."

"Come right back."

"Yes sir."

And Pickens Freeman hustled off.

Said Mac: "Dan, listen up. Reference my last, cancel my last. We're not going downstream. Take your platoon and search this ridge." Mac indicated the next one, the one where the gunny had spent the night. "One hour."

"Aye aye sir," said Dan Shaw.

"Sergeant Graves, come here a minute."

Graves—a muscular man with fat red hands, a black mustache, whiskers, and glittering black eyes—approached and Mac showed him a third ridge on the map, that lay upstream, west of the one assigned to Dan Shaw.

Graves Registration nodded solemnly and bellowed for his platoon.

"Gunny, grab your gang from Third before they take off. Take the next ridge west."

Thus Mac set in motion a search of four ridges that descended from the hill mass to the level of the river.

Paul Adrano and Henry Bartholomew stood off to the side while 2nd Platoon was assembling.

Bartholomew said: "So Chaplain, are you still with us?"

"Certainly. What do you mean?"

"Are you sticking with Second Platoon? Come on, die with us."

"I don't expect to die today," Paul said looking at the corpsman for signs of fear.

"You must be an optimist. Me, I expect to die every day."

"Then you've been wrong every day." Paul placed his hand on Henry's shoulder saying, "Not today. No, I don't feel it coming, for me or you." The covered plate of the flak jacket intervened between Paul's hand and Henry's shoulder.

"Oh you don't? Jeez, didn't you see the gunships fly away home?"

"I saw them," Paul acknowledged, then asked: "How long will they be gone?"

"Long enough," said Henry with a kind of satisfaction. "Twenty or more minutes to Charlie Med, drop off the WIA, go to Ky Ha to refuel, and while they're at it they'll replenish ammo, fly back here—could be two hours. Time for Mr. Gook to surround us with a thousand martyrs doped to the eyeballs."

"Two hours," Paul repeated. His voice had neither tone nor inflection. And he watched the corpsman, whose skin shone with a metallic sheen of sweat, whose eyes were taut with the image of flying choppers.

"Isn't it beautiful, though? I mean, Chaplain, I know you're not a Jesuit but you've swum deep in theology, logic, Latin, Church history, and all. Am I right?"

"You know what I've studied because you studied it too."

"So isn't it hilarious?"

"What?"

"This day I'll be with you in Paradise to explain," Henry said lightly. "But are you sticking with Second Platoon?"

"I'll go with the command group and then later wherever I'm needed."

"Hey, Chappie, the command group is no safer than Second Platoon. And wow! Go where you're needed! That's a pretty dangerous program. Since you've got a choice, I suggest you go where you're not needed. But the whole thing is equally funny—throughout Delta—equally chucklesome."

"What is funny?" asked Paul patiently.

"Beautiful too."

"What is beautiful—Henry?"

"*Henry?* Careful there, Chaplain."

"What is hilarious?" Paul asked and sought the answer in Henry's eyes. Is fear hilarious or beautiful?

"Well didn't you notice?" Henry Bartholomew asked. "The skipper put a hundred and thirty men in jeopardy to save one."

"Yes," said Paul, who felt he was speaking now as a priest.

"Chaplain, would you mind taking your hand away?"

Paul did so—again, as a priest.

Henry continued: "He could have let the guy die and we keep the gunships. The guy would go quickly and nobody'd notice until somebody said, 'Hey, that guy is lying over there in his skivvies with his eyes full of flies.' It could happen like that."

"Yes, and what is hilarious or beautiful, Henry?"

"Open your eyes," Henry fired back. "Everybody said in the seminary that if Jesus returned, nobody would recognize him. O.K., you came here looking for God and here He is, see, here's the Old Man Himself and you can't see Him. You're blind.

"Anyway Chaplain, I'm off with Second Platoon and I hope I won't encounter any more proofs of divine love. Don't get me wrong. This is life as we know it and I personally wouldn't have it any other way."

Joining the command group, Paul Adrano began to see how the terrain was shaped. As they humped in the sun, Paul observed that the ridges of jungle descended like fingers to the flat sandy ground.

If you spread the fingers of your right hand and placed them on a sheet of paper, then traced the outline with a pencil, you would have a simplified map of the search area. Even simpler, the hand itself could serve as a map. Extend the right hand, palm toward you, spread the fingers, and you had a map.

The fingers or ridges pointed south toward the little river in lines that were more or less parallel. The spaces between the fingers were the flat sandy embayments, open at the river end and enclosed by jungle at the north end, nearest the hill mass.

The open spaces or bays were perhaps a hundred meters wide and two hundred long, and the ridges were of the same dimensions. The four ridges enclosed three bays. So Mac's search area consisted of ridges being combed by 1st, 2nd, and 3rd Platoons and by the gunny's gang of cutthroats.

Mac established his CP at the closed, north end of the middle bay, at the very edge of the screen of vegetation, in the very center of the search area. Here the command group set up its antennas.

Paul noticed there was no platoon or even a squad providing security. But he reflected that the CP was between 1st and 2nd Platoon, and he guessed that was good enough.

Paul had drunk river water purified with pills, while it was still cool, and he felt physically strong and was not afraid. He lay on his back in the shade and closed his eyes. He heard Graeser say:

"Battalion's on the line, Skipper."

"Goddamn," said Mac, then in a radio voice: "This is Striker Six Actual." A pause, then: "Negative." Then: "I could not be sure but that was my judgment." Then: "I'm glad to hear it." Then: "Negative."

There was a longer pause and then Paul Adrano heard Kindred asking: "Was he pissed?"

Mac: "He was pissed. He must think I'm a doctor. Was I sure the man couldn't wait an hour? *No.* Did I realize the risk I was running? *Yes.* Would I be so kind as to report to Battalion when we get back? *With pleasure.*"

"There goes your fitness report," said Kindred idly.

"Kinny, you are looking at a civilian temporarily caught in the Crotch."

A few minutes later Paul was awakened by flies, or the sound of Kindred on his radio:

"I'll take whatever you can give me. We were in contact with Victor Charlie half an hour ago and we're expecting another party." Then, like Mac, Kindred listened, and finally said: "I'll take a flyswatter if you can spare one." And in a different voice, as he evidently turned to Mac: "They'll see what they can do but they aren't making any promises. He said, 'I gave you some pretty good assets and you misused'm.'"

"Yeah," said Mac. "Tell him his ass sucks canal water."

"I think I'll wait till he gives us a couple Phantoms before I insult him," Captain Kindred replied.

"Yeah, mister," Mac fantasized, "four Phantoms—rockets, bombs, napalm!"

"Whoopee!" cried a voice Paul could not identify.

Paul sat up and looked around. The sun poured its rays vertically on the men of the command group in a spirit of vengeance. Paul was soaked, losing already the water he had just drunk. Mac stood with his hands on his pistol, on one side, and canteen on the other, elbows out, helmet cocked back, squinting against the glare. He lifted his face a little in greeting and said:

"I saw you filling your canteens at the river. You did put in the pills, didn't you? If not, your guts are Mount Vesuvius."

"Oh yes, absolutely," Paul said, thinking: "I'm not that green."

Paul was sitting, legs stretched in a V, leaning back on his elbows. Mac squatted beside him and said:

"Thanks for helping over there," indicating the other side of the river.

"It was nothing. The water was fine."

"There was nobody anchoring the lifeline," said Mac. "I don't understand how you got across."

"But there was," Paul told him. "We yelled and two men ran to the rope and held it taut and we crossed."

"I never heard that yell," Mac declared as if to himself.

"We made a heck of a noise but I'm not surprised you didn't hear."

"I can tell you, he was alive when they got him to Charlie Med."

"Then he'll be alive now," said Paul with assurance.

"Yes I think he will. Graeser"—over his shoulder—"check the gunny."

But Paul could see in Mac's face a flood of happiness.

Graeser clicked his key and drooped his mouth, staring, then said, "Sir, he said 'Alfa Sierra.' "

"O.K." said Mac, rising and looking around. "O.K.—O.K.—O.K." He checked his watch and looked inquiringly at the sky. He said to the exec: "It'll be a bastard, with the roots in this ground, but let's dig in."

The gunny's brain was buzzing.

"Yeah yeah I *know* what they call it, 'loyalty up,' that's when he decides and I execute. Without me nothing happens, which maybe at a time like this is just what ought to happen."

Gunnery Sergeant Hitchcock tramped in the middle of his little column of select bozos. Pretty soon he'd halt and shift to a skirmish line but in this leech- and snake-infested tropical paradise he'd keep'm in column till he came to—

"Yeah—'Hey Guns, it ain't so bad, naked as a jaybird, so? Hey! Marines are made to die.' Ain't that the meaning of Semper Fi?"

With this noise in his head the gunny stared at the bobbing pack in front, and at the ground. Watch the ground! Step quiet!

"So this is the idea, like this: O.K., you fuckin civilians, my policy is, hear that? *My* policy—well fuck-shit-piss-my-balls, suck the monster, we, I mean *we*—see what I'm trying to say? We gotta sorta more-or-less fuckin—*do it.*"

He stopped the column and crept forward and whispered to the Golden Greek: "Hey Valas. We go to a skirmish line now. You on the right, me on the left. First I want a look at that open ground on the left, that bay or whatever, then we turn and sweep over the ridge. We sweep across the ridge, got it?"

"Sure, Guns, what's mysterious about that?"

"O.K. you fuckers," he whispered and waved them forward. "O.K. you creeps, we snoop and poop. You fire your weapon and I don't see a dead gook, I cut yer balls off. Got it?"

They indicated in solemn silence that they got it.

"So you gotta scratch yer balls? Do it now. From here on I don't want to hear a hummingbird's fart. We scope out the bay. Stay hidden. Then we climb the ridge. We are strictly recon, everybody understand?"

They were formed just inside the cover of their assigned ridge, in a line abreast and ready to climb.

"So"—running in Hitchcock's mind—"all those orders in the exec's wheel book, pffft! Reference my last, cancel my last. He turns the whole thing around because *one guy sees one detail,* thanks to me if I do say so myself, and his jelly-pulp shakes and belches, out comes an idea, and the whole company does a one-eighty.

"I'll hand it to you, Skipper, you're not afraid to change your mind. Some officers only change their mind if a general says so. This guy's different. I think—

"Yeah, there's one problem. That's when he flinches. He's a good battle leader on the outside; inside he's got a little soft place. I hate to say it, and if a snuffie said it I'd ream his ass, but yeah, it's true."

The sailor beckoned and the gunny crept to him, placing every step with utmost care.

"What?" Gunnery Sergeant Hitchcock demanded irritably.

"I saw a flash."

"What kind of flash?"

The two were whispering, bent close.

Said Collins: "The sun flashed on metal or glass. See that hill?"

They peered through the vegetation and out across the bay to a steep hill some thousand meters away, across the river. It was covered by bright-green jungle.

For several minutes they watched. The other men stood patiently. Valas could see only one man to his left. The gunny and sailor had a longer view on either side. The flash did not repeat itself.

Hitchcock, in a painstaking series of slow silent strides, made his way to his radioman and whispered a message: "We saw a sun flash." He gave the coordinates, resumed his place, glancing once through the lacework at the open sky, gave a hand signal, and inched the line forward.

But—looking between leafy branches into the bay—he stopped his troops immediately and, repeating the same laborious and patient stride, went again to the radioman. The gunny thought: "Thank you eyes, thank you brain, but be quicker next time." First the flash and now this. Holy mackerel! He would never admit it but his heart was racing. He peered again into the bay to be sure he'd seen what he'd seen, then took the handset extended to him by Hippo.

Hitchcock whispered into the mike: "Grass. Got that? Fuckin *grass* in the bay. Tell the Skipper grass, grass, grass-grass!"

He tapped Hippo on the shoulder and saw the man's hand appear to receive the handset. The gunny had started the handset on its journey of a few inches toward the black man's open hand when he saw something that was out of place.

It was a horizontal line, maybe ten feet long, and it was three paces from his eyes in the tall grass and bamboo. "Holy fuckin banana shit!" His view was obscured, but piecing it together he could make out the line and something dark.

He keyed the handset. "Bunker," he breathed. "I'm lookin at a bunker. If it's manned—"

He placed his hand on Hippo's helmet and pushed steadily down, and the radioman and gunnery sergeant went slowly to earth. Seeing this, the men on either side did the same, expressionlessly.

"If it's manned," the gunny whispered into the handset, "I'm Christopher Columbus. Made a great discovery and I'm dead."

Chapter 10

Dragon's Head

At the new CP the fighting holes were only half dug. The exposed roots displayed hacks and scars showing how tenaciously they had resisted every inch of depth achieved by the marines wielding entrenching tools.

The wind was calm. Many insects who might otherwise have set up a buzz were sleeping, as if the sun had overpowered even them. Yet the soft air conveyed a low seething of the kind that charms the ear of one who sits far from any known sound source, and listens.

The perimeter brushed the edge of the clearing, and here the fighting holes offered a clear view and field of fire into the open sandy area, the middle bay. From these holes, half-concealed in vegetation, the defenders of the Delta command function could have seen all along both tree lines, all the way to the brim of the little river.

This place was far from ideal as a night defensive position but in choosing it for his command post Mac had never intended to stay. As a temporary stopping place to be occupied while Delta searched the ridges, it had several advantages and only one disadvantage. This was the difficulty of digging in, because of the roots. Knowing the price the men would pay in energy and sweat, Mac had been reluctant to give the order to dig in; and therefore doubly reluctant to order them

to move out when he received the gunny's report of a concealed bunker. Mac felt compelled to see this thing with his own eyes and to place it in a tactical context. So he set out with his command group.

Now in each hole the roots stretched inward like tortured arms; and some of the marines as they marched away looked at these costly holes as if at a lost home.

While marching, Mac transmitted two orders to Gunnery Sergeant Hitchcock: establish a defensive position around the bunker—not in it—and send a three-man team outward along the edge of the ridge.

Hitchcock asked: "Looking for what?"

"I don't know," said Mac. "Let's just see what they see."

And so the sailor and two others began feeling their way along the base of the ridge, going toward the river, with the open bay on their left and the ridge rising on the right. Meanwhile Mac and the command group bashed their way through tangled brush and thickset trees, and in fifteen minutes reached the bunker, where Mac congratulated Hitchcock.

"Yeah. Sir. See how it's angled?"

The structure sat at a forty-five-degree angle to the open bay, facing half south.

Mac pondered this. He squatted and discovered that the brush grew up in multistemmed shafts, most of them growing out of little square-cut stumps very near ground level. The place had been cleared, probably last summer.

"They had a clear field of fire here," Mac concluded.

"And two men swinging machetes could clear it again in ten minutes," Hitchcock declared.

The bunker could then lay fire in and across the bay.

A man came crashing through the bamboo and brush. Gunny Hitchcock shouted: "Hold your fire!" and the marines crouching along the defense line unshouldered their weapons, and saw their buddy Gonzalez, a member of the sailor's patrol.

"Gonny!—Captain!" Gonzalez cried as he emerged cut, bleeding, sweating from his race through the vegetation. "We find another. Just like thees. Earth an logs. Nobody home."

"Facing the same way?" Mac asked.

"At the same angle?" the gunny pressed him.

"Yeah, Guns. Yes sir."

"Christ," said Mac and his eyes seemed to be waiting for more.

"What if they've got the same stuff across the clearing?" said the gunny, marveling.

Mac turned to the exec and told him to order Sergeant Graves of 3rd Platoon to concentrate its search on the tree line where his ridge met the open bay. Thus the gunny's men were searching one side of the bay while 3rd Platoon searched the other.

The newly discovered bunker, Gonzalez reported, was built a hundred meters farther along the tree line on this side of the bay. If 3rd Platoon were to find a similar arrangement of defenses on the other side, it would signify that the builders had something important to defend, and that the something, whatever it was, was nearby.

"Gunny," said Mac after due deliberation, "let's send the sailor all the way." Turning to the runner, Mac said: "Can you make it back?"

"Sure, Skipper."

Gonzalez turned to sprint away and Mac said, "Wait a second—please." To the gunny: "What do you think?"

"I think, Christ if they've built a string of these things we are in the belly of the beast."

"Roger that," said Mac.

On receiving an affirmative nod from Mac, Gunnery Sergeant Hitchcock said to the runner:

"O.K. Gonzalez, tell the sailor, 'Go to the end of the ridge, no farther.' Hear me?"

"Yes, Guns."

"And stay concealed. That's an absolute."

"*Sí*, Guns."

"And what are you looking for?" the gunny prompted.

"Signs of foot or vehicular trahffic."

"Yeah. *Y que massomucho?*"

"Bunkers, trenches, holes."

"Good. *Hasta la shove off.*"

Gonzalez spun around and ducked and bobbed into the thicket.

Mac spread the fingers of his right hand and held it out with the palm toward him, and studied it—and then he opened his map, which was folded in clear plastic. He had placed a red dot on the hilltop where the gunny had reported the flash. The place where Mac, the gunny, and the command group were now located was not visible from the dot, owing to the intervening rise of the ridge opposite—the one being searched by Sergeant Graves and 3rd Platoon.

But the newly reported bunker, had the vegetation been stripped away, would be in plain sight of an observer on the hill.

"Jesus," Gunnery Sergeant Hitchcock moaned. "If Graves finds one of these across the bay—holy shit!"

"Right," said Mac. "Interlocking fields of fire. All of it laid out to stop anybody coming this way from the river. Ollie"—and Mac turned and looked for the artilleryman.

"Yes sir," said Ollie coming forward.

"If I asked you to take the roof off this bunker, could you do it?"

"Sure, Skipper."

"Fine. How many like this could you blow?"

It was an earth-and-log bunker sunk about two feet into the ground, with a low wall two feet high, surmounted by a shaggy roof. The firing port was at eye height for a machine gunner sitting inside. Thus the thing was designed for grazing fire—fire skimming the earth at knee height.

"Well," Ollie said, "blow the roof, I could do ten of these maybe."

"Rig this one to blow," said Mac. "Use as little as possible."

Ollie and his radioman stacked their gear and set to work in the bunker with pliers, C4 blocks, wire, and detonators.

Mac again held out his hand as a map. The bunker was located at a point corresponding to the first knuckle of the index finger. The bay was the open space between the index and middle fingers. Now 3rd Platoon was searching the edge of the middle finger bordering the open space, and the sailor was searching the tip of the index finger.

If the enemy had built bunkers on both fingers, he intended to defend the area above the apex of the bay, an area in the hand proper, with interlocking fields of fire. That these defenses were unmanned suggested that nothing remained to be defended, or that defenders would move into prepared positions if their caches were threatened.

On the hill where the sailor had seen the flash stood a young man who was far from home—six hundred miles and more, and half of it trav-

212

eled under a rain of terror from the American B52's. He had learned the difference between fear and terror. To him at least, if not to his comrades, fear was the persisting condition of life during those weeks trudging south. The object of fear, unexpectedly, was not death but terror. He could not conceive of death; he was too young. The corpses he saw along the trail, and the graves, told him that others died. He knew he could die too, but it was not a knowledge he could feel. But when the terror struck him it throttled his body and unloosed his mind. He believed in an abstract way that death would be no worse than this. The object of his fear was not the death he had never experienced but the terror that he had.

You could not see, and usually could not even hear, the bombers. But they could hear you. The Americans had sown the land through which the trail passed with listening devices and it was said that the officers listening, in Saigon or wherever they might be, could hear the screams of the dying. Of course that was only a side show. What they wanted to hear was the engine noise from the Chinese and Russian trucks. This told them which segments were in heaviest use.

But to the man on the hill, who had carelessly let his glasses pass through a bar of sunshine, their listening to the screams removed them from the human race and placed them in a category he could not name.

Amid his memories of the march from Hanoi, two were conspicuous. The first was of a night when a driver had given up his truck cab. The man who was now the observer on the hill had slept in the cab from just after dark till dawn. The cab sheltered him from the rain, and the rain kept the B52's at home, on Guam, he believed. This was not his only night of peace; there were others. But this was the one that seemed blessed by a spirit of mercy in the universe, because of the way the rain smothered the cab, and imparted the feeling that he was, for those hours, in a place set aside from strife.

The other clear memory was in the form of a picture. As he walked in the mud, pausing to allow trucks and carts to pass, he saw an unexploded 500-pound bomb. At least so he was told by a man who knew. The tracks parted, carving grooves on either side of the glistening gray steel. Then they rejoined on the other side. There was a certain grace in the way the tracks diverged and reunited. The bomb itself was without grace, even though its lines were simple and softly curved, and its skin shone under the rain. Often when the observer looked at the photograph of his sweetheart he couldn't concentrate on her face, because the other picture intruded. The bomb had bounced, it hadn't dug itself in, and the base lay lower than the nose, so passersby could admire the ogive and the blunt nose.

Walking close to it, the observer passed through an aura of death. It would be a death that enveloped its victims in a blinding, annihilating burst of immeasurable energy. Then he passed out of the zone and knew he was alive, one of the living who has seen death and would never forget. He told himself that such a death would be almost painless and perhaps devoid of fear. There would be no terror. But the bomb tortured him.

Its image robbed him of a proper sense of what life should be. He could imagine the end of the war, but as he slogged south he grew ever more doubtful that he would see it.

When he arrived in the South and was ordered to his present duty, he discovered that he was able to hope again. Even if he didn't survive, he hoped to find intervals of quiet in which to sit in solitude and meditate on his life and its feeling. How did it feel to be alive and to be who he was? The trail stood between him and his past life. The bomb stood between him and his future. He could not visualize his sweetheart's face, and could not believe in survival. But he did hope. Here at his observation post he was at least alone, and he attempted to put his solitude to good use by trying to recapture his true self.

The shooting down by the river last night had awakened him and he couldn't go back to sleep. In the morning, dizzy from fatigue and tormented by the rash on his skin, a flaming scall that sent cracks across the insides of his elbows and knees, that exuded serum and blood— beset by this affliction and sick of rifle fire and explosions, sick of the machinelike repetition of everything that destroyed his peace—in the morning after the firefight at the river he went to his mortars.

He talked to the crew chief and derived some comfort from merely talking with this simple man, even though all their talk was about how to kill the Americans with more explosions. Then, having eaten rice and fish heads with the men in the village, he climbed his hill, his little principality, carrying his own radio and binoculars. For a while he rested in the shade, listening; he heard some gunfire and didn't know who was shooting. Some people just did whatever came into their heads. But the observer was not one of these. The guerrillas were almost free. Shoot at random and run at will. But the observer was no guerrilla. He was an officer in the NVA, assigned to the unit commanded by a maniac major who took as his primary mission the breaking of his men's will. For the major, winning the war came second.

This major would demand a report loaded with detail and free of mere opinion. So the observer had to put aside the quest for his own humanity, a trifle, and do his job. He knew the Americans were down there, and he raised his binoculars to have a look.

And there they were, the big fools, standing around in a cluster of antennas. He had only to speak ten words on his radio and they would all die in his first salvo. He watched; he couldn't see it all but he knew they were searching the ridges, and thought they would probably find the access road from the south, even though it was nearly grown over. He believed they had already found the bridge. Why else would so many of them be so close to the access road? He had plenty of time. He watched out of pure curiosity. Who were these big rich people who came twelve thousand miles to jam their fingers into the gears of destiny? He focused his glasses on the obvious leader, the one the others kept approaching as if for decisions and orders. When this personage removed his helmet he revealed a head of bronze hair, almost red. And his face was red too.

Then the observer saw that they'd found the boat. A load of soldiers in green shorts crossed the river, then another, and the observer decided to act. He consulted his map, plotted his fire mission from one of his battery's registration points, and was about to transmit when a puff and then a billow of smoke rose up and sent them scattering. That put an end to his nice concentrated target. He felt the guilt of a man who has wasted an opportunity. He watched and waited.

Pretty soon the group re-formed around the red top man, but much looser, not so good a target, and marched up the sandy lane between two arms of jungle. They went into the trees but only a few paces. He could still see one tall antenna in there; then it disappeared. Undoubtedly the radioman had rigged his short antenna. The observer decided to study the pattern of their search, for his report.

He dreaded the major more than he hated the Americans. But he called his battery and gave the chief the coordinates, telling him to stand by for the order to fire. He said to the chief: "We will cut off this dragon's head."

Turning to the exec, Mac said: "If Sergeant Graves finds—"

He did not finish. He went silent when the air pulsed with three thumps, overlain by three others. They were soft on the ears but loud in the brain. Every man knew their message. Since sound travels straight while mortar projectiles describe an arc, there was still time to take cover.

There was no cover to be found. Some of the men thought, with a twinge of regret, of the half-dug holes at the CP they had abandoned when the gunny reported the bunker. They flattened themselves and went through the supernatural experience known as burrowing into the earth, which has never saved anybody.

Next they heard the bursting charges and knew the tubes were aimed elsewhere; then, mixing with the bursting charges, six more propelling charges, then a cacophony, consisting of more of both. To one man it was not a cacophony but a legible record.

Lieutenant Oliver—Ollie, the forward observer—dropped his wire cutters and raised his Rolex. Being inside the bunker he could not stand upright. He bent over the watch, placing his index finger on the start button. He closed his eyes, listening with care. At a certain moment he started the stopwatch. A few seconds later he hit stop. He had time to do this twice before the eighteen rounds had been fired and silence ensued.

But the silence was short. From one of the other ridges came a sudden wave of small-arms fire and the periodic thump of grenades. Auditing this noise, Mac surmised that the enemy was armed with old M1's and a few AK-47's on automatic, but no machine guns.

"Sir, Second says it's First Platoon that's in contact."

Mac took the handset and spoke with Lieutenant Dan Shaw of 2nd Platoon. Shaw told him there was no action on his ridge but 1st was in a fight. And Dan Shaw said: "Those mortars creamed your old CP. The angels were with you when you skeedaddled out of that dump."

Mac saw that Ollie was bursting with an idea. He nodded that he was listening and Ollie proposed:

"Skipper, lemme do a crater analysis. I could be there and back in twenty minutes. I already got the time of flight."

Mac looked at Ollie, trying to see if he understood the hazard; he looked for ten seconds; Ollie grinned and crossed his eyes.

Mac said: "Take two men. Snoop and poop, got it?"

"Yes sir. Quiet as mice."

"Go."

Mac raised Kim Kolias, who said he was being harassed by a squad-size unit of VC.

"Easy on the ammo," said Mac. "How's the chaplain?"

"Fine, sir. Want to talk to him?"

"No. Consolidate. Pull back. Stay in the woods."

He called for Kindred and said: "Hey Kinny, get us some air. Tell him his ass does not suck canal water."

While Kindred got on his radio Mac, the exec, and the gunnery sergeant sat in a close triangle near the enemy bunker and deliberated.

Mac declared as a fact: "Mr. Big knows we're working our way, ridge by ridge, to the gold mine."

"Yeah sir. Right."

"The attack on First is to pull us away."

"Yeah."

"He wants us to ride to the rescue," Mac speculated, "in the wrong direction."

"The big guy is coming," said the exec as if it were proven.

"Maybe," said Mac. "I wish we had some air."

The exec: "Don't worry, Skipper, we'll get some."

"Yeah, Skipper," the gunny added, "we support your decision, we make the best of it, we don't bitch about it."

The small-arms fusillade intensified.

"Those gooks are gonna run out of ammo in five minutes. They are fuckin desperate. It's a fuckin demonstration," the gunny asserted.

"So—I agree, that's a demonstration, and the Big Guy is coming. He may be right over the ridge," said Mac. "We have to assume he's on his way."

"Good! We'll kill'm from their own bunkers," the gunny exulted.

Mac demurred. "Not unless he gives us a wet dream by marching in formation up the bay. The bunkers are oriented all wrong if he comes over the ridge."

There was a silence and Mac's mind presented him with a nervous blank. But a second later he saw the immediate need. He said: "We'll pull in a platoon."

The exec poured out his advice: "Second Platoon. Leave First where it is, in reserve, pull Second up here through the woods."

"That leaves First isolated," Mac objected.

"Sir, it's Sergeant Graves," said Graeser, Mac's radioman, holding out the handset, and Graves said to Mac:

"We got a bunker—halfway down the tree line."

"O.K. Search to the tip. Occupy the bunker but watch your rear."

"Fuck!" said the gunny when Mac had told him what Graves had found. "Wouldn't I like to see that gook battalion marching up the bay. Interlocking fields of fire, you fuckin monkeys."

"No," said Mac reasoning as he spoke, "they'll come from—from Five B or Ambush Alley, or downriver."

As Mac pondered, Jake the exec declared confidently: "Five B, sir."

"Why?"

"If he was up Ambush Alley he would have hit us this morning. The river—too complicated, boats and fords and all that. But Five B— that's his route from the Ho Chi Minh Trail. He's an NVA battalion or regimental commander and he's based near the Trail, miles from us. That's why he's not all over us right now."

"Go on."

"So he'll come over this ridge," Jake concluded, his eyes glowing with moisture, with a nod toward the woods behind the bunker. "He'll try to occupy these bunkers."

A few minutes later, as Mac awaited word from the sailor, Graeser passed him the handset. It was Ollie, the forward observer.

"The old CP is a beaten zone straight out of a textbook. Half the rounds detonated in the trees, so you could've died at the bottom of a hole ten feet deep. The others chewed up a bunch of dirt, snakes, and roots. I'm chewing on a snake right now. A little on the rare side. Yikes! Just swallowed the head. Anyway, Skipper, I can tell you where those mortars are."

And he told him. The tubes were either in the vill beyond the bridge or just outside it.

"Good job, Ollie. Get your ass back here."

"Hey, Six, I'm halfway there already."

Next Mac heard a voice in the earpiece: "Striker Six, Striker Three."

"Go, Three," said Mac.

"Got us another bunker right near the tip of the ridge," said Graves Registration.

And Mac said: "Hasty defense around the first bunker. Patrol the whole ridge. Hundred percent alert. Stay concealed."

And Staff Sergeant Reggie Graves said coolly, "Roger, out."

Returning the handset to Graeser, Mac said: "See if you can raise Battalion." And over his shoulder: "Kindred!"

"Yeah boss."

"Get us some air, man. One canister of napalm for that genius on the hill."

Minutes later Kindred cried: "Hey wow! They found us a guy with heavy wings. Needs to dump ordnance. Heading for the ocean."

"What's he got?" asked Mac.

"Napalm of course."

"Turn him back!"

"A man is much heavier than I thought," Paul mused.

He filled his lungs with air that did him no good. He stumbled on a boulder concealed by ferns. The whole team lurched. The poncho sagged and the body of the wounded man swung forward and hit Michelson behind his knee. Michelson almost buckled, then the team lost its stride and the wounded man hit the ground.

"Aaaah! My God it hurts. God God God!"

"Sorry!" Paul cried. "My fault. These damned rocks."

"Don't drop me! Where's my dad? How did this happen? Where's my dad? Dad!"

One man on each corner of this bloody poncho—a man slung in the middle crying for his father—swinging along with this bloody man—in this blood-boiling overheated sun in this pathless choking jungle—and Paul had a flash: that this could go on for days!

Paul's senses had been distorted by the fight, so it was impossible to say: Was he numb as a stone or hypersensitive as a quivering nerve?

His hearing especially was fouled up, for he seemed to hear in his brain sounds that had never reached his ears, a queer sensation, and there was also the ringing, which was starting to annoy him—at first it was entertaining; and between the phantom sounds and the real ringing he didn't know what to credit.

"Where's my dad for Christ's sake? I want my dad."

"We're with you," said Paul, and his own voice struck him as grotesque. "Four of us. Don't you see us?"

"Aiiiihhh—Jesus Christ!"

Suddenly Paul thought: "Shut up!" He didn't regret thinking it. He felt for this man absolutely nothing. What an odd fact.

It reminded him of yesterday when he and Doc Bartholomew helped Corporal Sedgwick limp along as his "Navy escort." The love Paul felt for the skinny black shambling man with the corrugated face contrasted with his present indifference to this—whining—man, who scarcely registered in his mind as a man—more as an inconvenient object. For his sake they had let themselves be separated from the platoon. For his sake they had consumed most of their water and were sinking fast into heat exhaustion. Paul was quite sure the man was in no danger of death, whereas he himself could still see his last glimpse of the platoon disappearing into the green.

The carriers staggered under their load and when they dropped the man again Paul heard more anger than pain in his howl of protest. And Paul saw the image of the column—going away.

They came to a better-lighted place and he recognized the old CP. The trees and ground had been ripped up by an agency strong enough to claw holes in the cover above and the ground below, but too weak to tear the roof off the forest.

They lay the man gently down. They flopped on the ground and opened their canteens. Paul's first was already empty and a few sips were all that remained of his second, yet going to the river was not to be considered. He drank it all.

He thought: "When will I get used to this heat?"

Lieutenant Kolias had admonished them not to lose contact with the column, then marched off too fast. Here lay five men sprawled among the half-dug fighting holes, the earthen craters and twisted roots.

Paul asked: "Who's senior?"

A man said he was a lance corporal.

"Shouldn't we move?" Paul suggested.

"Yes sir." He stood up.

Paul stood up.

A new sound. He wished his ears were working. What was this?

As if a piece of thick cardboard were being ripped, an ever-stronger tearing—which grew so loud that Paul finally recognized it—a jet aircraft. It came in low and fast and Paul looked down the open bay, toward the river, through a gap in the foliage. He saw a Phantom streaking past, so close he saw the red arrow and the word "Danger" printed on its side, and the pilot himself in profile, his head forward; and a second man behind him looking Paul's way. A horrific roar swept along with the silver plane and a flash of blue fire at its tail; then a dark object like a Tootsie Roll appeared in the sky beneath the plane, lagging behind it.

The plane swept up and away and the Tootsie Roll tumbled down the sky and plunged into the jungled hilltop.

For an instant nothing happened. The delay was long enough for Paul to cringe in anticipation of an explosion, and a close one at that—but none occurred.

The trees on the hill puffed out in a quick little wave. A black ball erupted. Red and orange fire swirled inside the ball and pressed outward, covering the black with globes of rounded flame, globes within globes of fire, globes surpassing globes of dark red fire.

At the edge of this expanding inferno the foliage withered and then caught fire and fed the balls as they rolled out and rose higher. Smoke rose over the whole mass and just then the tree skeletons began to materialize as obscure black sticks in the whirling smoke.

A wave of heat ran over the sun-cooked bay and swept through the old CP, where Paul stood stunned. He had seen exactly this on television night after night in the rectory in Fall River—but he realized he had seen nothing. Now he saw.

A noise from the right—part roar and part scream—signaled the approach of another aircraft. Paul saw the lethal-looking down-slope of the plane's tail. He concentrated on the image of the pilot—who looked to the left—and for a flash the two men might have been watching each other—till another canister came tumbling down.

The jet strained and climbed at an impossible angle. The sun flashed on its tubular body and outstretched, swept wings. A new gas wave puffed the smoke and flame still roiling from the first strike. A new fireball swirled in the midst of the old one.

"Ready, Chaplain?" Michelson inquired, and Paul said hastily: "Yes. Sorry."

He grabbed his corner and the four lifted together. He thought: "I'm out of water. Where can I get more water?"

Yes he thought of water, but it might also be truthfully said that he imagined fire and only fire. No amount of water could quench the fire that he saw; it was too alive, too red, intense, and rolling. At one moment his skin crawled with prickly heat. Next a shivering chill passed all down his spine.

Paul walked at the left rear corner, the last man to leave the ring of spiderweb holes, and by one millisecond the first to feel on his back the shock wave of an 82-millimeter mortar projectile detonating against the earth. Fragments streaked through the trees all around him and little branches and leaves floated sweetly down in shafts of sunlight turned gold by the ambient dust and pollen. The blast was mediated by the tone in his ears and the blended ringing, but it was terribly loud all the same—and Paul found himself face down in the ferns. He never saw the twigs floating.

Where was he? No knowledge. Who was he? Irrelevant question. Was he alive? Yes! A bunch of shocks followed and Paul burrowed into the earth. He did not understand anything.

The enemy gun crew in the vill had seen their observation post incinerated and took revenge on the CP of the enemy. Their data were still good—no changes in weather—and so they fired the same mission again to give the enemy what he had given their forward observer. Or so they believed.

"*Di-di-mau—di mau di!*" cried the senior marine, and the bearers rose and grabbed the corners of the poncho and staggered forward. The wounded man looked up at Paul with wild white eyes.

When he spoke with the wounded, Paul would crouch down—squat, actually; he didn't want to cause a panic by kneeling—and ask how they felt, did they hurt, were they thirsty? He had found some men who would share water—but his mind was not focused on this pastoral work, and he opened his eyes and ears, trying to figure out what was happening.

Obviously there was a mortar attack hitting somebody, each impact coming in two strokes, the second harsher than the first, a growl more than a bang—and it amazed him that Mac and the officers around him stood quite fearlessly in front of the bunker, apparently discussing what they should do about the mortars.

A dozen men had just run by the bunker, passing between its firing port and the little group of officers gathered in the newly cut grass, near the bamboo shafts cut off low. A working party had been mowing these down when Paul and the other bearers arrived with the wounded man—twenty minutes ago.

Here came a dozen more marines, running, soaked in sweat, their equipment clanging, and from Paul's low perspective they looked huge and out of control. He called: "What platoon?" and a man answered, "First." It was the very platoon Paul had lost in the jungle.

He moved among the little group of wounded, eight men, some of whom lay under IV drips secured to rifles, their bayonets driven into the earth. Paul stood up and a man gave him two full canteens and took his empties. Paul said: "What's this?"

"Resupply, sir. We got ammo and water."

Paul had not observed this miracle. It must have occurred while he was with 1st Platoon in the firefight that produced the wounded. Now he heard the pounding of mortars very close. The noise shook the leaves and it shook Paul.

He stepped boldly to the edge of the trees and looked across the bay to the ridge opposite, where 3rd Platoon was deployed—he knew that much. There was a shocking detonation near the tree line on the other side, and the woods exploded. Paul heard Captain Kindred speaking and drew nearer and listened.

"Yeah yeah, we think it's unobserved fire. We took out their OP and we think they're just firing preplanned concentrations blind." After a pause Kindred continued: "So can you shut'm up? We've got a whole platoon over there, and the fuckers are going to kill somebody before too long." New pause, and then: "I recommend you approach on a course of, say, One Eight Zero grid. The fuckers are shooting right now. We think they're within a hundred meters of the west edge of the vill. Christ!"

There was a brutal slam across the bay and Kindred said: "Take'm out, take'm out!"

Paul heard a chopper driving from north to south, low, and Kindred saying: "Great. That's a good approach. Hit'm!"

Paul could see nothing. Everyone stood in suspense—Kindred, Mac, Hitchcock, Ollie, the exec, and several troopers. The next crash did not seem to jolt any of them: they listened for the noise of salvation and it soon came, a long ripping sound, surprisingly low in pitch—long, long—then a detonation, and another. Then a new chopper sailing in the wake of the first, and four more rockets launched and landed, and the mortars of the enemy had nothing more to offer.

Paul heard the choppers climbing.

"Hey you did?" Kindred cried. "No shit, man!" Turning to Mac, Kindred said: "They saw the gooks working their guns. They never even took cover! Kept on dropping rounds till you know what!"

Paul Adrano asked Kindred: "So your helicopters hit the mortars?"

"So he says."

"The pilot?"

"Yes, the pilots say they hit with half their rockets."

"But I thought the mortars were in a village," Paul persisted.

"In it, near it, one or the other," Kindred declared looking straight at Paul.

"But which is it?"

"How would I know?"

"Ask the pilot," said Paul.

Paul now felt himself the focus of all eyes. Mac was standing near, and Paul turned to him.

Never before had this man seemed so hard. He was regarding Paul calmly, with eyes that were not malevolent—but there was a certain tinge of contempt in them, Paul believed.

Said Mac to the forward air controller: "Go ahead, Kinny, ask."

Kindred did, and reported: "He says it was at the west edge of the vill."

"What's that smoke?" Paul asked.

All eyes turned. There were two kinds of smoke rising from across the little river—a thin puff of gray-black, and a billowy pile of white.

Kindred said into his handset: "Can you give us a damage assessment?"

A few moments later the birds were over the target again, at a safe altitude. Kindred pressed the handset to his ear, listened, then said:

"They hit the target, the gun position is burning, and a couple hooches are burning."

"Thank you," said Paul in a flat voice.

"Any more questions, Chaplain?" Mac asked.

Paul met his blue cold eyes—at least a cold feeling entered Paul's mind, seeing those eyes, and that big-shouldered torso, the heat-reddened face, and straight-down nose. Paul met Mac's eyes, and held them, or was held by them, and said:

"No. I have no more questions."

Said Mac to Paul Adrano: "I have a question."

"Ask it."

"Do you know why those people set up their mortars in a village?"

"Yes, I think I do."

They still locked eyes—till Mac turned and said:

"Graeser, ask Graves Registration where the hell he is."

And Graeser, who had been watching the chaplain, said to his radio: "Striker Three, Striker Six, your position."

Paul returned to the wounded—seething—trembling. But exactly why he should *tremble* he did not know.

After Mac had deployed the company for night defense, two or three hours of daylight yet remained. He sent two squads into the woods to search for caches.

The squads came from Dan Shaw's 2nd Platoon and were led by Dan Shaw. Paul Adrano sought and received Mac's permission to accompany the search troops.

As they were stepping out they could hear a helicopter landing to evacuate the wounded, just a hundred meters behind them. When the chopper departed, all was quiet.

The searchers moved into the woods on a line abreast, slowly. On the hand map they were moving toward the palm, away from the junction of the index and middle fingers. On the printed map they were moving toward the hill mass and Ambush Alley, away from the flat sandy ground along the little river. On the earth itself they were moving northeast, and the sun was dropping behind their left shoulder.

They had not traveled as much as two hundred meters when Dan Shaw stopped the line and gave the signal to stand at ease. The men collapsed in the ferns. Paul and Michelson went to find Dan Shaw.

A trooper told Paul that Shaw was off to the right of center. Paul therefore went right, walking to the rear of the line, occasionally losing touch with it, since many of the men could not be seen in the ferns and brush. But the forest floor was sheltered from the sun and so the underbrush was not especially thick or high. One could wade through it almost freely.

Paul soon saw Lieutenant Dan Shaw and Branoff, his radioman, standing conspicuously in knee-deep grass among tall-shafted trees. The sunlight patterned Dan Shaw's shoulders and helmet, and Paul caught a glimpse of sunshine on the short flexible antenna shaped like a strip of tape.

Paul approached Dan Shaw and was pleased to see a smile of greeting. Here apparently was a man who liked him. Dan Shaw was built like a fireplug, although not as compact and powerful as Paul.

One difference was that Shaw was used to the heat, and for that reason he seemed, and was, more able than Paul. He was also smaller. And compared to Paul's gladiator face with its sharp dark eyes and coal-black brows and lashes, and his thick stubble of unshaven whiskers, Dan Shaw's features were mild and easy.

Even when he had fumed over Ollie's initial refusal of his requests for artillery—during the recoilless rifle attack yesterday—Dan Shaw's eyes, and his attitude, suggested he believed there was a joke behind the roll of the universe.

He gestured for Paul to approach. Since he had issued an order for a quiet march he did not have to signal silence. Paul came without a word.

Dan Shaw, signaling the radioman to come along, led Paul forward two or three paces, stopped, and looked at Paul as if to say: "What about this!"

Paul looked for something remarkable. He was about to ask, when he saw that they were standing in a road. Clogged with low ferns and fallen trees, yes, but it was certainly a road, a work of man amid jungle. Dappled by broken sunlight, curving gently, with wheel ruts gouged under the greenery, as Paul discovered when he dragged his feet—yes, a road.

Looking at Paul in triumph, waving for the handset, which Branoff proffered, Dan Shaw straddled the middle of the road with a huge smile breaking out on his face. He accepted the handset from Branoff but on second thought returned it and whispered:

"You tell'm, Branoff."

Branoff raised the handset to his head.

Paul was puzzled. Why had he not seen the road when he helped carry the wounded man? He must surely have crossed it. He was working on this, watching Branoff, whose features showed his appreciation of Shaw's consideration in allowing him to break the news.

And all this formed an indelible pattern of memory and meaning in Paul Adrano's mind—the puzzle, the face, the hand.

Branoff's hand turned red and exploded blood and bones. Shock waves stunned Paul's senses. Sound and shock pierced his eardrums. Branoff's face disappeared in a hideous instantaneous mutilation. The man himself sunk out of sight. A scorching stream of energy passed between Paul and Dan Shaw. Paul saw the surprise on Shaw's face and then all he saw was green and brown. He was down and squirming in a wheel rut, getting out of the road, going, he hoped, away—but his mind or conscience plucked at his sleeve and he stopped.

The heat stream streaked over his head; and by means of the shock he knew it was a weapon firing on automatic. What kind of weapon he had no idea but the impact was huge and hot.

He grabbed Branoff's foot and tried to pull him but he was in the wheel rut, and heavy. In a normal world Paul would now stand up, plant his feet for leverage, and pull the man, or the body, into the concealment of the nearby brush and trees. But in such a world there'd be no need to do that. Paul's predicament did not strike him as anything but natural.

By some means forever unknown to him, Paul and Michelson did pull Branoff's body into the woods, while two or more weapons sought their lives and the marine line exploded in fire. He remembered seeing the coiled wire straightening and re-coiling, and the handset jumping along in pursuit of the radio on Branoff's backboard.

Paul had gained concealment, not cover. He thought: "Grenade." They could loft a grenade. Here came Dan Shaw digging on his elbows. He was shouting, but Paul did not track his words.

The scene was bright enough, there was sunlight scattered among the trees, branches, and leaves, so Paul could see, but his mind darkened. He felt he had been here before, but could not recognize the place. In this place life was infinitely intensified but infinitely perilous; he'd be justified in thinking "I am alive" but knew he could be dead the next second. He swelled with a thrill of self-affirmation. A man escaping death does not feel insignificant.

Dan Shaw was forming the squads for defense and Paul began to understand. He grabbed the handset intending to tell Mac what was happening, but the handset, like Branoff, was smashed and bloody.

He felt an icy liquid cold in his bowels and gut, and could not move. His heart went mad. He stared and saw nothing, and didn't know where he was.

Dan Shaw was shouting, and the firing accelerated. Paul heard a man cry, "They got me," and he tried to get into the bosom of the earth.

"Fix bayonets!" Dan Shaw hollered.

This Paul could not believe, but he saw Shaw ripping the bayonet from its scabbard on his belt and slipping it into place on his rifle—and Shaw was twisting on the ground, either writhing in agony or just changing his position. Paul did not know but he twisted in the same direction, thinking: "Better face them." He did not want to be bayoneted in the back.

Paul thought: "God, are they coming? Where's Mac?"

Dan Shaw shouted to the men to form a wedge but Paul dared not move. To rise was to die. To crawl was to get nowhere, and even crawling meant rising too high. But he feared one thing more than the liquid fire above, and that was being separated from Dan Shaw and Michelson.

A soldier in khaki—the unfamiliar color sent a yelp of terror through Paul's brain—a man with black hair and no hat, came forcing his way through the grass, swinging an assault rifle at chest height, and Paul recognized the AK-47 by the backward slanting metal on top of the barrel and its banana-curved magazine. The man saw Paul. He brought his rifle partway up. His face was full of fear and rage.

A burst of fire split Paul's ears and the enemy dropped, with a different expression on his face and blood all over his front.

Paul watched as Dan Shaw rose and threw a grenade, then Shaw hollered: "LAW, LAW!" It never crossed Paul's mind that he didn't know what this was. Somebody shouted, "Yeah, Lieutenant!" and then a crack and whoosh came and then a piercing blast very close to Dan Shaw in front.

"Drag him," said Dan Shaw to Paul, then Shaw began running zigzag, and the little chopping sounds chased him through the foliage.

Next, with his mind flashing in and out, Paul and Michelson took Branoff's body by the arms. Paul heard another shouted "LAW" and another whoosh, then Paul—and this somehow seemed like madness—began dragging. He didn't know where Michelson was.

He found himself among marines in a confused cluster with nobody in charge. They peered out in all directions and sometimes fired off a burst to no apparent purpose. They paid no attention to Paul or to Branoff's body. A man stood erect and fired off a full magazine and flopped down and said that he could not see anything but fucking trees. Another flung a grenade with a straight swinging arm. Then Paul learned what a LAW was.

A man with a short metal tube, a light antitank weapon, stood up placed it over his shoulder, paused, and fired it. A backflash and then a terrific concussion. He hit the deck and flung the hot tube away. Somebody complained, "If you fire a LAW, muddah, you warn us."

Dan Shaw came piling in. An NVA hero-maniac burst into the little circle firing his AK-47 single-shot, trying to pick targets, and he did hit two men before he dropped with a dozen rounds pounding his shuddering body. A marine rolled Branoff over and took the radio and hacked at it with a machete, then hammered the battery terminals with its butt—the big knife pumping up and down—and said, "O.K., done, Lieutenant."

Dan Shaw hollered, "Wedge, goddamn it," and said to somebody, "Gotta locate his flank," and the group began moving, hauling the wounded, with Dan Shaw on the point and Paul and Michelson still dragging Branoff, but he was easier to move without the pack and radio.

The next thing Paul fully understood was that he and Michelson were in a circle with the wounded and Branoff's body, guarded by a fire team. A corporal said, "Lieutenant Shaw said wait here, sir."

Paul asked the corporal: "Where's Doc Bartholomew?"

"With the lieutenant."

Paul began to help the wounded. He paused and turned again to the corporal and asked: "How is the lieutenant going to find us?"

Because to Paul it was all jungle.

Dan Shaw maintained contact with the enemy long enough to locate his left flank, some fifty meters right of the road. He then disengaged, pulled back, retrieved his casualties, and rejoined Delta at dusk.

Shaw told Mac he had seen cleared fields of fire where all the foliage below waist level had been trimmed and the higher stuff left untouched. It was something a trooper might not see. He could walk into a cleared field of fire and never know it.

Dan Shaw guessed that the farmers intercepted by the gunny's team last night had been bound for the woods to do this kind of work.

"Why at night?" Jake the exec wanted to know.

Dan Shaw had an answer ready. "They didn't want to cross the river in daylight. Cross in the dark, sleep, work in—"

The exec interrupted to dispute this, but Mac said:

"Save it." He told the exec to blow up the bunkers 3rd Platoon had searched. "We'll concentrate the troops on this ridge right here," Mac said.

He consulted the brain trust on the night's patrol and ambush plan. The effect of his decisions was to place a mobile screen between his night position and the NVA positions Dan Shaw had discovered.

Mac reported to Battalion and asked for the quick-reaction company. He requested medevac birds, resupply of ammo, rations, water, C4, and bangalore torpedoes. Battalion said: "In the morning. You're on your own tonight but we are requesting Puff."

On hearing this, the forward air controller, Kindred, began singing, "Puff the Magic Dragon, come and play with me," smiling like a maniac.

In the first hour of darkness the patrols got bit on the nose twice, but Mac heard good news. The Air Force was sending Puff.

Kindred said: "For the first time in my Marine Corps career I talked respectfully to an Air Force man. They'll be here in twenty-five minutes. Batten down the hatches."

Mac pulled in the screen and told Jake: "Troop the line. Talk to every squad leader and make sure everybody's home. Nobody out from now on." And to Captain Kindred: "Hose the bastards, Kinny."

So it was that Father Paul Adrano saw more fire in the sky.

Somebody called: "Come on up, Chaplain." Paul climbed to the top of the bunker, which had now been named the Holiday Inn.

"Make a hole for the chaplain, you snuffies," somebody said in the dark, and Paul took his seat in the grandstand.

"I read you five by five and we hear you coming." It was Captain Kindred, seated near Paul, talking to Puff.

The droning of the old prop-driven plane made its way through the ringing in Paul's ears—high in altitude, distinct, invisible. The night was almost black.

Kindred read off the friendly front lines in plain English. He encrypted the CP location. Then he started rattling off target coordinates, again in plain English. The drone grew louder, from above and rumbling off the mountain. The men on the bunker roof toned down; pretty soon they were perfectly quiet.

Into this void came the voice of Gunny Hitchcock: "One tracer in this bunker, Captain, and we go sky-high."

Said Kindred: "These guys are accurate, Guns. He can lay that stuff twenty-five meters from your ass and never crack it."

"Hey Captain, now I feel safe. Twenty-five meters."

"Just watch," said Kindred. "He'll scorch the whole grid square."

From the sound Paul judged the plane to be circling overhead, quite high. The enemy opened up with small arms and machine guns and the droning continued undisturbed.

"Sure, sure," said Kindred, evidently to his radio, "counterbattery first."

A stream of fire poured down. It went on and on. Paul's ears were educated by this time to expect machine guns to fire in short bursts, but this was a torrent that did not cease. The men around Paul uttered awed exclamations, and Paul himself felt a hollow, echoing shudder in his heart. Through the gun noise, which, being so high, was not very loud, Paul heard strange squeaking or yodeling sounds.

"Jesus Christ they're screaming," somebody said.

"Don't say Jesus Christ in front of the chaplain," said someone else.

Paul did not comment.

The "hosing" continued.

Kindred spoke, not to his radio but to the men in the grandstand. "One round in five is a tracer. What you're seeing is just every fifth round. Gatling guns. Max rate of fire, six thousand rounds a minute, and I did say six thousand. And—he's firing three guns. Do the arithmetic."

The Gatling guns sent down wide streams of red liquid fire—which stopped altogether and left the sky black. Paul's eyes when he shut them repeated the image of jetting fire in green.

In this private world of the image, Paul listened to the screams and cries from just beyond the perimeter.

It seemed to Paul that if he could listen and make no protest he was no priest. Fear hollowed out his insides, and he jerked forward as if to get up and leave, the minimal gesture, but he sat back trembling.

He imagined he could see the bullets striking the soldier who had tried to kill him. He understood why all this was necessary. This was a war. He had thanked Dan Shaw, but Shaw said, "Hey, Padre, it wasn't me." So he thanked Michelson, who seemed pleased.

The men had heard that Paul and Michelson dragged Branoff's body out of the road and Paul knew within five minutes of returning to the company that he was now regarded almost as a marine. A chaplain to be sure, but a special kind. He could tell by the way they looked, by their voices when they greeted him, and even by Michelson's bearing, that he would never have to worry about being addressed by the dread title of "Chappie." Michelson was proud to be his bodyguard.

Paul thought of trading his life for that of the man who tried to kill him, but it was an academic exercise. He knew he was more valuable than the other. He had God's work to do.

But all the fire, blood, exhaustion, thirst—all his—frenzy—fear—

He needed an interval to pray, an interval of peace in which to recapture his former self by opening his soul once more to God. He cried peace, peace, but there was no peace, and, actually, trying to be honest, he realized he did not cry peace at all.

He stayed with the rest and watched Puff darting fire on the enemy. A white flare popped and swung gently on its parachute cords, then steadied and descended slantwise, streaming white smoke up through its own light as it floated down. Paul lost sight of it among the trees. Another popped, and a second or two later there was a crash and some shouting from the perimeter.

Kindred cried: "Canister, canister! Your canister hit inside our line." A pause, and then: "Negative. I didn't say check fire, just watch the flares is all. Go to it, buddy."

The fire stream shot down the sky. Another flare popped above the trees that cut off Paul's view at the bottom. The blue-white lamp swung serenely on its cords, drifting in the breeze and trailing white smoke as it descended. Paul could see the slopes of Nui Gio in its light, strangely shaded and colorless.

The Puff went silent for a minute except for the slow drone of its engines, then another flare was born and commenced its brief drifting life in a world defended by darkness: the terrain stood revealed, clothed in rounded trees, in a ghostly gray light that threw tremendous shadows.

A new stream of red fire sought the ground below the trees.

Speaking in murmurs some of the men claimed they still heard screams. Paul concentrated, and though the ringing in his ears had subsided, it still persisted faintly. He did not hear screams. He imagined them. A new flare popped. New jets of fire probed the earth.

Then a different quality of light erupted, from the ground up, first as a small white flash that leapt up and spread in one thrust through the layer of smoking dust that overlay the hillside, then as another leap of white light chasing the first. Then a mammoth ball of red fire arose with a puff of rushing gas. It spat jets of white fire and smoke beyond its red circumference. This sphere expanded so fast the eye could barely keep track. Then a wave of energy struck Paul's chest. His shirt waved and he felt it in his lungs. A concussion of sound passed over him and echoed against the hills across the river.

"Secondary!" Kindred cried.

MacHugh Clare said calmly, "Graeser, see if you can raise Battalion."

Kindred again: "Can you give us coordinates? That was enough ammo to win the war."

A new eruption stopped him. The sky turned white with a blinding light, then settled on red. It burned red for several minutes, pulsing and blowing like sunspots, all in the same area, then paled to orange and began to spread like an ordinary fire. It lost its spherical shape and roamed here and there igniting new explosions that leapt now and then in small jets and balls.

Mac was speaking to Battalion: ". . . two secondary explosions and a fire. Obviously an ammo dump, and a big one."

The troops were talking excitedly. One said: "Bingo!" and Paul understood they had found what they were searching for.

But seeing the rain of red which still continued, thinking again of Branoff's hand turning red, he underwent a basic change. He said to himself: "It doesn't make any difference." There was no arguing against that. "Whether God exists or not, whether He cares or not, makes no difference. All this is happening." From his parish work, from reading, from life, he knew about poverty and cancer, and even war. Never before had he said that God's presence "makes no difference." He said in his mind: "I must be wrong." But he watched the torrents of fire, and he listened.

The weather changed and that changed everything. Puff received a storm warning and departed early. Battalion sent a message, first about nine o'clock at night, that tomorrow's reinforcement, medevac, and resupply might not be possible; then, a little after midnight, Battalion said all aircraft had been grounded. By that time every man in the company already knew what Mac told the brain trust at one o'clock in the morning:

"We could be alone out here for three or four days."

They were assembled around a candle in the Holiday Inn. The roof kept the rain off their backs but their feet were in water. Being half in the ground and built of earth and logs, the bunker could not tremble. But it lay submissive under the pressures of wind and the weight of falling water.

"Gentlemen," Mac said, "I have only one idea and it is not a good one, but I am going to decide this in the next ten minutes."

A gust slipped in by the firing port and extinguished the candle. Graeser struck a match.

Over the last quarter-hour—amid their tactical analysis—the brain trusters had exhausted their supply of jokes about Graeser's lighting the wrong wick and blowing the Holiday Inn to atoms.

Graeser cupped his hands and shepherded the little flame to the candle. A feeble yellow ellipse rose up and trembled. Graeser shook the match out. A man shifted his body to shelter the candle, and the little flame stood straighter.

Mac spoke somewhat louder than usual to be heard above the roar outside. This was not "molecular" rain but a wind-driven monsoon storm. Mac said: "Ollie, please summarize your comments on the NVA mortars."

"Well, Skipper, like I said, the choppers shut'm down, we all know that, but I doubt they actually ruined the tubes. I mean how do you smash a steel tube except with a direct hit? You can fire an eighty-two with a busted sight if you're desperate. So I'd say we could see more trouble from those same tubes. Different gooks of course."

"O.K.," said Mac, pondering. "We're good on ammo—all the C4 we're likely to need—LAWs, sixties, machine-gun ammo—but the other guy can figure all this as accurately as he needs to. He knows how many we are, how we're armed, and exactly where we are. He knows we're naked, no air, no arty.—Doc Bartholomew?"

"Sir."

"Welcome to the brain trust."

"My privilege, sir."

"Can we move the wounded?"

"If you mean would it kill anybody, the answer is, no sir."

"Chaplain?"

"Yes?"

"How's morale among the wounded?"

"They seem brave and cheerful to me, except one who is moaning a lot."

"From pain?"

"I don't think it's pain."

The gunny cut in: "Reminds me of that sissy who wanted his daddy. That's a new one. Me, I want my mommy."

"What about it, Doc?" Mac asked. "Can you give him some morphine?"

"He doesn't need it, sir."

"What does he need?"

"It's called courage," Paul Adrano cut in.

"So," Mac surmised, "as far as you both are concerned we can move out at first light if we so decide, and nobody dies."

"Nobody dies of wounds they already have," said Henry Bartholomew, correcting his superior.

"No," said Mac with the utmost calm, "but the wounds we already have are nothing compared to those we could face tomorrow. We are sitting on what Sun Tzu calls death ground. Oddly enough, so is the enemy. All right, gents, we've gabbed enough. First light, what do we do? Junior first."

Staff Sergeant Reggie Graves of 3rd Platoon said: "Dig in till the skies clear."

The gunny said: "I don't know what Sun Tzu says about death ground—but the mission of Marine Corps infantry is to close with the enemy and destroy him by fire and maneuver. That's all I'm going to say about that."

Lieutenant Kim Kolias said: "Dig in right here. Wait for air."

Lieutenant Dan Shaw said: Attack.

Lieutenant Oliver the FO said: Go for the fan of fire.

The weapons platoon leader said: Attack.

Jake the exec said: "Attack while dragging wounded?" He advocated the company avoid contact until it had established itself within the fan of fire.

Captain Kindred said: "I'll check the weather again in the morning. If the forecast is more of the same, we've got no choice. Attack."

Mac said: "I hear three options. Dig in here, go for the fan of fire by the safest route, and attack. Is that a fair summary?"

"I didn't say go by the safest route, sir," Jake objected uneasily. "I said avoid contact, get inside that fan, then we can establish a good defensive position for the wounded and the command group and send out patrols from there."

"All right, Jake," said Mac, and it struck the exec that Mac had called him by name.

And Jake thought: "I must be doing O.K." He said: "We've got to get out of here, that's for sure."

"Yes," said Mac, and went silent. He was listening to the wind and rain, thinking: "It is not easy to walk in this kind of storm, or to think clearly."

The gunny broke the silence. "This is a friggin storm, Skipper. We make a plan then we execute it. Blab on this side of the LOD, fight on the other."

"Exactly," said Mac. "I did not hear a terrific idea. I heard three I don't especially like.

"If we dig in here we get pounded tomorrow or the next day by eighty-twos and maybe big rockets or heavy mortars, certainly by light mortars and the reckless rifles they fired at Dan. We give him all the time he needs to assemble a big force. We give him the incentive too. We sit here in our holes, starving and saying, 'Attack me please.' In two days' time we could be saying hi to a thousand of Ho Chi Minh's finest. Worse yet, we become bait for bigger game. They use us to pull the battalion into a sack.

"If we march inside the fan of fire, avoiding contact, we literally march right by the caches we were sent here to destroy."

"I withdraw that, sir," said Jake the exec in a chagrined voice.

"That's O.K., Jake. It's no worse than digging in."

There was a heated agitation in Mac's body. The skin of his face burned. He was glad it was dark. He spoke slowly to keep his voice steady. At a moment like this, he knew his voice might break if he spoke too fast.

"Suppose we attack at o-dark-thirty. We stand a fifty percent watch tonight, hold reveille at 0500, eat a meal, fill our canteens, and cross the line of departure just before full daylight.

"We head straight for those secondaries. My guess is that the enemy took shelter in their bunkers, the only escape from Puff's guns. And I think we'll find that four or five bunkers loaded with ammo exploded and burned last night. If I had to guess I'd say the enemy lost half his defending force in the secondaries. Do we give him time to summon a reaction force or do we attack?"

"Attack!" growled Gunnery Sergeant Hitchcock.

"If we do," Mac continued, "we face an experienced enemy in a prepared defensive position. And we are carrying wounded. I do not like this. But we have LAWs against the bunkers, and sixties and bloopers against the troops dug in with no overhead cover.

"I think they are going to start dragging bodies up there at dawn. I think he will expect us to dig in here and wait for air. His experience must tell him that's what Americans do. The NVA sends men, we send steel.

"But if we advance quickly we'll be on them while they're still frazzled from last night's raid. Think of it as a prep fire, gentlemen. I am not saying we can surprise them, although it's possible. I *am* saying they will never be weaker than they are now and could be stronger as early as tomorrow afternoon.

"If there's a regiment up there we are going to need a miracle, but think a minute. If there's a regiment, do you want to fight tomorrow while they're bleeding, or wait here till they consolidate their force and swarm over this little ridge of ours like the Chinese at Chosin. Which is better and which is worse?

"One more factor. Those secondaries—the caches—I suspect—lie exactly on our direct route to artillery support. If this thing works, we attack, play hell with the caches, pass through the gook positions, then swing back and start burning.

"We march another thousand meters—less, about six hundred— and we set in to a defensive position inside the fan of fire before noon tomorrow, and Ollie gives the enemy what they would give us if we stayed here.

"So that's the decision. We attack." Trying to see the faces around him, Mac said: "Let's get some sleep. Reveille at 0500. I'll issue orders at 0530."

In this man's words, in his logic, in his attitude, Paul Adrano believed he heard himself sentenced to death.

In the facts as he arranged them, in his reasoning over the facts, in his assumptions, in his decision, MacHugh Clare believed he had sentenced himself and half his men to death.

But on death ground you must fight.

Chapter 11

The Beaten Zone

If this was to be the last night of his life he didn't notice. If he was never to see Sarah again or live with her and their child, he felt no loss. She was perhaps waiting for him. He was not waiting for her.

He was utterly absorbed in the plan of battle, his thoughts moving in thrilling unexpected jumps. He did not want to lose, or see his men die. Any image of his own death lay concealed in the drama of his planning. His guiding idea crept in unseen. Absent this idea he would never have attempted what he did plan to attempt. Yet it was a mere idea. If knowledge is "justified true belief," this so-called guiding idea was not knowledge. It had no such dignity.

He alone was still awake in the Holiday Inn, bent over a candle, writing in his wheel book.

Being out of the action as forward air controller and artillery forward observer, Kindred and Ollie had volunteered to join the perimeter watch. Mac thanked them and accepted. So these two and their radiomen had departed into the storm with the rest of the brain trust.

Encrypting his message to Battalion, writing on his knee with his boots buried in six inches of muck, Mac had looked up at some time around one-thirty or two in the morning to find everyone else asleep—Graeser, the exec, Pickens Freeman the company runner,

Michelson, and Paul Adrano. Nor did they wake when Mac got on the radio and succeeded in raising Battalion. He had to repeat portions of his message two or three times, to press it through the storm. He had copied it from the wheel book into the message book without the crossouts and corrections. The key to the message was that it didn't carry the word "attack." Speaking in plain English for most of it, and in cipher for the geographic coordinates, he had merely said he would be in a certain place tomorrow.

The question was whether Battalion would see the significance of his move into the beaten zone of the air strike.

Thirty minutes later, as Mac began to nod, Battalion came back with an order that he call again at ten tomorrow, two hours earlier than usual. They had not understood, or, having understood all too well, they had decided to put his company's fate entirely in his hands.

Mac woke Graeser and gave him the radio. He slid onto a sleeping shelf still warm from Graeser's body. He lay back and let a rush of good feeling rise through his legs. He marveled at the narcotic pleasure in his brain of lying flat and closing his eyes. He slid his hands into his belt to keep them from dropping into the muck. This position suppressed his breathing and helped put him into a turbulent wild sleep charged with unhinged dreams—set loose from whatever in the world of men and nature was rational and calculable.

He realized later he had a plan. It heaved up in the confusion of the dreams to shake him. It was a coldly rational plan concocted to get him out of death ground and turn danger into safety. It had probably come about more or less like this.

He had been lecturing himself on his principal weakness, his ungovernable temper and impulsiveness. He kept these weaknesses almost always under strong control. Sun Tzu would say: Never yield to anger or impulse. Anger and hatred may unify troops and motivate them to kill in battle, but for a tactician the passions are a dangerous intoxicant. Your anger is the enemy's advantage; your impulse, his opportunity. In the course of these lectures Mac had a surprising thought: that his adversary must have a weakness too.

"I have seen him up to now as a pure soldier, but he is also a man."

Among the several weaknesses this man might have, Mac chose one. He had no proof, in fact no evidence. But imagining him and his troops withering under the spewing fire, and adding what everybody knew about the American way of fighting—Mac had said it last night, "The enemy sends men, we send steel"—thinking of all this, Mac could almost feel his adversary's respect for American firepower and contempt for the soldiers who hide behind it.

Here was an officer who had walked for weeks through the jungle down the Ho Chi Minh Trail under frequent bombardment—and when he finally reaches the field of battle he encounters an army of men who huddle in their holes while their forward observers direct the artillery, air and naval gunfire that do their killing for them.

The greater this adversary's experience of the Americans, Mac believed, the more likely it was that he held the marines and all Americans in contempt. It was doubtful that Sun Tzu's earnest warnings about assessing your enemy objectively could overcome the experience of fighting a nation that was so exquisitely stingy in expending its soldiers' lives.

So Mac more or less consciously admitted the "guiding idea" into his mental process. The adversary was perhaps indulging in scorn and contempt. It was the corrosive contempt of an officer who sends men into battle for an enemy who sends steel. And possibly, knowing Mac was without his supporting arms, the adversary was a little too confident besides.

At 0530, after Kindred got a weather report from the Wing predicting more of the same, Mac issued his orders: the gunny, with the sailor, the Greek, and Hippo, would reconnoiter the enemy's right edge; Ollie would lead a squad from 3rd Platoon, plus a gun and two bloopers, find the center of the enemy's perimeter, and stand by to make a demonstration; Mac would lead the Main Body on a course tangential to the enemy's left edge as discovered yesterday by Dan Shaw.

Thus when they reached their new phase line, Delta Company would be deployed in three units—a fast recon team on the left, a well-armed but fast demonstration force in the center, and the Main Body on the right.

What Mac did next would depend on the gunny's report on the enemy's disposition and strength, but Mac told the exec to be ready to assist 1st and 2nd Platoons in a wheeling maneuver.

If Mac ordered the wheel it would work like this. The Main Body, with 1st Platoon in the lead and 2nd following in column, would move up the left edge of the enemy's perimeter. If the enemy followed Sun Tzu's advice and let the marines continue their supposed retreat—and when the lead platoon had moved fifty meters beyond the enemy's flank—the whole Main Body would stop.

The lead platoon, 1st, under Kim Kolias, would be like the minute hand and the following platoon, 2nd, under Dan Shaw, like the hour hand of a clock stuck at 6:00. Then on order, the minute hand would wheel back to 5:45. The exec as pivot would hold the two hands of the clock together.

When the maneuver was completed the two platoons would be facing the enemy on two fronts, creating a kill zone with interlocking fires in the angle between them. The exec must make certain that no gap opened at the apex of the right angle formed by the maneuver.

Dan Shaw would issue a "nothing right" firing order to prevent his men from firing on 1st Platoon; Kim Kolias would order "nothing left."

Mac told Ollie that if he ordered a demonstration he wanted it to be obvious to the enemy that it was a fake.

"Eh? Skipper?"

"Yes, Ollie. Fake it and act like a fake."

"Like?"

"Be incompetent. You won't have any trouble at it."

"Ouch!" cried Ollie, and the assembled officers and platoon sergeants laughed, and Ollie did a little spinning dance of fake pain.

To the gunny Mac said: "Snoop and poop, Guns. Low and slow."

"Aye aye sir. Anybody sees us, you can have my stripes."

To Kim Kolias, Dan Shaw, and the exec: "If I give the word, we make noise like a bunch of civilians. We carry some able-bodied men in ponchos as if they were wounded. We limp and whine and act tired and hungry."

"That'll be easy," Ollie cracked.

Gunnery Sergeant Hitchcock cut in: "I get it, Skipper. You're the wounded bird."

"Right," Mac confirmed. "We're hurting and we're running for the fan of fire. But don't count on anything. This is one possibility among several. If necessary we go hi-diddle-diddle right up the middle."

"Ugh," was Ollie's comment.

Mac continued: "If we draw him out of his perimeter, if he sends troops to stop us or chase us, we have split his force and pulled some of his troops out of prepared positions."

"The dogs of war come howling out of their kennels," said Ollie.

Jake the exec said: "Shut up, Ollie."

Said Mac: "It'll be better than facing those prepared defenses. Now, gentlemen, understand that we are going to improvise if necessary, and use this plan only if it seems good at the critical moment. If he comes after us we ambush his ass. Remember we've still got Third Platoon in reserve. And after the demonstration, we'll have Ollie's gang plus the recon team moving from left to right. Gunny, Ollie, link up with the Main Body as soon as you can. Join the command group.

"And Ollie," Mac concluded, "not a shot, not a sound till I say so."

"Yes sir."

This conference had been conducted in the rain. It still came down, as the light grew upon the scene.

As the trees and faces gained clarity Mac ordered: "Smash batteries. Blow the Holiday Inn. Blow the other bunker. We cross the LOD in five minutes."

The three units of Delta—the gunny's recon team, the demonstration team led by Ollie, and the Main Body led by Mac—crossed the line of departure simultaneously and diverged gradually. Two great blasting shocks signaled the end of the bunkers. Parts of the Holiday Inn scattered into the sky and joined the rain falling to earth.

The gunny and his men soon disappeared in the trees and rain. Mac watched the demonstration force for several minutes as it moved straight forward, till he lost it in the elements. Then in a few steps the Main Body—moving slowly, carrying the wounded—entered the beaten zone.

Doc Bartholomew bent down and whispered to a man who had groaned in the night: "Be quiet now, marine. We're tactical."

The ragged wounds opened in the jungle by the Gatling guns reduced concealment and forced Mac to lengthen the interval between men from three to six meters. This diluted his firepower and made him uneasy but he drove on toward the phase line.

The Main Body could move no faster than the slowest bearers. The rain laid its weight on everything, and set silver halos dancing on the men's helmets and shoulders.

Coming after several minutes to a little cove of chopped vegetation surrounded by higher brush, Mac halted the column and crouched down with Graeser, the coiled wire connecting the two. Mac raised the gunny.

"Buzzbomb, this is Striker Six. Are you ready to talk?"

"Wait." This was the voice of Hippo-I'm-Great-In-Dayton, the gunny's radioman.

Next came the gunny's voice whispering: "Six, Buzzbomb, how do you read?"

"Loud and clear, go," said Mac.

The gunny responded: "O.K., your essential elements of information. One, a hundred to a hundred and fifty gook-type regulars. EEI Number Two, perimeter circular, maybe a hundred meters across, bunch a craters, two strong points intact, plus the army ants are rebuilding the ones that blew last night, and more ants coming in all the time from Ambush Alley. And there's oxcarts up here, Skipper. I think there's an access road from Five B.

"Everything's oriented for an all-around defense and there's maybe a command bunker in the middle, made it through the night just fine. I guess the boss gook let his peons hide in the ammo bunkers, and he took one of the inerts. Rank has its privileges.

"Three, damage assessment: in-fuckin-credible. You got zombies staggering around the place falling in holes and this little rooster comes up and slaps the shit outa their faces and screams *hong-fong-dong-ow-bow-cow* and cracks their fuckin face with his stick, and they, I swear, they just stand there and look lost.

"So then the rooster turns and screams at the gang of slaves digging a mass grave and rolling the vanguard of the revolution into it. There's a whole army of these barefoot human miracles, most of'm look a hundred years old. Jabbering, dragging the heroes to their last resting place—and these old dudes in black pajamas just keep on digging and dragging. Must be fifty of these old coots, no teeth, old biddies with red around their mouths, guys so old you can't find their eyes—women with knockers around their knees—

"I mean I was real close, less than two hundred meters I'd say, and I scoped 'em out with my glasses and I says, 'Hey Pop, where's your eyes?' All as he's got is two little black dots in his brown face. But the old papa-san could swing a pick better'n ever I could, mister."

Mac said: "Describe the rooster."

"Uh—I'd guess he was a major or light colonel—never went to charm school. Carries a swagger stick with a leather thong, it swings and dangles from his right wrist when he's not swatting zombies. Short—a cocky little shit—bowlegged, little knobby knees to his curved brown legs—the kind of guy could march all day on a drop a water and a grain a rice—holds his elbows out, struts around hell like he was the boss devil—almost naked, black shorts, Ho Chi Minh shoes—no gun—mean little beady black eyes, lotsa jet black hair, pretty long actually, the guy could use a haircut. I'd put him on report for bad grooming."

"Describe his voice," said Mac patiently.

"Well at two hundred meters—except for the rain I'd bet a gook could've understood every word. Kinda squeaks and pipes. This is no John Wayne. Jabber-jabber-scream."

"So, a hundred to a hundred fifty effectives, regulars," said Mac in a different tone.

"At least."

"Did you see any heavy weapons?"

"Oh yeah! In one bunker they've got some back-to-Bataan monster, ain't no fifty, could be some kinda twelve mike-mike but it's a big mamma and it's automatic; and I hate to say it but they got at least two reckless rifles, including one of our 106's.

"And they've got an aid station, guys carrying bodies in and out, who's dead, who's alive, search me. I'll tell you, Six, this is the cinders of hell, this place. I never saw flies before in rain like this, and you don't have to search for drag marks in the jungle, just follow the hands, or feet, take your choice. I mean, when you see this you won't have any more questions. This is the big EEI."

It wasn't possible now to pick out the road Dan Shaw had found. And there was no concealment here, it had all been laid open by shock and combustion. Underfoot, a black carbon soup; at man level, black trunks and splintered blasted sticks; overhead, a network of bony charred fingers interlocking. The wind carried the rain freely through the vegetable wreckage.

Most of the mines in a beaten zone so intensely chopped as this one would have been detonated by the Gatling guns. This surmise was confirmed when Mac noted, at intervals along the route of march, small shallow craters and patterns of fragmentation on the blackened trunks.

He remembered the Bouncing Betty and the blood trickling down his leg, and the startling report so typical of what the manuals quaintly call "bounding munitions." He could feel the blood moving down again.

So it was that terror inserted its digits into his entrails and sent an injection straight to his heart.

His legs took him off the route, to the right, and this caused confusion among the men marching behind him. Naturally they followed, but they could also see the men ahead still taking the original path, and so the Main Body broke in two. Jake the exec ran forward and stopped the lead platoon, but Mac was still moving to the right, leading 2nd Platoon, the command group, the wounded, and the reserve, 3rd Platoon, off and away. The exec was dumbfounded. He told 1st to stand fast, and he chased Mac through the black trunks, up a little hill—but Mac had passed over the top and for a moment the exec lost sight of him. Jake ran, slipping in the ooze, scrambling up the slope.

On the other side Mac dived in fear for his life and lay prone and tried to merge with the mud. He pressed himself into the ooze, he forced his cheek into the mud. A threat, a threat! But a voice in his mind asked what he was doing—but he knew the answer. The voice said, "Get up," but he began to curl his knees into the fetal position— it was safer!—rolling on his side but the voice spoke adamantly, "No!" and he did not curl all the way up, not quite.

Rolling on his back he uncurled his legs but it was the hardest thing he ever did. It increased his fear. The sky as he stared wildly into its featureless gray terrified him. He was vulnerable in his exposed chest and belly, and his genitals. From a stiffened immobility he shifted in an instant to a shaking that made his teeth clatter and dried his mouth.

In this moment he could lose everything—reputation, respect, self-respect, and all that made life worth living. His life would be unendurable, his identity destroyed.

He had but a second remaining. Get up now or live the unlivable for the rest of your life. In fact he knew the only recourse would be suicide. He realized that he'd rather die. If he could not live as a coward, either in the Marine Corps or at home—which would be worse?—he'd better die. His mind cleared.

He crawled forward dragging his rifle and dipped his hands to the elbows in a puddle, and probed the bottom. His eyes darted left and right. He hoped to catch sight of somebody without appearing to look. He flipped his helmet off, to appear casual and absorbed in his probing.

"Are you O.K., Skipper?" It was Jake speaking in a baffled but cautious voice.

Mac could not produce a sound. He tried, and a grunt came out, then he was able to say, "Fine, Jake. Give me a second." He resumed his probing. He knew his voice had sounded odd but maybe Jake would attribute that to his lying on his chest.

He felt around the bottom: muck and small stones. He rose to his knees and shook water off his arms and looked around at a sight such as he had never seen before. It looked even worse now. If hell existed, this was it. If he couldn't make up a suitable lie here he couldn't do it anywhere.

He said: "Jake, there is no fuze well in this goddamn crater."

"Sir?"

"Right, no fuze well," Mac repeated hoping Jake didn't know much about crater analysis.

Mac got to his feet, held his rifle out, and stared at it angrily and said with disgust: "I'll have to clean this thing."

Jake was still looking at him oddly.

Mac feared he was not carrying it off but he went ahead, saying: "This is no mortar crater." He thought: "Of course it's not." He said: "It's a mine, goddamn it."

"Yes sir," said Jake.

"So—pass the word to look out for mines. There must still be some that are—pass the word."

"Aye aye sir."

"And I'm going forward," Mac said on a sudden inspiration. "I'm taking the point till we find his left flank. Graeser—" and Mac looked around and discovered Graeser at his side, where he must have witnessed the whole thing. "Stay with the exec," Mac said calmly.

"Yes sir"—and Mac could read nothing in the laconic Graeser's face except automatic compliance.

"God, I curled up!" he thought with self-hate. He came up with another lie: "Christ, I'm freezing. Are you cold?"

Graeser said he was actually pretty hot.

"I've got the chills," Mac continued as the inner voice told him to shut up. He seemed to know that lies should be simple. Where had he learned that? To Jake he said: "When I find his flank I'll come back and we'll start the demonstration."

"Yes sir," said Jake enigmatically.

So Mac started forward not knowing whether he'd been caught. The two parts of the Delta Main Body knit together and he heard the men passing the word about mines, and he felt more secure and more shamed.

The men greeted him and smiled—their spirit was strong, and he took strength from them. He strode on toward the point, thinking:

"Hungry, sleepless, rattled, foggy in the head, and I was—paralyzed! But I'll be O.K. when the shooting starts. If that Rooster Major doesn't light the fuze, I will."

Mac's veering out of line put Paul in a quandary. He was in charge of the group carrying the wounded, and, anticipating an exhausting day's work, quite aside from any fighting the bearers might have to do, he wanted to conserve their energy. Since he was a bearer himself he knew how exhausting it was. So he did not intend to lead the group off the track if Mac was simply making a detour.

Paul said to Henry Bartholomew: "Do you think we should wait here?"

The chaplain and corpsman decided that Paul should follow Mac with the rest of the command group and ascertain whether this was a change of course or a detour for some unknown cause. Most causes out here were unknown. He could see 1st Platoon standing fast—uneasily casting alert glances all around—so it seemed reasonable to wait. Paul went off after Mac.

When he topped the rise he saw that the command group had paused and gathered in a little knot, tighter than usual. Paul asked his question and Captain Kindred said he didn't know what was going on, but the exec had gone forward to find the skipper. Paul continued forward, slipping among the charred trees, leaping over severed branches, wading through the muck and denuded brush—and he soon saw the exec. The man was standing with his back to Paul.

Graeser was looking inquisitively at something on the ground. Approaching him Paul saw what he was looking at. A thrill of horror leaped up in Paul as he saw Mac rolling and uncurling his body. That Mac should die so soon, when he was needed, and when his replacement, the exec, was so patently unfit for command—that he should die just before seeing his wife, when he was so young, so powerful, so muscular and fearless—

Now Paul saw him crawl and plunge his hands into a big puddle, and Paul watched stunned with disbelief and incomprehension.

What was he doing? Graeser and the exec exchanged a glance.

Mac rose and faced the exec—and evidently did not see Paul through the trees and off to the side. Paul believed he had witnessed the breakdown of the only man whose intelligence and resolution could guide Delta Company through this day. His shoulders were as huge as ever and his "military bearing," a great subject in chaplain school, was undiminished.

Paul could hear their voices but it was some kind of technical talk about a fuze and he turned back.

"What's going on?" Henry Bartholomew asked when Paul returned.

"I don't know but I think we should wait here."

Henry and Paul walked ten or twelve paces to a fallen tree and sat down.

Looking keenly at Paul's staring eyes Henry Bartholomew thought: "This guy is coming apart."

Paul was indeed paler than usual; and he had something in his face that could have been despair.

"He's giving up," Henry Bartholomew thought. "You look like you need a doctor," he said, "or a chaplain."

"Is that so?"

Paul Adrano sat with his back straight, hands on his knees, looking straight ahead.

"It's true I missed my vocation, or never had one," Henry ventured, "but I've still got the urge to give spiritual advice."

"And what advice is it you feel inclined to give?"

"It's straight out of Scripture. Sorry I can't cite chapter and verse but you'll recognize it when you hear it."

Paul sat silent. All he presented to Henry was an indifferent profile.

"You came here looking for a sign. Which is explicitly condemned. Thou shalt not seek a sign."

"Yes," the priest admitted. "I was looking for a sign. I was very stupid."

"But isn't it a good joke on you, Father? You finally see a sign—I mean, Puff the Magic Dragon—and it's not exactly what—"

"It is a very good joke. I expect I'll break out laughing at any moment."

"But you should be thrilled. We are free to make our own world. The only trouble is, this is the world we make. Did you know this place is called a beaten zone?"

"Military people have a way with language," Paul commented.

Henry looked at him but the priest was still offering only his profile.

Henry said: "Yes, we have entered the beaten zone from the air strike. The skipper saw a sign in the heavens that said, 'Illumination Go On.' Did you ever hear that one?"

"No. That too has its own kind of interest."

"Listen to a naval gunfire man calling in a night mission sometime. You'll hear it. Do you know what the skipper's plan is?"

"More or less, insofar as he has one."

"Oh hey, Father, he's got one. We're attacking."

"So I understand."

"Because if we sit still they clobber us," Henry pursued. "By attacking we get to die fighting, instead of cringing. A far far better thing."

"Maybe it is," Paul said.

"And maybe it's not. Those gooks are bleeding and won't be in any shape to attack anybody for a day or two at least. We should have stayed at the Holiday Inn. You could've saved us all by praying for clear weather."

"I don't believe I would," said Paul.

"You wouldn't pray to be saved?"

"Saved from death? No."

"Chaplain, you are, in your own way, what these jarheads call hard-core."

"Oh, but I am soft."

"Meaning?"

"It is a thought of my own I don't want to share with you."

"Oh, sorry. Your most private thought."

"One of them."

"Well I'll tell you my private thoughts."

"That won't be necessary."

"What? I thought you were a priest."

"Thanks for reminding me. If you approach me as a chaplain then of course you may speak. Do you want to make your confession?"

"I do, Padre, but not the one you expect. I have no sins to confess."

"Ah, the perfect man, the first since Jesus."

"I am the worst coward ever born."

"That's no sin. Anyway you told me that the day we went through the wall," said the chaplain.

"Oh I was just about normal then. Now—I know I'm going to die."

"So you said yesterday."

"Yesterday I was wrong, today I'm right. My guts are liquid jelly, my heart is wild, and I hate, hate, hate the thought of the eternal nothing."

Paul interrupted, saying: "But the philosophers deny that death is an appropriate object of fear. Secular philosophers, learned men with long hair and mistresses."

"What do they know that I don't? I am terrified, I can't stand it, Father, I can't go on, I'm going to explode, I love life, I even love it now in this—goddamn beaten zone—and I—that's it. That's my confession."

"I see that you believe in hell, at any rate. All is not lost." Paul turned to face him and his black eyes and brows stood out stark amid the pallor; his brush of black hair glistened.

Henry thought he was crazy; certainly not a priest. "And so do you," Henry said.

"Well at least we have—don't we?—on that side of the question, a sign?" said Paul, looking around him.

And Henry thought: "He can't stand this." Henry said: "So it makes more sense to die in this place than at home surrounded by those you love."

"Certainly," Paul assented.

"And it's better to die knowing what a coward you are, than if you still were nursing all your stupid illusions."

"Which illusions do you mean?" asked Paul. "Mine, about God, eternal life, the reunion of souls, the illusion that my mother is not and cannot be truly dead?"

"No. The one that says I'm a man, a real man."

"Surely, Henry, you are that."

"Surely, Chaplain, I am not. You want to see one? Look at the skipper."

Ollie was having a brisk little chat with the father he had lost when he was still a child.

"Will you look at that needle!" Ollie exclaimed. "Did you ever see— must be a concentration of iron around here. I'll just say I've been humping on this bearing for three hundred meters minimum, and if I'm not smack in the middle of Slope City by now I don't know where I am. Dad, I admit it—I'm lost."

Lieutenant Calvin Oliver, artillery forward observer, closed his compass and his eyes and communed with his wise and patient parent.

"O.K., try again," Ollie decided after taking counsel.

He opened the compass and lay it flat in his hand. The needle trembled and swung just as before. Ollie found a chip of wood (courtesy of Puff) and set the instrument down. The needle settled immediately.

"Do you see that? Know why it was jumping? I'm shaking, that's why." He thought: Breakdown. The idea entered him not as a word but an opening-up of his belly.

"I'll control that, Dad, don't worry." He wanted his father to be proud, and have good reason for pride. "I will provide that," he said with calm assurance, looking at his hands. "Honesty, clear thinking, truth. I crack jokes and play roles and everybody thinks I'm somebody

252

else. You know who I am. I am a plodder, so who cares about these hands? Do I plod to the right place and do the right thing when I get there, that's what counts.

"But why'd he pick me? I don't know where he gets his confidence. Sure it's a tribute, and I want you to understand that. He's a damn good skipper. The whole company knows this man is the true sterling. The question is, Why does he trust me? I've never led a fire team, let alone a reinforced squad with a mission like this. I'm a cannon-cocker, for pity's sake. I'm supposed to walk in the charmed circle, every marine my own personal bodyguard. I'm the last guy they want killed. I save their nuts with the big stuff.

"Now here I am, a troop commander all of a sudden. Recon, I could do that. Just snoop and poop, nothing to it. The sensible thing would be, the gunny takes my job and I take his."

Ollie waved the troops forward but it suffocated his courage, walking in the burnt woods where they could see him fifty meters away and cut him up before his men could react. So he waved the squad down again and lay on his front in a depressed place and peeked over the rise into a scene of broken terrain in the carbonized forest.

"He chose me because an FO never gets lost. I've had helicopter pilots land and come up to me and say 'Hey, bub, where am I?' Now I've got a squad and a gun crew wedged behind me and five minutes to make the phase line. So Dad, am I—you know—incompetent?"

After crossing the line of departure, Ollie had led his men through a jungle till he reached the burnt part. There he changed from a column to a wedge—his own perhaps unique idea of a wedge. He stayed on the point to show his courage and brought up a three-man line abreast behind him, with a blooper in the center, then a long line abreast with a gun. He moved the whole contraption forward slowly, explaining his predicament to his father.

"All I had to do was move out on Zero Four Five magnetic and within three hundred meters I'd reach the outskirts of Slope City. Hunker down and wait for the skipper's call. At which my guys let go a mighty boom and convince the boss gook that we are a demonstration force.

"Then he thinks, Mr. Gook thinks, 'Ah so. Amellicans feint heal, attack somewhell else!' Then he sees the wounded bird hobbling up his left flank and his brain goes: 'Ah so! Amellicans free to fahn of file!'—Then something happens, but I have no idea what."

He saw something that brought out a little moan, something round and dark out there in the carbon wasteland. Now it was still. Now it moved. It told Ollie he could not reach the phase line and get into position without fighting. Very too bad. He squinted the rain away. He listened. It moved slightly. He thought: "Maybe I could hit him." Ollie had fired expert at Lejeune with both rifle and pistol but the rifle had been an M14 and this was an M16, which had yet to earn his respect. The head reared up close in his sights at a range of less than one hundred meters. He steadied the weapon. One thing he never liked about the M16 was its lightness, especially at the muzzle. He wanted some weight to steady the front sight.

Ollie was a one-eyed shooter. He squinted his left eye, brought the sights into correct alignment, and focused hard on the front post sight. He shifted the black hemisphere of his target into its correct position, blurred, sitting on the post like a fuzzy ball balancing there. Ollie settled into his squeeze.

He remembered the order: no shooting. He exhaled, let the rifle down, and then saw what his target was.

It was the head of a black man; it was Hippo-I'm-Great-In-Dayton.

"I had you right here," said Ollie to Hippo three minutes later, touching his front sight.

Hippo, who was not known for his flow of eloquence, frowned.

Gunny Hitchcock said to him: "Gimme the phone, Hippo." And to the handset: "Striker Six, Buzzbomb. We have linked up but we need five more minutes." And looking at Ollie with extreme reserve he said: "You're way off, Lieutenant."

"O.K., Guns, don't rub it in, get us to the phase line, you take the point, CSMO on outa here."

The combined recon and demonstration force was about to rise and expose itself fully when the gunny waved everybody down. Flopping on his face, believing it was all over—from the ferocity of the gunny's eyes—Ollie peered over a hump of earth and saw what the gunny had seen, an NVA soldier in khaki, hatless in the rain, with a rifle and bandoliers—no pack or rice roll, no chicken dangling by its legs on his back—in short, a soldier in tactical mode—then one, two, four, six more—a whole squad, armed with assault rifles and RPGs.

Knowing you are in hell does not tell you where you are on the map, and Ollie had not asked the gunny. But the patrol was to Ollie's right, moving toward the Holiday Inn. This put the enemy between Ollie and the place he should have been; and assuming he let the enemy pass unchallenged and later went through with the demonstration, the enemy would be behind him when the time came to rejoin the Main Body.

Gunny Hitchcock whispered: "They heard us blow the bunkers. The little rooster sent them to scope us out."

Ollie thought: "Little rooster?" He said: "Let's hit the fuckers now." He was thrilled, as who wouldn't be, by the idea of opening up on an enemy who hadn't seen him.

"No, Lieutenant. We got our orders."

Mortified at having forgotten the orders again, Ollie protested: "They'll be in our rear, for Christ's sake, Guns."

"We'll worry about that later."

"Goddamn it, Guns!"

After a barely perceptible pause the gunny said: "Aye aye sir" in a tone of practiced resignation to the will of a fool, and the gunny shouldered his rifle and settled into his aim.

"Take the point!" Ollie hissed, covering the sight with his hand.

Paul trudged on, holding one corner of the poncho in which a pale gray face rode in misery and cold fear. Paul said, "You're doing fine," and the man knew he was lying.

When the command group halted Paul didn't even look for a log or other seat, but collapsed in the ooze and acquiesced as it entered his pants and chilled his anus and genitals, and they shriveled in the cold.

He looked into the sky, the rain, and he could see drops in their thousands driving down in circular yet wavy patterns composed of sheetlike masses all of which, coming from different origins, seemed nonetheless to end up in his face.

"So—a man—for Christ's sake," he pondered. Here it came again. All the time, nearly every day—he was dragged through the scene with his father when he had told him "I am going to be a priest."

In the clash of wills that severed the father and son forever, the elder Adrano had said with bitter shame: "Why can't you be a man, for

Christ's sake," and Paul retorted, "I intend to be a man—for Christ's sake."

Now this "man" suspected a sniper behind every tree trunk and a mine in every puddle—and he saw fear all around him, fear in Mr. Invincible himself.

At just that moment Mr. Invincible came back from the point and his blue or gray eyes were terrible. Paul said to himself: "May I not see what he has just seen." He got up and went close, to hear what was being said. Mac talked with the exec in that rumbling Please Step Aside voice, the one he had used to tell Henry Bartholomew: "Go back to your platoon." But now Paul had seen him on the ground and he could hear the voice of fear within the rumbling. He could almost see fear in Mac's eyes.

Paul thought he had the answer to the question he had asked Mac before they came to the S-curve: "Why are you here?"

Even such a skeptic as Henry Bartholomew, who had been humiliated by him, defined Mac as a real man.

"Define all you want," thought Paul, "I saw him rolling in the mud, with his legs curled, cringing like a dog—I saw—"

Paul was not unaware of the note of vindictive triumph in his voice. But he refused to let guilt deflect him. He's here to prove his manhood! An adolescent project. The decisiveness, the voice of command in which he uttered his orders—orders that translated: "Die if you must. What's that to me?"—all this, said Paul, was façade. Inside crouched a terrified creature pretending to be a "real man." Pitiful!

But Paul swung back to his father's shame. If Paul did not believe in the Promise, then his father was right. He was throwing his life away on a fairy tale propagated by capons for the comfort of old ladies clicking their false teeth over their beads.

He pulled Doc Bartholomew aside and whispered: "Would you be afraid if you still believed in life after death?"

Henry's green eyes showed a keen amusement under the brim of his helmet, with its "green side out" camouflage cover; he answered: "Of course."

"But why?"

"Why? I'm human! What a question!"

"I heard you," Mac said, and Paul spun around, but Mac was speaking into his handset.

"I heard you but there's nothing I can do. You'll have to deal with it."

Turning to the exec, Mac explained: "He says he just let a heavy-armed patrol pass and they might come up behind him if he carries out the demonstration."

Paul listened with the most intense curiosity, thinking that these were men he knew—Ollie, the gunny, Hippo the blackest of the black.

To the handset Mac said in his "roll on" voice, rumbling and perfectly calm amid danger to somebody else: "Stand by for my mark." To the exec: "Are you ready?"

"Yes sir," said Jake, whose own handset was half raised.

Mac lifted his watch and, with his eyes on it, said, "Stand by—mark."

And Jake said, "Mark."

"Execute in two minutes," said Mac to Ollie. And to Jake: "Execute in three minutes."

Paul was piecing this together as the start of the demonstration and the "wounded bird" when the exec said in a normal voice:

"Saddle up."

Paul asked: "Where are we going?"

And Jake said: "To Slope City."

So now Paul would see the fortified position of the "slopes"; he would see what Mac had seen, and he did not know what that would be.

The Main Body crawled ponderously toward Slope City and the rain pounded deafeningly down, and it seemed to Paul that a normal mind would not function in a place like this.

When the demonstration started, his guts leapt inside him, it sounded so close. He'd thought of Ollie as being a mile away. But he couldn't be more than two hundred meters, and the noise was that piercing kind that you hear when weapons are aimed in your direction. The grenades and the machine gun commenced a hacking, tubercular coughing in quick wild rips. The M16's began chopping—and at length the enemy responded but meekly, with only three or four weapons so far as Paul could tell.

The white-gray face in the hollow of the poncho had turned red and puffy, and the man seemed to be talking to himself in slurred syllables, and waving his arms weakly. He disturbed the dressings on his chest and shoulder, which were disintegrating in the rain anyway, and suddenly Paul thought: "He's in trouble!"

Explain that in your letter of condolence. "Your son died of cold in one of the hottest countries on the globe." Paul shouted: "Corpsman up!"

They broke into the open, beside a huge shallow crater from whose rim the bodies had been removed but all around to a distance of fifty meters lay arms and legs and bodies, or rather trunks—it seemed to Paul there were many feet—and charred shreds of clothing, a scalp—his eyes refused further duty.

Forward a few men began shouting. There were bearers and wounded up there, where none had been before, and thus the wounded bird began its charade. Men yodeled and one man screamed "I want my mommie!" and another cried "Wha cha gonna do when the well runs dry?"—"We're traveling through the jungle on the Wabash Cannonball."—"Congressman, can they make me do this?"

Everybody staggered on and Paul, having shut out the crater, not daring to look beyond it to his left toward Slope City, just struggled along staring at the cold man—his face was losing its color—saw the shuddering jaw, and said, "It's O.K."

The enemy opened up from the left and people pitched to the ground. A wounded man who had been dropped howled, but not the cold man. Paul hugged the muck. A hideous energy stream cut through the rain above him and he thought: "Death."

A sergeant came trotting along hollering: "Move, move!"

Men lurched to their feet and bent double and began to run, including the bearers, bouncing the wounded unmercifully. Paul looked left and saw rounded black humps—the lips of craters, stick trees and fallen trunks, and charred branches lying in profusion all across a burnt landscape, but he saw no soldiers or muzzle flashes. Then he discerned a hump with a firing slit and a flash in the shadow. The fire increased.

In front a man fell; another ran past him; it was Dan Shaw. The platoon halted and in response to a shout the men faced left and flopped down and began firing prone, and Dan Shaw shouted for LAWs and bloopers.

The exec cried from somewhere ahead, "Wheel!" and Paul saw him running back down the line shouting, "Maintain your interval," and slapping men on their packs, and looking ahead, Paul saw 1st Platoon disappearing—walking at a measured pace, wheeling left into Slope City.

"What is it?" asked Henry Bartholomew, crouching.

Paul had no recollection of summoning a corpsman but pointed automatically to the cold man.

Henry bent forward and said: "Hey, marine, how are you feeling?"

The man was shivering violently. "Cold—my God—wrong—" His syllables lost distinction, his voice lost timbre; his eyes were fixed on Henry but his head trembled. He said, "Wet—Christ—"

In the seminary Paul's young imagination, heated by his most intense passion and by prolonged continence, had fantasized a centurion of the Roman Empire trying to extract from him, by torture, a denial of his Savior.

The Roman was armored, sweaty, muscular, and merciless. He squeezed Paul's testicles and rammed a glowing poker into his body.

"I could endure that—long enough to deserve my martyrdom."

That was a torture he could understand. An empire seeking to protect its dying gods from the new, true God. But this—

He looked around him at the tortured forest, at the men of 2nd Platoon crawling through the black muck toward Slope City, at the shivering marine in the poncho—

Dan Shaw came running along the line shouting: "Nothing right! Second Platoon! Nothing right."

Mac realized he was wrong to adopt the gunny's nickname for his adversary, the "Little Rooster."

He pictured the man striding among his exploded bunkers as the gunny had described him, in shorts and sandals, with the rain flying off his bare shoulders—and imagined him returning to his command bunker, where his cowboy would have a C4 fire going and a can of hot tea ready—and he saw the man strip and wipe himself with an old gray towel, put on his khakis, and squat at the firing port, and survey his situation with intelligent patient eyes, as he drank his tea.

He would see the upheaved earth and twisted trees; the conscript porters bringing ammo on their backs; the coolies burying what remained of men he needed. He would see his supply dump half destroyed but also half surviving. He would assess his losses in men and matériel, and he would plan the rebuilding of his defenses. Or—plan an attack. Mac decided to call him "the Major."

Given one antiaircraft gun, Major Pham could have brought down the dragon ship—one gun, six men—and this loss would never have occurred.

Major Pham had recommended, then requested, then pleaded, and then demanded. He had threatened to resign his commission and serve in the ranks. The colonel only told him to do his best with what he had. The major resumed his demands and persisted and began to shout, and the colonel admonished him that flying spit did not win arguments or obtain unavailable equipment and weapons. The colonel finally said, in English: "Shut up." He had an English vocabulary that stretched all the way from "shut up" to "bullshit."

So now Major Pham had the satisfaction of a man who can see how right he was, and the consequences of his superior's stupidity. Staring from his bunker, he sent his embittered gaze over the proof: suffering, smoke, and cinders.

The major had taken two blows. First the artillery forward observer was burned alive—a promising young lieutenant whom he treated virtually as a son; then this incendiary attack on his depot, a strike at the very locus of his ambitions. He was to have been the quartermaster who delivered all that was needed to destroy the 2nd ARVN Division in the spring. In Quang Ngai if anywhere, the people would rise up and throw off the bourgeois collaborators, and the major would be advanced to colonel and given a post in the new government. With a little luck—as soon as the revolutionary government took over the city—he would avenge himself on a certain family who had fled south in 1954 from his home province in the North.

Thinking of these people he seethed with fury. He saw them as they had appeared thirteen years ago—young, successful, and disloyal. He knew they were in Quang Ngai; he knew what he would do when he found them.

And besides the two misfortunes, any idiot could predict the next blow. Having plotted the secondary explosions of last night's disaster on their maps, the Americans, as soon as the skies cleared, would launch one of their air armadas heavy with 1,000-pound bombs, with mixed quick and delay fuzes, to complete the destruction of the major's depot and his forces.

But the major was preparing a surprise for the big noses. He was already resupplying ammo and augmenting his troop roster with a Trail company and a company of Local Force VC stiffened by an infusion of noncommissioned officers from the NVA garrison upcountry. He had already deactivated three of his decimated companies in order to reconstitute two new ones; and he would soon command a force approximating a battalion—perhaps as early as noon. He checked his watch: soon, quite soon.

The major intended to attack the round-eyes as soon as his big mortars and ammo arrived. He wouldn't wait for all the replacement troops. Strike! They thought he was finished. Strike! The only question was whether to feed the troops first or to seize the earliest opportunity—to march when he had the mortars.

He had given his orders. The laborers were burying the dead, the medics were saving the most promising of the wounded, and the NCOs were supervising battle preparations. He anticipated a one-day engagement but could sustain the fight for two if the sky remained sealed. If it opened, he would have no recourse but to hide in the canopy and husband his resources.

There was one other thing on his mind. He had to do it! Before another hour passed! It was a debt he owed to men who could very well die today—five or six such men. His mind was not altogether clear as to who they were, owing to his customary lapse of perception at certain critical moments. He believed there were six of them. It was essential to find them—but he could not recall their faces. He concentrated on associated memories—places, the rain, the smoke. But it had been so intense, too blinding, too mad. Of course the major was not insane but in every man there is a spirit of madness that is either suppressed utterly, resulting in torpidity and predictability, or else it is harbored, even nurtured, certainly not disowned. It is a source of energy and fire. Do not try to extinguish it.

In imagination he saw spurting blood, then he could see the face and remember where the thing had happened. Yes, the man was on the burial crew; the major knew exactly where. He went there and saw him, recognized him by the purple mark of the blow to the face.

Seeing the major coming toward him with his swagger stick swinging from the cord around his right wrist, the man shrank away, holding up a hand to ward off another blow. The major ordered him to stand, and the man obeyed, the fear in his eyes turning to hate. They faced each other.

"I was wrong," said Major Pham, and he felt as if he spoke uphill, to a man standing higher than he. "I had no right. I am ashamed before you. Now you have the right to hit me. Do it, hit me."

Slowly the man comprehended, slowly he arrived at the appropriate attitude. He said in halting, humble tones: "Do not be ashamed. We have lost so many of our comrades, we need a strong commander."

"You have the right to strike me with this stick," Major Pham persisted, half in a frenzy. He slid the leather thong over his hand and offered the stick.

"No, Major."

In a solemn voice the major said, "I respect you."

He passed his hand again through the loop and walked off in search of another of the six, and as he walked, the swagger stick whirled in a circle around his hand and made a whistling sound.

To the next man, after offering himself for chastisement, the major confessed: "I have been a man of violence for too long. But I will kill the Americans."

"Good," the second man said. "So will I."

Major Pham tramped off amid the chaos of his smoking depot, thinking: "I will be a man of violence still, but not of cruelty. I will control my rage." He feared his own emotions. He himself was their chief victim.

When the American attack began on his southern flank he knew immediately it was a demonstration, but he also knew they intended to bring the battle to him. Too soon! He thought of his replacement troops, his mortars. He began running and shouting orders. A grenade exploded and red-hot fragments pierced his leg and side, but he experienced the impacts without fear. Running, organizing, he screamed, but not with pain.

He saw some men tumbling into a crater and huddling there, cowering. The major slid down the side into the water at the bottom, wading, laying about him with his stick, calling them cowards and leeches, smiting them on their heads and on the pitiful hands that sought to protect their skulls. He was blind, he was enraged, he hated their cowardice. He drove them out and harried them as they stumbled to their positions in the defensive line.

Mac halted the demonstration. He raised Kim Kolias and Dan Shaw. Both were ready.

"O.K.," said Mac, "attack by fire. Do not advance."

Thus began a drum-tearing storm of fire from the two platoons.

If the major's position was circular, then 1st and 2nd Platoons were pouring fire into the top-right quadrant. The demonstration fire had been aimed into the bottom center at about 6 o'clock. And Ollie and the gunny should now be moving right, to come up the edge of the circle to where Mac had set up his CP, at 2 o'clock.

The command group including the wounded lay behind 2nd Platoon; the reserve, 3rd, was deployed defensively behind the wounded.

Mac took the handset and said: "Striker One and Two, this is Six."

Both lieutenants rogered and Mac said: "One, hold your position and cease fire. Two, advance on your objective."

The snapping shots on the right from Kim Kolias's 1st Platoon ceased at a stroke—very satisfying to Mac—and the men of Dan Shaw's 2nd rose and began walking forward, firing, flinging grenades ahead, and rushing craters. The enemy's big gun that Hitchcock had seen suddenly opened up and Mac saw three men fall, and all dived for cover.

Mac couldn't catch Dan Shaw's shouted words but the shouts were cool—Dan Shaw was in command not only of his troops but himself.

A LAW whooshed. Dan Shaw shouted again—Mac could not see him—and the men began to advance by bounds. But the return fire was intense and two more marines fell.

A soft whump, a sound that seemed to pound the earth, struck Mac's ear from the left, then again and again, and soon Delta's 60-millimeter mortars had heaved six rounds into the air, and the bursts blew up ahead of Dan Shaw's men as they advanced inexorably.

Then a new firefight broke out about a hundred meters to Mac's left. He could not see any troops down there but the firing was hot. Looking around, Mac happened to see Doc Bartholomew and the chaplain working over a wounded marine. They were spreading a poncho and letting it settle on him.

Hippo-I'm-Great-In-Dayton called. "I supposed to tell you we cut off. They between us and you. Can you hit the gooks in the rear?"

Mac hesitated. To win you go up; and from there the people down below may look small. Mac understood this but had never before experienced it.

He said: "How's your ammo?" and Hippo said it was O.K.

Mac surmised that Ollie had run into the patrol he let pass ten minutes before. The patrol must have turned around when it heard the demonstration fires.

Mac said: "Break on through." To say this is different from hearing it said to you.

Hippo said nothing for ten or twenty seconds, then: "They right in front of us."

The enemy's big 12.7-millimeter resumed its thudding fire and slugs and green tracers skimmed over Mac's head.

He repeated calmly: "I said break on through."

"Roger that," Hippo murmured, disconsolate.

Mac said to his runner: "Tell Doc Bartholomew to go forward with his platoon."

The runner took off and Mac raised Kim Kolias: "Form a skirmish line right of Striker Two and advance with him."

There was a new source of firing off to the right suddenly. Kim Kolias yelled into the radio:

"I'm under attack from the rear."

Mac thought: "What?" He told Kolias to turn and defend himself and he stood to his full height and searched for Graves Registration. He hollered for him and strode back through the wounded and saw that Doc Bartholomew was still there. He shouted for Graves Registration—and then after a moment Graves came up and Mac told him to get ready to move to the relief of 1st Platoon.

Said Mac: "Be alert for my signal. Go in on the enemy left and pour it into him. Careful. Nothing left."

Graves Registration nodded his large and hairy head; Mac's eyes settled for a second on the man's big red hands. Graves returned unhurriedly to his line and Mac, passing through the little circle of WIAs again, saw the doc crouched over a man. The rage flooded Mac's chest but he had no time to push the doc to his duty.

"We're moving," he called and led the command group forward ten paces to where he could crouch in a crater and peer over its rim. Mac was now in the kill zone of the wheel movement and it was strewn with bodies.

Captain Kindred said: "What can I do?"

"Just stick with me a while," said Mac. "Makes me feel powerful to have an air liaison officer."

Kindred sat on the slope and folded his arms and looked around, laughing. He proposed: "I could scope out your right flank."

"Good idea. O.K. the big EEI is, how many gooks against Kim? Go with Graves Registration."

Mac rose and looked back. A rocket-propelled grenade that had sailed harmlessly over 2nd Platoon on the attacking front skimmed over Mac and detonated in the air between him and the WIAs. Mac didn't wince or even blink. He shouted, and Graves Registration popped up like a rabbit out of a hat. Mac gave an arm signal. Captain Kindred and his radioman sprinted out of the crater. At the same moment the men of 3rd rose out of the scarred earth and followed Staff Sergeant Graves. He began trotting toward the right flank. A recoilless rifle flashed out and streamed fire over Mac's head and landed at the place Mac had just vacated.

"Pickens Freeman!" Mac shouted.

"Here sir!" Freeman came splashing toward Mac with his long limbs flopping in the muck.

"Tell the doc to join his platoon."

"Already tole him," Freeman protested.

"Tell him again," said Mac evenly.

Freeman slid over the rear rim and was on his way running zigzag, leaping over downed trees and the bodies of NVA, losing his helmet. Mac saw it bounce and roll.

Crouching again he separated the noise of Ollie's fight from the rest. Ollie was making very heavy use of his machine gun and Mac feared he'd damage the barrel. Mac couldn't afford to lose that M60. There was a cluster of grenade booms under the machine-gun music, and Mac believed both sides were throwing. This was a chilling surmise, meaning they were too close to fire the 40-millimeter grenades from the bloopers.

The exec landed heavily at Mac's side.

"So how are you, Jake?" asked Mac cordially.

"Good, good."

"Alive, I see."

"Yes sir."

"Good job on that wheel, Jake."

"Thank you, sir."

"O.K. here it is. Ollie is blocked. I've told him to break through. First is getting hit from behind and can't join Second in the advance. Third is moving in to take the pressure off First. Kindred is out with Third to tell me what's happening, if he can figure it out."

Jake's eyes were ablaze but not with fear. He cried: "I can take the pressure off Ollie. Give me a squad."

"Damn it, Jake," Mac said laughing, "you weren't listening. I haven't got a squad. I haven't even got a fire team."

From the left Mac heard short bursts of M16 fire—and nothing in response from the enemy.

Pickens Freeman, an Ichabod Crane from South Carolina, flopped his limbs into the crater. "Sir, the doc's looking at the ape. I done tole him twice and he just eyeballs the ape."

"There are wounded men from his platoon lying in front of us."

"Yes sir, Ah know and Ah tole him."

"O.K. Pick. Lie low."

"They're quiet on the left," Jake observed with interest.

Mac nodded and said, "Let's go." He rose, his head exceeding the height of the rim, ran up the slope and over into the open, and dodged forward ten or twenty yards and flopped by a downed marine. His men dropped in around him and he told Jake to check the marine.

Jake rolled the body over. It did not look promising. Mac saw Jake's fingers sink into the man's neck, then turned to Graeser, who was holding out the handset.

"Hey, Six!" cried Ollie in triumph. "We are with the doc and chaplain. We fuckin made it!"

"Damn your no-good ass, Ollie!"

"Yeah yeah. Nobody got a scratch. This friggin Hippo's a maniac!"

"O.K., Ollie," said Mac, breaking for a second time the rule against using names on the air. "Keep your troops there and guard the wounded. Send Doc Bartholomew forward. And tell the gunny I want him here."

"Roger, Six," said Ollie and his elation still lifted his voice.

"Puke!" cried Pickens Freeman and let go a burst from his rifle. Slugs thudded into the mud six feet from Mac and Graeser.

The exec cried out, startled and angry, and the big Ichabod explained:

"A rat, sir, big as a cat!"

"I didn't see any rat," cried Jake. "Watch your damned fire."

"Yeah, well sir, I missed im. Sorry bout that." But he let out a huge laugh. He ejected his magazine and refilled it from single rounds that he took in handfuls from his cargo pockets.

A loony thought crossed Mac's mind, to tell Pickens Freeman to stick his head up and scope out the terrain. Instead he said: "CSMO. Pickens, you lay down a base of fire. Everybody else follow me."

Mac leaped up and ran forward, scouting the humps, holes, and runnels for a good place. He dived into the biggest crater he'd ever seen, a depression on the scale of a 2,000-pound bomb hole. Pickens Freeman's fire had chopped to his left and right, and now ceased. Mac and Graeser laid down fire for the Ichabod Crane of South Carolina and he came flying in like a ballplayer sliding, splattering mud and water over everybody and hollering:

"Whoopee!"

"Pick," said Graeser, who seldom spoke except on the radio, "I'd call you an animal but animals have brains."

"Ha ha ha," Pick chuckled and rammed in a new magazine.

In this run Mac had seen Dan Shaw's men prone on the slopes of two more deep craters, and beyond these he had seen another crater of equal size. A new thought occurred: that nobody in a hundred-meter radius could have survived the big secondaries and fires. Did this mean that the major had come here this morning from somewhere else? If so, was he much stronger than Mac had assumed?

"O.K., O.K., reassess," he thought, almost with joy. This fact or guess, which should have shaken his bones in their bag, thrilled him instead. He had told himself to reassess but forgot to do so. He called Kindred: "Hey, Kinny, what can you tell me?"

"Nothing yet, Six. We're all alone out here. We're looking for the flank but I think we're too far right."

"Striker Three, are you listening?"

"Affirmative," said Graves Registration.

"I think our friends from up north might have another base between here and Ambush Alley. Pull in a little to your left. Link up with One. Watch for another defense perimeter. In other words, Three, watch your step."

Somewhere nearby a marine called for a corpsman. The voice was stretched as taut as a wire. The cacophony from the right (1st Platoon) was quite fierce. Mac distinguished Kim Kolias's machine guns, but, on the enemy side, nothing like a big 12.7 mike-mike and no recoilless rifles.

"One, this is Six. How's it going?"

The radioman of 1st Platoon responded: "We're taking casualties. We're in jungle and can't see the gooks."

"Have you completed your turn?"

"What turn?"

"Are you now facing the enemy?" Mac asked with perfect calm.

"That's affirmative but we're pinned down."

"Tell One Actual that Three is coming in on his right flank. Do not fire at targets you can't see."

"Roger."

"Tell him."

"I will."

To Graves Registration, Mac said: "Are you in open terrain or jungle?"

"Open, burned out."

"One is in jungle," said Mac. He gave Three a bearing and said: "Try that for about a hundred more meters."

Mac thought: "I can't control this." But this realization left him as calm as before.

He did a three-sixty scan and saw two marines wrestling. In this hellscape you might see anything. They moved closer, oblivious of the enemy's bullets and grenades, and now it seemed that one, the stronger, was dragging and pushing the other and catching him if he tried to break loose. Mac figured it out.

"Get in there!" Gunnery Sergeant Hitchcock snarled, and pushed Doc Bartholomew so hard he careened down the crater slope on his chest and landed in a wave of muck at the bottom.

The gunny grabbed him by the arm holes of his flak jacket and lifted him and said to his face, but speaking to Mac: "Bartholomew, HM Three, U.S. Navy, reporting for duty, sir."

Bartholomew's head hung. No one could see his eyes and he was panting. Everything about him from his helmet to his trousers trembled.

A blast, sharp and huge, rolled over the rumpled landscape and through the denuded trees. It came from behind the old pivot point. Then another and another, to a total of a dozen. The men in the command group looked at one another as if the phone had rung and each was saying to the rest: "Are you going to get it?"

Mac said into his handset: "Kinny, what's going on?"

"Don't know, Skipper. They were close but not too close. Off to our right."

There came another series, deep-throated and majestic.

Said Captain Kindred: "Those hit up the hill a ways. They're on a line. The line runs—I'd say—across—"

"They're eighty-twos," said Mac quickly. "Blocking fires or channeling fires."

"Hey," Kindred protested, "you're talking to an aviator."

"Blocking fires to keep us where we are," Mac explained. "Channeling fires to allow us to move, if we insist on moving, along a predetermined path."

"Oh boy," Kindred replied.

"Kinny, I need to know everything you see, hear, or smell."

"Right now I smell trouble. That's a big boomer."

"Tell Graves Registration to carry on.—Break.—Striker One, Striker Six, over."

"This is One."

"Let me speak to your Actual."

In the interval, Mac noticed that Hitchcock was watching him with an unrelenting eye.

"This is Striker One Actual," said Kim Kolias in the voice of the inexperienced officer at the LP.

"Listen," said Mac, gentling a little. "They are trying to block us. Link up with Striker Three."

"I'm trying. I can't move."

"You have to move. Press to your right. Link up, man, link up."

Mac leaned a little forward, passing the handset to Graeser, and placed a hand on Doc Bartholomew's shoulder. Mac could feel the stiff, curved flak jacket and the tremors beneath.

"Do you hear that man?" he asked. The cry of "Corpsman" had recurred at just that moment.

Mac said: "You'd better go help him."

Henry Bartholomew rose to full height. His face was gray as a dead man's and his eyes dull. He began climbing, slipping to his knees. He topped the rim, looked around blankly, listened, and walked away amid the zipping and whining of the small arms and booming of grenades.

Chapter 12

Mac versus the Major

"O.K. Guns, listen, listen." Mac heard the repetition. Who cares! He was flying too high and knew it. Don't come down! He hadn't made a mistake yet. Win this thing! He was sleep-deprived, hungry, half-blind with fatigue, and when he picked up a grease pencil he couldn't feel it between his numb fingers. He never said, "Careful, go slow," and he never came down.

The gunny fixed his eager eyes on Mac. The gunny was flying too. "I hope you got it figured out."

"I don't, but you can help."

"Yeah yeah."

"Take the Greek, the sailor, and Hippo. Takes lots of ammo. Leave your packs with the wounded."

"Hot damn, no packs." The gunny thought: "We can slither like snakes, fast snakes." He didn't notice how odd this was.

"I have to know what's happening up on the slope between that firefight," and Mac gestured toward 1st Platoon, "and Ambush Alley. This stretch here." And he marked the hillside on the acetate cover of the gunny's map.

"Activity," the gunny recited, "installations, fortified positions, caches, roads and trails, troops movements, a regular VR."

"Yes. Because here's what I think."

Mac was cut off by another set of blocking fires roaring out of the enemy's mortars. He waited, and he and Hitchcock locked eyes.

Mac continued: "I think the major's getting greedy."

"What major?"

"The rooster."

"Oh, him! The fucker's crazier than Hippo."

"I think he's jacking himself up from one mission to two. He came here to protect the caches and now he's trying to bait a trap for Battalion."

"We're the bait."

"So I need to know, has he got a reserve up there? The demonstration and that wounded-bird routine—I was hoping to pull a chase platoon out of his defense, and at first I thought it worked. Now I don't know. The unit that's hitting First Platoon might have come down from Ambush Alley. I need to know if he's got another base up there."

"You'll know in fifteen minutes, sir."

"Don't be a hero. I need you more than I need answers."

"Hero? Me? Har-dee-har-har.—Valas! Sailor! Hippo-I'm-A-Dork-In-New-York! Saddle up, you marines, we're going for a walk in the sun. Full ammo, no packs. Hustle, you fuckin turtles."

"Wait," said Mac taking him by the arm, which he had never done before. "Think about this. He's firing two or three dozen rounds of eighty-two into the bush. We are here and he knows it, but he's firing these blocking fires. He could be dumping that stuff on us. Think about it."

The two men seemed to search for the answer in each other's eyes.

Said the gunny: "He's fat with ammo, that's for sure."

"Yes, or he wants us to think he is."

"Would he spend his ammo just to fuck up your brain?"

"I don't know," said Mac. "Think about it."

Mac looked at each man—didn't smile—nodded to Hitchcock—and the team was over and gone.

Mac thought: "He thinks he could blow us to hell in ten minutes but he doesn't want to do that. He wants to prolong this till the weather improves enough to allow Battalion to pile in. Then he springs it. He must have—Christ, he's got huge reserves or he's expecting a regiment to come marching down 5B to augment his force. But Major, if you can knock us off, you better do it now. By God, you better do it!"

Mac slapped a fist into a hand—and men looked at him but he didn't know it. He was in his own brain. The world out there seemed unreal, like a huge game where only death counts.

"Or—or he's all cut to ribbons—and has zero reserve and no reinforcements, he's been told he's on his own—for days—he's, yes, trying to 'fuck up my mind,' thanks, Guns. I'm deep into his perimeter. By God! And I've never seen anything like this."

The sky, air, rain, and muck all the same color; actually no color; the trees that still stood offered the only contrast, black on gray, with a little sprinkle of blood that you'd kick up sometimes walking, and limbs, bones.

"As soon as I can pull One and Three down here—" His mind jumped ahead of his language until he said: "Right. Right. Continue the attack on what he has to defend. Sun Tzu. Go for his nuts."

He heard firing from a new quarter and said to Graeser: "Is Three in contact?"

Graeser talked as Mac brought out his map again, then Graeser said:

"Sir, Three is in contact with the enemy and can't find First Platoon. He says what should he do."

"Fix and destroy," said Mac without hesitation.

"Fix and destroy," Graeser repeated with evident satisfaction.

"O.K., Graeser, I want a green flare from One and a red from Three. I'll give you a mark."

When this had been arranged two flares shot up, streaming colored light, smoke, and white steam as they rose in the pale sky; and Mac thought: "What's going on?" Neither flare was where it should be.

Taking the handset he said, "Three, this is Six. Do you see One's flare?"

"That's affirmative."

"Move toward it when you can but first kill NVA so they don't swing around and hit your rear."

"Roger, Six."

The fight noise reached Mac once again through the radio and the air as if he were listening to a radio drama in which he was playing a role. For a moment he could not distinguish the three fights—all blended into the metallic drumming of the rain on his helmet and the rush of wind around his ears.

Neither Kim Kolias of 1st Platoon nor Graves Registration of 3rd had gone where Mac thought he had sent him. If Mac was high, which he was, it was the illusion of control.

"Those flares—how did they get there? Think, plan, deploy, ha!"

He crawled up the edge and looked toward the center of the objective, across the wreckage of earthen structures now reduced to their original atoms, with splintered and burned timbers flung as if weightless here and there, and he thought:

"No. It's going well. Dan Shaw's advancing."

He saw a marine rise out of a depression and dash forward, dive, and cautiously raise his head. A screen of fire burned the air near him and two more advanced, and Mac thought: "We'll hit his command bunker in a few minutes."

He got on the radio to Dan Shaw. "Two, this is Six, over."

"This is Two, go." It was Dan Shaw himself.

"Straighten your line. Hasty defense. Report in five minutes."

"Roger, Six. Thanks."

"One, this is Six, over."

"This is One, go."

"Listen Kim, fall back into the beaten zone if you can find some good cover. You've got to link up."

"Roger," said Kim Kolias.

"Three, this is Six. Did you monitor?"

"Affirmative. I've got these monkeys howling."

"Good. Watch for One. When you see him, break contact and link up."

Mac gave the handset to Graeser and noticed the man's look—he was watching Mac as a dog watches its master. As soon as this thought flashed through his mind Mac recoiled from it almost in fear. He said by way of compensation: "Graeser, I'm buying you a beer when we get back."

"Hey, roger that, Skipper."

An explosion, a big secondary, lifted a portion of the earth whose edge lay under Mac's knees, and the crater rose and subsided hastily into its original shape. Fragments of earth, trees, trash, and bodies splattered in the puddle and Mac heard the buzzing in his ears, and knew that henceforth, for hours or maybe days, all of reality would reach him through a filter. He would understand words, but all words and sounds would be inflected by an intruder in his brain. The ringing made it harder to distinguish what was going on inside from events in the world. A brain that rings like this is not your own familiar one. Even his sight was affected. When he looked out toward the secondary explosion, debris was still falling but he imagined it was also rising in a cloud of vapor and dirt.

"Two, this is Six. Congratulations on that secondary. Report when you can."

Then a pregnant silence fell on the men and the crater where Mac squatted with the command group. Mac recalled that he had told Three to fix and destroy the enemy, and five minutes later to break contact if necessary to link up with One. This switch seemed to be all right. Perhaps it was, perhaps it was not; it didn't disturb him.

"Sir, here's Two," Graeser said, passing the handset.

"Hey, Six," cried Dan Shaw. "Sitrep follows. Balls in my belly. Otherwise all secure. Everybody's stunned but not as stunned as the gooks. Our line's pretty straight and we're in defense till further orders." He pronounced it *de*fense like the Tennessee football player he was.

"Hey Two, damn your ass!" Mac exclaimed.

"Roger that," said Dan Shaw irrationally. "One a my guys put a LAW right through the mail slot. I'm lookin for the command bunker but ain't found it yet. Can you pick up my WIAs?"

"I'm working on that," said Mac, who had been listening with an edge of pain in his attention to the men crying for help.

"Six, this is One, over." It was Kim Kolias, sounding excited. "We've linked up!"

"Good job," Mac said. "Now fix and destroy.—Break.—Three, did you monitor?"

"Sure did," said Graves Registration, and the reverberations in his barrel chest carried across the air waves. "Find, fix, and destroy. Rape, pillage, and plunder."

"Slow, careful, but unstoppable," said Mac. "Do not go beyond Ambush Alley." Turning to the exec beside him Mac said: "Bring up Ollie's squad and the wounded. We've advanced too far. I want Ollie and that gun right here and we'll set up a new aid station. This'll be our CP for a while." Mac saw some uncertainty in Jake's eyes and said: "This is our CP, this crater."

"Yes sir."

"Ollie's got the demonstration squad and a gun and I think two bloopers. Pretty good security, right?"

"Yes sir."

"O.K. Order him up here. When he gets here send some men out to help Doc Bartholomew drag in wounded."

"Uh—where are you going to be?" Jake asked, and Mac thought he saw the famous "dread of command."

"I'm going to get Dan Shaw set for a counterattack, then I'll be back. Five minutes."

"Counterattack, sir?"

"Yes, Jake. I think that's what those blocking fires are telling us."

Jake looked like a man who has just been mugged.

"Ready, Freeman?" Mac asked.

"Ready for what?" asked the Ichabod Crane of the Southland even as he unfolded his spidery legs for traction.

"A walk in the sun," said Mac.

"Yes sir!" Freeman popped his eyes and showed his big white teeth in something akin to a smile. The red in his skin all but covered his freckles.

Mac told Graeser to stay with Jake. Then he tilted his head a little toward the forward rim, smiled at Freeman, and sprang. The two men crossed the rim together and twenty rifles sought their lives.

"Shit fire and save the matches!" Pickens Freeman bellowed—actually "shit *far*"—and he flopped down beside Lieutenant Dan Shaw.

"Freeman, what the hell!" cried the lieutenant.

"Me'n the skipper," Freeman panted. "Just out for a thrill. Ain't no demolition derby round here, so we just showed ourselves to the gooks—and the bastards!—not very friendly! Darn near—"

"Where's the skipper?" cried Dan Shaw, shaking him.

"Comin, Lieutenant. For crap sakes, you don't have to beat me. It's against Marine Corps regulations, I believe, corporal punishment of an enlisted man by an officer. He's on down the line there. You'll see him."

The big machine gun sent shock waves over their heads and Freeman was impressed.

Dan lifted his head gingerly and saw Mac crouched beside one of his troopers four or five spaces down. They were talking and Mac was gesturing to the front. Mac made his way space by space and man by man toward Dan Shaw and soon hit the deck beside him.

"What's that?" Freeman kept saying. "That's a big pig. That's a big pig."

Lying prone, the officers conversed while Freeman kept watch.

"Danny, you see how I've moved your line on an angle, a little forward?"

"Yes sir." Dan Shaw was not pleased at this intervention.

"Sorry, but I wanted to show you. Dress it up on the left with the same angle and interval, please."

"Aye aye sir."

"You see what he's doing," said Mac. "He's recalibrating his blocking fires, stepping those rounds between us and the other two platoons."

Both men watched the bursts coughing across the dead ground behind the crater CP. The bursts formed a ragged barrier between 2nd Platoon and the crater on one side, and 1st and 3rd Platoons on the other.

Dan Shaw shouted: "That's pretty good shootin, if I do say so myself." His helmet and shoulders were draining mud and ashes as the rain washed away the fallout. "My ears!" Dan shouted.

Mac yelled, "Can you understand me?"

"Yes sir. Just yell like hell."

"Counterattack," Mac yelled.

"You want me to—huh? Holy shit!"

"No, dammit. Dan, the enemy is going to counterattack."

Behind them the thud of mortar projectiles continued in two-syllable exclamations, crump-*bam*. The rounds were hopping down a line to separate one segment of Delta from the other, but their timing seemed to be random.

Dan's eyes flicked left and right along his defense line and he shouted, "Can you fellas hear me?" There were some scattered replies and Dan yelled:

"Stand by for a swarm of screaming gooks. Sector fire on my command. Fix bayonets." Turning to Mac he hollered: "I'll correct that line, Skipper."

"Bye, Danny. More for the Corps," said Mac, banging him on the helmet. "Freeman! Off your ass!"

Mac and Freeman rose—and the rifles of the enemy coughed in furious surprise. This time the marines laid down a cover fire that shut up every enemy gun except the big "Back to Bataan" monster the gunny had glimpsed. This was, Mac surmised, a Soviet 12.7-millimeter dual-purpose machine gun.

"The fool's hah," Freeman exulted, meaning "high."

In the midst of his dash Mac remembered his rifle was mucked up. Ninety seconds later he was crouched in the crater CP, no Holiday Inn, cleaning the rifle and watching the demonstration squad, the wounded and their bearers, and Chaplain Paul Adrano taking cover behind the rear rim. If a mortar round landed in the crater these would survive while the command group perished.

Mac passed the brass brush through the bore of his MI6 and said suddenly, looking up, "Get him, Freeman."

Pickens Freeman jumped up and fired off a quick burst, plopped down, and said, "By Jesus, got the poor little fella."

The heavy mortars crept closer but Mac doubted their observer had located him. He said belatedly to Graeser: "Keep that antenna flat."

This reminded Mac to report to Battalion. First he raised Captain Kindred at 3rd Platoon and asked for his observations.

"I think we've been tangling assholes with a platoon, nothing bigger," Kindred reported. "Where they came from I have no idea but I know where they went. Man, they went down."

"O.K., Kinny, will you make my ten hundred report to Battalion? Just say 'engaging enemy' and give the coordinates in the clear and say 'sitrep to follow at twelve hundred.' Got it?"

"Sure, and tell the bastards to leave us alone. I tell you, Mac, I think we're going to be O.K. on this flank and I think the rear's just fine. I mean it. He thinks he split us and I think we split him."

"I hope you're right. Will you be my deputy up there?"

"Sure, boss," said the aviator.

"Do as much damage as you can and then break clear. Establish a rear guard and move down the slope to join me. Can you find me?"

"We'll find you," a different voice intervened; it was Graves Registration.

"O.K.," Mac continued. "Keep One and Three together at all costs. Advance on us but don't fire—I mean no unaimed fire. There are marines all over the place down here, both effectives and WIAs. Form up behind us and cover down on Second. Got it?"

"Not exactly," said Kindred.

"We got it, Skipper," said Graves Registration. Like most staff NCOs he was adept at handling officers.

"I guess we got it," Kindred assented. "I'll ask Graves Registration what to do and then I'll fuckin order him to do it."

"Excellent system," said Mac. "Break.—One, this is Six, did you monitor?"

"That's affirmative. Gold Wings in tactical command up here. We kill these gooks and drop down behind you, and fall in behind Second."

"Go," said Mac.

A horrific blast shook him to the eyeballs and he froze physically, then breathed deep, his mind hyperalert. Ringing ringing ringing. He touched his jaw and cheekbones, to place himself. It all came back: who he was, and where. Then he concentrated on hearing and sight. He paused, and breathed, and looked at the men around him. He crawled up to the rim and peered over.

"You guys O.K.?" he asked.

Paul Adrano looked up. He held the ends of a nylon line. He jerked it tight and it creased the flesh of a man with a bare bleeding arm. Adrano said: "We're O.K. here. How are you?" Mac slid back into the hole. Taking the handset he called Dan Shaw of 2nd Platoon: "Danny, I think you better get ready."

"Here they come!" Dan Shaw cried and Mac heard him shouting to his men: the defense line erupted. Rifles, machine guns, bloopers, LAWs, and light mortars set up a death screen, and the NVA flung themselves into it.

Mac said coolly to Captain Kindred: "Show's starting. Break off, Kinny, break off. Come on down."

When Doc Bartholomew had left the command group in Mac's crater he slouched around aimlessly looking for the man who had ceased calling. Every step you take in an upright posture is a step toward death. Death is not to be feared. If he could find the man he would perhaps learn if this were true. A man staring it in the face (it must have a face, which is why the ancients said "the angel of death")—a man staring at it would perhaps show fear or the lack of fear. And the doc could learn from this. Learn what? And what's the point now?

What Henry Bartholomew saw, in his stumbling around, could not be explained. Everybody wanted the Big Explanation, but if you took one glance you'd see there is no explanation. So get used to it.

Doc Bartholomew saw a man in the mud and dropped to his knees beside him.

"Doc! I—no!—no!" Complete with gasps and bubbles.

"You're O.K. Quit yelling, will you?" said the doc, asking himself why we always lie to the dying.

He did a fast head-to-toe and felt the pulse and saw it was pointless. It reminded him of a man who had it all, in a sense, a man who had given up nothing, but everything that was supposed to be inside was outside, and everything that was supposed to be outside—air, dirt, a little steel—was inside; so it was pointless.

Just ask him if he wants a chaplain and go on to the next one. But that was not the procedure.

"You're fine, marine," said Doc Bartholomew, "just relax, I've got to fix up some guy who needs it more than you do, because you're fine, then I'll be back."

You could see doubt and hope in his eyes. Why hope? If death is not to be feared, as a philosopher claims.

The man's helmet was crooked on his head and the doc set it straight and looked at his worried face. Doc almost couldn't hear the guns and grenades. There was the big one again. He heard a voice and rose. He did not hate the gunny, as he got to his feet. The gunny's game was, he wanted Henry to hate himself, but Henry had no hate, not even for himself.

At the sound of the new voice he came to life. He was sprinting, as if he were racing for his school team again, wearing shorts and his school colors, no pack, flak jacket, or pistol, no web belt, pack, or canteens. He felt the canteens flop but did not mind their weight. Maybe they were empty. "Empty canteens!" Who cares?

He saw the man rolling in agony. He himself did not feel the man's agony, or expect to. He saw the man, the man only, and a few feet of surrounding muck and sticks, humps and hollows. He thought of a kid in his high school who defined sex, about which nobody knew anything worth knowing, as all humps and hollows. Henry didn't know.

In Henry's mind there was no perception of rain, nor any knowledge that there was no rain. He got a shock in his leg like a bolt of electricity, and he spun down on the leg. He knew what it was but he had a flak jacket. Then the big gun hit him and he knew it was all over. "It." The 12.7's hitting at a right angle would go right through a flak jacket. He got pounded and it was stunning, it shook him and made his head snap forward on his neck.

He lay still for a minute and looked up and saw the rain but could not feel it striking his face. He rose to his knees to find the man but the big one hit him again and that meant he hadn't much time left.

He was not cold and didn't feel wet. He felt warm with a mantle of cold. He retreated into his mind.

He said, "Just lie here. I'll be right back."

It was quite true. It was no appropriate object of fear. "It."

When his canoe tipped over in the Manistee River in Michigan— he was eleven—he could not believe such a thing was happening to him. When a car hit his bicycle and threw him ten yards he could not believe it. When he walked out of the seminary he could not believe he was doing it. When he mocked Father Adrano about the "divine presence" he could not believe that he, Henry Bartholomew, was talking so smart.

But of course he believed he had been hit by the big gun and would

Rostraver Public Library
800 Fellsburg Road
Rostraver, PA 15012
724-379-5511

have been dead a long time ago but for his jacket. Now he had to decide whether he'd been right to leave the seminary. Was he right to accept No Explanation as the basis of his life?

He thought: "People die this way." Killed by guns. But that didn't scare him. He'd lived in terror but that was a long time ago.

One last conversation with the chaplain, that's all he wanted. If he could demolish the chaplain's absurd beliefs he'd feel better. But it was obvious the chaplain held his beliefs unsteadily. So he and the chaplain were the same, or nearly so—he and—I—

"If I call him will he hear me?"

Doc Bartholomew was lifted on a rising wave of oceanic curves—of deep power rising from within—a wave of love. He rose in a bliss of love for the chaplain, for the skipper, the man he had left and the one he had never reached—for the cold marine, who had ceased shivering, so probably he'd live—for his mother and father and sister—love for—he called for the chaplain in a pleading, cracking, high voice. Rising, bearing him upward, bliss, love. His mind darkened.

"Hey Six, this is Buzzbomb. You're making a hell of a racket down there."

"So we are, Guns. Wish you were here," said Mac. He was among the few who could speak in a low tone into his handset while guns, grenades, and 82's were blowing up the air around him.

"Be down in a minute," said Hitchcock, "but I thought I'd give you the news first. What if they killed me, you know, you'd never hear my news."

"Let's hear it then, Guns, while you're still alive."

"O.K.," said Gunnery Sergeant Hitchcock, "it's my professional opinion that the gooks who bit First Platoon in the ass came out of the major's left, or as I'd rather call him, right out of the Rooster's feathers."

"That'd be beautiful," Mac declared.

"I waltzed across his left flank on my way up here and nobody fired a round at me. I say again, nobody. I think his left flank, boss, is totally gookless. You could turn it with a screwdriver. And we found a cut trail up here that they used to circle our guys.

"But except for that, there's nothing up here but trees and monkey shit. No bunkers, holes, strong points, or trails, nothin. It's pure jungle all the way to Ambush Alley."

"Thank you, Guns. Before you come down, talk to Striker One. I don't want you killing each other."

"I'm ready to come home."

"O.K., do it. Report to me and I'll give you another interesting job."

"Hey, Six, love the Corps, pray for war."

Mac shouted to Ollie: "All around defense of the CP. Aimed fire only. No grenades. Hear that, everybody? There are marines all over the place."

"Fix bayonets," Ollie hollered and began deploying his rifles, bloopers, and gun to defend the command group and the WIAs, who crouched behind the upraised rim of the crater.

Seeing the men deftly slide their bayonets home—seeing this ominous action for the second time in two days—Paul Adrano shuddered. He bent over the cold man and looked into his dull eyes.

Paul bent lower and began to pray close to the man. The color of his ear unnerved Paul. He dragged him across the rim and down into the crater.

Mac saw with irritation that Ollie's mast antenna was still up, sticking well above the rim. He shouted at the radioman to rig his short antenna, and at the same moment somebody yelled "Gooks in the perimeter" and Mac turned to see three soldiers in khaki running toward him. They had AK-47's across their chests and bush hats making low circles over their heads. One made a swift twisting motion and a Chicom grenade flew end over end, like a truncheon.

Two of Ollie's men opened up and two of the enemy fell. The third was still coming. Mac flattened out and the Chicom detonated, bashing his ears and sending frags ripping the air. A marine cried out. Mac stood erect and stared for a split second at a soldier ten meters away who stopped—stood, irresolute—looked at Mac with fear-struck young eyes, and raised his assault rifle, but Mac began his burst low—and lifted it into the man. He twitched and danced and Mac kept it up. The man fell convulsing and Mac dropped to his knees, only his head and shoulders in the danger zone, released his magazine while looking all around, inserted a fresh magazine, and stripped the remaining two rounds from the old one. He dropped these in a pocket of his utility pants.

He made a mental note: rounds in the pocket. He imagined the difficulty of feeding them into a magazine when his fingers might be hard to control.

Graeser passed him the handset, looking into his eyes. "It's Lieutenant Shaw," Graeser said.

"Hi, Danny," said Mac.

"Hey, Six, tell those fucking idiots they almost killed my guys."

"Sorry, we'll be more careful." And Mac called out in a huge voice: "Aimed fire only. Marines all around us."

"Hey, Six," Dan Shaw said again, "here's what they're doing. They send six or eight men at one of mine, and he kills three or four and the rest rush on through without stopping. They're after you, Skipper. They located you by your bloomin antennas."

"Roger. How you doing?"

"We're O.K. We're piling the fuckers up like cordwood. If it's a war of attrition, we won—but I hope I don't make my hometown paper."

"You won't, Danny. Never in a hundred years. Hold your line. We'll give the major a surprise in a minute here."

Mac called Captain Kindred: "Hey, Kinny, I need your guys down here. Double time."

To win you must go high; and from up there, the people down below may look small.

Kindred said: "We got you spotted. We'll be there in a—two, three minutes. We're scattered though. This is no guard mount, more like a mob, except a mob has a leader."

"Just hurry," said Mac.

Ollie's gun hammered away and several more infiltrators dropped out of sight, either hit or, more likely, seeking cover. Mac couldn't use the 60's or bloopers because the wounded of 2nd Platoon were scattered over the ground between the crater and Dan Shaw's defense line.

Some marines came running in from the right rear and identified themselves as part of 3rd Platoon. Mac sent the exec to deploy 3rd and, when it should arrive, 1st. Glancing back he could see scattered men beginning to converge on him. The enemy's mortars were firing long, and the men scampered, sailing through the smoke and the flying dirt.

Mac strode back to the exec, to within ten meters of him, and shouted: "First on the right and ready to counterattack. Third in reserve, hasty defense oriented that way," pointing back. As he walked quickly to his former place he saw a man run in from the right hollering:

"Where's the chaplain? Doc Bartholomew's hollering for the chaplain!"

Paul Adrano rose—slowly—in the crater—and looked at Mac with stricken eyes—large, black, questioning.

The marine shouted to Paul: "There's a guy out there calling you."

"Thank you," Paul said and Mac could barely hear him. But Paul looked at Mac, standing somewhat higher than he, on the slope, and the two held each other in a terrible gaze. Then they heard it, the voice. Doc Bartholomew was calling the chaplain.

The NVA big gun started thudding again with malignant pride and the marines responded with wild wasted fire, for nobody knew exactly where it was, and they were shooting over 2nd Platoon anyway, and thus couldn't possibly hit it. This was mere "pissing your pants" fire and Mac hollered in anger against it; it cooled; and for a second all was silent, but nobody's ears were sensitive enough to hear the rain. And when Mac looked again he saw Paul still staring at him with huge terrified eyes.

Paul lowered himself trembling beside the cold man and in the silence Mac heard him saying:

"Our Father, Who art in Heaven—" his voice struggling to escape his throat.

The cold man cried: "You aren't my brother. You can go to hell!"

Paul bent lower and his mind was ice, his legs were jelly. His mouth was a petrified waste and he could not speak. He could still see the gunny pushing Doc Bartholomew and yelling, "They need you up there, you fucking squid."

Mac said: "Stay here, Graeser" and started up the slope.

"There's one!" cried Ollie pointing.

A man fired off a burst.

"You missed!" Ollie said. "Hold your fire!"

Ollie ran wildly out of the circle and a corporal shouted, "Cease fire!" and Paul in disbelief watched Ollie leaping and dashing into the hurricane, and saw him stop, aim, and fire, then turn and look around with a worried expression.

"Base of fire!" a corporal shouted and marines creased the air with a scorching fire that embraced Ollie like a loving mother. He walked back, reloading, and Paul heard a fragment:

". . . so, Dad, how'd you like that?"

And Paul thought of his father and "Why can't you be a man, for Christ's sake?"

A form—a body—a man—came flying at Paul, and Paul saw the face of death, and his mind yielded, and it seemed for an instant that all he need do was wait.

Michelson made a thrust and the man gasped, and his mouth opened, revealing rotted teeth, and he rose a little on Michelson's bayonet. Michelson pulled the trigger and the body convulsed, and the man was no more. Paul sat beside the cold marine and forgot to pray, for the marine, for the NVA soldier, for Michelson, or himself. He just sat there up to his genitals in mucky water.

As though it were still happening Mac saw the soldier twitch as he fired into him—saw this, and saw it again. It thrilled and transformed him.

Paul thought about it—going out there and looking for Doc Bartholomew. He saw himself stumbling around out there beyond this circle of marines—and it was not possible. He could not do it, even for Doc Bartholomew. He heard the call but could not answer it. "Impossible!" he murmured and no one heard him.

MacHugh Clare stood on the rim, fully exposed, while the big gun thumped regularly. Mac was waving his arms and shouting words Paul didn't take in. Paul was hypnotized by disbelief and death.

The next thing Paul knew, a man came along carrying another. Mac was shouting at this man. The man being carried had been stripped of flak jacket, pack, canteens, and web belt. The carrier crossed the small rise and slid in, and with a shrug of his shoulder lay the other man out, with his feet and legs in the water and his torso on the slope, arms thrown to the sides. The carrier was Gunnery Sergeant Hitchcock and the carried man was Henry Bartholomew, Hospitalman Third Class, U.S. Navy.

"He's all yours, Chaplain," said the gunny. "He wants to confess."

Paul crawled over toward the bloody body.

"But he's dead," said Paul.

"Yeah. He sure is," said Gunnery Sergeant Hitchcock contemptuously.

"Cut the shit, Guns," Mac intervened. "I've got a job for you."

Mac would attack with 1st Platoon on the right. In reserve, 3rd Platoon would prepare for a frontal assault should 1st succeed in turning the enemy's left. As it swept forward 3rd would pick up the squad and gun it had loaned to Ollie for the demonstration. Mac would displace the CP forward just behind 3rd moving through 2nd Platoon's old defense line, and establishing a new CP and aid station somewhere deeper inside the enemy's perimeter; 2nd Platoon would collect the wounded and bring them to the new aid station, mark the dead, and defend the CP.

Gunnery Sergeant Hitchcock would accompany 3rd Platoon in its attack and coordinate the fires of the 60-millimeter mortars with the weapons platoon leader, who would remain with his mortars. The gunny would try to guide 3rd to the major's command bunker. In giving these orders Mac assumed the major was directing his defense from a bunker. The territorial objective was the entire cache complex. The tactical objective was the destruction of the major's force.

At ten minutes past eleven, after giving the troops a few minutes to eat, drink, clean weapons, and restrap gear, Mac set 1st Platoon in motion. Then he moved a few meters back to talk with Graves Registration.

The enemy's left was weak, as the gunny had said, and 1st Platoon advanced with a light expenditure of ammunition and no casualties.

Mac was standing beside Graves Registration, whose thick torso, fat red hands, black mustache, and glittering black eyes always impressed him. Here was a gladiator.

Said Mac: "O.K., Sergeant Graves, attack, and tell me when you establish an unbroken line with First."

Graves Registration nodded his head and bellowed to his troops.

Mac and Captain Kindred walked with 3rd as far as the existing crater CP, where Mac ordered the command group forward. He had intended to tell the chaplain to move the wounded—he had assigned a working party as bearers—but the chaplain was standing at the rear of the crater, with Michelson holding his arm, and a dull, dead look in his eyes.

Michelson looked at Mac in a silent confused appeal.

"Kinny," said Mac, "I know it's not your job, but could you take charge of moving the wounded?"

Captain Kindred took in the situation and shepherded the bearers along. Mac led the command group, and Jake brought up the rear.

Second Platoon roared away and suppressed the enemy's fire, and opened its intervals for 3rd to pass through. Initially, 3rd walked in a line abreast, till Graves Registration ordered them to advance by bounds, and they made steady progress behind the curtain of USMC blooper and 60-millimeter fire.

Third and 1st formed a solid line with an obtuse angle at the junction, and 2nd formed a mobile security perimeter for the command group and wounded, and everything proceeded according to plan for several minutes.

Dan Shaw was supposed to be soldiering but in fact he was singing.

> *Had me a dog named ole Ramblin Roy,*
> *Taught me to fetch when I was a boy,*
> *Pick his burrs and fix his evening stew.*
> *Ole Roy was an easy master*
> *But dogs grow old much faster*
> *Than boys who love'm ever do.*

And Dan Shaw recalled how Roy's muzzle grew white with age, and his joints painful and stiff, his eyes timid and rheumy. Dan said: "I remember that old guy—when his joints hurt and his—"

Dan looked around in surprise. He shouted angrily: "Watch your ammo, you fuckin civilians!"

When he was about sixty meters forward of the 2nd Platoon line, Mac stopped the command group and set up a defensive position. The attack platoons crept forward under strong supporting fires, and the enemy fell back, leaving scores of wounded and dead.

"Advance with caution," Mac told Graves Registration. "Do not walk into a sack."

Checking his local security Mac happened to see the chaplain sitting cross-legged among the wounded. He was reading from a small black book, with his head bent to shelter it from the rain. Michelson crouched beside him with his rifle across his knees.

Mac worried about the left flank, and his worry amounted almost to fear. But he pressed 3rd forward, making sure its link with 1st on the right was closed. Kim Kolias continued to report a clear right, and light resistance, or none at all. Mac called a halt and ordered Graves Registration to send flankers left. The enemy kept up a drumming small-arms fire but his 82's were silent and Mac allowed himself to hope that the Puff raid had cut deeply into the major's mortar ammo.

Lieutenant Kim Kolias reported that a fire team he had sent into the jungle on the right had discovered an unexploded bunker. The men had not entered, and when they threw in a tear-gas grenade nobody came out. Mac began to ponder a new approach—but he wanted above all to smash the major's command bunker. So he pressed the attack and drew 2nd Platoon tighter around the command group and aid station.

It was now about 1125. Mac had forgotten to refill his canteens. He accepted Graeser's offer and drank from his canteen, an experience that told him how thirsty he was.

Kindred and a corpsman on loan from 2nd Platoon were making some kind of fuss over a wounded man, and Mac noted somewhere in his mind that something was going on back there, but he did not shift his attention. He now opened in his mind the subject of a counterattack by the major, either on the right, in the rear of 1st, or on the left, in the flank of 3rd.

"We hold the command bunker visually," Graves Registration reported as if with indifference.

Mac pressed the earpiece closer and said: "Can you hit it with LAWs?"

"I'll send two out," said the sergeant.

"Wait," said Mac. "What's the range?"

"Oh, less than two hundred meters."

"Hold what you've got," Mac ordered. "I'm coming up."

"Roger, Six, but keep your head down."

Mac informed the exec, signed to Graeser and Pickens Freeman, and started running a zigzag course through the humps and debris, sailing over downed branches like a hurdler—in high school he had run the 110 highs and 220 lows—past and around dead NVA. The volume of enemy fire remained unchanged and Mac believed the major must have pulled troops back to defend the bunker.

Graves Registration and Hitchcock crouched behind three stacked NVA bodies. Mac placed Graeser about six meters on the left and Freeman on the right, and still it seemed crowded behind the dead pile.

"Yes, I see it," said Mac. He pondered, staring at the black slit in the black mound, where a split log still retained a streak of yellow bordered by carbon.

Said Mac: "What if we treat it like a tank."

"Sir?" said Graves Registration without tone or impatience.

"The gunny strips away the infantry with mortar fire, point-detonating fuze, and we advance with LAWs on his flanks and a squad up the middle. We send two LAW teams at once, while the squad in the middle pours fire into the slit. Then your LAW men fire simultaneously while we pour in more small-arms fire."

Graves Registration caressed his mustache, and his black quick eyes darted around the whole scene, glittering dimly in their pockets of flesh. He said: "Yes sir."

"Guns?"

"Yes sir."

"O.K. start the mortars," Mac said. "I'm going with that center squad."

"Jesus, Skipper," the gunny protested.

"Hey, Guns, 'more for the Corps.'" And to Graves Registration: "Which squad?"

Sergeant Graves pointed solemnly and Mac waved to his two men and they all took off, and this time the NVA snapped at them desperately, but they reached the squad, said their hellos, and waited for Graves Registration to signal the advance.

His voice boomed through the rain and gunfire—the rain had gone thin and weak. The LAW teams spread out to both sides and moved forward, crouching and dodging. Mac, Graeser, Freeman, and the infantry squad went up the middle, covering themselves and the LAW teams as they advanced by bounds against the small arms and the big 12.7 mike-mike.

Its orange jets flashed rhythmically in the dark slit. Green tracers streaked past on either side, and Mac seemed to sense that men were falling, but it made no difference, he still advanced. He was hot and automatic and devoid of sympathy or fear. Graeser and Freeman were on either side, and the squad was still functioning as a unit, it still existed even though smaller. The noise and ripping of the air, the evil orange-yellow flashes in the slit, and the green streaks combined to suppress Mac's capacity for fresh thought. The only idea was the last one: get closer, get to a good place. And then: silence that fucking gun. Give the LAW men a chance to take an aimed shot.

Then a strange picture flashed in his mind and was gone: of Paul ruining his book by reading it in this rain. Mac saw it disintegrating in Paul's hands. Mac glanced around and saw Pickens Freeman and the laconic Graeser, the squad leader, and one or two men. Mac pointed to a low depression ahead—the squad leader saw his meaning, and the squad, Mac, Freeman, and Graeser hit the deck behind scant cover—some fallen logs and a low rise of the earth—and they ate mud. They waited for the LAW teams to catch up, taking turns firing suppressing fire, two riflemen at a time.

If you should close your eyes, in such a position, and listen, you might think all you have to do is stay right there, and all will be well. The flat-trajectory missiles fly over—but grenades and airbursts are different. Soon enough you remember, and your hollow haven is no longer secure.

Mac and the squad leader were close enough to talk but there was not much to say. Neither would know it when the alignment of LAW teams and the squad reached the optimum.

"We'll give the LAWs two more minutes," said Mac.

The minutes passed without the slightest concession to Mac's sense of urgency. Two RPGs exploded behind him. Finally he said: "O.K. let's hit it."

The squad leader shouted to his men, and everybody, including Mac, began slamming the bunker. Like a quick-witted robot the big gun instantly redirected its fire and chewed the earth and logs and bodies the men were using for cover. The squad leader flipped backward like a man who takes a hard punch in the face. Freeman shouted something and rolled, and the dirt spewed at his former location. Mac checked his "auto" lever, formed a mental picture of the bunker as he had last seen it five seconds ago, rolled over once, exposed his head and face, fired a burst, and rolled back. He was sure he had poured poison in the bunker's mouth. He rolled in the other direction but the ground was humped and he didn't have a clear shot. He cursed and found a better place, slithering, took deliberate aim, saw the devil smile, and emptied his magazine. This time he saw his rounds thudding and raising splats of mud above the slit. The smile of those yellow teeth had thrown him off aim.

He pocketed his empty magazine and rammed a new one in, breathed, and repeated his last maneuver more consciously. This time he was on, and the 12.7 went silent.

Ahead and to the right a marine's helmet rose quickly out of the ashes. A slender tube lay over the man's shoulder. Mac and the squad set up a storm of fire to give the LAW man an extra moment to aim. Fire shot out of the back of the tube and the rocket streaked away and blasted up against the top lip of the bunker. It had hit the bunker but Mac counted it a miss. He wanted LAWs inside—to kill the major or drive him out.

A LAW man on the left fired one that sailed clean over the bunker, a flinch, a wild wasted shot. Two more whooshed out and neither penetrated. But both of these had struck the bunker and life inside could not be very happy. Then Mac knew, or felt certain—that the major had run out the back. He had left the big gun there only because it was a slow carry for a team; but the major was off somewhere, contriving something new.

"Hit it again!" Mac shouted and the LAW men complied. One of these rounds threaded the needle and the firing slit puffed smoke and dirt.

Mac rolled toward Graeser, who listened with ears and eyes grown large, while Mac hollered:

"Tell Graves Registration I'm going back to the command group. Tell him, 'Go on, but watch your left.' "

Graeser talked to his handset, nodded to Mac, and Mac, Graeser, and Freeman went back.

The exec told Mac that Lieutenant Kim Kolias was being attacked from the rear, and that in turning to repel this attack he had allowed a gap of some fifty meters to open between his 1st Platoon and 3rd.

Jake delivered this report in an excessively loud voice, with Mac two feet away. Then Jake changed in a stroke.

"They'll drive a wedge through us," he screamed sobbing. "We're all going to die!"

Mac scarcely recognized him. Sobs distorted his face and wrinkled his voice. He covered his face, his shoulders heaved.

Mac led him away from the men and said quietly: "You're wrong. This is not a disaster, it's the beginning of the end and we are winning."

Jake sobbed and tried to choke out something about dying, and Mac grew calmer, more clear in his own conviction.

He said: "We'll close the gap. Then we sic the reserve on the gooks harassing Kim and we—"

"Harassing! What do you mean, harassing? They're wiping him out!"

"Be quiet," said Mac, still speaking with a sovereign certainty. "If the enemy had a reserve he would have hit Graves Registration. Those gooks hitting Kim are the leftovers from their first shot at him. Don't let the men see you like this, Jake."

"I'm going to die!" Jake shrieked, twisting his head and giving Mac a disconcerting view of his open mouth. His eyes were rimmed in pink and the eyeballs were shot through with red veins.

Mac stood there, held the man by both shoulders, and saw it was useless. Had nobody witnessed this he could have offered him another chance but everybody was watching. For some reason Mac took Jake's hand and began to shake hands, as if in farewell. Jake pulled violently and Mac suddenly felt a rush, like black lava, in his mind. He seemed to slide into a river of lava, and he clenched his right fist, which was now free; he nearly slugged Jake in his distorted mouth; but he stopped at the last instant. He waved a corpsman over, and walked back to where Graeser, Freeman, Kindred, the weapons platoon leader, and the gunny stood like a bunch of pallbearers.

"Guns," said Mac, but his voice was not yet recovered from the flow of black in his heart.

"More for the Corps?" said Gunnery Sergeant Hitchcock with his unlovely smile.

"Just a little. Ask Lieutenant Shaw to give you a squad, and go plug that gap. Ask Shaw to come see me right away."

"Aye aye sir," and the gunny strolled off with his cocky swinging gait, joined by the sailor, the Greek, and Hippo.

Hitchcock halted, turned, and asked: "Do I get a gun?"

"Ask Lieutenant Shaw," said Mac.

The gunny tilted his head, regarded Mac closely, as if deciding whether he should demand a gun or let it ride. Then he turned, and the lethal combination of men and steel wended its way through the debris to 2nd Platoon.

Mac ordered Dan Shaw to attack the NVA who were attacking Kim Kolias, and suggested he try to pour in enfilading fire from the NVA left. He cautioned Dan against friendly fire, incoming and outgoing, and sent him on his way.

Mac took a turn among the wounded, and Captain Kindred showed him the man they had covered with ponchos. Mac crouched and searched for a radial pulse. Finding none, he tried the carotid artery, and this too was unresponsive. The raindrops slid down the man's face and formed little reservoirs at the corners of his eyes.

Mac spoke to several men. To one he said: "Thank you, marine. We'll get you to Charlie Med as soon as the birds fly. Thank you." The man smiled.

Another on hearing a similar message did not smile.

For several minutes, although the firing continued both forward and on the right, Mac did not hear it. He believed he must speak to these men but it was difficult to do. If he said, "We are winning," would a dying man care? Would he hate Mac, the Marine Corps, and the country which didn't care? For a single moment Mac descended into an irrational rage and thought: "You can take it and stick it up Lyndon Johnson's ass." He was not sure what "it" was, but he was poised on the edge of a razor; on one side lay an abyss of hatred for the politicians he was already calling in his mind "the blood-soaked buffoons."

Graeser came up and gave him the handset. It was Graves Registration calling.

"Six, this is Three. We have secured the objective."

"Roger, Three. Hasty defense. Throw tear gas in all bunkers and tunnels and keep your troops out." The words ran through his mind: "We have secured the objective."

As he walked out of the circle of wounded he saw the chaplain kneeling, with a hand on a man's chest, holding his book in the other hand, his closed eyes raised to the sky and the rain. He wore no helmet. His clipped, soaked hair was pure black. Mac walked on. He had to assess the situation of 1st Platoon.

Thirty minutes later Mac was compelled to conclude that he had won. The NVA survivors had fled.

He got the camera out of its plastic bag in Jake's pack and told the weapons platoon leader to photograph everything of intelligence value. He set Ollie to the task of rigging the remaining bunkers for demolition.

He assigned working parties to bring the wounded to the aid station and to lay out the dead. A third party gathered the weapons left on the battlefield by the NVA, counted the enemy dead, and pulled the enemy wounded into one location. Mac ordered a guard on these men.

The rain was abating as Delta Company, 1st Battalion, Nth Marines, heavily encumbered, entered the jungle and began to climb toward the fan of fire. Mac halted the company and told Ollie he could proceed with the demolition. In ten huge reports, the whole complex—what had been discovered in the last two hours and what had survived Puff—was reduced to a scattering of dark depressions in the devastated earth. The men of Delta saw a black cloud rise over the battlefield.

Mac called a conference. Neither the exec nor the chaplain attended.

"Kinny," said Mac, "please repeat what you told me."

"Sure, boss. The weather is improving but Wing can't promise me a gunship for tonight. They can't promise anything."

"Therefore, gentlemen," said Mac, "we must decide: Do we go back down to the beaten zone for tonight, hoping we get a gunship, or do we climb for an hour and place ourselves inside the fan of fire? Any comments before I ask for recommendations?"

"Question, sir." It was Ollie. "Why would we want to go back?"

"Because," said Mac, "when the birds come, that'll be their landing zone."

"So we get arty support if we just hump an hour?" Ollie said. "Hell that's easy."

Mac solicited recommendations in the usual order. Most wanted to climb. Mac pronounced:

"Ollie, tell your cannon cockers we'll be asking for plenty of H and I's tonight. Gentlemen, saddle up."

Delta had lost eleven killed; one died of the cold; twenty-three were wounded. They counted 103 NVA bodies and carried six NVA wounded. They took seventy-nine AK-47 assault rifles, several SKS carbines, two Chicom pistols, and one Soviet 12.7-millimeter machine gun. They did not find the 82's.

When they were well set for the night, the rain having stopped altogether and the heat having come back, Mac led Gunnery Sergeant Hitchcock to a place of privacy and said:

"Guns, the exec will be leaving Delta. But the chaplain will undoubtedly remain in this regiment. He may someday return to Delta. Do not think I will tolerate any disrespect for the chaplain."

"No sir. I can only respect who I respect."

"I am not speaking of your state of mind, but of your attitude and conduct."

"Sir, my attitude is my state of mind."

"Your attitude is one of open disrespect and I will not have it in this company."

"Sir, are you threatening to throw me out of Delta Company to make room for a coward?"

"Gunnery Sergeant Hitchcock, you are a valuable man."

"Thank you, Captain Clare."

"But if you express disrespect for the chaplain by word, deed, or facial ticks your value to this company will drop to zero."

"How so, sir?"

"Gunny, do not press me. The chaplain is a lieutenant in the Navy. The Marine Corps, as you well know, is part of the Navy Department. I expect you to accord him all the respect that is due his rank and position."

"And his conspicuous gallantry on the field of battle," the gunny put in.

Mac said: "Gunny, please. I ask you only to be the best marine you can be. Nothing more or less."

Hitchcock—standing small next to the tall and muscular captain—but with latent power in his rounded shoulders, with a vertical crease between brown eyes like those of a bird of prey on a bad day—Hitchcock stood and said nothing, but stared at his captain provocatively.

Mac stared back—at first in mute appeal, then harder, and finally with open anger.

"What will it be?" Mac demanded.

"Aye aye sir."

"Answer my question."

"Yes sir."

"Meaning you will respect him as an officer."

"Not as a man but as an officer, yes sir."

"Very well, Gunny, carry on."

The next day a Huey slick braved marginal weather to evacuate the seriously wounded. The day after that, under gray but tranquil skies, four Huey gunships conducted a prep fire on the periphery of the old beaten zone. Delta moved down to secure the LZ and a new company was landed. Mac's walking wounded were lifted out. Mac gave the battalion commander a guided tour and listened to his congratulations. The regimental 6 was quite satisfied, therefore the battalion Six was equally satisfied.

By 1600 another company and a battery of 81-millimeter mortars had been inserted and Delta was lifted out. Mac rode in the last bird. He sat in the open doorway of a Huey with his feet dangling out while two men held him by the belt.

It was molecular rain but he could see for a distance of four or five kilometers. The bird described a helix path straight above the beaten zone and Mac saw the battlefield rotating and growing smaller. But in his mind, deep in the identity of mind and spirit, it grew larger. Either the wind or his sorrow for the dead men set his eyes streaming. The air grew frigid and the coldness seemed like a scene of death, and he thought of Doc Bartholomew, whom he had twice ordered into danger. But he was proud. His sorrow and remorse could not suppress it or drive it out—his pride.

He was hungry and his mind was mixing everything up, as if an evil magician were tampering with his brain. He needed sleep but he was stretched high. To win you must go high.

"Ah! You've come for your shirts," said Father Paul Adrano. He searched and found two green T-shirts in a pile of clean laundry on his cot, folded them, and held them out to MacHugh Clare.

"That's not why I came."

"Well, take the shirts with my thanks."

"I do not give a damn about the shirts," said Mac.

But as the priest still stood proffering the shirts Mac took them. He sat on the other cot, the one recently vacated by the exec.

Delta now occupied a position to the rear of the regimental CP, where for two or three days the troops could enjoy showers, A rats, beer, and movies.

Paul was still standing and Mac said patiently:

"Sit down, Paul."

"You invite me to sit down in my own hooch?"

Looking up to his face, Mac saw both determination and torment.

Mac said: "The S One says you've asked him to find a substitute chaplain to conduct the memorial service for our dead."

"True."

Mac just looked at him. And Paul looked back as if to prove he could stare as stubbornly as anybody. On his fresh utility shirt Paul wore neither his Navy lieutenant's railroad tracks nor his cross.

"You're out of uniform, mister," Mac cracked.

Paul stared.

"You could come to the O Club, you know, and have a drink. I'll be there after evening chow," Mac proposed.

"I could. Thank you. But I will not."

"Will you please sit down so we can talk this over?"

"I have reported to Regiment," Paul Adrano informed him. "I am not with Delta Company anymore."

"God, what a sea lawyer."

"One learns the ins and outs of military life."

"Paul, will you stop this? My guys deserve a memorial service and you are the one to conduct it."

"I am the last one is what you mean," said Paul but he did sit down on his cot—back straight, hands on knees—and met Mac's eyes from there.

"If a substitute conducts the service he won't know anything," said Mac. "He'll be reduced to saying, 'Of course I never met these men, but . . .' It will be an empty exercise."

"And if I conduct it, it will be a hypocritical exercise."

"Not necessarily."

"What do you know about it, if I may ask? No—no." Paul continued in a lecturer's voice: "You see, there are certain reasons to conduct a memorial service. The first is to pray for the souls of the dead. You of course don't believe in souls but some people are stuck in a time capsule and still do."

Said Mac: "If you mean immortal beings plucking harps for the delight of a music-loving Creator, no, I don't believe in that."

"See? You not only don't credit the underlying purpose, you speak of it with contempt. But whatever you may believe or not believe, I can pray in private, in fact I have been so doing for days now, even when I don't know why I should."

Mac sat in silence. He held two cold cans of Coca-Cola, a luxury not to be despised. He passed one to Paul and opened and drank from the other. Then he tossed the opener on Paul's cot.

Mac examined that funny script that he had been seeing since childhood, and at first it took him back—then made him feel older than he had ever expected to feel. It seemed absurd that people would still be reading "Coca-Cola" in that silly script after he was dead. Used-car dealers, the Sentry Insurance Company in Stevens Point would still be operating when his life had terminated.

"The other reason," said Paul, "is to memorialize and honor the dead, to help the living cope with their loss. The living need a reason, an explanation, a statement of faith, a sustaining image of the men who have been taken from us. That image helps the survivors to be reconciled to the hazards and losses of human life, to see them not as blind cruelty but as part of the fabric of life as it is lived and must be lived on this earth."

Mac listened to the stilted phrases with full attention.

"By exhibiting the dead as they were when alive, by honoring their devotion to duty and their courage, we confront the mourners with a solemn paradox. Pardon my hermeneutics, but would you care to know what the paradox is? Or have you no interest in the sublime and mysterious?"

"What is the paradox, Father?"

"This. The nobler the men who were killed, the better for us. So I trust you see now why I must leave the conduct of the memorial service to somebody else."

Mac said briefly, "Sorry, Paul, I don't."

"I'll spell it out then. These men died," Paul said with a voice that had turned raspy, and a hard stress on *died,* "in the course of doing their duty. Had they skillfully evaded their duty they would be alive now and going to the movies tonight to see Roy Rogers frisking with his horse, Trigger. They were brave and did their duty and are dead. I was a coward and evaded my duty and am alive. My presence at the service, let alone my presence as officiating chaplain, would be an insult to the memory of the dead. I will not officiate. I will not attend."

After another season of staring at Mac with bold defiant eyes he took up the opener that Mac had tossed, opened his Coke, and drank, and said, "That's a treat."

"You'll call me a liar," said Mac, "but I have tried to put myself in your place and imagine I was you conducting the service. I doubt I would have the strength to appear before the men and—"

"Audacity," Paul corrected him, "not strength."

"I don't know if I could do it."

"I know I cannot," said Paul categorically.

"But to me it's a question of personal courage."

"Please, Captain, none of that."

"May I go on?"

"I'd rather you didn't. You overcame your fear. My fear overcame me. A man called me. I had a sacred obligation to that man above all others. How can you expect me to sit here and listen?"

"I once told you," said Mac carefully, "that I had never been afraid."

"I remember."

Encouraged by this, Mac continued: "I could not say that today."

"I know."

"Oh?"

"I saw you in the grip of fear."

"Then you must—you saw me, so—do you think you were the only man out there who was afraid? I'd guess half the men saw the ape or at least got a glimpse of him."

"Half the men did not refuse to do their duty."

"You did your duty a hundred times and failed to do it once."

"Look, if anybody should ever write the history of cowardice, that will be the defense offered more than any other by the cowards."

"You are our chaplain," Mac persisted, "or at least our Catholic chaplain. We are entitled to a chaplain; we are not entitled to a perfect man."

"You come as close to being the perfect company commander as the troops will ever see," said Paul without envy.

Mac exploded with laughter. "Paul, if you can say that, you are a man of very limited experience."

"I was a man of limited experience. Not anymore. Anyway let's face it. You did it and I failed to do it."

"I'm not very sure what it is I did," said Mac.

"What you did will mark you, darken you. So you can observe the neat symmetry of it all. I failed in my duty and am marked for life. You succeeded in yours and you are marked for life."

"Paul," said Mac standing, "when will you come back to the company?"

"Never."

"You've got to. You don't realize it now but you've got to."

"I don't and I won't. I wish you a joyous reunion with your wife and lots of little babies. Now I've got to pack and get out of here."

Mac didn't leave. He noticed it was hotter standing, with his head near the canvas. He said: "You have to come back to Delta."

"There are other chaplains."

"Delta is the only place where you can change this."

Said Paul: "It cannot be changed."

Striding alone down the regimental main street, Mac saw a naked man white with soap, standing under a barrel perched on a little scaffold. He was about to pull a rope. As Mac passed, the man pulled and Mac heard him say, "Damn, she's dry." Mac thought: "It's soap, mister. It won't mark you for life."

He suddenly saw Doc Bartholomew's body all riddled and bloody as the gunny dumped it in the crater. The blood was diluted by rain and muck; the face was dirty, gray, and expressionless. It was no record of fear or pain.

Mac stopped and held out both his hands to catch the rain, so he could bathe his face. But there was no rain. He cursed and went on.

"So Paul thinks it's better—to go through that—and come out unmarked? Does he really? We lose eleven men—Christ knows if we've got a paraplegic or some guy without his arm, or missing his nuts— Marked? O.K., marked!"

He forgot where he was going. Some goddamn office, some tent where bureaucracy planted itself in the so-called war zone. This was the place to rest, but he couldn't sleep, hadn't had a good sleep since he brought the company in. On Nui Gio he could sleep anytime. Now if he drifted off amid a clamor of weird voices prophesying Armageddon he awoke with a start, almost a leap, and a hammering heart. Sitting on his cot, soaking in cold sweat, with his teeth chattering, he thought of the man they had covered with ponchos who died anyway—after he quit shivering. Mac concentrated on controlling his teeth and stopping the shivers, and succeeded for seconds at a time. He didn't want Sarah to see him like this.

People called it madness. That was a dodge. They had never lived it.

"Isolate it and I admit it looks like madness; take it in context, I'm not so sure. If you could stop in the middle of it—but I couldn't, I was flying, nothing but a gang of reflexes. No, wait. I was aware, sharp. With all that racket in my head I was able to keep hold. I had to win and I knew how to win. But suppose you could pause and look around, you'd say these men were mad, crazier every minute, vicious bloodthirsty criminal lunatics. No, be truthful. They are not bloodthirsty or vicious—almost never—maybe sometimes—the point is they want to live. They are in a fight and only fighters will live.

"If you pull back you see it's one element in a titanic struggle, and I have no doubt which side is right. Of course the struggle could be sane and just, yet this particular fragment crazy and wrong. But what do we do? Throw the people of South Vietnam to the wolves? What if they want freedom? I wonder if it could be both right and mad. No. Ridiculous!"

Narrowing his eyes, looking deeper into this—vision, this hallucination—he saw that Doc Bartholomew's face wasn't quite human in death—rather, he was human with the humanity gone. That's what "gone" means. My uncle is gone, my friend is gone. The face of Bartholomew was not at all like an ape's but for some reason Mac went in that direction and thought of Pickens Freeman reporting that Bartholomew was looking at the ape. A gray face without humanity but with a human structure.

"I saw the ape too, I'm marked, I won the damned battle, we lost eleven men, Hitchcock despises the chaplain—and should despise me too. Christ, if this is victory I'd hate to meet up with defeat."

That night at the O Club some officers asked his pleasure and he said Hennessy. The first was like a fire on a winter night at a snowy camp, the next was like a woman's hand caressing his forehead, and the third was like a narcotic, easing out all trouble.

"If I could only hold her," he thought. "If I could just—hug her."

Then: "Maybe what I really mean is, if she could hold me." He said in his mind: "Sarah, I love you. Do you love me? I'll see you next week!" Thinking: "God can that be true?" True that he would see her, true that she existed.

Chapter 13

Fatherly Advice

Seated in a leather chair in the den of his house in River Hills, Warren Woodley, aged sixty-one, sipped brandy, smoked a Chesterfield, and waited for his daughter. She had excused herself a moment ago, in the midst of a conversation that Mr. Woodley was anxious to continue.

His thoughts shifted from Sarah, his younger daughter, to his late wife, Carol. He did not turn to her photograph, standing on the bookcase to his left. He did not need to. His desire was for Carol. He was conscious of an ever deeper loneliness, now that both daughters were grown and married and neither one living nearby, and his wife quite suddenly dead.

Mr. Woodley's white hair and eyebrows, his outdoorsman's complexion, his puritanically hooked nose and wide mouth, all this plus a striking intelligence together with a trace of aggressiveness in his pale blue eyes, had contributed immeasurably to his success as a trial lawyer. Starting poor helped too. He knew how to talk to a jury.

Turning his mind to MacHugh Clare he seemed to examine that young man down to his shoes, to evaluate him, in fact to judge him; while in the powder room down the hall, Sarah cooled her eyes with water and combed her hair. The woman who faced her was very like herself. This woman looked pale but calm. Sarah said: "I am a match for him. I have always done what I wanted to do."

Observing her face Sarah could not resist a sensation of approval. She took a hand mirror from the drawer, intending to glance at her profile, but it was a mirror of her mother's, and she stopped, and looked instead at the mirror itself, its ornate pewter frame. The object seemed familiar but her hand did not. The hand looked strong.

When she told him she would be flying to Honolulu via military air he had invited her to stop on the way. And when she said it would be difficult to catch a hop that took her near Milwaukee he sent a commercial airline ticket. She returned to the den ready to continue the conversation.

"We could talk about something else," her father offered. "We could go to a movie, it's still early."

"Let's talk about this," Sarah said, taking her former seat. Her glass of brandy stood untouched, and she let it stand.

"All right, if you are willing to go on—" said Mr. Woodley tentatively.

"I am."

"—then we might as well face the issue squarely."

"Yes, let's do."

"Please don't be testy. I'd much rather drop the subject."

"You would not. Neither do I want to drop it, so please, make your point. I know you have one ready."

"In fact I have," said the father. He aimed a cloud of smoke upward and then his eyes darted from one point on the ceiling to another, his head still lifted. This was a piece of trial lawyer's theatrics she had noticed as a young girl and tried for a time to adopt as her own.

He said: "Anybody can name ten or twenty famous actresses. How many playwrights can you name?"

"Tennessee Williams, George Bernard Shaw—"

"Living playwrights."

"Edward Albee—"

"Never heard of him."

"Arthur Miller," Sarah added.

"*Death of a Salesman.* A vastly overrated piece. I'll bet you never get to ten."

"What's your point, Daddy?"

"I suspect you know. The odds of your making a dollar on your play, or other plays you might write if you write till you're seventy years old—"

Sarah heard the note of derision.

"—are very long odds indeed."

"If I were writing the play to get rich I'd be a very naïve and silly girl." She said this even though she doubted he'd catch the spirit in which she used the phrase "silly girl."

He went right on: "Isn't it possible that the play is an expression of your reluctance to give up altogether on your dream of a career in the theater?"

"Quite possible," she conceded as if it were no concession at all.

"I suspect," Mr. Woodley continued, "that your odds were better as an actress."

She did not respond, except to meet his eyes. And she didn't touch the brandy. She would do it pure, without props or artificial pauses for a drink or a drag on a cigarette. So far she felt satisfied with her performance.

Mr. Woodley snubbed out his cigarette as if there were wisdom or restraint in the action, then looked up and smiled. In this smile she saw both power and love.

He said, "Of course there's no crime in writing for a hobby, but to write plays seriously—and I don't denigrate the profession of Mr. William Shakespeare, not in the least—but to devote oneself to writing plays in this modern age, when the great plays and books have already been written—entails one of two conditions. The first would be to live in utter poverty and obscurity, wasting one's talents, looking forward to final failure as a virtual certainty—"

"Virtual," she interrupted.

"Precisely what I said—to see yourself at the age, say, of sixty or seventy, sitting on a straight chair in a very austere apartment in New York with no money and one bottle of sour milk in the icebox."

"Daddy, you are a playwright yourself."

"The other—thank you—the other, the alternative condition, is money to support the habit. I myself could never consent to finance such an unpromising venture."

"I haven't asked."

"And if I should offer, I know you would refuse me."

"Probably," she said. Then laughed. "Maybe not!"

He smiled his courtroom smile and elaborated: "In your case the only way to pursue such an ambition would be as the wife of a man who made enough money to support you, your children, and a flock of babysitters. In short, your despised middle-class life, while married to an appropriate husband."

"Mary Chase," Sarah said.

"Who is Mary Chase?"

"She wrote *Harvey*. She is a wife and mother and she has talent."

"And is her husband a carefree hippie wandering the Green Mountains of Vermont?"

Controlling her anger she cautioned him: "I will not listen to—"

"Forgive me!"

"You mean 'strike it from the record,' but you have said it, it cannot be unsaid. Daddy, you must not slip into the habit of being witty and cutting at Mac's expense when he is not here to defend himself. That's a style of wit I do not appreciate."

"I intended no disrespect."

"Yes you did. You took a dislike to Mac from the day he quit law school, and I know why."

"I wish I knew why you believed that, I could have—"

She cut in: "You decided to be insulted, because you were set on believing that his decision implied disrespect for you."

"Is that what I was set on believing? Thank you for informing me."

"You think Mac is contemptuous of lawyers, but I have tried time and again to tell you—"

"Oh, I remember what you've told me. No need to repeat it."

"He simply did not want that life for himself. He is made for a different kind of life."

"May I ask what kind that is? Since my daughter is married to him, do I have standing to ask: What niche does he intend to fill in the American economy?"

"He planned to go into his father's business but—"

"House builder?"

"He builds houses and digs wells and sets up irrigation—"

"Ah! He wants to be a well digger!"

"Daddy, be careful. The short answer is yes, he did."

"All right, so we come to your famous peace treaty. I know the terms only in the vaguest way."

Sarah said: "I told him I'd die in Stevens Point. Digging wells was O.K. but not in the middle of Wisconsin."

"Maybe we need wells in Milwaukee."

"Stop it. I said I didn't want to live in New York or San Francisco, that I loved Vermont when—"

"You were a child."

"I don't care. We made our treaty on that basis. We are going up there to try it out."

"You will find it no more thrilling than central Wisconsin. But shall we take a step back?"

"Meaning?"

"Look again at the treaty. Do you really want this life you've described—children, poverty, however temporary, for the sake of what he calls freedom? Poverty even for a year or two could be quite unpleasant. You have never known it. I do not recommend it."

"And we cannot let our lives be ruled by the fear of it," she said defiantly.

"Do not let your life be ruled by the fear of anything. Fear is an unreliable counselor."

"What is it you want to say, Daddy?"

"I pose you a question. You've told me Mac has decided to quit the service."

"Yes."

"Why? Military service is a good career path."

"He's had enough of that life, I suppose. He feels oppressed by the regimentation. I'm not sure he's cut out to be a military man, and I am not ready to spend my life as the wife of a marine who's gone half the time."

"Nor was he cut out to be a lawyer."

The father looked at his daughter with a closer scrutiny and waited. Sarah experienced this pause as coercive.

Mr. Woodley said: "There are other careers, certainly, but how many opportunities will this young man throw away?"

"Speak more clearly, Daddy."

"I cannot make it any clearer. I am worried about your marriage from the material standpoint."

"Because we reject the suburban middle-class life? Because we think it would be a mistake for us? Not for you and Mother, but for us."

"Your mother and I were born poor, Sarah-Dove. To us Whitefish Bay and then, later, River Hills, didn't look so bad."

"We have to live our lives, not yours."

"Agreed. And I won't argue the merits of middle-class existence or even wealth. It's part of my life's achievement, however, that you and your sister are able to approach these questions with a range of choices that was not available to your mother and me."

"I think you know that I appreciate that, Daddy."

The father was emboldened to say: "Just consider a different plan."

"We are going to Vermont and live where we can see—"

"Cows."

"All right, yes, cows, forests, fields, hills."

"But you are not going to be farmers?"

"I don't know."

"To start a farm takes money, and to make one go takes knowledge, of which neither you nor your husband has even the barest rudiments."

"That is true. I never said we'd start a farm. I know nothing about farming."

"I know this," said her father. "Farming is dangerous, backbreaking, endless work. It is dark-to-dark work in the winter and five in the morning till eight at night in summer. I know all this from my boyhood, till I almost—"

"Yes! Stop! I said we do not plan—"

"Listen to me, Sarah. Living on Marine Corps bases for the past four years you have missed something. The world is changing around you. Will you listen to me quietly?"

"Go on. Just nothing about farming please. That's your nightmare, not mine. What am I missing?"

"I'll begin with a number. Last autumn the University of Wisconsin Law School admitted *eight* women, in a class of one hundred sixty-five. This fall the number is ten, in a class of two hundred seventy-two, very low numbers."

Said Sarah quietly: "Now I see what you're up to."

"As you know, UW is my school. The dean happens to be my classmate and I called him after you and I spoke on the phone. Now I come to a different number altogether. Next fall, Sarah, they will double the number of women. They will admit twenty or thirty. And the year after that they plan another increase. When I say the world is changing, I mean changing in a way that could transform your life. You know Miss Timmerman in my office?"

"Of course, I've known her since I was a child."

"Miss Timmerman knows more law than any of the partners, myself included. She runs the office and she is perhaps the smartest person in the place. But she is a secretary, she has no law degree, she will never be allowed to argue to a court or sign a legal document as counsel. That is what's changing. There will be no Miss Timmermans in the coming generation of women, that is to say, in your generation. The new women will paint their names on the door, Sarah. Your name, if you act decisively, could be painted on the door."

Sarah rose from her chair and approached her father, who looked up in surprise and smiled when she placed her hands on the satin shoulders of his old smoking jacket and bent to kiss him. She returned to her chair, crossed her legs, straightened her skirt, and said calmly:

"Go on."

Mr. Woodley lit another Chesterfield and blew the smoke up and looked at the ceiling, and darted his eyes. He said: "I happen to believe—and this isn't necessarily a reflection on your husband—that people who say money is unimportant are seriously misinformed."

"Mac doesn't say that," Sarah insisted.

"All but," said Mr. Woodley.

"No, he does not *all but* say it either."

"Well you have one opinion and I have another. I love my girl and seek her happiness, and fear her possible misery and dejection."

"Daddy—misery?"

"Sarah my dear, my dear dear woman, for all your intelligence you are living your life for the first time, as everyone does, but this means that you can see only what lies immediately before you. You are a mariner sailing up an unknown channel and you cannot see around the curves."

"Neither could you and Mother."

"True but our course was set for us by two strong influences, poverty and ambition. It is entirely due to our grit, if I may say so, and of course good fortune, that yours is a more complicated problem. But here is my point," he continued. And lifting both arms—the cigarette smoking in his right hand—he said, "Now I don my preaching robe."

"It looks like your old smoking jacket to me," said Sarah, smiling affectionately.

"Yes. My relic of prewar elegance."

It was a faded velvet jacket, maroon with black buttons and black silk piping on the sleeves and pockets.

"I don't need a sermon, Daddy, but it's true I am going around in circles. I don't expect money to bring me happiness. It would be enough if it liberated me from drudgery. I do not need to be free like a bird, but I have recently been learning all I ever want to know about wage slavery and the life of a drudge. Since Mac went over I've had three jobs around the base, three utterly stupid jobs, simply to get out of the house. I quit them all."

"I see," he said with a glint of satisfaction in his pale eyes.

"Drudgery does two things," she asserted. "It wastes my life and drags me down somehow."

Said her father: "If I were an Englishman—I knew them in the war, you remember—I would now say: Quite."

"Yes, old chap, quite."

Mr. Woodley began: "But I should think, with your education—"

"Oh no. They want skills and training. Education is of no interest to them."

"Of course if you were a man, educated as you are, you could start in a brokerage house, peddling stocks—or banking; bankers don't really know anything at the start—real estate, advertising, executive training programs, whatnot."

"Excellent. I am not a man."

"Teaching, nursing, social work."

"Daddy, please."

"Forgive me." He smiled again and looked up and flicked his keen pale eyes back and forth, and so doing, said: "But I let go my thread. Now here it is."

Henceforth he spoke directly to Sarah and sought to get behind her attentive eyes. He said:

"No, you cannot see around the curves, you have never navigated that channel, but I have, and I'll tell you what I see."

"Misery? Poverty? Dependency on you?"

"I don't see that far. All I can tell you is that you are coming to a parting."

"Not from Mac! I love him! You may not understand that, Daddy, and I don't know why you refuse to believe it."

"I do believe it and that's the source of the trouble."

"It is not *trouble* when you love the man you married. His indifference to money, to being a cog in the corporate machine, his independence—I may as well tell you that was the first thing that drew me to him. He is a man who refuses to trade his life for money. Tell me what's wrong with that!"

He replied coolly: "I did not say a parting from Mac. Calm yourself, Sarah. I was about to say you are approaching a parting of the waters. The river of your life now reaches a place where various branches lead away in different directions. Some of these tempting branches will run dry after the first curve and leave you grounded, perhaps for life. A decision suggests an opportunity, and some opportunities come only once. Mac is about to quit the Marine Corps, as you inform me."

"Thank God."

"Is it really such a good thing? I gather he is something of a success as a military officer—so now he's dying to throw away that career too. But when he gets out he'll have to do something."

"I'm sure he will do something."

"And so must you," insisted Mr. Woodley.

"You mean law school."

"That's one possibility. What's wrong with it?"

"Nothing so far as I know. I've never given it a minute's thought. That's a lie."

"Give it a minute's thought now."

On an impulse Mr. Woodley got up and went to the bookshelf. He handed Sarah an old blue book, saying: "A gift."

Sarah opened it and read on the inside cover, in a flowing script: "Warren Woodley, UW Law School, 1932." She looked up, smiled, and turned to the title page. It was Justice Cardozo's *Law and Literature and Other Essays*. "Thank you, Daddy. What a fine gift."

Mr. Woodley said: "It will give me pleasure to know you own it. Now. If your husband retreats to the forest primeval I promise you, you will not be enjoying Sunday brunch at Boder's nor will Mac be buying his suits at MacNeil and Moore's."

"He won't be buying suits anywhere."

"Exactly. And if you have a child, two, three children, then the life of a woodland hippie or neophyte farmer may prove other than what you expect. There is another life besides poverty and aimlessness. Get a law degree at Madison or Marquette. You could live with me while you're in school. This is a large house, and Mac and I have always gotten on well enough.

"Then if ten years from now you are still married to him, and he wants to go back to Stevens Point and dig wells, because he associates menial work with freedom, even though it is money that sets a man free, let him. You'll be practicing law and making good money for yourself and your children. You need not depend on him. You are not helpless, you are not even dependent."

"Stop a second, Daddy," said Sarah with a slight drop of her head, glancing at the book in her lap—but then she faced him with wide-open eyes. "Why would you say *if* we are still married?"

"Sarah-Dove, this retreat to the hills, this naïve ideal of freedom, as if country people enjoy a pure and carefree existence compared to the pampered slaves of the suburban middle class, where did he get that? Children, my girl, require clothing, food, and schooling. When your children are eighteen, are you going to tell them they can't go to college because their father spent his time walking in the woods?"

She exclaimed: "I love him!"

Mr. Woodley looked at his daughter with worry, or fear, in his eyes. "Of course you do, Sarah-Dove, and I have always—"

"I love him!" she cried out. "The pain of this separation—the visions I have of his body mutilated and bleeding, of his *eyes* on me while he bleeds to death, his trousers soaked in blood, his eyes blinded, his hands—"

"Sarah-Dove, please, I—"

"—his legs and arms gone. That has happened—legs and arms! And he sits there too proud to ask me to feed him. I simply can't stand—I want him! I want to hold him, I want his arms around me, I want to hear his voice saying, 'I'm here, let me take you in my arms.' I can't—Daddy!"

Seeing her father's face, aghast and pleading, Sarah stopped; her voice died in her throat. She trembled all over.

Chapter 14

Rest and Recreation

Mac had failed to stop Hitchcock bullying Doc Bartholomew. He forgot that. He forgot his shame. He forgot being "high." He forgot the wounded, the blood and the dead, and the cold man, and the *necessary conviction* that somebody had to die. He thought only of Sarah—with an intensity that was all but unbearable.

The engines ceased to strain, and the plane began to descend. You knew the moment the big engines realized the hard part was done. The plane was drawing near Honolulu and everybody knew it, even the ones who had just awakened. Now everybody was awake. The men grew turbulent and noisy. Mac could hardly believe she'd be there. It's a long way from North Carolina—something would delay or stop her, or she just wouldn't come.

To embrace Sarah, to clasp her to his chest, to look into her deep dark brown eyes; to hold, embrace, and touch her, and see her happy eyes lifted to his. He wanted Sarah and he would soon have her.

He saw her, quite close. He tried to slip by the men in front but the gap closed on him. He tried the left, then the right. They were widened, and so was he, by the bags they carried. He moved within the mass of uniformed men, Navy and Marine Corps, but those in front who had already found their women had stopped the parade.

But she was here again; their eyes met and he felt the sudden release. She loved him. It was in her eyes. He would hold her. After six months, it was a matter of seconds. It was already having its effect, as if he already held her against his body.

Catching another glimpse he realized she was not waiting. She ducked under the rope and began pressing toward him, running as best she could in the crowd.

He ran too, trying not to knock anybody over. He weaved among the men, the whole mass moving again somehow, and he passed through an opening, then another, and they nearly missed each other. They met, here she was, neither spoke, she was in his arms and he pressed her to his chest. He was embracing his entire world, his life, all that he cared for.

Sarah said, "I want to be conscious, not delirious. For God's sake let's jump in bed and I don't care what happens next."

They lay down and he felt her quivering in his hands. He began to apologize for the accident that he predicted would happen before he could bring her with him, but she said:

"Mac, just come to me. I only want you."

He said: "I was half afraid you wouldn't be here."

"Not be here! Oh, how little you understand.—Yes. Just that. Oh Mac, I have longed for you. I love you so much."

"May I just look into your eyes for a minute?"

"Of course, show me the blue lamps but I will have to close my eyes soon, you know. I am dying for you."

So he began, mindful of all she had ever said about the gentle and the thoughtful, but this time she urged him on and exclaimed, "There!" and smiled up at him, opening her eyes in amazement.

She tightened her grip on him, with both her arms curving under his, and her hands circling his shoulders from behind. This seemed to free her lower body.

It would not have been unusual if she had talked; she often described what was happening to her, using a vocabulary he knew by heart; but today she did not, and Mac believed she could not. Nor did she ask him, as she often did, to tell what he was doing, or intended to do.

316

Except for her breathing she made no sound, and he had hope for a completion that would include her. He did not want to use the permission she had given him. He was full of desire to carry her to the end, together with a doubt that he could do it. The moment came when, if he looked in her eyes, it would all be over, so he closed his eyes and controlled himself, to bring her forward if he could.

She cried that she loved him, and this was more than he could withstand. His stream rushed into her in jets that seemed all the wilder for having originated in his effort to restrain and guide himself. He lost all control, and as a couple they lost harmony. Mac went wild and Sarah stopped gently, and held his shoulders in a strong grip and crooned her approval.

"Lovely strong beautiful man," she whispered in his ear.

"I wanted—" he started, but could not speak yet.

She said, "I know, dear. Next time. Soon. Don't apologize for giving me what I wanted. I love the intimacy and trust. Just stay where you are, just be with me."

While they were showering she congratulated him on his animal abundance, but he heard this with a certain apprehension. It was probable Sarah would ask him to tell the story of his experience. If she ran true to form she would want to know where it originated, why it began when it did, and where it made itself most intensely felt. Often she wanted to know what she had done to forestall or hasten its coming. He had never satisfied her wish to know what it felt like. That lay beyond speech.

It was a story he did not want to tell. In the midst of the part no man can control, Mac had seen a vision. The vision blotted out all feeling. He saw Doc Bartholomew going over the rim, standing irresolute, and walking out.

She would not be surprised if he told her his experience was too intense for feeling. This she had learned to accept. It did not mean he felt nothing; it meant the center of the experience was a sensation other than pleasure, more like oblivion. He would tell her that now. He didn't want to reveal the truth to her. What he didn't know was why he should conceal it. There was a flicker of fear in him, and he hoped she wouldn't ask.

As they stood under the shower, holding each other in what otherwise would have been perfect love, and this false design lodged in his mind, he asked:

"Are you frustrated?"

"Oh no. I'm human again. No dearest, I am well and happy and we'll sleep together tonight."

Each one spoke again of love, and when they drew back to look at each other, Mac told her that he had never seen anything as beautiful as she was. He gazed at her and could not believe such beauty existed, but there it was and he kept on gazing. Her eyes showed a strong interest in his. She smiled and kissed him, and kissed him again, softly.

As they dressed, Mac looked around the hotel room for the first time. They were not in the armed forces hotel but in an oceanfront room on Waikiki Beach at a fancy resort, courtesy of Mr. Woodley.

Mac said: "Thank you, Warren Woodley, for liberating us from Uncle Sam for five days."

The room was spacious, with a large bed, reading chairs, a desk, and balcony. The surf foamed barely fifty meters away. It sent into their room a rushing, advancing whir and subsidence, like flocks of wide-winged birds descending among the treetops. The crash and tumble of Atlantic surf, which they expected to hear, was absent. In its stead came the long-drawn rush of foaming waves, and the silence of their withdrawal.

"Can I take this?" Mac asked. "Chairs, a table, carpet, a bed, a bathroom and shower—where has all this stuff been? I could have a sensual experience just walking barefoot on this carpet."

"The world goes on," Sarah said. "You're the one who has stepped out of it."

"Sweetheart, I think I stepped *in* it."

"Well—leaving that for later," Sarah said, "what were you starting to say about a shirt?"

He told her, "I'm tired of saluting. We've got to get me some civvies."

So after lunch they bought him three Hawaiian shirts, Bermuda shorts, and canvas sneakers. Attiring himself in festive colors had a strange effect. The cloth was loose and light, the colors garish. He looked in the mirror and laughed.

Then they separated to do their Christmas shopping. Christmas was two days away.

. . .

Walking among the shops, Sarah said to herself: "He has not men-tioned the baby." She could not find among the clothes and trinkets anything suitable, so she went to a bookstore and scanned the titles in fiction and history. She said again, almost in the same words, that he had not brought up the subject of a baby, nor had he asked if she had taken her usual precautions. She chose *Zorba the Greek; Look Home-ward, Angel; Adam Bede,* for its carpenter hero; and Morison's history of the American people.

She now felt she had an excellent Christmas morning in her bag, and it was light enough to carry back to Vietnam. The name of that place passed through her mind and left a kind of shadow. She went early to their rendezvous and sat in the shade of the palms, looking toward the ocean.

As he approached—wearing his new shorts—she noticed the scar and asked:

"What happened to your leg?"

He looked down at the Bouncing Betty scar and said that he had slipped on a wet rock. He sat beside her and they gazed at the sea, holding hands, till Mac said:

"It is very hard to live without you, Woody."

"Yes."

"Very hard."

"Yes, my love."

"I picture you—such a good swimmer, your figure, that queenly carriage, the dark hair, the brown eyes—I see your eyes a lot, your shoulders. I often see you swimming in that pond, where the water was so clear and you swam around the dock and I was looking down on you, and your skin was turned pure white by the water. You told me it wasn't at all cold, and I dived in and damn near froze."

Mac tried to describe his loneliness but it eluded him. She listened with care to his halting efforts, leaning forward and to one side, facing him and nodding gravely. Her eyes had a devouring quality, as if his every word and thought confirmed and justified her love. There was no tension in her eyes; a keenness and insatiability, but no anxiety.

He spoke with a certain—almost—anguish, it seemed to Sarah. He was not just telling how precious she was to him, and how her image

319

came to him sometimes; he also tried to describe the competition be-tween his love of her and the demands of his "job." She noticed he avoided the word "duty." This competition awakened a strange excite-ment in her breast and she listened intently, eagerly.

He said it made him feel strange to dream and plan their life to-gether—and yet, while still being the man who intended to live that life, to order an attack and watch his troops advance, and some of them fall. Sarah's eyes never left him. When he looked away she made certain her eyes would be full upon his when he looked back.

"I wonder if I'm two men," said Mac.

"This war will not go on forever. You'll be out soon, free to be your real self."

"Maybe that's my real self. I wouldn't walk away from it if I could. I've never done anything in my life half so important as being CO of Delta Company. I look around this place—cars, women, people in clean clothes strolling around in pleasant weather, nobody worried about snipers or land mines—I can't take it in. I keep feeling exposed to snipers. I love you, Woody, and I want our life together. But I go for days, sometimes longer, when I forget that this world exists."

"You forget me?"

"Yes. I mentioned the fight at the S-curve—"

"You must tell me about it."

"Maybe later. But during that whole operation I was not two men, I was one. It doesn't mean I love you any less now."

"Of course not.—You mean—"

"A lot depended on—I shouldn't say it, but a lot depended on my judgment."

"And so I just flew out of your head?" She was not alarmed but she did not like it.

"Yes. I'm sorry."

"Don't be sorry!" she exclaimed, not quite sure why.

"Then we were lifted out and I saw the hill mass from the air, the black smudge where the Holiday Inn had been"—he explained about the Holiday Inn and continued—"and the river from the air, and we were safe and gone—"

"And then?"

"It took two or three days, but I woke up in the middle of the night and felt a terrible sorrow when I found you weren't beside me. I felt you were dead and buried. It hit me. You were dead, and I thought I might as well be dead myself. Then I thought, 'This will kill me.' "

Sarah sat back in her chair, looked away, and pondered this. She said with slow deliberation: "But you love me now?"

"More than ever. I live for the moment when we'll be together again, to go up to Vermont and find a place, maybe a run-down old farm. I got a letter from a broker who said a farm with a good house, barn, and eighty acres just sold for twenty thousand dollars, a good place. I can picture myself fixing up an old barn, but here I sit in Honolulu and there's Waikiki Beach and I can't figure it out."

She leaned forward and took his hand.

"This is an interlude, an oasis in the desert," she said. "It's not real life. We are real enough but this R and R is a dream."

"A desert, O.K., I loved you when I was in the desert and I'll love you when I come out of it." But he was thinking: "It's not a desert"—seeing jungle and a trail.

Said Sarah: "You said you forgot me. I don't blame you but it seems I have a very strong competitor."

He smiled, and Sarah said, "A powerful competitor."

"Yes. But how can you ask if I love you? You must feel it. I was in a—goddamn battle—and to do my job I had to be a certain kind of man. You either hide or you fight. You either make your men fight or face disaster. All I mean is that the fighting, while it lasted, took my whole brain. Now I'm here—with you—"

At that moment he almost told her what he was sure she wanted to know. The impulse took him, almost. But it would have thrown too much weight into one conversation. He'd tell her—confess—when she asked for the "story." It always seemed that she wanted, so far as she could, to experience their love from his side as well as her own.

But Sarah was not thinking about that. She wondered if there really were two of him, if the two could coexist—and which was real. The way he had said 'a goddamn battle' disturbed her.

Certainly a battle would change a man. The question of their lives was whether the change was permanent. It was one thing to tell her father that Mac might come home a screamer or a drunk, and quite another to live with him if he did. But she thought: "He's so honest.

He forgets me for days at a time, probably weeks! And—he imagined me dead!"

"Your shoulders are warm," he said, covering both with his hands.

"Yes. Isn't the breeze nice?" She lifted her head from the pillow, kissed him lightly, and relaxed. "I have been longing to have you where you are now."

Here began a series of light, chaste kisses which had an effect on Mac not altogether chaste. He was required to change his position, a change that must have affected Sarah. She began to kiss him in a different way, and to look at him earnestly between kisses; but these intervals grew shorter and her kisses longer and hotter, so that both Mac and Sarah began to forget who they were, and ceased to know whether they had given a kiss or received one. To kiss her was the same as to receive her kiss.

"This," said Mac, "is very—"

"Intimate."

"Yes."

"Doing this, I can taste and smell you as well as—caress you—with—"

"Yes," she said, "it isn't just kisses, it's—God—when you—please, please."

Thus began their loss of personal identity, and they proceeded steadily into it, as if they were experimenting, as if they were surprised at the power of it to transform them.

Her taste changed as the minutes passed. She was just as desirable, but different. She became more earthy, more ripe. He felt her hand take his hair in a strong grip and turn his head. She whispered in his ear:

"Dear Mac, I love you, love you."

"I love you, Sarah."

"While you're kissing my face I feel how big and hard you've grown. It is a joy to lie under you, a joy! Give me your tongue."

She flung the blanket away and went down and kissed his ankles and his knees.

When she resurfaced, they began again but it was different, since it was not possible now for him to keep his hungry hands off her bare flesh. He pressed her against his chest and she was warm, and her skin was a surprise to his own. She gave a cry of delight and renewed her kisses with warmer passion.

She whispered, "I want to make you happy!" desperately, and kissed and kissed him. "Go ahead, be a rampaging bull, I don't care!"

It was becoming harder for Mac to remember his duty. It didn't seem possible she could be behind him. All he could believe was that they were together, because his personality was constantly being lost in their kisses, and in the warmth and ripeness of her body in his hands. Yet somewhere in his alien mind he knew that she was a different person, and almost certainly lagging behind him, so he tried again to concentrate and to encourage her. It was easy to make the cardinal error of moving too soon, and this would snap her out of the ecstasy that he believed was taking her. If he moved too soon it would seem like force to her. He knew this, or the man he had been when he approached the bed knew it. He went down and licked her nipples with loving gentleness, and felt them respond. He heard her giving voice, as if, to her, voice was part of the sensation, and he continued, tenderly but with the authority conferred by his muscular arms, which held her just as he wanted her to be.

But when she tried to escape he let her go. He came back up and they lay side by side, gazing at each other.

"We will never part," said Sarah.

"I will love you all my life," said Mac.

Then he touched her thighs, and in a little while he perceived that they were opening. She was giving voice again. Hearing her, listening to this soft unique music, he caressed her inner thigh with love and care. He had no idea of going ahead, did not know what "ahead" might mean. He listened and the music was his guide. How long this went on he would never know. Again he felt that this by itself was enough, that there was nothing more or better to be sought. They were not going anywhere. The music and the touch of her flesh was his happiness, and only a fool would demand more.

But when almost by accident he brushed over her mons, and then touched her deliberately and lingeringly lower down, and found that his fingers were moist, he was suddenly carried back to his identity as her lover. He felt such tender and compassionate love—it exalted him—he was indeed the very man who placed this woman above life itself—he wanted to pour forth the love overflowing his soul—he wanted the joy that he already had, of hearing the music and sensing her hand as she took him—

And for a few seconds he knew exactly who he was and what he must do—for her sake—for the ecstasy of this beloved Sarah. He was the man to whom she opened her legs. This knowledge blazed in his mind and further exalted him. The music—the sound of her breathing merging with the music—the way she moved under his hand—her own gently fondling hand—

He concentrated. His mind was fully present and dedicated. But the more clearly he could read the signs of his success as her lover, the stronger grew the pressure of something wild inside him, which could banish his dedication. He felt the advent of this wildness, and knew he could still decide. He could choose between being her lover and going wild. It was very odd, not quite believable, that it was presented to him as a decision, he could do one or the other.

Then he realized she was speaking, and had already spoken several words which he missed. Words now instead of music. He listened. She was saying, "Please" and tugging at him. "Please," she said breathlessly, "take me now."

He found the portal and advanced carefully but she cried: "Slow, dearest, slow!" He went deeper but not very, and looked down at her. She was smiling up at him, and she nodded approval, and he advanced again but as slowly as he could, and stayed, and then withdrew part way. She smiled again—having momentarily turned her face aside. She sighed, and pressed on his rear, and said clearly, "Yes, oh my King Kong." Her jokes, coming at a time like this, always startled him. He was the serious one. He began the gentle slow opening that would precede the oceanic motion.

Now he looked "ahead." Their common motion could be seen as a dance in movements, and they were beginning the final movement, which he called the oceanic. The knowledge of his duty, and his role as her lover, dissolved in the waters of this ocean, and left behind it no knowledge at all. Who he was, who she was, were equally unknown and irrelevant. He had no duty because he had no partner, and there was no "he." They were one, but not one person. They were not dancers but the dance.

And yet this motion began to change, and to change him. The change came very gradually like a mist imperceptibly introduced into a vale of pure darkness, and the observer, without sensing when it begins, and doubting the report of his senses at first, finally admits that the black is not pure anymore, that the mist has made its entrance. A mist gathered in his loins.

Its ever more intense concentration proved to Mac that he had a body after all. And he began to realize that this body of his was being influenced by another, by Sarah's, where a change was also going on. This was the end of the oceanic, this new gripping of Sarah's. She seemed now to penetrate him even as he penetrated her. Her power was subtler and went deeper than his; it reached very deep, all the way to a region of which he was never conscious except under her influence, to a place below his spine.

And her music had become a gasping series of soft, self-abandoned cries. One hand held his shoulder, the other measured his movements by holding his rear in a firm grip. The cries came faster and it was joy to hear them—triumphant joy—but the next triumph was the victory of his wild body over whatever remained of his mission as her lover.

Here was another leap. Starting from deep inside his loins, where Sarah's influence beckoned the wild spirit out of its deepest recess, the wildness leapt toward the woman who called to it.

Mac entered the true oblivion. He passed its threshold, which was a series of throbs so violent he had to catch his breath when he could—for long intervals he didn't breathe at all—and it was bliss, yes, a bliss of the senses—but also a blank unconsciousness, an emptiness.

He lost his mind again and again, and reentered oblivion without knowing how, without memory or consciousness.

At some point he heard Sarah's moans, heard his own groaning voice, and covered her ear with a considerate hand. He let the bliss continue—its throbbing intervals of sense and oblivion—and he saw the trail in the green brush. This image rushed in to fill the void. Dawn was turning to full daylight. He couldn't put out flankers because the brush was impenetrable. But they had taken this trail to avoid repeating the route they had followed on their way out, and to check the bicycle tracks. The three miscreants who had slept at the LP marched ahead, slouching with shame and apprehension. Mac's radioman, Graeser, followed five meters behind him; the chaplain was back there somewhere. They marched silently but Mac hated it, hated this trail.

He was trying to work out the problem of what to do with the three dumb shits. His preference was to let Gunny Hitchcock handle it but if—he was conjuring up the worst possibilities—if somebody were wounded or killed on the way in he might have to file charges of sleeping on watch.

The trail ran straight through deep brush about ten feet high. Just before he reached a curve Mac looked back and his eyes and the chaplain's met. Then the curve. Paul Adrano had seen him with those sharp black eyes. The air was humid, close, and hot already, down in this bush.

Mac heard a sound and knew he'd done it and it was too late. A tug on his boot. A simultaneous pop like the report of a 20-gauge shotgun—and he was diving, sailing through the air desperate to hit ground—but if you're diving it's already too late. He took a blow on the knee. His mind still worked, and it told him he was dead.

He hit the deck and rolled. He rolled clear of the trail and into the brush but it stopped him. It was like rolling against a wall. He was still alive. Men were flattened up and down the trail and he heard somebody cry halt in the rear. That'd be Gunny Hitchcock.

A few minutes later, four or five men were gathered around it—looking down at it like it was a death's head—and Paul Adrano said:

"What is it?"

Mac didn't answer right away. He was looking now at his right leg, where the faded green trouser was dripping blood onto his boot and the corpsman worked to stop the bleeding, pressing a soaked cloth against the gash.

The thing lying there was a cylinder with a little round chimney.

Mac looked up at Paul Adrano and caught him looking at the bloody trouser with eyes somewhat enlarged. Then their eyes met, and held.

In the background Graeser breathed: "Jesus, Skipper."

Mac said: "It's a Bouncing Betty. A dud." And he repeated: "A dud."

Then there was something—different, tender; it was Sarah's kiss. Her eyes shone with love and happiness.

He thought: "Look at her. Is this real?"

"Hell, I can swim in these," Mac said, meaning his new Bermuda shorts.

"Let's buy you a swimming suit," Sarah urged. "You'd look so spiffy."

"I'd rather save the money. What did your plane ticket cost?"

"It cost us nothing," she said, a little uneasily.

"Your father?" Mac guessed, looking closely at her.

"Yes," she said. "So you see we can afford five dollars for a swimming suit."

Mac pondered, turning away from her, and sat in one of the easy chairs, and stared. He turned his gaze to Sarah, who stood in a swimming suit covered by Mac's military shirt. As he continued to stare, she opened the shirt and swayed.

"Careful," he cautioned her.

"Don't tell me! The archbishop can't possibly be ready to conduct divine services."

"No, he's not. You are the loveliest tall girl I ever saw. What's it like to have what you've got?"

"I am seldom conscious that I *have* anything. Only you bring it out."

"I can't believe that. I know what effect you have on men.—Hey, let's go!" he cried, leaping up, and so they descended in the elevator and went to the little shelter on the beach where the hotel guests could get surfboards, swim fins, and such. Mac asked for two surfboards, all the while examining the bamboo-and-palm shelter with special curiosity.

A young man of twenty or twenty-two brought the surfboards and asked if they were experienced surfers.

Mac turned his attention from the shelter to the young man, whose muscles were somewhat heavy and smooth and blending, not sharply differentiated. He had a swimmer's body. He was a Caucasian, in fact a blonde with sharp confident eyes, but his skin was dark as a Hawaiian's and his eyebrows and hair were bleached white.

Mac said they were not experienced.

So the young man gave a few pointers, like placing your weight on the centerline, doing a push-up as you move outward through a wave, and so forth.

Mac listened, his eyes never moving from the young man's face. Seeing what was in Mac's eyes, Sarah tried to bring the conversation to an end.

She said, "We'll just see what happens, thank you," and picked up her board. "Come on, Mac."

He lifted his board and they went out toward the water.

"Well you certainly despised him!" she exclaimed.

"Did I? Do you think he noticed?"

"I hope not."

"Funny, I hope he did."

Sarah dropped her shirt, sandals, and hat, and Mac let go his gear in the same pile, and they went in the water to their knees, and watched the better surfers, studying their methods.

"It looks impossible," said Mac.

"So graceful! Look at that man!"

A surfer who proved to be a kid of about twelve, deeply tanned and slender, was riding in from a distance of 150 yards, balancing effortlessly, extending his arms but otherwise seeming to stand on a motionless platform.

"Why," said Sarah, pausing and turning from the view of the open ocean to face Mac, "why did you take such a dislike to that man?"

"Oh—the shelter reminds me of a hooch in Vietnam, is all."

"It's not all. Your antipathy was so intense—"

"I wonder why he's here surfing while my guys are in Vietnam."

"It's the luck of the draw, isn't it?"

"It's anything but luck. It's the law. College boys get a pass. Blue-collar kids get drafted—according to laws written by the daddies of the college boys. Tell me, does it make you sick?"

"So—you'd have him go over, whether he has to go or not?"

"You'll disagree of course, but yes, I would. I don't see how any military-aged man can stay home and let others do the fighting."

"But Mac, let me quote from one of your letters. You wrote that the politicians send men over there with clear instructions. Fight, swat mosquitoes, get your legs blown off, die, do anything but win. Did you write that?"

"Yes."

"So why should this boy go, if he isn't compelled?"

"If he has no pride, shame, or courage, maybe he shouldn't."

"Mac, my dearest, not everyone thinks as you do."

"Hardly anybody thinks as I do."

"Actually," she said, "my attitude is similar to yours, but perhaps a bit less severe."

"I'm too severe?"

"You are a man of conviction and you sometimes seem cut off from—you seem to me to be unable to enter into somebody else's circumstances."

"A lack of empathy maybe?"

"No—you are capable of empathy but maybe less on this subject than some others."

"That guy can walk down the street of his hometown because, nine chances out of ten, he lives in someplace like Whitefish Bay. If he lived in South Milwaukee he'd be ashamed to show his face."

She didn't answer. He was right on the last point but she feared where this exchange might lead.

Mac said: "It is a dishonorable system."

"Yes, Mac. As you may have noticed, there is a lot of dishonor and injustice, more than enough to go around."

"I have noticed.—There's a guy doing a push-up."

They watched a skilled surfer take an incoming wave head-on, by straightening his arms vertically and lifting his body on his toes, just as the wave engulfed his bow. The foam rushed back between his body and his board, and he proceeded outbound, dropping on his chest and paddling vigorously.

Mac and Sarah waded out side by side, flopped on their boards, and began stroking. They took the first mild waves easily, but then a wave flipped Mac's board by the bow and threw him off. He remounted, they grew more cautious, and both tried the push-up method on the next wave. Mac made it through the foam but Sarah's board lifted and knocked her gently in the forehead.

"Oh! It hit me!" she cried as she resurfaced, gasping. Mac circled and went in pursuit of her board. She treaded water, watching him skim along with powerful strokes till he caught her board. She could see he was puzzled what to do next. After a minute he rolled off, hitting the water on his back, and kicked to seaward, holding a board in each hand.

Sarah remounted and they paddled out, negotiating two foaming waves by the push-up method. They were now some 150 or 200 yards offshore. Most of the waves broke and began boiling at about this range.

They turned toward the beach and went dead in the water, paddling only so much as was necessary to keep their bows pointing in. A few waves lifted them, rather too gently, and Sarah proposed they go out farther. They did a one-eighty and resumed paddling to seaward, but immediately faced a big standing wave that threw them both.

They surfaced quite close to each other and Mac observed the quick practiced motion with which Sarah drew the hair back out of her eyes. They swam in search of the boards, and five minutes later, without having touched bottom, they were paddling abreast, outbound.

"What was the boat," Sarah asked panting, "that Kennedy had during the war?"

"Patrol Torpedo Boat 109," said Mac without hesitation.

"That's you. A regular PT 109 when you skim along. But I am keeping up with you, Mr. Mac!"

"Hey, Woody, I can just barely keep up with you," he said, then: "Here comes one."

It toppled both, and they surfaced and swam close to each other, and Mac kissed her, and tasted her mouth after the salt.

"Now, *land the landing party,*" he hollered, imitating the loudspeaker on an amphibious ship.

They swam after their boards again, taking the lift offered by each incoming swell, and turned again out to sea in the blinding glitter of the high sun.

"I don't exactly know why," Sarah ventured, "but I am enjoying this."

"Me too. It's the form of the waves, big but not vicious like the ones on the Outer Bank. Remember our ride on the rubber ladies?"

They had paddled out from the beach at Surf City, south of Onslow Beach at Camp Lejeune, each one riding a rubber lady (Marine Corps talk for air mattress) and as they reached the break line, or what should have been the break line, a wave twice as high as the rest broke over them and tumbled. It flipped and drove them both headfirst into the sand six or eight feet down. Neither would ever forget the force and violence of it. In a wave like that you are a chip of wood.

It was at the same beach, just by Barnacle Bill's fishing pier, that a marine had been knocked out by a tumbling comber and drowned. His dead body was the first Sarah had ever seen outside a funeral parlor.

They were now keeping station, glancing back, and both cried that the next wave was *the* wave. They paddled hard till the last second, then jumped to their knees. Mac looked aside to see her, and she was kneeling forward, and the thrill was in her face.

Mac jumped to his feet, planted himself in the center, and slowly stood full upright as the wave carried him up and on. His feet sank in the boiling white foam and he got the sensation of sailing while balanced, and of steady velocity. He looked around for Sarah, the sky flipped, and he was in the wave, lost in the foam, down in the pure heaving water. He dropped a few feet, found the vertical by finding the sunlight beaming down like a rain of light rays, then propelled himself up and broke the surface, coughing the snorting salt water.

All he saw was ocean. He spun to landward and beheld the athletic Miss Woodley, sailing like a low-flying gull, wings spread and bent, motionless, knees flexed, head up.

When they joined up for the next foray Mac said:

"Now I know your secret. It's all in your butt. If I had a butt like yours—"

"You have a boy's butt. A grown man, buttless! But I like you as you are."

And this caused her to think of him as he was. She realized she had a fear deep inside her mind that he would cease to be "as he was," or had already ceased. In the past he would shout and curse and laugh, getting knocked over by waves, seeing his feet fly. Today he was saying very little. She wasn't sure he was really enjoying it. She said as they rode up a high crest, "Do you hear? *As you are.*"

He thought of her *as she was* and realized how good and nearly perfect she was from his point of view. He saw again the sailing gull. He admired her for standing fast against him, as she had over the (presumably) draft-dodging young man. He was still, in a different way, riding in her body and immersing his identity and passions in her person.

"O.K.," he shouted with gusto, "here comes my ride."

He spun his board, paddled furiously, cast a quick look back, and hopped to his knees, felt the lift and thrust under him, and jumped to his feet.

It centered in his chest. He thought that if he could keep this center of force poised above his knees, let it sway however it might, then he'd sail as she had done. In fact he was sailing, a bird-mariner on a foaming crest of white, running shoreward in the bright sun, atop a wave that passed over the water without moving it, as a wind-wave traverses a field of wheat.

It lasted, and lasted, and was a sharp thrill in his mind, but something went suddenly wrong, and he had to force his balance. This was fatal. The board flipped, his feet flew, and he plunged sideways with his arms flailing and sunk into the wave. He surfaced in a deep trough with a new and stronger wave looming over him. He dropped but too late. The boiling, moving crest caught him and bore him along, and he, having lost all sense of up or down, closed his eyes and let himself be rushed along. After a second, out of shame, he opened his eyes and saw white chaos, and heard it in his ears, and tried to swim. He was running out of air but he kept trying to find the level and to swim to the top and catch a breath.

His lungs wanted to burst—he realized with a little ray of fear that his lungs wanted to suck in—and his heart pounded. With a series of strong strokes, on his last air, he dived and swam down, into the darker element. He whirled, and stroked up. He broke the surface and gulped air, then went down again before the next one hit.

After this he swam shoreward to find his board, and there he met Sarah. She had ridden all the way in and was flushed with her accomplishment. They paddled seaward again, lying prone and arching their backs and stroking together to one rhythm. He observed the curve of her back, where it was crossed by a narrow strip of gold cloth, and it swooped down from the shoulders and up at the gold cloth that covered her buttocks.

Seeing his eye on her, Sarah said: "You've lost weight. Your muscles don't bulge as much. They are tighter and harder. You look all tight and wiry."

He said: "Yep. You look like a queen."

She smiled and they stroked seaward.

Late in the afternoon while walking along the crescent beach they came upon a gang of military men, with many wives and girlfriends, playing volleyball. The players had erected a net and scraped boundaries in the sand but as far as rules, they seemed to have none. The ball went flying and sometimes was set up four or five times before someone spiked it like a rifle shot, yet nobody complained.

Attracted by the boisterous energy and exuberance, Mac and Sarah stopped to watch. It was already five o'clock and many players had partaken of the beer supply that was cooling in a galvanized tub full of ice on a picnic table. Dozens of cans, full and empty, stood lined up like soldiers on the redwood planks.

If a player trotted over to the table and lifted a can the game continued uninterrupted. Mac cast a thirsty glance at the tub, but he had not eaten since noon and a beer now could make him dizzy.

He tried to guess if the men were soldiers or marines, and decided it was a motley collection. There were men in the crowd with cantilevered guts who could not be marines, and others with farmer suntans and lean muscular bodies who might be.

It must have been obvious from Sarah's shirt that Mac and Sarah were a military couple. A chant arose: "Join up, join up," first from two or three voices, then from the half-drunken mob. Sarah, with a daring glance at Mac, kicked off her sandals and ran into the game. They greeted her with whoops. Mac slipped off his new shirt and sneakers and joined the other side. So Mac and Sarah faced each other through the net.

Sarah cried: "Look out, Red!"

And Mac retorted: "Look out yourself, Woody!"

Nobody knew the score or cared to know it till a man named Sam proposed they start over. The ball flew. Sarah's team won the volley and they tossed the ball to Sarah to serve.

Sensible of this honor, she stood leaning over the back line, her eyes shifting from the ball to the court and back, then she fell forward, popped the ball, and watched it arc away. Somebody on Mac's side set it up and Mac spiked it with expert force, and the serve shifted to his side.

"No fair!" a girl shouted indignantly, "they're sober!"

At this a man dashed to the picnic table, and threw a can toward Sarah and another toward Mac. Somebody supplied a church key and they both drank. Sarah took hers back to the table but Mac drained his in a single chugalug, threw it toward the tub, and was cheered like a hero. He squinted into the low sun and shouted some "go team" phrases, and his teammates set up a husky chatter. The sun glittered on the ocean and a mild breeze swept over the game.

There were upward of fifteen players on each side so people kept bumping one another, and often two or three ganged up on one flying ball. Mac, from a back row, set up a shot and a forward teammate spiked it for a point, and Mac's team started jeering and boasting.

Across the net Sarah crouched like a tiger and pounced on every shot that came within her reach. When he had the chance Mac fired his shots toward her, and she proved a formidable opponent, either setting up a second shot with casual skill or screwing the shot back at him. Her returns often flew just outside his reach, and in his zeal to return her shots he sometimes lunged into and toppled his teammates. But mostly he played team ball, setting up spikes for the front line when he was not able to spike a shot himself.

Now the game turned serious. Mac's head was clear and he forgot his hunger.

Sarah was happy, almost drunk with it. Seeing that some of the men were tanned all over and others had Mac's "farmer suntan"—face, neck, and arms only—she could assign them to the two main categories of combat soldier or rear-echelon pogue.

"So, Captain," she had said earlier that day when Mac was throwing those terms around, "are you contemptuous of rear-echelon pogues too? Is going to Vietnam and doing your duty—if it's not as a frontline fighter—is that not enough? I mean, Captain, is *nobody* worth his salt except a combat marine?"

"She's got it!" he roared and took her by the shoulders and kissed her, and she saw a flush of genuine hilarity in his face.

With this in her mind she glanced from man to man and noticed that many of the supposed combat soldier and marines—the ones with farmer suntans—were far from being the Adonises she expected. Because her own Adonis was a combat marine she had too facilely concluded that the men who did the fighting must be tough and muscular, the kind of man the world stands away from.

Looking with avid curiosity at these men and women Sarah felt, despite the differences, that she belonged among them. Their rough gusto answered some call in her spirit. She didn't know the name of it, but some kind of power or drive in her called out and received its answer. She came from a different kind of place, almost a different society, but she was with them.

Sarah saw Mac squinting against the sun, which made him look serious, almost fierce. She knew he would not want to be identified by his rank so she suppressed her egotistical urge to shout "Captain" to him. She cried: "I'm sending one your way, Red!"

He stiffened, stood straight, pointed at her threateningly, and called: "Watch your nose, Woody!"

The game proceeded. The two sides were evenly matched. And suddenly everybody was crazy to win. Mac kept slamming his shots toward Sarah wherever she happened to be placed, and she as competently returned them and even outperformed him. This drove him to pound harder and spike faster, and he lost part of his team consciousness, and lunged for shots he should have left to others. But he was one of the best on the court and nobody complained.

One of the shots he fired at Sarah was intercepted by a lithe and aggressive man who leapt in front of her and tripped the ball up for a spike return by a front-row player. With the sun glaring in his eyes Mac could not clearly see the man's features but his body and smoothly coordinated movements were those of a self-confident aggressive athlete. He was a good player—too crashing and a little wild, not a team player but one who wanted to win the game by himself rather than let the drunken sots lose it. Mac recognized a competitor.

Suddenly a shout went up, exclamations of amazed admiration as people pointed toward the ocean and cried, "Look at him!" Sarah saw a brown-skinned man in a tight swimsuit riding a surfboard in at unusual speed. He was standing on his head with his straight legs pointed to the sky. The military mob cheered beerily and went a little crazier. The surfer seemed to elevate, then flipped neatly sideways. He stepped forward in the shallows like a prince condescending to greet the rabble, and he made a slight bow, and lifted his board and waded ashore, turning his back and departing without a word.

Now the players stretched out. It became a mark of valor to lunge for a ball and collide with your teammates, a show of daring to knock somebody down. Still the game retained a kind of order, and the scorekeeper called out the numbers.

Sarah observed that Mac was playing superaggressive ball. On her own side the man who had taken away her shot was perhaps the most reckless and aggressive one. In grabbing one shot he gave her a bump that didn't quite knock her over, and then he wasted the shot by driving it into the net. She said nothing but resolved to claim her own shots.

She saw Mac give the man a hard stare, stopping the game while he held the ball and stuck out his neck and glared. The man, the competitor, paid no attention, but clapped his hands and hollered, "Drive on, drive on!"

He was almost Mac's size, well built, and quick. For one his size and weight he was in fact very quick. His chest and shoulders were burned by the sun and their color had begun to blend into this farmer's tan. He had a sharp face and deep-set dark eyes. Mac appraised him, and a kind of dark flow began in his mind, a specific force tending in a certain direction.

Mac took a time-out, downed another beer, and trotted back to the game. The service passed from his team to Sarah's, and the next event was that Sarah's side scored a point, and the scorekeeper shouted: "Nineteen-seventeen." The ball came flying, and a teammate of Mac's set it up for Mac, who spiked it with more force than accuracy.

As he hit the ground somewhat off balance Mac saw through the net that Sarah was hustling forward to spike a setup. Mac had not seen the setup but there was the ball hanging in the air, with Sarah poised to return it. Her body sprang and stretched, and she hovered.

The competitor leaped and struck her with his shoulder and she flew, and dropped with a whiplash motion, and her head hit the sand hard. Mac saw the whiplash and saw the force of it. She didn't fall, she hit the deck with the velocity of the whiplash.

Mac ducked under the net and crouched beside her and said, "Woody, are you all right?"

Sarah said yes, but not immediately. She rested her head on the sand, looked at Mac equivocally, shut her eyes, then held out her hand. He pulled her to a sitting position, where she again paused, lowering her head between her knees. She took two or three breaths, looked up, smiled, and said, "O.K.," and he pulled her to her feet.

Mac met the competitor's eyes and went back to his side, and the game resumed.

But after two minutes Mac again crossed under the net, as if unaware there was a game going on. He went to the competitor and stood facing him. The man did not move back, and he stood, loose and derisive, with his weight on one hip. His wet pectorals and shoulders, specked with sand, picked up the gleam of the low sun.

Mac said: "Are you a marine?"

Everybody was now paying attention.

"Who wants to know?"

"My name is Clare and I asked you, are you a marine."

The man said: "Do I look that stupid?"

"You don't look stupid at all," said Mac.

And each man took a half-step closer and Mac's eyes poured a warning.

A deep voice from somewhere in the mob drummed out: "U!-S!-M!-C! U!-S!-M!-C!"

In ten seconds the mob reorganized itself, men shifting position and getting their bearings, exchanging looks of recognition. And Sarah's stomach heaved with fear. Instead of two volleyball teams she now beheld a group of about ten men facing a group of about twenty, marines against soldiers.

"You'd better apologize to the lady," Mac rumbled.

Sarah cried: "Mac! Stop it! He did not hurt me."

Mac repeated, without turning his head or shifting his eyes: "Apologize to the lady."

"I am not a *lady*! Stop this, Mac!"

Said the competitor, whom everybody now clearly understood to be a soldier—that is to say, Army: "I guess she's not a lady."

In the indecisive pause that followed this, a voice raised a chant: "Airborne! Airborne!" And a shouting chorus echoed it.

A man near Mac began barking derisively, and soon all the marines were barking in derision of the "dogfaces" of the Army. Sarah realized there was only one person who could stop it, and that she had a second to act.

She stepped between Mac and the soldier, took Mac's hand and pulled, looking at him with peremptory anger. He stood. She stretched his arm and said:

"Mac, this is stupid."

And Mac yielded. He turned from the soldier and followed his wife, and some of the marines groaned.

The soldier crowed: "Hundred and Seventy-Third Airborne says— bye-bye!—to pussy marines!"

Mac halted. He looked at Sarah's hand on his arm. She did not release him.

Three minutes ago, when he first saw the man bump Sarah, and while he stared at him, Mac felt the dark flow moving inside him. It was like an overflow of lava, and it was hot. If he got into a fight and the Military Police filed a report, it was conceivable the report would reach his regiment, and he might be relieved of his command. He enjoyed the confidence of the regimental commander, and since the S-curve he had been regarded as the outstanding company commander in the regiment. But officers do not brawl with enlisted men, or encourage marines to attack the U.S. Army. So Mac had feared what seemed to be going on in his mind as he watched the competitor.

Then when the man knocked Sarah down he feared she was injured. More fear. When he helped her to her feet his love took him over with cutting power. What—for Christ's sake—what if something happened to her? But then he stumbled into the question—was the competitor a marine? If he was, Mac could not touch him. So his mind seemed to have decided to beat the man if he was not. But this could entail the loss of what, after Sarah, he cared about most.

As Mac stared the man down and got his answer, he was almost trembling with fear and rage. To lose Delta Company! He had to pull back!

Then Sarah took his arm and pulled him and said, quite sensibly, that this was stupid. So he went with her.

But now, with the marines barking like rabid dogs and the soldiers calling "Airborne, airborne!" Mac cooled. He cooled to the point of ice. He had no choice now. It was as good as done. He looked at Sarah, and saw her despair, but there was nothing he could do about it. He gently but forcibly pulled his arm free.

Approaching the soldier he felt the good confidence: he could keep his temper, that is to say, his clarity. Mac was not a habitual brawler but he held in his memory a paradigm fight. It occurred in the summer between his junior and senior years at UW, at a construction site in Stevens Point where his father was excavation contractor and Mac was driving a bulldozer. It was a two-man fistfight and Mac had won against a heavier but slower opponent, and won decisively. The soldier wasn't the only man on the beach who was quick.

The din of the barking rose to a new pitch as Mac came slowly forward. He took a subtly conscious pleasure in his strength. He flicked his shoulders. The barking grew frenzied. They were squealing like little poodles and booming like shepherds and howling like huskies. The paratroopers were thudding out: "Airborne, airborne!" There was no point in talking, nobody would hear.

The soldier stepped dangerously close and tried to hold Mac's eyes, but Mac knew all about the knee in the groin delivered under cover of a defiant stare. At this point, anyway, it didn't matter who went first.

Mac spun a quarter-turn right and jabbed back with his left elbow. The soldier deflected a blow that would have knocked him flat. He swung at Mac's neck but Mac dropped into a crouch and shot up on the power of his knees, thrusting both fists straight up. One connected, and the soldier's head flipped back, reminding Mac of the platoon sergeant's head flying during the attack on the bunker. He pounded the soldier's solar plexus and took a stout blow to his left ear, absorbed it, and jabbed at the man's face. This blow was on target but too light for the damage needed, which was above all shock, violence. Both men swung with wild malice and neither was scoring. Then Mac connected with a strong right to the man's face, which spurted blood, and an eye closed almost instantly.

Then Mac let fly a left that also scored. The bleeding soldier wobbled and went bleary. A mental clearing opened and allowed Mac to realize that a general brawl was going on all around him. Two men were trying to grab his arms. He struck one a good blow with a fist and caught the other in the face with an elbow.

The soldier was upon him again but Mac had no fear of him. He danced back—he had done this at Stevens Point—and the soldier let fly while he was not firmly grounded. His fist hit Mac's eye socket. Mac simply planted himself and sent back a javelin right that struck the soldier square in the chin. Mac next swung a haymaker from the left that jerked the man's head sharply, and when Mac saw the twist of this one he stopped. He could have dropped him now but didn't. Mac took a blow from behind and paid no attention.

Somebody shouted that the MPs were coming. Mac said loudly, "Knock if off, marines." The men scattered and the women lingered to greet the two MPs running toward the scene.

Mac took Sarah's hand and they walked quickly to the water and waded away into the evening combers, and swam out, and Mac breathed heavily, and turned and watched the MPs talking with the women. Mac guessed they were two very relieved MPs.

He asked Sarah if she was O.K. and she said she was. Was he? He said yes. Mac floated on his back to take the weight of the water off his chest, and he breathed deeply. His left ear hurt but his eye was fine. He looked at Sarah. She was not smiling.

"I'm trying," said Sarah.

"But not succeeding."

"I can't help it."

"How many hours have we got left?" Mac asked. "And we just lost twenty-four, a whole goddamn day."

"I am really trying, but it's as if you gave me an injection of ice water."

"Jesus!"

"It's spreading inside me and it's not getting any better."

"Then for God's sake we have got to talk."

"And say what? I've already told you ten times, I feel chilled."

"Then tell me again. I want my wife back."

"And I want my life back."

"Sarah, for Christ's sake what does *that* mean? I took your life away when I punched that dogface?"

"Mac, do you think you could control your swearing? I know you don't mean anything by it but it upsets me sometimes, taken together with everything else."

"Fine, I'll stop swearing, but what is *everything else?*"

"You were in the middle of it, so you maybe can't understand. You didn't see what I saw."

"Good, we've gotten beyond the 'chill.' What is it you saw that I didn't?"

"I think you were blind to everything but your temper. I saw a strong, intelligent man fly into a fury, and that man was my husband."

They were walking along one of the commercial streets of Honolulu. It was Christmas Eve and Mac was still looking for a present he really wanted to give her. But upon hearing this "fury" statement he halted and took her hand, but then released it when he felt no response. It didn't even feel like her hand.

He said: "A guy knocks my wife for a loop and then calls me a pussy, and I'm supposed to walk away."

"Was it better to do what you did? I tell you, Mac, I watched you lose control, and I heard a fiendish voice in my ear. Oh God, I don't want to tell you!"

"Tell me."

Now he took both her hands. She looked aside and shook her head in negation and pain.

He said: "Sarah. Tell me. What did this voice say—that I was a—"

"It said, 'Is that your idea of a husband?' And you are, Mac, you are exactly, my only idea, but when you flipped out, and now when you use me as an excuse, I can't accept it."

"Use you as an excuse?"

"Yes. I was not your motive when you fought that soldier. You are dishonest to say I was. You smashed his face and walked away unharmed, so you're quite satisfied. But you did it for your own satisfaction. I told you, he didn't hurt me."

"So we get a divorce because I got into a fight that didn't amount to a hill of beans? It was nothing, Woody, absolutely nothing."

"If it was nothing why did you say you had to do it?"

"Did I say that?"

"You said, 'Am I supposed to let a guy knock my wife for a loop and call me a pussy?' You mean you had to fight him. So which is it? Did you have to do it or was it nothing?"

"O.K., you win the argument. What does that prove?"

"Oh, we reach that old familiar point. Whenever I *win the argument* it proves you are right. You are too simple and noble to win an argument. Let's walk. People are staring at us."

Mac said: "All it proves is that, for you, winning the argument is the most important thing."

"It proves no such thing," she insisted. "Anyway I haven't won this argument because you are still convinced of two contradictory propositions."

"Woody, quit it! *Contradictory propositions.*"

"Sorry. Let me just say then, you can't have it both ways."

"What's the difference which way I have it. I don't care! I want my wife back."

"And I want a husband I can live with!"

For the first time he felt the fear, not of divorce, which was inconceivable, but of an estrangement such as they had never experienced. He said, "O.K., tell me what I have to do. Tell me and I'll see if I can do it."

"About the fight?"

"Yes."

"There's nothing to be done. You smashed your enemy and rescued your 'lady' and showed true Marine Corps spirit. Semper Fi! What's left to be done?"

"I mean, what must I do to satisfy Your Royal Turbulence?"

"Just—Mac—just love me, O.K.?"

"Woody, I love you down to the ground, but I think you're saying I have to do or quit doing *something* to get rid of the chill. I—it sounds like—did I scare you?"

"It was a coldness."

"Cold toward me?"

"Yes. I lost all feeling except a kind of cold foreboding."

He was just absorbing this when they were interrupted by a couple they knew from Camp Lejeune, and, to Mac's consternation, Sarah proposed all four meet for dinner. The couple said they had already made plans to meet another couple whose names were unknown to

Mac and Sarah; and Sarah quickly asked if she and Mac could join the party. They were accepted and the date was made. To hide his irritation Mac set off to find her a present, and they agreed to meet at the hotel. Mac found a present but not peace. Thus they spent the evening with four others, ate dinner, went to a music bar, and returned to their room at midnight having had no opportunity to go deeper into their problem.

Sarah was moving toward confession. She went to sleep believing that since she had to confess anyway it would be well to confess in the midst of this alienation, and that perhaps her confession would heal it. She expected to be understood and forgiven. She believed she had not offended, therefore all she needed was understanding. But she was willing to allow him the consciousness of forgiveness if that would heal the rift.

He went to sleep believing he had not offended by fighting, but would not be forgiven. He believed her all too deeply when she said she had lost all feeling for him, and he decided he must confess the "empty center"—what happened in the oblivion at the center of his climax. This too was not an offense but it was a secret and he wanted to confess it. He could not stand the rift between them, or her coldness. He thought if he told her about the empty center, and the images that filled it, she would understand, and this understanding would encompass the problem of the brawl, he'd be forgiven and the rift healed.

He was withholding, which was a kind of falseness, and he wanted to come clean. As this desire to be honest gained a foothold he felt his resolution grow stronger, to confess the empty center; but he forgot the black flow in his mind, the sensation of being carried by a malign force he could not understand or control.

The next morning was Christmas. Mac was set on confessing but Sarah spoke first. They were dressed for breakfast but Sarah took his hand as he was about to open the door.

"I can see that you might not understand why I am so upset. Am I right? You say, 'Nothing happened,' and therefore I should roll with the punch, so to speak."

He said, "I know you are upset. I don't know why."

"Right. I'll tell you why and I promise not to sound like a stuffed shirt."

343

"I apologize for that. Use all the 'contradictory propositions' you want."

Passing this over Sarah said: "You were in the middle of the fight, pushing your face two inches from that man's, and I assume this is a rather intense experience, a semicrazy minute. Am I right?"

"More or less," he said and thought of the black flow. It was like a cataract of liquid tar in which his volition slipped and rode. But he didn't speak of it.

Sarah continued: "But I was outside the action."

"Go on," said Mac when she paused and glanced at him, awaiting a sign to continue.

"And here's what I have to offer," she said. "I hope by telling you this I don't ruin our vacation."

He said quietly, "Go on."

"Believe me, I hesitate to say it. I don't want to say it. But you will never understand me if I don't. When I saw you in a fury, temporarily mad, and capable of—I thank God the other guy was nearly as big and strong as you. Had he been smaller and weaker—"

"Then I would never have—"

"Yes, yes, but are you listening to me? I'm not interested in your code of conduct on who you will clobber and who you won't. I am trying to tell you something about me, not you. Do you realize? I was frightened! I am still chilled by it, it makes me go cold inside. If I sound stiff and strange it's because I am stiff with fear, Mac."

"Christ! Fear of me?"

"I don't know! Please forgive me for being so formal and detached, but I can only explain it this way. If I'd simply blubbered like a baby seal I don't think I could have made myself half so clear."

"But are you afraid of me? That's incredible."

"I told you I don't know."

He saw tears filling her eyes and it made him feel like a criminal. He took her in his arms and began trying to tell how sorry and wretched he was, but she stopped him.

"Don't apologize! I am not entitled to an apology. I just want you to know, Mac, I was—"

They embraced and neither spoke for a while, till Sarah said:

"I have so much to tell you, Mac my love. My love! O.K., I have to go all the way! Let's not forget we love each other—in the next minute. We have discovered how awful life is alone, at least I have, let's remember—not having a 'goddamn battle' to keep me company—I mean, we are married! We are together for life, we decided, we fell in love, I love you still—"

She was getting more and more distraught and Mac said:

"Sarah, I love you, you know I do, I couldn't ever be happy without you."

"Stop. Here it comes. Are you feeling strong?"

"No."

"Here it comes anyway. When I saw you carried away by fury I heard the little fiendish voice say, 'Is he your idea of a husband?' I didn't answer, but I listened! And Mac—no, please, let me finish. I have another thing to say, then we'll go down to breakfast and then we'll exchange Christmas presents and go surfing and forget the war." She drew back, and regarded him with hopeful, glowing eyes.

He watched her patiently.

She said: "Mac, I'm on the Pill." She could see that he didn't grasp it right away and she said: "I am taking birth-control pills."

He said, looking level at her eyes, "I know what 'the Pill' means."

She watched his face and it seemed to reflect a burden of painful thought. She continued: "I couldn't discuss it with you. I wanted to, but I had to decide for both of us, the way you decided for both of us. I gave it careful—I tried to see it from all angles and to consider your wishes, but I decided I didn't want to get pregnant. Can you understand?"

She saw the terrible shock in his face. She felt his hand stiffen in hers and she squeezed, and got no response other than the stiffness.

He said, "No," but he could hardly speak.

"Mac, my love, it isn't as simple as you might think. You're going to be over there six more months. How can you expect me—"

"Don't say any more."

His tone stunned her. He turned the doorknob but she slammed the door and cried:

"What are you doing!"

He said, "I'm going down to breakfast."

"No! You act as if I have no right to decide this with you."

"You have no right to decide it without me."

"Which is exactly what you did. You decided you wanted the baby immediately, so you wrote a little cheery note *announcing* that I would become pregnant on this trip, and, as I have already said, I *wanted* to discuss it with you but what chance did I have?"

"Wait," he said in a voice she could scarcely hear.

"So I went to a doctor and got pills, because I want you with me during pregnancy and delivery. What is so wrong with that?"

She watched in a fury as he sank onto the bed and held his head in his hands. She noticed the short military haircut and the red knuckles. She was still going; she said:

"I took your note seriously and I sympathize with you, you want a child this minute, and so do I! But I had to decide by myself. And I decided it would not matter if we waited six more months. We've already waited so long, on account of this horrible war, and I wanted you with me, and you said you wanted to be with me, you said you wanted to see the baby born. You remember? 'I am going to see that miracle.' Remember?"

"Yes," and he looked up and she was astounded to see tears on his face.

She sat beside him and took him in her arms.

He said, "Forgive me, Woody. I thought you meant something else."

"What, Red, what else could I mean?"

"When you said you were on the Pill."

She was rocking back and forth, and he perforce rocked with her, but she stopped—and it hit her what he meant. She cried: "Oh no Red, no, no, never!"

"I know. Please forgive me, please. I was a weak and stupid fool."

Mac looked into her eyes and saw her love and forgiveness welling up without pause or judgment. He touched her face on both sides and said:

"Please, please forgive me. I am a goddamn jerk. Yes. You were right. We aren't even sure I'm coming home, are we?"

"Oh yes, Mac, we are sure. You'll come home and we'll have a healthy happy baby and we'll be together and live as a family. But Mac—that other—*suspicion*—"

346

"I'm sorry, I'm so goddamn sorry."

"No, no more. Just—that's impossible Mac, inconceivable."

They went down to their Christmas breakfast.

Sitting on the bed, drinking coffee, flipping through one of his new books, Mac thought Sarah was changing into her swimming suit. But sensing motion he looked up and saw her dancing, in the nightgown he had just given her as a Christmas present, to a cadenced music audible only to herself, with her eyes almost closed and her lips smiling. It was a shortie nightgown of black silk and lace, with narrow shoulder straps.

Turning in her dance, and without looking at him, she asked if he liked it. He said he definitely liked it. She moved toward the bed and picked up the box containing the gold necklace, and linked it around her throat.

"I want you to see me," Sarah said. "I love to see you looking at me—this way."

He replied: "I love to look."

Approaching the bed, still smiling, she gradually resumed her day-to-day persona. Leaning over and peering into the ditty bag from which he had taken her gifts, she asked, "What's this?" She took out a small package.

"Open it," he said. "I got that for your father. Will you send it to him?"

She examined a brass buckle with five stars, a big numeral 1 and the word "Guadalcanal," the emblem of the 1st Marine Division. She said, "He'll like this. He'll wear it. And what's this other one?" She took out a larger package and handed it to Mac.

He unwrapped a green canvas-bound notebook with a leather loop holding a stainless-steel pencil. Giving it to her he said: "It's for a man named Paul Adrano."

As she turned it over he told her the story of Paul's fear at the S-curve, and of his departure from the regiment. He also told her about his own moment of fear.

Leafing through the notebook she pondered, as if trying to imagine what Paul Adrano might write there. She gave it back and asked: "Where is he now?"

"I heard he was at the naval support hospital in Da Nang."

"Support hospital—meaning—"

"I believe it's like an Army evac hospital, a place where they save the guy and then send him up the chain if he needs more sophisticated surgery. The naval support hospital at Da Nang probably sends hard cases to the hospital ship lying off Da Nang Harbor."

"I see. So this Paul Adrano, who calls himself a coward, is ministering to men on the brink of death."

"Some of them, yes."

"And he chose that assignment?"

"I expect he did."

"He must be a strong man—who uses his strength against himself."

"I think that's it. He couldn't forgive himself, if that's the word, for his moment of paralysis. He saw mine and he called me 'victorious.' But he calls himself a coward."

Sarah searched his eyes as if to make certain she understood, then said: "He sees your fear as an episode, and his own as a permanent condition."

"Evidently."

"Is he right?"

"About me, yes. About himself, I don't know. Had the fight lasted a day longer, or an hour, I think he would have conquered it."

"Can it be conquered—by lesser men than you?"

"Paul is not a lesser man than I. And you give me too much credit. I make no claim to courage because I do not feel courage within me, and I know now that I can be taken by the throat and shaken to pieces. But could Paul conquer it? I think so."

Sarah turned her back and Mac, knowing she would prefer he look elsewhere, returned to *Adam Bede*.

Attired now in her swimming suit, she pulled on Mac's Marine Corps shirt, slipped into her sandals with a lifting first of one hip, then the other, and said she was ready.

In the elevator she asked: "Do you like this man Paul Adrano?"

"Oh yes, I more than like him. To me he's an exceptional man."

"How so?"

"Physical strength, endurance, courage, intelligence, humor—everything that makes a man, and the sympathy and charity that make the man human, he has all that."

She nodded gravely, lifted her face unexpectedly, and kissed him on the lips. Mac responded to the kiss, and they drew apart just as the doors opened on the lobby.

Mac said: "He asked me—this was before we went out to the S-curve—what I was doing in Vietnam. I think now he knows."

Said she: "I'd like to know myself."

"I asked him the same question," said Mac, "and I think I know."

"And what is the answer?"

"He went there to serve."

"Isn't that obvious?"

"No."

They were now crossing the terrace, under a canvas awning, and could see and smell the ocean.

Mac said: "Plenty of men are there under compulsion. Many are trying to make careers. Others are running from life. Some take war as a drug. No. Very few go there to serve, and fewer still can offer exactly what's needed."

"How strange," she said. "How strange it must be, to be over there among those men, every one so different from the other yet all trying to act like men, to be men."

They put their shirts and shoes in a pile and walked toward the surf but Mac took her hand, and stopped her. To him she seemed utterly truthful and loving. He was secure in her love.

"Woody—about that brawl."

"Forget it," she laughed. "You're an animal but you're mine."

"No, I think I better remember it. I did lose control. I couldn't stop myself. That's not an excuse, it's a confession of a deeper crime."

"Crime, Mac! Please."

"It was as if I had been thrown into a river. I could swim anywhere except against the current." He thought: "Black flow," but it was too dramatic to say aloud. Still it was the name he used in his thoughts. "And if you doubt that I am anybody's idea of a husband, I doubt it sometimes myself."

"Mac, I do not doubt it. That was a passing fear."

He said: "*My* fear is just coming on. Except for one moment I was never afraid at the S-curve, but I am afraid now." He dared not tell her about the images in the "empty center."

She looked at him with earnest, troubled eyes. "My dearest Red, I love you so intensely, so gloriously and painfully, I love you with all my heart, I—"

"Yes," he said, "I understand what you're saying. Don't worry, I'll control it, I'll conquer it."

Hand in hand they walked into the surf. And she tried to answer a question: What was the "it" that he would conquer? There was in her mind a shadow of a tremor. What if he couldn't conquer it?

Chapter 15

Paul at the Hospital

In high school Paul Adrano had twice made love to a girl called Monica. He did it clumsily and perhaps for that reason she rejected his third advance. But the experience was an omen of something powerful beyond the senses. It promised a mystical bliss such as he had never known. He failed with Monica, and it was only her kindness and naïveté that saved him from humiliation. But from the age of seventeen he began associating or confounding mystery and bliss, and to believe that each contained the other.

He made the mistake of obeying the stern teaching of the church and never sought out another girl. His sense of vocation gained upon him and seemed to offer a different and elevated form of mystical bliss. He read Teresa of Avila and St. John of the Cross, and it was their path, surely the nobler path, that he followed.

His father railed against it and Paul saw that he could preserve his family and save his aunt from his father's wrath—she defended his plan to enter the seminary—or he could follow the new vocation. He could not do both. It presented itself to him as a choice between his father and God. This was his first consciousness of a moral dilemma with two goods. Because he believed there must be a profound meaning to life, he chose God. His father tortured his aunt with denunciations. Paul felt exactly as he would feel it if were he himself inflicting this abuse on the woman who had served him as a mother. But he did not back off.

Nor did he find bliss. He did find satisfaction, but satisfaction is not bliss. His energies from the very beginning were divided between God's work and the struggle against nature. He was a virile man, or so nature had intended, but from his thirtieth birthday onward he had been haunted by fear of impotence and atrophy. In one limited sense he was forced to stay in adolescence because the only other course available was surely the path to atrophy. He would look in the mirror to see if he was getting smaller. This shamed him without reassuring him.

While he was at the S-curve with Delta Company he ran on adrenaline. His adversaries were fear, horror, and exhaustion. Now he was at the naval support hospital at Da Nang, sheltered from wind and rain, decently fed, and safe—and the old implacable enemy was at him again.

He had seen a woman's smile. This woman was a star member of a group of doctors and nurses who drank together at the Officers' Club, growing more boisterous and profane as the night wore on. Paul loved the O Club but usually left early to get out of the way of his friends' pleasure. He believed the cross on his lapel would sour their evenings. But one woman, Rebecca Vanburen, a lieutenant junior grade in the Navy Nurse Corps, smiled at him not once but often. She lit up with a smile on seeing him—or so he thought. It was she who came to the bar one night when Paul stood more or less alone and insisted he join the group. She was half drunk but Paul went along, and became more than half drunk himself, before leaving an hour later than usual.

Like the other nurses, Rebecca Vanburen wore jungle utilities—a baggy green shirt that buttoned down the front, with pockets at the chest and sides. This shirt hung over the trousers, as low as the hips, thus concealing from view the only portion of the uniform that was at all snug, the hips. The trousers had the usual side pockets high up, plus cargo pockets on the sides of the legs above the knee. Becka's stethoscope and blood-pressure cuff could usually be seen hanging from the cargo pockets. What could not be seen was any clear outline of the body beneath the uniform. But Paul's uncontrollable mind made certain deductions from the vague creases and eminences of the cloth as it moved in harmony with Becka's movements. He did not see her naked in his mind, but he virtually knew her efficient muscular figure.

She was a trifle shorter than Paul, quick and limber. Even during the "mass casualty" events that lasted from twenty-four to forty-eight hours, when no one slept or even took regular meals, when some of the nurses claimed they had not seen a bathroom all day and all night, when the medevac birds arrived outside in a steady procession delivering blood and breakage as to a storm-wracked shore—even after twenty-four hours of unremitting work, Paul saw that she was able to do what she must do. Her skin—subject to flushing at the slightest provocation, for she was a redhead—would turn gradually pale, and then paler; so by the middle of the second day she seemed to shuffle semiconsciously from one patient to the next; but she endured. Paul observed this as if with pride.

Her red hair was cut close, almost like a man's, and her skin was pink when she was rested and vital; her dark blue eyes, wide set, narrowed when she smiled or laughed. She was trim and athletic, with small breasts so far as Paul could surmise. He had seen the scissors flash in her quick skilled hands when she cut away the shredded trousers of a man who had tripped a mine. At such times her face went dark with a kind of fury.

At about the twentieth hour of a mass casualty event, when Paul still had his wits about him and when his feet still told him the approximate level of the floor, he purposely began walking toward Triage.

He was two men at that moment, antagonists, one going forward, the other trying to stop the madman. But he proceeded forward and his chest, his guts, and his mind protested and pounded at the walker—but he went on, and came to Triage, where he knew he would find her. He insisted he was innocent. It is not a violation of any just law to look at a woman you see every day or to say hello to a friend in the midst of such an ordeal as this.

Just as Paul arrived a corpsman walked through announcing in a ringing voice: "Two more birds, ladies. ETA five minutes."

Becka was bent over a man strapped to a cart, holding his hands in both her own, whispering in his ear. He was a "gorp"—gray clammy skin, glass eyes, afflicted in his limbs with a steely stiffness.

She was saying, "Charles, Charles, I am Rebecca, a nurse, can you hear me?"

Paul saw a pool of blood and something else under Charles's neck.

Rebecca said, "I know you can hear me, Charles."

She ran her right hand under his neck and up his skull slowly, and stared at the blood on the tips of her white-gloved fingers. She bent even closer and turned his face toward hers, and Paul saw her eyes grow hard as she examined the gash. Looking up she saw Paul and a strange expression came into her eyes, as if to say "Do you see what has happened to him? Do you see!" Her gaze lingered on Paul for a moment, changing all the while, till it seemed to emanate sympathy for Paul.

Then she stepped back half a step, surveyed the body, and suddenly ripped Charles's shirt. The buttons flew and Paul heard them hit the plywood floor. Charles's exposed chest was free of marks except for a necklace of dried blood streaked by sweat and dirt. Rebecca applied her stethoscope, and her blue eyes lifted again to meet Paul's, and their expression was unreadable yet Paul thought she was communicating something intense and—it seemed to him—brave, defiant.

She took a full set of vitals and showed no sign of emotion. For all Paul could tell the findings were quite normal. She started an IV with a deft thrust of the needle and one careless turn of the drip control. She glanced at Paul again, as if to maintain their connection.

Then she applied her lips lightly but for a full second to Charles's forehead.

She placed her hand on Paul's, evidently forgetting it was bloody, and asked him to stay with Charles, then she ran off, and Paul began to pray for Charles.

When she came back five minutes later she was walking. At that moment a corpsman was passing. There was a surprising amount of noise in the ward, squeaking wheels, voices, a cry of pain, moans, the humming of the air conditioners.

Becka caught the corpsman and said: "Nathan, this man's an Expectant." Nathan paused, giving her time to change her mind, then shrugged and wheeled Charles away.

Rebecca looked at Paul and a tremor went through her body. He saw her shoulders move and then, turning, he watched Nathan pushing the cart through a curtain into the "Parking Lot." Paul followed. When he looked back, just as he was parting the curtain, Rebecca had already begun cutting away the trousers of another man on another cart—legs and boots all shredded.

Paul watched as she quickly scissored and ripped—with the red fury in her face. He went into the Parking Lot.

And so Paul had in his mind the shredded trousers when he confronted the dark space where five or six carts had been shunted. One of the men was convulsing, the rest were still, but he heard stertorous breathing from somewhere. It was then he felt the question bounce off one side of his brain and hit the other: "What kind of God is this?" If life is like this, all right, let it be so—but what has God got to do with it?

But Paul dropped to his knees at Charles's cart and folded one of Charles's hands into his own and his mind and soul let him pray with sincerity and love, for Charles's soul and for his family's peace. He did not think to pray for peace in the world. That was receding farther and farther from serious consideration.

Within his folded hands Paul felt a jerk and a relaxation of Charles's stiff fingers. He completed the prayers of extreme unction and rose stiffly, his knees aching from contact with the wood floor. There was Rebecca watching him rise.

She pressed her fingertips into Charles's neck at the angle of the jaw, closed her eyes and waited, then withdrew her hand, looking at Paul, and turned to go.

Paul took from his right cargo pocket the green notebook and read, as he always did, the inscription inside the cover. "To the man Delta needs most, from Sarah and Mac—Christmas 1967." Paul wrote down Charles's full name and service number and left a space for the name and address of his next of kin. He would write a letter tonight— instead of going to the O Club.

· · ·

355

He did write the letter, and there was still time to visit the club. But he did not go. And there was no struggle of two men, the goer and the stayer. He turned a fresh page and wrote:

"After years of straining to believe, it should be easy to play with reasoning.

"I will start with my fear. I clearly remember when I was a teenager and had no fear of death at all, in fact in those days I thought of *life* as an obstacle between me and God's paradise. If God had ordained that I should live, I was willing, but I was impatient. But now at the age of thirty-four, when faced with death on the battlefield—because Doc Bartholomew's call was nothing other than his call for me to *die now*—I could not move.

"But *reasoning* carries me to a new question. Why am I so shocked? Why did Puff the Magic Dragon, why does the suffering in this hospital shock me so? I must be thinking at some primitive level that suffering and death *do not belong*. They are out of place in this world.

"But suppose a world existed in which people lived forever in perfect happiness. No suffering, no death. Of course this is ridiculous. More than that, it's an affront to mankind. What would a man do, what would I do, for all eternity? It would be unendurable. In that world happiness and satiety would be the same, an exhaustion of the senses and the mind. Suppose one form of happiness were the sensual experiences we have on earth, say the most intense one, the act of love. So we have an act of sexual intercourse that goes on for thirty-five years and six days. Utter horror. Life itself would be reduced to a perpetual shuddering and corruption, and a cry for release.

"Or take love itself. If everybody is in love with everybody (universal brotherhood), love would lose its value by being distributed across all humanity. Nobody would be special. If love were limited to a small circle, nobody could live happily in the knowledge that he lacked the heart to love all mankind.

"And in this world there would be no courage, nor any real goodness, nor any call for trust, hope, regret, remorse, resolve, or anything. Truth itself would be defined out of existence. First it would be boring like everything else. And if anyone should speak the only truth worthy of the name, that this was a hideous world, he'd be, well, not killed, that would be impossible, but silenced.

"As for an eternity adoring God, I can't imagine a God who would arrange the whole universe around that.

"This is where reasoning takes me. This must be what Doc Bartholomew meant when he said he wouldn't have it any other way. He accepted our world as it is given to us. It is the only conceivable world in which men and women are real. Death and suffering, it seems, are necessary. So why am I shocked at what I see every day?

"It's only because I keep trying to fit a loving God into the picture. It's a coherent and natural picture, except that He doesn't belong in it."

Having written this he thought of Rebecca Vanburen as she bent over Charles and whispered, and of her eyes when she glared at the gash. He thought of her kissing Charles's forehead, and dwelt on the thought.

Somebody told Paul the sun was shining. He staggered up the ramp and out the double doors. Another bird was clattering down to the helipad and it was true, the rain had ceased, the sky opened, and a white sun burned down out of the atmosphere. Paul closed his eyes against the glare and lifted his face and let the hot rays beat upon his cheeks and forehead. He listened to the helicopter's engine go through its sequence of changes as it bellied down, and when the engine subsided Paul opened his eyes and saw the corpsmen running with their stretchers. He ran after them and ducked as he entered the circle under the props. The run made him gasp for breath; he had neither slept nor eaten for he didn't know how long. The sweat on his face was cooled by the gentle rotation of the props. He approached the open side of the chopper. It was an old bulb-nosed machine of a kind the Army had discarded years before, but which the Marine Corps still relied on. It could carry only six or eight WIAs. The corpsmen worked in silence. Several had jumped into the bird and were lifting the wounded onto stretchers, which they then passed out to their mates on the ground. There were six prostrate wounded and three who sat on the canvas bench and huddled, still shivering from their drenched ride into the cold air aloft. These three rose slowly and, crouching, made their own way out.

Paul was seething in his mind. His brain was overcharged like one of those old automobile batteries that had no way of limiting the amount of voltage coming in. Paul looked at one of the walking wounded for any sign of injury and, seeing none, trotted to catch one of the stretchers. Soon he was walking beside a man slobbering blood. The corpsmen had rolled him on his side and he flopped dangerously. At one point they stopped and Paul rolled him back to his side and the blood drooled out. They took him to Triage.

There Paul saw Becka already applying her stethoscope to a man's black heaving chest, while the man stared up at her with amazed eyes. Paul heard somebody say "Sir" timidly and turned and saw the walking wounded man he had examined for injury.

He said, "Hello, I'm Chaplain Adrano. May I help you?"

"Yes." But the man said nothing more.

Paul said, "Do you need a doctor?" but he knew they were all gone to Receiving and the operating rooms.

The marine was a gaunt, bent, pale trembling man whose jungle utilities hung loose on his angular frame. He said: "I don't know." His brow was all furrows that looked as if they had been sprinkled with coal dust. He smelled of rice-paddy mud, that is to say, mold and excrement.

"Tell me what's wrong," said Paul gently.

People were crossing back and forth past them. Some were calling out for help, or giving commands, or demanding supplies. Again Paul noticed the squeaking wheels of the carts as the corpsmen pushed them from station to station.

The marine said to Paul: "I can't tie my shoes."

Paul drew closer, placed his hand on the man's shoulder, and looked into his eyes as if he could instill courage. Paul said, "We can help you."

The marine went on: "I asked the battalion doctor and he said to come here. He put me on the chopper."

"Yes, he was right, you came to the right place," said Paul earnestly, and did not say: "the antechamber of hell."

The marine looked at Paul's hand, then into Paul's generous eyes. He began to weep, he covered his face and sobbed convulsively. Paul gathered him into his arm and led him to a chair. The man's shoulders inside the curve of Paul's arm were hot and wet. When Paul had seated him he looked at the top of his head, at the place near the crown where the wet brown hair whirled in a pinwheel pattern. Paul saw that his boots were neatly laced and the trousers bloused in regulation style, and then Paul imagined the man sitting somewhere, looking down at a doctor or corpsman crouched before him, lacing up his boots for him.

An hour, perhaps two hours later, forcing his legs forward, ignoring the aching of his feet and the brain fatigue, when even more casualties had just been wheeled in, Paul found himself in Triage again and he saw Rebecca turning from a cart and the supine form on it. She was carrying a marine's boot, all marked by blood and mud. He saw her throw it into a trash barrel. From the sound it made hitting bottom he knew it was not empty. The look she gave him with her sincere eyes was like a cry for understanding. He wanted to take her out of this place and—he had a mad idea—and enter some kind of warm bath, bathe her with a soft sponge. He gave what must have been a crooked smile but she lit up with a smile that was really a smile. There was no gaiety in it, only—affection! He was sure of it.

Over the next twelve hours, or maybe fourteen or sixteen—he seemed to be in a dream of this woman, her presence being suppressed by his work and prayer, but always returning to the footlights when his mind completed its task of the moment. He saw her expression as she threw the boot, and her eyes seemed to register the thud; and now Paul began to worry about her drinking. Where this came from he didn't know.

He did know that when the pressure eased and the medical staff were allowed to rest she would sleep for eight or ten hours, and wake up ravenously hungry—as she had one day when she and Paul and three others had persuaded the cooks to serve breakfast at three in the afternoon.

Then she would return to duty for a couple of hours, and during this time Paul could hope to see her and possibly speak with her. And then at the evening meal she would scarcely touch her food. But the moment the club opened she'd be there in the center of the "elite" drinking group, and she'd be relaxed and laughing after the first drink. He had seen all this before. During a mass casualty her drugs were sleeplessness and adrenaline; during normal times, alcohol and maybe pot.

The trouble evidently with pot was that the drinkers dared not consume it at the club. There was a nurse lieutenant commander called The Destroyer who wouldn't tolerate it. So they would disappear now and then, and return gliding and smiling. But Rebecca and one or two others seemed to prefer the noise, music, smoke, and cheap booze of the club to the satisfactions of the weed in somebody's dismal hooch.

The music was part of it. Why they liked it, how they could stand it, Paul could not tell, but they did. He saw the appeal of the groaning singer whose best line was "Mike me, mike me your bye-bee," but the senseless tuneless music of alienation repelled him. Rebecca never seemed to be listening, but when a tape ended she was among the first to shout for another.

As to the music, Paul was an outsider. Two others who seemed to be with him were Doc Regnary, the star surgeon of the place, a man who needed to shave twice a day but seldom did, and The Destroyer, whose real name was Evelyn Maddox. There was a rather famous destroyer in the Pacific Fleet, the USS *Maddox*. And Evelyn Maddox was a go-ahead military kind of person as well as head nurse—hence the nickname.

These four, Rebecca Vanburen, lieutenant junior grade, who was twenty-five at the oldest, and three who were about eight years older—Doc Regnary, The Destroyer, and Paul—these four had become the nucleus of the elite bunch. Paul drank less than the others but more than he ever had. He often left early, but his restraints were weakening. It was hard enough to leave the glare, smoke, and noise of the club with its boozy comradeship, after resting from a mass casualty—and harder still to leave Rebecca.

More than food, more than laughter or sunshine, Paul needed sleep. But when finally he lay down with a groan on his cot, and sat up again to take off his boots—and even when he was enjoying the liberation of his swollen feet from their prison—even then he realized how elusive sleep can be for the one who needs it most.

While praying with a wounded marine he could look at the man's face, smile at him with encouragement, listen to his voice to learn if his heart was in the prayer. Then while walking here he could keep his eyes on the duckboards, and observe the droplets hopping in their quick startled way out of the puddles. He could marvel at this simple show of nature and his mind was content.

On entering his room he could rearrange his sleeping-bag cover and anticipate the slide into sleep. All these activities occupied his mind so that it ran at a regulated pace. But now as he lay on his back, wearing only his skivvies, his brain went half mad. His consciousness flooded with an unintelligible blare of memories, fears, and dreams assailing it from all directions and for all purposes. It was almost funny and some of the images and dialogue were insane, and instantly forgotten. It was a wild outcry of mental fugitives. Each stupid idea claimed the privilege of conscious examination and, if not acceptance, at least a decent burial.

After a few minutes Paul began to see the pattern. He doubted his perception at first. But he was soon persuaded (by a specific idea, that MacHugh Clare had a good life)—persuaded that the subject and the question behind the whole gang of demands was celibacy. He realized he was questioning his vow. What if, after all, this Christian system were another iteration of the same impossible longing that had produced the Greek and Roman gods and all the other weird religions present and past—all of which would pass into dust as they deserved to do, leaving space in the mind of the race for a new and even more absurd opera. This at least was true: he was trying to live a medieval life in the midst of a war being fought with radars and computers.

He groaned that he was too tired to explore this old enigma. But his mind marched right into it, and his thoughts grew gradually more ordered and clear. This was not the show of colors and the lunatic speeches of his usual falling to sleep. No, it was beginning to look like full consciousness returning. Not that he wanted to be conscious.

He laced his boots with special care, thinking of the marine who could not, and of his face when he looked at the doc doing it for him. Then he, Paul, went out into the night.

It was probably about three in the morning. He was situated between two rather distant diesel generators pumping power to the hospital and surrounding Quonset huts and tents. He tried to listen first to one then the other generator, and found he could do this only by turning his head. He walked in a dark mist—and tried to distinguish the breeze from the mechanical rushing sound of the generators.

A sentry challenged him and Paul shined his own flashlight on himself and said he was Chaplain Adrano from the hospital. When the sentry cleared him Paul felt an inexplicable happiness. How strange. He walked on, splashing through a puddle and feeling the cold water flooding his boots, and imagining it rushing out again through the little circular metal sand screens on the sides of the boots. He needed sleep; he thought of those screens for a full minute, couldn't kick his mind ahead. But he kept walking.

Suppose he lost his sexual prowess. He had no need of it of course, so why care—but suppose he lost it. It tormented him. So long as he knew he could call upon it he still felt himself a man. But lose it altogether because of pure atrophy—he couldn't bear that.

He compared his case to Mac's. Mac was free to love a woman and live a sexual and family life with her. Paul had seen Sarah's picture and could well imagine what such a life would be. But his vow stood between him and a life like that. By his vow he had sacrificed what was "normal" in order to serve God by serving His people. Excellent idea, excellent life. Paul could not imagine himself married and committed as he was now to that degree of devotion. You must deny yourself riches in one form to attain them in another; deny what is perhaps most difficult and you attain the greater store of riches. That was the idea. Celibacy was the only way to concentrate his whole body and soul, his life, on his vocation.

But for the first time he could imagine himself married and living the sexual and family life he had renounced. He had taken vows in full awareness but not full knowledge. His "awareness" had been more like a delirium and he was learning only now what full knowledge was. He had only to think of Becka roaming his "interior castle" as she did all the time. Now he knew.

This didn't shake his conviction that life can have a profound meaning. He knew why he had chosen the life he chose. Between his father and God, between vacuity and God, he chose God. Now suddenly he was asking "What kind of God is this?" He thought of Becka kissing the forehead of the gorp marine and it seemed he sensed on his own lips that same cold salt.

Trying to exert control over himself, Paul left the club early that night, went to his office, a corner lit by a kerosene lamp, and wrote a letter of condolence to the parents of a marine. Few men died at this hospital but many would later wish they had. Paul could not use that argument on bereaved parents, and did not know how a profession of faith would affect them, so he was reduced to writing a lame, essentially false letter stressing the imponderability of human events, the will of God, and other bromides. It was letters like this that comforted the weak and disgusted the strong. He sealed it and instead of making his night rounds went back to the O Club.

"Our spiritual leader, our wise counselor—have a seat!" cried Doc Regnary, who always took the role of host.

Paul had already sat down. He was uncertain about the surgeon's welcome, in which there was perhaps a concealed blade of sarcasm.

Regnary said: "Do you have a drink? You need a drink, everybody needs a drink!" He was drunker than Paul had ever seen him.

Paul said, lifting his glass one inch off the table and looking straight at Doc Regnary: "As you see."

"Ah! I didn't see! Well since you have a drink suppose you get one for me." He held an empty glass across the table.

The Destroyer and Rebecca Vanburen exchanged a glance but neither spoke. Paul accepted the glass from the surgeon's hand and rose somewhat deliberately. Paul turned and Regnary called:

"Double scotch and fizz water if you please."

Paul showed Regnary his back, then made his way through the boom and blast, finally reaching the bar a full minute later. He resolved on patience and charity, but felt a rising of the kind of heat that precedes anger. Regnary lived in the room next to Paul's, and Paul regarded him as a friend.

Paul's social life here was so much richer than in Fall River and his pleasure in his new friendships so unexpected that he gave Regnary and many others the benefit of the doubt. This was, maybe, Regnary's idea of a rough-and-ready military comradeship.

Except that Regnary, like himself, was a civilian in uniform. In fact, a draftee, and very vocal and bitter about the injustice of it. College boys studying marketing or poetry were exempt but he, *a surgeon,* was not! When The Destroyer had said quite succinctly, "We need surgeons," it had made no impression. The consensus was that there was no winning an argument with Dr. John Regnary.

When Paul put his drink in front of him Regnary simply continued his conversation, not even looking at Paul. He completed his sentence, which was: "With all respect, Commander, that is romantic nonsense." He then thanked Paul with a silent nod.

As a lieutenant commander, The Destroyer outranked the surgeon, who was a lieutenant. On the other hand she was a nurse and he a medical doctor.

The Destroyer replied: "It isn't nonsense or sense either one, it's the way I feel."

"Oh, the way you *feel!*" the doctor retorted. "Tell the chaplain and let's see if he feels the same way."

Paul turned reluctantly to The Destroyer, a woman with blotched skin, a troubled face, pale blue eyes, and hair dyed blond, a chain smoker and steady drinker (never a binge, but never a dry day)—and a head nurse, it was often said, without a peer in the Navy.

She now said: "I think I'll drop it."

But the doc said: "Drop it? My God, Commander, we can't drop it! Tell him."

"No," was all she said.

"Becka, you tell him," the surgeon urged and he nudged Rebecca with his arm. The two sat side by side across the circular table from Paul. Besides Becka, Regnary, Lieutenant Commander Evelyn Maddox, and Paul there were three other nurses and one physician present, but they were not regarded as among the elite.

Becka said, "Maybe she understands better than the rest of us."

"Oh Christ!" Regnary exclaimed—and Paul was stone-faced.

"The commander *feels* the presence of a Death Force, Chaplain, and *believes* we are all lined up in battle order to resist it."

Paul stared into the doc's bloodshot, moist, sleep-deprived eyes and did not comment.

One of the other nurses seconded Rebecca, and Regnary ignored her. He was watching Paul.

"Well, Chaplain?" He held out his hand as if to offer Paul the floor. "Well, Chaplain?" he repeated more quietly.

"I don't see anything strange about that," Paul said.

Regnary stared at Paul as if to say, "I knew you'd say that," drank his scotch, and looked around. His gaze paused on Rebecca but she, with somewhat enlarged eyes, was studying the tabletop with its litter of cigarette packs, empty glasses, and swizzle sticks. Her eye rested on a bright object, The Destroyer's Zippo lighter. She seemed lost in her own thoughts.

Paul saw in her eyes her exhaustion and—he hazarded—the boot that was not empty.

Regnary persisted: "You think there's a Death Force, Chaplain, a Death Devil?"

"No," said Paul.

"What about other devils?"

"No," Paul repeated, staring the surgeon level in the eyes.

"There are devils in the Bible," Dr. Regnary insisted, lifting his black eyebrows.

"The Bible was written by men who lived in their own times, as we live in ours. They saw devils, we do not. A devil—"

"You're contradicting your own Bible!"

"Let me finish please. A 'devil' is a reality, not an imaginary creature with a forked tail. A devil is the spear, made of our own bone, which we turn upon ourselves."

"You are a well-trained Jesuit."

"I am not a Jesuit."

"Well, the equivalent," the doc persisted.

"Not the equivalent either. And Evelyn never said 'devil,' you did."

" 'Evelyn'! Let's have a little respect for her military rank, Chaplain!"

"I respect her rank a good deal more than you do."

"Oho! The clergyman has claws. He is not necessarily guided by the principle of Christian charity."

Said Paul: "Not always, no. But tell me, what's bothering you?"

"Why not say, 'What's bothering you, *John*?' My name is John, and you can call me John. We're practically roommates."

"What's bothering you, John?"

"Not a damned thing."

Rebecca cut in: "He is tired and drunk."

"True enough," Doc Regnary said, "but when drunk I see the world with a more intelligent perspective. I forget my lessons in civilization. Those are the lessons that twist everything and apply a sticky coating of sugar that won't blow away in the cosmic wind. The sugar, Chaplain, is your specialty."

Paul's eyes glowed with suppressed anger and Becka saw it.

She said to Regnary, "Don't say that to him."

"Say whatever you like," said Paul to Regnary.

"I will say what I like and I don't need a clergyman's permission."

"John, be quiet," Rebecca urged with some distress.

Said the surgeon, "Sugar, exactly. And the lies of civilization. Romantic nonsense. Self-deception and, let's face it, fear. That's the driving force, Chaplain, fear."

"I agree with you," said Paul. "Perhaps not the only one but certainly one of the driving forces."

"Forces driving what?" Becka demanded. "What are you two talking about?"

"By God, he's a freethinker," Regnary piped, ignoring Becka. "No sir, *the* force, fear, call it horror, everywhere you look."

"I am not afraid," The Destroyer interposed. "You obviously are, but not me. I know the score too."

"Oh shit! I can smell your fear like a wind wafted from Graves Registration and see it in your face when those red spots bloom like flowers in the springtime."

"What you see on my face, Doctor, is rosacea, as you must know. There is an obvious medical explanation."

"Excuse me, Commander, the medical explanation only goes so deep. You did not dream up your Battle Against Death because you suffer from rosacea. Anyway, the Chaplain thinks you're telling a fairy tale, he's just too polite to admit it."

"What do you think?" Rebecca asked Paul, and he saw with a deep pleasure the earnest expression when she narrowed her eyes and leaned toward him.

Everyone was sweating and Paul noticed that the collar of Becka's shirt was dark, and the hair on her temples turned from red to almost black; and once when she turned to speak to somebody he saw the dark wet curls at the nape of her neck. Still he saw her as if she had just emerged from the shower. To Paul her flushed skin was fresh and vital, and the exhaustion in her face bore a stamp of nobility. He knew so much about her; he knew exactly how her energy was spent.

He answered: "I heard you laugh yesterday. I'd like to hear that again."

But it was Regnary who laughed, a great long bellow in which nobody else joined. Paul heard no humor in it, only derision. Becka was smiling at Paul and he drank in the affection he believed he saw in her eyes.

Paul said, "I think the commander has found a way to explain her life and live it. I think it's not such a bad explanation."

"Balls!" cried Doc Regnary indignantly. "It doesn't explain anything; it drives out explanation."

"And I think," Paul continued, addressing Rebecca, who watched him intently, "that she's right, it is a kind of battle. The troops out there are engaged in a battle, and we in this place are engaged in a struggle against a different enemy. I might favor another explanation," Paul added, turning to the reddened, combative face of The Destroyer, "but I respect yours."

"He respects a fairy tale," Doc Regnary muttered to himself.

"I believe," Becka began—and hesitated, and grew redder—"that she's right. *Something* kills and maims the marines."

"It's called war," Regnary asserted. "Which is to say, human nature."

"Agreed," said Paul.

"And it is pointless," the surgeon went on, "perfectly useless."

"Do you mean pointless or useless?" asked Paul.

"What's the difference, Jesuit?"

"People are constantly saying wars accomplish nothing, because they hate war, but it's not true," Paul argued cooly. "Wars change the way people live, so they are not useless. Terrible but useful for those who win them."

"I wasn't talking about the war, Chaplain. You are slipping off the point. I was talking about whatever it is that forced the commander, an otherwise intelligent woman"—here The Destroyer exhaled a cloud of thick smoke in the doctor's direction—"and Rebecca, an otherwise brilliant, unconventional, and rebellious young woman, to go for this Titanic Battle bullshit."

"I wish you wouldn't describe me," Rebecca said.

"It is my right to *describe* anybody I choose to describe, within the law of slander. I say you are—"

"Shut up," Becka snapped.

"I'm a lieutenant and you're a lieutenant junior grade and you tell me 'shut up'? You make a poor sailor, miss."

"So do you."

"No," said the surgeon. "Pointless and useless. So wars change the way people live, do they? Well so what? You see the men's bodies from the outside, Chaplain, and I see them from the inside, and I claim superior knowledge. And what I say is: pointless. Or if you drive me to the wall, 'Yes, there is a point to it after all!' And that is, young men are blown to smithereens, civilians are systematically murdered by the Communists or barbecued by American napalm. People like the commander are infantilized by what they see, and people like you, Chaplain, fall on their knees and pray, against all the evidence, for a little mercy.

"There it is right there," the surgeon went rattling on, "now I see. I was wrong before. 'Was blind but now I see.' Sure, yes—" He stopped and sat there drinking as if he were alone. He looked around the booming, smoking room with keen curiosity.

"All right, what do you see?" Paul asked patiently.

"Shit, I forget," said the doc and finished his drink. He held the glass out to Paul.

A siren moaned outside, the lights flashed inside, and an officer wearing the brassard of the Officer of the Day ordered everybody to the bunkers.

Paul took Becka's arm as they went into the rain and said quietly, urgently, "All we have is hope."

"I heard that!" Doc Regnary cried from behind. "You're corrupting a virgin!"

Without a moon, saturated by rain and fog, the sky trembled with distant white flashes over the air base. The rocket detonations went *rup-*

rup as the enemy fired on the parked aircraft, but most of these were slotted in revetted bays that protected them from all but a direct hit. The flashes resembled a far-off heat lightning refracting through the dim-dark heavens.

Paul slipped away and made for the wards. There was still time to walk his night rounds. He recoiled from the idea of sitting in a bunker till the all-clear was sounded. If the rockets landed far away nobody needed to die of boredom sitting on a hard bench in a hole. If they landed here, his place was in the wards.

The hospital was blacked out. The men who could move had been ordered to get under their beds. As Paul made his way through the familiar halls by flashlight, and his beam bounced off glass cabinets with their glass shelves of surgical instruments, and swept past steel frameworks for the spinal cases, he could see what kind of place this was.

Reaching the patient wards he walked more slowly, keeping the beam down, pausing to read charts and sometimes talking with the men who were still in bed. He took longest when he sensed that a man truly welcomed him. He had encountered in some few men a bias against him, not as a man but as a chaplain. To these, a chaplain was an officer who pampered the whiners and protected the cowardly. Paul never forced himself on such men.

He sat on the floor between two beds, leaning against the wall and talking quietly with two marines who had dragged their sheets and pillows under their beds. One would soon be transferred to the hospital ship offshore; the other was about to return to his unit.

The men told Paul what they had heard on Armed Forces Radio— that the Communists in northern I Corps had mounted dozens of attacks on U.S. and ARVN positions and district and province administrative centers. Yet the remainder of the country was quiet and the truce honoring the Tet holiday was holding.

From time to time the three paused their conversation to listen to the rocketing. A man said that this truce like all others was a farce. There came a low rumble and he said, "They got a plane with that one."

Moving on, Paul wondered why this ministry was so much more satisfying than the parish in Fall River. The death of a shriveled old woman full of complaints, toothless, giving off an odor of uncleanness and incontinence, aware that nobody much cared whether she lived or died, this was the same death that Doc Bartholomew had met, or perhaps a more desolating one. But Paul remembered one old man, and the memory of the smell that rose from his cracked lips, the sight of his teeth all broken and brown, his livid eyes like two globs of pastel gelatin—and the way he took Paul's hand—it nauseated the young priest, the supposed servant of God's people.

Paul clicked off his flashlight. Nobody saw him stop or heard what he was saying in his mind.

"Yes, Mac can look forward to a full life—'they shall be one flesh'— children—he fathers children upon his loving wife who wants him and wants the children, she wants them, wants *him*! They live as a family and he, after his RTD, he's home, released from active duty— a place in the—what did he say? Where the farms and hills come together. What a lovely woman she is, judging from that picture. Yes, a full and active and *normal* life! They make love—man and woman—

"But I— One thing is clear, I can't stand to be in this war forever— the strain—I wish I could talk to Corporal Sedgwick again. There's a guy with his feet on the ground. And he faces prejudice as a black man and derision as a Christian—a solid stable man! What I should be! And a sense of humor to go with it all. 'Hey you muddahs of Second Platoon, eat dirt!' Wham wham wham. Good thing we did eat dirt or we'd all be under these beds right now. Sedgwick will marry, for sure.

"I vowed in a passion of devotion and—ego. I could do it! I knew so little then. Now, I have met her—"

She appeared to his warm imagination, with the smile she had given him tonight, and she did not look drunk, not at all, and Paul looked closer and taxed his memory, and ended up thinking that he'd been unfair to her. Doc Regnary was certainly drunk and that had given Paul the wrong cue, so he had been too ready to see drunkenness in others, even Rebecca. No, she was just exhausted, and why not?

"That boot! God, let her forget it, cleanse her memory of knowledge none of us can bear.

"Why is it necessary that I be alone? Why? Sedgwick's faith is stronger than mine and he will surely marry. Faith and service are not incompatible with—"

He moved unconsciously from prayer to inner speech addressed mainly to himself. He said, "I can believe and serve as a married man. Actually I could believe more fervently and serve more effectively as a complete man, a normal man. We are sexual creatures! If God made us, this is the way He made us! Why can't I just say, 'Here! I throw away this cross. Marry me!'"

A voice said from very close: "Is that you, Father?"

"What?"

Paul flicked on his light, still at floor level, and saw a pair of legs and white sneakers and got a start, but it turned out to be The Destroyer.

She said: "The alert's over. The lights will come on in a minute."

The ward lights flickered into full brightness and men began crawling out from under their beds, and talking more loudly than before, when their voices had been a murmur, and the stronger ones laughed and joked about the alert.

In the face of The Destroyer Paul saw a record of twenty years' consumption of cigarettes and booze.

She was saying: "I thought I'd find you here."

Said Paul: "Are you going back to work at this hour?"

"No, just checking up."

"I heard," Paul began, "that you went home two months ago after a full tour of duty and came right back."

She said: "I did my year and was dying to get out of this place. I said another week would kill me. When I got home, though, I realized—I never knew how it was changing at home. There's still a country on the map called the U.S. of A., but America, as far as I'm concerned, has ceased to exist."

Paul did not ask what she meant; he knew. He said: "But somebody told me you—well, you just said it, that another week would kill you, and yet you came back for another year."

"I found myself among the wrong people. When you go home you'll see for yourself. They have no idea. Believe me, Paul, they just have no idea. I couldn't stand it. I certainly couldn't tell everybody; they can't hear. I couldn't even tell my own brother. So I came back here. This is where I belong, and if it kills me, it kills me."

They walked to a more private place and Paul spoke as a chaplain: "And how are you holding up?"

"Oh, I know the dangers, cigarettes and whiskey and the loss of professional detachment—getting sucked in—I forget little things. Can't remember their names—and I must have left my lighter in the bunker. It was a special lighter, a Zippo with the insignia of the USS *Maddox* sent to me by the crew. But look at my hands."

She held them out and they were almost steady.

Paul said: "Not bad, Commander."

"When you know what you should do," said The Destroyer, "I say you better do it. And I found out what I had to do when I spent two months trying not to do it. Don't worry about me, Paul, worry about Doc Regnary. That man needs help."

Returning to his quarters Paul had a sudden idea and turned toward the bunker. He took out his flashlight and played the beam forward, searching for the sandbagged entrance ramp. He went slowly down, keeping the light on his footing, and followed the right-angle turn of the narrow corridor with sandbag walls.

As he made the second turn into the bunker itself he shone the beam to the right, toward the bench on that side. As the beam skimmed the floor he heard a quick, half-suppressed scream of fear or alarm. He turned the light toward it.

He saw clothing and boots scattered on the floor. Then the beam struck Rebecca full in the face, and encompassed the startled, angry face of Doc Regnary above Rebecca's.

"Get out!" the surgeon hissed.

Paul played the beam slowly down their bodies, and returned it to Rebecca's face. She lay, staring upward.

As he backed out, Paul kept the light aimed into the doc's eyes, blinding him.

Some time later as Paul lunged along the alleyway between the Quonset huts, wiping rain from his eyes, he was challenged by a sentry.

"I am Chaplain Adrano," he responded in a voice he had never heard before.

He splashed through a puddle, stumbled on some obstacle, and kept going.

• • •

372

The sentry saw a figure slouching through the rain, furtively, it seemed. True, he was wet, cold, and bored, but he saw this approaching figure as an ape. He stepped into the middle of the alleyway and challenged it. The figure responded:

"It's me again."

"Chaplain Adrano?"

"Yes, out for a stroll."

He staggered on, and the sentry wondered if something was wrong, he seemed to be lurching, swinging.

A spear fashioned of his own bone found its mark in Paul. It was jagged and it spread the wound throughout his heart and across his chest. It burned his eyes with images. He saw the bluebeard face of Doc Regnary, unshaven for two days, twisted by surprise and rage, and heard him hiss "Get out!"

He saw Rebecca's eyes stare emptily up toward the black ceiling, and her body lie inert under the naked weight of the surgeon, quiescent as a body on an operating table.

The spear twisted and he saw Rebecca lying naked on a stone floor with her knees bent and drawn up, and both hands buried in her vulvae. She cried out a kind of shriek, and then he saw her pull the surgeon down upon her and writhe with joy under his huge body. She shrieked in ecstasy and cried, "More, more," and Paul heard the doc call her bitch, whore, and cunt. The doc's body heaved above her and a beam of electric light swung up and down to display the spectacle in all its ghastly reality.

Paul staggered on. He was half-conscious that he was passing the sentry again; he must be going in circles. The marine seemed to peer at him out of the shadow; his rifle glinted in the driving rain.

Paul came to some object, and felt it with his hands. It must have been a stack of wooden pallets. Maybe he was near the mess hall. Naturally his brain said, "Take up thy pallet and walk," but instead he sat down and grew colder and colder, but he welcomed his trembling and the absurd chattering of his teeth. He sank into a despairing self-hatred and shouted, "Fool, fool, fool," a hundred times. The sentry or some other marine approached cautiously and asked if he was O.K. and Paul said: "I'm praying, leave me alone."

In a torrent of damning sentences Paul attacked himself as a hyp-

Rostraver Public Library
800 Fellsburg Road
Rostraver, PA 15012
724-879-5511

ocrite, dunce, clown, buffoon, and fraud. He dug deep into the idea that he was a fraud. The bone burned into his brain—and he hated Doc Regnary. He said, "I want to murder him." He did not repent this, but said it again and again. The image rose up anew, Becka digging her fingers into her vagina and screaming with pain and joy. He heard her words and could hardly believe they issued from her lips, or from his own brain. He listened, panting, while she shouted what bliss it was that she possessed this supernatural organ. Then again she screamed in agony, and next Doc Regnary pulled her hands apart and flopped his weighty body upon her and found her with his thrust. She cried out her lust. Paul buried his face in his hands and wept, and moaned that he loved her.

He was shaken by a terrific blast which he never heard. But a flash of white light surrounded him. He found himself on the ground in the water, and the pallets scattered over and beside him, with some splintered boards on top of his legs. His flash-blinded eyes were useless for several seconds during which he concluded he must be dead. Then he heard somebody groan.

He pulled free and looked toward the groan, only to behold a series of white flashes, some of them having orange at the core, illuminating the alley and cracking his eardrums. He crawled toward a downed man and realized it was the sentry, but it seemed he was missing an arm. Was this water or blood? Paul patted the man's chest, trying to determine which it was.

"Chaplain," said the marine with a kind of hush in his voice.

"Yes, yes, I'm here." Paul leaned toward the pale smudge that was all he could see of the man's face, but in a new white flash he saw the stricken great eyes of the man trying to find him.

"Our Father," said Paul, bringing his face closer, "Who art in Heaven, hallowed be Thy name."

"Thy kingdom come," the marine panted.

"Thy will be done," said Paul as if pronouncing the man's fate.

"—on earth," said the marine faintly, and Paul waited for more.

The man shivered and his legs began twitching, kicking.

"No!" Paul cried. "Don't do this."

. . .

374

Rockville Pu... ... Library
900 Fallsgrove Road
Rockville, MD 20851
240-876-8311

The Communists launched the Tet Offensive with scattered attacks in northern I Corps. They hit Da Nang—the city, port, air base, and naval complex including the hospital—with rockets and heavy mortars. This occurred in the early hours of 30 January 1968, and it was the opening salvo of this bombardment that knocked Chaplain Paul Adrano off the stack of pallets where he sat damning himself.

Next day the full extent of the Communist offensive revealed itself. The VC and NVA attacked every major city, town, and ARVN command center up and down the country, from I Corps in the north to the mouths of the Mekong in the south. They got inside the wall of the U.S. Embassy in Saigon and they took Hue City. U.S. and ARVN casualties were severe, but the loss of life on the Communist side was staggering. The Communist high command in Hanoi poured its entire reservoir of southern guerrilla manpower into the thrust, plus heavy reinforcements of regulars from the North.

The objectives of the Tet Offensive were to inflict casualties on U.S. forces, cause a revolt of the ARVN, and trigger the "general uprising" of the people against the government of the Republic of Vietnam.

Initially the Allied forces were slow to respond because many of the ARVN officers and senior NCOs were suckered by the truce and had left their units to celebrate Tet at home. But after the first shock, the U.S., ARVN, and Vietnamese Marine Corps struck back hard. In many places the Communists were driven out and left a carpet of bodies behind them. The squad of sappers attacking the U.S. Embassy was obliterated.

American commanders began moving units where the need was greatest. MacHugh Clare's battalion, 1st Battalion, Nth Marines, was ordered into action.

For two days in the maelstrom of a mass-casualty event Paul had not slept or taken a complete meal. From the look of her, neither had Rebecca.

She was standing before his desk. He had just now sensed someone's presence and looked up from the letter he was writing. He lay down his pen and stared at it—picked it up and capped it—and took in a huge breath.

He rose and said hello, and waited.

Rebecca said she had to talk with him. He led her to the counseling room that he shared with the Protestant chaplain and saw by the open door that it was free—a private place—but she said:

"Not here."

"Well—where then?"

They tried the officers' mess but it was secured for cleaning, the O Club but it was closed. At this point they exchanged a tentative glance and Paul was struck by a pain so sharp he was not sure he could conceal it. Rebecca said she did not mind walking in the rain, so each went to get a poncho and they met outside the door of Receiving. Across the sweep of cement they could see the helipad and curtains of wind-driven rain.

Paul said that she should be using the lull to rest, that a new wave would arrive as soon as the birds could fly. But she shook her head, and they started along one of the alleyways between Quonset huts.

He could not see her face now, only her hood and the silver nimbus of rain pelting down on it. He watched her feet in their white sneakers swinging rhythmically.

"Are you cold?" he inquired in a sort of professional voice.

"Yes, are you?"

He said, "Should we go back?"

"No."

He was anything but cold. He imagined her damp hair and her ears inside the hood, and her clasped hands freezing under her poncho.

Rebecca said: "The new chaplain said he was here to relieve you. Is that true?"

"Yes, I leave tonight. That's why I had to leave the ward to write letters."

"You leave tonight? For good?"

"Yes, for good."

"But why?"

"Several reasons. One is that I don't want to stay here and sleep in a cot under canvas, and drink brandy at the club, while the marines are out there fighting. It makes me feel that I'm missing something."

"You can do more good here," she asserted.

"Maybe. How would you measure how much good a chaplain does?"

"I don't care. You know I'm right. I think you're leaving for the wrong reason. I heard you had asked to be sent back to your old regiment."

"True. Where did you hear that?"

"Everybody knows it."

"What else does everybody know?"

"That you are going back to prove something."

"I see. Well then I guess the gossips can explain it all."

"No. I don't think so. But is it true?"

"Actually yes," Paul said. "I have to prove something." He began to tell her how Doc Bartholomew had called for him, and he had refused to leave the crater, but she said she knew that already.

He had half-guessed that this too was something everybody knew.

Rebecca said, "I know you for a brave man."

"No. You don't know me at all."

"I see you every day. I work with you. I know you very well, Paul. You are not aware of it."

"Aware—of—"

"That I am conscious of your presence whenever you come on the ward, of how you conduct yourself, and that I admire you."

"Thank you. No, I was not aware." But now he was.

"So, you asked—I mean, you volunteered."

"Of course."

"As soon as the offensive began."

"On that very day, yes."

"In order," she ventured, "to wipe out some imaginary stain."

"And the other reason too."

She said, "What other reason?"

"As I said, how can I stay here in safety while the men of my regiment are fighting?"

"And how can you leave these men?" She indicated the hospital, and as she turned her head he caught a look at her face.

This made it a little harder to say, "I've made my choice. I can't be in two places at once."

"You face death here," she declared.

"Not my own. I have always found it relatively easy to endure somebody else's death. I have done that many times and I'm not aware of any change it has produced in me."

Rebecca said, stopping and turning again to face him, "Paul, you could be killed."

"I doubt it," he said.

By now they had turned a corner in the maze. Two men approached and greeted Paul and perhaps recognized Becka but did not speak to her. Paul thought they must have been wondering something. He said she had been recognized and she replied:

"It is O.K. for me to talk with a chaplain."

He said, "You should beware of gossips. They might whisper that we are having an affair."

She stopped, then looked at him. Her face was pale with the cold, her lips were turning blue, and she was shivering. She said with a trace of anger or defiance: "Maybe I wish we were."

"Nonsense," said Paul dogmatically.

She said: "Paul, I have a problem."

"What is your problem?"

His tone gave her pause, and she looked unsure of herself, but said: "I'm doing what I should, and what I want to do. Shouldn't that be enough?"

"Tell me what you mean by enough."

"You talk to the men, you say that they will live and all the other things you say, and they die anyway, or are wrecked for life, but it doesn't kill you. You carry on. For you it seems to be enough that you're doing all you can. But I do all I can too, and it's grinding me down. I don't know how much more I can take. Don't tell me to pray. I don't believe what you believe. I see that you take strength from it but I couldn't."

"What do you believe?" Paul asked.

"I don't know. Sometimes I wish I had what you've got but mostly I don't even want it. I don't see how it could be true, you know? My life is, a guy gets his hand blown off by his own grenade and I just think, 'O.K., bleeding, shock, sepsis, all that.' That's all I think."

"You are caught in a struggle," Paul said in a dead voice. "Your mind is consumed with the battle to help your patients. Someday you'll take a breather, you'll be glad you could nurse these men."

"Oh I'm glad already, but the more I do the emptier I get. If The Destroyer is right I should get stronger. We are on the side of the men, and the other side is the damaging force. The Destroyer is a little crazy but we're for life and the other force is for death, but I am not getting stronger."

Paul said: "This work gives meaning to your life," thinking: "and takes all the meaning from mine." He said, "I respect The Destroyer and don't think she is crazy."

"I just meant, she's an oddball."

"But I like her."

"Me too. Is it true you can't get married?"

He thought: "Can she be so ignorant?" He responded: "I've taken a vow of celibacy, yes."

"What does that mean? No marriage, or no anything?"

"It means no anything."

"So this vow is forever?"

"For my lifetime."

"Forever," she said simply. "Would you do it again?"

"I have done it and that's all that matters."

"I would never never say this back home! But Paul," she said hurriedly and covered her face momentarily, then faced him with exceedingly bright and hopeful eyes, and said: "if you and I had met before you took the vow, what would you do?"

"Of course I'd take the vow anyway. It is part of my vocation."

"Oh!" she said. She tossed back her hood, and he saw a painful smile on her lips.

They walked back toward the door of Receiving. She was on the point of entering when he detained her.

He said, "No, if I had known I was going to meet you here, I would never have taken the vow."

"Paul, please don't go. Please stay."

He said, "It's done. I leave tonight."

Chapter 16

On the Eve

"So it was pretty hard," said MacHugh Clare with conscious understatement.

"It wasn't pretty hard," said Paul Adrano, "it was very hard."

"I couldn't handle it," Mac said after deliberation. "It'd tear me apart."

"It all but wrecked me." As Paul said this he was aware of its inaccuracy, in that he spoke as if it were over.

"But you've got a way to get through it," Mac declared, and he was thinking: "I'm on my own." This was a little frightening, with death so close, but he was proud.

Said Paul: "There is no way to get through it. I'm still in it."

"I mean you've got a way to explain it, a reason for everything."

"I see, but you're mistaken if you think a way to explain it, as you call it, can get anybody through it, if you mean—unscathed."

"O.K.," said Mac, chastened.

"I had six years of pastoral work in Fall River, which is a poverty-stricken place, believe me, and poverty doesn't help. I've tended the sick and dying. I am no novice is what I'm trying to say, but I never saw such an intensity of suffering, maiming, horror. I know we're not supposed to use words like 'horror' and 'unbearable' and so forth."

"Use the words that fit."

"No words really fit," said Paul. And he said almost in surprise: "If this were a nightmare, one of those dreams that cannot be real, you would ask yourself what put such cruel images in your mind. Where did they come from?"

"And you'd be glad they weren't real," Mac offered.

Paul ruminated, then went on to a new thought: "The notebook you gave me, I started out by writing the names of the dead in it, and addresses of their next of kin. I had to write dozens of letters of condolence to parents and wives, an impossible task."

"I know it is." Mac's cigar grew brighter and more yellow as he pulled on it. "I've written a few letters myself."

They were in a dark but well-built hooch, sheltered from the rain, with a blackout baffle and an angled ventilation sheet—all this erected over a hole by the resourceful Michelson. The rain pressed in a waveless hum on the canvas overhead.

"If angels exist," Paul said, "it's they who should write such letters. I started using the notebook as a journal for my thoughts. When I opened it I always looked at the inscription, 'from Sarah and Mac,' and I tried to picture her, but all I could do in my imagination was reproduce the photograph you showed me, which is not the same."

"But you get the idea."

"Yes, a tall willowy woman who gives an impression of personal strength. What color is her hair?"

"Brown to black. Dark brown eyes. A figure. She can run like hell, a terrific swimmer"—Mac thought of her as she swam naked, underwater in the pond in northern Wisconsin. The black water turned her skin an ivory white. "And the weather never bothers her," he continued. "Hot, cold, wind, rain, snow, makes no difference to her. She wants to meet you. I told her about you," said Mac.

Paul wondered if he meant "told her about the crater." He said: "I'd like to meet her."

"By the time you get home," said Mac, "we'll be living up in Vermont on a farm or in a cabin in the woods, and there'll be a baby on the rug or on the way. We'll feed you steak and corn and home-baked bread and French brandy and we'll all three stay up till dawn talking about the Packers, which is the only team worth talking about."

"Does Sarah follow the Packers?"

"Paul, everybody from Wisconsin follows the Packers."

"What I'd prefer," said Paul, "is a walk along some road that's covered with snow, new snow, hard and crunchy with the cold, on a night with a full moon."

"We'll do it. So—what did you learn in Da Nang?"

"Learn? You think there must be a lesson?"

"I'm just asking, did you learn anything? You said, 'blood and breakage,' but did it have any redeeming value?"

"Even if I learned something," said Paul, "that wouldn't *redeem* it. What do you mean by 'redeem'?"

"Man, I don't know. Did it change you?"

"Yes."

And Mac said, "How?"

"I'm not sure I can put it in words. Or trace a cause."

"Well, try."

Paul sat silent, fanning cigar smoke away from his face in the dark. They were in bivouac near Route 1, in the pine belt that runs along the coast. Their candle flickered on a box placed in the center of the hole by Michelson. Besides the candle, the box held the parts of the rifle Mac was cleaning. Paul heard the copper brush passing through the barrel. He smelled, besides the cigar, the banana smell of powder solvent.

"I learned that I was right to leave Fall River to come here. I learned a kind of love for the men."

"Well, then," said Mac, "how would you like my job?"

"Never," said Paul instantly.

"Why not?"

"You know why not. At daylight we'll go up Route One, and you know better than I what's going to happen. But even I know that something will happen, and when it does you'll give orders, and—"
He stopped and Mac said:

"Men will die." Mac held his ramrod close to the candle, affixed a cloth patch, and passed it back and forth through the bore. He repeated this with a fresh patch, examining it as best he could in the dim illumination, till he had a clean patch. He began reassembling the weapon.

Paul remained silent, listening to the clicks and rubbings of Mac's work. A cloud of smoke found Mac's eyes and he removed the cigar from his teeth and blinked away his tears.

Mac said: "If I gave no orders at all, more men would die."

"Quite probably. That only means," said Paul Adrano, "that you are forced to send men into battle and possibly to their death. I can't believe that makes it any easier."

"Oh hell, forced. I want to do it. Don't forget that."

"Certainly. You have a zest for this business, but I have seen the other side of your zeal. I know the effect it has."

"On me?"

"Yes."

"What makes you think it has any effect on me."

"I know," said Paul without insistence.

"What are you talking about, Chaplain?"

"I saw you go berserk at your exec when he broke down at Slope City, when he screamed he was going to die, we were all going to die."

"You call that berserk? I chewed him out is all. As the troops say, 'It don't mean nothin.' "

Paul responded: "Yes, but when they say 'It don't mean nothin,' they mean it means everything. You give an order, a man dies, or several men, on our side or the other, a legitimate order—"

"A necessary order. You don't have to be Eisenhower to see that."

"And you ask how I know it affects you. Are you serious?"

"I'm serious as hell. I did it at the S-curve and came back to the rear and Regiment praised me. If I do it again tomorrow to the same degree of success they'll praise me again."

"As a combat leader," said Paul as if to restrict Mac's meaning.

"What else?"

"Well, you deserved the praise, I'm sure, and that has nothing to do with it."

"With what?" Mac asked, but Paul noted a special timbre or stress in his voice.

Paul said, "Are you playing a game with me? What are you resisting here?"

"I'm not resisting anything. You want to believe it'll kill a normal man, I'm telling you it won't kill me, and that's what you can't stand to hear. Do you know why? Because it might shatter your world, and your idea of what a man is."

"I never claimed it'd kill you," Paul protested mildly. "But I don't see how a man preserves his soul in the midst of all this. But then you don't recognize the soul."

"I mourn our losses," said Mac as if making a great concession, "and I miss those who are gone, of course, but that's not what I mean."

"I don't think you know what you mean," said Paul.

"I know all right."

"Then what?" Paul pressed on.

"I can do this," Mac declared as if to himself, "and hang on to who I am."

Paul was leaning toward the candle, with his arms on his knees, glancing at Mac, then back to the candle, which shuddered in the draft.

"O.K., let it pass," Paul said. "I heard that Corporal Sedgwick has rejoined Delta."

"You'll see him in the morning. He asked about you. He's fine; he's the same guy. Walks with a limp, otherwise—"

Paul said: "By the way, several of the men have come up to shake my hand."

"A few will brand you," Mac said, "but most will accept you and even like you. Everybody, or almost everybody's seen the ape. The men are glad you're human. They probably wouldn't know a saint if they saw one."

"A saint and a brave man are not the same," said Paul. "But why did you ask if I wanted your job?"

Mac answered: "You said you'd learned to love the troops. I assume you meant the wounded."

"So it naturally came into your head, How would I like to be the one who sends them into battle."

Mac replied: "It naturally came into my head." He had by now re-assembled his rifle, and thrust home a loaded magazine. He continued: "I'll tell you another part of it. These guys want to fight. These guys are marines."

"So are you," Paul said. "You and Hitchcock. But tell me what happens tomorrow. All I know is we move out."

"The battalion moves and we move with it. You know the Communists have taken all but one corner of Hue City."

"Yes."

"And the marines and ARVN up there are fighting to take back
every street and every building."

"Yes," Paul said solemnly.

"We're going up to Hue. About fifty miles north."

"By truck?"

"We'll go as far as we can in trucks. All the bridges were blown on
the thirty-first but the Marine Corps and Army engineers are laying
pontoons and repairing what they can. We'll be lifted out by chopper
from someplace up the road. But yes, we start in trucks.

"Our job is to help liberate Hue. Either we jump into the fight in
the city itself or we interdict and destroy the NVA relief force outside
the city, if there is one. And you're coming along?"

Paul answered: "That's why I'm here."

Mac smiled again. He held out his hand and Paul took it, still wishing he could see Mac's expressions more clearly. Mac noticed that
Paul's hand did not slap into his, as it had when they first met at the O
Club at Regiment; the thick strong hand, rather, awaited Mac's, and
took it firmly.

Mac said, "Glad you're back." He dropped his cigar and ground it
out with his heel, and slipped out.

Paul lay back and tried to arrange the sleeping-bag cover that was
his only bedding. His poncho formed part of the shelter. He left the
candle burning for Michelson. His mind turned immediately to Rebecca, and he knew the bitter joy of pretending she was with him, and
that he had a right to her company.

Mac walked five paces and stood in the rain listening. Here he
could be alone for some minutes. Unconscious of the rain, he enveloped himself in the dark. He saw Sarah swimming in the pond.

The death voice spoke to Mac as he slept and it spoke simply: "You
will kill again and you will die." It did not say the word "tomorrow" but
Mac understood. But he also knew that the voice had spoken falsely to
his father during the war against Japan.

The elder Clare had been sleeping in a tent on Guadalcanal, in relative security, after the Marine Corps had established the air base. The enemy still controlled half the island but Clare was with a well-protected engineer unit, sleeping dry and safe, except for a few bombing raids by the crippled Japanese air force. But the voice told him he would never leave the island. The voice was punishing and vindictive. "It wanted me to die and was glad I was going to die," his father had said.

The voice that awakened Mac was vindictive too. Mac believed it instantly and was afraid. He admitted that in some sense he deserved to die, but it seemed a twisted kind of justice that would sentence to death a man who led his troops to the best of his ability and never killed or ordered killed anybody but those he must kill, either to protect his own men or to win, which was the same thing. If he deserved death then so did everybody else.

With a power he had never known before he gave himself up to the vision of living a life with Sarah. He sensed that seeing her in Hawaii had weakened him by presenting a view of something so precious and good that to be denied it, after seeing it, would seem doubly cruel. Their five days together, of course, could never be lived again. Married life on his return could never be like that. It made no difference. He knew her in a better way now, and he kept seeing her and hearing her voice as she told him she could never betray him. It still made him writhe to remember how he had misinterpreted her declaration that she was taking the Pill. He felt a kind of stifled joy to realize she had never chastised him for his low opinion of her. No, he did not want to die tomorrow. As a wheel that's bent cannot be pounded back to true, as it will always wobble however slightly, so Mac's fearless confidence in his survival would not run true tonight, or maybe ever again. He was a killer, and in a just world he would get what he gave.

He thought of his advance on "the major's" bunker, how he and Freeman went forward with the squad, and the squad sergeant suddenly flipped backward. He had died without a word of self-pity or protest. He was still, and always would be, dead. That was the meaning of eternity. He thought of the screams of the enemy during the Puff strike. No longer the hot data of battle, they now suggested a greater meaning. He did not articulate "greater meaning" but his intellect wanted to assign to these cries a meaning they did not convey when first heard.

He thought that if he could get home and live with Sarah, preferably in a remote place where he could support her and the baby by farming or logging or construction, that then he could begin to think clearly. It was not possible to think clearly here.

He felt his will bending. It was a tempting thought, to be like Paul, to embrace a universal illusion and perform simple acts of innocent charity in its service. But he was commander of Delta Company and had to be a certain kind of man, one of the best kinds, and he did not intend to be any other kind. And if he could go back five or more years and change history by staying in law school, dodging the draft, and starting a career in law, he would not do it. No, he would make the same decisions, even if it meant—

A man of the kind he wished to be would say "even if it meant death." Next he thought: "Maybe I won't die, maybe I'll slip through one more time." He consulted his watch. It was 2330.

The image of Sarah's face came searingly close, into his mind yet somehow throughout his body too. His hopes expanded to the point of certainty. He would live, and see her again, and they would begin a sane and happy life in the summer.

He lit the candle, peering across the darkness to see if Graeser or Freeman stirred. They did not, and Mac scooped out a little shelf in the sand and placed the candle at his elbow, and began to write in his wheel book.

"Dearest Sarah, We are going north to Hue tomorrow and I will ask Paul Adrano to send this to you if I am not able to send it myself."

He paused, and weighed the implication of this "if." It was only half real but all too real.

"I am sorry for the time I lost my temper and shouted at the dog like a madman, and made you cry. I know you cried in fear of the kind of man you had married, and knowing how courageous you are only serves to make it worse. I will never do anything like that again.

"I wanted to be the best man you could possibly have, and I am sorry I failed. But I have loved you and love you now with all the power of caring and sympathy and love that I possess. And to me it seems infinite."

387

He carefully ripped these pages from the little memo book, folded them, and wrote her address on the outside: Sarah Woodley Clare, Hagaru Dr., Tarawa Terrace, Camp Lejeune, NC. He wrapped the letter in a battery envelope and slipped it into his shirt pocket. He doused the candle and lay down to sleep.

There was no rain. The radio gave off a steady purr, and all else was silence.

Chapter 17

A Perfect Day
for an Ambush

Hippo-I'm-Great-In-Dayton wasn't a hostile character; he didn't hate anybody. He suspected the gunny was a secret racist and maybe not so very secret among his own kind. He knew the sailor was prejudiced just because he was an Irish fighter from Boston. He'd heard all about Boston from his cousin, who went to school there. And Valas—Valas the Golden Greek was probably an easy kind of white guy and therefore O.K. No point in looking for prejudice in every heart because too damn often you'll find it. So, no, Hippo wasn't boiling with hate because in a way he liked the other guys in the squad. This little bunch was known throughout Delta as a special unit—"the gunny's fuckups."

Just the same, Hippo ate his breakfast alone. He didn't even want to eat with any brothers. When he said "alone" he really meant "by himself," which wasn't the same thing. It meant he had himself with him. He could calm down and listen to the voice that he believed was his own true voice, and work on the problem of who you are when you're a marine. Jarhead, snuffie, trooper. He wasn't even sure it was a problem but it certainly was a puzzle.

Did he like it? No, really, did he love it? He had really cut loose at the S-curve when the skipper said "Break on through." As if it was like punching your fist through a paper bag. Sure, Skipper. So he'd passed it on to the gunny: "Skipper says break on through." That is, don't hunker down, don't turn back: break through. And the gunny answered: "Fuckin A." So it seemed O.K. by the gunny. Lieutenant Oliver looked a little nauseous, like Hippo's cousin talking about Boston.

Then came Hippo's—higher than a kite—his first battle. Little, short, deadly. For the gooks. Hippo saw two or three gooks crumple. For some reason now he wanted to know if he could still go to college after this. His teachers at Dunbar, especially Mrs. Shipman, told him he had to go. "Dr. King says it's terrible to waste a mind, David." His real name was David Hounsley. "You make your plans right now," Mrs. Shipman urged him. "Get your GI Bill and then, college, young man, college because you can benefit from it. I'll write you the best reference any student of mine ever got."

Mrs. Shipman was the math teacher. She was famous throughout Dunbar and the West Side as a kind of high queen, a person of character. Would she write that reference if she knew how Hippo felt "breaking through"?

He could see the fight best while alone, or "by himself." It was like watching a log burn, with the colors and the flare-ups, and it never seemed to end, the log never burned up. The voice that he knew, the one he believed spoke for him, tried to explain but it sounded like excuses; the voice was unrecognizable, almost phony. In short it didn't come across as his own true voice anymore.

"See, this is war. You are in the marines, not the movies. You never did it before but now you are."

Not really a voice he could respect. So he listened with suspicion— something like the feeling he had about the gunny.

When they policed the bodies the gunny took a little folder from one of the gooks and they all peeked at the pictures of men in cheap suits like the ones they sell on West 3rd Street, not the downtown kind; women and girls in flowered dresses, grinning—and the voice shut up. As soon as he saw the pictures, silence.

What he wanted—and he sat on his helmet and started to open the brown cardboard C-rat box—was a voice that sounded the same note as he heard in Mrs. Shipman's voice—to explain the rush, the spurting force, the kind of—happiness—was that possible?—when he laid a gook down with a burst from his M16. That's what he wanted and didn't get. He knew what the special note was, it was a voice speaking truth. That was what he listened for.

He took out his heavy and frowned. He would not—damn it to hell—*not*—eat this heavy! Ham and lima beans, the worst in the whole batch. No sir!

He felt around in his pack and found his trove of cigarettes. He went canvassing throughout Delta and finally found a guy in the 60-millimeter mortars who'd trade. So he came back with a can of chicken and noodles, the best heavy of all, and pound cake, the best dessert. He lit a heat tab and cooked the heavy.

He ate with slow appreciation. Then all of a sudden, instead of a voice he heard trucks rumbling and treads clanking. The convoy was assembling along Route 1. Holy shit. He bolted the chicken and noodles. Troopers were kicking sand on their fires and hollering, putting on a big show of how gung ho they were. Scared of going to Hue? Ha, not me! Well if not, why not? Hippo wanted to know. He kicked sand, he grabbed his gear, he hefted his pack and slung his rifle.

Here came the new exec, whatever his name was, hollering to saddle up. And then the skipper came through, quiet, calm, and his eyes met Hippo's. He seemed to say, "Hippo, you're my man." And Hippo actually opened his mouth and said, "Ready, Skipper."

He dropped the can of pound cake into his shirt pocket—and five minutes later, sitting on an idling truck, he saw a bunch of kids trotting along from truck to truck calling "Hey Joe!" and "Hey O.K." and "VC Number Ten."

Hippo said, "Yeah, VC Number Ten," and without thinking he threw the pound cake to one of the kids. She caught it and laughed, screamed,

"VC Number Ten!"

The engine revved up, the truck jerked, and Hippo and all Delta Company started for Hue.

Scarcely three hundred meters away, in a hooch in a dense little village near the highway, an NVA captain was constructing a picture that promised to give him perfect satisfaction.

The marine convoy now idling its engines comprised about fifty vehicles and stretched to a length of fifteen hundred meters along Route 1, and he knew it. It carried a battalion, or at the least a battalion minus, and he knew that. It was pointed north and, given the tactical situation up there, he surmised it was going to the battle in Hue. It was protected by three "ontos" tank killers; it had artillery and naval gunfire observers and air controllers; it had a water trailer and the usual machine guns, grenade launchers, rockets, mortars, and such, and he knew all that. He drew a sketch and studied it carefully before arranging his orders in his mind.

He was especially pleased by the report that the tracked vehicles were ontos and not tanks. He could damage a tank with a mine but could not be certain of stopping it. An ontos was an easier job. He could make excellent use of an ontos.

The captain had questioned the little girl with the patience of a mentor. After all, she was only twelve, and many adults could not distinguish an ontos from a tank. But the girl was quite certain. She spoke the word "ontos" clearly, then described it: like a tank but smaller, with three long tubes on either side instead of one in the middle. These were the six 106-millimeter recoilless rifles, a terrible array of weapons to be sure, but the vehicle itself was lightly armored and the captain could easily stop it, cripple it, set it afire, and let it blow itself to pieces. Yes, he was very glad the convoy was to be escorted by ontos instead of tanks.

During her walk along the highway the girl had collected a hatful of candy, gum, and other goodies that the marines threw to her whenever she cried "Hey O.K.! Hey Joe!" She now selected from her conical hat a small can containing American pound cake and gave it to the captain as a delicacy. He accepted gratefully and resumed his questions.

He asked her about the jeeps with the long antennas, and she said distinctly: "Six." This meant, at least, a battalion command group. He asked again about the "water buffalo," because he hoped she was mistaking fuel for water. But her description was unmistakable: it was a water trailer and nothing more. He asked about the big trucks with the fat double wheels in back and she said: "Forty-four." Certainly a battalion minus; perhaps a full battalion.

He thanked her with a kiss and called to the old lady, who had opened her house to him. She approached him with a degree of ceremony, gave him a betel-nut smile as she served his tea, and brought an opener for the pound cake. Tasting the cake, tasting the tea, he contemplated his sketch. It showed an ontos leading the parade, then, next in line, an infantry company and a bunch of radio jeeps, then some construction troops to rebuild bridges, then another ontos and one or two more infantry companies, and finally another ontos at the stinger end.

He wished he could show the sketch to his superiors. He folded it and put it in his pocket.

He proceeded to his radio and his orders. Everything he had to say to his team was positive except his own report that he had seen an American destroyer lying in the fog just off the coast. The captain surmised that this ship with its long-range guns had been assigned to escort the motor convoy as it crawled up Route 1.

The captain said to his battery commander: "Do not worry about the destroyer; you are behind a steep hill and you are in defilade. Just keep the mortars where they are, and you will be perfectly safe." His men possessed an unexploded American 105-millimeter howitzer round. He ordered that it be placed in its cradle in the highway, covered with dirt and wired up; that the attack platoon of infantry take position along the seaward slope of the railway embankment, peering west over the rim at the highway; and that the forward observer and the boom boy move to their assigned places.

The trap the captain was setting looked like this.

His sketch showed three parallel lines: a raised railway embankment on the right, the east; the highway in the center; and the ridge line on the left, the west. He had ordered his infantry platoon to a concealed position on the seaward, right side of the railway. These troops could lay fire on the road, and they would be very hard to counterattack except from the air. The captain had looked at the sky only five minutes before transmitting his orders, and he was satisfied.

The convoy would creep up the middle line, the highway.

Behind the third line, the ridge running parallel to the highway on its left, the captain's mortars were in defilade and could never be detected except from the air.

The captain found that the old lady's tea and the pound cake made a refreshing dish.

In his imagination he saw his forward observer climbing the path to the ridge line. He would be moving from the three mortar pits eastward toward the sea, up the hill to the crest from which he could view the entire scene. And the man the captain was thinking of—the forward observer—was thinking of the captain.

The forward observer was a rice farmer in his late sixties who was supposed to be the local guide, and no more. That was what he had agreed to be. But he had been ashamed to hide the fact that he was an experienced FO. On learning this the captain had appointed him to the most dangerous job in the whole mission; and now, as he neared the crest, he set his radio against a rock slab, uncoiled his comm wire, and began unreeling it as he crawled forward. The terrain was open, rocky, and brushy. If the cloud cover should go, the marine bird dog buzzing around up there would spot him in a minute. The forward observer lay at the very crest, hoping his head and shoulders would be lost among the rocks and bushes. The whole scene was visible to him now. It reminded him of the early days, when he and his teammates would spend hours, in fact days, building sand models and rehearsing. Here before him lay not a model but the scene itself. The difference was his age and his solitude; his old friends were nearly all dead, and the living were being finished off in the Tet attacks and their disastrous aftermath.

Since the start of the General Offensive, which was supposed to lead to the General Uprising, he had been hearing stories of the slaughter of his old units. And he could now plainly see there would be no uprising. What, then, was to be gained by the sacrifice of the best cadre the revolution had produced? Who would carry on the struggle after this? It occurred to him that of course the Northerners would carry on. And then it occurred to him that perhaps this was just as the Northerners wished it to be.

But the observer wanted to live. He wanted, above all else, to be alive to see the Americans driven out and the puppet army defeated. He hoped that after the glorious victory he would be a man of influence, so that he could save his wife's brother and his own cousin, both of them officers in the ARVN. And he began to doubt he would live.

The captain's plan protected the mortars but not the forward observer.

The captain meanwhile was talking by radio with the leader of the infantry platoon assigned to protect the mortars. These were big 120's, three of them, capable not just of harassing and delaying the convoy but of destroying it. They had been loaned by an artillery regiment newly arrived from the North and if they were lost the captain's reputation would go with them. So he emphasized to the leader of the defense platoon how precious they were, and that his job was not just to kill a few Americans and retreat, but to protect the big tubes at any cost. The captain described how the marines might, with excellent leadership, close on the mortars via the low saddle in the ridge. The platoon leader assured him he understood his assignment, as well as the meaning of "at any cost."

The captain signed off, returned the radio to its hiding place, and sipped his tea. He observed the old lady, and noted that she was not so very old. But he had no time. She refilled his cup. Her teeth might be red and crooked but her eyes were young and lonely. The captain gave himself over, for a moment, to the gift of her image naked, and drank his tea. He listened to the marines' engines revving and shifting, and the sound was a new source of satisfaction.

He dwelt again on the excellence of his decisions and dispositions. He listened to the Marine bird dog circling up there above the clouds. May the clouds remain, he thought, and fully expected they would. He rinsed his cup, told the woman where she could get a fresh battery for the radio, and went outside and mounted his motorbike. The woman's body seemed younger and more willing the farther away he rode.

The forward observer too was contemplating an image of youth. Below him, just at the bottom of the steep hill that ran down to the paddies and highway, a young boy was taking up his post. He sat cross-legged behind a dike—behind it, that is to say, from the perspective of the road. But the observer saw the boy from above and behind, saw him bent forward. He knew that in his hands the boy held two little black wires stripped at the ends, so their clean copper would shine in his little brown fingers.

The surrounding paddies were all but deserted, although people still hurried along the highway, walking, pushing bicycles, carrying poles, hustling past the sapper crew which had already come out of the elephant grass on the other side of the road. The crew were shoveling swiftly and as the observer watched, they lowered the 105 projectile into the prepared hole, and a man bent down to wire it. The man looked up as he worked, and the observer imagined him looking directly at the boy, two hundred meters away in the paddy. In two more minutes the sappers had covered the 105 projectile and completed their work; they disappeared over the rim of the road into the elephant grass on the other side; and the hole looked like a thousand others.

Looking down the hill, the observer saw the boy's back and his black head bent down; he saw the road crossing his view sideways, then the belt of abandoned paddies now grown thick with elephant grass twelve feet tall; and then, also running left and right, he saw the railroad, beyond which the infantry attack platoon lay crouched. And beyond the railroad he could make out the humping forms of the dunes; and beyond these he could almost see the gray ocean lost in the gray haze. He could imagine the destroyer cutting a path northward.

And the observer thought of the three 120-millimeter mortars his comrades were preparing at the bottom of the hill behind him. And he imagined the air observer circling above. But his mind kept returning to the image of the unseen ship. He had seen one of these destroyers firing once, flashing out its greenish-yellow flames. He had no desire to see that again.

The people were really hopping now, in both directions. Here came the old blue rattletrap bus with "Sai Gon–Da Nang–Hue" on its fading sides. He couldn't read the letters but he knew them.

Chugging through a village off the highway, the NVA captain acknowledged that the marines had a formidable battery of weapons at their disposal but they also had two big disadvantages.

First, he reflected, they couldn't fire their ship against the attack platoon on the railway embankment because the destroyer's guns were 5-inch 54's, a terrible weapon, surely, but the features that made it so terrible also made it useless against the attack platoon. He had figured this all out. The 5-inch 54 was a high-velocity, flat-trajectory naval rifle that could not be trusted to hit the rim of the railway embankment; more likely some rounds would sail over and fall among the marines on the highway beyond. So the marines would not use it. The captain was certain of that. They would go after the railway platoon with their mortars. No, the captain's men would not hear that hideous *yap* of naval rifles this morning.

Second, he thought, if the weather remained closed, and the ceiling so low (not much higher than the observer's hill) the marines would not even find the 120's.

All in all, not a good morning to be a marine riding up this road to Hue.

For his part, the forward observer was more worried than the captain. The marines of course would be damaged by the mine, by the mortar salvos, and by the fires of the attack platoon, not to mention the other little surprises buried alongside the road. But they would—somebody among them surely would still be able to think—there is almost always *one man* who keeps his wits—and that man would turn after a very few seconds to the hill on which the observer lay. Certainly after the observer had made one or two adjustments, that calm and thinking man would turn his eyes to the hill.

At length, out of the haze and around the curve from the right, an ontos came into view. The observer's heart beat against the earth. He keyed his mike and told the mortars to stand by.

Whoever named the ontos was a joker. The word can be translated from the Greek as "thing," or, more informatively, "that which exists."

There is an "ontological" argument for the existence of God but the ontos does not participate in it. However if it can't prove divinity it can go a long way toward proving something just as important, namely existence. Who doubts this? Improbably, a whole school of philosophers, who are paid by universities to argue over whether we can verify the presence of objects other than ourselves. One way to settle the argument would be to pick a philosopher at random, stand him in front of an ontos, and ask if he thought it was capable of proving its existence to him.

When going down a pockmarked road an ontos sounds like a junk-yard being inverted by the devil. But its name gives it a metaphysical beard. Why this name? Looking like a monster machine out of fantasy fiction, the ontos at first asks to be dismissed as impossibly ungainly and overarmed. It seems to represent unreality.

Now the first ontos rumbled forward pointing its six recoilless rifles into the future—each one capable of obliterating a Soviet battle tank. As it moved it vibrated in its whole frame, encountering the filled holes and cuts in the road in their thousands.

And the ship, a destroyer of the Sherman class eight thousand yards to the east in the South China Sea, with a length ten times her width and 70,000 horsepower behind her, went knifing gracefully through the purling water, throwing a white bow wave—while down be-lowdecks in the fire-control room a chief in wrinkled khakis leaned over a computer cabinet.

Like all chiefs in the U.S. Navy this one held a cup of coffee in his hand, and took his time sipping from it thoughtfully. He gave a six-teenth of a turn to a little wheel. Thus he entered the new ACTH, or "arbitrary correction to hit," to improve first-salvo accuracy. The ACTH is not derived mathematically. It is nonrational. It represents the computer's respect for an input that has no scientific justification whatever.

As he had a right to do, though only a corporal, the ontos driver stopped his vehicle and thus halted the whole convoy. When the battalion commander came forward he saw the same pattern of menace the corporal had seen, and for a minute the young corporal and the middle-aged lieutenant colonel stared silently at the road ahead, not for the pleasure of it, but for something very nearly the opposite.

This lieutenant colonel, commanding officer of 1st Battalion, Nth Marines, and thus MacHugh Clare's immediate superior, was the very man who had obtained a Honolulu R and R slot for Mac six weeks ago. He had proved an effective regimental 5, and his boss rewarded him with command of 1st Battalion.

He studied the road, the terrain. His eyes seemed tired but were actually very acute. Although he spent more time in the sun now, his drooping and benign face still had the noncolor of dishwater.

A battalion command is the best billet in the Marine Corps for a man of his rank, and he was cautious by nature. He called forward his naval gunfire and artillery liaison officers. The weather was socked in and there'd be no need for the air liaison officer.

Now the three officers stood by the idling ontos, studying the prospect and finding something within themselves confirmed by its haunted emptiness. The road and the paddies were utterly deserted.

"What I'd like," said the colonel, "is exactly what you gents can't give me."

The two junior officers, a Marine Corps captain and a Navy lieutenant, scanned the colonel's features, anxiously awaiting his expression of a wish they could fulfill.

The colonel stared at the bleak scene before him: the highway curving into the mist with the ridge looming on the left, set back some three or four hundred meters, and on the right, the abandoned paddies thick with new-growth elephant grass twice as tall as a man, and the railway embankment farther right, curving parallel to the road—and then the fogbound sea. And not a Vietnamese in sight.

"I'd like to take a *rake*," said the colonel in a dreamlike way, "and *rake* the seaward slope of the railroad. That's what I'd like to do."

Mr. Greenlee, the naval gunfire liaison officer, said confidently: "I can do that, sir."

"And then I want," continued the colonel, turning to the artillery officer, "say, approximately *thirty* rounds of 105 dropped on the reverse slope of that ridge because I'll bet my balls there's mortars over there."

The artilleryman said he could do that, not with 105's but with 4.2-inch mortars, which was just as good. So they began.

Mr. Greenlee climbed to the top of the nearest six-by truck and spoke with meticulous precision to his radioman on the ground. He called for one gun in adjustment, high explosive, fuze time. Few of the listening marines had ever seen a naval rifle fire timed fuzes—nor, if the truth were known, had Mr. Greenlee ever shot such a mission except at the range at Vieques Island, Puerto Rico. But he remembered that he had to place those dumbbell-shaped black clouds twenty yards above his target, and then woe unto those below.

The first detonation bloomed directly above the highway but it didn't matter because the highway was deserted. Mr. Greenlee then adjusted eastward, moving the rounds left, right, back, forth, and up and down till he could place his little clouds exactly over the seaward slope of the railway embankment. He then shifted to two guns and the *yap, yap, yap* of the 5-inch 54's barked insolently out of the fog, and the black dumbbells puffed in quick succession all up and down the railway.

Sometimes he used his 6 × 30 spotting glasses and sometimes he did it with the naked eye, but in either mode Mr. Greenlee knew his business.

When the artilleryman got word that the bird dog had moved safely north, he began chewing on the elephant grass with the four-deuces. Great gouts of mud and greenery rose and fell, sighing up and down the abandoned paddies, and the marines of the convoy took their ease, listening to the music of survival.

Next, the 4.2-inch mortars began dropping rounds along the top of the observer's hill, working slowly up and down the ridge line. The ship moved closer to the beach and fired a high-angle mission onto the reverse slope of the ridge, striking terrain that would have been safe in defilade had Mr. Greenlee not attempted a high-angle mission. But the ship's guns had the necessary reach, Greenlee did attempt it, and it was working.

The ship's ordnance dug up a long rectangular beaten zone at the base of the reverse slope, where a reasonable artilleryman would emplace his guns if he intended to hit the convoy. The four-deuce mortars did the same job on adjoining real estate.

To the enemy observer on the hill it was obvious this was all precautionary fire. The marines were so rich in ammunition they could fire off a hundred rounds on suspicion alone. Nonetheless the effect was terrific. He was certain they had killed half the attack platoon crouching behind the embankment. Even as the big mortar rounds dropped all around him on the hill, the observer listened with pained concentration for a secondary explosion from behind him. The Americans would quit this stupidity soon enough, and with luck all three 120's would still be ready, and he himself still alive. But the damage to the attack platoon laid out in the grass along the railway was very disheartening. The observer dared not raise his glasses; he could only guess. In any event the Americans had marched their big rounds within sixty meters of him and he still lived, as they would soon discover. His eyes blinked grit and the detonations howled in his head, his clothes were torn bloody, but he still lived.

As for the boy, he had thought the first round from the ship was intended for him. His insides had embarrassed him. When the yapping, a sound he had never heard, moved away, he knew he would live, that the convoy would move, and that he would realize the dream of starting a battle by touching his two wires one to the other. He held them now. He dared not move despite his discomfort. The explosions in front and behind him were frightening but he knew that noise and death were two different things. He looked at the bare copper ends, and saw them tremble. He thought of the observer behind him, and hoped. Even if the attack platoon were destroyed, the observer killed, and the mortar crews dying of wounds, the boy knew what he would do. He had orders to destroy the second ontos and he intended to do it.

The shaky shining copper ends of the two black wires fascinated him. He could hardly believe he held them in his hands.

Traveling by an unmapped and circuitous route, the NVA captain had reached the mortar emplacements while all was still peace in the valley. He and the battery commander, a young lieutenant, exchanged greetings and expressions of confidence about the visibility and the ceiling. They were so engaged when the observer called from the hill to report that an ontos had come into view on the right and stopped. They agreed there could be a dozen reasons for this, most of them quite innocent, but on the whole, the captain said, yielding to an urge to express himself, he didn't like it. It bespoke an excess of caution in the officer commanding the convoy. "He will have to move," said the captain to his junior. "He cannot just sit there." The lieutenant assented. He told the captain he could not hit the convoy where it was unless he relaid his guns. The captain said he already knew that and had no intention of ordering anybody to relay the guns.

The officers heard the first *yap*. They felt as a man might feel who wades into a brawl in the belief that everybody else is armed as he is, with fists only, when he suddenly sees a flash of brass knuckles.

Nor could the captain understand it. But for his responsibilities he would have climbed the hill to see for himself. The observer reported that the railway was under naval gunfire attack, but the captain dismissed this as impossible. He was sure the rounds must be either landing harmlessly short or flying over the railway. Then the four-deuces began hammering the elephant grass. Being unable to see any of this, he had to guess, and he guessed right. The marines were thrashing the abandoned paddies purely on a hunch. Since the sappers had departed he assured the lieutenant that the operation could proceed as soon as the Americans quit wasting their ammunition and resumed their march. And he added: "Don't worry. You are in defilade to all but his mortars, and he cannot adjust because he cannot see." This was a case of a man repeating himself to reinforce belief.

Then the captain heard a new and strange sound. A projectile of some kind had burst in the sky overhead—too high to hurt anybody but too ominous to be ignored. The captain did not know what was going on.

The lieutenant said: "I am afraid the ship is firing variable time-fuzed projectiles."

"At who?" said the captain.

"At us," said the lieutenant.

"And what," demanded the captain, "is a variable time fuze?"

"It is an antiaircraft projectile that detonates on proximity, not contact. It does not have to score a hit."

The captain still wanted to believe all would be well, since they were, after all, in defilade. The rounds would sail overhead.

But the artillery lieutenant said: "If he is firing a high-angle mission, these naval projectiles will rain down on us in a minute."

"But they are exploding in the sky!" cried the captain.

"Some of them, yes, because they are pinging off the clouds. Many will get through, perhaps half, perhaps more."

As the captain tried to remember something about high-angle fire, he was forced to listen to the *yap yap yap yap* of the naval guns. These always speak with a high-pitched semimaniacal barking and a malevolence all their own. And then the lieutenant's prophesy proved true.

A storm of concussions exploded at treetop level and the Victor Tango projectiles sent down a hail of vertical hell in hot hissing streaks of red. The mortar crews cried out and the men dropped, trying to make themselves small.

The captain grabbed the leader of the defense platoon charged with keeping the marines away from the mortars. He shouted that when the 120's hit the convoy, the marines would send a platoon or even a company. "They will come through the saddle!" screamed the captain. "You ambush them! Kill the capitalist pigs! Ambush them! Move your men now!"

The trees, the earth jumped and puffed in the steel storm, and the clouds boomed with explosions and flashed yellow (but nobody was looking up). The defense troops scurried toward the saddle to lay their ambush. The mortar crews crouched and reduced themselves in size as far as they could, and dreamed of overhead cover, of which there was none. The captain shouted to the defense platoon leader one last time:

"At any cost! Do not let a single marine through the saddle."

Shouting this deadly order the captain felt large. And when he dropped to the ground and tried to curl small (another problem in geometry) he still felt large, but he didn't feel good.

In all but the details, the NVA captain had sketched the convoy accurately. An ontos led the way, followed by Alfa Company, the battalion command group, an engineer detachment with basic bridging equipment, and a flatbed trailer carrying a small dozer; then Bravo, the middle ontos, and then Delta Company, and finally the last ontos and the stinger. The fourth company, Charlie, was already at Hue under the operational control of a different battalion.

Within Delta, Mac had placed Kim Kolias and his platoon first, then the company command group including Mac and Paul, then

Dan Shaw's platoon, then Graves's, and finally the gunny's gang as stinger.

The convoy rattled forward into the haze and smoke hanging in the air from the naval guns and the four-deuces. To the eye the highway presented a gray smear; to the ear, a certain exhausted stillness after the bombardment; to the nostrils, something of the sickening decadence of spent munitions.

Mac rode in the passenger seat of a jeep, with Graeser and the radio in the back. He had taken off his flak jacket and sat on it. Better risk hot fragments flying horizontally than the ones coming straight up. He was watching the ridge on the left, a low, rounded eminence rising some sixty or seventy meters above the level of the paddies. The artillery and the ship had hammered it hard, but no infantry officer is ever fully confident of unobserved fire—and all the rounds placed behind the ridge had been unobserved. Mac looked on it with an untrusting eye.

He felt the wave hit his face before he heard the sound. The mine lifted the middle ontos, and at the same time distorted it. The shock swept back through the column. Ahead he saw peripheral blast effects, smoke and flames and debris waves but not the ontos itself. A metallic crash followed the first blast, and then a new explosion of a lower order; and then the carcass shook with a cacophony of lesser blasts until after about two seconds it settled onto the road to burn itself and its crew into oblivion.

Mac leapt out—being on the passenger side he was on the right side of the convoy—and ran forward at mid speed. A man fell and jerked on the road surface. There was a clanging on Mac's left as a machine gun sought the fuel tank of the truck he was passing. He understood that enemy troops on the right were attacking by fire. He stopped and stood quite still, full upright, and looked. He saw a pale yellow flash in the weeds along the railroad, 250 meters away. He shouted for Graeser, who was nowhere in sight. He ran forward and passed one or two more trucks, with the machine-gun and rifle fire zipping before and behind him. He saw a stream spewing out of the water buffalo.

When the heat threatened to burn him he stopped. Now he could see the ontos consuming itself in yellow, red, and blue flames, and the six-by just behind it also burning—and there were no marines near it. The fuel tanks had not yet caught.

Mac forgot he was the company commander. He began dragging a man back by his arm, knowing he was dead and evidently not caring. He left the body between two six-by's and ran into the heat again and looked for men. He was still aware of the firing from the railroad, and automatically evaluated it, but he didn't take command. He guessed there was one light machine gun—certainly not a 12.7—and two or three rifles—five or six men at most. Had this been a full platoon he would have behaved differently, but somehow he reached the conclusion that this problem needn't claim his attention now. His men were firing in accordance with the doctrine of "instant action" anyway. He pulled on the leg of a man lying under the second truck behind the pyre and dragged this man too, leaving him with the body of the first. Whether he was alive or dead Mac never ascertained.

He saw a man skip and fall. He heard shouting which his brain never decoded. He hated the flames, and was cautious with his hands. He did not touch the door handle of the burning truck. He saw a piece of jagged metal smoking white on the ground and recognized it as a chunk of a 106 rocket from the ontos. He looked forward and saw chaos ahead of the pyre-ontos, among the men of Bravo Company. For an instant he didn't care what happened to Bravo Company. But his mind did not quite click back into its assigned role as CO of Delta. He saw one of his men leap into the grass on the left of the road, apparently to escape the firing from the right, but the man was enveloped in a gray explosion.

Mac shouted his first order: "Stay out of the grass on the left, it's mined!"—knowing hardly anybody would hear.

He waded into this same grass and pulled the man out, shouting for a corpsman—a useless thing to do. But he was moving toward clarity. He knew that a command-detonated mine had struck the ontos traveling between Bravo and Delta; a squad of enemy infantry then began firing from prepared positions along the railroad. Yes, he understood it. Now he began to think about what to do.

He was stopped by two nearly simultaneous explosions in the paddies on the left. It was big stuff—heavy mortars. He looked through the dirt, rice, and water descending from these detonations as through a transparent screen, and what he saw was the hill. He connected the detonations and the hill, and the connection seemed natural. He knew that a man on that hill would now adjust the mortars toward the convoy.

He shouted "Incoming!" and trotted back, hoping to find Graeser. He called his name and the man appeared with wild eyes—unhurt. Mac grabbed the handset.

"Platoon leaders, answer up fast," he said.

"Striker Three here," said Graves Registration's radioman.

"Striker Two, we're O.K.," said Dan Shaw's radioman.

Mac said, "Striker One, do you read?"

Silence.

"Striker One, how do you read me?"

Silence.

Mac said, "O.K., Two and Three, listen up. Keep your men out of the grass on the left because it's fucking mined. Move away from burning vehicles. Stand by for heavy incoming. Holler it now, 'Incoming!' Go ahead, holler it. Striker Three, suppress the fire from the railway. Striker Two, keep your men down and spread out, and don't expend any ammo. Break. Buzzbomb, how do you read?"

Gunnery Sergeant Hitchcock said cooly: "I read you five by five. All secure back here."

Mac said: "Keep your team intact and ready to move out. I plan on going after those fucking mortars."

Mac was standing straight on the left side of a six-by, with the cab between his body and the gunners on the railroad. His flak jacket was still in the jeep. He noticed a man beside him—his new executive officer, First Lieutenant Wozniak. The man looked at Mac burningly, with a suppressed eagerness compromised by fear.

Mac said: "Go forward and take over First Platoon—wait—I mean, go see what's up with Kolias. If he's—burned up—take over First Platoon. Find a radio somewhere and get back to me fast. Now go."

"Aye aye sir"—and Wozniak was gone running.

"Sir, the chaplain wants to know—"

Mac looked in another direction and saw Michelson soaked in blood. Mac said: "Are you O.K.?"

"Yes sir. The chaplain says to tell you he's setting up an aid station with a couple a docs and he can't find the other doc and he's got two guys really bad off."

"Tell him, 'Incoming.' Tell him—go!"

Michelson stared blankly, then dashed off forward. A mammoth concussion knocked him off his feet and he hit shoulder first against the wheel of a truck.

Mac felt himself waver and he held out his hands as if to grasp something but he was no longer vertical. He was in a concussion without sound, and he saw a white flash. A while later he rolled on his side, looked up, and saw flames licking the bottom of a truck, and he began crawling away. He hollered for Graeser and Graeser said:

"Right behind you, Skipper."

Then came a blank time, which Mac knew only by inference, having found himself where he had not been. Graeser crouched behind a double wheel, and Mac seemed to be standing upright somewhere, thinking. All around him men were lying on the road, under trucks or trailers, firing toward the railroad. Mac cried, "Go, Delta! Kill the fuckers!" It never occurred to him that these men might be from the platoon that he had ordered to save its ammo.

Graeser crawled toward him and held out the handset: "Sir, it's Battalion."

"This is Striker Six," said Mac. He heard his voice and realized he was sounding quite composed.

The battalion commander was not shaking either. He said, almost slowly, deliberately: "O.K. Mac, how many WIA and KIA?"

"Don't know," said Mac. "Several of both."

"Can you hold your piece of the string?"

"Affirmative," said Mac.

"Good," replied the colonel. "Now tell me, have you got a good crater? Can you find a good crater?"

Mac answered: "Wait two."

"Make that one, I'll wait one," said the colonel.

Mac gave the handset to Graeser and trotted along the string of trucks hollering for Ollie.

Corporal Sedgwick popped up from under a truck and cried, "Lieutenant Oliver way forward."

To Mac this implied that Ollie was dead.

Mac grabbed Sedgwick and looked into the bloodshot eyes of the black man, perceiving his entire character from his eyes, his wrinkled brow, and grim depressed mouth. It was a fearless man Mac saw.

Mac said: "Come here, Sedgwick."

He trotted forward and squatted beside a crater still smoking from a detonation and said: "Give me a back azimuth on this, quick."

Sedgwick's sagging features concentrated as he began the process of reading the hieroglyphic before him. He spent three seconds looking at the hole, then ran his hand along under the lip of the side toward the railroad, cried out in surprise, and quickly withdrew his hand. He dropped to his knees.

Another massive detonation shook the road and vehicles but Sedgwick, with care and sensitivity, and after only a second's hesitation, drove his bunched fingertips deep into the hole, cried aloud, pulled his hand back and shook it, and then drove it in again. He stood up, spitting on his fingers, turned to Mac, and said: "Got the fuze well. Just a minute now, Skipper."

Sedgwick opened his compass. He went around the hole and lay the compass flat on his outstretched hand and slowly squatted. His grave eyes darted from the hole to the compass and back and he said: "Back azimuth Four Seven Hundred mils magnetic. Right behine that hill." He rose to his full height and said, "Sure thing," and snapped the compass closed.

Mac clapped him on the shoulder and smiled, and Sedgwick looked at Mac with a conspiratorial smile.

"Sir," Mac radioed the battalion commander, "we did a crater analysis and those mortars are behind that hill almost straight west."

"O.K., O.K.," said the colonel, "are you ready for a frag order?"

"Affirmative."

"Take a platoon and FO and go get those mortars. We'll prep the saddle with 105's and run unobserved fire from the four-deuces on the reverse slope. Keep us apprised of your movements and position at all times. Tell me when to shift control of the fire missions to your FO. And I'm sending you the Navy gunshot. His name is Greenlee, Navy lieutenant. Use the ship if you can, I like the sound of those five-inch 54's. Greenlee's on his way. Got it?"

Mac said he had got it. He strode down the line and found Dan Shaw. He gave the gunny his orders. He delegated the defense of the road position to the exec, who, having failed to locate Kim Kolias, had taken over 1st Platoon.

Mr. Greenlee arrived running, with his radioman; the gunny briefed his team on its role; Dan Shaw pronounced 2nd Platoon ready to rumble.

Mac said: "Wait!" He slid down the left bank, through the weeds and over the first dike into the flooded paddy. He shouted: "Single file, keep in my trace."

Second Platoon filed down the bank. As each man passed him Mac slapped him on the back and said, "Good job" or "We've got to stop those mortars."

The four-deuces started pounding behind the hill, the 105's thudded into the saddle with a whipping sound as they lashed the trees, and the enemy mortars kept firing.

Mac and Mr. Greenlee were walking abreast, actually trotting, and this was unnerving. It meant two pairs of boots trolling for mines. But they had no choice. They had to talk, and stopping was out of the question.

"Can you pound the reverse slope again?" Mac asked.

"Sure," Greenlee said, puffing and jogging along. "But right now we're on the gun-target line and I—"

"Yeah. But we're humping toward that saddle. See it?"

Greenlee looked ahead and a little left, to where the saddle cut the height of the ridge by half.

"O.K.," said Greenlee, "if we keep on this course we'll be safe in a couple minutes. I'll fire the same concentration as before. I told the ship to record the data."

"Do it!" Mac cried.

"Yeah, yeah—" and Greenlee grabbed the handset and stretched the coiled wire taut while his radioman, a marine private, trotted with the two officers.

Greenlee said to the ship: "I want you to refire Target Number Zero Four Dash Two, but! But! Keep the gun-target line as it was. Can you do that, I hope?"

After a pause for consultation with the conning officer the ship's gun boss said he could.

Greenlee continued: "We are moving under that GTL right now. I'll tell you when to shoot. We are under attack from heavy mortars located somewhere in the box I drew for you the first time you shot this target. We are pretty sure that's where they are. We are humping right now, we'll soon be out of the way. Can you fire in say five minutes—HE, Victor Tango, saturate the box with a hundred rounds."

Mac exclaimed: "Jesus Christ!—May I speak to him?"

Greenlee passed the handset and Mac said: "This is Striker Six Actual. Those mortars are tearing hell out of the convoy. Please give us all you can."

A very deep calm voice responded: "We are on station and ready for call for fire."

Taking the mike, Greenlee said: "When we get off the GTL I'll ask you for a spotting round but I might lose it. I want you then to shoot unobserved fire if necessary. USMC arty is firing four-deuces at the adjacent box."

Said the voice: "We'll be ready when you call. We will maintain the old gun-target line."

Greenlee shouted to Mac: "He can keep the GTL the same. We'll be in Safe City."

Mac ordered the gunny's team to break away. Following orders Mac had issued before they left the highway, the gunny headed south; the platoon continued north. If Mac's plan worked, the gunny would reach the south flank of the ridge line at the same time Mac reached the approach to the saddle on the north. Diverging from each other, the two units both moved toward the hill, in full view of the enemy observer. Mac was virtually certain such an observer existed and could see both the Main Body and the gunny's gang. If so, the observer would report that the main body was headed toward the saddle. The gunny's team was headed for the south shoulder of the hill, some three hundred meters south of the saddle.

The enemy mortars boomed and the projectiles struck among the vehicles behind Mac. He didn't turn to look. He was setting a brutal pace.

Corporal Sedgwick said to Mac, "Ain't but two a those gook-type tubes, Skipper."

Mac nodded and kept humping. Turning, he shouted: "Faster, marines! Don't bunch up! Faster!" Mac was on the point, Greenlee following in trace.

A man cried, "Look at that!" and Mac saw a figure in black pajamas 150 meters away running up the gravelly brushy hill beyond the paddies. He was distancing the marines.

Mac shouted: "Get him, Danny!"

Dan Shaw's voice rose from the middle of the column and one fire team of four rifles cracked out on slow fire six, eight shots, and the figure dropped.

Shaw shouted: "Should we check him out?"

"Forget him," Mac called and they plunged on through the paddy, sending water flying about their churning knees.

The 105's were raising a cloud of smoke and dust from the tree-clogged saddle which lay ahead of Mac, uphill to the left. Mac and the platoon were still at sea level, splashing through the paddy.

Mac said, twisting to look at Greenlee: "Why don't those mortars go after us?"

Greenlee was soaked from the waist down, his legs raising waves and screens of paddy water, his mouth open to gulp air, his bulging brown eyes watching Mac. He was crimson in the face and his teeth displayed white enamel. He was keeping the pace.

Greenlee panted out his answer: "He'd rather pound the convoy, I guess."

"Yeah," said Mac.

Both men were breathing heavily and Mac felt strong. Mac added: "And he's not worried about us yet."

Greenlee asked why not and Mac said he didn't know, but he did: the NVA gunners believed they had all the protection they needed against attacking infantry.

Mac called back: "Sedgwick, take over both arty missions."

"Y'all give me these here fire missions," Sedgwick's voice cried out as he yelled into his mike. "Don't truss y'all no longer." A moment later Mac heard him cry: "Check fire why don't you? Juss check fire so I know you can do it."

The platoon was drawing near the saddle, to the point where they could hear the fragments ripping through the air. The 105's suddenly ceased. The four-deuces continued, and Sedgwick talked to the fire direction center. The dust cloud lay suspended over the saddle.

Mac shifted the platoon from a column to a skirmish line and moved to within 150 meters of the place where the saddle debouched into the paddy, then set into cover behind a dike. Mac was deployed not to enter the saddle but to bring fire on it. He called Dan Shaw to the center.

Mr. Greenlee said to his radio: "One gun, main armament, high-explosive, fuze Victor Tango, will adjust, over."

After about thirty seconds the ship said: "Ready four eight, over."

"Roger, ready four eight," said Greenlee, "shoot."

"Shot," said the voice on Greenlee's radio. After forty-three seconds precisely the ship said: "Stand by, out."

The forty-three seconds had been long ones; the next five would be longer.

Said Greenlee softly, "Five seconds."

The *yap* of the naval gun came rolling in, and soon they heard a detonation somewhere in the air above the hill.

Said Greenlee: "Lost. Drop one hundred."

The ship fired again and everybody listened as you listen when you think you hear a sound in the night. Then came a muffled detonation lower down and Corporal Sedgwick said to Greenlee:

"That was a good one, Lieutenant."

"Fire for effect," said Greenlee. "Two guns, as many salvos short of fifty as you can give me."

The ship's guns began a wild barking out of the fog.

Then the various sounds—the yapping from the sea, the shuttle rumble from the sky as the projectiles climbed a parabola and then a faint whine as they descended at terrific velocity, and then the detonations high and low, above and behind the hill—all this impressed the men of Delta as a message either of predominance or waste. Either the enemy was suffering or laughing; but in either case his 120's kept firing.

During this interval of listening Mac realized his head was splitting and his inner ears plaguing him with a ringing that never quit. Everything that reached his mind had to pass through the screen of pain and noise, yet he had not known it till this minute.

He said to Corporal Sedgwick: "Prep that saddle but keep it all in the saddle."

"Huh?"

"What are you firing?" Mac asked.

Sedgwick said he would fire 105's.

"Hit the saddle but nothing south. Because," said Mac, "we are going up the hill now."

Dan Shaw cried: "We're not going through the saddle?"

"Not on your life," Mac said. "Skirmishers right, Danny. Let's move out."

The platoon re-formed and pivoted, and started angling up the hill, while the 105's thudded into the brush and trees choking the saddle. The formation had pivoted left and was now leaving the paddies, climbing at a diagonal with the hilltop on the right and the saddle falling out of view over the curve of the hill. The platoon was moving again toward the gun-target line from the ship.

Greenlee cautioned: "No closer, Skipper. I've got a long range-dispersion pattern, plus Victor Tango fuzes, it's too chancy."

"O.K.," said Mac, "stop it."

Greenlee said, "Check fire," and the yapping stopped after thirty seconds, but the chugging of flying projectiles and the thudding of the bursts opening beyond the hill continued another minute.

The group around Mac crouched and listened as the naval gunfire subsided, but the 105's in the saddle, the four-deuces, and evidently the NVA 120's continued to bang away at their eardrums. In the midst of this Graeser was trying to raise the gunny. In one of the silences after Graeser had said, "Buzzbomb, talk to me," a voice spoke near Mac's ear.

It was Corporal Sedgwick saying, "Ain't but one a those NVA shootin now, Skipper."

Mac and Sedgwick faced each other and neither could conceal the hope in his eyes. Mac was fascinated by Sedgwick's face, by the lugubrious droop of his skin, as if Nature had bestowed on him a face that was one size too big. His eyes too were larger than life, and very bright and liquid, and bloodshot. His skin shone with a sheen of sweat.

"Sir," said Graeser, "here's the gunny."

413

Mac told Sedgwick to check fire in the saddle, then took the mike: "Hey Buzzbomb, *re*-port."

"Just like always, Mr. Six," the gunny said smoothly, "we're making John Wayne look like a pussy."

"I guess you mean I'd be happy if you told me what you've seen on your walk."

"You have every reason to be happy," said the gunny, meaning he had seen no dinks on his side of the hill.

"O.K., you know the rest," Mac said.

"That's a rodge. I go ahead, right?"

"You go ahead," Mac said.

Gunnery Sergeant Hitchcock led his team along a contour line circling the hill with the summit above his right. As he rounded the shoulder he looked back at the convoy, of which he had an unobstructed view, and saw the smoke and leaping flames; he heard the firing of small arms from the marines and the enemy squad on the railroad. But he did not have any sense of calamity. He saw it, he registered it; he guessed that Bravo and Delta had lost maybe ten men killed in the initial blast and the secondaries and fires it ignited. But now it was just a fight and he knew it would soon be over. The NVA would run or die.

When he had rounded the southern shoulder of the hill he stopped and waved Hippo forward.

"I gotta talk to your blood brother from the artillery," said the gunny.

Hippo squinted at him, paused, and decided the gunny was just a kind of white dolt who meant no harm—and changed the frequency on his PRC 25 from the company tactical net to the artillery net. He passed the handset and the gunny said:

"Hey, Bub, when're you gonna stop the friggin boom-boom. You want me to walk right into it?"

Said Corporal Sedgwick: "Wait one, Mr. Guns," and later: "When y'all want me to stop?"

"Five minutes," said Hitchcock. And to his team: "Bring the gun up. Hippo, stick by me."

So the team moved out in this order: the gunny, Hippo with the radio and a blooper, the M60 gunner and his assistant, Gonzalez the runner, Collins the sailor, and Valas the Golden Greek.

Dropping lower as they completed their circuit, they entered a bamboo woods and marched toward the naval gunfire beaten zone. Just beyond this was the beaten zone of the four-deuce mortars; here the projectiles still fell; these were point-detonating fuzed shells that burst on contact with trees or the earth. With each step the team moved deeper into the zone of blast and shock wave.

At length the gunny lifted his hand, then signaled a hasty defense with the gun forward. The men crouched and waited for Sedgwick to stop the four-deuces firing.

Hitchcock observed with satisfaction the multiple effects around him of the naval gunfire mission. There were no craters, just a general shredding of foliage and scarring and splitting of the hollow trunks of bamboo. He peered inquisitively at a bamboo stalk opened with geometric precision by a fragment from one of the 5-inch 54's. All the while his mind analyzed the sounds coming from 150 to 200 meters ahead—or less. He thought he had come a little too close but what the fuck. He concluded that the NVA mortar, probably a 120, was still getting off about two rounds a minute—but he heard none of the shouted commands and adjustments he had expected to hear.

With the silence of the four-deuces came a shower of rain, a heavy shower of vertical rain as heavy as lead. This did not irritate the gunny. All in all he would prefer to be dry. But what he really cared about was getting the 120.

"We've got no time," said Mac speaking fast. "We go over the top. If their defense force was waiting for us in the saddle they must be pretty messed up by now."

He saw in his mind a flash of blood and breaking bones.

"But they'll soon figure out what we're doing. They may run to their guns. That means that we pour it on from the hill as we go down. While the gunny takes'm with enfilading fire from the left. But suppose they climb the hill following us as we go up? And take us in the rear? How bout that?"

415

Greenlee, Sedgwick, Dan Shaw, and Graeser did not approve.

"Bad," said Dan Shaw. "Cowardly. Attacking American freedom fighters from the rear."

"So, Danny, take three men, go off to the right, line abreast. Any NVA come up the hill from the saddle, open up, then run and join us on the top, or over the top. Don't take a radio, it'd slow you down. Got it, son?"

"Yes sir. If I see gooks I shoot like hell and chase you."

"Right. Remember we may be in the middle of a big noise too, so make a racket, then run! And you take over my rear defense."

Dan Shaw got three men and jogged off toward the slope that fell into the saddle.

Mac arrayed the rest of the platoon for offensive fire straight ahead and resumed the ascent. As he climbed, he waved Mr. Greenlee close and asked:

"Can you lay down a blocking fire about four hundred meters beyond the base of this hill?"

"You mean on the other side?"

"Yes."

"With us on top of the hill?"

"Yes," said Mac, checking his flanks and waving the left a little forward.

"No. You mean just four hundred meters horizontal distance beyond us when we hit the top of the hill?"

"I mean," said Mac panting, wondering why the man didn't get it, "four hundred meters from the place where the ground levels out—the bottom of the goddamn hill, for Christ's sake." But he realized he hadn't made it clear. He said, "We top the hill. You call in a blocking fire on a crossing line four hundred meters that way"—gesturing ahead—"from the place where—Christ, forget it."

Greenlee pondered, he consulted his map, wiping the rain away, and said: "No."

"Goddamn it," said Mac.

"Sorry."

They pushed on until a man on the left called Mac. With extreme reluctance he halted the advance and ran down the line. There was the body of the man in black pajamas, only he wasn't a man but a ten-

or twelve-year-old boy. His shirt was ripped by bullets and one arm was splintered. His eyes were black with flies. He smelled of shit. The rain fell thinly on the corpse.

As the platoon neared the top, three or four men at once saw a man in black pajamas pop up from among the bushes and run. He was carrying something in his hand and trailing a black string or wire—this later proved to be his microphone. They dropped him and he looked as if some invisible adversary had pulled him back by the hair.

The line reached the crest.

Mac said to Corporal Sedgwick: "Can you lay down a blocking fire—" and he indicated where.

Sedgwick cranked up the four-deuces and the rain-deadened explosions began rumbling up from the flat ground below. The four-deuces were laying down a blocking fire across the NVA's probable bugout route.

Mac looked in both directions—raised his arm, and paused, and all eyes were on him—and signaled the advance. The marines descended toward the NVA position at a steady pace and then heard rifle fire on full automatic from their rear. Dan Shaw was busting his primers.

Mac increased the pace without going to double-time and the men went lunging and crashing down through the brush and around big boulders. A bamboo forest lay some hundred meters ahead. Men looked with fear and uncertainty toward the center to see what Mac would do and he pressed on even faster. Nobody wavered but many wished they could. They entered the woods and Mac felt he was slipping into chaos. What if the platoon reached the bottom before the gunny started firing, and he took them from the left? What if the NVA roared after Dan Shaw and took them from the rear? What if the NVA down below let his men pass through and then attacked from behind? What if the gunny had gone off track? What if Dan Shaw were killed? An unknown welling, an expansion, took command of Mac's innards and he realized that total ruin and death lay just ahead among the bamboo shafts. He went ahead anyway, looking left and right and keeping the nearest two men in sight. The 120 boomed and Mac signaled a change of course toward the sound. The firing above came closer. Mac halted the formation, called the gunny, and said, "Both of us aim toward that mortar. Fire away."

The gunny's team ripped open its fire box and Mac opened fire with rifles but held the bloopers and machine guns. Mac marched carefully forward. There was no return fire. The gunny's men, still invisible, hammered away, and a man cried out in shock and pain—an enemy. The fire doubled as both formations, Mac's and the gunny's, advanced by short careful steps, till they could see one another.

"Here's a mortar pit," a man called out, and there was a quick furious exchange of fire. Mac halted the gunny and led the main body forward into the kill zone. He saw an NVA mortarman raising a projectile to drop into the mouth of a 120-millimeter tube. Mac and Graeser fired on automatic through the trees and cut the man down.

Some NVA defenders rushed in from the right, but they were running right in front of the right half of Mac's line, and several of them flopped under the fusillade, either hit or diving for cover. Mac now lost control of his right; everything had worked pretty well up to now but suddenly he couldn't exert any influence, men on both sides were firing wildly. It seemed a new flow of enemy troops was coming in from the saddle but many of them were wounded or dazed, they seemed to stagger and fire and whirl in search of danger; and the marines gained fire superiority in a matter of two or three hellish minutes. The firing subsided but continued. The men around Mac killed the mortar crew.

Looking down the slope Mac could see through the trees that the ground leveled out in paddies. From the rear Dan Shaw hollered to one of his squads. Seeing himself among his platoon, Dan would be taking control of the defense to the rear, or so Mac hoped.

Mac hollered to the gunny and got a reply. He told him to sweep toward the paddies. There was firing from all sides and in all directions and Mac did not know what to do next, or where anybody was, except the gunny. He saw the gunny making hand signals. Mac shouted to fire only on visible targets and the shooting diminished radically. But Mac was in a woods and could see very little, just shafts and some clusters of banana leaves, and smoke. The four-deuces were still laying down a blocking fire but Mac sensed they were conserving ammo; he tried to concentrate; he tried to conquer the thing in his mind that had gone wild.

He saw a Vietnamese in a green uniform and helmet with an assault rifle stalking him. As he leveled his rifle Mac realized the man had not taken an opportunity to fire. Graeser was turning. Mac thought no more, he cut the man down and watched him twitch and fall with the same expression on his face as Lee Harvey Oswald when Jack Ruby shot him in the gut.

Mac raised Dan Shaw's radioman and found that he and Dan were together. He made sure that Dan had control of the rear, and that all was well in that sector. Mac strode right and organized the flank for defense. Then he knit the platoon together—when no new attack came—and swept down the slope to the paddy. He halted the blocking fire. He left two men to guard the 120. At the edge of the paddies by a footpath they found a pile of a dozen NVA bodies ready for evacuation, and the base plate of another mortar. Mac did not look for very long at the pile of dead men.

Across the paddies, as the rain thickened, they could not see much, but one man said loudly: "Somebody just started up a motorbike." And Mac heard the little engine rev and take off.

The gunny's men found a third gun pit minus the gun. The blood trails were dissolving in the rain. Mac thought it was over but a Chicom grenade flew in out of nowhere and landed near him and he saw it bounce. A blast of machine-gun fire severed a tree near his face and he dropped to his knees and returned the fire. A dozen marines joined in; two marines fell; and Mac forgot the grenade. There was a great yelling and a report of a blooper, then a wallop in the brush, and several marine rifles were spitting out fury in three directions, and nobody knew what was going on except maybe the other side.

Mac saw the grenade down there among the leaves, and wished the U.S. grenades were made on the same pattern. The unconscious mental background to this wish was a boyhood memory of throwing fat sticks that flipped end over end, it seemed, under their own power. Mac found himself firing at movement among the bamboo shafts, where some banana leaves occupied an open space, and he saw how dark the rain had made the leaves and tree trunks. He forgot about the grenade and concluded, a day or two later, that it had never detonated.

A marine hollered "grenade" and let one fly. His partner threw one too. The things detonated together with their peculiar chuffing sound, modified in some undefinable way by the thick continuous rain.

Mac could see no more movement by the banana leaves. He called a cease-fire and everything went silent, they could all listen to the rain and sniff the sulfur.

The platoon sergeant organized a work party to cut bamboo shafts, so teams of two men could carry out the mortar tube and the two baseplates suspended from poles between them. He asked for volunteers to tend the wounded since the corpsman was dead. He split the men into teams to carry the wounded and the two KIAs.

Mac ran another sweep of the woods and found five more NVA bodies and three AK-47's. He counted the discarded ammo boxes and estimated that three mortars had fired about forty rounds. He reported to Battalion.

Mac took the point; the platoon loaded up and began climbing the hill along the same path the forward observer had followed an hour before. Near the top Mac ordered everybody down. Mr. Greenlee talked to his ship and soon the yapping started up. The ship was pounding the NVA escape routes with flat-trajectory fire, using point-detonating fuzes, the projectiles streaming overhead as fast as meteors.

Mac crawled toward the wounded and spoke to every man who could understand. Corporal Sedgwick was spread on a smeared poncho and his legs were bloody rags and his head rolled. He did not see Mac but Mac drew very close and said:

"Does it hurt, old man?"

In the past when he bent over wounded men Mac experienced something like despair in his idea of himself, because he did it too easily. He could touch a man's shoulder and speak encouragingly and tell optimistic lies, and never feel the man's pain or fear. Therefore he was a heartless man. But speaking to Sedgwick he could not control his voice. He knew this man's death would take a part of his soul from him.

Corporal Sedgwick turned his eyes toward Mac as if in surprise, as if he had believed he was alone.

Mac said: "We'll have you on a medevac bird in half an hour." This might even be true, but Sedgwick did not have a half an hour.

Sedgwick looked at Mac as if he wanted to detect every nuance and consider every syllable that Mac spoke, but he did not speak.

Mac lied: "You look pretty good." He was fumbling for the pulse in the skinny black wrist. "You've got a good strong pulse—"

Something fierce came into the wounded man's eyes and Mac kept their eyes together, and he grasped and regrasped the wrist, still seeking the tiny jolt on his finger ends. He broke the stare because the tension was too acute. He did not want to sob or weep. He looked down at Sedgwick's wrist.

Sedgwick moved his free hand and covered Mac's. He made a sound in his throat.

Mac thought: "Live, please live."

"Skipper, be reasonable," said Dan Shaw boldly. "I've got two willing men, plus me makes three, and we could all trade off."

If all four took turns walking point they would spread the risk.

"No, Danny," Mac replied. "No, but thanks. These guys have got to fight but they don't have to walk point."

So Mac again walked point, directing Dan Shaw to array the platoon in a column to minimize the danger of mines.

And Mac turned his back on the fight scene and climbed up the hill feeling fairly safe, but this feeling waned with each step, until on reaching the crest he felt the presence of mines as a man walking a bad neighborhood might feel menace in the street. He looked down at the highway curtained in shrouds of rain and fog, and saw the devastation, the smoke and black smudges on the road, but he wished he was there and not here.

Even at this distance he could see a gang of marines toppling the hulk of a six-by. It flopped down the bank, rearing its smoking black wheels and settling with a gently rolling motion at the edge of the paddy. On careful inspection Mac saw that Delta Company was still viable and mobile. Besides the middle ontos only three trucks had burned, and the pattern of craters in the road told him that the enemy gunners had spread their fire all up and down the column, and so had scored few hits on Delta's segment.

Mac guessed that the enemy had intended to disable several vehicles at wide intervals to trap the entire convoy. His next step would have been to pound the battalion into the earth; but he had not been given time to do that.

As Mac dropped lower and approached the edge of the flooded paddies, he stopped again. For some reason he did not want to walk the next thirty meters. Then he realized he was following a faint trail. He veered right and pressed through brush and bulging bushes, deliberately plowing through vegetation that he could easily circumvent.

He decided to go through the flooded fields rather than walk a wall. The wounded needed immediate attention and his decision would double the crossing time, but the paddies were safer and the four-man teams carrying WIAs in ponchos could not walk on a dike anyway.

Mac stepped on the first dike and jumped into the paddy. He slogged forward. He was not thinking of Sarah, but of life itself. He would try to find the trail the platoon had trampled when it followed him down the bank from highway to paddy.

Now he was low, drawing near the highway, and could not see the railway or the mists of the sea. All he could see across his front was the smoking roadway and, increasingly, the figures and faces of the men of Delta Company. The dozer was pushing a black hulk that bumped reluctantly along on its bare blackened wheels. Graves Registration and another sergeant were clearing men away from the rim in case the falling truck should set off a mine.

When the truck was out of the way the men on the road saw the platoon approaching, and a few started up a cheer, perhaps noticing the big mortar tube and the baseplates suspended on ropes from bamboo poles—but the cheer died as more and more troopers saw the bearers bringing in the wounded and dead.

So when Mac began climbing the bank, having located the dark mark in the brush made by the platoon on its way down, all was silence. As his eye reached road level, and then rose higher, he surveyed his company from side to side—and men looked at him, and some looked into his eyes as if they wished to speak. He went among them and spoke quietly, and listened.

Michelson led the bearers forward to the aid station. Mac commended the exec on the cleanup and received his report: five dead and eleven seriously wounded—then Mac ordered a 100-percent alert. He told Graeser to stay with the exec, and he walked forward.

He met Paul Adrano. The priest's sleeves were rolled up, his hands and forearms colored with blood, his eyes glowing with an unnamable emotion.

"Did he say anything to you?" Mac asked.

Both knew that "he" meant Sedgwick.

Paul Adrano replied: "I think he was trying to tell me something at the end."

At that moment, as the two stood over the body, a corpsman covered the face with a poncho. Now the face was neither so black nor so wrinkled as before, nor so intelligent. The eyes were open but had nothing to tell or ask.

Mac watched Paul for a sign that he had more to say. Paul's deep brown eyes as they turned on Mac seemed to understand something that lay beyond Mac's reach. Over Paul's shoulder Mac saw the hulk of the ontos and it drew his eye for a second. Paul turned and saw it too.

Paul said, "They must have burned to death."

"I hope they died sooner," Mac said.

"Yes, we can hope that."

The battalion trekked northward, and that night it reached the marine base at Phu Bai, eight miles south of Hue. Mac and Paul drank at the tent of some base officers, then walked in the rain.

Paul said: "Tomorrow more hell, I suppose."

"Right."

"You envy me," said Paul Adrano, "because you think I have an explanation, as you call it. I envy you because you have a wife you are free to love."

Mac didn't respond and they kept walking.

Paul said, "When I saw it was Sedgwick, I said to myself, 'Now I'll find out if he believes what he said he did.' Do you believe on the threshold of death the things you tell yourself you believe during life, or does fear just grab you by the throat?"

Mac said: "Fear grabs you by the throat."

"But Sedgwick was unconscious."

"Eventually, yes." And Mac went on: "When we were on the hill he looked at me as if I were the one with the answers."

"A creature from another world, to him," Paul supplied. "He looked at me the same way. But until I realized he couldn't or wouldn't speak I wanted him to tell me something that only he could know."

"A very naïve desire."

"Yes."

After a minute Mac asked: "Did you ever try to imagine what it'd be like—to be in that ontos?"

"I am thinking of it right now."

"And does it seem real?"

"You mean do I have the power of imagination?"

"I just mean that supposing you can imagine it," said Mac, "does it seem real?"

"If I follow you," said Paul carefully, "assuming I understand you, you must be saying, does death seem real. I have to say I can see myself in the ontos and see my own death, yes."

"Real, then," said Mac. "Your own death."

"Very real."

Mac grunted and threw away his cigar, which had been extinguished by the rain. He suggested, "Let's get another drink."

"No, I don't need anymore."

So they walked on, and Paul thought of his walk in the rain with Becka. He said:

"I cannot believe this is all. This can't be it."

"It'd be pretty ugly, wouldn't it?"

After several minutes, when they had found a place to sit under the flap of a tent, Mac said:

"I keep thinking of Sedgwick when he looked at me. I went over to him when we were in defilade and I said, 'You're looking good' or something. He was spread out on the poncho, and he looked up and he seemed to think it was O.K. that I should lie, he wouldn't hold it against me. I couldn't see any fear, regret, or affection in his eyes. Just—knowledge."

Paul said out of nowhere, "If you were in that ontos, would you be thinking about Sarah?"

"I don't know. I guess I'd think about my own—myself."

Paul nodded. He said, "Well—I have a request."

"O.K.," said Mac.

"If I am killed, please go to the naval hospital at Da Nang. Find a nurse named Rebecca Vanburen. Can you remember the name?"

"Certainly."

"Tell her this, only this: that I thank God I met her."

"O.K. And you'll mail my letter?"

"If necessary, yes," said Paul.

"And I'll carry your message to Da Nang."

Chapter 18

The Corridor

Corporal Sedgwick looked at his hand against the sky. His eyes saw it but his heart did not own it. He had been struck by some invincible force, with violence, that would deprive him of life and had begun by depriving him of the feeling that he inhabited his own body. It was like being drunk. That was one reason Sedgwick had quit drinking even before he was born again, because he had once, while drunk, seen a man's foot protruding from under a table and realized a minute later it was his own. He let his hand fall, and let it lie on his chest, trying to learn if the hand and chest were acquainted with each other.

The fear came when he saw the faces of the marines standing around him. If they were standing like that, upright, it meant he had not been shot. He must have tripped a mine. He did recall a pink cloud and a big blast. They were looking down at him with shock, horror that was not terror, and, already, dismissal. They cared but they could not afford to care too much. As soon as he saw their faces he knew he was already dying. He looked down his body and saw two men doing something to him down there. He felt a kind of thrusting and twisting. One of the men was covered with blood to his shoulders.

Sedgwick's fear was like a lion whose footsteps he could plainly hear through the screaming in his ears. The beast paced around him. He feared the lion and he was the lion, the predator and the prey. When the beast had devoured him, neither he nor his attacker would survive.

He cried out, and the two marines down there shot a glance at him, but continued their futile work.

For Sedgwick it was already too late. This seemed perfect and just, a rare certainty in a chaotic world. It proved that this world is but a prelude. And if that were true then Sedgwick had nothing to fear. But he was terrified of being devoured, dismembered and strewn over the jungle while retaining for a period of unspeakable pain the capacity to see, feel, and understand. After that, no fear, no pain.

Had he sustained a trauma like this at home or in school he could not have believed it. He would have tried to deny it. But here it was the natural thing. There need be no protest or confusion. All he had to do was say, "My turn." But the truth was, he was just as confused as if this had happened to him on the playground at school. Why should he lie here while the lion prowled? Why should he feel the same hunger for death that the lion felt? He tried to scream but nothing came, not, at least, any sound that he could hear.

Sedgwick began to dream he was talking to his little sister, trying to explain to her. His point was that she would be cut to pieces in an indifferent world unless she put on the armor of faith. "I wear the armor of faith," he said. She had already had one baby. She so loved the child that it was impossible to make her see that anything was wrong. She never contradicted him because she loved him too. But she didn't listen; or she listened just in order to smile in pretty much the same way she smiled at her baby.

Sedgwick was cramped by fear for his sister. He didn't think God would damn her; she was not really evil and God was not that stern. But he feared that a life of spiritual starvation lay before her. When he tried to describe what she was missing she looked skeptical, then said, "I have everything I need." She hugged her baby. Thus by reason of her own neglect and ignorance she would live all her life as if sex, alcohol, television, boyfriends with cars, and babies were her all in all. He could see her at forty, an addict living in a squalid apartment, setting a bad example for her children. God would allow that to happen. It happened all the time because God lets you make your own decisions. Sedgwick's sister would mistake the indifference of the world for God's indifference. All He does is set you free, then He watches.

"God loves you!" he shouted in his dream.

She smiled at her older brother as if he were a child.

The jolting and jostling ceased, and Sedgwick knew he was lying on his back looking into the rain. There was no sun but the glare hurt his eyes. He was in a clear place now on a steep slope. He believed something grave and serious had happened to him, something impossible to understand. His senses distorted everything. He felt a flooding within, of despair. He could read his fate in the skipper's eyes.

Seeing the skipper's tears he realized he was as good as gone. He had been given an interval of ease but now the strain had returned. Now he must face death. But instead he searched the skipper's eyes for another reprieve. He tried to read the skipper's lips. He imagined he was saying, "You'll be O.K., just hang on. All you need is a medevac bird and you'll be fine. You'll live!" The skipper's lips moved and maybe he was saying that. But his eyes said something else. Despair drove Sedgwick into the ground as he saw the skipper weep.

He had a vision of his father lying drunk on the living room floor. He was a skinny man with a drunkard's little potbelly, and when he lay on his back and snored the belly sank and almost disappeared. His head was by the sofa and his feet by the TV, so Sedgwick had to step over him. This had happened many times but the boy remembered one time in particular when a little smear of vomit glistened on the carpet beside his father's head. This picture stayed alive and influenced him. From then on it was a struggle against hate, and he never really won it. He was supposed to do God's will, and God has commanded us to love one another and honor our fathers, but Sedgwick could not love or honor his father. "God, you know I tried."

He went back to a day when they let the black kids swim at the YMCA. His friend Clayton Briscoe explained why they could swim there only once a week. "Iss cause they cleans the pool after we swims and it takes all week. They thinks we is dirty."

"Rev Jameson say we is washed in the blood of the lamb."

"What he know," Clayton retorted.

But Sedgwick believed the Reverend Mr. Jameson. Belief turned to certainty when he was about seventeen and was touched by grace.

428

From his rebirth to the present moment he had walked in a cleansing faith and feared nothing. He was certain. The exception was a short period when his intellect, only his intellect, was confused on the question whether it was God's will that he look forward to salvation with confidence or try to consider himself unworthy of it, so as to be surprised by joy when it came. At length he surrendered to his belief that God was good and merciful. He would be saved, so long as he acknowledged he didn't deserve it. He must strive—but in the end only grace would be sufficient.

As his life ran out he waited fearfully for grace. It lay within God's power, not his own.

He must have fallen asleep. He awoke in pain. The pain grew more acute and soon it grew terrible. He couldn't endure it. He had been marveling at how little it hurt, and thanking God, and now this. He struggled—and then saw a good face, the chaplain's face, and he too was near tears. Now came terror.

He saw the chaplain fold his hands and look to the sky and pray, and realized that everybody was giving him up for dead. He cried out loud and the chaplain placed his hand on his head and went on praying. Sedgwick could hear nothing but the mechanical scream in his skull. He groped for the chaplain's hand and grasped it, he thought.

The chaplain looked down. He spoke, he smiled, he was a man of God. Sedgwick waited for grace, for bliss. The pain was too much and he tried to scream.

To his horror he saw a corpsman lifting a needle. The rain and blood ran down the corpsman's arm and the little point glinted. Sedgwick tried to cry out, No!—but the corpsman stabbed him, and that meant the end of his pain, and of his mind.

He gazed at the loving face of the chaplain and he felt his own love, but now he would never know what he desperately wanted to know, wouldn't know ever, unless—he was touched by grace again. Yes! If God touched him with His grace, that would be the answer. The pain faded. He either closed his eyes or went blind.

Chapter 19

Sarah's Letter

Dearest Mac—

Of course I was warned—every woman is—but the beauty and strangeness of it have taken me by surprise. I really don't know what I expected because it never seemed real to me—the possibility—so with every new sign I denied it more dogmatically. The more *obvious* it was the hotter my denials—I played tricks on myself—and as the days passed and still no period, I was more certain—not less!—that I could not possibly be pregnant. I believed that I knew who I was, and that that woman was not careless enough to end up pregnant while her husband was where you are. The doctor said to use two methods on my first cycle, the Pill itself and my diaphragm, but I recoiled because I remember how you howled once when you collided with it. So—to save your Donkey I left my kit at home and now here I stand. Pregnant!

So you've got your way and it seems our Treaty is ratified indeed. What else can I do now except go anywhere you like and be your childbearing, child-rearing, cooking, cleaning wife? I don't say drudge, but do you think I planned this? To be a housewife? Denise said, and I quote: Your head's in the toilet for twenty years.

Denise and I have been exploring the question of how to live a

430

woman's life, and I am listening—not swallowing but considering—even her most radical proposals and also one astounding suggestion of my father's which I have never mentioned to you, it's so extreme. But since *now* is new and different, a fresh deal of the cards and the whole idea is purely academic now, I can say it—in a minute. These two different souls almost sound to me like conspirators, they are in such perfect harmony despite the contrast in age, outlook, and worldly knowledge—with their jeering and catcalling—and the object of their scorn, my dear, is none other than the solemn Treaty that is the plan of our future life. And when I psychoanalyze myself I discover that half the joy and beauty I feel within, the luster and magic about our wee babe, is that I must now fall back to the original position—fall back on the Treaty. Relief!

I have felt that I stood in the center of a triangle of forces with my father, Denise, and *my own ambitions* at the points, beaming red-hot rays at me and addling my brain. I began to see myself strutting around a courtroom in a clinging dress, astounding the jury with my wit, command of facts, stage presence, and of course legal knowledge and my passionate sincerity on behalf of my client—so I was living in a fantasy encouraged by the Triangle of Forces; and the deeper I went into it the more plausible it began to seem. Not ridiculous, plausible! I gave up writing my play—I must tell you about the play, which is my other secret—no. 1, pregnant; no. 2, writing a play; no. 3, fantasy lawyer—anyway I shut the play in my drawer because my whole imagination was caught up in the lawyer opera.

I got a casebook from the base library and what do you think? It was boring. A man trips over a brick and blames the city for his broken leg. The lawsuit shows the tripper to be a con artist, the city a lumbering bureaucracy, the judge a nitwit, and the jurors a bunch of credulous boobies. Having read four of these "slip-and-fall" tragedies I realized in a blaze of self-awareness that *I could never be a lawyer.* Lawyers burrow in musty fact-heaps and actually have to master the facts of the case. What a cool job. But these facts, taken outside the case, are pointless. You devote hours or days to learning a case that doesn't enlighten your mind by even 20 watts but leaves your life shorter, all for the sake of arguing issues that have no conceivable interest to anybody but the parties. So I knew it was not for me. I have a life to live.

But that very night I couldn't sleep for the booming of the opera in my head. I made speeches. I gesticulated, argued, pleaded. My client had slipped on the ice and was a paraplegic, ended his career on the Packers—and I sued the homeowner who had failed to shovel his sidewalk, and reduced him to tears and poverty—somehow insurance didn't figure in the case. I was on top!

It is pathetic but I have to inform you I am still dazzled, astounded, seduced by this drama. Undoubtedly tonight in my lonely bed it will roll right over me again. I want to remind you that lawyers get paid and playwrights—as my father sympathetically tells me—starve. Unless they are waitresses. But the new horizons, Mac—this is the trouble—scare me. Law school, where the order of the day is for sadistic professors to humiliate students, scares me. Trying to master some complex antitrust or contract case would reduce me to a puddle. *That* is the "magic" of being pregnant, I fear. I simply can't picture myself in a law school class with a baby at my breast!

I hatched a saving idea. I could write my play or some future play while you chop down trees, feed the cows, and split firewood. That's Denise's scenario: I freeze in a shack while you play at being a lumberjack. But I could find a couple of hours every day to write. I must admit my powers of imagination do not go so far as to show me my name in lights. I am afraid my father is right. I had a better chance as an actress. Or: my chance in either role is virtually zero. So what a relief it is to find I am pregnant and out of the game.

I have now covered all three points and perhaps your mind is prepared for a confession of a different order. I told you on our fateful and joyous day—while we watched the fountains spouting in the sunshine—that I would wait for you. I did—happily, gladly, with my whole heart—I waited and I have the reward of my loneliness, you are my husband, I am your wife, and I will never wish to change that. But as I get nearer to the actual execution of the Treaty I begin to wonder if a remote farm or cabin in the country, however lovely, will satisfy me. My father said—perhaps wisely—that if I couldn't stand Stevens Point, what makes me think Vermont would be any better? One is flat, the other hilly. Neither one is New York City. And I do not want to be poor, or married to a man who gradually loses his pride because he sees his family suffering.

Please don't think I mean to withdraw from the Treaty. Like you, I do not want to live in Milwaukee and certainly not New York. (Although maybe I'm kidding myself on that one.) I still believe in the Treaty. I will not push for Boston or San Francisco if you agree not to insist on Stevens Point—and I do know, dearest Mac, that working with your father is what you really want to do—and that he too would be very happy if you became his partner—and that you will give up that dream for me. I make bold to ask you to give it up! For my sake! And my compromise is to forget my adored San Francisco—which I admit I have seen only once, for two whole days—so please hear me when I say I still agree to the Treaty. But I felt you should know that I am worried. Also pregnant. I am now a pregnant woman, soon to be a mother. I know exactly what I'll be doing with 90% of my time for the next several years. But—

Well, you know the "but." I just told you.

And now, my hunk of sweet power, please consider this letter as strictly business, and tomorrow I'll pour forth my passion and devotion, or do I mean lust, and describe my other fantasies, which do not take me into a courtroom; rather they admit you into an antechamber, then to the innermost place. Your performance is superb, utterly peerless, and drives me to the brink of a sublime insanity. If you knew how I long for your touch on my body you'd pity me and rush home today. You have hungry hands, you've told me. I tell you: I don't know how I can wait till June, my body is one great hunger. And so tomorrow a love letter. I know you are safe because you are constantly in my heart, where no harm can come to you. I favor the name Hugh for a boy and Dawn for a girl.

Your Sarah

Chapter 20

Bound for Hue

M ac knew he could be paralyzed, killed, castrated, driven crazy. But he burned with a different flame, his image of a life with Sarah. He wanted to see her belly grow, and to lay his hand on her shoulder, and take her lovely face in his gentle hands, to feel the hunger of his hands satisfied. But the city of Hue lay only three or four kilometers ahead and the rattling of small arms and the voices of rockets and grenades shook the monsoon sky.

He felt no fear—although he searched for it—it simply wasn't present. But something other than fear had taken hold when he saw the lower half of Sedgwick's body and then, with this impression on his soul, he looked into Sedgwick's eyes. He turned away saying, "Live, Sedgwick, live," and it seemed he faced a different world than the one he had known; or it was the same world but now he understood it. This was a dark knowledge.

Deeper than this lay his understanding of his role as company commander. Below the level of conscious thought he knew that power has a price. He could command Delta only if he paid with a portion of his innate identity. It is quite true that a combat leader can be a fully alive human being. The contradiction is that the combat leader must control his humane instincts. He cares for his men—up to a point. He acknowledges the enemy's humanity—up to a point. He dreams of his wife and home—but he must wake up before it's too late.

He may think that if he leads effectively and escapes with his life all will be well. This is an incoherent thought. To lead he may be required to burn half his nerves. Having done this he can never be quite the same. He may not even want to be the same. He may place such a value on his experience that he would choose to do it again. It confers a kind of knowledge that cannot be forgotten and a character that cannot be eradicated. But he has lost a portion of his system of nerves. What's left is powerful and quick, but what's lost is lost.

Within the intoxication there is this burning and cauterizing of the nerves. To command Delta Company was to be drunk, and burned.

Mac's mind carried him away to a cabin in the woods in some northern place in America. Sarah lay on a cot and he placed his hand on her belly to feel the baby kick and roll. He lit a kerosene lamp and fed the wood fire in the stove. The snowstorm flew against the window.

He was distracted by a familiar sound, a rifle shot, and his body went stiff. Two or three more shots cracked in his ears and set a kind of drum roll going in his skull—but that was the end of it. His internal drum roll continued for a time, with kettledrums and cymbals, plus a blaring as of horns, but it all calmed down and he almost relaxed. Stray shots, inexplicable noise.

He was starting to overreact to gunfire. At quiet times he grew edgy, expecting it. When the guns opened their mouths he wanted to ask for a little mercy. The feeling was like self-pity. Why must this happen again? But it passed, and he slipped into the skin of the man he had to be, the skipper of Delta Company, 1st Battalion, Nth Marines.

Except that Delta had been detached from its parent battalion. The commanding general, Task Force X-ray, at Phu Bai, ordered that Delta be sent north to reinforce a battalion that had already lost the equivalent of a company in the fighting in Hue.

A major from Task Force X-ray told Mac that the general had chosen him because of Delta's performance at the S-curve.

And Mac said: "Thank you, Major."

The engineers had reopened the road from Phu Bai to the Perfume

River. Delta was riding this road, going north toward the river, through the southern suburbs of the city. So far nobody had tried to stop them.

Looking back Mac saw the last vehicle in line, a U.S. Army duster with quad fifties, rise from the pontoons to the earthen edge of the canal that Delta had just crossed. Looking ahead he saw the derelicts and hulks of a previous Marine Corps convoy, blasted and burned and washed of blood by the monsoon. These vehicles sat stalled with hatches open and doors standing stiff in the wind, and despite the weather it was a poisonous envelope of bad air that the moving convoy passed through. The bodies of the VC and NVA ambushers must still be strewn among the brush and trees alongside the road. The marine bodies had all been taken away. This was enemy smell. But marines had died here; the wounded had gasped here.

Passing these vehicles strung out in a dead parade, swerving to get around them one by one, the convoy marines gazed on the detritus of disaster and every man was thinking some variant of one thought: "Our guys."

And Mac thought: "I could be crippled, I could be castrated, I could be—" But these were mere words. As for going crazy, it was easier to imagine losing his balls than his mind. He had a firm grasp of reality, firmer than ever before. He lived with the objects of fear as if they were mere objects. He remembered Corporal Sedgwick. Kim Kolias he had all but forgotten, but he remembered Sedgwick.

Passing the hulk of an ontos Mac thought of the rockets and fuel that must have been ignited in this ambush as in the earlier one. This ontos had perhaps been hit by a B40 rocket, quite equal to its task. Mac thought of the crew, as he and Paul Adrano had thought of the other crew, men they knew. He felt he knew these men also.

It made his own death seem plausible. Under the influence of the blackened and ripped ontos, he regained some suppressed sensitivity. He could hear the men yelling, but only for a moment. It would be a mistake to go on listening, and he tried to turn it off.

The 6 × 6 lurched, the big tires hissed as they spun over the mud surface shining in the wind and rain. Mac's mind went back again to Sedgwick. The man had called himself a moron but he was rare and gifted, maybe not an academic genius but a life genius.

"Like you," Mac thought, "I am a sack of guts walking around on sticks—just waiting to be punctured in a hundred little places so my life's blood can leak out."

As if it followed logically he thought: "If I fuck up in Hue I'm finished." If his marines died unnecessarily—and he paused to smile over that word "unnecessarily"—if he quit or cracked or vacillated, and they died, he would never get over it. If he failed, his only option was suicide. Leave her behind. Renounce life because you failed at killing. Stick the .45 in your mouth and blow the roof off. One mistake, one moment of weakness.

Now Mac saw that Gunnery Sergeant Hitchcock, sitting aft, was surreptitiously beckoning. That was odd. If the gunny wanted to talk he should crawl up here.

Mac got to his feet, lurching and almost falling. The truck heaved, and Mac held on, steadying himself, and squatted beside the gunny.

"I couldn't move, sir," said Hitchcock, and with a sly look he lifted a poncho that covered some kind of pile beside him, revealing a segmented steel tube and some wooden crates.

"Hitchcock, you're a criminal," said Mac with admiration.

"Right, Skipper. Not a word. The driver might squeal when he gets back to Phu Bai."

Mac asked how Hitchcock had acquired his contraband.

"A quart bottle of Jack Daniel's to the right man," Hitchcock informed him.

"And where'd you get the whiskey?"

"That was the hard part, Captain. Can't tell anybody, not even you."

"Guns, you are a master of the art of comeshaw."

"Thank you, sir."

The gunny had "comeshawed" a 3.5-inch rocket launcher and ammo boxes from some supply sergeant at Task Force X-ray. The 3.5 was an old weapon that had been replaced in the inventory by the LAW rocket—the light antitank weapon—because LAWs were lighter, smaller, and disposable.

The gunny said: "Fuckin LAWs'll never open a hole in a thick masonry wall. You know, Skipper, the whole city of Hue is masonry houses and brick and cement walls and terraces and all."

"Yes, I know."

437

"So now," said the gunny, smiling as much as he ever did, "onward to Hue."

"I've got a surprise for you too," said Mac.

"Wow, it ain't even my birthday."

"The weapons company commander," Mac began, drawing his sentence out for effect, "has promised us a—mechanical mule—"

"Jesus! With a 106!"

"Right."

"Skipper, we'll blast the fuckin monkeys outa their trees."

"And out of their houses," Mac added.

Paul Adrano rode a truck two or three spaces back in the convoy. He sat on a sandbag to protect the genitals he would never need, but everybody wants to keep his body more or less intact, and Paul's vows and his departure from the hospital at Da Nang did not change this. They were his by gift of nature and he had as much right to a sandbag as any other man. In fact there were several extra sandbags scattered in the bed of the 6 × 6 so he could cuddle his useless stones with a clear conscience.

He sat with his arms crossed on his upturned knees and his head buried. Let them think he was trying to sleep. He was far from sleep. He was proceeding slowly into a scene of lacerating self-torture. With a purpose. He intended to press his guts against the knife until he had driven out love and admitted hate. When the truck lurched and the cargo of barbed-wire coils and water cans shifted, when the floor vibrated, when a man guffawed over some joke told in a whisper to keep dirt out of the chaplain's ears—Paul was unaware. He was deep in his mental drama.

For the ten-thousandth time he crouched to enter the bunker, and he saw in his imagination the Zippo lighter left behind by The Destroyer. It lay faintly gleaming on the dirt deck. This dirt had absorbed atmospheric moisture out of the monsoon but it wasn't yet mud. They could throw their clothes down, their boots and socks, and still expect to dress again later without having to scrape off a film of mud. This would be an important consideration for people who madly strip off their clothes and throw them in the dark. Or maybe not so important after all. Maybe they strip in such a passion of desire that neither mud nor the night's monsoon chill nor the danger of discovery even enters their minds.

All they know is desire. They are mad. All they want is more madness, and each other.

Therefore Paul, thinking of how his flashlight would pick up the gleam of The Destroyer's Zippo with USS *Maddox* stamped on its case, and only of this image, experienced again the moment when he stooped under the lintel to enter the bunker, then stood to his full height and switched the flashlight on. He sent the beam right, along the wall, intending to search for the lighter on the bench and the earthen deck. He heard a suppressed cry of alarm, a whisper, and pulled the light left, where it shone on a disordered pile of clothing and one white sneaker. The scattering of these articles would later suggest to his fertile brain a whole scene of its own.

As if involuntarily he lifted the beam to reveal the lovers spread out on the bench with Doc Regnary above Lieutenant (junior grade) Rebecca Vanburen. Regnary stared in surprise and fury. Becka stared straight up into the darkness. Paul saw in her eyes, or created there, a look of wretched surrender.

At this point in the scene Paul always had trouble fixing on the truth. Had she bent her face slowly toward him and allowed a smile to lift the corners of her happy lips?

"Happy lips! You fool, you idiot!"

Or had she really been all but killed by being discovered? Was she staring upward in a paralysis of fear and humiliation?

And did the doc really smile and say, "Hello, Chaplain. Would you care to join us?"

When Paul ranged back and forth over the scene it always changed, but never for the better. He saw the doc's buttocks pumping and heard a cry of—a moan of deep pleasure escape Rebecca, as they went right on in plain view. He saw her body pinned down by the weight—her breasts in repose and her legs bent, but he never saw her hands. He wished he could find out what she was doing with her hands.

He thought of her rank, lieutenant (junior grade), and wondered why he should focus on this irrelevant fact. He remembered she was a nurse. He could see the freckles on her shoulders, and the red in her hair (surely not visible in his flashlight). He seemed to construct a full physical and mental identity for her, with emphasis on the boot; then he saw the sneaker again; but he feared he would never learn what her hands were doing. Then suddenly and for the first time he saw that she was gripping the doc's buttocks. He felt sick with disbelief.

"Go on," he said bitterly. "More. Take more, you slut."

He tried it again, "Slut, slut," and even if it seemed true it didn't kill his love. He loved her all the more! He had chosen God over this woman but he loved her all the more!

Crouching, backing out of the bunker, with his light trained on the doc and Lieutenant (junior grade) Vanburen, he knew he would never really get out. He was in the bunker with the lovers for the rest of his life.

Chapter 21

Forget Hue

Embarked in cargo boats and escorted by one heavy-armed Swift boat, Delta pressed along the black river surface under a dark dome of sky lighted from time to time by flares. Collins the sailor spoke authoritatively of Mike boats, LCUs, and Swifts but when Hippo asked how the real sailor guiding their craft could see where he was going Collins had no answer.

"He got radar?" asked Hippo.

And Collins said, "Radar is for pussies."

Valas cut in: "You call him 'cocks.' He's got more than one?"

"He's the coxswain, you moron."

"So two cocks, cool, man, but how's he see?" Hippo insisted.

"Shut the fuck up," Gunnery Sergeant Hitchcock hissed.

Hitchcock then stumbled across to the other gunwale and told the marines manning the rail there: "O.K. you snuffies, we're in the shooting gallery. When they hit us I want you to fire low and lift gradually. Got it? There's a mountain of ammo where we're going so I want the usual: instant action and fire superiority. Aim at their muzzle flashes. Hit the shore right and left of the red tracers, outgoing. You see a stream of green tracers incoming, kill him!"

A man Hitchcock could barely see told him they knew all that. Red is us, green is the gooks.

The gunny disdained to answer this. He worked his way back over the cargo, squeezing between jerry cans full of gasoline, and returned to the starboard gunwale where his ruffians made room for him, and he peered off into the night.

Valas said: "Yeah, yeah, skim'm off the water and lift slow. We're not morons, Guns."

"True. A moron has a brain. Just remember: instant action. Fire superiority. The Navy says it'll only last about five minutes."

The Mike boat shoved its blunt bow over the flat surface, chugging in the wake of a big LCU that was also loaded deep with men and flammables. The banks on either side were shrouded with thick vegetation that the marines could not see. The city loomed in the distance on the left, but a city without electricity is a ghostly presence, illuminated in this case by an occasional, weak, swaying flare.

Standing aft in a protective steel box shaped like an upright coffin, the coxswain repeated his instructions to the marines about cease-fire left and cease-fire right. The gunny went over it all again, threatening anybody who shot the Swift boat with life in the Portsmouth Naval Prison.

Then the Mike boat went quiet—except for the low howl of its engine and the rush of the Perfume River under the hull. There were three Mike boats, one much larger LCU, and the Swift boat. Delta was headed for the north corner of Hue, the only portion of the city under Allied control.

The marines watched the shadows of buildings on the left bank slide astern.

"So this speedy boat—" Valas began.

"Swift boat," Collins corrected him.

"O.K. What's he got?"

"A fifty, bloopers, maybe an eighty-one."

"He's got a fifty?" said Gunnery Sergeant Hitchcock with respect.

"Maybe two," said Collins.

"Number One!" Hippo exclaimed with enthusiasm.

The Swift boat had made a turn and now came up on their port side, passing forward along the line of landing craft. The stubborn Mike boats had to push water that the Swiftie sliced.

Here the river was about 175 meters wide, both banks held by the enemy.

"So why don't they blast our ass?" Valas demanded.

"They will," the gunny assured him.

Their rifles had iron sights, hard to see in the dark, and their M16 ammo had no tracers.

"Tell you what I don't want," Valas offered after a while. "When the gooks sink us and I'm swimming for my life, I don't want that fuckin speedy boat draggin his propeller over my skull."

"You won't be swimming," said the gunny.

But Valas cheered up. "*Cocks*. What about you guys calling me Cock? I only got one but its reputation is enormous."

"How bout we call you Weenie," said the gunny. "Did you clean that M16 like I told you?"

"Yes, Guns. Jesus, show a little respect."

Hippo said: "I clean my 16, I put a new battery in my Prick 25. In Phu Bai they got *beaucoup* batteries."

Hitchcock said: "In Phu Bai they got everything but a mess hall. Did you see that place?"

"I hope the gook that splattered that mess hall went on vacation," said Valas. "All they got left down there now's a bent fork." And he whispered into the darkness: "Come on, you fuckin slopes."

For a moment no one spoke. They heard the muted talk of the men at the other gunwale; they heard the throb of the engine blending with the tones of the boats ahead; and they could distinguish an irregular plangent lapping as the river yielded to the thrust of the boxy Mike boat.

Hippo was imagining the moment when the boat would press its square bow against the bank and drop its ramp, and the marines would wade out into water of unknown depth. He had heard of men stepping into holes and sinking. He thought of his rifle, pack, and radio, of their weight and the awkwardness of getting rid of the whole load in one twist. He imagined himself underwater in the dark, and a puff of fear expanded inside him.

The lead boat must have slowed. The whole convoy went dead in the water and dead in the dark. To show how salty he was Collins said, "We are Delta in the Whiskey." A searchlight flicked on downriver and cut off just as quickly. The engines went back to work. The Mike boat resumed its throbbing progress.

Then came an ear-assaulting *crack* and a white light streaking toward them from the right bank, then the whole bank lit up with orange and green flashes. Green lines zipped overhead. The left bank erupted with the same conjunction of light and menace. The night was creased with green streaks and red, white, and yellow rocket trails.

Something blasted the water and showered the gunny and his men, and split their eardrums. The gunny's team and Delta Company in all the boats opened up like lunatics, aiming for the muzzle flashes on shore or following the red tracers of their own machine guns into the dim target area. But much of the M16 fire was wasted in the water or the trees. The machine guns, however, took the élan out of the enemy attack, and the bloopers began to find the range with their 40-millimeter grenades. The grenadiers could often see the flash of their own rounds hitting and could adjust accordingly.

A loudspeaker crackling from the Swift boat ordered, "Cease-fire starboard!" and the coxswain shouted from his pedestal: "Cease-fire right!" The gunny added his thunder, and the starboard side went silent just as the Swift boat came roaring up on the right, pounding the shore with his big 50 and bloopers, sending flaming-red goof balls and bursting grenades into the brushy bank. A careful eye could discern the general shape of the enemy's position from all the flashes. An enemy rocket streaked out but missed the Swiftie by a meter or two. It sent a plume rising on the opposite shore, which the gunny observed because he had followed the rocket out of curiosity.

Now he studied the situation. He saw that the enemy fires were angled to prevent the murder of their compatriots on the opposite shore. There was a blank in their beaten zone on the right shore, which he could locate by its immunity to the green tracer fire of the enemy guns on the left bank. This could be a sanctuary for weapons whose muzzle flashes the enemy could conceal—such as mortars. A yawning canyon opened in the gunny's gut, back to his rectum. He grabbed the machine gun, giving his M16 to the gunner, and placed the bipod on the gunwale. He waited.

The instant the coxswain cried "Resume fire right" the gunny set the machine gun chattering, pouring its red arcs into the blank space and screaming at his men to pile their fire on his own. A rocket creased the velvet blackness, then another, sailing over the boat and impacting in the trees on the opposite bank. The gunny shouted for more fire.

While the marines sent hell to the right bank, the Swift boat made a hazardous 180, swinging perilously close to the shallows, beating the trees and houses with his big gun all the while, then throttled up and set to work on the left bank. The Swiftie's engine and his ordnance howled behind the gunny and his team. The gunny hollered again, "Pour it on, you marines!"

There was no mortar fire but an enemy gunner found the elevation and put a burst, then another, into the side of the Mike boat. The hammering made more noise in the gunny's mind than in his ears, but he was wild, and the idea that formed in his mind, of a fireball with himself at the center, simply had no effect on his actions. He saw the flash quite plainly, but he let his bore cool—all the while watching the flash as if it were a snake's tongue—and when the time was right, which coincided with the enemy's blinking off—undoubtedly cooling his own bore—the gunny set his gun dancing on its bipod.

The red zips probed the bank in response to the gunny's skilled, small adjustments; the A-gunner kept up a steady feed of belted ammo; and the black place on the bank gradually receded to the right, astern, without further mischief. The gunny felt O.K.

The firing on both sides diminished as the convoy churned downstream at six or seven knots, much too fast, but without mishap. An odor of burnt powder pervaded the air. This was only to be expected; but the gasoline smell was now much stronger.

The gunny addressed the men on the port side. "You snuffies better thank God I didn't use this." He tapped the 3.5-inch rocket launcher propped against the gunwale.

"Use what?" a man asked. He couldn't see what the gunny meant, and the 3.5 was, in any case, still in its folded position and perhaps hard to recognize in the dark—still the gunny's secret weapon.

He lifted it high, saying, "I almost fired this baby."

A voice from across the boat exclaimed: "You wouldna!"

The backblast from the 3.5 would have engulfed the gas cans packed into the center of the boat.

Another man said, "Hell, die now and forget fuckin Hue."

Somebody asked if anyone was hit.

A man said, "Yeah. Yeah."

"O.K., what's up?" Hitchcock growled. "Goddamn it, who's hit?"

They disembarked at a Navy landing where you could hardly put your feet on the ground for the barrels and wheels and tank treads and ammo boxes scattered around. They carried the wounded and asked directions to the aid station. A corpsman named Doc Sobieski, who had replaced Doc Bartholomew, bossed the detail, and they went humping off through one of the gigantic gates and entered the walled citadel.

Paul Adrano marched with them. When his group stopped to breathe, Paul realized what felt strange. They were in a city.

Paul and Doc Sobieski conferred, and settled on a direction, and the raggedy detail pulled on, sixteen men carrying four wounded. Approaching a long low building silhouetted against the sheen of a lake, they stopped. Paul heard the steady puffing of a generator behind the building, and a murmur of voices from within. Coming closer he saw an aluminum shutter made of the same material as the building and propped open just enough to admit a stream of air. He found a canvas flap and pulled it aside, and they entered the aid station.

Paul found himself under an aluminum roof stretching for fifty yards over a sand deck. The air inside was hot and charged with humidity, almost liquid, and big drops fell from the roof on Paul's helmet and shoulders. The place was lit dimly by a line of bulbs suspended from a black wire running under the ridge pole. Two corners to Paul's right, however, were much brighter. Each was screened off by sheets of plywood and illuminated by blazing lights hanging from wires dropped from an overhead beam.

Paul guessed these were operating rooms. He saw rows of cots, and dark figures wrapped in blankets. He decided to come back in the morning to hear confessions and celebrate Mass.

A surgeon came out of a cubicle, and began removing his gloves and mask. Paul approached him as he was bending over a big metal box with a hose feeding water into it. Paul introduced himself and told the man his intention.

The surgeon looked sideways at Paul in a peculiar way and asked if he was going into the city.

"I thought this was the city," said Paul.

"I guess," said the surgeon as he wiped his hands. "At least we're inside the citadel wall. I mean, are you—is your company going down to attack the NVA?"

"I'm here with the reinforcing company."

"Does that mean you're going out into the city with the company?" asked the doctor, still eyeing Paul in some strange way.

"The company commander told me to be ready to move at ten in the morning. I really don't know anything."

"Come with me," said the doctor. He was a man of Paul's own age, about thirty-five, with a fair skin and balding head marked with scattered freckles, puffy lips that he never closed, a rounded nose in which the red showed the beginnings of a purple hue, pale blue eyes that snapped this way and that, and a stocky muscular body going to fat. When he was buttoning his utility shirt Paul saw that he was a Navy lieutenant commander. Paul followed him into his sleeping quarters. He offered Paul the only chair, plastic webbing of various colors rigged on a frame of aluminum tubes.

The doctor took a bottle from beneath his cot. The bending caused him to breathe audibly, as if he had climbed a hill. He held two shot glasses in one hand while pouring with the other. Paul drank his off and the doctor, before drinking his own, refilled Paul's. He smiled and said it was good stuff. Paul agreed.

The doctor began: "I want to tell you two things, Chaplain. A, we have no chaplain in this aid station and we could surely use one. B, don't go out there." He watched Paul react. Or fail to react. He saw in Paul a young black-haired man built like a prizefighter, with thick arms and a blocky head, almost massive—bright inquisitive eyes, thin lips, with dark whiskers beginning to mark his upper lip, close-cut hair, and a sunburned face. And he saw that Paul did not intend to be his chaplain.

He continued: "Let me state my case."

"Go ahead," said Paul.

The doctor held out the bottle and Paul accepted a third ration. The doctor drank his second then said:

"There was an Army chaplain around here for a couple of days. Nobody knows exactly why but he showed up and offered his services to the marines. The colonel said, 'It's your funeral,' and so he attached himself to one of our companies.

"The troops are not accustomed to seeing a chaplain crawling through the rubble beside them, or riding around on a mechanical mule smiling and waving—eating C rations and claiming he never tasted such excellent food—walking down the street! This chaplain walked down the middle of the street! There's a commercial district a little south of here, he walked along, looking in the shop windows, when all he could hope to see was a total smash. Anything that the NVA or Marine Corps had not destroyed had already been looted by the ARVN, but there he was, peering into broken windows and shell holes in the walls.

"Then they found him in a residential neighborhood checking out the houses that were still smoking, you know, and finally some marines hustled him to safety and he protested. 'You boys don't understand. I have a mission, just like you.' And they said, 'No, Reverend, *you* don't understand. The NVA will, you know, sort of *kill you.*' So the next day—"

"What was he looking for?" Paul interrupted.

"I thought you'd know."

"Maybe I do."

"He must have had a good-shepherd complex, don't you think? Looking for his lost sheep?"

"Why," said Paul hesitantly, "why don't we ask him?"

"You're getting ahead of me," said the doctor. He drained his glass and said, "More?"

"No thank you. It was very good though."

"Oh yes, it keeps me going."

"I see."

"So the next day, after the window-shopping thing, a guy riding a mechanical mule, you know, those little topless buggies—"

"Yes," Paul said.

"A golf cart without the fringe on top. Anyway, we have a marine who runs back and forth between the fighting line and this CP, delivering ammo, water, rations, and such, entirely by himself, a perfect madman named Terwilliger—

"Anyway, Terwilliger gets lost! He looks around and sees the houses are intact! There's a car sitting in a driveway. A garden wall with flowerpots on top. A house with windows still in place, unheard of! Our genius realizes he's in a neighborhood that the fighting has not yet reached, enemy territory, forward of the fighting line, all alone! While he's shitting his britches he happens to see an NVA standing in somebody's doorway smoking a cigarette. He can smell the smoke. French, black tobacco. Terwilliger pulls a U-turn, the cargo spills all over the street, and a whole squad of NVA open up with about ten thousand rounds and twenty RPGs and Terwilliger escapes unscathed.

"And while driving out of the jaws of death he finds himself in the midst of utter devastation, not a stone standing upon a stone or whatever the saying is—"

"No stone shall stand upon another," Paul said.

"Suddenly Terwilliger sees a guy strolling down the street toward the jaws. He stops and says, 'Hi there, Major.' It's of course a guy in U.S. Army uniform with a major's leaf on one collar and a cross on the other. Terwilliger says, 'Don't take another step.' The chaplain says in all innocence, 'Why not?' Terwilliger says, 'Because the gooks are right behind me,' and the chaplain scolds him for calling a fellow man a gook. But he accepts Terwilliger's invitation and hops aboard."

The surgeon, reversing an earlier decision, reached down and withdrew the bottle again. "More?" he asked, breathing audibly.

Paul declined.

After drinking and staring at Paul inquisitively the doctor said: "The next day, which was yesterday, the marines found his body in a house the NVA had been using as a battalion command post. He'd been shot through the forehead, obviously looking straight at the guy who shot him. Picture that. We think he was captured, interrogated, and executed."

"Do you think he was aware of—the danger?"

"How do I know? Terwilliger said he told him, 'I go where I am needed.' "

"I see. Of course," said Paul quietly.

"He should have stayed with his unit. His cross didn't save him. Why should the Communists respect a cross?"

"He was with one unit," Paul said rapidly, "then he wanted to spread his influence, so he went searching for another, and became confused, because nobody knows what's going on anyway, or where they are, I mean, you don't really know what's happening or why. He took a wrong turn and met the wrong people. So I'd say, no, he wasn't truly aware. He was—a chaplain."

"And you," the doctor concluded, "are a chaplain and you are needed right here. We've got one paraplegic for sure and another maybe, we've got a triple amputee that we can't ship out because of the weather, we've got a man with his jaw shot away. When the wind blows from the right quarter this place reeks of dead bodies stacked in the next building. That's dead marines. Do you understand?"

Paul said: "I understand you and I understand your need."

"I don't know what denomination you are and I don't care."

Said Paul as if to himself, "They need a chaplain, any chaplain."

"I'd like somebody to tell these marines—" The doctor hesitated.

"Tell them what?"

"That's for you to figure out."

Paul rose, thanked him for the drink, and said: "We'll talk in the morning."

"Bring your gear. We've got a cot and a roof to keep the rain off."

"I'll think it over," said Paul.

The briefing officer was a captain about Mac's own age, perhaps younger, and from his language, from what might be called his bookishness, Mac surmised that he'd never fought. The others attending the briefing—Mac's platoon leaders, the exec, Ollie the artilleryman, Kindred, Hitchcock, and Paul Adrano—were moving toward a similar opinion. The man was the kind of staff officer who would never admit that the war, to him, was only a game. He played it as a rule-driven procedure rather than a piece of chaos. He played with arrows and lines, advances and withdrawals, blocks and drives, all actuated by voice and written messages, and displayed in two dimensions on a map.

Because of all this Mac thought he lacked the reality dimension. But Mac misjudged. The briefer was in one sense actually more impressed with the reality of the war than Mac was. The man was terrified. With every sentence, with every touch of his pointer on the map, he uttered a silent prayer for Mac's life. If Mac should be killed, he, as the only infantry captain remaining in the battalion, would certainly be shifted from his job as operations officer to command of Delta Company, a ragged gang of hungry, strange, violent, contemptuous men who would resist him and maybe even plot his death.

When pointing to the map on its easel he had to press the end of the stick firmly against the surface to keep it from shaking. He had to speak slowly to control his voice. Gunnery Sergeant Hitchcock suspected something but even the gunny was off the mark. He thought the nervous ticks were the effect of the captain's faking it: so many officers masked their lack of experience with a cloak of bravado or intellectual superiority, which they could barely sustain. This little puke was trying to put on a military bearing as if he knew the answers. He didn't know shit. He was a Basic School commando. So the gunny listened with contempt and a curled lip, which he did not feel compelled to conceal. The gunny was never insubordinate, and never forgiving.

The briefer set out the tactical situation, starting with terrain. The Perfume River divided the city into north and south sections. The north was The Citadel, a self-contained walled city roughly three kilometers square. Inside the Citadel wall, at its southern end, where it was bordered by the river, stood a fort within a fort. This inner fortress was The Palace. The Citadel, although it was square, presented itself on a map as a diamond tilted slightly right. What the briefer called the "east wall" was actually a wall running northwest-southeast. This east wall would become an important terrain feature for Delta Company.

The sheer size of The Citadel surprised Mac. Each of its four walls was six to seven meters high and anywhere from five to ten meters thick. They were thickened every two hundred to three hundred running meters by bastions jutting outward, designed to give the defenders clear angles of fire against attackers near the walls. Besides the bastions, the walls were strengthened in a few places with massive towers, huge squat thicknesses affording the defenders clear fields of fire, a height advantage, and ample cover. Especially at the towers the enemy had dug into the walls to create strongpoints that were very hard to eradicate.

Thus a fortress designed to defend against attack from outside was now occupied by NVA troops defending against a Marine Corps attack from the inside. And this interior comprised a city complete with airstrip, parks, ponds, residential and business districts, much of it intensely planted with trees and gardens.

The Allies—the USMC and ARVN—controlled the north corner of The Citadel, where the ARVN occupied a safe, walled position (the third fort within the fort), and where the Americans had sited an aid station, command post, and logistics facility. The briefing took place within this north corner fort.

Delta was tasked to relieve Mike Company, which had lost half its men, killed or wounded. Delta would then link up with Kilo and Lima Companies, now on the line, and attack south with the east wall on its left. The wall, then, would stand on the left of Delta's axis of attack. This was bad enough, since the enemy had dug fighting holes into the top of the wall as well, giving him clear fields of fire into the streets below.

What made it worse, the briefer said candidly, was that farther to the left, outside The Citadel and across a moat, the whole scene was overlooked by blocks of three-, four-, and five-story buildings. Snipers and machine gunners in these high windows could bring fire to bear on any Delta marines who tried to attack along the top of the wall and even, depending on the street layout, on Delta men as they advanced south through the city.

The objective, said the briefer, was to drive the NVA out of the houses and shops that lay between the outer wall and the inner wall, between the Citadel wall and the Palace wall. This Palace wall, which would stand on the right of the attack, was every bit as formidable as the Citadel wall, with this additional complication: the U.S. and ARVN command in Da Nang had forbidden the marines to fire heavy ordnance at The Palace or its wall. It was a historic, even sacred, place to the Vietnamese.

Mac said: "Wait a minute."

The briefer was shocked at the interruption. He added quickly that III MAF (Third Marine Amphibious Force, the top command in Da Nang) had lifted the prohibition and would now allow the marines to hit the Palace wall with artillery "under certain circumstances."

"How many marines died as a result of that no-fire order?" Mac asked.

Said the briefer, turning red, "I don't know. Nobody knows."

Mac said: "The NVA are dug in at The Palace—cover and conceal-ment, clear fields of fire from fortified positions—and Three MAF told your men to walk by it without artillery, air, or naval gunfire."

"Air—well—the weather— We haven't used much air."

"Is that why we're relieving Mike Company, because they were cut up under that rule?"

"They took a lot of casualties," said the briefer, still boiling red.

The room went silent. Mac stared at the briefer for a full five sec-onds and the man played with his stick, looking at his hands, and when he looked up, Mac's eyes were still on him. The briefer saw those fierce blue eyes and that hulking set of shoulders and said:

"I did not give that order."

Mac said: "Of course you didn't. Go ahead."

"You *can* call in arty and naval gunfire. Did I make that clear?"

"You said 'under certain circumstances.' What circumstances?"

"I don't know precisely. You have to request a mission. It'll go from us to Task Force X-ray to Division to Three MAF in Da Nang. If it's approved at the top it comes back down to us and we give you the clearance."

"Tell me you're making this up."

Gunny Hitchcock, while this was going on, had nobody to speak to, so he spoke to himself: "This is a fuckin war?"

"Let me ask you to clarify something," Mac said and his men lis-tened with life-death interest. "May I shoot an eighty-one on my own authority?"

"Yes," said the briefer.

And Mac continued: "May I shoot a three-point-five rocket launcher?"

"Yes."

"May I shoot a 106 reckless rifle?"

"Yes. Anything bigger, you come to us."

"To Battalion."

"Right."

"O.K., now I see the picture. Four echelons of control. Brilliant. Please proceed."

Scrutinizing the briefing officer, Hitchcock couldn't tell whether he was smoldering or trembling.

The briefer said: "You'll advance southward on a line abreast with Kilo on your right and Lima on Kilo's right."

"My left is against the Citadel wall."

"That's correct."

"Is there a reserve?"

"No. Or Mike's in reserve, theoretically. Mike will be here at the CP."

"And they're all shot up," said Mac.

"That's why you're here." Consulting his notes the officer went on: "You must keep contact with Kilo, and keep the line straight. This will not be as easy as you might expect, given all the rubble, the trees and alleys, and houses. The alleys between houses are narrow and thick with vegetation. We call it an alley but you could not drive an ontos through. If he got in he couldn't turn around. Most of the yards of the better houses are walled, walls about four feet high, made of brick, block, stone, masonry. Some higher. There are lots of trees. You will have a hard time seeing your own men, let alone Kilo's. But we must keep the line straight for obvious reasons."

"Obviously," said Mac.

"Battalion will control your movements and your assets. When I give you a tank-ontos team, you control it. But you must relinquish it when the colonel needs to shift it somewhere else. Do you roger that?"

"Of course," said Mac.

Paul Adrano knew what Mac was thinking about the high command and its rescinded order against employing artillery and naval gunfire on The Palace. Vietnamese bricks were valued above American lives. Now the briefer was into another subject and Paul had missed the beginning. He was trying to grasp what kind of man the general commanding III MAF must be. What kind of man issues an order that will lead to certain death for his own men, when that order is a political gesture? Paul heard:

". . . a lot of our casualties that way. I understand your concern. You'll have to use your judgment."

"Are you talking about frontal assaults?" Mac asked.

"Yes. We would assault across a street—this has happened any number of times in the last couple of days—and two or three men would go down—they're lying in the street. Our guys go after them—

454

in some cases they even went after dead men, that they knew were dead—and they got creamed."

The briefing officer was holding his pointer across his belt buckle and the knuckles gripping it were yellow, his face was livid red, and his shirt was darkened with sweat. He continued, or repeated: "A marine is lying in the middle of the street. His squad lays down a massive base of fire—six, seven, eight men firing on full automatic, plus a machine gun, you'd think nothing could be safer than to run out and drag him back—but there's always one enemy gunner that we don't see—and so—"

A contraction almost like pain struck Paul's heart as he visualized marines and corpsmen running a gauntlet of fire to drag in the wounded. Rebecca rose in his mind and he suddenly realized he was a complete man, that his completeness derived from a source other than sacrifice, that he loved her as a man loves a woman. A killing sorrow invaded him—that the "complete man" would lose her at the moment of discovery, that this was the end.

The briefer was saying: "The ontos goes first. He can drive thirty, forty miles an hour if you clear the street of rubble. He charges into the intersection and lets go all six rifles at once, then jams it into reverse and pulls back to find cover. Meanwhile the tank is coming up. He gets as close as he can and hits the same house with his fifty and his ninety mike-mike cannon. Then he pulls back." He paused, and Mac supplied the next sentence:

"And then we assault frontally." No one could have sensed any emotion in Mac's voice now.

"Yes. If you can take a corner house, or any house, that way, you're in a position to direct flanking fire on the house next door. So you do it that way, one house at a time till you own the whole street."

They discussed the use of smoke, which Paul did not follow. He was imagining a wounded marine in a rubble-strewn street—the difficulty of running and hopping through the rubble to reach him.

Gunnery Sergeant Hitchcock was working out the best way to use the 3.5. He was glad he had obtained two cases of white phosphorus rockets along with the HE. He thought: "The gooks'll wish they were back in Hanoi."

But the gunny felt an undercurrent of apprehension. Lots of men were going to buy the farm today. But the gunny knew one thing. He wasn't dying.

Graves Registration was trying to remember everything he had ever learned about urban combat, but it was all so long ago.

Lieutenant Wozniak, the new exec, had an empty space in his guts.

Ollie was trying to figure out how he was going to adjust artillery fire when he couldn't see the fall of shot, and the reports would bounce every which way off walls and buildings.

Dan Shaw was humming "Fire in the County Jail," his favorite disaster song. "Deputy home for lunch with the key / Prisoners screamin 'Set us free!' "

Russell Falk, age twenty-three, the second lieutenant who had replaced Kim Kolias at 1st Platoon, was experiencing pregame turmoil. Lieutenant Falk had been a wide receiver on the Naval Academy football team: he could run forty yards in 4.5 seconds, 100 yards in 9.6; he was six feet one and weighed 185 pounds; he could block, catch, run a broken field. But here his prowess didn't mean a thing.

"We dig the NVA out of every house and hole," the briefing officer was saying, "and we pin the bastards against the south wall."

Ollie thought: "Say, Dad, who's he mean by *we*?"

Mac reached under the bench for his helmet and flak jacket— paused—confronted the briefing officer, and said: "So—we talk to you on thirty-eight point four, and the secondary freek is forty-three point eight. Left to right, Delta, Kilo, Lima, south in a line abreast. Cleanout, house to house, street by street. We request supporting arms through you."

Ollie thought: "And the request goes to X-ray, then Division, then Three MAF, and they stew over it for ten minutes and maybe send it back down through the same stations. Approved. Thanks, you fucking pussies, too late, I'm fucking dead."

The briefer said: "One more thing. You may find the NVA defending every other street. They've been skipping streets. But look out."

The gunny thought: "Thanks a million, you fucking puke."

The briefer asked for questions but Mac was already standing up. He said to Lieutenant Wozniak:

"Assemble the company."

And to the briefer: "Thank you, Captain. I realize you don't write the rules of engagement."

Mac detained Paul; and when the last man had left the room he faced him and took him by the upper arm. Mac thought that this was a man of muscle who dug more holes, trenches, and 1-2-3 ditches than any enlisted man in the company. As somebody had said, the chaplain was built out of steel rods and cement. But his eyes were not cement.

Mac said: "You should have stayed in Phu Bai. I should have ordered you to stay."

Paul smiled enigmatically.

"If I think a man is placing himself in harm's way I sure as hell can order him to the rear."

"You should have thought of that before we left Phu Bai," Paul said.

"I didn't understand the situation. Now I do."

"Well, Captain—too late."

Mac persisted: "There's an aid station here, almost a hospital. Maybe they could use a chaplain."

"I turned down that job this morning," said Paul and the whole scene bounced back at him—himself bluntly refusing the doctor's repeated requests and standing there while the doctor accused him of indifference to the wounded.

"You belong to our battalion," said Mac, heating up. "You work directly for our regimental CO."

"And since he's not here," Paul returned in a mild voice, "I will go where I think best, which is where I am most needed."

"If I say so, you go to the rear," said Mac.

"You have no right," Paul retorted bitterly.

"Paul," said Mac, "for Christ's sake—"

"Exactly," said Paul.

But nothing fit "exactly." Paul was walking by himself to the company meeting, in a state of confusion. For the first time in his life he saw death as final. But he had said with such passion and assurance to Becka: "All we have is hope," when hope seemed true, and sufficient. Now he dreaded life without her. Therefore in some half-secret way he had refused to give her up. He had chosen faith, rejected Rebecca. He would never give up hope. "All we have is hope." Live without her? Never. But then he thought: "It happens I won't have to face that."

He arrived a couple of minutes late. Mac was already speaking to the company, gathered under the aluminum roof of a warehouse or garage of some kind, where the ARVN kept spare tires, truck parts, old motors, and other junk.

Before sending Delta to Hue the staff of Task Force X-ray had augmented the company with four extra machine guns and crews, and nearly sixty riflemen. Thus the company Mac addressed now mustered almost 190 men. A third were new.

"I want to speak to the new men in particular," Mac said. "In this company there is no such thing as a 'fuckin new guy.' I have heard this phrase used in other outfits. It is stupid. We are glad you're with us. We need you. Just remember that the man on your left and the man on your right are Delta Company marines, and so are you. Be there for Delta Company.

"And to the old hands let me say that this is a company of marines— and a few sailors."

A man in the crowd said: "And one ex-sailor."

Collins raised his rifle and acknowledged the scattered cheers and jeers.

Mac continued, smiling: "Be there for the new men. Show them that I'm not mistaken when I say we are all one company—marines and corpsmen, new men and old hands.

"We are going into a hell of a fight. You can hear it right now. We'll relieve a company that has been hit hard. If they follow Marine Corps tradition they're going to chant, or catcall, a message to us as we take their place on the line. They're going to chant, 'You'll be sorry.' That's their privilege. It dates from the Chosin Reservoir. But don't take it too seriously.

"Maybe we'll be sorry but I think we'll be proud. I think we'll fight like marines—as marines fought against the Chinese at Chosin, as they fought against the Japanese at Tarawa and against the Germans at Belleau Wood. Those men will be watching us today, those veterans.

"New men, old hands, officers, NCOs, corporals, and privates, we are the United States Marines. There's a man on your left and a man on your right, and they count on you. And you can count on them, because we are Delta Company marines. Now the chaplain will say a word."

Paul stood in the crowd baffled. He couldn't move. He thought: "Should I tell them they don't have to listen?" Then he began making his way forward and a path opened. He turned and faced the men, looking from face to face with a mind perfectly empty of words, filled with an emotion so powerful it drove out fear and loss. The men seemed ready to wait for five minutes, ten minutes, an hour if necessary, in patient silence. Every man was watching him—some with a kind of awe, as if for the first time realizing that they stood on the brink; some with charity or kindness in their young eyes; and there were a few, he thought, who were irritated at the prospect of a sermon. Paul could hear the far-off rattling of machine guns and the wallop of something bigger.

He resisted an impulse to express his emotion—then yielded to it. He said: "In trying to serve God and his people I have seen bravery, fear, suffering, loss, and joy. I have always considered my work a blessing. I have been blessed in a hundred ways but never more than at this minute. Though I am not worthy to be your chaplain today, it happens that I am. I would not change places today with any man on earth.

"You remember that when the lake was calm Jesus said to his friends, 'Let us cross to the other side.' They began to cross. The water grew rough, Jesus was tired and went to sleep on a blanket in the stern of the boat. But a storm arose and the boat began shipping water. The sailors woke Jesus and said, 'How can you sleep when we are sinking?' Throwing the blanket aside He stood facing the storm and shouted, 'Be calm!'—and a great peace descended and the water grew smooth. His friends whispered among themselves, saying, 'What kind of man is this, whom the sea obeys?'

"My friends, it seems probable that we will soon face a terrible storm. We can hear the thunder of it right now. But Jesus said: 'If you listen to what I say, and act according to my teaching, you will be like the man who builds his house upon a rock. Neither hurricane nor flood can prevail against it.'

459

"You know the Sermon on the Mount, you've all heard it. When Jesus had finished that sermon and was walking down from the mount a leper accosted Him and said, 'Lord, if you will do it, you can cure my disease.' Jesus said, 'I will do it.' He didn't ask what the man deserved, He said 'I will do it.' He stretched out His hand and touched the leper, and he was cured.

"None of us is building a house today, but each of us is building a life. None of us is a leper, but we all could be better men if we tried. So let us build our lives on the rock of faith which alone gives hope. Let us ask Jesus to make us more courageous in the storm that awaits us, more willing to sacrifice our own good for the good of our fellow marines. If we ask, who can doubt that He will respond to us as He responded to the leper?

"In the long hours of this day," said Paul, "you will forget about God in the stress of battle. But my friends, marines and sailors, God will not forget you."

Paul stepped aside. Mac was again asking himself how a man like Paul could believe that fairy tale. Mac resumed his place and let his gaze roam over the faces before him. A perceptive marine might have seen in Mac's eyes, in addition to his fixity of purpose, a glint of exaltation, or pride. Mac said in a low voice:

"Lieutenant Wozniak, CSMO in ten minutes."

The exec boomed: "Platoon leaders! Close Station March Order, ten minutes! Company, dismissed!"

Delta marched to the line and relieved Mike Company. And the marines of Mike Company did not jeer or call out "You'll be sorry." They walked to the rear, to life, as those who were able walked away from a medieval town struck with plague.

Mac established his CP in a blasted house that smelled of shit and death. Drag marks through the plaster dust showed where the NVA had removed their wounded. They had left the dead. But Mac chose the house for its view of an intersection. A street a few houses to the right marked the boundary between Delta and Kilo. The one on the left was Mac's tank and ontos route. The street crossing his view to the front was the border between the marines and the NVA. The pavement of that street was no-man's-land.

The front and side windows offered the views Mac needed, with this disadvantage: to look out could give you a bullet in the face.

He left Graeser, the exec, and one fire team in the house and met the tank and ontos crew chiefs in the safe street to the rear. They conferred, and Mac returned. He asked Graeser for the handset. Sitting on the floor and unfolding his map—an unusual 1:25,000 map showing extraordinary detail—he conferred with the CO of Kilo Company and they agreed on a coordinated plan.

Then, listening to the clanking and whining of the ontos as it rattled along at terrific speed, the men in the room began showing a crazy happiness. The ontos raced toward the intersection. Delta sent forth a torrent of fire against the houses across the street. This base of fire emboldened Mac and he rushed to a window in time to see the ontos jam its tracks and come to a lurching halt. The six recoilless rifles, three on a side and each one over six feet long, trembled as the vehicle made quick adjustments, then all six screamed at once. The rockets streaked away and the machine pivoted on its left tread and retreated into its own backblast where it was invisible. The enemy RPGs and tracers flew in pursuit into the dust and debris but Mac could tell by the engine noise that the ontos had escaped.

Not so the house across the street, the objective house, which had been the target of the six 106's. It was a smoking shambles, a one-story bungalow reduced to half a story by the partial collapse of its roof and front wall. But amid the smoke and ruin Mac could see the muzzle flashes of NVA troops still firing. That this was a human marvel did not occur to Mac till later.

On came the tank, rumbling up the same street toward the intersection. It was an M48 mounting a .50-caliber machine gun and a 90-millimeter cannon, and it made the ontos look like a toy insect with six rigid feelers. The hulking, rounded, mammoth tank shook the pavement as its turret began to rotate with incongruous dignity. It came to the intersection and stopped, and shrugged off a B40 rocket that would have vaporized the ontos; then another B40 ricocheted off its turret and exploded in the air. The gunner took his time, although he was in grave danger that the next B40 would hit his treads. The turret jerked ever so slightly, jerked again, the cannon with its recoil suppressor shaped like a junction of water pipes lifted an inch, then calmly let out a belching blast of flame. Then the monster took fright, wheeled on its left tread, and hurried down the street like a fleeing rooster.

A squad from 1st Platoon charged across the pavement under covering fire from the rest of the platoon. Mac watched with narrowed eyes burning from the dust as a grenade detonated somewhere. He watched, and not a man fell. He shouted with mad joy.

The friendly fire on the objective house ceased just as the 1st Platoon team slipped over a low courtyard wall, and now the only shooting over there was the team's own, as they rolled in through the front window after tossing in two grenades, one through the door and one through the window.

Lieutenant Russell Falk, the ex-football player, dashed across the street with his radioman and they entered the house, even as a new detonation sounded in one of its back rooms. The search continued—but within two minutes Falk's radioman was telling Graeser that the house was secured.

Said Mac to Graeser: "Tell those guys Bravo Zulu."

And Graeser said in his handset: "Skipper says good job."

Mac to Wozniak: "O.K. Woz, next phase."

Wozniak stuck his head out a side window, lifted his leg, and rolled out. Mac saw him struggling over the courtyard wall at the side of the house. "Now he's crossing the street," Mac thought and waited in suspense.

The men in the house opposite Mac's in front should now be setting up to fire on the house next to theirs, the one to the left, from Mac's perspective. This was the next objective. Mac could hear an occasional shout from there. He waited. There was no shooting now, except from the right, where Kilo Company was doing something.

Graeser said: "Sir, Lieutenant Wozniak says he's ready."

Said Mac: "Tell him to throw it."

"Throw it," said Graeser, then: "There she goes, sir."

A furious fusillade broke out. Lieutenant Wozniak had thrown a smoke grenade into the street between his house and Mac's. Believing the smoke masked a dash by marines, the enemy was firing blindly into the white cloud. In so doing they revealed the position of their machine gun low in the brush between houses. The gunny had set up his 3.5 two doors down from Wozniak, and now a rocket whooshed and Mac watched as it traced its own path with fire and smoke then slammed into the brush, satisfactorily close to the gun. A horrific blast sent a wave of heat, energy, and debris through the window of Mac's house and the men shouted in surprise and rage; but the enemy gun went silent.

"Flanking fire," said Mac.

Graeser passed this on, using the same two words, and the marines in Falk's house poured sound and fire into the new objective. On this signal, Mac's, Wozniak's, and the gunny's men all spewed forth a huge volume of fire, including two rockets from the 3.5 and several LAWs. Next the gunny sent a rocket against the wall the attackers would have to cross. A four-man fire team from Wozniak's house, hunching low, scurried to the wall and crouched on either side of the breach. The marines' fire grew more intense. A man half-rose, aimed his blooper through the breach, and sent a grenade into the front door of this second objective. Wozniak directed the fire, now, at the front window, and the gunny launched another rocket, which struck just below the sill, to expand the opening, making it easier to climb in. The blooper man put a shot through the window and Mac said:

"Cease fire."

The shooting stuttered to a halt. The fire team climbed through the breach in the wall, providing its own base of fire in relays. A new fire team ran through the alleyway between the first objective house and the present one. The through-the-wall team rushed the house, and entered by the window and door simultaneously, after throwing two more grenades. Firing broke out behind the house as the kill-zone team reached the back entrance at precisely the moment the occupants were dragging their wounded out the back. There were several bursts of M16 fire, then silence.

"Sir," said Graeser, "they've got a WIA."

"Tell Wozniak."

Graeser did so, and in a moment a corpsman dashed across the street, dived through the wall, picked himself up, and sprinted to the window. A marine hauled him in.

Said Graeser: "Sir, it's too late."

"Tell Wozniak to get some men to haul the body to the rear. Tell those guys across the street Bravo Zulu."

Mac wanted to know who the KIA was but couldn't ask for a name over the radio. He went out into the side street and waited beside the tracks left in the dust by the tank and ontos. The man was a new man; Mac looked down on him for several seconds, and it never entered his mind that death was anything other than death. Mac took the man's dog tag in his hand and read his name and the abbreviation CATH.

He said, "Does anybody know where the chaplain is?"

"I'm here," said Paul. He took a corner of the poncho and set off with the bearers.

When they reached the safe street to the rear they lay the man down, and Paul knelt beside him to administer the last rites. A stone pressed sharply into his knee and he shifted his position while praying. The men stood by and listened. When Paul had finished and the group started back he stopped the corpsman. This was Jake Sobieski, Hospitalman 2nd Class, U.S. Navy.

Paul said: "Are we just going to leave him lying there?"

Doc Sobieski replied: "As soon as we get some WIAs I'll send them to the battalion aid station. I'll pick him up then."

"You're going to carry WIAs to the aid station? It must be two kilometers."

"No sir. They'll send a truck. I'll call for a truck."

"I see," said Paul. "So this man lies there until—"

"Yes sir."

For want of a better idea Paul acquiesced. The corpsman and bearers began walking, with no great show of haste, back to the line where the gunny was coordinating the attack on the third house. Paul decided to join 1st Platoon because Russell Falk was so inexperienced.

Lieutenant Russell Falk tried to roll under Paul's hands but Paul held him down. On a sudden impulse Paul ripped the shirt and laid bare the mutilated chest. The corpsman—not Doc Sobieski, somebody Paul had never met—who had taken forever to get rid of the suspender straps, the dispatch case, and binoculars that crisscrossed the bloody shirt—said in a rush, "No, let him roll over."

As Falk rolled and groaned the corpsman pushed him, and Falk lay now on his front.

"My God," the corpsman whispered. There was an exit wound in the back, a big one.

"Roll him!" the corpsman cried and Paul and the corpsman exposed the chest again. Lieutenant Falk lay panting, staring at Paul with terror in his wide-open eyes. The corpsman began applying dressings and Paul pressed a piece of plastic sheeting against a wound in the chest that had just sent up a pink bubble. To Paul they looked like fragmentation wounds—and he couldn't explain the exit wound.

Lieutenant Falk coughed, choked, and beheld Paul above him as though he were either an angel of death or a savior. He grasped him by the arm and squeezed and began to shake him, pulling the arm this way and that. Paul taped the plastic down and the corpsman, observing this, said, "That's no good. He's too wet." Then the corpsman who, like Paul, was kneeling, reared up and threw back his head and screamed at the sky.

Paul took dressings out of the bag and began trying to tape them to Falk's heaving chest. His hairy skin was slick with rain, sweat, and blood.

"That's all wrong," the corpsman cried.

"Then do it!" said Paul under his breath.

They were crouching behind a wall. The firing all around had shut down Paul's senses. He knew nothing. If it rained, if a man shouted, if a mortar exploded nearby he didn't know it. He saw the plastic puff ever so gently, lifting off Falk's chest.

There was a rubber strap around the corpsman's helmet, holding a little white plastic bottle of bug repellent. Paul felt a shock in his ear and across his face, the bottle exploded (although he didn't see this), and the fluid splattered in his face. The corpsman was oblivious, he kept working, but he was sobbing, "He'll die, he'll die on my hands."

Paul wiped the burning fluid from his eyes and had a quick flash of Becka ripping a man's shirt. Then he saw Becka bent over a cart and lifting a man's hands and heard her whisper, "I am Rebecca. I will help you." Of course that man went to the Parking Lot. Another bullet thudded with sudden force into the wall just as the corpsman started to get to his feet. Paul said, "Where are you going?"

The corpsman stared at him with a terror in his eyes different from

Falk's. In the lieutenant's eyes Paul saw a question. The corpsman's displayed only fear.

Another bullet, a single shot, skipped on a piece of concrete by Paul's knee and caromed into the wall.

"Help me," said Paul as he pulled Lieutenant Falk up by his armpits.

The corpsman tried to comply but the two men interfered with each other and the corpsman slipped and sat down. Paul said in a fury, "Get out of my way!"

He dragged Falk over a low place in the wall, to the other side. The corpsman remained sitting. He was still on the house side while Paul was now on the street side. Paul called to him but got no answer. Paul insisted, "This is better. Come over here."

The corpsman dived through the opening and rolled away and ran across the street, back toward the house from which 1st Platoon had just launched an assault. He darted through a gateless opening in the wall and into the house. Paul crouched over the wounded lieutenant and asked: "How are you feeling?"

Falk coughed and Paul looked for blood on his lips but there was none.

Paul said: "You'll be all right. I'll get you out of here."

Falk whispered: "What's wrong with me?"

But Paul lost these words in the din. He wasted precious time asking Falk what he had said. Again the blue lips moved and again Paul missed the words. This futile exchange woke Paul up to the blasting, crashing, and singing of the fusillade, and he realized his man was momentarily safe but perhaps dying.

Unconscious of danger, Paul shouldered the huge athlete, staggered into the street, and fell sprawling when his foot struck a jagged chunk of cement. He lay for a second in the middle of the street, halfway under the lieutenant's body, with the rubble so close to his eyes that he couldn't focus on it. He struggled to his knees. He got all the way up, believing this was it, and began dragging Falk to a burnt car and propped him up against the door and said: "Lift your arms." Falk just stared at him, as if breaking contact with Paul's eyes would be a step toward death. Paul grabbed Falk's hand and pulled it up, and dug his shoulder into Falk's body, and strained upward.

For several seconds Paul was a man without a mind, straining to the utmost limit, staggering, then falling. Next he was dragging Falk by one arm and Michelson was pulling on the other, and some man was walking cooly beside him firing short bursts from an M60 machine gun from his hip. Paul reflected that he had never seen this done. The firing hurt his ears. He saw the ammo belt swinging at the feed port, shortening itself as it quivered in eager dusty little jerks, moving up toward the gun. The corpsman was not there.

The gunner stopped, allowing Paul and Michelson to precede him through the gateless opening. Paul saw him looking down at his gun, and there was no belt and no more ammo. Paul and Michelson dragged the lieutenant up two steps and into the house and the gunner ran in just as a rain of heavy bullets battered the walls and zipped through the front window.

They spread Falk on the floor. His chest wounds were clogged with brick dust and dirt, and the dressings lay in tatters in all directions.

With relief Paul saw Doc Sobieski kneeling beside an unconscious man. The doc drew his pistol, removed its plastic battery bag, and passed the bag to Paul. He looked into Paul's eyes but said nothing. Paul slapped the plastic against the bubble that was forming at the main wound. He looked around for help and somebody threw a roll of gauze. With help, Paul wound it around Falk's body, trying to fix the plastic to make an airtight seal, but it turned into a mess. He was not controlling his hands; he had no dexterity in his fingers. And the plastic wrinkled. The unknown corpsman was there again suddenly, inexplicably, kneeling beside Paul, and he set an IV. Paul held the drip bottle above Falk's chest and somebody somewhere said, "CSMO on outa here," but the machine gunner hollered: "I need an A-gunner! Who's gonna be my A-gunner?"

Everybody looked at everybody else till Michelson volunteered, asking Paul for approval. Paul said, "Stay with this platoon and I'll find you." The gunner pulled an ammo belt out of a steel box and handed it to Michelson. A terrific racket pounded the walls and everybody shrunk back even farther from the window. They knew this new fusillade could be the prep for a counterattack, and nobody knew quite what to do about it.

The nameless corpsmen, the rest of the marines, and Paul began stumbling through the wreck of some family's furniture and the remains of the collapsed ceiling, carrying the two wounded men. The gunner and Michelson approached the window, the gunner firing from the hip, then they crouched and started putting out aimed short bursts.

When Paul and the bearers were outside, Paul spotted Doc Sobieski and shouted: "Where'd we leave that guy?"

Staggering, stumbling, gasping for breath, Paul could picture the gap in a wall where they had left the body but, looking around him, he saw nothing familiar. Sobieski pulled on his corner of a poncho, and the whole bunch veered right, into a shambles of a street. They plunged into a gap between houses where the trees were thick. One house was joined to another by a kind of chicken coop. A rusty motor scooter hidden in the weeds tripped the man in front, and then tripped Paul, but he kept his footing. The adrenaline rush set his skin prickling.

The rain had stopped and Paul went from a shivering wreck to a man in a fever. He pressed on. They came out on a street and all at once Paul knew where they were. He shouted, "Left!" and the gang turned and soon came upon the body. They lay the two WIAs down beside it but Paul still had to hold the serum bottle.

He sat beside Lieutenant Falk and his legs rejoiced at being relieved of his weight. He breathed easily, and looked around. A city, a neighborhood, houses, streets, a row of slender graceful trees, all of it ugly and some of it smashed.

They heard a sputtering, like an outboard motor, and here came a mechanical mule. The driver wore black leather gloves. No shirt, no helmet, plenty of black uncut hair and unshaven whiskers, and his rifle slung over his shoulder, his dog tags swinging on a beaded chain. He had the face and eyes of a daredevil. The open flak jacket flopped at his hairy chest. Not even the Marine Corps could control him.

Paul asked: "Are you Terwilliger?"

"Yes, yes, he'll live all right," the surgeon reported. "My colleague is seeing to that right now. His vital signs are good. He'll absolutely live."

Paul said to himself, "Thank God, thank God, thank God." His head went dizzy suddenly and he caught hold of the surgeon's shoulder, leaned forward, and lowered his head for several seconds. The surgeon observed this and made no comment, but stood solid, supporting Paul.

Lieutenant Falk would live! They were operating right now. The man who had fixed his eyes on Paul's. Paul would never forget those eyes full of desperate hope and terror. He said to the surgeon, "Thank you for helping him and the other man. I can't thank you enough."

"Oh yes you can," the doctor parried, and Paul knew what was coming.

Paul stood straight, glanced up at the colorless sky for a second, and said hastily, "I'm sorry, I have to go back."

"Stay!" cried the doctor, grasping Paul's arm. "I just amputated a man's leg. Stay and talk to him, do something for him."

"I can't stay." But the guilt hit him and Paul stammered: "Is he— O.K., where is he?"

"He's in recovery but—"

"Not conscious?"

"No, but in the meantime you could—"

"I've got to go back," Paul cried.

"My God, why can't you talk to these men? Just go up and down the rows and give them whatever it is you give. Don't leave it all to me, my God we need a chaplain, for God's sake stay!"

Paul looked at the man, stunned, at his crimson face and wild eyes. Paul pulled his arm free but the surgeon raved:

"Persuade a man on the threshold of life, with everything before him, eager and ready to open a new life—into a pure and free life in which he can do—or anyway try to do—what he *wants* to do—and I'm going to persuade him that his desires, his dream of sleeping in a bed again, only now with his girlfriend beside him, in peace—that this is all unreasonable and even selfish—

"Life in a wheelchair—I—a triple amputee— Do you see? Are you made of wood for God's sake?"

Paul said, "Doctor, may God bless you and your work." He extended his hand and the surgeon gaped at him, then took the hand reluctantly, and the two men shook hands. Paul went out into the rain.

He set out for the boat landing but stopped after a few steps and looked back, not knowing exactly why. He rested his gaze on a placid lake, on its level surface enlivened as it was by the beating rain—a pond, a thing of gentle nature.

Paul hurried through a wide quadrangle with long buildings on three sides and stately trees scattered over its parklike space. For a moment he was unaware of the sounds of the fighting two thousand meters to the south.

He found Terwilliger with two sailors shifting ammo boxes from a landing craft onto the mechanical mule. Carrying a box, he read the stenciling: it contained 7.62-millimeter belted ammo for an M60 machine gun, and was heavy for its size.

Terwilliger kicked the little engine into life and Paul jumped on the cargo. The vehicle sputtered toward the big gate. An ARVN soldier smiling hugely waved them through, and Paul and Terwilliger raced into the city.

Gripping the wheel with both his gloved hands, Terwilliger turned to Paul and gave him an evaluative look and said, "So you're a chaplain?"

"That's right. My name is Paul Adrano."

"Hi. You already told me your name."

"O.K."

"My name's Terwilliger, lance corporal, U.S. muddah-friggin Crotch."

"Right," said Paul. "I know."

"Yeah, I'm famous. Listen, where can I drop you?"

"Thanks, but I'll help you with this load."

"I can handle it," said Terwilliger.

"Of course you can. I want to see the city."

Terwilliger banged the wheel with both hands and cried: "Ha! See the city! Cool!" and he drove on, weaving among the heaps of rubble and pulverized glass.

He stopped when they reached an impassable obstacle, and he and Paul lifted a long section of wall, several blocks still cemented together, and heaved it aside.

"So," said Terwilliger, "are they alive? Those WIAs we brought in?"

"Yes, they'll both live."

Terwilliger nodded as if to approve this report, and both men bent to the heap of loose brick and block and began throwing pieces with gusto. As they remounted, Terwilliger gave Paul a merry smile. A moment later, sensing a subtle change in the light, Paul looked up and saw a break in the overcast, with a flaglike spread of blue.

There was something cynical or mocking in Terwilliger's smile now, or maybe just mischievous. He said: "So why are you out here?"

"I'm a tourist," said Paul.

"Hey, outa the church, into the street, huh?"

"Right."

"A street priest! Got any dope?"

Paul laughed and Terwilliger roared with heavy, chest-shaking laughter. He slammed his foot down and the mule spewed noise like a suburbanite's lawn mower, but didn't gain much speed.

"My Mercedes," Terwilliger shouted, bouncing in his seat, wiping sweat from his forehead with the back of his glove. He was a tautly built, short man. As he leaned into his wheel his stomach didn't show any sag. He put one dog tag between his teeth; the other tag and the beaded chain flopped in a loop under his chin. Turning to Paul he bared his teeth in a grin, let the dog tag drop, and said: "Want a beer?"

"Sure," said Paul.

Terwilliger pulled a can of Schlitz from a haversack at his feet. The can all but burned Paul's hand. Terwilliger passed him a church key and Paul held the can to the side, popped it, and let the spray fly.

Said Terwilliger: "Nothing like a cold brew on a hot day, eh, Chaplain? Ha ha ha."

They chugged south on a commercial street where the trees on either side were mostly denuded or charred, or ripped half apart by slugs. The sidewalks were strewn with junk, glass, boxes, and ruined shop goods. But now they turned right into a narrower street and suddenly saw the Palace wall at the end of their view, some three hundred meters ahead, a solid low mass, blank, cutting off the view. They bounced along, passing between rows of trees and walled houses on either side. The trees lifted their tops gracefully above roof level. Most of the houses were intact except for the windows. The air was almost cool against Paul's skin. He looked up for the blue space and it was still there. There were no people to be seen. Through the clattering of the little engine Paul could still hear automatic-weapons fire and one big boom.

"That's a 106," Terwilliger informed him.

Paul had known this but said, "Ah," as if enlightened. He threw the beer can into the window of a car hulk as they passed it. It was a pleasing sight—to see the can sailing into the car and bouncing off the steering wheel, and to hear it hit the floor, or the exposed seat springs of the burnt interior. Paul felt lighthearted, like a boy experimenting with a trifling kind of wrongdoing. But it didn't last.

A shock wave hit Paul, as if a tiger had clamped its jaws an inch from his face. He saw Terwilliger's head twist and split open above the ear. Terwilliger was now falling forward as the mule struck something and veered off course. Then Paul found himself in a clump of brush, on his back. A string of dusty eruptions which he imagined rather than saw disturbed the dirt somewhere nearby and he could feel the snap of each concussion. He knew he was O.K. but he was missing several seconds. He started to roll over.

He wasn't grateful. He had a sense of grave misfortune. He saw blood on his forearm (his sleeves were rolled up) and knew it was not his own. His arm and all the rest of him felt fine. He felt very good, now that he noticed. Yes, good! He touched the cargo pocket of his right trouser leg, to make contact with his missal, then his left, to touch the two cans of C-rats. He reached for his helmet and slapped it on.

He stood up, his upper body emerging from the brush, and saw the mule rammed against a wall. The ammo boxes lay scattered over the street. He felt another tiger snap and dropped. He never heard the shot. He was down in the brush again. If the shooter didn't rake the brush it meant he was low on ammo or playing a game, or that Paul was protected by the wall, so long as he stayed down. Paul began crawling, pushing the brush aside, cutting his face—he was plowing right through the stems and stalks and branches, till he came upon Terwilliger's body after crawling ten meters. The ominous feeling came back, all over him, seeing the wound. One small portion of the man's body had been parted and that was sufficient.

Paul lay still and the gun that was after him waited too. Paul panted, pulling in oxygen at a steady clip, looking at a strange pattern on Terwilliger's shoulder. It was a shadow. The sun was shining! Paul was utterly amazed, and almost stood up to see it. The little bristles and sprouts of vegetation threw shadows on Terwilliger's shoulder. Paul spread his hand and made a shadow.

An icicle of fear stood erect in his chest. He worked quickly, collecting Terwilliger's dog tags. He put one in Terwilliger's mouth and the other in the wallet that he removed from a pocket. He unsnapped the wristwatch and pocketed that too. He checked for rings; there were none. He squeezed Terwilliger's hand and perceived the absence of life.

Then he searched down the wall on his belly and found Terwilliger's rifle. Peering out, he saw a sling of M16 magazines at the edge of the street. The rifle itself had a magazine in the slot and another taped upside down to the slotted one. Forty rounds, if Paul remembered correctly. He stared in perplexity at the rifle, trying to find the safety. Would the thing blow up on him? In one big heave he jumped up and rolled over the wall. He felt the shock waves but never heard the shots; he ran like a man fleeing a blowtorch.

Chapter 22

The 12.7

"Sir, he refuses," Ollie shouted with tremor in his voice. "He says he already relayed our request to X-ray, and if everybody repeated their—"

"He won't let us fire? Christ, did you tell him we're getting plastered by fuckin rockets? Tell him!"

"Sir, I already told him and he says he's gotta send it up to X-ray and there's nothing—"

"Screw him!" Mac shouted in the din.

Mac's men were dying. They had taken shelter in a car-repair shop with a grease pit filled with rubbish and an oil-soaked cement floor. The cinder-block walls spattered chips and dust when hit by heavy weapons and they opened in funnel-shaped holes when a rocket struck. There was no place to go. If you were looking for the "last good place," this one might be last but it wasn't good.

Mac and Ollie were crouched helmet to helmet. It was hard to kneel unless you wanted to jam rocks into your knees. The noise was like the breath of a monster breaking the building apart and bellowing with calculated rage.

Mac said, "What about naval gunfire?"

"Impossible," said Ollie. "It's a flat-trajectory weapon and—"

"Yeah, yeah. Goddamn it!"

Watching Mac's eyes, Ollie for the first time in his career was glad he wasn't a company commander. That was his whole ambition, company or battery commander. Now he didn't know what to do and he was watching Mac to see if he did.

"Kinny!" Mac shouted and Captain Kindred came slithering across the deck like an arthritic snake.

He spoke before Mac could: "I got no birds. Not a single fucking bird."

"Christ, why not?" said Mac in a fury. "The sun's shining out there. See it? Jesus!"

Another screamer hit the wall and sent chips and fragments flying across the little space occupied by the command group. A man cried, "Ah" and writhed on the floor, and a new hole shed a better light on the whole scene. Now the air was a gray mist and the floor was white with cement dust, heaped with shards of the east wall and ceiling.

Said Captain Kindred: "Wing won't launch any birds if it's going to start raining again, which they say it is, so no fucking air, brother."

Mac repeated his unnecessary report that the sun was actually shining for the first time in a week. Another rocket hit the building and Mac shouted, "Out of here! Kinny take the lead. Back, back!"

The men dragged wounded toward the door. Somebody was pulling on a body half covered with rubble and Mac paused to look at the face—covered with white dust except for the wet lips and eyes. He said, "We'll get him later." Led by Kindred the command group stumbled out into the open space in back. "Left!" Mac shouted and Kindred led the group around the corner of the building, where they crouched against the west wall even as another rocket spewed its gases overheard and smashed into a building to the west.

Mac stood upright and walked to Ollie, who was crouching inside a car without doors or hood. Its engine was gone, so were the wheels. Mac squatted and told Ollie to try again. Ollie repeated his request, listened, then said to Mac:

"They're still waiting."

Mac looked around, looked at the ground soaked with grease, smelled the familiar garage smells of gasoline and lubricants, a reminder of his father's equipment shed in Stevens Point, and suddenly stepped out of his rage. He rose again, and it felt good to stand. He returned to the wall where Graeser was watching, and took the handset.

"Hey Buzzbomb, this is Six."

The gunny responded immediately and Mac asked:

"Do you see the source of these rockets?"

"That's affirmative. I mean I don't see the launch site but I see the fuckers flying. They're fuckin goin right over my head."

"Can you shut him up with your three-point-five?"

"I'm on my way. Gotta get some height. Give me five minutes."

Mac said: "He'll be moving from window to window. So don't use HE. Give him some Willie Peter."

"I'll put some Willie Peter up his nose," the gunny boasted.

"First, two rounds on the floor below him," Mac counseled.

"O.K., white phosphorus cocktail—for the—" Hitchcock was panting, apparently running.

Mac sat down, leaned against the wall, and took a deep breath. Then he crawled to a wounded man. Without speaking, looking the man in the eyes, Mac took his wrist and felt the fluttery pulse. The man's eyes never left Mac and Mac's eyes did not lie.

A little east of Mac, Hitchcock and his gang searched for a multi-story structure. They ran around aimlessly for several minutes, during which another rocket streaked overhead, till they found a good house, then they stopped. They were about fifty meters from a big white house with a projecting balcony on the right side, a place the troops would call a mansion to distinguish it from the common run of bungalows, and they blew off the door. Hitchcock sent Collins to one side and Valas to the other and they blew out the windows then threw grenades more or less simultaneously. The gunny approached the house, walking behind the machine gunner, who prepped the place with ten or fifteen short bursts. The gunny entered first, with a drawn pistol, followed by the machine gunner and his A-gunner, then the gunny's A-gunner for the 3.5, who carried the launcher. The gunny himself was weighted down with three rockets. Every man except the machine gunner carried at least two, and there were two ammo bearers. Thus the gunny had an ample supply of high explosive and white phosphorus.

He climbed to the second floor and went out a French door to the open balcony. He crouched to peer over a wall of fretted woodwork, holding his hand out behind him to keep the other men back, and another rocket flew. He saw its source, a second-floor window in a white apartment building. Nobody was showing himself now but the shutters closed as if automatically.

"Load me a Willie Peter round," said Hitchcock to the sailor.

Collins crawled to the gunny and slid a white phosphorous rocket into the breech of the launcher.

"Did you twist it?" the gunny demanded.

"Oh! No! Yeah! You gotta twist'm," said Collins as if discovering a surprising new feature of the weapon. The magneto, armature, and coils in the firing mechanism were all terra incognita to the sailor. He gave the rocket a twist to ensure electrical contact.

The gunny hollered: "Valas!" and the Golden Greek appeared in the doorway and announced himself. By then the gunny was in a crouch with the launcher on his shoulder. Without turning he said:

"Did you search this whole floor?"

"Yes, Mr. Guns. Nobody home and no jewelry. Ha ha ha."

"Get yer asses downstairs. Three-sixty defense."

The Golden Greek and the others went down, leaving only the gunny, the sailor, and the 3.5 A-gunner. The gunny hitched the launcher to a firm position on his shoulder, took the pistol grip in his right hand, and rested the monopod on his left. He rose and viewed the sight through his right eye. He had estimated the range at two hundred yards so he set the pointer at the 0–450 position. He brought the vertical line on the reticule to his target, then the two-hundred-yard horizontal line. He said quietly, "Stay forward, you morons."

For reply the sailor tapped him on the helmet, the signal that he could fire.

Hitchcock fired. A plume of fire streaked backward as the rocket screamed forward, sailing over the trees and rooftops and zooming without any sign of desperation or animosity toward the apartment house. It smashed through a set of elegant wooden shutters on the second floor, sending splinters in all directions, and detonated inside with a burst of supernatural whiteness and embedded yellow streaks.

"Load me," said the gunny as a white cloud billowed from the hole in the shutters.

477

"HE or Willie Peter?" asked Collins.

"Willie Peter. We cook this gook's goose."

"Hey, a tongue twister," said Collins. "Cook this goose's gook? Cook this—"

"Load the fuckin gun."

"Yes, Mr. Guns."

They put two rockets on the lower floor—a third spent itself against the exterior of the building—and then the gunny scored two more hits through the windows of the floor above, plus two misses that didn't seem to perturb him in the slightest. The apartment building was engulfed in smoke.

"Hey, Guns, we're on fire, you know," said Collins.

The gunny didn't even look. He coughed in the smoke and blinked his bloodshot eyes. He ordered up another rocket and blasted the apartment house again. From the floor below him he heard the Golden Greek shout:

"Guns, can we go now? Go out and get shot? I mean wouldn't you rather—"

The gunny and his crew leapt clear of the flames playing on the wall behind them. They hopped through the French doors and clattered down the stairs, while the gunny bellowed, "CSMO, you fuckin civilians." And they poured out of the house with the machine gunner leading the way, blasting the garden and bushes, till they reached the street, and everybody, as if by agreement, turned to the burning house.

Valas said: "Guns, you are one careless guy."

"Rape, pillage, and plunder," the gunny said. "Hippo, tell the skipper, target neutralized."

Hearing these words on his radio Mac felt himself free to attack the houses across from the workshop. He moved laterally to a safe house—actually a bordello that smelled even now of beer and perfume—from which he could view the action. He gave Dan Shaw the attack order, and after a heavy prep, Dan sent a four-man fire team that shot its way into the house directly across from Mac's vantage point.

The team leader appeared in the front window and waved to Dan Shaw and Mac. Then the house exploded and its façade disappeared, along with the team leader.

. . .

Paul dodged into a doorway, a shop of some kind. He stood there panting—exulting. "The bastard missed me!" he cried, and immediately his brain punished him with an image of Terwilliger's wound. The bastard had not missed Terwilliger. "But he missed me!" Paul repeated, out of control. He stomped to the rear of the place, over crushed boxes and fields of glass and china. He bent to examine the stuff and saw any number of empty boxes with illustrations of short candles in red, green, and blue. There were candles and china all over the floor. Paul had heard all about the ARVN and their depredations, had even seen truckloads of soldiers and heard their whoops as they sped through the business district, away from the marines' fighting line and toward their own CP.

"Oh!" he said with a jolt. He had forgotten to pray for Terwilliger, had not even blessed him in those precious minutes right after death. "I forgot—Terwilliger," he said aloud. He peered around to see if anybody else was hiding here. He couldn't be certain, it was too dark in the corners and the back. There was a merchant's counter—somebody could be crouching behind it. The shelves had been pulled down, and blocked his way—so he didn't check the counter, he just stood among the ruins of somebody's business.

He pulled out Terwilliger's dog tag. It didn't say CATH; it said NO PREF, a very unusual dog tag. All the more reason to pray for his soul. But at just this moment, with his chest and legs still aching from his insane dash, and his ears still ringing, with a perfect geometrical diagram of the line of fire against him, and an aerial view of his stupendous escape—escape!—at just this moment in his intellectual life Paul Adrano suddenly decided it was silly, ridiculous that Terwilliger's soul should be hanging around in the air somewhere hoping somebody would pray for him to a God he had denied, and that this Exalted Personage would then break down and admit the sinner into Paradise.

If irreligious men like Terwilliger or Mac get in, why shouldn't I catch the next bird to Da Nang and tell Becka the whole truth? Pour it out! He thought all this without the language to express it, but the significance of it was strong. Why not tell her! "Yes," he said eagerly, "it's her decision. I've got a good reason to survive this battle and that reason is Becka."

Of course something else stirred in the background.

Five minutes ago he was mad to escape death and there was no reality except reality. Now he was standing in a pile of candle bones spouting heresy. "I forgot Terwilliger," he said, but what he meant and half knew was that he forgot God. If he listened to his own sermonizing, God would not forget him. But maybe—"Maybe I wish He would," said Paul in surprise. "Now that I know what life is, maybe I wish I—yes, leave me alone! I'll beg forgiveness when I've lived a life! If she rejects me I go off in a corner and eat worms. Ha!"

Still laughing, he tried again to figure out the M16. He went to the front and turned the accursed thing every which way in the light. Suppose he had to fire off all twenty rounds in the magazine. How do you eject the empty one so you can push in a full one? He pulled the trigger and nothing happened.

He saw Rebecca bending with angelic compassion over the unconscious man. I am Rebecca, a nurse, I will help you. And then he saw her staring blankly up while Doc Regnary's body crushed hers, and he cried, "I don't care!"

Now he knew what they were talking about. Thirty-four years old and now he finds out. He saw real life beckoning, and the loss of it. Now he realized that there is an inner life that cannot be suppressed by vows, sacrifices, denials, and bleakness. Or by affirmations of holy faith. It was irrepressible and it was taking control of him. He stood in a wrecked shop, in a wrecked city, in a wrecked country, his left shoulder sticky with somebody else's blood, and he suddenly cried, "Thank you, God, for showing me! Now I know!—Get out of here," he whispered and peered out in both directions. He knew this much: the men going down the right side of the street watch the left; the men on the left watch the right. He was one man. Go anyway. So he went, but got a bad surprise.

"What's that?" he hissed. He slipped between buildings. They had seen him. But they were—surely they were harmless, a bunch of ragtag refugees. Yes but they'd seen him and hesitated; they feared him. A looter or rapist, with a gun. He pounded down a path between buildings and the path smelled of excrement, urine, garbage, and death. A florist's funeral of sick smells.

If the refugees could circle around from the south of The Citadel to the north, get through or over the wall, and end up here, then the NVA and VC being driven south by the marines' advance could do it too. And if they saw him, *zap-zap*.

He determined to find out how to shoot the M16. After a minute of puzzling over it he flicked a little lever; a red mark appeared. He pointed the gun up and pulled the trigger and the report cracked in his right ear and crashed between the walls on either side. "O.K.," Paul shouted. He reset the lever to *safe* and pushed on. He was not very worried. Who else had ever seen Hue as he was seeing it now? He didn't think God would forget him. "No, ha ha! but He might kill me." But a thrill lifted him and he ran a few yards simply from excess energy.

"I'm not dying today. I will survive," he said, "and clear my mind, confess, clear my conscience, take absolution—purge these selfish thoughts, and *decide*. Every man must decide his own fate, which I define as discovering the will of God. If I see that God still wants me to be his devoted servant despite my—fantasies—so be it! But if there is no reason why I shouldn't go to her, I will go!"

He was walking in some kind of alley between houses. He was searching for a clear route east to rejoin Delta and this might be it. But he came across a pile—a pile of, as he finally realized, corpses, overflowing from some kind of outbuilding, a gardner's shed or something. They were civilians, all of them with hands roped behind their backs. Bloated and turning black; some of them in Western-style business suits. There was one who might have been a Caucasian. The rest had the straight shining black hair of the Vietnamese. Ten or a dozen people, but Paul didn't look too deeply into the little shed—but he did look into—he gasped and he was seeing the bunker again, still searching for The Destroyer's lighter—and he cried, "I don't care!"

With twenty men for every woman there was only one way for an attractive woman to have any peace—and with the loneliness, the harrowing *experience* every day and night, how can a person withstand— He looked into the bunker almost as if he wanted to watch.

He thought he must be going south now; he'd made enough progress east to line him up behind Delta. So now, press south. At a cross street he saw a wall and some tall buildings to his left, which had to be the Citadel wall and the buildings. He kept hoping for Americans. It was rough walking and the noise of the fighting drew closer. Yes, he was nearer the battle. He wasn't scared but he was fierce for life. He decided he would do his duty and no more. There was no dishonor in that. "Just do your duty. You're still the chaplain around here, not a corpsman or marine, so act like a chaplain! That's enough! I see. You want only one thing. And what is that one thing?" Paul cried: "Becka!"

Now it was almost deafening. He strode on. He saw some tank or ontos tracks in the film of white mud and his heart jumped. Marines! He started trotting and scarcely noticed the jiggling of the flak jacket on his shoulders. He clapped his free hand on his helmet and kept trotting, holding Terwilliger's rifle in his other hand. Small-arms fire, a blooper, then a grenade detonation—all so familiar and hellish.

Ahead, less than a block away, he glimpsed a man in a dark-green uniform, certainly a marine. He ran faster. The man, who was perhaps a sentry with orders to guard the rear, saw him and came to a menacing alert. Paul was now only about three houses up the street from this man. He halted, waved his rifle and called "Hey! Marine!" He moved to the middle of the street and walked boldly forward. The man maintained his position at the corner of a small building.

Unnerved, breaking a sweat, Paul stopped and called, "I am Chaplain Adrano, Delta Company."

The sentry waved him forward and, as Paul approached, stood out from the building and leveled his rifle. Paul stopped. He was less than fifty meters away. He could plainly see that the man was a black marine armed with an M16.

"I am Chaplain Adrano," Paul repeated in a carrying voice. "I am looking for Delta Company."

"Advance and be recognized."

Paul heaved a huge breath and approached.

The marine said, "If you're a chaplain how come you're carrying that weapon?"

"Oh this! This gun," said Paul speaking in a normal voice now and smiling at the sentry's suspicious eyes. "This is Terwilliger's rifle. Do you know Terwilliger?"

"Maybe I do," said the sentry without altering the aim of his M16.

Said Paul patiently, "Would you please point that thing somewhere else?"

"You stop."

Paul was already stopped.

The marine came forward and walked slowly around Paul. Completing the circle he said, "Where's Williger?"

"Dead," Paul answered, hearing a surprising tone in his own voice. "I was riding with him. This is his blood." Paul wondered why he was blabbing like this. Growing testy he said: "Who do I look like? Ho Chi Minh? Tell me where Delta Company is."

A great explosion rocked the earth.

In Mac's mind the house was still falling. He ordered everybody to stay away from it because he suspected this was the first part of a "two-part invention." The marines who rushed in to help their buddies would be clobbered themselves.

Mac said: "I'm going over there, Graeser. You don't have to come."

"I'm coming, sir," Graeser said, and Mac saw he meant it.

Mac turned toward the others in the room. Captain Kindred unhesitatingly raised his hand and said he would come. Ollie said, "I'm with you, Skipper." Doc Sobieski said he would come, so did two troopers. Mac said, "That's enough." He averted his eyes from those who had not spoken.

He ordered the exec to lay suppressive fires on every point where the enemy might have a machine gun that could hit the house. Then, turning to the volunteers, he said:

"O.K. One at a time, Captain Kindred first. I go last."

Mac, turning again toward the street, was astounded to see a marine running toward the house. In fact the man was running right down the middle of the street, from the right.

Mac shouted: "Stop!" The man looked startled, confused. He stopped and stared toward Mac. He wore a flak jacket and helmet, so Mac couldn't be certain, but he looked a lot like Paul Adrano—except he was carrying a rifle.

Mac boomed out: "Go back to your unit."

The man hesitated, then turned and ran through the gate in the wall that surrounded the demolished, smoking house across the street. Mac cursed. Turning to Kinny he said, "Go, Kinny," and Kindred ran out. Mac sent the others one by one at varying intervals. The Delta suppressive fire reached a horrific crescendo. It came Mac's turn and he scissored out the front window, landed on both feet, staggered, and began to run. He ran like a greyhound, with long reaching strides, crossed the street in three steps and passed through the gate into the yard. Coming to the pile of rubble in front of the house he scrambled up on all fours, cutting both hands and knees. He saw the blood and the rips in his trousers, and registered these in some meaningless way against the background of the machine guns and mortars of Delta's suppressive fires.

When he could stand upright in what had been the front room he saw that Kindred and two others were trying to lift a section of the ceiling that lay on the floor. Somewhere a man was saying, "Good, good."

Mac recognized the voice. It had to be Paul Adrano's. He bent down and looked at the soles of a man's boots—a man on his knees—amid the rubble of the ceiling and walls, and then his brain adjusted the picture and he realized that somebody was down there on hands and knees holding up a section of the ceiling with his back. This was the man saying "Good," and now Mac was certain the voice was Paul's.

Paul said, "Lift, quick!"

The group led by Kinny struggled but the piece broke, Kinny staggered and fell, still holding a chunk in his hands, and half the section crashed down on Paul's back. But Paul did not give way. Mac could see the rubble lifting and dropping as Paul breathed.

Men began to shout contradictory ideas and orders. Three of them again got together to lift a considerable chunk, it held together, and they swung it aside.

"Hurry," said Paul, "he's bleeding."

Mac and others grabbed whatever they could in bleeding hands, and heaved and pitched till Paul was uncovered. Under him lay a bloody mess like a chalk man streaked with crimson.

Paul said, "This man's alive."

Worried about the ammo, Mac said, "Graeser, tell Lieutenant Wozniak to suspend fire." After a while the firing, which Mac had not noticed since he entered the house, came to a stuttering halt, and he heard that. "Graeser, tell Lieutenant Wozniak to alert the gunners to resume fire at my command."

They carried the wounded marine to the front of the pile and Mac said to Doc Sobieski, "Wait, Doc." He joined Paul and Ollie where they were digging with the desperate fury of men who can hear the voice of one who is trapped. Mac too heard this weak and tremulous voice with a thin thread of hope. Mac saw that Paul Adrano's hands were dripping, streaming, and that Paul grabbed a splintered board, pulled it from a heap, and flung it across the room without wincing.

They uncovered the man but he died in their lacerated hands. Paul lifted his torso, and his head flopped back, his mouth opened, and he exhaled, never to inhale again. Paul whispered a prayer—his helmet was gone and his wet black hair held the gray dust, the color of the dead marine's skin.

Said Mac: "Graeser, tell Kilo Company we will hold what we've got for a few minutes. Ask them not to advance."

Graeser said a minute later: "Sir, he says they'll wait for us."

"Thank you, Graeser."

They carried the body to the front and as they lay it down, Graeser called: "Sir, Battalion wants you to explain the delay."

"Tell Battalion," said Mac, thinking of the briefer, "that we'll resume the advance in five minutes."

"There are two more men in here," said Mac, holding up his hand for silence. But nobody could hear any voice or motion in the debris. The dust hung in the silent air. Some distant gunfire rumbled down the street.

Mac had an idea that didn't quite work. He thought that if all the parts were put in one place he could deduce whether a man who could be saved lay somewhere under the rubble. But as the parts piled up he suspected he would never know. He had just reached that conclusion when Paul appeared and they faced each other.

"The wounded man has got to move!" said Paul almost in a shout. He gripped Mac with a dripping hand; his eyes grew huge and urgent.

"Yes," said Mac calmly. "Take him to the rear, but wait just a second."

Mac ordered that the suppressive fire be resumed. When the cacophony reached full throat he nodded to Paul and said softly, but his words were drowned out: "Go ahead." Paul read his lips.

Taking a poncho and two men, Paul Adrano slung the bleeding marine in a kind of sack and they struggled down the rubble slope, exercising great care, and no one fell, and they reached the front yard and moved toward the wall. They passed through the gate and into the street with Delta's suppressive fire in full roar, and Mac watched them over the top of the wall.

As they reached the middle of the street Mac heard something ominous, as it seemed, in the distance—but he also felt the shocks of a heavy weapon aimed almost directly at him. He saw Paul and the others spin and writhe, and fall. The slugs of a 12.7 ripped into the sheet of rubber that had been the cradle of the wounded man. The marines' flak jackets offered no protection from the 12.7. This was the second part of the two-part invention.

He could not locate the gun but it certainly wasn't close. On a guess he told Graeser to order the company's 106-millimeter recoilless rifle to bash the high buildings to the east, but he didn't know how long it would take to bring the 106 into battery. He didn't wait for a reply. He ran sliding and skidding down the debris slope, kept his balance, and ran into the street. The 12.7 was at that moment pounding the house that Mac and the others had left ten minutes ago.

Mac grabbed Paul by the arm holes of his flak jacket and began dragging. He discovered that he wasn't alone. Ollie was also dragging a man back to the wall, leaving trails in the rubble, and blood in the trails. They laid the men in the yard, in the shelter of the wall, then went back to the street where by now the 12.7 was chewing the earth.

Mac saw Paul Adrano, wearing the face of death, with one arm swinging limp, staggering back into the street from which Mac had just removed him. Paul's eyes met Mac's for one brief moment and Mac saw their message. Paul shivered and lurched toward a downed man, and went down on his knees. His head flopped back and he collapsed forward.

Mac yanked him up. Pulling backward, watching the feet flop, he pulled Paul into the yard and stretched him out on his back under the wall.

He unsnapped the flak jacket. Paul's chest was bubbling blood in two places. His face was gray and his lips blue, and his dark brown eyes were wide with alarm. He was looking at the sky.

Mac said, "Hey Paul." He covered one hole with the flat of his hand and felt the warm blood explode against his palm. It caressed his hand in slight, swift pops.

Paul seemed to notice Mac. He took his arm, gripped it strongly, shifted to Mac's wrist, and tried to pull him down. He looked into Mac's eyes as through a window—as if he wanted to see what was on the other side. His eyes lost their fear, then their curiosity, their desire to know. They lost all desire. His grip lost its strength. One moment he was there and the next he was gone. Mac howled like a wounded dog, with pain and rage. As in a dream he heard the howling. As in a dream he saw the blank eyes, searching no more, and felt the hand slide down, and saw it flop on the chest and cover one of the wounds. But in this dream Mac's pain was real. It lodged in his throat and chest, as if his howling would break something inside him. He howled inhumanly. It was something to inspire fear. But stopping it offered him no relief. There was no relief anywhere.

"Sir," Graeser pleaded, "the exec wants you. Talk to him."

"Haven't got time," said Mac as he stuffed two grenades into each cargo pocket.

Graeser murmured in the dark and came back to say, "Sir, he says to tell you he insists."

Mac looked up quickly as if he'd heard a strange noise, and in the wavering candlelight Graeser saw his indifferent eyes. He knew what Mac would say.

"Tell him I'll be back at first light. All he has to do is hold this position. No patrols. Tell him." Mac spoke as a man who has more important things on his mind.

"I told him and he says—"

"Christ, Skipper, what are you doing?" Gunny Hitchcock cut in.

"I told you what I'm doing and you said, 'Count me out.' O.K. Guns, you're out." Mac slung a loop of M16 magazines over his shoulder. He fastened his helmet strap, which the gunny had never before seen him do.

"With respect, sir," said Hitchcock from the floor—he was still sitting on his helmet whereas Mac was now standing—"with respect"—and Mac could see the whites of his eyes when he looked up—"you're a company commander, not some wild-ass squad leader."

"With respect, you're a gunnery sergeant and I'm a captain."

"That's just it. I wouldn't let a corporal do what you're doing."

"Fine. You keep the corporals in line while I'm gone."

"Sir," the gunny pressed on, in a conciliatory tone now, "you're responsible for the company. You can't go off on personal business. You're the company commander, the best job in the fuckin Marine Corps." Veering off on a new track, the gunny said: "You'll never find the bastard anyway. You know you'll never find him."

Hitchcock stood up now and faced his captain from a range of six inches. He watched the man he sometimes called "Big Face" and looked into the deep blue eyes, saw the lips changing with a crooked smile. The gunny was not pleased to see disrespect in the captain's expression.

"Wherever he was when he hit those guys," the gunny persisted, "he's somewhere else now. You got a twelve-point-seven, you keep it moving. You don't park a twelve-point-seven." To Hitchcock it was clear the captain was not thinking as a company commander or even an officer. Hitchcock said: "Skipper, maybe you need a rest."

Mac was straightening the twists out of a belt to which he had attached two LAW rockets, using long strips of electrician's tape. Now he slung it over his left shoulder.

Hitchcock pleaded: "Skipper, for Christ's sake." He sought Mac's eyes and found nothing.

Hitchcock pressed on: "Since you'll never find the guy or his gun, why not wait till tomorrow. We advance in a line abreast and we kill a hundred fuckin NVA. What's wrong with that?"

"Nothing. I intend to do that too," Mac replied. He turned to Graeser and, placing his hand on Graeser's shoulder, he said, "No, no, no. Stay here and—"

Graeser said with anguish in his voice, "Sir, I—"

"No, Graeser. Stay with the command group. They need you."

Mac started toward the door. Hitchcock sprang forward and blocked the way.

Said Mac, "What the fuck do you think you're doing?"

"Hippo, Sailor, Valas," Hitchcock called over Mac's shoulder, "saddle up. All the ammo you can carry. Leave the three-point-five, bring some LAWs and a bushel of grenades."

"Get out of my way," said Mac.

Hitchcock was blocking the door with his body. Behind Mac the gunny's three men were loading up and strapping up. The gunny was snapping his flak jacket.

"I don't want you," said Mac. "I misjudged you. Stay here."

"Everybody, two full canteens," said Hitchcock, ignoring Mac.

The sailor complained that he had only one. He asked somebody for a canteen. Mac slammed Hitchcock against the door frame. Hitchcock had seldom been so impressed with another man's strength. He caught his breath, signed to his men, and they went out into the night.

When the gunny caught up, Mac was walking down the middle of the street. Back in the house Graeser was notifying Lieutenant Wozniak that Mac had taken a patrol out and that he had requested that nobody fire forward of the line. Graeser did this on his own initiative. He asked the lieutenant to join the command group. Lieutenant Wozniak asked where Mac was going and Graeser said he didn't know. Lieutenant Wozniak said, "What is going on?" Then Graeser heard Wozniak's voice on the company net saying: "Friendlies forward of the line. Do not fire unless you can positively identify your target. Friendlies, friendlies."

Mac, the gunny, the sailor, the Golden Greek, and Hippo humped down the street, stumbling on debris. They were going east toward the Citadel wall. The gunny signaled his men to follow in column, and he walked to Mac's right and one pace behind. Mac had not acknowledged his presence. Hitchcock drew abreast and gradually moved closer. Neither man spoke. Hitchcock saw a match flare on the right, the NVA side. The street was a vague pathway, poorly bounded, of a lesser darkness than the rest. Hitchcock knew that multistory buildings stood in their path ahead and he could almost see their black shapes. He knew the wall was up there somewhere. An engine intruded on the silence, a boat or maybe a generator, somewhere ahead; a faint gleam filled the sky, possibly light refracted upward from a generator-served building. Hitchcock resolved to count blocks and houses. So many streets this way, so many that way; so many houses in a row. He had no hope of finding the house from which they had set out, but he wanted at the least to be able to locate the Delta defensive line when the captain's "patrol" was over.

As they were leaving the house Hitchcock had noticed that Hippo was not carrying his PRC 25. He must have taken the gunny's order to load up ammo to mean he should leave the radio behind. The gunny did not regret this. He'd rather have the extra ammo. So: the captain was a one-man arsenal; Hitchcock, Valas, and Collins toted M16's, grenades, and LAWs; and Hippo carried a blooper and a pistol. The gunny felt a surge within him, a thrill that almost lifted him off the ground. His whole life had pointed to this night. But he did want to live. "I will make goddamn sure of that," he thought. He almost believed he could share the skipper's lunacy and live.

Suddenly the skipper grabbed his arm in a sharp grip and stopped. The men seemed to catch on fast and they all stopped without a sound and without bunching up. Mac whispered in the gunny's ear: "Has Hippo got a blooper?"

"Yes sir."

"Hippo comes with me. You take Valas and Collins and go down this alley."

The gunny sensed that they were between houses, still on the street, with NVA territory on their right. The alley ran off to the right.

Mac continued: "Down the alley, got it? Set up a kill zone behind the house. Hippo and I'll drive the bastards out of the house. You set up a kill zone in back. Do you fuckin understand?"

"I understand."

Hitchcock took his two men and disappeared. Mac and Hippo stood together in the street.

"We advance together. We blow the shit out of the house."

Hippo nodded.

"Keep three or four meters on my right. Do not go in the house unless I call you. Do not fire into the house after I say 'I'm in.' Got it?"

"I got it," assented Hippo-I'm-Great-In-Dayton. And he thought: "Here comes a spree."

They moved toward the wall and scrambled over. A burst of fire struck the wall between them. They crouched and went still. After a few seconds of warm silence Mac fired a burst on automatic, they diverged, Hippo let fly a grenade, and they advanced frontally, blasting continuously. Mac hollered "I'm in" and rushed the door, chopping first the door and then the front windows. He sent two blasts through the wood-and-glass door, then kicked it in and leveled his M16 and swept the room. Then he heard a lot of chaotic firing from the back. In the muzzle flashes of his weapon he determined there was nobody left in the main room. He called to Hippo. They joined in the middle of the room and felt their way carefully back.

"Hey, Buzzbomb!" Mac shouted, and ducked with Hippo into a side room in order to be someplace his voice had not been.

From the rear of the house the gunny hollered, "Alfa Sierra back here. Three dead gook-types."

"Do not go back into the alley," Mac called.

"Kee-rist no."

The gunny and his men came into the house via the back door. Mac told Hippo to blast the houses on either side with his blooper, so Hippo lined a 40-millimeter grenade into each dwelling. Nobody fired back. They stood there, all of them, sweating, panting, waiting. Mac's heart was rapping its cage like a gorilla. He didn't feel good, he didn't feel relief, but then again it wasn't so bad either. He was drenched and breathless. His whole consciousness was given over to a repetition of the muzzle flashes and grenade bursts, blossoming orange and streaking out in yellow.

Valas whispered, "Sir, there's a man over here asking to meet you. Wants to shake your hand."

Mac followed the Golden Greek and nudged the body with the toe of his boot. He stood over it and somebody watching might have thought he was pondering death. In fact he was thinking what next.

He could not go out the way he came in. That would be asking for it. He moved to the center of the group and allowed a minute for the men to adjust their gear and replace magazines. Then he started out the back door, and the gunny thought, "No, goddamn it, no," but he followed.

They paused in the yard, then headed straight back—deeper into NVA land. The gunny cursed but chalked it on his memory board: three blocks east, half a block south, then another block south. If the

house was a link in the enemy's defensive line they were already behind it and going deeper. Under an impulse of fear and rage, Gunnery
Sergeant Hitchcock grabbed his company commander and spun him
around.

"What the fuck!" the gunny hissed.

Mac broke his grip and said, "Go back."

"Quiet!" Hitchcock hissed.

And Mac said again without lowering his voice, "Go back to the
command group."

Then he was gone. Hitchcock stood there for a full minute knowing
it was death to follow. He looked at his men but they were mere shadows, bunched up like sheep. One grenade could kill them all. Hitchcock knew he'd lose Mac in the dark if he didn't pursue him. In a rage
he ran after Mac and the others ran after him.

Mac was on hyperalert.

"The right place, belly of the beast. They won't shoot at movement
here, they'll have to challenge. Just as well I sent Hitchcock back. I
can do this alone.

"New magazine. Click. There she is, twenty more and plenty where
that came from." He threw the empty magazine and listened to it
strike on a rock or something. "O.K., stealth and silence now. Must be
two blocks in. Hey! the walking's easy, no rubble. Swing feet swing.
Christ, I move in the dark, marine alone, slip along, soundless, brain-
less. Well shit, turn here.

"Bushes, trees, holy shit, what's this, a friggin jungle in the middle
of the city. Make progress toward the wall. I never did shake hands
with that man. He seemed a little soft against my toe. I'm ugly and re-
pulsive, and I never expected that. Thought I'd be a good man, maybe
like Paul, good but strong, a searcher. O.K., a few more blocks east
but—God, the smell.

"A man who tries to go beyond—that's Paul—beyond what we can
know for sure. What's obvious is fine as far as it goes but a man—a
man like Paul is a— What's out there where Paul was searching? You
can never find it, so—give up? We are animals, of course, and animals
die, but is—take this goddamn war. Is this it? Is this the definition?

"Must be bodies everywhere but I can't figure it out, there hasn't been any fighting in this neighborhood, they just overran the area. Maybe it's dogs and cats. They like dog meat, so they shoot a dog, skin him, and toss the offal, that'd account for the smell I suppose. Well for all I know dogs taste all right but I doubt it. Anyway I love dogs. Good old Clinker! I can say that, I love a dog, but Christ, maybe Jack the Ripper loved a dog.

"You know, I don't see why it had to be so quick. That little pop in my hand, and when he grabbed my arm I was sure he had some time, I mean he seemed so strong—desperate, terrified, but surely he had a minute, two minutes. God, I wish he had ten seconds, five seconds!

Mac squinted away the tears and rubbed the pain in his throat, remembering the howl, his howl like a loon in a swamp.

"I wish he'd spoken just five words, two words. I want to know, was it victory. I mean in his own terms. You live a difficult life in accord with your vision or hope. You try to live a better life, you strive. I don't strive, I just live. Paul was a striver. So is it victory? I have to say, about his eyes, it certainly wasn't some kind of ecstasy of the spirit. I believe it was fear. All that striving and probing, all that agony about faith, I think it must have been agony, and in the end what have you got but fear? If there ever was a time for honesty this is it. So I saw—what? Not a fearless man, that's for sure. God, I believe it was one part hope and nine parts fear of the abyss. But really, I don't know. Was he fearless? A man like me, how could I see the truth of a man like him? But I've got my truth too. That can't be any good, a separate truth for everybody, how can that be any good?"

He stopped and removed his helmet to listen. Maybe he heard footsteps, but maybe not. Certainly no voices, no music. "Hey, give me some revolutionary music! Ha! They say revolution and they mean tyranny. I guess that's what they want." A small engine humming, a little louder now, toward the wall. The darkness less than perfect. A smell of river or rot—he was evidently out of the dead-dog neighborhood—no, here's a whiff again, decomposition. "I will decompose too."

"I wish I could see into his mind. What did he think when—*could* he think?"

Mac found himself on his knees sobbing, covering his face with both hands. His rifle lay beside him and he remembered placing it there—that in dropping to his knees he had not lost all precaution. But the sobbing and shakes engulfed him now in an agony like death. He staggered to his feet. He was standing but mentally he was still down on the ground blind. Blindness! He knew a darkness and hurt in life that he had covered up with blind ignorance.

He walked east searching for a light, listening for a sound of any kind that would betray the presence of the enemy. He stopped to let his strength gather in his chest and legs. He sensed, but did not comprehend, a crisis. If this was the crisis why was he filling its void with hate? Marked forever. Right. He paused, a momentary weakness. Within the pause he recognized the mark and hailed it. Then came the rush, the ferocity. If only he could kill right now. If only he could get beyond the searching and finding, the *tactics.* If he could spew a magazine in one hot burst—charge their position flinging grenades— if he could catch one by the throat—"I'd do it!" And mentally he did it, *in his heart he did it,* he strangled a man and shook him as a dog shakes a woodchuck to snap its spinal cord, shaking, screaming, then quitting the scream to listen for the crack. But the victim was somehow innocent and it was a self-inflicted horror, but he kept it up.

Coming to a wider street with taller buildings on the left, he turned south again and made another two blocks into their domain before crouching under a wall to listen. Then he had an inspiration. He would go for the generator, which must be a center of enemy presence and activity. He went east. He imagined that the throb of the machine was bouncing off the inner surface of the east wall. So he was close. A steady rush of engine noise and now it was closer. Now it grew louder with every step.

Mac saw a little bar of light, very narrow, with a right angle in it. He thought it must be a corner of a blackout curtain. He waited by a truck. He lowered himself to the ground and peered around the double wheels. Nobody looks for a head at wheel level. The truck was intact, a captured ARVN vehicle for sure. Mac could hear nothing but the generator and see nothing but a vague and high shape, a building, and the bar of yellow light, on the ground floor. He was in a parking lot or some kind of open space.

He had no plan, no step two, but he did have step one, which was

494

"Kill." He had a lust, not the same as the necessity of fighting, of conquering an objective or defending a perimeter. This was stronger. He shivered. He felt weak and confused, as if he were inhabiting somebody else's body or some other mind possessed his mind. But he knew how to cope with that. He rose and walked toward the little bar of amber light.

Valas halted and by reflex the others did too.

The gunny said irritably: "What's up?"

Said Valas: "This is as far as I go."

The gunny was stunned into silence.

Valas said: "We're not a mob. We're a lower form of social life. Like they say, a mob has a leader."

"I'm your leader," the gunny snapped.

"Then I bet you know where we're going."

"Yes I do."

"Right into an NVA battalion. I'm going back, is where I'm going."

Because it was dark, and because Hitchcock was fast with his fists, Valas never saw the blow that found the soft place between his flak jacket and helmet. A sensual explosion in his eyes, bones, lips, teeth, and ears. He knew what it was but had a hard time believing it. He lost orientation; he lost up and down. He was still trying to believe it, or trying not to, when he felt both his wrists seized by strong hands that lifted him to his feet. The sailor stood on one side and Hippo on the other. The gunny handed him his weapon.

"Listen up, marines. I think he'll home in on that generator. So that's where we're going." Hitchcock slapped himself in the chest with a whack. "See me?" he demanded in a harsh whisper. "See me? You fuckin keep me in sight! We are staying together and we're finding the skipper. He's out of his fuckin mind and what happens to berserk lunatics is they get killed. We lose the skipper and we get that little Basic School puke from Battalion. Understand? Forget about interval and everything I ever said about bunching up. We search as a team."

"One mortar round could kill us all," Collins tossed in satirically.

"Shut the fuck up."

"Yes sir."

"Don't sir me, you squid. Twelve years in the Corps and I never been behind bars yet. Now, if I get hit you're in charge. We are going to find the skipper. Got it, sailor?"

"Sure, Guns."

"Got it, Hippo?"

"Yes, Mr. Guns."

"Got it, Valas?"

Valas was stubbornly silent and the gunny grabbed his throat.

"Yes, yes, for Christ's sake."

"O.K.," said Hitchcock. "Semper Fi. More for the Corps. New magazines everybody."

They ejected the half-spent magazines and pocketed them and rammed in new ones. As they were completing this task they heard a rush and a blast.

"That's a LAW," said Hippo in disbelief. "That's a blessed LAW."

"That's the skipper," said the gunny. "Move out," and they strode off toward the sound.

Mac had already taken several steps when he realized he didn't know what he was doing. He faced a dark building that was obviously lit in at least one room, the light being masked. He stood in the parking lot or whatever it was. On his left a street ran toward the Citadel wall. Judging from the volume of generator sound, the wall must be just beyond the lighted building. He thought of creeping closer and peeking into the room. This seemed necessary but stupid. He stood frozen, pondering. He heard shrill laughter from the lighted room, and a whack, as if a man had downed a drink and slammed his glass on a wooden tabletop. Then came two or three more whacks of the same kind, and the scene spread itself before Mac's imagination. He listened to their laughter with a keen appreciation. It told him he was very deep in their territory. And he thought: "Laugh, go on, laugh."

He remembered an artillery forward observer, Steven Matthew, who had called a mission one night, and his target description was "voices in the dark." Listening to the laughter in the dark, Mac still hesitated.

He judged there were five or ten of them and maybe they were eating a late supper. He sniffed the air but all he could pick up was a whiff of generator exhaust. He wanted to tear their throats out for laughing.

His hate was stealthy. He was not fully aware of its power. It took him to the brink of a very foolish action. He raised his M16 to his shoulder, aimed at the middle of the blackout curtain, and began his trigger squeeze. Instead of completing it he let his finger relax, and he withdrew ten paces to lean against the wall of the building behind him. He watched the bent bar of amber light as if he expected it to move, and it did. It waved, then lost and gradually resumed its shape. Somebody had brushed against it from inside.

The building appeared to be made of cement blocks faced with stucco. If this were true Mac could penetrate it with a LAW striking the surface at a right angle—but then what?

He contemplated an approach from the front. He could burst in and fire off a magazine, and probably be killed while reloading. He ran through several possibilities. He crossed the open space and crouched to peer under the blackout curtain.

It was a big room. A bunch of office furniture had been shoved against the wall to the left, under a window that must open on the street. This window too was draped. Just in front of him, in the center of his view, stood a stack of ammo cases nearly five feet high. The cases were painted olive drab and labeled in yellow Chinese characters. He searched for Arabic numerals, for the numerals "12.7," but found none. It was all Chinese. There was an open door and evidently a corridor beyond, and another open door farther right, giving on the same corridor. Near the second door stood a steel desk heaped with military gear—and his search this time was for officers' accouterments such as binoculars, dispatch cases, pistols; but there were none. It was a heap of packs and web gear.

Next, to the right, partially obscured by the desk, a row of a dozen AK-47 assault rifles leaned against the wall.

Here Mac's view ended. There was a brighter light farther to the right but its source was hidden from him. The voices and laughter came from there.

"Do not kill these men," said a voice in his mind. He knew why it spoke. Because they were men, and because Paul would condemn it.

Taking all the time and care necessary, he examined the position of the ammo stack in relation to the window, which was open—he could smell their cook pot of rice and fish heads—then he slowly backed away, and strode across the open place and pressed his back against the wall of the opposite building.

Looking all ways—doing the whole circuit from the street on the left to the truck-sized opening in the low wall to the right, and all along the wall he was leaning on—scanning this little universe, the only one of any interest, he must have reached a decision. He set his rifle against the wall, an action perhaps suggested by his seeing the row of AK-47's, and unshouldered the belt holding his LAW rockets. He unsheathed his K-Bar and sliced the tape that held one rocket. He prepared it to fire, propped it against the wall a foot from his rifle, and quickly prepared the second LAW for firing.

He stepped several paces forward and shouldered the first LAW. To launch it would change his life or end it. What was the correct angle of fire to strike the cache of ammo? If he hit it, it would almost certainly explode and kill every man in the room, and spout flame and fragments back at him. A miss would give him away without perhaps killing more than one or two.

He prepared for a startling experience—the takeoff of a rocket shooting flame back at him, the whoosh of the backblast behind him, the detonation of the projectile, and possibly the mammoth explosion when the ammo pile blew. He instructed himself to close his eyes at the last second and save his night vision. To be night-blind even for half a minute could be fatal. But this word did not deter him.

He fired the LAW. The tail plume turned his closed eyelids pink. The thing exploded somewhere in the building. Mac flung the spent casing left, and it skidded across the street. He grabbed his rifle and the other rocket, and trotted a few steps farther right. He laid his rifle down carefully, shouldered the launcher, and adjusted his aim to hit at a right angle. He aimed at the point behind which, he estimated, the enemy's rifles stood. He imagined them going for their weapons, since the ammo stack had not detonated. He let the rocket go.

He forgot to close his eyes and saw a blindingly brilliant streak and a halo of smoke, dust puffing where the rocket struck the wall, and a flash the size of a softball.

Then all he could see was a bright-green sort of flower that faded to red. He fumbled for his rifle, caught it up, and tried to aim it, but the hole in the building was too small, it was covered by his visual impairment. He darted forward, crouched under the window, pulled the pin on a grenade, and let go the spoon. He counted four and hooked it into the window, but it bounced back at him. A man had been standing in the window and the grenade had hit him in the chest. The grenade lay between Mac's knees. He dashed away, along the wall, and threw himself forward. The thing boomed and Mac heard fragments spray against the wall beside him and the one ahead, the one with the truck gate.

The question was whether the man was still in the window. Would he lean out and fire? Mac rolled tighter to the building and looked toward the window. Enough light came out to show him his rifle lying three or four paces back. He watched, and nobody leaned out. It flashed in his mind that the blast had killed the man. He got to his feet full of this hopeful idea and he was quite unconscious of any pain or disability; he grabbed his rifle and ran out the truck gate. He heard screams and shouts as he passed the small hole his LAW had opened in the wall. His eyes were getting better. He knew that he hadn't escaped the grenade altogether but he seemed to be running and thinking. He ran left around the building, halting when he reached the street.

He expected to see or hear soldiers—but no. He was alone. He dropped to the deck and tried to peer around the corner but his view was blocked. He would have to stand up. He did—but an idea caught hold of him, an incredible observation. The lights were still on in the room. He had seen light coming out through the remains of the blackout curtain.

Looking around the corner, he saw a man run out of the building and turn left, away from him, and go into the street where he had thrown the rocket casing. In service to his main idea, Mac wanted this man to conclude that somebody had fired two rockets and run. He thought there was a good chance he'd conclude just that.

Mac forgot about the man who leaned out the window. He forgot everything else. If, from this point on, he did anything right it was not because he remembered his training, which in any case had never

499

prepared him for this. Forgetting everything, he acted automatically. He even forgot about life. Nothing was precious to him except what was lost. Some of his actions would have seemed reasonable to a man who intended to survive, and some would not. But everything he did was reasonable when set against his aim, his purpose. He was given over, body and soul, to that.

He became aware of a sound on his right. With a minimum of display he looked that way. Two soldiers were running toward him along the street. He waited till they were level with him and cut them down with a long burst from his M16. He stood still, watching the street. He dropped the half-empty magazine in his pocket and jammed in a full one. He slung the rifle on his left shoulder and went out to the bodies. Crouching, glancing quickly up and down the street, he ejected the magazine from one of the dead men's AK-47's, hefted it and judged it was full, dropped it in a different pocket, and picked up the other corpse's AK-47. He checked its magazine too.

Now he was armed with a hard-hitting rifle. He looked at the inanimate face of one of the dead men, and paraded a familiar sentence through his mind: "This is death." It meant death was death. This was anything but a circular statement. He didn't go through their pockets and such to find more ammo because he knew the bodies would be warm and feel alive.

Carrying the AK-47 at the ready he walked toward the door. Just as he reached it and mounted its two stone steps—just as he reached the porch and turned to face right, for an unknown reason—a man appeared from the street where he had tossed the casing. They saw each other at the same time but Mac was ready and the other was not, so the man went down.

The body made a dark shapeless something on the asphalt. A bad presence entered Mac's mind. He thought of going close. Then: "Generator." Just that one word. He leapt from the porch and raced into the street, down an alley toward the sound till he saw a lighted doorway. A man armed with an AK-47 was just coming out and Mac killed him. Now he felt blood trickling down his left leg; and it was hard to lift his left arm. He jogged back to the porch and entered the building.

He walked into a dark corridor hoping to find the interior door on his right. This would be the first door he had seen while looking under the blackout curtain; and there should be another door just beyond it, also on his right. After a few paces he saw light falling on a smoking beaten zone on his left. His first LAW must have sailed right through a door and detonated in the unlighted office on the left. It had missed the stacked ammo completely. Mac stopped to listen. He heard groans and a kind of pitiful crying. He walked closer, and looked through the second door and saw the blackout curtains hanging in shreds and a body beneath the sill. Mac paused again, listening to the unholy music of suffering and death. He advanced a step into the lighted room and saw the ammo boxes, dusted with powdered plaster and chips of lath. He took another slow step, still listening, then another.

He stepped clear into the room and swept it with his eyes. The dust was dancing in the visible cone from one remaining light in the ceiling. On the left he saw a small black hole in the wall surrounded by a larger, shallow crater produced by the shaped charge of his second LAW. The dead and wounded lay among the jumbled furniture. One man rolled over and looked at him. There was a marked absence of fear in his black eyes.

The assault rifles were scattered all along the wall. Mac stepped over a body and kicked the weapons into a heap and skidded them one by one to the front, where he kicked them under the window. Then he looked for a light switch, found it by the door, and flicked it.

The room went dark, but not totally; it was a gray, not a black place. He went to the corridor, which gave him a clear view of the street door. He noted that the light in the street, however dim it was, was still brighter than the corridor. Anyone entering would be backlighted. So Mac waited.

He had a clear field of fire and cover if he needed it for reloading. He had an AK-47 man-stopper, an M16 spray gun, six grenades, and a K-Bar knife. He fixed the bayonet on his M16. He realized they might send medics, not fighters. In that case he would treat their medics as they had treated his.

Gunnery Sergeant Hitchcock was familiar with the military maxim "When in doubt, do something." But the gunny was not in doubt. He was convinced that the best thing for him to do right now was nothing.

The sailor had reported two dead NVA in the street south of the entrance to the lighted building. The gunny himself had seen the window at the back, where yellow light filtered through some hanging rags. Valas had reported one dead gook at the corner, and the gunny himself had found another dead one at the generator. Hippo had circled around and returned with the report that there was a spent LAW casing in the street. The gunny had to assume that the captain had fired his LAWs and run like hell—or was still snooping and pooping around here somewhere.

It was too early to withdraw if he still hoped to find the captain, and not too late to wait for developments. Hitchcock had a military maxim of his own. Developments have a way of developing if you let them. He told Hippo to sling his blooper and grab an AK-47 from a dead gook. Then he deployed his men around the intersection and placed himself a few paces back from the window of some kind of shop or tearoom. From here he could see the entrance of the lighted building and dim light passing through some shreds of a curtain across from his point of vantage. He would wait three or four minutes, then holler for the captain. Then if he got no answer he'd gather his men and light out for the territory.

Only a minute had passed when the building across the street went dim. It had seemed pretty dark before, but now at a stroke it was darker. Here was a what-the-fuck development. Exciting to the testicles but—what the fuck did it mean? The generator was still puffing away, the body still lay at the corner. Hitchcock decided to go on doing nothing.

If some Basic School commando had demanded: "What are you doing, Hitchcock?" he would have replied, "If you've got to give it a name, call it an ambush." He'd give it, say, two minutes and then— that would be time to "do something." What a waste of piss and sweat to quit without killing any more gooks.

"Thank God there's four and not forty," Hitchcock said two minutes later as they came trotting down the street from his left, with their AK-47's at port arms like a fucking Chinese Communist military parade. Trot-trot-trot. Then they got confused. They didn't know what to do. "Hey, you slopes, when in doubt do something." Their idea of something was to mill around the intersection. What the marines call a group grope. Maybe they'd been told to find a lighted or damaged building, but from the street there wasn't any such thing. So the gunny watched the drones who were certainly no credit to the People's Army of Vietnam. And how they jabbered. *Ong-gong-bong-dong.* The leader waved his arms like a scarecrow in the wind, pointed his rifle, and one of the soldiers slouched toward the door. The Door. Obviously not too thrilled with his assignment. The others headed for various other doors including the one that led straight to Gunnery Sergeant Hitchcock, his mama's little brat. The gunny thought, "Come and die for the revolution."

But it didn't happen that way. The one across the street slouched to The Door, hesitated, looked back as if to ask if this was far enough, then took another step—and *blam,* he got blasted right out again. He came flying backward and spread himself all over the street. He wasn't granted a death agony, only death.

The gunny, the gunny's men in their various places of concealment, the lead gook, and his two remaining drones reached the same conclusion at the same moment. There was a capitalist pig in the building and he didn't want any company. The gunny was fuckin thundered in his brain. "That fucker!" he cried, referring to his company commander and thereby violating the article of the Uniform Code of Military Justice mandating respect for superiors. Or maybe validating it. In any case the gunny was flabbergasted. Each and every one of his flabbers was fucking gasted. "Would you believe?" he exclaimed half aloud. Of course this meant the skipper was deeper into mayhem than sanity.

The gooks held a jabbery conclave and the gunny noted with relief that they had no radio. He saw—he moved closer to the window glass. But what's the point of listening to gook talk? He saw that the leader was trying to send the others in and they were refusing. The leader suddenly faced the door, and began pounding the place with quick bursts from his AK-47, marching in. He stopped, ducked aside, inserted a fresh magazine, and marched in blasting.

The muzzle flashes lighted the vestibule and the reports bounced off the walls everywhere. The lead gook ducked and one of his stooges threw a grenade. When it blew the big gook went deeper into the darkness.

All the gunny could hear was a hell of AK-47 talk. The guy was inside, chopping the place to pieces, but it was all AK-47, whereas the gunny was waiting to hear the more shrill and quicker chatter of an American M16. Then it hit the gunny that the first gook, the one lying in the street, had been hit with a high-impact round—in fact, with an AK-47. Now the gunny's flabbers were gasted on a truly cosmic scale. "Holy shit, he's got a forty-seven," the gunny crowed in admiration.

The shooting stopped. The two gooks in the street plastered themselves against the wall, one on either side of the door, and the gunny realized the time had come to "do something." Placing himself as close as possible to a ninety-degree angle to the glass, he hit the gook on the left with a long burst, then shifted to the one on the right; but the shattered glass ruined his sight picture, and he ripped off a burst more or less at the world, knowing he'd missed.

But Hippo did not miss. From his hideaway he sent hellfire at this figure frozen by terror and the man danced and threw his gun and quivered in midair, then fell like a wet rag, a long rag. Hippo walked slowly into the street and the gunny watched him through the broken glass, but the gunny could not see into his mind.

All the wickedness in Hippo came to a boil and drove all his goodness into a cave. Approaching the body, he breathed the fumes of the triumph of fury. He had his desire. He was a killer and it was all legitimate.

Looking out from his little tearoom at his man lying there like an object that had never known or deserved life, the gunny felt a jolt of confirmation. The gunny thought something like: "I am more than anybody knows; I am more than I knew."

He stepped out into the street and waved to Collins and Valas, who joined him and Hippo and they all made a team, aiming their weapons outboard, crossing toward the door. Hitchcock shouted: "Striker Six! This is Buzzbomb!"

The four marines waited. The generator chuffed; the sailor looked down the street, the gunny repeated his call—and was amazed when a light flicked on. He saw it through the busted glass and rags in the front window.

Valas was so surprised he forgot that he hated both the gunny and the captain. He even forgot he was about to lose the only life in the world that he valued. "The fuckin lights went on," he said in awe.

Gunny to Hippo: "Check the back window. Be careful."

Hippo disappeared around the corner.

Gunny to the sailor and the Golden Greek: "Watch the street. I'm going in."

Forgetting that he had vowed to live, the gunny started toward the door. He could see weak light ahead, but light. He stepped around the body in the street. He mounted the two steps and dropped to a squat on the porch. Nothing happened. He knew he was backlighted and wide open. He duck-walked in a little ways. In here, where the generator noise was muted, he could hear a dying man dying, or wishing he could. The gunny duck-walked to the interior door, but kept his head lower than knee level. The door led into a dimly lighted room that smelled of explosive gases. He listened intently and heard a crunching step. Now he had to decide whether to get a better look, and remembered he didn't plan on dying tonight. So—turn around. His knees objected to the duck-walking and his brain was shocked at the idea that Hippo might shoot him in the ass. Would Hippo shoot at movement? What the gunny needed was an American flag.

Mac heard the words spoken, or maybe he was the speaker. He knew the urge the words expressed. He had always recognized a separation between what stirred the mind and the words that issued forth; but there always seemed to be a harmony between the two, as if the separation were a medium of transmittal. The urge, the separation, then the words: "Get one more."

Just now the whole process was squeezed by the screaming in his skull. And of course by the pain. But the pain wasn't the worst of it.

He wiped blood from his eyes and tried to steady himself on his feet. He walked as if barefoot over broken glass, and wobbled as if his soles were rounded and tender. He held his arms out for balance despite the pain. On the left the rifle with its bayonet. On the right his cupped hand with the leaking blood. He lifted the hand to his wound, one of them, and held it there to stanch the bleeding, and it did not help. It hurt, but he held it there even though more blood seeped down into his eyes. His arm hurt.

He still had a purpose to be accomplished before he gave out. That he would give out he was quite certain. He knew by the screaming, and by the way the room whirled—a dark space turning invisibly. And through it all he still heard: "One more." So he staggered along the wall, turned on the lights, and searched for the man with no fear in his eyes.

They were still dying. Mac heard the groans and saw some feeble movement among the scattered wreckage of their jolly dinner. He shook his right hand and wiped his eyes again, and his vision cleared for a second and he saw the green uniform of the man he was seeking. He went there asking if he was still alive and fearless. He paid no attention to the others. He saw the man's black hair, brown skin, shiny teeth—the man strained to breathe, and that seemed to produce a grin—and his fierce, free, fearless black eyes. There he was.

The floor flew up and struck Mac in the face with tremendous violence. He lay still for a moment, remembered his rifle, remembered the bayonet, and pulled himself to his feet by holding the leg of an upturned table. He reached down to retrieve the rifle and when he straightened up the room whirled. He waited for it to settle.

The man looked up at Mac, and his eyes moved from the point of the bayonet to Mac's eyes and back.

Mac said, "Are you ready to die?" At least he intended to say it. He thought he said it.

By this time the eyes of the Vietnamese had steadied on the point of the bayonet that hovered over his neck. His mouth was turned down with the effort to see an object so close to his throat. He was in a river of pain and had the expression of a drowning man but not of a frightened one. For one second his eyes flicked up and met Mac's. A trace, maybe a trace of regret, but no fear.

Mac was losing track of the situation. It wasn't obvious why he was here or who this man was. He remembered "Get one more," but the underlying urge had changed. What stirred his mind now would not be in harmony with those words—or maybe it would. Mac was losing his reality. He lifted the bayonet by two inches, to give the man a better view, or to withdraw it.

Hitchcock crawled past the interior door, flattened his body, and with his face on the ground took one quick look through the door. He saw a mess, but nobody. He gave himself two more inches and did it again, and he saw a bigger mess, and nobody. He rose quietly, breathed quietly, and listened. He heard a voice that was familiar but inarticulate. He jumped into the room and there stood the captain. At least it was a big man, too big for a Vietnamese, and he had the captain's wide shoulders and red hair. No helmet. This man who was facing away from him turned at his call, but very slowly. His face and the front of his flak jacket were covered with blood and his trousers were ripped and bloody. His eyes were dull and for a second Hitchcock thought it must be somebody else. The big man looked at the gunny, showing no sign of recognition. His head went back even as his body dropped forward, his eyes rolled up, and he hit the deck with a whiplash motion.

Hitchcock checked the room for enemy effectives, then called his men.

They stripped off Mac's flak jacket, web belt, magazine sling, and boots. Hitchcock gave Mac's rifle and magazines to Hippo and his grenades to Valas. They rolled him onto a blackout curtain and carried him out.

They paused long enough to put a LAW through the back window. The ammo pile took it, and the whole room, in fact that whole corner of the building, was an inferno. But before it ever became an inferno, for a second or two, it enjoyed a brief career as a ball of fire, metal, and gas, expanding so rapidly it resounded across the city, and its shock waves were still bouncing off the Citadel walls eight seconds later.

Four men, carrying a fifth, stumbled through the darkness.

Chapter 23

Lost History

"Please slow down," said Mac, pressing words out with difficulty. "Doctor—" he added in a separate breath.

"Regnary, John Regnary. I'm the one who patched you up."

"Thank you. Excuse me. My brain isn't ready for conversation."

Doc Regnary said: "Did a lot of scalp work. Nothing very challenging but the scalp is not to be ignored. When we take off those bandages you'll see what I mean. Your left ear won't ever be quite the same, but then ears are a pretty foolish-looking creation anyway, don't you agree?"

"So long as I can hear," Mac said.

"You seem to be hearing me O.K."

"Yes."

"It was your scalp, your ear, the concussion. Half an inch left with the big fragment, though, and you'd be feeding maggots. Of course maggots have a right to eat, but they won't be eating you just yet. You are one lucky man, Captain. One inch, half an inch. And then your leg. We worked on your left leg, arm, and side. I saw a leg recently with one little slit a half an inch long near the groin, and the man was dead as a dodo. So would you be if one, just one little fragment had nicked your inferior vena cava. But they all got buried in muscle. You

508

have all the muscle any man will ever need, and evidently all the luck."

"But I want to ask you—" Mac tried to say.

Doc Regnary, standing by the bed, looking darkly down from his wide-set black eyes beneath his black hair—his skin was pale as a dead man's and his virile beard had gone a considerable distance toward blackening his cheeks and chin—standing there as if something about Mac fascinated him—

Doc Regnary said: "Ask, ask me anything."

"You said—did you say, they had all been killed?"

"That's what I heard at the O Club. You were still out, but already quite a celebrity. It isn't every day we get a patient who's being nominated for the Navy Cross."

"But did you say all of them?"

"The story is the marines found a whole slew of dead NVA in the corner of the building that you attacked. Some might have crawled away, I suppose. There's no ruling that out."

"So all of them," Mac repeated with a curious sense of foreboding. "Doctor—"

"John. John Regnary, M.D. Call me John. What should I call you?"

But Mac was trying to concentrate on the main thing. He said: "I'm—please go at my pace. I'm sorry."

"Don't sweat it. Your mind'll be O.K. soon and so will your body."

"The thing is," said Mac, "I can't remember all of it."

"Oh! I should have mentioned that. That's the concussion. Perfectly normal and predictable. Whatever it was, it's unrecorded. Tell me what you do remember and we'll work from there forward."

Mac's memory was actually quite clear, up to a point. He remembered walking across the room in the dusky electric light. Carrying his rifle. With the bayonet still fixed. And he saw the fearless man watching him. He stood over him and said, "Are you ready to die?" He lowered the point, and the man's eyes tracked it. All this was sharply etched but silent. The noise was all in his skull, a fearful screeching. The memory stopped there.

Mac responded: "I was in a dark place, I remember that."

"Yes, you talked a lot about muzzle flashes in the dark. That's something I'd like to see if I could do it and live. You almost make me jealous, but then I do plan on going home and making pots of money, and living in some uncrowded suburb with the wife and kiddies."

"I don't remember talking about this to anybody."

"You weren't exactly talking to anybody. More like telling yourself."

Mac said: "A man came in and threw a grenade. I was knocked down and my helmet was blown off. I don't understand it. I had the chin strap secured."

"Sure. That's why your jaw is swollen and you'll have a few facial scars. Luck again. By rights you should be both blind and dead. Did you ever sit down and try to get to the bottom of it? Oh, sweet mystery of life. But what's so sweet about it, except you-know-what. Without you-know-what this'd be a pretty grim existence, right?

"Just think about the chances of it. One guy is splattered by fragments the way you were and he's killed five times over. Another walks away pissed because he's got a temporary ringing in his ears."

"I saw him coming," said Mac as if he hadn't been listening, "and we both opened up. Jesus!" He was thinking of the difference between the kick of the AK-47 and the nudging of the M16. This stimulated his prejudice against the M16, a weapon adopted not for its reach, accuracy, or striking power, but for the lightness of its ammunition. If you fire off ten rounds where one would do, what happens to the weight advantage? But it was great for laying down a base of fire or chopping bushes. Mac's mind skipped down this well-worn path as an interval of relief from what was really bothering him.

"Yeah," Doc Regnary was saying, "he hit you at least twice. Your body armor saved you. Chance again, luck. Many slugs do get through. If your chest is sore just consider it a cheap price to pay for your life. Next time you screw a broad, eat a steak, or drink a beer, remember that."

"I killed him," said Mac.

"If one of you had to die," Regnary began but thought it superfluous to finish.

Mac tried to fill his lungs but he couldn't quite expand his chest for the pain. He saw the man walking into his muzzle flashes. He saw him jolt with the impact of the heavy slugs from Mac's AK-47. Mac must have emptied the 47 because next he was crossing the room carrying the 16.

"So," said Doc Regnary, "what you want to know is, what happened to the stuff you don't remember. All that data."

"Yes. Please."

"You haven't forgotten it," said the doctor, "you never knew it. You did it, whatever it was, but you never recorded it so you can't recover it. If some centurion in Caesar's army woke up on some battlefield in Gaul or Thrace and found himself under a pile of dead horses and barbarians with their throats slit, and had no idea what happened, we would consider it lost history. Ninety-nine percent of history is lost. Who needs it? We don't know who the centurion was, let alone what he did. Lost. It might as well not exist."

"But it happened," Mac tried to insist.

"Yeah, I guess. So did all the fear and agony of a million times a million women giving birth. You want to bring it all back?"

"If they were all killed—" Mac began.

"So what? You are alive and so are your men."

"Yes. I sent them back, thank God."

"What do you mean, sent them back?"

"I'm so damned tired," said Mac.

"Who says you sent them back?"

"I was alone," Mac declared as if to no one in particular, and his eyes were wandering. But he heard in memory a burst, then another, from outside the building. They seemed to require explaining. Somebody was firing something that wasn't an AK-47—and Mac could not distinguish an SKS from a 47—so he didn't know what weapon this was, but it was quick and sharp like an M16.

"Jesus!" Doc Regnary cried. "Here comes the wild woman of Borneo!" He slipped out of the curtained alcove. Mac looked up and there stood a young nurse.

She was not happy. Her face was flushed with anger or perhaps the heat. But it was a face Mac wanted to look at, a face he could watch for hours. As the seconds passed, her expression softened, her tension eased, and though she didn't smile she seemed to look at Mac as if she too wanted to see more.

She said, "Are you MacHugh Clare?"

"Yes. Are you Rebecca Vanburen?"

"Yes"—and she slowly and almost solemnly extended her hand, and

Mac found strength to take it. For another moment they regarded each other with mutual interest.

Rebecca said: "You asked to see me."

"I want to know," said Mac, still pressing his words out as if each one was resisting him, "if you have heard about Paul Adrano."

She nodded but did not speak—a quick, minimal nod. Her eyes were luminous but they didn't tell him what he needed to know, so he was forced to ask outright:

"I'm sorry, please forgive me, but do you know that Paul is dead?"

"I know it," she responded, and her earnest eyes rested on him as if it were up to him to continue.

He tried again to heave a big breath but it didn't work. She slid her hand behind his back and lifted, so that his body curved gently forward, and she said: "Relax your belly and try again."

He did and this time he felt a pleasant rush of air into his lungs. She eased him back against his pillow and smiled, but she did not speak.

Mac said: "Paul asked me to give you a message. This was several days ago. What's the date today, do you know?"

"This is the twentieth of February."

"How can that be?"

She smiled and said, "It is."

"Before we went up to Hue," said Mac, "I gave him a letter for my wife, just in case, and he asked me to speak to you, just in case. He asked me, if he was killed, to go to the naval hospital in Da Nang and find a nurse named Rebecca Vanburen."

Mac paused to breathe. Rebecca's glowing eyes rested on him and he watched to be sure she could take it.

He proceeded: "His message was: 'Tell her I thank God I met her.' He told me not to add or subtract from that sentence."

Her face flushed and her eyes grew brighter as they filled with tears. She said: "How did he die?"

Mac saw the street and he paused as if listening to the hammering of the 12.7. He described it to Rebecca who then asked:

"You were near him? I mean is this something you actually saw happen?"

"I was near him, in the house he had just left. I dragged him out of the street to a place where the gun couldn't reach him. But he went into the street again, and was hit again. He had only a few seconds left. He didn't speak. He looked at me and I saw that his life was dear to him, and was being withdrawn from him. I saw the life go out of his eyes. I wish I could tell you his last words. I—wait—his last words were: 'That man needs help, we've got to get him out of here'—something like that. But as to any—words of wisdom—or what he was thinking, no. He died too soon."

Later Mac thought it was unnecessary and maybe even cruel to say to Rebecca, "He died too soon."

She said with a certain thickness in her voice: "I'll come back tomorrow." And she left quickly.

Closing his eyes he saw the NVA man jolting in the weak light of the flashes. He remembered pain, and to some degree he felt it. He remembered unconsciousness as though he had been aware of it—the slipping away into it. He saw the black bayonet plunging into the throat of the fearless man.

His mind raced ahead into the midst of what it believed was the new life, the furtive, self-accusing, and self-justifying existence of the murderer. It trampled on his old identity of a fighter and created in its place the new identity of the man who said, "Are you ready to die."

The racing mind was honest, merciless, serving truth as it understood truth. Murderer. Berserker. Madman. This mind in striving to create the new identity smothered not just the fighter but the husband and lover. It screamed that he had not given Sarah a single thought or the baby she carried—since the beginning of the Hue action. Nor had he taken any of several opportunities since he regained consciousness to spare her the anxiety of uncertainty. Apparently he didn't care if she knew the extent and limits of his injuries. He could have asked Dr. Regnary to send a message following on the original, routine notification that he had been wounded; he could have asked Rebecca Vanburen. He did not. He had forgotten his pregnant wife! Or perhaps in some secret chamber of what remained of a normal mind he feared that Sarah could never love a murderer.

It wasn't exactly sleep. He was awake but lying in the dark, trying to give his body the sleep it craved. In his mental wilderness there were pictures all over the place—the bayonet and the brown skin of the throat, the film of terror that finally slipped over the man's eyes as the point came down—

He was swept along in a river of loss and horror—he was the object of his own horrid revulsion. He compared himself to Paul. If Paul's faith was an illusion springing from hope and fear, if it was false, still it sustained him. In striving to believe in it against the evidence Paul was a better man. Or maybe he actually believed it. Illusion served a man better than truth. Mac clung to the truth and was a murderer. Clinging to an illusion Paul died a good man.

He kept seeing the bayonet enter the throat of the fearless man, and the man's accusing eyes. How can you do this? Yes—how?

He knew every step he had taken after Paul died. He carried the body to the rear, knowing exactly what he would do. He would kill them. And having killed as many as he could find, he would search for more and kill them too. His brain was ice, then it burned. Then again, cold and crystal. *Kill.* A crystalline word, simple and consuming. Then he and Hippo blasting the house—and fire in the mind—orange flames melting the eyes—he kicked the door and cleared the room with two sweeps of his M16. What a consummation. What splendor. You would never call it beauty but it had the effects of the sublime, the ecstatic. A thrill passed down the front of his body. He was driving them out to the gunny's kill zone. Go there and die. Die! They could not resist his fire. This was the—gushing stream—the sweep, the discharge, the ejaculation of mind.

Next morning Rebecca Vanburen appeared at his bedside with a corpsman and a wheelchair. They helped Mac into the chair and the corpsman left. Rebecca pushed him smoothly down an aisle between beds and outside into the muggy, sun-suffused, ovenlike air, then through a door into an empty mess hall. She navigated between benches and set the chair beside a table near enough to a fan to provide a steady breeze. The monsoon was in abeyance; now and again a white blinding sun cleared the zenith and shed a hazy light down on the ocean and the earth. Mac blinked at the sun. He surveyed the room. There is a certain atmospheric signature of a Navy or Marine Corps mess hall no matter where found, and this one had it. While Becka fetched coffee Mac listened to the mess crew banging pots somewhere and shouting over the bangs. He watched her crossing toward him from the coffee urn and could not but admire her.

She gave him a pleasant, appreciative smile, and sat sideways on a bench with her legs crossed and her right arm resting on the table. The white cup steamed in the damp air. She remarked that it was crazy to drink hot coffee in this climate and Mac said he understood, he was an addict too, and hadn't tasted good coffee since Christmas. She warned him not to expect too much. Neither spoke for a while; they let their coffee cool in the breeze. Mac shivered but Becka did not see; she was looking, perhaps, at her knees, with wide, abstracted eyes. He guessed she was with Paul at that moment.

She asked him to tell her about Paul. Yesterday's tears were gone, and though she was not cheerful she seemed calm. He noticed how her left hand lay in her lap with the palm and fingers up. He had not seen a beautiful woman since Honolulu, and this unconscious way of placing her hand drew his attention to the gentle and feminine quality in her.

Believing she knew Paul better than he did, Mac did not try to describe his character. Rather he told several stories, starting with the first night, when they went out to the listening post, telling how Paul had volunteered before he knew anything about the mission.

"I said, 'Do you know where we're going?' And Paul said he did not. I said, 'But you want to come anyway?' And he said he did."

She smiled in a half-melancholy way and nodded.

Mac told how Paul had come charging to the point upon hearing the false report that he, Mac, had been hit. She asked about the rumor, vaguely confirmed by Paul himself, that he had cringed in a shell crater while a man called for him. Mac recounted that event, and Paul's refusal to conduct the memorial service.

"I told him he owed it to the men and to himself," said Mac. "He thought he was unworthy. When I look back on it now I think I was too assertive. I should have let him decide without butting in."

Rebecca listened with her entire being. But Mac noted that her left hand lay in the same relaxed posture. Her eyes all but burned with empathy.

While speaking about Paul, Mac was carried away by his subject. He forgot the "murderer" and the exile, was free of the fog in which he could see nothing but the moving bayonet, and was eager to find stories that would convey to his listener his own image of the man. He stated that he was virtually ignorant of the critical part of Paul, his belief. Mac also admitted his ignorance on another material point: Was Paul trying to prove something in Hue or had a natural courage grown in him after the crater incident? Was his the kind of courage that overpowers fear, or the kind that does not know it?

"And which kind do you have?" Rebecca interrupted.

Mac declared he had been terrified once for one minute, and never before or since. He offered no explanation and she asked for none.

He did say: "It's not because I have nothing to lose." For the first time since they rode into Hue he saw a living picture of Sarah. "I have plenty to lose," he said and thought: "And I have lost it." He knew that some Indian tribes punished murder by casting out the murderer. He almost said aloud, "I killed a defenseless man." It was as if his feet were slipping and his head going dizzy.

"When you say 'nothing to lose,' " Becka began tentatively, "I know what that means. I'd almost say I had nothing to lose until I met Paul."

Mac suppressed all the questions this suggested. He sat and listened.

"He had his vows," Becka said.

"Yes."

"So you say you're ignorant of his beliefs, but you know he was bound by vows."

"Yes. I suppose. No. Actually I don't know how bound he was, how bound he thought himself to be."

"Maybe the vows were an excuse. I more or less threw myself at him, which is what I always do because I always have more feeling than the man. I sort of fling myself on the railroad tracks and look up and say, 'Save me, don't just stand there.' But this time—you were his friend. He told me so. You are the one I want to tell. This time it was different. I didn't realize it right away but pretty soon, after I began to notice and to listen to him and watch him with the wounded—pretty soon, but not soon enough—God, not soon enough, I did notice him, and I was a goner the minute I saw him like that, do you know what I mean?"

"Yes."

"Like falling down an elevator shaft only in reverse. So I went to him sort of as a patient, if that's what they call the ones who consult a chaplain. It was genuine enough, my ailment. Actually two ailments. I was buckling. I'm supposed to be a nurse and it was ruining me. I don't expect anything, I don't say we're entitled to any particular kind of life one way or another, but still it was wrecking my whole idea of what life is. Not what it should be. I have no idea of that, do you?"

"I do have an idea," Mac responded but left it there.

"We'll never meet again, but if we did, you could tell me. That's something I'd like to hear. The one thing that ever sort of guided me was that I'd have children someday. I figured babies, kids, a house, or at least apartment, a car, a man who doesn't cheat on you. That was my picture. Lots of people would be bored stiff. But with me it was babies, so I worked in the pedie ward in Cleveland and I thought, this is making me strong, this is making me competent, I am cool under fire. And it's true, I still am, but sometime around my third mass casualty event in this place I could almost hear the little cracks cracking in my head.

"I thought, you know, 'professional detachment,' " she continued. "They insist on that and of course they should. You can't let the little end of the wedge in. Let it in, just a bit, and you'll be sorry. Also less effective. They can't have nurses bawling on the ward. But it found its way in somehow, the little end. About that same time I had started to see Paul not as a chaplain but as a man. It made me believe I had never seen anybody really as a man before. It was kind of surprising. I had a pretty good reason to try to figure out what a good man looks like.

"As soon as I said, 'There's a man, this Paul Adrano is a man,' my feet left the ground. I broke up with a guy and went to Paul, not that I had any hope because after all he was the chaplain, but I needed to ask about this wedge thing. I had seen his courage. Of course he wouldn't call it that, he thinks courage is jumping out of the hole. So I went to him and ended up practically asking him to notice that I was a woman. Just, 'I am a woman, Paul.' But he had his vows.

"I'm glad he left. I might have done the worst thing in my life if he hadn't. So he saved me from that. But the way it turned out, maybe I wouldn't—my plan—maybe, wouldn't—"

She stopped and Mac did not disturb the silence for a full minute. Then he said:

"I don't know what you mean by the worst thing you ever did, or didn't do, but I know this: he cared for you. Not that he ever said it. He didn't have to."

"Did he talk about me?"

"Never, except that one time."

"He wouldn't care for me now."

"What do you mean?"

"You haven't heard? They're throwing me out of the Navy for pregnancy. They got the result yesterday and they've booked me a space on a flight to Okinawa tomorrow. Then Treasure Island, then out."

Guessing Mac's thought, she added quickly: "Paul is not the father. If Paul was the father I would be as happy as I could be under the circumstances. I wish Paul was the father. To have Paul's baby would—my future would be different if I could have Paul's baby. This is somebody else's."

Mac was silent—staring at her and wanting to help somehow. He believed it was best to say nothing. They sat in silence and let the fan sweep humid air across them. At length Mac asked:

"Will you go back to Cleveland?"

"I don't know. I might even live at home—no, I just don't know. I love my dad but it's not clear how—you know."

For the next several minutes she spoke in short, disconnected and repetitive sentences. She said that she had broken with her baby's father and now felt "better and worse," that it wasn't till she met Paul that she recognized the kind of man she could love—that Paul had told her he must keep his vows—that she wished he had told her something else—that Paul was in her mind all the time, and that his being there was her only pleasure, so she let it continue, she even said, "Now I can think about Paul." This sometimes even made her happy.

She would love the child but wished it was Paul's. She repeated this wish several times. She told Mac that she had seen through the priest to the man. But as soon as she declared this indirectly to Paul he had

518

announced he must leave. That was when he went back to his old regiment.

"I asked him not to go. I said he could be killed. Now I think that was exactly what I shouldn't have said."

Listening, Mac almost forgot that he belonged outside the human race. For that reason or some other he decided to tell the truth.

"I killed a defenseless man," he said.

To his surprise she looked at him steadily with patient expectant eyes, and then sipped her coffee without breaking her gaze. She waited.

"He was wounded and evidently unable to move except to roll a bit," said Mac more freely than he had expected. "I was in a little firefight and got this"—indicating his bandages—"and I turned on the lights, because I wanted to find him. If the lights had not worked I would have done something else, I don't know what. But I remembered him and decided to kill him too. And the lights worked. I walked over toward him and looked around in the mess—"

"What mess?" She wore a worried, frowning expression as if she must visualize every detail.

He explained, omitting only the single fact that he and this man had looked deep into each other's eyes—and the other fact, that what he saw in those eyes was courage.

"I think I fell or almost fell, I was kind of harassed by the noise in my head and the trouble from the frag wounds. I wasn't quite all there. That's not—I don't say that to excuse myself."

She had put down her cup and was now leaning with her head propped on her right hand, concentrating on his eyes.

"So I put the bayonet down by his throat, and we looked at each other. It was like a silent debate." At this point Mac realized he had no further memory. He said, "Then I must have stabbed him, which is what I went over there to do. I know I did because the doctor told me they were all killed, and I think this man was one of the last alive. But my memory ends right there. I don't know how I got out of the building."

She was pondering. Once she even closed her eyes, and he watched anxiously as if she were a member of some jury.

Rebecca said: "You have to find out how you escaped."

519

"The doctor said I'll never remember because I never knew. But the gunny's coming tomorrow," Mac reported. "He might know. I assume they found me when the company swept south."

"Who is this gunny?"

"My company gunnery sergeant, Hitchcock is his name. He knows everything that goes on in Delta Company."

"I'm wondering who wrote you up for the Navy Cross."

"I'm wondering that too."

"But you're sure you stabbed him. You didn't shoot him. That's a terrible thing. How could you forget it? You might have been temporarily insane."

"I intended to stab him. Maybe I shot him, I don't know. Paul would say the intent is the same as the act."

"Well it isn't."

"I'm not so sure."

Again she sat there pondering with her warm eyes fixed on Mac's. He looked at her as if she could suggest a way out.

She said, "I don't understand how you happened to be in that building alone, just you and all those enemy troops."

Mac explained, telling about the attack on the house, his dismissal of the gunny's team, and his decision to attack the building with rockets.

"All alone?" she asked incredulously.

"Yes."

"Then you must have been out of your mind."

"Not quite."

"I have an idea," she said slowly. "First tell me when Paul died."

"He died that afternoon."

"The afternoon before or after?"

"Before."

"So you were out there to pay them back."

"It was more complicated than that," said Mac, not knowing exactly what he meant, but it couldn't be mere vengeance.

"Paul was your friend."

"Of course."

"And they killed him. So you killed them. That's revenge."

"It was more than that."

"What more?"

Mac looked away.

"And the doctor—do you mean John Regnary?"

"Yes, I think that was his name."

"How much can he know?"

"He said he heard it at the club. So it's just rumor, I guess."

Becka said enigmatically: "Be careful. Be very careful what you do with this." A second or two passed, then she said, "Now please—tell me more about Paul."

They talked for another hour, till the place began to fill up with men getting their midday meal. As they talked Mac realized that he was opening at the seams because of Paul's death, yet he could not grasp it as fact. But something else agitated him.

He asked: "What did you mean, you might have done the worst thing in your life?"

"I've done it before," she said with a smile or a grimace of some kind. "More than once. But if I did it with Paul that'd be a different kind of thing."

"If you did what?"

"You know, use my female powers. Play to his weakness. Draw him into my net."

"Maybe you have a weakness of your own," Mac proposed.

"I do. I told you about it. But Paul would never take advantage of me."

"Probably not, but if he loved you he would want you, and I bet he'd go after you."

"Right, and then maybe he'd break his vows, but he didn't love me."

"Maybe he didn't have time," said Mac.

"No—he would need more time than we had. But his vows came from his true self, don't you think?"

He didn't sleep—or maybe he did. Here was another piece of lost history. He would never know whether he was dreaming or his mind was running wild while he lay half awake. In stabbing the other he had stabbed himself, and his spirit was bleeding.

He crossed the littered room in the dim and dusty electric light, to shoot the fearless man. Suddenly a better idea thrilled him. Here's a bayonet. You'll feel it go in, you'll know in your fingers and palms all about the twist, and maybe you'll hit a nerve that throws the body into convulsions. God! And you can watch his eyes as he sees it coming closer.

Mac wasn't creating this but remembering it. This was recorded, this was history recovered: the grisly plan and the premonitory fantasy, all occurring in the five or ten seconds before he came up to the paralyzed man amid the rubble.

He woke up and saw Rebecca Vanburen. She wore a crisp clean uniform; her hair in its tight curls lay wet against her head. A black leather bag hung from her shoulder on a strap.

She apologized for waking him and said: "I thought you'd want to see this."

And to his shame she showed him a copy of the message sent by the hospital's comm unit to Camp Lejeune asking that his next of kin be informed of the extent of his wounds.

She told him: "We always send these out, and I asked the comm officer to update your condition every few days."

Meeting her steady calm eyes, he wondered what she was thinking.

She said: "Are there any calls I can make when I get to CONUS?"

He gave her Sarah's name and number, which she wrote in a little notebook that she slipped into her shoulder bag. She said she was glad that Paul had a friend in his final minutes. He half expected some elaboration, but that was all she said. As they clasped hands her eyes filled with tears and she smiled and rocked his hand gently back and forth. When she released him she lowered her face and kissed him lightly on the forehead.

Departing, she said, "I'll tell her you're doing fine."

He was astounded at the kiss, chaste as it was. He thought something like: "I'll ask Paul to tell me more about her." But a depression came rolling in, together with reality in all its forms.

An hour later the gunny showed up and handed him a packet of letters from Sarah.

Conscious that his hand touched papers that had been touched by Sarah, he held the packet against his side while the gunny told his story.

"So no, we didn't go back, we disobeyed your order. Violation of Article Ump-de-ump of the UCMJ. Hope you won't put me on report. So I figured you'd make for the generator—you know we lost you in the dark, you went charging off by yourself—so I said the generator would be a sure gook magnet, that's where you'll head, otherwise you'd be groping in the dark. We got there and circled the place expecting you'd take us for gooks and kill us all—but what? I'm going to holler 'Hey Skipper!' No way. So we pretty well established you were somewhere else, we'd been wrong, or you were inside the building looking for a flush toilet. I already knew you were fuckin berserk, temporarily of course, sir.

"So I found the idiot guarding the generator who probably didn't understand he couldn't hear anybody coming and I said, 'The maniac'—meaning you, in all respect—'waltzed up to this moron and unzipped him and now he's gotta be inside the big building and do I really want to fight the entire NVA tonight?' Which I did not. Then a gook goes in to snuff out your precious life and there's all this booming and I do not mean sexual intercourse. I think I've got this mixed up. Anyhow at some point I said, 'O.K., the gooks are not fighting each other. Plenty of time for intergook recognition signals. And there's the LAW casing. There's one dead gook on the corner that we didn't kill, plus the generator man.' That was going through my Einstein brain. So I reached the conclusion: 'The skipper's in there and he'll die in there if we don't get him out and take him to the nearest mental hospital.' Plus we die too if we hang around, so I—

"Then the lights come on and I said, 'What the fuckin hell?' Or else four gooks come down the pike, I forget which comes first. One gook goes in and gets his ticket to the Hall of Fame, and right then I knew, A) you were in there for sure, and B) you'd got yourself an AK-47, and I said, 'Carramba!' Is that what Gonzo says? Carramba! The skipper is setting up a kind of Alamo situation and I asked myself 'Does the fucker—I mean, the skipper—really intend to buy the farm tonight?' Cause that's how it looked.

"Then we shot, me and Hippo shot us each a gook and I knew we had H Hour in our fuckin laps. So I squatted down and quack-quacked in and sniffed the hellhole smell and saw where the LAW had hit, and this other body lying there kinda disappointed, and then I saw you. Standing there like a hopeless drunk and kind of wavin your

M16 around like a magic wand. Next thing, you fell like a mighty oak and for all I knew you was Kilo in the Alfalfa, because you were the bluest red-haired man I ever saw, with pale lipstick and goggle eyes and red paint all over your face, a real sight. We didn't take any pictures to send your grandmother.

"You maybe don't know it, Skipper, but you are one heavy muddah. We dropped you about ten times. Sorry about that."

Mac asked if all four men were O.K.

"Valas got it," said the gunny.

This hit Mac like a kick from a bull, and he could not speak or breathe.

"Yeah," Hitchcock elaborated, "got hit with about half the payload of a B40. He was a good field marine. Tried to start a mutiny till I administered a little nonjudicial punishment, then he squared away. Hate to lose a man like the Golden Greek. He pulled his weight."

But Mac could not pull his. He did not see Valas or hear his wiseass comments. It was all abstract. Valas had died so Mac could peel out of formation to kill a few NVA. He stared at Hitchcock out of a profound fear and still he couldn't speak. Which was no loss since he had nothing to say. Mac was like a man in shock who sees and hears but can't put it together. He noticed that Hitchcock was actually a pretty small man—all brown and dressed in faded green—a suntanned skin, receding brown hair, small protuberant ears, black brows, and liquid brown eyes that looked inward rather than out, and darted here and there when he wasn't speaking. Although sometimes he listened with strenuous concentration. He had a voice that ranged over the treble from high to low.

At length Mac asked him to go back to the part where they dropped him ten times.

The request seemed to perturb him. He went silent, eyed Mac with a gaze that was part critical and part quizzical, and said: "Are you picking this up, Skipper?"

"Yes. My mind wandered for a second but I—please—"

"O.K. Let's see. We got to the phase line and the question was, would you bleed to death if we waited till morning or should we enter our own lines and get shot by our pals. So Valas took your pulse and said it was pretty strong, not that he knows shit about it. And I looked you over and took your pulse and you seemed pretty alive to me, in fact I'd gladly trade places at that point—so what we did, we crawled into some bushes that smelled like an outhouse in the summer and waited for the dawn's early light. Rain, cold, shivers, I was so stiff by daylight I could hardly talk. Pissed on my hands to warm my fingers.

"We see these fuckin jarheads moving on the other side, obviously getting ready to pound the shit out of our side of the street. Oh boy. If we holler maybe the gooks next door blow us out of the water. If we hunker down the USMC does the same thing. What to do? Pray for guidance from above? I asked myself what would Chesty Puller do? Answer: people like him don't get into a mess like this. You were sleeping like a little lamb, a two-hundred-and-ten-pound lamb, so no help there."

"What did you do?" Mac asked.

"I screamed bloody murder and after a second this voice across the street says, 'Sounds like the gunny. Let's shoot him.' So I bellow my lungs out, 'I heard that, you fuckin civilian,' and then we dragged you across. We were too tired to carry you and you didn't appreciate it anyway. Then the people all cheer, 'They got the skipper, they got the skipper!' What a patriotic scene."

Mac held up his right hand. The left would not go up without pain. He said: "What about Valas?"

"He dragged you too. We all did."

"When did he get hit?"

"Two, three hours later, when we were pushing the gallant NVA toward the south wall."

Mac proceeded cautiously. "He did not get hit till after you got me back to Delta?"

"No. We turned you over to some corpsmen from the battalion aid station and me and my guys stayed with the company. I found Lieutenant Wozniak and told him about the Alamo. He says, 'Let me see it,' and I said, 'O.K., Lieutenant, follow me, you'll love the neighborhood.'

"I told him the whole story and he says, 'I gotta see that building, the LAW casing, the dead gooks.' And I says, 'Follow me.' I knew right then he was thinking about writing you up for maybe the Bronze Star with Combat V. But the Navy Cross? Practically nobody and maybe zero people since the fuckin war began in the whole regiment has got a Navy Cross. Do you realize that? Not taking anything away from your heroic exploits, but holy shit, we both know the difference between Chesty Puller and some lunatic—with respect.

"So we drove south pushing the gooks, and me and my guys stayed with the command group."

Mac was thinking: "He didn't die until three hours later. He died the next day. He didn't die that night."

"About fifteen hundred," Hitchcock was saying, "we came to the building. The dead gooks were gone of course, but your LAW casing was still there—blood all over the place—a second LAW that we missed in the dark, and—"

"So—all the NVA were dead?" Mac interrupted. "There were no survivors."

"Not after we lit off the ammo cases," Hitchcock confirmed. "They had to be dead after that. I didn't go back. In a weak moment I decided I loved life."

"This is new," said Mac as if to himself.

"That I love life?"

"You never mentioned the stack of ammo cases till now," said Mac. "You mean the ones in the lighted room?"

"Yes sir. I didn't see any others."

"O.K., Guns. Tell me about that."

"What it was was a pretty lucrative target. We lugged your ass out and we stopped about a hundred meters away and I wanted to ask you, but you were asleep at your post, so I decided to put a LAW through the back window. So we fired one—I hate to say it but we fired three and they all missed the window. Talk about marksmanship. Then I gave it to Collins and he got a bull's-eye, she went kaboom, and we hauled ass."

"I see." Mac paused, and lifted his torso off the pillow and drew a chest-filling breath (and thought of Rebecca Vanburen) and then asked: "Will you tell me again what you saw when you came into the lighted room?"

"I'll sit here and talk about it all day if you ask me. What else have I got to do but go back to Dirty Delta."

"All right," said Mac trying to draw another deep breath, "you figured I had to be in there. You came into the lighted room."

"Yeah, smoky as hell. If I saw that room when I was ten years old and under the influence of the fire eaters I'd of said this is fuckin hell for certain. Except I didn't use that naughty word when I was a little boy in church. Anyhow—when I think of all the nookie I missed during my Christian adolescence. Jesus! Anyhow, smoke and dust and a caved-in wall and messed-up furniture, noise like rats moving somewhere. That was the wounded doing their dying thing, I guess."

"You saw wounded NVA?"

"That's real affirmative, sir. You were sort of swaying in the breeze with your mouth open and your eyes half shut, and like I said, you flopped and it was a cement floor, remember, and your skull whacked that ole cement! I thought, 'If the gooks didn't kill him, that will.' Cause at that point you looked deader than any living man I ever saw. So I hollered for the Yankees and they came in, gawking and whistling. We reduced weight and wrapped you up and you know the rest."

Mac again raised his hand to ask for time. Eventually he said: "How many dead NVA were there?"

"I told Lieutenant Wozniak twelve. It was more like six but this is war."

"And how many wounded?" Mac asked as if it were an afterthought.

"Oh—three, four."

"Did you notice a wounded man in a green NVA uniform who seemed to be paralyzed, who was conscious and alert?"

"Yes sir. Him and I had a whole conversation together. He was watching like he was my supervisor and after we got you ready I went over to him—he was the closest one—"

"Right," Mac interjected.

"—only a step away—a guy with pretty round eyes for a slope? Brand-new haircut? Is that the one?"

"Yes. He had big eyes, almost Caucasian eyes."

"Yeah. Probably his momma collaborated with a Frenchman. He'd'a looked pretty squared away except for the drool. I said, 'Gunnery Sergeant Hitchcock, USMC. You wouldn't happen to be the mastermind of the big massacre, would you sir?' That's what I asked him."

Mac said: "What massacre?"

"The VC and NVA, they've been shooting civilians by the hundreds, people in Hue, hands tied behind their backs. All in a day's work for the vanguard of the proletariat. So I says to Dark Eyes, 'Remember Hitchcock for the rest of your life. It'll be easy.' And I grinned at him, just to return the silly grin he was giving me. Not that I saw anything funny but I make a rule to smile at least once a month. Oh, and I said, 'If I were you, sir, I'd get the fuck out of this building.' He didn't take my advice. But he should've."

Mac said carefully, "He was alive, and there were no visible wounds?"

"He was alive all right, and no, I didn't see any. His eyes kept shifting from me to you, like he hated to see you go. I don't know, maybe he saw you fall and was thinking, 'That running dog of capitalism is gonna have a hell of a headache.' Beats me. Anyway, he did his bit for the revolution, I saw to that."

Reluctantly Mac asked: "You didn't shoot him, did you?"

"Me? Shoot the wounded? Christ no, I blew him up."

When Hitchcock was gone and Mac was alone, and Rebecca was gone, and Sarah ten thousand miles away, he opened her first letter, the one she had written first, postmarked 8 February—and began to read—but stopped, and looked up from the page and said aloud: "Not a murderer. A fighter, yes, but not a murderer."

Then, with a fresh feeling of—being married, of being her partner in life—he turned to the beloved script and read:

"Dearest Mac—Where are you? I keep reading about the Tet Offensive and seeing it on television, and I know you're in the middle of it—but I am here alone dying for you—please, Red, please!"

Chapter 24

A Circle of Friends

They gave him a cane and sent him back to his old job as assistant operations officer at Regiment. When he stumped into the club on his first night the officers clapped and cheered, and the bartender set before him a glass of Hennessy. Mac enjoyed this treatment well enough to stay till his lips tingled and the floor moved, then he climbed a slippery path to his hooch, dropped onto a cot, and allowed the world to spin around him.

Next morning the 6 summoned him and told him he would not sign the recommendation for a Navy Cross, and Mac replied through his headache:

"Fine, Sir. I don't deserve a Navy Cross."

The 6 said: "Nobody living does. But I'll get you a Silver Star for the S-curve."

"Sir, I don't deserve a Silver Star either but I'm writing up three of my men who do, and the chaplain for the Navy Cross."

The 6, a full colonel in the prime of his career and his existence, who had fought at Iwo Jima and in Korea, said he would sign that one. "So he walked right back into it?" the 6 asked, narrowing his hooded eyes at Mac.

"Yes sir."

"He must have been a man without fear—at that moment."

"He was, sir."

"And you, maybe you're pretty gung ho too, Clare, but don't let it swell your head. You'll get the Silver Star for the S-curve, but for Hue I'm awarding you this one single sentence. 'You walked away from your troops.' I'm not writing it in your service record as I should because you're the best company commander in the regiment, but I'm telling you to your face, Captain, and if you're not ashamed then I've misjudged you. Are you listening?"

"Yes sir," Mac said through the flaring pains behind his eyes.

"A company commander is responsible for his company. Do I have to make it plainer?"

"Sir, I went a little crazy. I have no excuse."

"You left your troopers, Captain," said the 6, bearing down harder. "I'll say that again. You went off on personal business."

Mac stood silent. The 6 had not given him an "at ease," so he was still at attention with his fissured head up in the hot zone near the canvas.

The colonel went on. "You made a grave error, but I didn't pull you back here to punish you. You're here because you already had five and a half months in command of Delta Company and as you know, nobody gets more than six. You know that."

"Yes sir."

"So you have not been relieved for disciplinary reasons but in accordance with Three MAF policy."

This policy was called "ticket punching." It applied in the Army and Marine Corps both and meant the high command was keen on nurturing careers and indifferent to winning the war. Mac kept this opinion to himself, and thirsted for water, ginger ale, beer, anything.

"So you had your time as a company commander and now we need your experience in the Three Shop. Dismissed."

Mac's reputation had preceded him and it was three nights before he could buy a drink at the club. Then he put a wad of military payment certificates on the bar and bought for the house.

He did not disparage medals, and he was not ashamed. He would wear a Silver Star proudly and make sure that Doc Bartholomew's mother got the doc's to hang by his picture.

Now it was Mac who drew little arrows on a map. Men could die following his arrows, but once drawn they must be followed. That was the problem with staff work. Staff officers made decisions that other men had to live with. Mac would have walked every step along his arrows if he could. And the other problem was that in the rear time stopped. In forward units it marched. In combat it flew.

That was the reason he asked to be sent to 3rd Battalion when its operations officer, a captain, rotated home. So long as he could hear the artillery and air, and see the star shells at night, no matter how distant, he must be as far forward as they would let him go. The colonel reluctantly assented and Mac moved one echelon forward. As part of a battalion command group he had a fair chance of getting back into the action. Chance favored him twice and he nearly died once, but in June 1968, his tour completed, he departed Vietnam for the Marine Corps base at Okinawa.

There he spent thirty-six hours in a state of surprise and elation— surprised to be alive, elated to be walking on streets that were not mined or stalked by snipers. He found he could step wherever he wished without fear; he could walk upright without asking for a sniper's bullet. For a year and four days neither had been possible, but he had not realized how guarded he had become. A distant tree line did not conceal a machine gun, and a glob of dung on the road did not cover a mine.

At the supply depot he drew the seabag he had left a year ago and found in it all the familiar mundane objects he had packed into it, including the kind of uniform you wear with a necktie. He took his wash khakis to a laundry, stuffed his jungle utilities into a trash container, and emerged into the sunshine in a clean summer uniform and low-cut shoes that made his feet weightless. That night he stood in a shower, naked and cool but not cold, then slept between clean sheets, and when he awoke his mind was dancing to a song of life.

At breakfast he overheard two master sergeants conversing. They were evidently members of the garrison who had been living, as many did, with Japanese girls. One said, "How can we go back to those middle-aged women?" Mac thought of Sarah, not yet thirty, and six months pregnant, and he tried to imagine the changes in her. He went for coffee, returned to the same table, and sat down to keep on thinking of Sarah. The two others had gone, and he felt fortunate in his solitude, and in his wife.

The next morning, however you compute time when flying against the course of the sun at 450 miles an hour, he awoke to see a jagged white line bounding a green continent. It was California. The cliffs lay in shadow below a plateau of luminescent grass, and the surf marked the edge of the shadow. The plane descended and Mac could see waves crashing into a cliff wall. It leaned into a slow turn and he saw San Francisco with its towers, the Golden Gate, the bay, and the Bay Bridge, and the runways of the Alameda Naval Air Station at the water's edge in Oakland.

Here he got a room and a seat on a Navy flight east the next morning, and because he had not slept above twelve hours in the last five days he did only one thing before going to bed: he called Sarah, but received no answer. He dropped through a cacophony of strange voices into a silent sleep. In late afternoon, having risen, showered, and dressed in wash khakis and one of his Hawaiian shirts, he tried Sarah's line again, with the same result. Then he made a mistake and called a law school classmate. The man said that he and his wife were throwing a dinner party that night. Would Mac come? The phrase "dinner party" had a certain ring to it, carrying him back to former times, and he accepted. He thought he was reentering normal social life.

Crossing the Bay Bridge in a cab Mac listened to the driver rail against the hippies and peaceniks. Mac had read about the polarization of the country but this was his first experience of it. He alighted from the cab and knocked at his friend's door. His initiation into the politics of America in 1968 occurred when he entered that house and shook hands with his friend. The man's greeting was loud and forced, but the wife stood mute. Mac, who had known her distantly at Madison, thought she was shy, and he spent an extra moment greeting her. The host then introduced him to a couple named Bert and Jennifer.

The sounds of vigorous conversation, mixed with laughter, drifted in from an adjoining room, and Mac's attention was divided, so he couldn't be sure—but he wondered if Bert and Jennifer had forced themselves to shake his hand. He was in this state of uncertainty when

Jennifer clarified everything by announcing, with mixed pride and defiance, that she and her husband were peace activists.

It was as if a clock had stopped ticking. Mac looked down at a small, pale, black-haired woman with piercing black eyes fixed on him.

He paused before speaking, because his chest was sending rage signals and his mind yelled beware.

He said cautiously: "By peace—what do you mean by peace?"

"We stop the killing. We mind our own business. We pull out."

"I see. We pull out. And you think that would bring peace to Vietnam."

"It is not our business. We must stop the killing."

"Not our business if South Vietnam is conquered by the North."

"No. Yes. What are we doing there? What did you do over there besides kill people?"

Mac turned to his host and extended his hand again. The man in confusion took Mac's hand a second time. Mac turned without speaking and left the house. He heard his classmate say:

"Hey, buddy, what's this?"

But he kept going. He was already in the street when he felt a tug at his sleeve.

His classmate admonished him: "Hey, man, don't walk out on us. Some of us might want to hear what it's like over there."

"Not that woman," said Mac.

"Not her, but maybe I do."

"Sorry. I couldn't trust myself in the same room with her."

And he walked away, downhill toward the bay. It was his only way to escape the black flow of fury. He had told his troops: "Someday somebody will ask you what you did in this war," but he had not foreseen how the question would be turned on him.

His night walk through the crowded streets near Fisherman's Wharf was his first venture into an America where that question could be turned into an accusation. He kept seeing military-aged men, and it flashed in his mind that those with a sense of honor would have to find a justification for standing aside.

He stopped in a bar and watched a ball game while he consumed his beer and hamburger. The game was being played on the East Coast and ended quite early, so he stayed to watch the news, his second mistake. Sick with what he saw—protesters crying for peace, when peace could have only one meaning for the people of the South—he went back into the street. A passerby would have seen a tall well-built man striding along with his hands thrust deep in his pockets, leaning into the hill, his eyes cast down—a man hurrying somewhere who in fact was going no place in particular, who seemed self-absorbed, but would have been glad to talk with just about anybody; who actually was talking to himself.

"They'll spend the rest of their lives with the knowledge that they lived in comfort while others did the fighting. They've only got one choice. They have to denounce the war as immoral."

But he heard the screams of the dying. He saw red streaks in a black sky and heard the monkey chatter of the Puff guns.

"Wait! Be fair. If you had a younger brother would you tell him to go? If the enterprise is doomed and the country divided, why not dodge the draft? But—what a difference!—between Sedgwick and a draft dodger. But no—I might even say, 'Hell no, don't go.' Still I'd hope a brother of mine would decide: 'I belong over there with those guys.'

"Fine. A man of honor. So he goes and gets his legs blown off like Sedgwick. Christ!"

He walked on, through the night, till he crested a high street and turned to look out over the city and the bay. He could see Treasure Island, where Rebecca Vanburen had stopped over to be discharged from the Navy. He saw these two places, Naval Air Station Alameda and Treasure Island, as sanctuaries where he could drink with friendly strangers rather than with friends who had become strange. He gazed at the city lights and the blackness of the bay, and he found it thrilling, a testimony of grandeur and a statement about human will. Exactly why it was beautiful, rather than a desecration of nature, Mac did not know, but he received the sight of it as something benign; it contrasted so evenly with a rain of fire. And yet this place had been seized from Mexico by force; and the new occupants, the new sovereign, had built something magnificent and humane, where people could make a good life and sometimes rise above the struggle for life to come out on a higher plane, where they could flourish in friendship, generosity, and peace.

It was growing late, already two o'clock in the East, but he stopped at a pay phone and called Sarah. Her voice was husky with sleep but she answered on the first ring and spoke before he did.

"Mac? Is that you, Mac?"

"It's me, babe. I love you and I'm almost there."

"Oh Mac," she cried, "come home!"

There was joy in it, and relief at being alive, and the ecstasy of taking Sarah into his arms again. There was a new awe in seeing the changes in her face and body, still subtle at this stage but already casting a mysterious question over their lives, and an even more mysterious answer. Henceforth they would be a family.

There was the physical comfort, the good food and drink, with a release from tension always on offer at the liquor cabinet; and there was the difference between sleeping in a warm bed with Sarah—today—and rolling up in a sheet of canvas to shiver under the monsoon—yesterday. On nights when they didn't make love, simply holding each other was enough. But such nights were few. She was experiencing a surge of energy and desire, and Mac's own desire kept pace.

There was all this in Mac's life—but something in the country was broken. He did not recognize it as his country now. Arriving at home, that is to say, in a split nation occupying the same ground as that once occupied by America, Mac felt as if he must explain something to anybody who would listen. Once or twice he tried. In a phone conversation with his father-in-law he limited himself to what seemed incontrovertible, that Tet was a massive Allied victory. But Mr. Woodley, anything but a peacenik, said, "It was a military victory perhaps for us but a propaganda victory for them."

"Why can't somebody explain that?" Mac demanded. "Why can't the president—"

"Nobody believes him anymore," Mr. Woodley interrupted, "and the media have turned. It's too late. You can't unbreak the egg."

Mr. Woodley then invited Mac and Sarah to meet him in Washington, where he had business. Mac was adrift for a few days at Lejeune anyway, and Sarah was joyous at the chance to see her father, so they drove north in the old ten-ton Buick and checked in at the Willard Hotel.

It turned out that Mr. Woodley had an agenda. He gave fair warning as they took their seats at a table brilliant with white cloth, silver, and white china.

He said, "You and I have got to talk seriously, Mac." And Mac responded, fine, let's talk, but Mr. Woodley insisted they eat and drink first.

Mac stopped at one bourbon on the rocks, and ate his dinner in the belief that his father-in-law was about to spring his favorite thesis— that Mac was formed by nature to be a lawyer.

"There are certain attitudes and prejudices," Mr. Woodley said over coffee, "that are appropriate for a college man but limiting, sometimes even crippling, for a mature adult." He tapped the ash off his cigarette and looked benignly at Mac.

Sarah ventured: "Daddy, let's enjoy ourselves tonight."

"I am enjoying myself," her father declared blandly.

"And I'll be having a barrel of fun in just about a minute, I can feel it coming," Mac added.

"Oh it won't be so terrible," Mr. Woodley assured him. "Now let me say that you, Mac, have seen more of a certain aspect of life on this bedeviled planet than I will ever see, or hope to see. In your world somebody is always dying somewhere. Somebody is being betrayed, deserted, crushed, or simply killed. Everyone knows this, even people who love humanity. Statesmen lie and run amok. They create tremendous wars and let justice fly by the boards. Anybody who cannot contemplate this without losing his nerve was meant for another world. Since there is no other world, the ones who can't face it are pushed into the corners of this one; and those who can are loaded with rewards and responsibilities.

"Many of these responsible ones, as I'll call them, stand in no danger of buckling. They are made of cast iron and think accordingly. But there are a few who carry the burden of their duties on shoulders that chafe and bleed. They are not indifferent to suffering and injustice. They are capable of compassion, and they suffer with the sufferers. It would be an elegant fit if these, who are both brave and sympathetic, were also the best. But that is not always true. Some who are sane, brave, responsible, and sympathetic do eventually break. This may happen in the midst of war or elsewhere. But if you break you are perhaps not ready for more action, and you therefore cannot be called the best."

He paused and looked without irony from Sarah to Mac, and leaned back to allow the waiter to refill his coffee cup. He took it black. He saw Mac's sharp concentrated eyes upon his and proceeded to his next point.

But Mac held up an arresting hand. With an edge in his voice he asked, "Are you trying to describe the combat experience for me?"

"Listen, both of you, can't you cool off?" Sarah interjected.

But without acknowledging her Mr. Woodley said to Mac, "No, I am speaking more broadly and humbly. May I go on?"

"Certainly, since we're both enjoying this so much," said Mac without breaking the interlocking stare that had taken hold between them.

And his father-in-law resumed: "The certain knowledge that somebody is dying somewhere, or justice is being raped, can sap your strength and break your will, by falsifying your belief that right will prevail. It may, or it may not. Often right is a mere product of the imagination."

Sarah broke in to ask her father to come to the point.

Mac began, "His point is—"

"I know what his point is!" She cut him off vehemently. She pushed her cup away, spilling some coffee on the tablecloth.

Mac was taking in every nuance of Mr. Woodley's mobile face.

Mac interpreted: "You're telling me the world is an arena."

"Not *telling* you," Mr. Woodley protested mildly. "I'm aware that you know it better than I do. I am saying I want you to be a player, Mac. You could do real work, you could pitch in with those who make the earth turn instead of being pushed to the margins."

"The ones who make the earth turn," Mac echoed enigmatically. "Like Lyndon Baines Johnson, like Robert Strange McNamara. Like that whole club of blood-soaked buffoons in this city who send marines and soldiers to die for nothing—because they are making the earth turn."

"You call it dying for nothing?"

"Don't misinterpret me," Mac said. "I believe in freedom for the people of Vietnam, but the buffoons have mismanaged and discredited that cause. Die now and you die for nothing."

"I agree, then," Mr. Woodley assented. "In that sense the dead have died in vain."

"So will thousands of others before it's over."

"Regrettably. The men dying over there are paying the price for the incompetence of statesmen. But Johnson is not a buffoon. He is a six-foot-three-inch man in seven feet of water. He has been a legislator and has never gone beyond the concept of the deal based on compromise. In his three years as commander-in-chief he has not learned that you can't win a war with preemptive concessions. At the fundamental level he doesn't know that if you will the end, you must will the means.

"But he has nothing whatever to do with your future, with the decision you must soon make about your career. You have—please hear me out, Mac."

Mac concentrated all the power of his eyes on him, and he held back the lava.

"You have discharged your responsibilities as a soldier with honor and courage, and, if I am not mistaken, with competence, possibly extraordinary ability. You have seen how far from perfect this world is, but you have carried the burden anyway. You are among the sane and the brave, Mac. You are among the best. Please don't feel compelled to deny it.

"But—do not let your knowledge that somebody has died in vain embitter you or keep you on the sidelines. Your life is young, your opportunities are ripening."

"You mean be a lawyer or a businessman," Mac said as if that summarized his father-in-law's entire argument.

"Those are two choices among many, yes."

Mac turned to Sarah and saw a glow of stress, possibly a query in her eyes.

Her father added his final touch: "If you fail to exercise your talents to their fullest extent," he declared, "you will have committed a grave sin, and you and your family will pay for it."

And Mac replied: "You may be right. But now I need to get my bearings. I want to live with Sarah and the baby, I want to live life, but I need to get my bearings."

On a sunny day favored by mild breezes rolling in from the ocean they decided to visit their beach. Mac sprawled in the passenger seat with his hand resting on her thigh, and Sarah piloted the old Buick in long sweeping curves through the forests of loblolly pines, to the south-bound highway, past the abandoned Army Air Corps strip and the Boomtown Grocery—where no town had existed since the end of the big war in 1945—then east through the sand country and over the In-tracoastal Waterway to Surf City. Turning left they passed along a row of ramshackle cottages to Barnacle Bill's Fishing Pier.

Mac put the frustrated Clinker on a leash, and they walked through a sparse crowd to the end of the pier and stood at the rail, where they had once seen whales churning the gray waves with their majestic copulations. Mac wanted exactly this, to stand and hold her hand, gaze at the water, and let the sun spread its silken blanket over his bare shoulders. Two boys were talking nearby and Mac heard them without listening. Clinker strained toward their bait bucket but Mac held him back.

Their household goods had been placed in storage that morning, and they had packed a few necessities into a U-haul trailer that stood in their driveway in Tarawa Terrace waiting to be hitched up and driven north. They had kept out a card table and three chairs, since they expected Denise for dinner. They would sleep on the floor tonight and Sarah had already shown him how comfortable she would be lying on a rubber lady. She lay on her side and rested her gently swelling belly on the air mattress, extended the lower leg and drew the upper one toward her chest. Mac saw this vision again, holding her hand, restraining Clinker, hearing the cry of the gulls. It was about three o'clock—on their last day in the Marine Corps.

As they walked north along the beach Mac set Clinker free. They took off their shoes and waded, till they climbed the dunes and visited the spot where Mac had shot a rattlesnake two years before. Turning their backs to the ocean, they heard how quickly the sound of the surf faded; then they took a meandering path that eventually led them seaward again and they picked up the distinct thud and breath of the waves, more clearly with every few steps. The sound increased faster than either expected. They topped a dune and there lay the ocean foaming twenty feet below. Clinker returned from some expedition of his own and dropped, panting, at Mac's feet, with his tongue racing in and out like a mechanical toy.

They sat on the edge and Mac stroked the happy dog's warm head. This was just what Mac wanted—to do nothing, and do it with Sarah.

Clinker stretched on his belly in the posture of a flying dog. His panting subsided and he reeled in his tongue part of the way, looking at Mac in hopes of new adventures. Eventually he stretched on his side, with his legs pointing toward Mac, and Mac studied his nearly hairless pink belly as it pumped in and out. His half-opened jaws lay on the sand and this didn't bother him. Nothing bothered him. His world was at peace.

Mac leaned back on his hands. Sarah rested her head in his lap and closed her eyes. Mac watched the gulls, the sea, and the surf, and thought of the empty bungalow and the awaiting trailer, and of becoming a civilian. It seemed necessary, but drab, perhaps lonely, and too easy. This morning he had said his goodbyes and returned at about ten to the bungalow. As he took off his uniform he realized that nobody would ever again see the Silver Star and Purple Heart on his chest and know what they meant. The men he cared most about were not at Camp Lejeune but in Vietnam, or scattered, or dead. There was nothing to keep him here, and he could not go back, and did not wish to go back, to Vietnam. Delta Company was not his to command and in any event would soon be transformed as men were rotated in and out. Without Delta Company he had no reason to stay in the Corps; and Sarah wanted out. But his separation order read like a passport to nowhere.

In imagination he saw Sarah laughing and settling on the floor, showing how comfortably she could rest her weight on the rubber lady. He took her hand as she lay there smiling and said:

"Do you know what this is? This is happiness."

Her flushed face, her smile, her eyes proved his point.

His mind presented a globe, with North Carolina on one side and Vietnam opposite, and he seemed to see how distant and different they were from each other, yet he felt almost as if he had never left the one, nor could he quite believe he was in the other. He caressed her hair and she smiled without opening her eyes. Clinker heaved a big sigh. The gulls called to one another, and the waves tumbled in. Here, instead of an assault, the sun offered a benediction.

Sarah lit a candle. Its flame stood up. Then she turned off the light in the kitchen, and the flame stood taller. There were no lamps left and this made it too dark. She went down the hall and turned on the ceiling light. A weak illumination found its way to the card table, where the candle burned between Mac and Denise. Sarah sat down in her chair and Mac began to cut the pizza. Sarah and Denise refused whiskey but popped their beer cans.

Denise announced that this was her last beer, and certainly her last taste of pizza, until Tommy came home in September. She would lose ten pounds a month for a total of thirty pounds, starting tomorrow.

"I will be a slithery sex object for Tommy," she said after she emptied a can of Carling Black Label in one long go.

Sarah could see her flushed features in the kind of light that candles throw over a circle of friends. She saw the pensive uncertainty that sometimes revealed itself in her friend's eyes, but only when she was silent, which was seldom. Just now she seemed to be doubting her vow. Sarah wondered how long Tommy would stay around if Denise continued gaining weight. She thought of Charles Dickens and Ernest Hemingway who, when their wives grew fat, took themselves elsewhere. To Sarah, Denise did not seem especially fat, but she knew her friend's fears. Denise had said that her mother, who started her womanhood as a beauty, was now obese. "She lost her face. It's buried." And her husband decamped.

Mac brought a new six-pack and set it on the table. He and Denise each popped a can, and all three fell to devouring the pizza. Mac was two shots of bourbon to the good and debating whether to make it three. Looking at Sarah he guessed she would disapprove. She had told him she was afraid of his drinking. "Afraid," he repeated to himself. He took the half-full bottle to the sink and poured it out, and splashed water in the sink, and dropped the empty bottle in the paper sack that served them as a wastebasket. Sarah's eyes met his and he saw approval and perhaps affection; he was glad of what he'd done. He marveled at how subtly she could express herself without words.

The three planned a reunion in Vermont when Tommy came marching home. Denise then spoke her two big fears—that Tommy would extend his tour of duty in Vietnam, and that he would stay in the Marine Corps.

"Augmenting," said Denise bitterly. "That's what they call it. Join for life and you've augmented. Where do they get these bloodless terms?"

"There's a language genius in Washington," said Sarah.

Denise said Washington was crawling with geniuses.

"Wait," Mac intervened. "No war talk. This'll be the only party in the country tonight where people don't talk about the fucking war."

They turned to the question whether they could watch *Shock Theater* in Vermont, at their reunion, as they had done here in Tarawa Terrace in olden days.

"Do they have television in Vermont?" Mac asked.

"There must be a station in Burlington," Sarah affirmed.

"But you could be in the shadow of a mountain," said Mac.

"The mountains are just big hills," said Sarah, who alone of the three had seen Vermont.

Denise concluded: "Then we can get plastered and holler 'Shock, shock!' "

Mac said, "Here's to Tommy, may he refuse to extend or augment."

They had set their table in the breakfast area, a part of the kitchen near the front door. They were surrounded by emptiness but could not see it. Much as Mac wanted out of the marines, he experienced a dull disturbance in his guts whenever he realized that the time had come. He could make a living anywhere; that didn't worry him. But to be a mere civilian was a demotion. The civilians were the people who didn't understand. He would soon live among them. And he knew—this was irrelevant—but he knew that in the darkness around him there was not a single familiar object except the rubber lady he had comeshawed as a place for Sarah to rest the weight of the baby.

In the morning they would load the card table and the folding chairs in the trailer, hitch up, and—as Sarah said—CSMO on outa here. Denise envied their luck. All she could look forward to was three months of hunger pangs to keep her mind off time.

There was a knock at the door.

Mac blasted out, "Advance and be recognized!"

There was a hesitation then a new and louder knocking.

Mac called, "Come on in!"

They all looked toward the door. They heard it open but could not quite see.

A young woman came slowly forward with guilt and fear in her eyes. She pointed.

Sarah said, "Hi Bev—what—" Bev was Denise's next-door neighbor.

Denise said hi also and found something amiss. Looking into Bev's sorrowing eyes, it flashed on her that Bev had just been told her husband was killed. Denise groped for his name—she had never met him—Karl, or Carl—

Bev stood there pointing, and although Denise did not comprehend it yet, Sarah saw that she was pointing at Denise.

A major in dress khakis stepped into the light. He fixed his eyes on Denise. A young lieutenant moved behind him.

The major said, "Excuse me," to Denise, and "Forgive me."

Denise screamed and lurched to her feet. The table shook and the beer cans toppled. Denise whirled, turning her back on the major. Mac rose and reached for her but she was gone. He followed and nearly tripped over her. She lay on the floor screaming in quick piercing gasps and her legs twitched like those of a man who has been shot and is in his death agony.

Mac said, "Help me," as he started to lift her. The major understood, and he and Mac lifted her while Sarah slid the rubber lady under her body. Neither her screaming nor her twitching stopped. They rested her on her side and Sarah knelt beside her and clasped her in an awkward embrace, and rocked with her, trying to do something.

Mac went aside with the major and asked, "WIA or KIA?"

The major said, "KIA," a little too loudly. Denise sent out a mad shriek and twisted out of Sarah's grasp and rolled along the floor, and Mac saw a ribbon of saliva trailing from her mouth. It seemed to him it was he, howling like a dog over Paul's body. He tried to protect her head but she had already smashed it on the floor twice before he dropped to his knees and got a grip on it. She screamed and he held her till her voice gave out.

Later that night Mac gathered Sarah's things from the bathroom and put them into her suitcase, which lay open on the bedroom floor. He carried the suitcase to Denise's bungalow and knocked softly.

Receiving no answer he entered and walked tentatively to the middle of the living room. It was dim but a light burned in the hall.

Sarah approached from that direction. At first she was backlighted but as she turned to him and they began to whisper he saw her face clearly. She looked like a woman who has been held down in cold water and half drowned.

"Call me," she said as if he'd fail to do it. "Here's the number." She gave him a folded paper.

"I'll call tomorrow."

"Yes. You have to call me."

"Don't worry. Are you O.K.?"

"Yes. When will you leave?"

"Right now," Mac said.

She protested: "You need to sleep."

"I couldn't sleep. Unless you need me here."

"No."

"How is she?"

"Not well," said Sarah. "She's dehydrating. I can guess that much."

"We should take her to the hospital."

"She refuses. I pleaded with her and she said no, no, no."

She took his hand and pressed it to her breast. They kissed and it sealed their love anew. They would never part. He inhaled her unique scent; his fingertips sensed the sweat in her hair.

He walked back and, working in the dark, he pulled the trailer to the rear of the car, found the ball of the hitch with his free hand, and lowered the tongue of the trailer. He secured the hitch and fastened the chains. He went into the bungalow and turned on the kitchen light to behold for the last time the scene of his past year's fantasies; it was bleak and dead. He lay the house keys on the counter and closed the door behind him.

An hour later, driving through a world of blackness and bright white lights while Clinker slept in the passenger seat, he passed a sentence through his mind deliberately. "We have no intention of winning, but you must die anyway." Then his thoughts shifted from Tommy to the paralyzed man with courage in his eyes. The man certainly thought he had something to die for. Whatever Tommy might have thought, he had nothing. Paul Adrano, Corporal Sedgwick, Doc Bartholomew—all had nothing.

But then—hadn't they actually died for one another? Amid the incompetence and perfidy of their leaders in Washington and Saigon, hadn't they died for one another? He thought of this, of course, but the other voice was still strong. They died for nothing.

He drove alone through the country that used to be America. He drove all night, aching for Sarah.

ABOUT THE AUTHOR

DONALD PFARRER was awarded the Bronze Star with Combat V and the Purple Heart for service in the Vietnam War. On returning from Vietnam, Pfarrer covered the antiwar movement for the *Milwaukee Journal*. He later became the *Journal's* senior political reporter. Pfarrer is a graduate of Harvard College and the author of three previous novels. He lives with his wife, Anne Burling, in Cambridge, Massachusetts.